a delicate balance

an introduction to american government

second | **edition**

paul c. light

The Brookings Institution

St. Martin's/WORTH

A Delicate Balance:
An Introduction to American Government, Second Edition

Copyright © 1999 by Worth Publishers, Inc.
All rights reserved.
Manufactured in the United States of America.
Library of Congress Catalog Card Number: 98–84991
ISBN: 0–312–19049–2
Printing: 1 2 3 4 5
Year: 02 01 00 99

Executive editor: James R. Headley
Project director: Scott E. Hitchcock
Editorial assistant: Brian Nobile
Development editor: Cecilia Gardner
Design director: Jennie R. Nichols
Production editor: Douglas Bell
Production manager: Barbara Anne Seixas
Project coordination: Ruttle, Shaw & Wetherill, Inc.
Text and cover design: Sandra Watanabe
Photo research manager: Deborah Goodsite
Photo research assistant: Treë
Cover photo: Underwood & Underwood/Corbis-Bettmann
Cover printer: Phoenix Color Corporation
Composition: Ruttle, Shaw & Wetherill, Inc.
Printing and binding: R. R. Donnelley & Sons Company

Worth Publishers
33 Irving Place
New York, NY 10003

www.worthpublishers.com

Acknowledgments

a delicate balance

an introduction to american government

To Kate, Max, and Wheeler

brief
contents

contents

preface

The goal in preparing this second edition of *A Delicate Balance: An Introduction to American Government* was the same as in the first edition: to write a concise introductory text that covers all the bases, carries a central theme, and is inviting to students and professors alike. The main difference between the first and second editions is in length and theme. The second edition has a full chapter on federalism, and it breaks two chapters from the first edition (Public Opinion and the Media, and Parties and Interest Groups) into four separate chapters. The result is a book that easily fits most introductory courses and covers the bases in more detail, yet still maintains a single author's writing integrity.

The second edition is also more rigorous about its central theme. Every chapter opens with a discussion of an aspect of the delicate balance between a government that would be strong enough to protect the nation from foreign and domestic threat, yet never so strong as to become a threat to liberty itself, and ends with a discussion of how American government does or does not maintain the balance today.

The text remains just as committed to providing up-to-the-minute examples, fresh writing, easy access, occasional humor, and comprehensive coverage and will appeal to students and instructors who want a thorough introduction to American government without all the clutter of the larger, more expensive textbooks currently available. Take away the endless boxes, special features, photos, tables, and full-color layouts of the bigger books and the second edition of *A Delicate Balance* will match every last one of them key term for key term, basics for basics, and fact for fact. The major difference is that students will be able to follow the main points in *A Delicate Balance* without getting lost in the kinds of extras that some publishers use to justify their higher prices. Moreover, because the second edition involves a complete, top-to-bottom revision, it is the most current book available today. Students will read it, enjoy it, and find plenty of examples from today's headlines, including the ones they find on the Internet.

REVISION HIGHLIGHTS

Like the first edition, this revision of *A Delicate Balance* is grounded in timely politics, yet remains tightly anchored to the leading scholarship in political science. It has many distinguishing characteristics that continue to make *A Delicate Balance* a different type of American government book.

Design and Format.   The second edition offers a clean, straightforward design that makes for easy reading. It looks and feels like a quality trade paperback, eschewing the trappings of a bulky hardcover textbook. Charts, boxes, and photographs are used sparingly, allowing readers to follow the flow of the text easily, without distraction. Pedagogy is kept to one place in each chapter, giving students quick and easy access to the information they need to review.

Consistent Voice.   Written by a single author, *A Delicate Balance* speaks in a consistent voice throughout. The writing style is smooth and comfortable, inviting students to stay with each chapter from beginning to end. Points are clearly made and stories well told. Chapter subtitles carry a punch. When taken all together, this text can claim what others cannot: this book is actually fun to read. Having begun his career as a newspaper reporter for the *Minneapolis Tribune,* the author knows what it takes to grab a reader's interest and hold it.

A Delicate Balance.   The second edition brings home the overall theme of the delicate balance between a government strong enough to ensure the liberty of the nation's citizens yet not so strong as to become a threat to that liberty. Each chapter opens with this theme and ends, in a new section called Maintaining the Balance, with insights into how today's government does or does not succeed in keeping the balance. In today's cynical environment, this theme should help keep the day-to-day frustrations of American government in perspective.

Expanded Coverage of American Government Essentials.   *A Delicate Balance,* Second Edition, provides expanded coverage of the essentials of any introductory American government course. As noted above, a full chapter has been given to a discussion of federalism. Public opinion, the media, political parties, and interest groups are now covered in four separate chapters instead of just two. The result is a fuller rendering of the basics that does not slow the narrative momentum.

"In a Different Light" Features.   This new edition continues to challenge students to think critically about up-to-the-minute controversies through "In a Different Light" discussions in every chapter. Drawing on nontraditional political topics such as gated communities, physician-assisted suicide, and negative campaign advertising, these features encourage students to think carefully about the issues that affect their own lives.

"Just the Facts" Sections.   Reformulated for the second edition, the "Just the Facts" section that ends each chapter brings home the points and theories presented in the text. The various elements—Terms to Remember, Facts and Interpretations, Open Questions, and For Further Study—enable students not only to review what they have just learned but also to deepen their understanding of it.

INSTRUCTIONAL PACKAGE

A Delicate Balance, Second Edition, stands by the premise that students won't learn what they won't read. So, in addition to this highly readable textbook, instructors have access to a package that makes teaching the American government course easier and more effective.

Instructor's Manual and Test Item File.   Like the text, these two supplements have been revised to meet the criteria for a full introductory course in American government. Using his experience as a professor of political science at Long Beach City College, Paul Savoie has combined the Instructor's Manual and Test Item File into a single volume. The comprehensive Instructor's Manual portion includes chapter overviews, discussion questions, classroom activities, and a series of lectures to accompany each chapter. The newly revised Test Item File offers close to one thousand multiple-choice, short-answer, and essay questions designed to ascertain a student's knowledge of the material presented. The computerized version of this Test Item File is available in three formats (DOS, Macintosh, and Windows) and has full authoring capabilities.

Web Site.   Found on the World Wide Web at <www.worthpublishers.com>, the *A Delicate Balance* Web site offers students a wealth of online resources, an electronic documents library, interactive study functions, annotated Web links, and more.

Also Available

Documents Collection. Compiled by Brian Fife of Indiana University–Purdue University at Fort Wayne, this volume contains a comprehensive collection of more than fifty primary source documents. Each document is preceded by a brief explanation of its context.

The St. Martin's/WORTH Resource Library in Political Science. St. Martin's/ WORTH offers the following brief, supplementary books on a range of topics:

- *Ralph Nader's Practicing Democracy: A Guide to Student Action,* Second Edition.— Katherine Isaac, Center for the Study of Responsive Law. This valuable resource contains biographical and contact information for more than four hundred political action groups. It empowers students to become politically active at the local, state, and federal levels.

- *Big Ideas: An Introduction to Ideologies in American Politics*—R. Mark Tiller, Houston Community College. This book presents an overview of political, social, and economic ideologies and their connection to politics and policy disputes.

- *The Real Thing: Contemporary Documents in American Government*—Fenyan Shi, Georgetown University. This anthology contains the texts of selected laws, letters, memos, grants, court opinions, and other documents that can be used for critical analysis.

- *Untangling the Web: A Beginner's Guide to Politics on the World Wide Web*—Brian Werner, St. John's University, New York. A thorough guide to using the Web to research politics.

ACKNOWLEDGMENTS

This second edition could not have come at a better moment for me. As the director of the public policy program at the Pew Charitable Trusts, I have been free to sample the leading scholarship in the field, to stay on top of the hottest controversies, and to remain in close contact with the best thinking in political science. I will always be grateful for the support of the Trusts and my talented staff: Jennifer Bolton, Elaine Casey, Elizabeth Hubbard, and Sean Treglia. They all have my deepest appreciation for their patience and encouragement.

I could not have done this work, however, without the support of my own family and wife. Sharon Light was unwavering in her willingness to enter the fray once again, acting as my own development editor, friend, researcher, and critic. Her contributions to this book can be found on every page, whether in her careful editing or her enlivening suggestions. Her contributions can also be found in the warmth that surrounded me from my three children, Kate, Max, and Wheeler, all of whom provided endless good humor, mostly welcome interruptions, and occasional reminders that this book is about helping readers learn.

Dozens of colleagues across the country helped in their own ways, too, whether in supplying answers to my pestering questions or the latest information on their own research. Kathleen Hall Jamieson of the University of Pennsylvania's Annenberg School of Communications proved a particularly encouraging colleague, as did Andy Kohut of the Pew Research Center for The People & The Press, Robert Katzmann of Georgetown University and the Governance Institute, Bill Galston of the University of Maryland, Burdett Loomis of the University of Kansas, Lawrence Jacobs of the University of Minnesota, G. Calvin Mackenzie of Colby College, and Dave Magleby of Brigham Young University. There are simply too many other grantees and friends to mention, but they all helped me achieve this revision in their own ways.

I would like to extend my sincere thanks to my colleagues who so carefully reviewed the manuscript for the first edition; their comments and suggestions were extremely helpful and appreciated. And thank you as well to the following individuals who reviewed the text for the second edition:

David L. Aronson	University of South Dakota
Debra August	Florida Atlantic University
Tom Baldino	Wilkes University
Christopher Carney	Pennsylvania State University, Worthington
Edward DeClair	Lynchburg College
Paul Goren	Southern Illinois University, Carbondale
Nirmal Goswami	Texas A&M University, Kingsville
Eric Heberlig	The Ohio State University
Thomas Michael Jackson	Marywood College
David Kimball	Southern Illinois University, Carbondale
Julie Lane	Western Wyoming Community College
Michael LeMay	California State University, San Bernardino
Brad Lockerbie	University of Georgia
Marsha Marotta	Westfield State College
Larry Martinez	California State University
Stephen K. Medvic	Old Dominion University
Bob Millar	Reading Area Community College
William Mishler	University of Arizona
Randall Newnham	Pennsylvania State University, Berks Campus
Scott A. Nikolai	Texas Tech University
John Norton	Lebanon Valley College
Jim Oxendale	West Virginia Institute of Technology
Rex Peebles	Austin Community College, Northridge
Dave Rausch	Fairmont State College
John David Rausch, Jr.	West Texas State University
Andrea Reeves	University of Alabama
John Reynolds	Moravian College
Robert P. Rhodes	Edinboro University of Pennsylvania
Cecilia Rodriquez	Southwest Texas State University

Brian Sanders	Evangel University
Paul Savoie	Long Beach City College
Stephanie A. Slocum-Schaffer	Gettysburg College
Sister Consuelo Sparks	Immaculata College
Donald Grier Stephenson, Jr.	Franklin and Marshall College
Bruce Stinebrickner	De Pauw University
Jerome Taylor	Cleveland State Community College
Roy Thoman	West Texas State University
Darcy Wudel	Averett College

The fact that this book is in final form is in no small part due to the editorial team at St. Martin's / Worth Publishers, who were far more enthusiastic about making the second edition a breakthrough project than I ever could have hoped. No author looks forward to the kind of editorial transition that I experienced in early 1998, when Worth Publishers became the lead in this project. But I cannot imagine a stronger commitment to excellence, a greater willingness to persevere, and a deeper faith in the potential for success from any other publisher. My deep appreciation must go to Susan Driscoll, James Headley, Barbara Militch, Scott Hitchcock, Cecilia Gardner, Douglas Bell, and Tom Conville, for helping me to undertake this revision.

Paul C. Light

about the
author

Paul C. Light is a popular instructor of political science and an award-winning writer who has spent almost half his career in the national policy process. He worked on the 1983 National Commission on Social Security Reform (Greenspan Commission) as an American Political Science Fellow assigned to Republican Representative Barber Conable, Jr., and then worked on Senator John Glenn's 1984 campaign for the Democratic presidential nomination. Light spent a year as guest scholar at The Brookings Institution, three years as director of research for the National Academy of Public Administration, and two years on Capitol Hill as a senior staffer with the U.S. Senate Government Affairs Committee. While at the Hubert H. Humphrey Institute as associate dean, he drafted the final reports of two blue-ribbon commissions on the public service (the Volcker and Winter Commissions). Light is former director of the public policy program at the Pew Charitable Trusts, where he helped design a new initiative on strengthening civic engagement and government performance in the United States. He is currently the Douglas Dillon Senior Fellow and founding director of the Center for Public Service at The Brookings Institution.

a delicate balance

an introduction to
american government

introduction

to build a government

This book is based on the simple notion that American government involves a balance between strength and limits on strength. The fifty-five delegates who gathered for the Constitutional Convention in the summer of 1787 wanted a government that would be strong enough to guide a fragile nation through an uncertain future, but limited enough that it would never threaten the liberty America had just won. Their government had to protect America as a nation even as it guaranteed the rights of every citizen as an individual.

The Founders' new government did not necessarily have to

be democratic, however. **Government** is simply a set of institutions (legislative, executive, and judicial) for making and executing the laws. As such, government is whatever a nation makes of it. It can be used for good or ill, to help the people or oppress them, to promote individual opportunity or suppress it. Even the most hateful dictatorship needs a government to execute its will. It was the government of Nazi Germany that organized the killing camps of the Holocaust, and the governments of colonial America that permitted slavery.

The choice between good and ill is made through **politics**, the process by which the people and their political parties, interest groups, and representatives decide who gets what, when, and how from government.[1] If government provides the playing field and sets the rules of the game—for example, by determining who can hold office, when elections are held, and how a bill becomes a law—politics determines the final score. Although the Founders were seasoned politicians in their own right, they gave the government the power to defend itself against political extremes. They wanted a government limited enough so that Americans would have the freedom to breathe as citizens, yet strong enough so that its citizens would always breathe free as Americans.

The search for balance is clear in the Preamble of the Constitution itself, which promises that the new government will create laws and courts ("establish Justice"), keep the peace ("insure domestic Tranquility"), defend the nation against foreign threats ("provide for the common defence"), and assure that every American has a chance at a better future ("promote the general Welfare"). To protect the young nation, America would need a government strong enough to raise taxes, tough enough to enforce the laws, and powerful enough to win wars.

Yet this same government would defend individual Americans from tyranny ("secure the Blessings of Liberty to ourselves and our Posterity"). To protect what Thomas Jefferson's Declaration of Independence deemed the "unalienable Rights" of "Life, Liberty and the pursuit of Happiness," America could never have a government so strong that it could be captured by a majority to be used against a minority. After all, the war for independence had been fueled by resentment toward the British government, which had stripped its American colonists of these unalienable rights.

The Founders understood that the delicate balance between strength and limits could not exist only on paper. They knew that government would be tested by history. Sometimes government would be too strong, other times too weak. Sometimes it would oppress minorities, other times it would ignore the majority. The best they could do was design a government that would seek equilibrium, or balance, whenever the balance of power shifted too far toward either strength or limits.

The Founders also knew that government could be used against the people. Having fought in British wars and paid British taxes, they had all once been loyal British citizens. But in the years leading to the Declaration of Independence, they came to believe that the British government had become more their oppressor than their ally. The Declaration of Independence, which was signed in Philadelphia on July 4, 1776, lists more than twenty-five "injuries and usurpations" by an increasingly hostile British government, ranging from "imposing taxes on us without our consent" to having "plundered our seas, ravaged our Coasts, burnt our towns, and destroyed the lives of our people" and "transporting large Armies of foreign Mercenaries to compleat the works of death, desolation and tyranny." The Declaration is the statement of a nation betrayed.

THE MISCHIEFS OF FACTION

The Founders faced many choices in building their new government, not the least of which was whether they wanted a democracy at all. Before turning to those choices, however, it is first important to understand that the Founders believed that human beings were mostly incapable of governing themselves. "If men were angels, no government would be necessary," Virginia's James Madison wrote in advertising the Constitution to the public in *Federalist Paper No. 51,* which can be read in full in Appendix C.[2] As the intellectual leader of the Constitutional Convention, Madison believed that human beings inevitably divide into **factions,** or groups, to impose their will on others, which is hardly angel-like behavior. A faction is a collection of people, large or small, that shares a common view of what government should do.

Because the Founders believed that this tendency toward faction was sown in human nature itself, they came to Philadelphia deeply concerned about what the people might do if given the power to govern themselves. They had no interest in building a modern version of ancient Athens, in which citizens had direct control of every government decision, large and small. Instead, they embraced a **republican form of government,** in which the people govern themselves through the election of representatives. In contrast to the British empire, which was ruled by a single king (at the time, King George III), or the future Soviet Union, which would be ruled by a single political party (the communists), the Founders' **republic** would be governed by those whom the people elected.

Even in 1787, when political campaigns consisted of town-square debates, pamphlets, and posters, the Founders saw people as easily manipulated by great orators and clever advertisers alike.[3] Surely, such a public could not be allowed to govern directly. Subject to "every sudden breeze of passion, or to every transient impulse," as Alexander Hamilton argued in *Federalist Paper No. 71,* the public was likely to sway back and forth with the promises of skillful tyrants.[4] As future president John Adams argued in 1787, "The proposition that [the people] are the best keepers of their liberties is not true. They are the worst conceivable; they are no keepers at all. They can neither act, judge, think, or will."[5] Convinced that human beings would fight about even the most trivial of issues, the Founders insulated government against public passions. The people would be asked to give their consent to be governed, but would not be given the power to actually govern themselves. That power would reside in a government that would separate, check, and balance public passions.

There were only two ways the Founders could cure what Madison called the "mischiefs of faction." They could either destroy the factions by creating an all-powerful government or convince every citizen to join the same faction. Since the first cure was worse than the disease and the second was impossible in a diverse nation, Madison and his colleagues designed a government that could never be used by the people *against* the people. In short, they designed government to make it difficult for any single majority to assert its will. This is one reason why government can sometimes be so frustrating. It will always be much more difficult to pass a law than to defeat one, even when most Americans want action.

Curious as it may sound, the Founders worried about protecting the people against government because government was, in fact, a product of the people. Americans were just as divided against one another in the 1780s as they seem to be today. The young nation came close to civil war twice and was plagued by deep social and economic divisions. It was also under nearly constant foreign threat, most notably from the British.

It is useful to consider two other points about how the Founders viewed the world before turning to a discussion of the choices they made. First, the Founders believed that some human beings could rise above faction. Even as Madison worried about the "degree of depravity in mankind," he celebrated the potential for virtue among America's future leaders. The mischiefs of faction could be solved in part, he wrote, by straining public opinion through the filter of "a chosen body of citizens" whose patriotism and love of justice would be so great that the new government could somehow rise above the petty conflicts of ordinary life.[6] That "chosen body" would be found in the Congress, the presidency, and the Supreme Court, all of which would be led by gifted patriots who would set aside their own interests for the greater good of the nation.

Second, even as they worried about protecting the public from government and vice versa, the Founders did not want government administration to be incompetent. They wanted the army and navy to be strong, the mail to be delivered on time, and the president to make sure the laws were faithfully executed. They certainly expected the three branches to disagree about **public policy,** which involves *what* government does. But they also wanted government to be effective at

The tendency of Americans to divide against each other usually expresses itself in legal activities such as voting and peaceful protest, but can also express itself in extremist acts such as the bombing of the Murrah Federal Building in Oklahoma City on April 19, 1995.

public administration, which involves *how* government implements public policy. Indeed, New York's Alexander Hamilton argued that a "government ill executed, whatever it may be in theory, must be in practice a bad government."[7] Occasional stalemate in protecting America from its enemies, both inside and outside, was unacceptable.

The rest of this chapter will take a closer look at the different choices the Founders faced as they built their new government. They had plenty of options from which to choose, running the gamut from giving Americans a direct say in every decision government would make to denying the people any say at all.

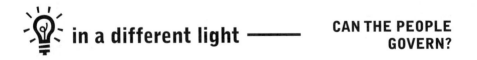 **in a different light** ——— CAN THE PEOPLE GOVERN?

America's current leaders appear to be just as skeptical about government by the people as the Founders were. Like the Founders, they simply do not believe Americans should have a direct voice in making public policy. According to a 1998 survey by the Pew Research Center for The People & The Press, most members of Congress, presidential appointees, and senior civil servants do not believe citizens know enough to form wise opinions about the issues that the nation faces.

As Box 1–1 shows, presidential appointees and senior civil servants have the least confidence in the American public, perhaps because they spend so little time with Americans who might persuade them otherwise. "I can only speak for the programs that I've been involved in," a senior Department of Justice official said. "I have found that the level of complexity is sometimes such that I think a lot of people would not be able to understand them."[8]

Even members of Congress, who spend weekend after weekend back in their districts, have doubts about the public. Perhaps it is because the citizens they meet are not always the ones with the wisdom. "We interact with the people

BOX **1-1**

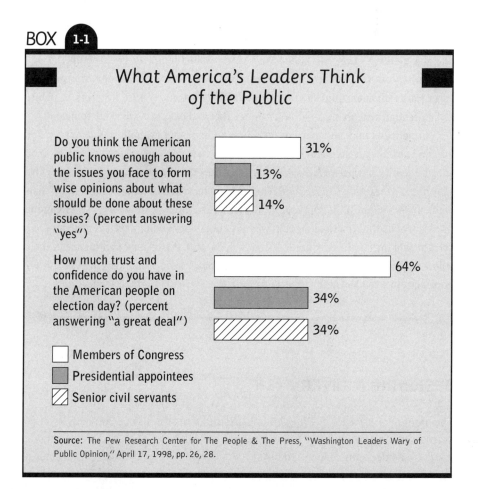

What America's Leaders Think of the Public

Do you think the American public knows enough about the issues you face to form wise opinions about what should be done about these issues? (percent answering "yes")

31%
13%
14%

How much trust and confidence do you have in the American people on election day? (percent answering "a great deal")

64%
34%
34%

☐ Members of Congress
◼ Presidential appointees
▨ Senior civil servants

Source: The Pew Research Center for The People & The Press, "Washington Leaders Wary of Public Opinion," April 17, 1998, pp. 26, 28.

who are angry," Representative David Skaggs (D-CO) noted. "People who are content—which would be the people from whom you would get a more balanced sense of this issue—tend to be cutting the grass on Saturday, not coming to town meetings. If most of what you encounter are gripes, [you'll think] the public is pretty gripish."

Whatever their doubts about the public's role in public policy, America's leaders have considerable confidence in the public's ability to make wise decisions on election day. Again like the Founders, they believe that Americans are perfectly capable of giving their consent to be governed. It is hardly surprising that members of Congress would have the greatest confidence in the electoral ability of the American people. After all, they would not be in Congress if they had not been elected.

America's leaders may not know as much about the people as they think, however. The Pew Center respondents consistently overestimated the public's antigovernment mood and underestimated the public's trust in government. At least inside the Beltway of interstate highway that surrounds Washington, DC., politicians tend to see the public as angrier than it really is. "The results underscore the problem inside the Beltway—that the public isn't really wise enough to understand the nuances of the water bill or a particular piece of legislation," Democratic pollster Peter Hart explained. "But in reality, the public is extremely wise in terms of pointing a direction and giving a set of attitudes that tell us where we want to head."

Americans may not know exactly how to implement a pollution program, but they do know they want clean air and water. They may not know exactly how the giant Social Security program works, but they do know they want it fixed in time for the baby boom generation's retirement. They may be far more rational in their views than the Founders might have guessed.[9] Americans seem to know it. Asked in 1998 about the wisdom of the American people when it comes to making political decisions, 64 percent said they had a very great deal or a good deal of trust and confidence in their fellow citizens.[10] Although that confidence was down from 77 percent in 1964, Americans continue to have much greater faith in themselves than their leaders do.

DESIGNING A GOVERNMENT

The Founders arrived in Philadelphia for the Constitutional Convention convinced that America needed a new national government. They had already made many of the decisions needed to build that government. They knew what kind of nation they had (a republic), what kind of government they wanted (a republican form of democracy), how that government would seek the consent of the governed (through representation), and how it would make most decisions about who gets what, when, and how (through majority rule).

What they did not know was how to convert their abstract belief in a **majoritarian representative democracy** into a set of specific institutions and rules that would maintain the delicate balance between a government strong enough to protect the nation, but not so strong as to threaten liberty. As shown in Chapter 2, it took a long summer to work out the details. But at least the Founders came to Philadelphia with broad answers to three key questions that any government builder must ask: (1) What kind of government did they want? (2) What kind of democracy did they favor? and (3) How would government decide? The one question they did not answer with absolute certainty was, (4) Who speaks for the people once the governing begins? That answer is constantly evolving.

What Kind of Government?

As noted at the very beginning of this chapter, American government did not have to be a democracy. The Founders could have created an **autocracy,** in which a single person has all the power to decide who gets what, when, and how from government, or an **oligarchy,** in which a handful of very powerful people rule the nation. They could even have created a **monarchy,** in which an autocracy resides by birth in a single royal family. Instead, they created a republican form of **democracy,** in which power resides with the people and is granted to government through the election of representatives of the people.

Abraham Lincoln gave America its most familiar definition of democracy in his 1863 Gettysburg Address: government of the people, by the people, and for the people. Although most Americans today would accept that definition, the Founders most certainly would not have. They may have believed in a government *for* the people, in which all Americans would receive the blessings of liberty. They may have also believed in a government *of* the people, in which Americans would give their consent to be governed through regularly scheduled elections. "I know of no safe depository of the ultimate powers of society," wrote Thomas Jefferson late in life, "but the people themselves."[11]

But the Founders did not believe in a government *by* the people. They simply did not trust the people to govern themselves. Indeed, they were so worried about government by the people that they never used the word "democracy" in the Constitution. And no wonder. The word is a combination of two ancient Greek words: *demos,* meaning the common people, and *kratos,* meaning rule. Putting the two parts together, *democracy* comes to mean "rule by the common people." Direct democracies can never work, Madison argued in *Federalist Paper No. 10,* because people are people. "Such democracies have ever been spectacles of turbulence and contention; have ever been found incompatible with personal security, or the rights of property; and have in general been as short in their lives, as they have been violent in their deaths."[12]

What Kind of Democracy?

Given a choice between what they saw as the tumult of a **direct democracy**, in which every citizen would have a say on every decision, no matter how trivial or complex, and the relative calm of a **representative democracy**, in which representatives would make the decisions on the people's behalf, the Founders clearly chose a representative system. The Founders defined government by the people as government by those *whom the people select* to be their representatives, and called it republican in part to make clear that the people were not to govern directly. The differences between direct and representative democracy are summarized in Box 1–2.

Even after defining democratic government in representative terms, the Founders still worried about what the people might do. They responded by reducing the public's opportunity to elect their representatives. Until the early 1900s, Americans were allowed to vote for only one set of representatives, members of the House of Representatives. Every other officeholder was selected through indirect means. Senators were elected by state legislatures, presidents were elected by the members of the Electoral College, and Supreme Court justices were appointed by the president with the advice and consent of the Senate.

Moreover, the Founders gave each set of representatives a different term of office (two years for House members, four years for presidents, six years for senators, and life appointments for Supreme Court justices), and a different base of voters (House members are elected by districts, senators by individual state legislatures, presidents by all the states together, and Supreme Court justices by no voters at all). The Founders did this to make certain that no single faction of the public could ever impose its will on the rest of the country by capturing one branch of government. The people may get to elect at least some of their representatives every few years, but otherwise have to trust that their elected leaders will act in the nation's best interest.

Representative democracy may be the only choice in a country as large and diverse as America. As political scientist E. E. Schattschneider wrote when America was just 230 million strong, "We ought to get rid of confusing language such as 'government by the people.' "[13] The fact is that Americans are spread out across 4 million square miles of national territory. Even if they could be brought together in one place, 270 million Americans would create a mosh pit covering 70 square miles, filling the entire District of Columbia.

Under the Constitution, states are free to make their own decisions about how to run government, provided they do not violate the basic rights of individual citizens. Although the Founders never gave citizens the opportunity to vote

BOX **1-2**

Who's in Charge? A Comparison of Direct and Representative Democracy

Direct Democracy	Representative Democracy
All eligible Americans have the opportunity to participate in every decision.	All eligible Americans have the opportunity to choose the representatives who will participate on their behalf in every decision.
Elections offer choices between candidates, as well as choices between different public policies.	Elections offer choices only between candidates.
The people have the opportunity to place public policies on the ballot.	The people have no opportunity to place public policies on the ballot.
Representatives of the people must always do exactly what the people want.	Representatives of the people are free to act according to their own views, which may or may not fit what the public wants them to do.
The agenda of government decisions about who gets what, when, and how is set by the people.	The agenda of government decisions about who gets what, when, and how is set by representatives according to their own views.
The majority rules in all decisions.	The will of the majority can be denied in order to protect the rights of minorities.

on national policy questions, many state and local governments allow a form of direct democracy through the *referendum* and *initiative*. In a **referendum**, a state or local government asks citizens to approve or reject a specific proposal, say, to build a new sports stadium, allow riverboat gambling, ban assisted suicide, or abolish English as a second language, all of which have been the subject of state or local referendums in recent years. In an **initiative**, citizens petition other citizens to ask a state or local government to allow a vote on a specific proposal, say, to ban gay and lesbian marriages, permit prayer in schools, impose term limits on the legislature, or cut taxes, all of which have been the subject of initiatives in recent years. Once citizens collect the minimum required number of signatures on the petition, the proposal is placed on the ballot for the next regularly scheduled election.

Whether the proposal is written by government (referendum) or citizens (initiative), the outcome is subject to majority rule. Because government must give its blessing to the referendum first, it is a more limited form of direct democracy than the initiative. Twenty-one states currently allow both referendums and initiatives; five more allow one or the other.

How Does Government Decide?

Once the Founders agreed on a representative democracy, they had to set the basic rules for making decisions. How many votes would elect a president? How many Senators or House members would pass a law? How many Supreme Court justices would decide a case? The Founders answered all of these questions with **majoritarianism,** which defines government by the people as government by the majority of the people (for elections) and the majority of the representatives whom the people select (for most government decisions).

Thus, American government makes most of its decisions by **majority rule,** which simply means that those who have half of the vote plus one have the greatest say over what government does. Majority rule holds in most elections, where the candidate who gets 50 percent of the vote plus one usually wins. Majority rule holds in Congress, where it always takes half of the Senate and House plus one to pass a bill, and sometimes takes a "supermajority" of three-fifths or more. Majority rule holds in the Supreme Court, where a majority of the nine justices determines the final opinion on most cases.

Even though the majority has the greatest influence in electing representatives and making government decisions, the Constitution also creates **minority rights** to protect those who do not happen to have the most popular position or the greatest number of supporters. The Constitution spells out these rights and limits in its first ten amendments, which are called the **Bill of Rights.** Together, the amendments in the Bill of Rights guarantee **civil liberties,** protecting individual citizens from their government, and **civil rights,** protecting individual citizens from each other.

Who Speaks for the People?

Governing does not end with an election, of course. Once the ballots are counted and the swearing-in occurs, government must make decisions on a host of questions, all of which involve politics. Where should the new highway be built? Who should be eligible for welfare and for how long? How much should be spent on foreign aid versus public schools? Because the people do not have a vote on such specific policy questions, the answers depend largely on who speaks for the people once the elections are over.

One option is to let property owners or other wealthy Americans speak for the people. As John Jay, one of the great champions of the Constitution in 1787, once said, "The people who own the country ought to govern it."[14] Although the Founders decided not to require property ownership as one of the qualifications to be president, wealth is an important asset in governing. It buys education, which buys information, which buys influence over who gets what, when, and how from government. Under **elitism,** government of the people becomes government of the people who have the resources and family ties to get to the top of the socioeconomic ladder.

The problem with letting elites speak for all Americans is that elites are largely isolated from the rest of America. They are not called elites for nothing. During the 1992 presidential campaign, for example, the public discovered that President George Bush did not know what a supermarket scanner was. He had not been grocery shopping in years, if ever, and could only marvel at the new invention that scanned bar codes on cans and packages.

Another option is to let **interest groups** speak for the people. Interest groups are collections, or groups, of people who join together to make their views known to government. Students, the elderly, women, small businesses, hospitals, corporations, doctors, veterans of foreign wars, trial lawyers, even political scientists and college professors have their own interest groups that try to influence government decisions. So, too, do people who care about food safety, dolphins, old-growth forests, children, abortion, and equal rights for women. Under **pluralism,** government of the people is defined as government of the many (or plural) interest groups the people join.

There are two problems with allowing interest groups to speak for all Americans. First, not all Americans belong to an interest group. Children do not join interest groups so they must rely on adults to make their case. Poor people do not join either, so they must hope that someone else speaks on their behalf. Second, interest groups do not necessarily believe in majority rule. Because they exist solely to serve their members or cause, they rarely take "no" for an answer, and often accept small compromises to keep their issue alive. They are also adept at exploiting opportunities to influence government wherever and whenever they can. As a result, a **pluralistic representative democracy** may have greater difficulty reaching final decisions than a majoritarian representative democracy.

It is not clear which theory the Founders intended their new government to apply. On the one hand, they hoped that the nation would be led by highly educated, virtuous elites, in part because that is exactly what they already were. On the other hand, they also believed that the nation would always be divided by *factions,* a term that is an acceptable synonym for interest groups. They expected factions to campaign for their favorite candidates, and designed the government as if factions would fight to impose their will on the rest of the country. Thus, even as they preferred elitism, they prepared for pluralism. They hoped for the best, but planned for the worst.

It may be that the Founders' worst-case scenario has come to pass. As the number of interest groups has grown in recent years, the pressure not to act has also increased. Congress often finds itself unable to make decisions because interest groups clog the system—a situation that suggests that government may have lost the delicate balance. Even though the Founders expected the people to divide into factions, they did not expect the divisions to continue to a point of perpetual stalemate, which so often appears to be the case today.

Whether led by elites or interest groups, however, the Founders did not believe the people could speak for themselves, at least not beyond casting a ballot every two years. The people would be free to petition government for action, assemble in protest, contribute money to campaigns, join interest groups, write letters to their congressional delegation, even burn the American flag (all of which are protected by the First Amendment), but they would never be given a chance to vote on a national referendum or initiative or cast a direct vote for the president or Supreme Court. The Founders built their new government to be *of* the people and *for* the people, but only by the most indirect means *by* the people.

in a different light ——— AN ELITE BUYS AN ELECTION

Under Article I of the Constitution, state governments are responsible for determining the manner of holding elections, whether for members of Congress, governor, mayor, or dog catcher, and whether for referendums or initiatives. That means state and local governments pay for printing the ballots, buying the polling machines, registering the voters, watching the polling places, and counting the votes. Imagine if a state or local government decided to cover those costs by finding a sponsor ("This election is brought to you by Duff Beer") or a rich benefactor ("This election is paid for by Daddy Warbucks"). Sound shocking? A violation of basic democratic procedures? It happened in Seattle in 1997 when Microsoft cofounder Paul Allen covered the costs of an election asking citizens to agree to pay for a new domed stadium for his latest purchase, the Seattle Seahawks professional football team.

By any measure, Paul Allen is an elite. He owned 100 million shares of Microsoft and was worth $11 billion when he bought the Seahawks in 1997 to keep them in his beloved city. His only condition for saving the team was that the city or state raise at least $300 million of the $425 million needed to build the kind of stadium that makes a professional team profitable, meaning luxury boxes, exploding scoreboards, four-star restaurants, sports bars, game arcades, and just about anything else to keep fans spending money.

Unfortunately for Allen, the city and state refused to either raise the $300 million in taxes or pay for a special election to approve a referendum. If Allen wanted his stadium, he would have to pay for the election himself. Since Seattle had already rejected a referendum on a new baseball stadium, Allen took his chances on a statewide vote. He spent $1.7 million lobbying the state government to call the referendum (recall that a referendum starts in government, while an initiative starts with citizens), another $3 million on a television advertising campaign, and $4 million to cover the costs of holding the special election. Washington State held Allen's election on June 17. The final tally was 820,000 in favor and 783,000 against, a margin of just 37,000 for the majority. Because majorities rule, even in very close elections, Allen got his stadium.

The irony is that the world's eighth richest man spent the money to give his fellow citizens a moment of direct democracy. On the one hand, it seems like a perfectly noble act: A concerned civic leader (Allen) decided to save a beloved institution (the Seahawks) and asked the citizens to help. On the other hand, Allen was hardly a disinterested elite. After all, he had already paid $200 million to purchase the Seahawks and clearly wanted to make money on the deal. He did not get to be the eighth richest man in the world by making bad investments. His neighbors would seem to be more civic-minded: they would get the "psychic income" of watching the Seahawks play, but they would not get any of Allen's profit. "I just don't recall ever seeing someone pick up a total tab for an election," a leading political scientist said at the time. "It bumps up against questions about just how far you can let democracy go. Do you then start letting some of the oil companies foot the bill for some referenda on cutting the gas tax?"[15]

HOW DEMOCRATIC IS AMERICAN GOVERNMENT?

Two hundred and twenty-five years after the founding of the United States, the Founders' new government is still standing mostly unchanged. The question is whether that government was and still is democratic. It is a difficult question to answer, if only because democracy depends on the consent of the governed and that consent is only given indirectly. Even voting is not a good measure of the consent of the governed. Many Americans stay home on election day because they are basically happy with the ways things are, others may see no real differences between the candidates; still others simply may not have the time to vote.

One way to test democracy is to measure it against procedures that are associated with the *possibility* of giving consent, even indirectly. Under the **procedural theory of democracy,** the focus is on *how* government makes decisions. Are all votes counted equally? Does the majority rule? Are elections fair? Consider the five tests used by political scientist G. Bingham Powell to measure democracies across the world:

1. *Most adults can participate in the electoral process.* Merely holding an election is not enough to guarantee democracy. The people must be able to participate. If the cost of voting in time and energy is too high, democracy cannot succeed.
2. *Voting is secret.* The people must be free to withhold their consent without fear that they will be punished by their own government. Dissent is essential to democracy.
3. *Leaders are chosen in free elections, contested by at least two political parties.* Democracy thrives on choices. Merely having an election does not make a democracy. Even dictatorships often hold elections.
4. *The government is required to act in response to elections.* Elections must make a difference in what government does. If a party loses, it must step down.
5. *There is freedom of speech, press, assembly, religion, and association.* Democracy also thrives when the people have the basic rights to make themselves heard (speech, assembly, and association), to inform themselves (press), and to hold their own beliefs (religion). Absent those rights, the people have no voice.[16]

Measured against these procedural tests, American democracy seems to be doing very well indeed. Most Americans *can* participate in elections; voting is entirely secret; most elections involve choices between two viable parties; the government does act in response to elections, as it did when Republicans became the majority party in Congress following their victories in the 1994 elections; and Americans enjoy all of the freedoms listed above. Indeed, Americans have never had more interest groups to join (freedom of assembly), more ways to influence government (freedom to petition), more sources of news (freedom of the press), more ways to speak, and more choices of religion than they do today.

One can celebrate the current possibilities for a vibrant democratic life, yet there is cause for concern. Americans may have the freedom to participate, but many refuse to exercise it. Most elections may involve two candidates, but there may be little difference between the two. Moreover, increasing numbers of elections are uncontested, meaning that only the incumbent officeholder is on the ballot. In 1998, for example, almost a quarter of the 435 elections for House seats were uncontested.

Homelessness can be seen as one measure of how well American government works in terms of the substantive theory of democracy. While the procedural theory of democracy might ask whether homeless people are allowed to vote and otherwise partici- pate freely in democratic life, the substantive theory would ask how a government founded on the notion that all people are created equal could allow homelessness to persist.

These numbers illustrate a second way to test democracy. Instead of asking whether democratic procedures are actually in place, the **substantive theory of democracy** asks whether the actual outcomes are democratic. The question is not whether all votes are equal in a specific congressional election, for example, but whether the House of Representatives as a whole represents the nation. It is en- tirely possible that every congressional election would be fair, every vote would be counted equally, and every American would vote, but that the House would end up being entirely composed of white, male, highly educated elites, which would hardly appear democratic to many Americans, who increasingly happen to be not white and anything but a majority male.

Consider the recent effort to measure the quality of American democratic life by the National Commission on Civic Renewal, which was chaired by former Sena- tor Sam Nunn, a Georgia Democrat, and former Reagan administration Secretary of Education William Bennett, a Republican. The commission clearly believed that the procedures of democracy were mostly intact. It was the actual participation that was in doubt. "Too many of us have become passive and disengaged," the commis- sion concluded in the summer of 1998. "Too many of us lack confidence in our ca- pacity to make basic moral and civic judgments, to join with our neighbors to do the work of community, to make a difference. . . . Never have we had so many op- portunities for participation, yet rarely have we felt so powerless. In a time that cries out for civic action, we are in danger of becoming a nation of spectators."[17]

The numbers seem to confirm the gap between the procedures and the substance of democracy. According to the commission's Index of National Civic Health (INCH), the substance of democracy can be measured by rates of political participation, political and social trust, membership in interest groups and other civic associations such as the League of Women Voters, family stability, and crime. The overall numbers diagrammed in Box 1–3 reflect sharp declines in all forms of political participation, some modest recent improvements in public trust in government, a leveling off of crime in all categories except for the rate of youth murders, a stabilization of divorce rates, and high numbers of out-of-marriage births.

BOX **1-3**

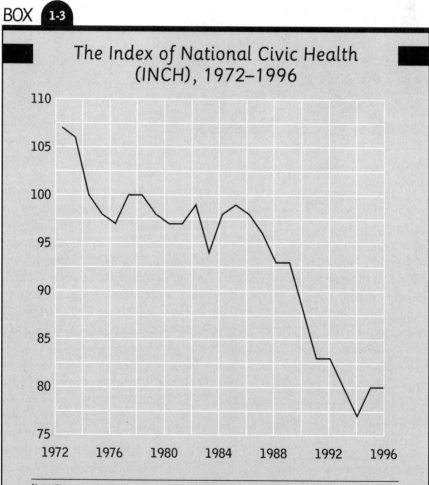

The Index of National Civic Health (INCH), 1972–1996

Note: The year 1974 is a baseline, set at 100. The graph shows change relative to that year.

Source: National Commission on Civic Renewal, *A Nation of Spectators* (Washington, D.C.: National Commission on Civic Renewal, 1998).

That the commission used divorce and out-of-marriage births in a general measure of civic health testifies to the problems in using the substantive theory of democracy. A different commission with different cochairs could just as easily have argued that the substance of democracy is to be found in the income gap between rich and poor Americans, which would have pushed the INCH even lower over time, or in the number of minority senators (exactly 2 out of 100), or in public support for abortion rights, or even in tolerance of gay and lesbian marriages. How one measures the substance of democracy depends largely on one's own view of how America should behave. Whether democracy passes that test depends largely on who has a voice in America's representative democracy.

☀ in a different light —— GATED COMMUNITIES

Every morning, tens of millions of schoolchildren start their day by reciting the Pledge of Allegiance: "I pledge allegiance to the flag of the United States of America, and to the republic for which it stands, one nation, under God, indivisible, with liberty and justice for all."

At the end of the day, however, increasing numbers of children go home to one of the 20,000 gated communities that have sprung up across a divided America. Gated communities, or residential community associations, as they are sometimes called, are higher-income, private housing developments whose residents usually pay a fee for common services such as garbage pickup, private police, and park maintenance.

Gated communities reject many of the basic procedures of democracy. Residents must abide by the covenant of the community, which governs everything from who can drive on the streets, to whether they can build basketball hoops in their driveways, to what color they can paint their shutters. Homeowners who break the rules can be fined by the development or forced to leave. People who live in these communities appear ready to surrender a great deal of their individual freedom in return for the safety and property value that come from building a wall around their communities.[18]

Gated communities have become particularly popular in large urban areas where crime and poor government services have led a growing number of Americans to leave their traditional neighborhoods. Roughly 28 million Americans now live in gated communities around the country, a number that may rise to 50 million by the year 2000. As many as eight out of every ten new inner-city real estate projects are gated, while a third of all new suburban developments in Southern California are what one pair of scholars describe as "fortified."[19] Some include private schools, grocery stores, and fitness centers, all of which are open only to homeowners in the development. Since the streets are all private, many gated communities do not even appear on the local road maps.

The rise of gated communities presents two challenges to the Founders' vision of democracy. First, residents are often separated from the rest of society, commuting to work in the morning and returning directly home at night. Cut off from the real problems of the cities and ongoing contact with people not like themselves, residents can lose touch with the "commons," that is, the shared concerns that affect all Americans.

Second, the residents may be unwilling to pay taxes to support their local or state governments. Why should they pay for public services they do not consume? The problem is that residents of gated communities are usually very well off financially. To the extent they are allowed to opt out of paying local taxes, the rest of the city suffers. The result may be a growing difference in the quality of the streets,

A guard checks all cars in and out of one of the nation's 20,000 gated communities. Like most gated communities, this one has private roads, sewer system, parks, and playgrounds. House colors and shrubbery heights are tightly regulated by the residents' association, which has the legal authority to enforce its rules.

parks, and services inside and outside the gated communities. And there is no wall high enough to keep out the social unrest that might eventually arise in response to these differences. Indeed, there is some evidence to suggest that gated communities are no safer than other communities. Nor do they appear to offer any greater return on real estate investment.

Alongside what may be a false sense of security and a false hope for higher property values, gated communities do not appear to have higher levels of political participation or any greater sense of community spirit. Once inside the gates, residents appear to be just as apathetic as they would have been outside. Although residents are clearly ready to pay for a higher quality of life within their gated communities, they do not appear ready to give their own time and energy to get it. Many are "checkbook citizens" who pay for the privilege of being left alone. As such, they may not be very different from the rest of America. Politics is becoming a spectator sport in almost every corner of the country.

Ultimately, the difference between gated communities and the rest of America is that the citizens inside the gates are pretty much the same. They may disagree about shrubbery height and acceptable paint color, but are very much alike in their overall view of the world. By debating only among themselves, they learn little about the quality of life in the rest of their cities, thereby widening the gap between life inside and outside the gates.

A Government of Which People?

Questions of who has a voice in democracy are played out every day in Washington, in who testifies before Congress, who serves as a presidential appointee in the executive branch, who brings a case before the Supreme Court, even who gets appointed to commissions such as the National Commission on Civic Renewal.[20] Even today, America's government of the people is not always a government of *all* the people.

George Washington had little trouble appointing a government that looked like "the people" as defined by the Constitution in 1789. He simply appointed white, male property owners. Those were the only people recognized as citizens under the state laws then in effect. New York voters had to own roughly $40 worth of property and voters in Massachusetts $120, a considerable amount of money at the time. Although the Constitution did not restrict the vote to property owners, it, too, defined "the people" as white males—thus ignoring the half of the

4 million Americans who happened to be women, as well as the one-sixth who were slaves.

America had clearly changed by the bicentennial of the Constitution in 1987. States had lowered the barriers to voting, sometimes on their own, sometimes under orders from the Supreme Court, sometimes under constitutional amendments. The Fifteenth Amendment (1870) gave the vote to males of all races; the Nineteenth (1920) to women; the Twenty-sixth (1971) to citizens over the age of eighteen.

Today, presidents not only are free to appoint women and minorities to their administrations but would be criticized if they did not. The face of American government has changed dramatically as a result. The first people President Bill Clinton appointed to office looked almost exactly like the rest of America: 13 percent were African American, compared to 12 percent of the general public; 46 percent were women, compared to 51 percent of the general public.

Nevertheless, America is still some distance from having a government of all the people. Most presidential appointees, members of Congress, and federal judges are highly educated, and many enter public service after high-paying careers in business. Clinton's first department secretaries may have looked like the rest of America, but almost half had done their undergraduate work at Harvard, Yale, or Stanford, and almost all had graduate degrees. Two-thirds were lawyers and one-fifth had doctorates.[21] As for income, the Clinton appointees hardly had bank accounts like most other Americans. All had made $200,000 or more in the year before joining the administration. Clinton's secretary of labor had made $540,000 and his secretary of education even more. Even the relatively young White House staff had substantial resources; thirty-something George Stephanopoulos was able to purchase an $835,000 Washington office building as an investment in 1994.[22]

As the Clinton appointments suggest, American government may look more like the rest of the country today, but may be just as unrepresentative of ordinary Americans as George Washington's administration was 225 years ago. The Americans who are most likely to have a voice in this representative democracy are the ones with the resources to participate, which means time, political skills, and money.

The Test of Time

If there is any absolute test of democracy, perhaps it is in sheer survival. A democracy that cannot pass the test of time is arguably a democracy that has failed. Much as the Founders wanted their new government to protect individual freedom, their first priority in going to Philadelphia was to protect the nation against a rising tide of internal dissent and clear threats from America's old enemy, Britain. Within a quarter century, America would go to war with Britain again, this time in the War of 1812.

The face of American government has changed dramatically since George Washington appointed all white males to his first Cabinet of department secretaries in 1789. Although Bill Clinton's first Cabinet appointees in 1993 were much more diverse in gender and race, they were also better educated and had higher incomes than Washington's appointees 200 years before, and therefore, perhaps just as out of touch with the lives of ordinary Americans.

That America survived its first thirty years is actually something of a miracle.[23] There were repeated threats to the new government: riots, highly unpopular government decisions, and at least two times when America came close to civil war, once surrounding preparations for a war with France and a second time over the deadlocked 1800 election.[24]

If only Americans understood what was at risk in the founding, perhaps they would be more engaged in democratic life today. Even as they celebrate the Fourth of July each summer, fully a quarter of Americans do not know just what happened more than 225 years ago to make the day special, and more than half see the holiday more as an opportunity to be with friends and families or just another day off from work than as a day to honor the history and freedoms of the country.[25] (July 4 did not become a holiday until 1783, seven years after the Declaration of Independence was signed. Until then, Independence Day was celebrated on March 5, marking the day in 1770 when British soldiers fired on unarmed protesters in the Boston Massacre, sparking the Revolutionary War.[26])

That American democracy has survived the past thirty years is also something of a miracle. The 1960s witnessed three assassinations (President John F. Kennedy, civil rights leader Rev. Martin Luther King, Jr., and Bobby Kennedy, a senator and presidential candidate), an unpopular war in Vietnam, and dozens of race riots in America's largest cities. The 1970s produced the Watergate scandal, the first president to resign in disgrace, economic chaos, and the Iranian hostage crisis, in which 90 U.S. diplomats were held captive for 444 days as their nation stood helpless. The 1980s produced more economic crisis, a soaring federal deficit, an international scandal involving the sale of arms to Iran in return for aid to the *contra* rebels in Nicaragua, and dozens of indictments of government officials for petty fraud. And the 1990s brought the Los Angeles riots in 1992, a rising tide of domestic terrorism that culminated in the Oklahoma City bombing in 1995, campaign finance scandals in 1996, and allegations about a sexual relationship between the president of the United States and a White House intern in 1998.

Yet, through it all, American democracy, and the liberty it both protects and reflects, endures at home and spreads to the rest of the world. At the end of the 1980s, it was the United States that remained standing and the repressive Soviet empire that lay in ruins.

Take away the computers, compact disks, and Rollerblades, and the America of today is strikingly similar to the America of the Founders. Colonial America was sharply divided on the issues of the day. The population was growing rapidly and was highly mobile. The economic "haves" tried to protect their interests as best they could; the "have-nots" wanted a piece of the growing economy. And civil unrest was frequent and violent—historian Richard Brown has counted at least twenty-eight riots between 1760 and 1775.[27] The same social and economic tensions are evident today, and may even be growing as America becomes more diverse and the distance between the richest and the poorest increases.

The nation is hardly bracing for another revolution. Americans remain too patriotic to engage in overthrows. At the same time, a 1997 survey by the Pew Research Center found that more than a quarter of Americans say that violent action against the government is justified under certain circumstances. The feeling is particularly pronounced among two groups of Americans: young men aged 18 to 29, and those who feel that the federal government controls too much of our daily lives. Roughly 40 percent of both groups said violent action can be justified in some cases.[28]

More important for testing the quality of democratic life is the fact that Americans remain remarkably distrustful toward government and each other. Just as the Founders felt the British government was unresponsive and oppressive in 1776, many Americans today believe that their government creates far more problems than it solves. In 1998, for example, only a quarter of Americans said that the federal government does an excellent or good job of running its programs, while just under 40 percent said that they could trust the government in Washington to do the right thing most or all of the time. At the same time, almost nine out of ten Americans said that politicians will say and do anything to get elected, then do pretty much whatever they want, while seven in ten agreed that government is run for the benefit of special interests. As for trusting each other, barely one in three Americans said most people can be trusted, while the rest say that "you can't be too careful in dealing with people."

Together, these parallels between the past and present suggest that striking a delicate balance is just as important today as it ever was. America has never had more factions, and James Madison's angels are in painfully short supply. It is precisely in moments of deep cynicism that American government seems to work best. As hard as Americans might push for immediate action to solve whatever problem might be at the top of the list, their government was designed to take its time. The delay may be frustrating, even enraging, but it prevents government from swinging too far in one direction or the other in times of great public passion. In such times, patience is very much a democratic virtue.

Whatever its flaws in giving each American a voice, the Founders' government has passed the survival test, at least so far. Although there have been times when it has clearly made terrible mistakes, such as allowing slavery to exist until the Civil War and suppressing free speech during the 1950s, American government has always been able to restore the delicate balance.

MAINTAINING THE BALANCE

It is no wonder that Americans are more frustrated than angered by the current stalemate and confusion in Washington. In their quest to create a government strong enough to protect a young nation, yet not so strong as to threaten liberty, the Founders created a government capable of absolute stalemate.

It is a government that can work very well, as it did during the Gulf War of 1991, and as it does every day in making sure the Social Security checks go out on time. But it is also a government that can teeter on the edge of what appears to be complete collapse, as it did in the fall and winter of 1995, when most federal departments and agencies were closed while Congress and the president battled over the federal budget. With the Washington Monument, the Statue of Liberty, the National Air and Space Museum, and Yellowstone Park all closed, and with federal workers standing in the unemployment lines, Americans had to wonder what kind of government they had. How can America be competitive in a global economy when its government cannot pass a budget on time?

The answer is that Americans have a democratic government that is constantly seeking balance. It was designed to work very well when the nation is threatened from inside or out, but not very well when the public is sharply divided. The fact is that a single committee of Congress, a single strong-willed president, a single federal court, even a single U.S. senator can sometimes bring the entire system to its knees. That is exactly what the Founders wanted. They were hardly perfect, but they did know how to design a government that would be easy to stalemate.

Thus, the Founders would not be troubled a bit by a government shutdown, not unless it threatened the safety of the nation as a whole. A few days without access to the Washington Monument to protect liberty? George Washington would hardly object. A few days without hot food at the Mount Rushmore snack bar to protect minority rights? Thomas Jefferson would be absolutely delighted.

But let that same shutdown weaken the government's ability to protect the nation, and the Founders would mind very much indeed. A few days without supplies for the Navy to score a political point? A week without cancer research to satisfy an interest group's demand? A month without food safety inspections to raise some campaign money? The Founders would be outraged. That is certainly how the American people felt when the shutdowns occurred. In fact, they were so angry that Congress and the president were actually forced to negotiate the first balanced budget agreement in nearly three decades. The key to maintaining the delicate balance is to recognize when government has gone too far in either threatening basic rights or threatening its own survival.

THE PLAN OF THE BOOK

Each chapter in this book will examine the delicate balance in more detail, asking how the search for balance continues today. Chapters 2 and 3 cover the basic structure of American government. Chapter 2 discusses the Constitution, asking why the Founders went to Philadelphia in the summer of 1787 and how they forged the compromises essential to building a democracy. Chapter 3 continues the discussion of the Founders' work by examining the ways in which national, state, and local governments fit together.

Chapters 4–9 focus on how the people participate in democratic life. Chapter 4 examines public opinion—where it comes from, how people organize ideas, and why they think what they think. Chapter 5 turns to the role of the media, both traditional media (newspapers and network television) and new media (cable television and the Internet), in shaping what people think about government and politics. Chapter 6 addresses the role of political parties in American government, whether in recruiting candidates before each campaign, shaping the platform of ideas at the nominating conventions, or organizing Congress after the ballots are counted. Chapter 7 explores the impact of interest groups as institutions that exist between the people and government, informing, interpreting, and even creating public pressure for action or inaction. Chapter 8 focuses on how citizens participate in democratic life, with a particular emphasis on the rules that affect who gets to vote, while Chapter 9 examines the role of campaigns in shaping how voters actually make the choice among candidates on election day.

Chapters 10–13 examine the institutions of government, asking how the legislative, executive, and judicial branches work. Although the four chapters treat Congress, the presidency, the federal bureaucracy, and the judiciary as separate institutions, each follows a similar outline, asking what the Founders intended in creating the institution, discussing the "real" institution as it exists today, and concluding with questions about recent trends that may be undermining the delicate balance.

The last two chapters of the book look at the key products of America's democracy: civil liberties and civil rights, and public policy. Chapter 14 asks how the people are protected against their government and each other through civil liberties and civil rights. Chapter 15 examines public policy, with a particular focus on the economic and social trends that are shaping America's future.

terms to remember

government (p. 1)
politics (p. 1)
factions (p. 2)
republican form of government
  (p. 2)
republic (p. 2)
public policy (p. 3)
public administration (p. 4)
majoritarian representative
  democracy (p. 7)
autocracy (p. 7)
oligarchy (p. 7)
monarchy (p. 7)
democracy (p. 7)
direct democracy (p. 8)
representative democracy
  (p. 8)

referendum (p. 9)
initiative (p. 9)
majoritarianism (p. 10)
majority rule (p. 10)
minority rights (p. 10)
Bill of Rights (p. 10)
civil liberties (p. 10)
civil rights (p. 10)
elitism (p. 11)
interest groups (p. 11)
pluralism (p. 11)
pluralistic representative
  democracy (p. 11)
procedural theory of democracy (p. 14)
substantive theory of democracy (p. 15)

facts and interpretations

- The Founders wanted a government that would be strong enough to protect a young nation against foreign and domestic threats, but not so strong that it could ever be used to oppress the people. They rejected direct democracy because they did not trust the American people to govern themselves. Since there was no cure for the basic human tendency to divide into factions, the Founders built a majoritarian representative democracy, which vested power in those whom the people elect. There is some evidence that American democracy is changing into a pluralistic representative democracy, in which interest groups resolve most disputes through bargaining rather than majority votes.

- There are two ways to measure the success of a democratic government. The first is to check for basic democratic procedures. Do all adults have the right to vote? Is the nation free? By most measures of the procedural method, American government is very democratic. The second is to look for basic democratic outcomes. Are elections actually fair? Does the government truly represent the people? Because the substantive method depends on one's own view of right and wrong, it is difficult to use. Some Americans would use the widening gap between the rich and the poor to show that our government is anything but democratic. Others would use the divorce rate or the number of out-of-marriage births as signs of a decline in civic health.

- American government is a set of institutions (legislative, executive, and judicial) that set the rules for politics, the process by which people decide who gets what, when, and how. Politics is not something that just happens in government, however. It occurs in every corner of life, even in debates about where to go for dinner and what kind of pizza to order.

27

open questions

- What kind of government would the Founders have designed if they had had greater faith in human beings to resist great orators and clever advertising? Were they right or wrong about the public's ability to resist such appeals? Just how much do people need to know about an issue such as Social Security or the environment to earn the chance to participate more directly in democracy?

- When does government become too strong or too weak? Are there any things government does that are so important that it should violate minority rights to get them done? Delivering the mail? Supervising nuclear power plants? Inspecting food? Funding student loans? Issuing passports? What offices of government should have been kept open when the government was shut down in 1995?

- Who are the people? Does the fact that many of America's leaders are wealthy matter? Are all the people represented in the Founders' government? And if not, does it matter?

for further study

Bowen, Catherine Drinker. *Miracle at Philadelphia: The Story of the Constitutional Convention, May to September 1787.* Boston: Little, Brown, 1966.

Fairfield, Roy P., ed. *The Federalist Papers.* Baltimore: Johns Hopkins University Press, 1981.

Morone, James A. *The Democratic Wish: Popular Participation and the Limits of American Government.* New York: Basic Books, 1990.

Pew Research Center for the People & the Press. *Deconstructing Distrust: How Americans View Government.* Washington, DC: Pew Research Center, 1998. All of the Pew surveys and reports are available on the Internet at www.people-press.org.

Sharp, James Roger. *American Politics in the Early Republic: The New Nation in Crisis.* New Haven, CT: Yale University Press, 1993.

endnotes for chapter 1

1. Harold D. Lasswell, *Politics: Who Gets What, When, and How* (New York: McGraw-Hill, 1938).
2. In Roy P. Fairfield, ed., *The Federalist Papers* (Baltimore: Johns Hopkins University Press, 1981), p. 160.
3. For an alternative view, see Benjamin Page and Robert Shapiro, *The Rational Public: Fifty Years of Trends in Americans' Policy Preferences* (Chicago: University of Chicago Press, 1992).
4. Fairfield, ed., *The Federalist Papers,* p. 206.
5. Quoted in James A. Morone, *The Democratic Wish: Popular Participation and the Limits of American Government* (New York: Basic Books, 1990), p. 33.
6. Fairfield, ed., *The Federalist Papers,* p. 22.
7. Fairfield, ed., *The Federalist Papers,* p. 198.
8. Alexis Simendinger, "Of the People, for the People," *National Journal,* April 18, 1998, p. 851; All quotes in this section are from this article.
9. See Page and Shapiro, *The Rational Public.*
10. Pew Research Center for The People & The Press, *Deconstructing Distrust: How Americans View Government* (Washington, DC: Pew Research Center, 1998). All of the Pew surveys and reports are available on the Internet at <www.people-press.org>.
11. Edward Dumbauld, ed., *The Political Writings of Thomas Jefferson: Representative Selections* (New York: Liberal Arts Press, 1955), p. 93.
12. Fairfield, ed., *The Federalist Papers,* p. 20.
13. E. E. Schattschneider, *Two Hundred Million Americans in Search of a Government* (New York: Holt, Rinehart and Winston, 1969), p. 63.
14. Catherine Drinker Bowen, *Miracle at Philadelphia: The Story of the Constitutional Convention, May to September 1787* (Boston: Little, Brown, 1966), p. 72.
15. The quote is from University of North Carolina political scientist Thad Beyle in Carey Goldberg, "Billionaire Finances a Vote About Replacing a Stadium," *New York Times,* May 25, 1997, p. A14.
16. G. Bingham Powell, Jr., *Contemporary Democracies* (Cambridge, MA: Harvard University Press, 1982), p. 3.

17. National Commission on Civic Renewal, *A Nation of Spectators* (Washington, DC: National Commission on Civic Renewal, 1998), p. 5.

18. Timothy Egan, "The Serene Fortress: A Special Report: Many Seek Security in Private Communities," *New York Times,* September 3, 1995, p. A1.

19. Edward J. Blakely and Mary Gail Snyder, *Fortress America: Gated Communities in the United States* (Washington, DC: Brookings Institution, 1997), p. 7.

20. The National Commission was funded under a grant from the Pew Charitable Trusts of Philadelphia, and was selected through a detailed review process conducted by former White House aide William Galston, a Democrat, with input from the two cochairs, Nunn and Bennett. I was the Pew official who oversaw the grant and had some input on the selection of the commission, but not on the development of or selection of indicators used in the Index of National Civic Health.

21. These figures are drawn from Martha Farnsworth Riche, "An Administration That Mirrors America," *Washington Post National Weekly Edition,* January 31–February 6, 1994, p. 25.

22. See Thomas Dye, "The Friends of Bill and Hillary," *PS: Political Science and Politics,* 26, no. 4 (December 1993): 1647–1661.

23. See James Roger Sharp, *American Politics in the Early Republic: The New Nation in Crisis* (New Haven, CT: Yale University Press, 1993).

24. See Sharp, *American Politics in the Early Republic,* Chapter One.

25. Survey conducted by the ABC News/*Washington Post* Poll on July 19, 1986.

26. Among the first to fall was a former slave named Crispus Attucks. For his story, see William C. Nell, *The Colored Patriots of the American Revolution* (New York: Arno Press and the *New York Times,* 1968, originally published in Boston, 1855).

27. Richard Brown, "Violence and the American Revolution," in S. Kurtz and J. Hutson, eds., *Essays on the American Revolution* (Chapel Hill: University of North Carolina Press, 1973), pp. 101 ff.

28. Pew Research Center, *Deconstructing Distrust,* p. 52.

the constitution

the revolutionary mind

The Founders of the United States of America arrived in Philadelphia for the Constitutional Convention in 1787 with strong opinions about government. As leaders of the American Revolution and future drafters of the Constitution, the Founders most certainly knew what they did not like about government. They had been oppressed for decades by a British government that was much too strong, but were being poorly served by a new American government that was much too weak. They understood the delicate balance between the two extremes.

They wanted a government that would be strong enough to hold the nation together as it grew and prospered, but would be limited enough to avoid the oppression that had sparked the American Revolution.

The Founders also knew what they liked about their own state and local governments. Many had helped draft their state constitutions, and all had some experience with the institutions of government. Eleven of the thirteen states had two-house, **bicameral legislatures** for making the laws; nine had a single executive for executing the laws; and all had state courts for protecting the rights of citizens and enforcing the laws. It is no surprise, therefore, that the Founders eventually gave their new government legislative, executive, and judicial powers. It was the prevailing wisdom of the time about how to build a government.

The Founders did not like everything about their state governments, however. Even though most states required their governors and legislators to own property as a condition of holding office, for example, the Founders rejected a similar requirement for the president and members of Congress. Members of the North Carolina legislature had to own at least 100 acres of land, while the governor of South Carolina had to have an estate worth at least 10,000 British pounds, a huge sum of money at that time. The Founders also decided not to include a bill of rights in their first draft of the Constitution, in part because most states already provided basic protections in their own constitutions. Although Virginia was the only state with a comprehensive Declaration of Rights, the Founders simply felt a national bill of rights was redundant. (As we will see later in this chapter, they added one later.)

Before turning to the Founders' work in more detail, it will be useful to make two points about the Constitutional Convention. The first is that the Founders did not go to Philadelphia with the explicit purpose of writing a new constitution. Rather, they were appointed by their states after the Continental Congress called a convention "for the sole and express purpose of revising the Articles of Confederation." One historian argues that two-thirds of the Founders would have stayed home had they known they would end up writing a new constitution.[1] Once in Philadelphia, however, the delegates soon concluded that the Articles could not be saved, for reasons that will be explained later. They would have to start over from scratch.

Drawing upon their own experience as pragmatic politicians, the Founders began building a new government. Some argued for a three-headed presidency; others for a single-house legislature; still others for the popular election of the president, a debate that was settled only after sixty ballots in the convention. The Founders generally agreed that they wanted the new government to have some kind of **legislative branch,** composed of a body of elected representatives to make the laws; an **executive branch,** composed of one or more presidents and their appointees to execute the laws; and a **judicial branch,** composed of a supreme court, and any other "inferior" courts the legislative branch might invent, to interpret the laws and protect individual rights.

Beyond these three basic components, the details were in flux. As the convention dragged on through the long summer, the debate pitched back and forth over a host of proposals, most of which sought to balance the power of the big states against the rights of the small ones. Ultimately, the debate turned on one central question: How could the new government be made strong enough to protect the young nation, yet not so strong as to threaten liberty itself? Although Americans frequently complain about how little gets done in Washington, the Founders arrived at an ingenious answer. Their new government would be able to act with surprising speed and strength in answering threats to its survival, but would otherwise be easy to stalemate. They created a government that would teeter precariously on the verge of complete frustration, but one that would be difficult for strong-willed majorities intent on oppression to capture. It would strike a balance between strength and limits on strength.

The second key point about the Constitutional Convention is that it was anything but an abstract intellectual exercise. Most of the Founders went to Philadelphia convinced that the nation was on the verge of collapse. America was hardly a superpower yet, and was saddled with a huge debt from fighting the Revolutionary War. The convention delegates were hard-nosed politicians who desperately needed some way to keep their young nation alive.

Because the Constitution would have to be approved by a two-thirds majority of the state legislatures, the Founders had to design a government that the country would support: one not so strong as to frighten an anxious public, but not so weak as to fail in the future. This chapter will review the compromises leading up to the final design, as well as the design itself. It will end by showing how the Constitution is a work in progress—that is, how the Founders always intended American government to change with the times.

PRELUDE TO A CONSTITUTION

It would have been easy for the Founders to build a government solely to defend the nation from foreign or domestic threat. They could have given it only the power to raise money, draft soldiers, and fight wars. Having fought for ten years to break free of just such an oppressive government, however, the Founders clearly understood that government could be used for good or ill. They also knew that a government built to simultaneously protect the nation as a whole and its citizens as individuals is quite different from a government built to do one or the other. Combining these two very different goals assured that American government would be relatively easy to stalemate.

Revolutionary Thinking

No single outrage sparked the American Revolution. Rather, the Revolution reflected what Thomas Jefferson called a long train of insults and injuries. Most of the insults and injuries involved British efforts to raise money from the colonies. The most infamous insult of all was the Tea Act of 1773, which raised the price of tea dramatically and prompted 150 colonists to disguise themselves as Mohawk Indians and dump three cargo holds of tea into Boston Harbor. (See Box 2–1 for a list of major events leading to the Revolution.)

Taken one by one, none of the insults and injuries was enough to cause a war. But together, each one added to the growing realization that America had to break free of British rule. "What do we mean by the American Revolution?" John Adams asked in 1818. "Do we mean the American war? The Revolution was effected before the war commenced. The Revolution was in the minds and hearts of the people; a change in their religious sentiments, of their duties and obligations . . . . This radical change in the principles, opinions, sentiments and affections of the people was the real American Revolution."[2]

No one was more important to this revolution of ideas than John Locke, an English political philosopher who had written his *Second Treatise of Government* in the 1600s. Locke had argued that people enjoyed certain natural, or unalienable, rights, which included "life, health, liberty, and possessions."[3] The role of government is not to give people these natural rights, but to protect the rights that people already have.

Locke had also argued that government was merely a mechanism created by the people for the people. Government retained its power only if it did not violate the natural rights of the people. People do not give up their rights just because they vote for a president or a member of Congress. Rather, the people give their *consent* to be governed, and always retain their absolute right to change their minds. The people, not the government, are always the best judges of their best interests. Government should be limited to what the people want, enact only those laws that are necessary and good for the people, and never raise taxes without the consent of the people, whether given directly or through their elected representatives.[4]

The colonists blended Locke's thinking with their own experience to create an image of government that was in direct contrast with what was happening in the 1760s and 1770s. It is not that the colonists wanted to fight the British. They had fought side by side with the British in the 1763 French and Indian War, which had given the British complete ownership of everything east of the Missis-

BOX **2-1**

Steps toward War

1763	The colonists and British celebrate their victory in the French and Indian War.
1764	The British Parliament passes the Sugar Act of 1764, placing a tax on sugar, coffee, wine and similar imports as a way to pay for the defense of the colonies and retire debt from the French and Indian War.
1765	Parliament passes the Stamp Act of 1765, placing a tax on all printed materials, from newspapers to playing cards.
1766	Parliament repeals the Stamp Act after the colonies stage a successful boycott of English goods.
1767	Parliament passes more taxes in the Townshend Revenue Acts. The colonies again boycott British goods, cutting imports by half.
1770	Tensions erupt in the March 5 Boston Massacre, leaving five colonists dead. Parliament rescinds the Townshend Acts and withdraws the troops. The boycotts also end.
1773	The calm lasts for three years, until Parliament imposes the Tea Act. Colonists hold the Boston Tea Party on December 16.
1774	To punish the colonies for the Tea Party, Parliament passes the Coercive Acts, which are quickly relabeled by the colonists as the Intolerable and Coercive Acts.
1774	From September 5 to October 26, 1774, the First Continental Congress meets in Philadelphia. The Congress adopts a resolution opposing the Coercive Acts.
1775	The Revolutionary War begins on April 18 with the Battle of Lexington and Concord. Eight Minutemen and seventy-three British soldiers die.
1775	The Second Continental Congress appoints George Washington to lead the Continental Army into war.
1776	The Congress appoints a committee to write a formal declaration of independence from England. On July 4, the Congress adopts Thomas Jefferson's draft of the Declaration of Independence.

sippi River. Rather, the colonists simply believed that they had the same unalienable rights to life, liberty, and the pursuit of happiness as all British citizens. As the British increased the troops and taxes, the colonists concluded that they would never be accepted as true citizens of England, but would always be subjects of an increasingly oppressive government.

Having decided that a separation from Britain was nearly inevitable, the Founders convened the **First Continental Congress** in September 1774. When most Americans think of Congress today, they think of a building in Washington or their own representative or senator. But in 1774, *Congress* was a term that meant an assembly of delegates from the colonies. Although it drew delegates to Philadelphia from every colony but Georgia, the First Continental Congress provided little drama. It stated its opposition to the latest British tax increase, supported a boycott of British products, passed a few other resolutions of minor note, and adjourned with plans to meet again in May 1775. It was the fact that it met that mattered most. The colonies were starting to come together to determine their future; they were asserting their right to legislate for themselves and denying England's right to do it for them.

By the time the **Second Continental Congress** met as scheduled the following year, the Revolutionary War had begun. In April 1775, British troops had marched from Boston to Concord, Massachusetts, in an effort to capture a stock of colonists' rifles and ammunition. They were intercepted in Lexington by a loosely formed group of seventy soldiers called the Minutemen, who had been alerted by Paul Revere's famous ride. As the British marched on, a single shot was fired (the shot heard 'round the world), the British fired back, and eight Minutemen were killed on the village green. The colonists quickly regrouped and killed seventy-three British soldiers on the road back to Boston.

Search as one may through the history books, one will never find a formal declaration of war. It would have taken weeks to convene an emergency session of the Continental Congress. Even without a declaration, the nation moved quickly onto a war footing. Some colonies began drafting their own constitutions, others convened their own legislatures to endorse independence from Britain, and still others began raising their own armies, which would later be unified into General George Washington's Continental Army.

The Declaration of Independence

The Revolution did have a defining moment, however, when the Second Continental Congress signed the **Declaration of Independence** on July 4, 1776. Written by Jefferson, a young Virginia farmer selected for both his intellect and his writing abilities, the Declaration became the centerpiece of a broad campaign to convince the colonists of the need for war, while showing Britain that the colonists were serious. The centerpiece of the declaration is a single sentence:

"We hold these truths to be self-evident, that all men are created equal, that they are endowed by their Creator with certain unalienable Rights, that among these are Life, Liberty and the pursuit of Happiness." It may be the most important sentence ever written in American political history, for it promised both a new society built on equality and a fundamental human right to freedom.

Jefferson's first draft of the Declaration was far from finished, however. It endured a series of heavy edits that whittled its length by nearly a third. Even then, politicians worried about holding the public's attention. Jefferson was outraged at the cuts, complaining later about the "mutilations" of his text. Instead of starting paragraph two with "We hold these truths to be sacred and undeniable," for example, the editing committee substituted "We hold these truths to be self-evident," removing an important reference to a higher power as the source of basic rights. Although most of the edits merely replaced one word with another, one of the lost passages clearly helped define what Jefferson meant in stating that "all men are created equal." Dropped from the list of insults was an attack on the King of England for having tolerated the slave trade:

> He has waged cruel war against human nature itself, violating its most sacred rights of life and liberty in the persons of a distant people who never offended him, captivating & carrying them into slavery in another hemisphere, or to incur miserable death in their transportation thither. . . . Determined to keep open a market where MEN should be bought & sold, he has [used his power to suppress] every legislative attempt to prohibit or restrain their execrable commerce.[5]

Did Jefferson mean that slaves were, in fact, people, as the first lost sentence implies (and as most slaveholders denied)? Did he also mean that women were, in fact, equal, as the use of the word *MEN* as a substitute for *humankind* in the second lost sentence seems to suggest? No one will ever know the answer, for the delegates from Georgia and South Carolina insisted that the paragraph be cut. It does seem reasonable to suggest, however, that the Constitution might not have so easily dismissed slaves and women ten years later had the Declaration been clearer in its choice of language.

The Declaration is best remembered as an invitation to revolution. The Second Continental Congress convened on July 2, 1776, with the express purpose of declaring independence, which it immediately did by a vote of 11 to 0 (Rhode Island's delegation was absent and New York's remained undecided on the issue until mid-August). John Adams predicted that July 2 would be celebrated by "succeeding generations as the great anniversary Festival. It ought to be solemnized with Pomp and Parades, with Shews, Games, Sports, Guns, Bells, Bonfires, and Illuminations from one End of this Continent to the other from this Time forward ever more." He had the right prediction, of course, just the wrong date. The actual document called the Declaration of Independence was adopted two days later as the stuff of which future anniversary festivals would be made.

in a different light ——

**THE RADICAL
REVOLUTION**

The American Revolution was about much more than "no taxation without repre-sentation" or the "long train of insults and injuries" listed in the Declaration of In-dependence. It was a fundamental break with all things British, and marked one of the most radical moments in political history. The Founders not only forged a new kind of government, they emphatically rejected the old.

They also created a unique revolution. Unlike the fall of the Soviet Union, which involved a tank battle in front of the Russian parliament, or the failed revolu-tion in China, which involved a massacre in Tiananmen Square, the American Revo-lution was launched with a barrage of ideas. "We cannot quite conceive of revolutionaries in powdered hair and knee breeches," writes Pulitzer Prize-winning historian Gordon S. Wood of the radicalism of the American Revolution. "They made speeches, not bombs; they wrote learned pamphlets, not manifestos."[6]

A solitary protester stops a Chinese tank in Tiananmen Square only hours before troops opened fire on the pro-democracy protesters. Most revolutions are violent, but the American Revolu-tion began with a barrage of ideas, not bombs.

Along the way, they also created a new society based on what Jefferson described as an "aristocracy of virtue and talent" to replace the British "aristocracy of wealth." Americans would be allowed to rise to their highest level on the basis of equality of opportunity, or so Jefferson hoped, not family connections or money. Gone would be the days when ordinary Americans would have to swear loyalty to a king to pursue their dreams; gone would be the days when they would have to stand aside when a "gentleman" passed on the street; gone would be any difference between the rulers and the ruled.

Thus, the Revolution marked a break not only with the British form of government, but also with the British form of social organization. Much as one can fault the Founders for ignoring slaves and women in their Republic, one cannot underemphasize how radical they were in declaring that all men are created equal. It was a statement that violated every principle governing British life, in which no one was equal to the King.

Viewed as such, the American Revolution lasted long after the war ended. "By the time the Revolution had run its course in the early nineteenth century," writes Wood, "American society had been radically and thoroughly transformed. One class did not overthrow another; the poor did not supplant the rich. But social relationships—the way people were connected one to another—were changed, and decisively so."[7] Once convinced that all men were, in fact, equal, Americans started behaving accordingly.

The changes can be seen to this day in Americans' overwhelming commitment to individual hard work. There are few things Americans admire more than people who get rich by working hard. In a November 1997 survey by the Pew Research Center for The People & The Press, two-thirds of a sample of Americans said that hard work is the best way to the top, and that success in life is mostly determined by forces within one's own control. Despite their faith in individual success, Americans do see a role for government in making sure everyone has a fair chance to make it to the top. Nine out of ten Americans believe that society should do what is necessary to make sure that everyone has an equal opportunity to succeed, while two-thirds say that it is the responsibility of government to take care of people who cannot take care of themselves.[8]

Wealth still plays a significant role in American society and politics, however. Witness the role of large campaign contributions in modern elections. But wealth is no guarantee of victory, and can create a backlash among voters. In the 1998 California governor's race, for example, Northwest Airlines owner Al Checci spent $40 million of his own money to win the Democratic nomination only to come in third in the election. Americans may admire self-made millionaires such as Checci, but they do not want elections to become auctions going to the highest bidder. Unfortunately, as Chapter 9 will suggest, America's elections may be heading in that direction.

War and Peace

Launched with the call to liberty, the **Revolutionary War** eventually became one of America's longest and costliest wars, lasting eight years (1775–1783), and creating a staggering debt for the new nation. (By comparison, the Civil War lasted five years, World War II less than four, Vietnam over ten, the 1991 Gulf War exactly 100 hours.) A quarter of a million colonists fought in the Revolutionary War, and casualties were often heavy. One-fourth of Washington's Continental Army froze to death at Valley Forge in the winter of 1778.

The war itself was an on-again/off-again event. There were years early on when the Continental Army was simply unable to fight. It was poorly equipped, poorly fed, and poorly paid. Many women followed their husbands, brothers, and fathers into the war. Some supported the troops by doing the laundry, cooking meals, and caring for the wounded. Others stood side by side with their husbands loading rifles and cannons. Still others fought in the war disguised as men. One woman, Deborah Sampson, eventually received a veteran's pension from the State of Massachusetts for her service; after she died, her husband was the first American to receive a pension as a soldier's widower. There was no controversy about women in combat in 1775. It was either pick up the rifle and reload the cannons of wounded or dead husbands or perish.[9]

What was remarkable was that the Continental Army was able to fight a war at all. The winter of 1778 was particularly demoralizing to the troops. According to one history of the war, Washington "wrote that the men starving at Valley Forge, leaving occasional bloody footprints in the snow for lack of shoes, would have been helpless against a British attack and unable to retreat for want of transport. The army was in even worse condition in 1780, when Washington wrote that the men had been 'five or six days together without meat; then as many without bread, and once or twice, two or three days without either. . . .'"[10]

The question, therefore, is how the Americans won the war. After all, the British had better training and weapons. They controlled the seas, and had more of just about everything a nation needs to win a war, including better uniforms. The one thing they did not have was leadership. They bungled nearly every engagement, while Washington seemed to make the most of whatever he had. Equally important, the British were absolutely unprepared for the American style of guerilla war. The British army was particularly skilled at fighting formal wars, forming ranks and firing in unison, while the colonists were gifted at hit-and-run tactics, moving quickly from skirmish to skirmish, rarely providing clean targets. As a result, the British were eventually worn down more by the nature of the conflict than by any stunning series of victories by the Continental Army. To be sure, they were defeated in key battles, including the final Battle of Yorktown. But they were also defeated by the sheer resolve of a newly independent nation. This was a war that America simply refused to lose.

A SUMMER OF REFORM

Even as the United States celebrated its hard-won victory, tensions across the thirteen newly independent states remained high. The tension culminated in a series of small "rebellions" against any kind of national government, be it strong or weak. The most infamous of the rebellions occurred in the summer of 1786, when a band of nearly one thousand men led by a former revolutionary soldier named Daniel Shays marched from Springfield, Massachusetts, to Boston in a violent protest about jobs and opportunity. The precise goals of the protest were unclear, yet four marchers died before it was over.

Troubling as it was as a sign of social unrest, **Shays's Rebellion** was just another in the long series of protests that had begun before the war and continued after it. Indeed, Jefferson remarked at the time that "A little rebellion now and then is a good thing. . . . God forbid that we should ever be twenty years without such a rebellion. . . . The tree of liberty must be refreshed from time to time with the blood of patriots and tyrants." This was easy for him to say, of course: he was in Paris at the time, serving as America's Ambassador to France.

Nevertheless, Shays's Rebellion convinced the Founders that America desperately needed a stronger national government than the one that had been established under the **Articles of Confederation.** Adopted in 1777 in the midst of war and ratified by all the states by 1781, the Articles of Confederation can be called America's first constitution. Under the Articles, the national government consisted of a single-house legislature with no formal executive or judicial branch. Most of the power remained in the thirteen states. Like the Declaration of Independence, the Articles were drafted in part to satisfy the public, which generally opposed any national government, and in part to satisfy the states. The result was a national government mostly incapable of protecting the nation from foreign or domestic threats. The problem was not a lack of either freedom or democracy, but an overabundance of both.

It was for the purpose of building a government that would balance strength and limits on strength that the fifty-five delegates went to Philadelphia in the summer of 1787.[11] Writers have usually described the summer as blistering hot, pre-

Washington presides over the Constitutional Convention in a painting by Stearns. The Founders had substantial experience in politics before coming to Philadelphia and organized the convention as a legislature, complete with committees, floor rules, and formal votes.

sumably to make drafting the Constitution seem an even more heroic act than it clearly was. In fact, the weather was rather cool as Philadelphia summers go. Temperatures were anything but cool in Independence Hall, however, as the delegates struggled to draft a new constitution in just four months, from May to September. The disagreements were sharp, dividing delegates of big and small states over who would control the new legislature, and between southern and northern states on how much power the new government would have to raise taxes.

How Strong a Government?

The first and most important debate centered on just how strong the new government should be. Led by James Madison, Virginia delegates offered their own vision, sometimes sharp and other times fuzzy, of a strong national government. Under what became known as the **Virginia Plan,** the new government would have three branches: a bicameral legislative branch to make the laws; an executive branch to implement and enforce the laws, led by an unspecified number of presidents appointed for a single term by the legislative branch; and a judicial branch to interpret the laws, composed of a supreme court and lower courts of some number and size. The people would elect one house of the new legislature; members of that chamber would select the members of the other house.

The national government would also have the power to reject, or **veto**, laws passed by the states, and a panel representing the executive and judicial branches would have the power to veto laws passed by the legislative branch, which would, in turn, have the power to overturn the veto (**veto override**). Although the convention would change parts of the plan, adding more specifics, the Virginia Plan set the basic agenda for what would be a much stronger national government.

The alternative vision was drafted by a single New Jersey delegate, William Paterson, in response. Under the **New Jersey Plan**, the national government would be far less powerful, perhaps even less powerful than it had been under the Articles of Confederation. The New Jersey Plan envisioned only two branches: a single-house, **unicameral legislature**, and a weak executive. There was no provision for a national court. Although the New Jersey Plan shared some features with the Virginia Plan, it represented a last gasp for supporters of a weak national government and was easily defeated at the beginning of the convention.

The New Jersey Plan did not disappear altogether, however. Unlike the Virginia Plan, which determined the number of seats in Congress by either the total population of or taxes paid by each state, the New Jersey Plan gave an equal number of slots to each state regardless of size. Small states were obviously drawn to the New Jersey view, while large states preferred the Virginia approach. The debate was finally resolved under the **Great Compromise** of early July, when the convention agreed to a two-house, bicameral legislature. Small states would be more heavily represented in the Senate (where each state would receive two seats regardless of size), large states would be more heavily represented in the House of Representatives (where seats would be apportioned, or granted, on the basis of population), and the power of taxation would be reserved for the House. Box 2–2 compares the Virginia and New Jersey Plans with the final compromise.

These compromises involved more than power politics between big states and small. In addition to their own experiences living under governments of one kind or another, the Founders read widely in the leading scholarship of their era. Benjamin Franklin was already an expert on the Iroquois Indian constitution, which had united the seven warring nations of the Iroquois; and James Madison quickly emerged as the convention's chief political philosopher. Before arriving in Philadelphia, he had asked Jefferson, who was still in Paris, to send "whatever may throw light on the general constitution."[12]

Founding Motives

The Founders had the education and income to be curious about different kinds of government. They did not get to be Founders without belonging to a distinguished elite. Forty-two of the original delegates had been members of the Continental Congress, thirty-one had attended college—Princeton claimed ten delegates among the fifty-five, William and Mary four, Yale three, Harvard two,

BOX **2-2**

The Constitution: The Great Compromise

	Virginia Plan	New Jersey Plan	The Constitution
Legislative authority	All national concerns	Limited	Broad
Type of legislature	Bicameral	Unicameral	Bicameral
Legislative power is derived from...	The people	The states	The people for the House and the states for the Senate
Each state is represented in the legislature...	Proportionally	Equally	Proportionally in the House and equally in the Senate
Number of executives	Unspecified	More than one	One
Legislature controlled by	Majority	Minority	Majority
Executive removed by	Congress	The states	Congress
Type of judiciary	National	No provision	National
Ratification required by	The people	The states	The people
Veto of executive decisions	By legislature and judicial panel	Not permitted	By legislature

and Columbia two—and thirty-four were practicing law. Although twenty-one of the delegates were under the age of forty, with the youngest twenty-six years old, most had accumulated at least some property along the way, including fifteen who owned slaves. They were, as historian James MacGregor Burns called them, "the well-bred, the well-fed, the well-read, and the well-wed."[13] Given their status and wealth, it is tempting to describe the origins of the Constitution in purely economic terms. Perhaps the Founders were concerned about protecting individual citizens because they were worried about their own economic interests.

That is exactly how historian Charles Beard described the founding in his 1913 book, *An Economic Interpretation of the Constitution.* According to Beard, there was no doubt about why the Founders worked through that long summer in Philadelphia: money. The Articles of Confederation had threatened the rich by giving the states too much power. No wonder the new government made passing legislation so difficult, Beard argued: the Founders did not want a popularly elected Congress and president forcing the rich to pay higher taxes or redistribute the wealth to the common people. In short, the Constitution could best be viewed as an economic document "drawn with superb skill by men whose property interests were immediately at stake."[14]

The only problem with Beard's interpretation is that it does not fit the facts. The Founders were certainly wealthier than average Americans, and more likely to own both land and slaves. And they were most certainly among the colonial elite. Yet there is little evidence that they schemed to protect their interests from an increasingly unhappy public. According to painstaking research by historian Forrest McDonald, the Founders did not act as a unified economic group, nor was ratification an expression of some great class struggle. Farmers, bankers, and merchants lined up on both sides of the ratification debate; so an economic interpretation is virtually useless in explaining the actual decisions in Philadelphia.[15]

The better explanation for what the Founders did rests in their worries about the future of the nation. Although their self-interest was obviously at stake if the young nation failed, the Founders went to Philadelphia because they believed that the nation was in crisis. Recalling the oppression of British rule, and having concluded that the Articles of Confederation had failed, the Founders set out to build a government strong enough to meet domestic and foreign threats, but not so strong as to threaten basic liberty.

 **in a different light** ——— **THE FOUNDERS AND SLAVERY**

A remarkable thing happened on the 200th anniversary of George Washington's inauguration as America's first president: the New Orleans school board prohibited any of its 121 schools to be named in honor of former slave owners. Most of the name changes involved switches from Confederate Civil War generals to African American heroes. Beauregard Junior High became Thurgood Marshall Middle School in honor of America's first African American Supreme Court justice; Robert

E. Lee Elementary became Ronald McNair Elementary in honor of the African American astronaut killed in the *Challenger* space shuttle explosion in 1986.

It all made sense in a modern context. "Why should African Americans want their kids to pay respect or pay homage to someone who enslaved their ancestors?" one advocate of the policy asked. "This was the most degrading thing that ever happened in North America." By applying today's standards to the past, which some historians call "presentism," New Orleans hoped to do the right thing for its student body, in which nine of ten students were African American.

The only problem was that one of the former slave owners caught in the name change was George Washington. In late 1997, George Washington Elementary became Dr. Charles Richard Drew Elementary. There is no question that Dr. Drew deserved honor, having invented the process for separating blood plasma. Nor is there any question that Washington owned as many as 316 slaves on his Mount Vernon plantation. He may have been troubled by slavery, and he may have ordered his slaves freed upon his death, but Washington was one of many Founders who benefited from the slave trade. So was Thomas Jefferson.

How could America's first president and its most eloquent champion of equality tolerate slavery? The simple answer is that both had economic interests in keeping slaves. Perhaps they tolerated the intolerable because they profited as a result. But that answer is much too simple. The reality is that the Founders would have lost the Constitution itself had they pushed for a final resolution of the slavery question. Even in 1787, southern states were willing to fight over the issue. If they had had to vote against the new Constitution to keep their slaves, they would have done so.

Slavery was hardly ignored at the Constitutional Convention. Southern states fought hard to defeat several motions to end slavery, and even managed to win a clause prohibiting Congress from taking any action to end the importation of slaves before 1808 (see Article I, Section 9, Subsection 1). Ironically, they also wanted to count every last slave in determining how many seats each state would earn in the new House of Representatives. If all slaves were counted as individual citizens, the South would have won more representatives; if they were not counted at all, the North would benefit. The Founders eventually agreed to the *three-fifths compromise,* which calculated each slave as three-fifths of a person toward the total population of a state.

Sadly, the Founders simply could not reach an agreement to end slavery. There is some confusion in the records as to what the passage in Article I meant. Some Founders thought the ban was a first step toward outright abolition of slavery after 1808; others, most notably Charles Pinckney of South Carolina, swore that no such agreement had been made. In the end, the ban may have been the kind of political agreement that allows each side to claim victory without making a final commitment at all, the kind made to this day by artful politicians who are not quite sure what they can deliver. Thus, the end of slavery was left to a future battlefield. Had the Founders known that so many thousands would die resolving the question in the Civil War, they might have tried harder to strike a compromise. Then again, such a compromise might have doomed the Constitution to defeat.

Looking back at the past with perfect hindsight is easy, of course, which is why New Orleans saw nothing wrong with changing the name of Washington Elementary. One cannot forgive Washington and Jefferson for their hypocrisy, but neither can one evaluate their contributions by a single fact. The Founders were just as human as today's leaders. Should they have freed their slaves immediately? Absolutely. But should their tolerance of slavery be the sole measure of their character? Absolutely not. Jefferson's greatest contribution to the end of slavery came when he crafted that one great sentence in the Declaration of Independence: "We hold these truths to be self-evident, that all men are created equal, that they are endowed by their Creator with certain unalienable Rights, that among these are Life, Liberty, and the pursuit of Happiness." It was and still is the kind of sentence worth trying to live up to.

A CONSTITUTIONAL PRIMER

Imagine designing a government based on the notion that the people, however defined, could not be trusted. Imagine worrying about the spread of what Alexander Hamilton called "the amazing violence & turbulence of the democratic spirit," or agreeing with John Jay that "The mass of men are neither wise nor good."[16] Imagine having watched democracy at work in events such as Shays's Rebellion, then concluding as Madison did that the life of true democracies is short and violent. Such imagining helps set the stage for understanding the Constitution, for the Founders were not imagining the threats to their young nation. They were seeking a way to address harsh reality.

Mugged by Reality

Although the Declaration of Independence and the Constitution were separated by only a decade, it was a decade of war, rising social and economic conflict, and a general awakening to the risks of pure democracy. In a sense, the Founders had been mugged by the democratic reality that had followed the Declaration of Independence.

By the time they arrived in Philadelphia, they were ready to abandon the utopian dreams of the prewar years for a government that could unite a divided nation. Their fears were well represented by Madison's *Federalist No. 10* (see Appendix C) Even the most dedicated supporters of liberty are complaining, he wrote, "that our governments are too unstable; that the public good is disregarded in the conflicts of rival parties; and that measures are too often decided, not according to the rules of justice, and the rights of the minor party, but by the superior force of an interested and overbearing majority." The Articles of Confederation were only partly to blame, for the tendency to divide into factions was sown in the nature of humankind. There was no sense pretending that enlightened statesmen could somehow subdue these tendencies through appeals to the greater good.

If factionalism could not be cured, perhaps it could be controlled. Madison was not worried about a minority faction, for the majority could simply defeat its "sinister views" by a majority vote. Rather, he worried most about a faction that consisted of a majority, particularly one that might want to oppress a minority. Madison was so frustrated by the musings of "theoretic politicians," whom he ridiculed for believing that perfect democratic equality would forge equally democratic citizens, that he wrote privately of the need to restore the good parts of the British monarchy. "That someone as moderate and committed to republicanism as Madison should speak even privately of the benefits of monarchy adhering in the Constitution of 1787," wrote historian Gordon S. Wood, "is a measure of how disillusioned many of the revolutionary gentry had become with the democratic consequences of the Revolution."[17] Madison longed for a government that would fly one flag, as monarchies do, even as it protected citizens against exploitation, as republics do. He hoped to combine the best of both options.

That meant creating a government with just enough power to act in crisis, but not so much power as to allow a majority to control the government during periods of calm. "You must first enable the government to control the governed," Madison explained in *Federalist No. 51,* "and in the next place, oblige it to control itself." Such a government might divide power among several branches, giving each one a stake in every decision. It might create competition among the branches through different terms of office and different constituencies, thereby allowing ambition to counteract ambition. It might reserve many decisions for states and localities in an effort to diffuse power even further. And it might even give each branch a way to check the other branches. Let the president cancel the Congress, let the Supreme Court cancel the president, give voters a bigger say in controlling some of the branches, but not all of them, and never, ever let any one person act alone. Such a government might occasionally drift into stalemate, but it would be far less of a threat to liberty.

That is just the kind of "limited" government the Founders wanted. As later chapters in this book will show, they struggled over the details—should there be a single president or a council of three? should there be a single chamber of Congress or two? But the Founders were always willing to accept occasional stalemate in making public policy to avoid the capture of government by strong-willed majorities, and they used four basic devices to raise the odds against oppression: separate powers, separate interests, separate layers, and checks and balances. (See Appendix B for the text of the Constitution.)

Separate Powers

The Founders did not want any single branch to control all decisions about who gets what, when, and how from government. To prevent such a concentration of strength, they created three separate branches, each with **separate powers** and enough authority to cancel a strong-willed majority in the other two. Article I created Congress, Article II created the presidency, and Article III created the Supreme Court. Roughly 80 percent of the Constitution is contained in these first three articles.

Article I.   Article I vests the legislative power in "a Congress of the United States." It is the most detailed of the three articles, in part because the Founders believed that the legislative branch would be the most powerful of the three and, therefore, the one with the greatest need for balance. That is why they divided the branch into two separate chambers, the House of Representatives and the Senate, each with enough authority to cancel a strong-willed majority in the other chamber.

They also gave Congress a long list of **enumerated powers,** which tell the House and Senate exactly what they can do. Congress is responsible, for example, for raising money to run the government, paying the government's debts, establishing post offices, creating and maintaining armies and navies, declaring war, and making rules for government. Under the **necessary and proper clause,** Congress is also responsible for making "all Laws which shall be necessary and proper for carrying into Execution" all of its enumerated powers. Because it appears to stretch to fit just about any situation, the clause is sometimes called the **elastic clause.** In addition, the House is to be the origin of all legislation dealing with raising taxes, largely reflecting the Founders' belief that the chamber closest to the people should be the one with the power to tax. In contrast, the Senate is to be responsible for giving its advice and consent on all treaties and presidential appointees, reflecting the Founders' belief that the upper chamber should be the one to cool public passions.

Article II.   Article II vests the executive power in "a President of the United States." The bulk of the article deals with the complicated process for electing the president. This process actually creates the possibility that a majority of the public might vote for one candidate only to have a majority of the **electoral college**

elect the other. The fact is that Americans do not vote for president at all, but for slates of electors who are elected by a majority vote in each state. A presidential candidate could win the popular vote by piling up huge margins in big states such as California, Texas, New York, and Florida only to lose in the electoral college on the basis of voting in the rest of the states.

The Founders also gave the president a list of enumerated powers. Under Article II, the president is to be commander in chief of the army and navy and has the power to make treaties and appoint ambassadors and judges. Under the **take care clause,** the president must also "take Care that the Laws be faithfully executed." The Founders may have divided the power to make the laws between the legislative and executive branches, but intended the laws to be faithfully implemented by the president once they were actually made.

Article III. Article III vests the judicial power "in one supreme Court, and in such inferior Courts as the Congress may from time to time ordain and establish." It is the shortest of the three articles, and left the design of the federal court system to future Congresses. It also makes clear that the judiciary's authority extends to "all Cases, in Law and Equity, arising under this Constitution, the Laws of the United States, and Treaties," thereby giving the Supreme Court the power to examine the constitutionality of legislation. The first Supreme Court used this power in establishing broad authority to check both Congress and the presidency.

Separate Interests

Having created the basic institutions of government, the Founders gave each branch and the two houses of Congress **separate interests,** which would be created by different sets of voters and different terms of office. Because members of Congress, presidents, and Supreme Court judges would focus on different parts of the public for different lengths of time, the Founders reduced the chances that any single group of Americans could capture all three branches with a call to public passions.

Legislative Interests. As if to assure constant conflict, the Founders created a Congress in which senators would represent the voters of their entire states, while representatives would represent the voters of smaller districts within the states. There would be *two* senators for *every state,* (an arrangement that would favor voters in smaller states, who get "more senator" per vote), but just *one* representative for what was every district containing roughly *30,000 voters* (an arrangement that would favor voters in larger states, who get more representatives per state).

Although the number of representatives per vote has changed over the past two hundred years as the population has grown—it was one representative per 570,000 voters in 1990—the basic principle has remained the same: small states have more power in the Senate, large states more power in the House. Some states with small populations—Wyoming and Vermont—have two senators and only one representative, while large states have two senators and dozens of representatives—California now has fifty-two House members, Texas thirty, New York thirty-one.

The Founders diffused power even more by giving the two chambers different terms of office. Senators would serve six-year terms, while representatives would serve two-year terms. Further, only one-third of the Senate would run for reelection in any one campaign, guaranteeing that no one election could sweep the Senate clean. Finally, senators would be selected by their state legislatures, further insulating the chamber from the public. It was only that under the Seventeenth Amendment to the Constitution, which was ratified in 1913, senators were subjected to direct election by popular vote.

Executive Interests.   As part of the Founders' effort to insulate the new government from the public, the president and vice president were given an entirely different election calendar. They would serve *four-year terms,* and campaign before the voters on a state-by-state basis. As noted above, presidents are not technically elected by the voters at all. Voters actually vote for their state's delegation to the electoral college. The number of electors on the ballot equals the number of senators plus representatives in a given state. It is the electors who then cast the ballots for the president and vice president.

Until the Twelfth Amendment took effect in 1804, presidential candidates did not run on a ticket together with their choice for vice president. The winner of the electoral college balloting became the president, while the runner-up became the vice president. Like the appointment of senators by state legislatures, the electoral college was designed to keep voters at a distance. Unlike the appointment of senators, the electoral college is still part of the process today.

Judicial Interests.   Supreme Court justices are appointed by the president with the consent of the Senate, not the House, and have no term at all. They can stay in office until they decide to retire, as long as they do not break the law themselves. Voters have no direct say in judicial decisions, and can influence the courts only by electing the president (through the electoral college), whose enumerated powers include making judicial nominations, and by electing their senators, whose enumerated powers include confirming the president's appointees. The lack of a direct say creates enormous independence for the courts, giving them the freedom to reject even the most popular laws.

Separate Layers of Government

The Founders clearly understood that the new government would not be the only government in the United States. After all, they cast their ballots at the Constitutional Convention state by state. Although the Constitution devotes the vast majority of its words to creating a national government, it does acknowledge the existance of government below the national level.

Beyond dividing control across the separate branches of the national government, the Founders also divided power vertically, in **separate layers,** between the national and state levels of government. They assumed that the states would continue to divide their power with local governments. These divisions create what is called a federalist system of government. As a result, the term *federal* can take on a very different meaning depending on how it is used in a sentence. When experts talk about **federalism** or the federalist system, the term *federal* refers to the American system of layers—that is, national, state, and local. But when they talk about the federal government, it is typically meant to refer to the national government located in Washington, D.C.

Although they acknowledged the importance of state government, the Founders were clear that the national government would be in charge. Article IV gives the national government the power to admit new states to the Union, while requiring it to protect individual states from invasion and domestic unrest, and to assure that each state will honor the public laws of every other state. Article VI contains the **supremacy clause,** which makes clear that the Constitution and all laws made under its auspices and institutions are to be the supreme "Law of the Land," no matter what states might say otherwise.

The Founders had no choice but to create a federal system, if only because the people would have a say on final approval of the Constitution through special state ratifying conventions. Facing strong opposition to the Constitution, the Founders eventually agreed to reserve for the states all powers *not* given explicitly to the national government. Under federalism, the Constitution created at least three kinds of enumerated powers: (1) **exclusive powers** given to the national government—for example, the power to declare war, make treaties with other governments, and create money; (2) **reserved powers** given to the states—such as the power to regulate commerce within state borders, police the public, and prosecute most crimes; and (3) **concurrent powers** shared by both—namely, the power to raise taxes. As Madison explained, the federal government has a very clear and short list of powers, while the states have everything else.[18]

Checks and Balances

Having separated the basic institutions of government, the Founders decided to give each branch a way to check, or stop, the others. Each branch would have its separate powers, but would also share power with the others, meaning that no single institution could ever act alone. These **checks and balances** are part of what many politicians now call *gridlock,* or stalemate between the branches, but they are essential for preventing any single branch or layer of government from overwhelming the rest. The Founders gave the president the power to veto legislation—the president can either sign an act of Congress into law or reject it with a stroke of the pen. The Founders then gave Congress the power to override the president's veto with a two-thirds majority. If the vote to override is successful, the bill becomes law without the president's signature. Otherwise, most legislation passes with a simple majority.

The Founders separated more than the legislative power, however. They gave the House the power to initiate the impeachment process to remove the president from office (by charging the president with "high crimes and misdemeanors"), but gave the Senate the power to convict. They gave the Senate the power to confirm presidential appointees to the court, but gave both chambers a say in how the courts would be designed. Moreover, because they knew the House would be closer to the people through direct elections, and because the nation had fought a war in part because of taxation without representation; they gave the House sole authority to author tax bills. The Senate would have a vote on all such bills as part of the normal legislative process, but could not start a tax bill on its legislative journey.

in a different light —— THE ODDS AGAINST ACTION

Insulating the government against capture by a strong-willed majority intent on oppression clearly increases the odds against action. Even routine ideas may have trouble winning passage into law. Congress will consider nearly eight thousand proposals, or bills, for new laws over the next two years. Of those, about three thousand will be considered good enough to be placed on the calendar for actual votes. Of those, only one thousand or so will be passed by either the House or the Senate. Of those, only five hundred will be passed by both, printed on parchment paper, and hand-carried to the president for signature into law. The odds that a bill will actually become law are only 1 in 15; the odds fall even further if an idea is particularly controversial.

The odds against passage have increased in recent decades. During the first years of Congress, almost every bill introduced was passed into law. Although the number fell steadily over the 1800s, Congress was still passing roughly one in five bills as late as the 1940s.

The odds are definitely *not* declining because Congress is overwhelmed by the sheer number of bills introduced. Back in the 1960s, for example, Congress handled over twenty thousand bills a year. However, as the number of bills introduced has declined, the number of pages of each bill has climbed dramatically. Whereas the average law in the 1960s was only three pages long, the average law today will top fifteen pages. Bills seem to be more complex now, thereby requiring more time and energy to pass.

The odds against passage create both pros and cons for American government. On the one hand, the nation is spared rapid changes in who gets what, when, and how from government. The fact that an idea is popular with the public or hot in one branch of government does not necessarily mean it is a good idea. The fact that major reforms are a long time coming also means that society has time to adjust to new ideas.

On the other hand, the odds against passage clearly protect the status quo. Although the Founders' government is very effective at meeting foreign threats such as the Gulf War of 1991, it may be less able to agree on just what constitutes a domestic threat. Problems such as racial inequality, ozone depletion, and inequities in health care may go unaddressed for decades as Americans debate whether a problem actually exists. This is one reason government can often be so frustrating to the public. The effort to protect the country from strong-willed majorities makes it less likely that even the most compelling action will be taken.

The effort to stop tobacco companies from selling cigarettes to young Americans is a classic example. There is no question that most Americans wanted such legislation passed. According to public opinion surveys conducted at the time, roughly five out of every six Americans thought tobacco companies should be prohibited from using cartoon characters such as Joe Camel to pitch cigarettes. They also agreed that the companies should be forced to pay higher taxes to cover the cost of treating tobacco-related illnesses such as lung cancer.

Despite what appeared to be overwhelming public support, the tobacco bill of 1998 was killed, in large part because the industry mounted a $40 million advertising campaign to convince Americans that it was a bad idea (see Chapter 15 for a further discussion of the campaign). The campaign exploited age-old public suspicions of big government. "Washington has gone haywire, proposing the same old tax and spend," one ad said. "Half a trillion dollars in new taxes . . . 17 new government bureaucracies. Cigarettes up to $5 a pack. . . . Huge job losses among farmers, retailers and small businesses." "Washington has gone cuckoo again," another ad started out in ridiculing the role of government bureaucrats in regulating what tobacco companies could say in their cigarette ads. "Washington is creating a serious new law enforcement problem," still another said in warning Americans about the cigarette smuggling that might follow an increase in prices.

Airing in as many as fifty television markets for the better part of three months, the ads clearly worked. Congress received 150,000 phone calls and letters, most of which came from cigarette smokers. "The message is bounced off the satellite—the satellite being the American people—and comes back to the member," one of the tobacco lobbyists argued. With an intense minority arguing against action and a nearly silent majority in favor, the tobacco bill was doomed.[19]

Winning Ratification

Despite the fact that the Founders had achieved their goals, their final signing of the Constitution on September 17, 1787, was anything but a great celebration. "Even now, at the very end, a half dozen men were wrangling about minor details," writes one historian of the final days, "and three others flatly refused to sign the instrument. Another group was already worrying about and planning for the strenuous campaign for ratification which lay ahead. Mostly, however, the atmosphere pervading the room was one of exhaustion and a sense of relief that the four month ordeal was over."[20]

Perhaps the Founders also recognized that the nation had to be persuaded that a stronger government made sense. Americans were hardly enthusiastic about a new national government, and remained much more loyal to their state and local governments than to the broad promises of the more perfect union envisioned in the Constitution. Mostly, Americans wanted to be left alone, particularly if a new government wanted to impose new taxes to pay off the war debt. Put to a national referendum, the Constitution probably would have failed, which may be one reason the Founders did not permit referendum or initiative in their design.

This opposition would not have mattered but for another protection against tyranny: **ratification,** or approval, of the Constitution itself. Under Article VII, the Constitution would need majority votes from nine state ratifying conventions, a number that constituted a three-fourths majority of the thirteen states. Part of the effort to win this "supermajority," as political scientists might call it today, was a public relations campaign built around eighty-four brief explanations of the Constitution that were written anonymously by New York's Alexander Hamilton and John Jay and Virginia's James Madison. These documents eventually became known as *The Federalist Papers*.

Ratification nevertheless remained very much in doubt. New York, Pennsylvania, and Virginia were sharply divided. The Founders would have to go back and redraft the Constitution or find some way to reassure the public. Taking the latter course, the Founders promised the states that the very first item on the agenda of the new federal government would be a list, or bill, of amendments guaranteeing basic freedoms. After all, they had established a process for adding amendments under Article V. Drawing from nearly two hundred proposals, the First Congress proposed ten amendments that became known as the Bill of Rights. The list was less an endorsement of new government powers than a statement of what the na-

Alexander Hamilton (left), John Jay (middle), and James Madison (right) wrote *The Federalist Papers* to advertise the Constitution as it moved through the states toward ratification.

tional government could *not* do. The amendments were passed in 1789 and ratified in 1791. Box 2–3 lists the limits on government imposed by the Bill of Rights.

Many of the amendments were designed to guarantee rights that had been violated under British rule. The British government had imprisoned colonists for assembling in public and publishing newspapers, forced them to house British soldiers against their will, searched their houses for arms, prosecuted them for false crimes, forced them to testify against themselves, imprisoned them without charges, held secret trials, and imposed excessive bail, unreasonable fines, and cruel and unusual punishment. Thus, alongside guaranteeing the basic freedoms of religion, speech, association, and assembly, the Bill of Rights protected the accused. It hardly made sense, for example, to guarantee free speech, then allow government to jail Americans for exercising that right. Providing due process, public trials, protection against being tried twice for the same crime, and so forth, made such political harassment much more difficult.

As a political strategy, the promised Bill of Rights succeeded: the Constitution was ratified in 1788, the Bill of Rights in 1791. Yet, by agreeing to the guarantees, the Founders also set a precedent in favor of change. The Constitution would be an evolving document. Madison had said as much at the Constitutional Convention: "In framing a system which we wish to last for ages, we should not lose sight of the changes which ages will produce."

A WORK IN PROGRESS

The Constitution was far from finished when New Hampshire became the ninth state to ratify it in June 1788, nor when Virginia became the last state needed to ratify the Bill of Rights in December 1791. Many countries create new govern-

BOX 2-3

Limits on Government in the Bill of Rights

(Passed by Congress on September 25, 1789. Ratified December 15, 1791.)

Limits on Congress

Amendment I: Congress shall not establish a religion or limit the free exercise of religion. It shall not limit the freedoms of speech, press, and peaceful assembly or the right to petition government for a redress of grievances.

Limits on the Executive Branch

Amendment II: The government shall not interfere with the right to keep and bear arms, "a well regulated Militia, being necessary to the security of a free State."

Amendment III: The government shall not arbitrarily force citizens to allow soldiers to live in their homes.

Amendment IV: The government shall not search for or seize evidence without first proving to a court that the search and seizure are reasonably linked to a crime.

Limits on the Federal Courts

Amendment V: The government shall not try someone for a crime unless there is a finding that such person might reasonably have committed that

ments only to lose them in the first crisis. Having created a new government, America had to keep it.

There have been plenty of tests over the years, of course, including a savage civil war over slavery and countless riots. The Constitution was tested almost immediately when western Pennsylvania farmers protested the federal government's new tax on whiskey by burning down the house of the local tax inspector. The 1794 "Whiskey Rebellion" bluntly asked whether the Constitution applied to every corner of the young nation.

The answer came fast and hard. President Washington ordered the states to assemble an army of twelve thousand men, far more than needed, to demonstrate crime; try someone twice for the same crime; force someone to testify against him- or herself; punish someone without due process of law; or take private property without paying a fair amount for it.

Amendment VI: The government shall not try someone for a serious crime unless the trial is speedy and public; the accused is informed of the charges; the accused is allowed to confront opposing witnesses and compel supporting witnesses to testify; the trial is held where the crime was committed and heard by an impartial jury; and an attorney is available to help with the defense.

Amendment VII: The government shall not deny the accused a trial by jury.

Amendment VIII: The government shall not impose excessive bail, unreasonable fines, or cruel and unusual punishments.

Limits on the Federal Government in General

Amendment IX: The federal government shall not assume the people have only those rights specified in the Constitution.

Amendment X: The federal government shall not exercise powers not delegated to it by the Constitution, because those powers belong to the states (unless the Constitution denies those powers to the states) or to the people.

the government's readiness to respond to any internal threat. The rebellion, if such a small collection of protestors can be called such, quickly evaporated. Nothing in the Constitution said the president had the power to order an army against the nation's own citizens to ensure domestic tranquility, but the precedent was set. The national government had the power, and military might, to enforce its will.

The fact is that the Founders had done the very best they could to create a new government but left many questions unanswered. Some of the answers have come in formal amendments to the Constitution; others from judicial review; still others from practice, practice, practice. Each will be examined next.

Amending the Constitution

At least one of the Founders' questions was answered almost two hundred years later by a college student at the University of Texas in Austin. The Bill of Rights had actually included twelve, not ten, amendments when first proposed. One of the two "lost" amendments was proposed by James Madison and prohibited Congress from raising its pay before an election; the other put a limit on the ultimate size of Congress.[21] Both failed to win ratification. The Madison pay amendment was approved by only six states between 1789 and 1791.

Except for ratification by the state of Ohio in 1873 and Wyoming in 1978, the pay amendment was all but dead, at least until a student named Gregory Watson found it while researching a paper for his American government course in 1982. Watson believed that the amendment was still alive—the fact that it had never passed did not mean it was dead. He said just that in his paper, only to get a C from his disbelieving professor.

What happened next is nothing short of amazing: Watson mounted a one-person campaign over the next ten years to get state legislatures to ratify Madi-

Gregory Watson, ten years after receiving a "C" for arguing that James Madison's proposed constitutional amendment limiting congressional pay was still alive. Watson led a successful campaign to ratify the Twenty-seventh Amendment, which was added to the Constitution 203 years after it was first passed by Congress.

son's pay ban. He had plenty of supporters, reflecting the growing public anger toward Congress. By 1990, for example, a Gallup poll found that almost half of Americans felt their members of Congress were paid "a lot too much," while another quarter said "a little too much."[22]

Passing the amendment became plain good politics. Maine ratified in 1983, Colorado in 1984. Five other states followed in 1985, another seventeen were added before 1990, and six more by 1992. Add up the numbers: six in the 1700s, plus one in the 1800s, thirty in the 1900s, and, by the time Michigan ratified the amendment in 1992, Watson had the thirty-eight, or three-fourths, needed to ratify. The Twenty-seventh Amendment became part of the Constitution 203 years after it was proposed. It was a hard way to protest a grade, but Watson had his amendment.

The Founders would have been pleased with Watson's success. They had never seen the Constitution as a perfect document and had provided a two-stage process for amending it. The first stage involves presenting a formal proposal, which can be made in two ways. In one, which has been used for all twenty-seven amendments, Congress passes a proposed amendment by a two-thirds vote in each house. In the other, which has never been used, Congress calls a national convention at the request of two-thirds of the state legislatures. The risk of a national convention is that it would open the entire Constitution for review. Apparently, the fear of changing the document too much has been enough to prevent such a convention from ever being called.

The second stage of the amendment process involves ratification, which can also occur in two ways. One, which has been used on twenty-six of the twenty-seven amendments, calls for a vote in three-fourths of the state legislatures. Because the Constitution itself does not say just how the state legislatures are to vote, some states use a simple majority to approve amendments, while others use a supermajority of either two-thirds or three-quarters. The other ratification device, used but once, calls for majority votes in three-fourths of state ratifying conventions, which is how the states passed the Twenty-first Amendment repealing the Eighteenth Amendment's prohibition on liquor.

Judicial Review

Under the new Constitution, Congress would make the laws, presidents would enforce them, and the federal courts would determine consistency with the Constitution. This power of **judicial review**, which gives federal courts the power to overturn an act of Congress, was far from automatic, however. After all, the courts had absolutely no way to enforce their decisions—no army, no special police. They would have to rely on Congress, presidents, and the public to accept their decisions as legitimate.

For the first decade, there were no opportunities to assert that power of review. As one political scientist writes, "The Supreme Court had little business, frequent turnover in personnel, no chambers or staff, no fixed customs, and no institutional identity."[23] At the time, there were very few laws to review, and the lower courts that now act as a "feeder" or source of cases were just getting under way. Not until 1803 did the Supreme Court have a case that would give it the chance to exercise judicial review to overturn an act of Congress. To this day, the federal courts can decide only the cases that are brought before them; they can give signals about what cases they might like to hear, but must wait until cases arrive before making a decision.

That 1803 case, known as *Marbury v. Madison,* was part of the continuing conflict over how much power states would have under the Constitution. The case began with the bitterly contested presidential election of 1800, one of only two elections ever decided by the House of Representatives. Thomas Jefferson won the election on the thirty-sixth ballot in the House, defeating the incumbent president, John Adams. (Chapter 9 looks at the election process in more detail).

The case turned on a simple problem of timing. In a last-minute effort to frustrate the incoming president, Adams and his Federalist Party supporters in Congress created a number of new judgeships, one of which was to be filled by a William Marbury. Seventeen new judges, including Marbury, had not received their papers of appointment by the time Jefferson was inaugurated as president. The papers were stuck in Washington. Acting on his authority as the new president, Jefferson immediately ordered his secretary of state, James Madison, not to issue the papers.

Marbury sued, arguing that Jefferson had no authority to undo the legal actions of a previous Congress and president, and asking the Supreme Court to use its power to force the president to release his appointment papers. It was a power that the Congress had clearly given the Supreme Court under the 1789 Judiciary Act, which had also created the federal court system.

The case offered a first test of the Supreme Court's authority to interpret the laws. On the one hand, the Supreme Court could not let a clearly illegal action stand, lest future presidents refuse to execute faithfully any law they did not like. On the other hand, the Supreme Court had no real power to make the president release the appointment papers. It had no army, no police, no history of making presidents obey. What if the president said, "Make me"? How could the Supreme Court do so?

The Supreme Court needed a way out of the dilemma. Chief Justice John Marshall soon found one. The Supreme Court would declare that Jefferson could not legally withhold the papers, but would simultaneously declare itself powerless to order the release. Writing for a unanimous 4–0 Supreme Court, Marshall first argued that Marbury deserved his appointment—Jefferson could not take advantage of administrative red tape to undo a legitimate act of Congress. However, Marshall also argued that Congress had violated the Constitution by expanding the Supreme Court's jurisdiction under a section of the 1789 Judiciary Act. Because Congress could not give the Supreme Court a jurisdiction that the

Constitution had clearly omitted, that section was unconstitutional. Lacking jurisdiction, the Supreme Court could not order the president to deliver Marbury's appointment.

The Supreme Court thereby declared one part of the 1789 act unconstitutional, trading a small congressionally derived power—the authority to order a specific member of the executive branch (in this case the secretary of state) to do something (in this case deliver a commission)—for the much larger constitutionally derived power of judicial review. In doing so, Marshall also avoided a confrontation with Jefferson, for it was almost certain that the new president would not have delivered the commission whatever the order.

Practice, Practice, Practice

The Constitution is actually a remarkably short document. It says much more about the overall design of American government than about the details. It says little about how the legislative branch should actually operate, and almost nothing about how the executive branch should look—nothing on congressional committees, nothing on the executive departments or White House staff. It left actual creation of the federal court system up to Congress. As for running the government, it merely asked the president to report from time to time to Congress on the state of the nation. Many of the details were left to the future.

Congress is one example. The Founders said virtually nothing about how the two parts of their bicameral legislature would work together. The Constitution requires only that Congress meet once every year on the first Monday in December, unless it decides on another date. Each chamber is to determine the rules of its own proceedings, keep a journal of its proceedings, and punish its own members. Beyond requiring that all tax bills originate in the House, and that each bill must pass both chambers before it can be delivered to the president, the Constitution leaves everything else up to practice.

The first Congress began inventing new governing devices almost immediately. In theory, for example, a bill could go to the president only after passing both chambers *in sequence*. One house would do its work, pass the bill to the other, wait for the return measure, do some more work if needed, pass it back, and so on. Members quickly decided that that was unnecessarily inefficient and created something called a **conference committee.** Members of conference committees would come from both chambers, and would have exactly two votes: one for the members appointed by the House and one for the members from the Senate. The committee would craft a final report, or bill, that would go to both chambers simultaneously for final action. Conference committee agreements are no guarantee that the House and Senate will go along. Conference committees certainly make the legislative process more efficient, but keep government working only well enough to get by.

The presidency is another example. Besides dictating the manner of election and specifying duties, the Constitution is absolutely silent on how the president would actually implement the laws. The Founders did give the president authority to recommend legislation and to call Congress back into session. And they did provide veto authority. After that, it was all up to practice.

The fourteen departments of government that exist today, which together employ roughly two million public employees, were created one by one over the years, starting with State, Treasury, and War (now Defense) in the 1790s. The **Executive Office of the President,** which contains the powerful Office of Management and Budget, as well as the assorted special assistants, press secretaries, and lawyers who get into the news from time to time, was not created until 1939. Until then, presidents did their work with one or two aides at most. President Lincoln wrote his famous Gettysburg Address without any speechwriters, and delivered it without a teleprompter to tell him exactly what to say.

Presidents today are surrounded by support. (Box 2–4 shows the inventory of people and equipment that followed President Bill Clinton to China in 1998.) This is not to suggest that the presidency should go back to two or three staffers, or that presidents should write every speech themselves. The world is much more complex today, and the pressures to make quick decisions much greater. Rather, it is to note the difference between what the Founders might have imagined and the reality that eventually emerged.

The federal courts are a final example. The Constitution requires only that the judicial power be vested in a supreme court and whatever "inferior," or lower, courts Congress wanted to create. Nothing about the number of justices on the Supreme Court; nothing about the federal system of district and appeals courts. In fact, the courts did not exist until Washington signed the Judiciary Act on September 24, 1789; this act required important concessions to win passage, not the least of which was a narrowing of federal court jurisdiction.

For now, it is useful to note that the act set up a supreme court with six justices, one for each of the six judicial circuits, or districts, covering the thirteen states (the number expanded with the number of districts until it was set at the current nine in 1870). Everything else—from the number of lower courts to the way the Supreme Court decides—has been resolved through legislation or custom.

MAINTAINING THE BALANCE

The Founders might be surprised that their constitutional framework has survived for more than two hundred years, and several might be disappointed. Washington, Adams, Hamilton, and Jefferson all ended their lives unsure about the American government they had helped create. Washington complained bitterly about the rise of political parties, arguing that any party could "set up a

BOX 2-4

Mr. Clinton Goes to Beijing

When President Clinton visited China in June 1998, he traveled with a retinue of more than 1,000 people.

President Clinton, Hillary and Chelsea Clinton

Secretary of State, Commerce, Treasury, Agriculture, U.S. Trade Representative

Six members of Congress

National security adviser and deputy, Chief of Staff and deputy, press secretary and deputy

Political aides and economic advisers

Senior Delegation (30)
Core party included president and cabinet officers. Official delegation made up of these 30 and the 70 senior aides and advisers.

70 Senior Aides and Advisers
Senior staff from the White House and cabinet deputies.

10 Armored Limousines for the Official Delegation (plus 350 rented cars)

150 Support Staff
Included White House press aides, travel aides, advance staff, translators, secretaries, speechwriters, and lower-level aides from all agencies.

150 Military
Included communications support, cable, transportation, baggage personnel, and drivers.

150 Security Personnel
Estimated 100–200 agents from the Secret Service and other departments.

200 News Media Personnel
An additional 175 news media personnel were accredited, but made their own way to China rather than travel with the official party.

Source: Adapted from *New York Times*, June 21, 1998, "Week in Review," p. 5.

 **in a different light** ———————

For the better part of two decades, presidents have been asking Congress for the power to veto pieces, or lines, of laws that control federal spending. President Reagan asked for that power during the 1980s, but was rebuked by a Democratic Congress that did not want a Republican rewriting its laws. When Clinton asked for the same power from the new Republican Congress elected in 1994, however, he got every president's wish. Under the *Line Item Veto Act of 1996*, the president was given the authority to cancel specific items, or lines, within any tax or spending bill, while letting the rest of the bill become law. The law merely gave the president of the United States what many state governors already had: the power to cancel unnecessary tax or spending items in otherwise necessary legislation. In passing the Line Item Veto Act, Congress was clearly admitting that it did not have the will to stop itself from passing wasteful projects. The act was the legislative equivalent of saying, "Stop me before I kill again."

Presidents already had the authority to veto tax and spending bills under Article II. They did not, however, have the power to sign a bill into law, then selectively veto items they did not like. Because the odds against action are so high, presidents rarely veto an entire tax or spending bill just because one or two items are wasteful. It was no surprise, therefore, that Clinton signed the bill into law on April 9, 1996. By the end of 1997, he had used the line item veto eighty-two times to cancel $1.9 billion in federal spending, a mere pittance in a federal budget of nearly $2 trillion.

The problem with the line item veto is that it altered the separation of powers between the legislative and executive branch. By giving the president the power to veto selected *parts* of a law after it was signed, the Line Item Veto Act rewrote the way a bill becomes a law. Although it certainly made the legislative process less frustrating and even saved taxpayers money, the act altered the delicate balance between strength and limits on strength. The president clearly gained an advantage over Congress that, as Senator Daniel Patrick Moynihan (D-NY) said in opposing the act, was "a formula for executive tyranny."

It was a point made by the City of New York, which sued Clinton on behalf of two hospital associations, one hospital, and two unions that represented the hospital employees, and by the Snake River Potato Growers, which sued Clinton on behalf of an association of Idaho farmers. The City of New York claimed that Clinton's line item veto of an increase in federal funding of health care for the poor would hurt its hospitals, while the Snake River Potato Growers argued that Clinton's line item veto of a special tax provision for agriculture companies would increase the cost of building a potato-processing plant. Both argued that the cancellations violated the constitutional separation of powers and should be overturned.

On February 12, 1998, U.S. District Court Judge Thomas F. Hogan agreed. The hospitals were to get their funding and the potato growers their tax break. Hogan's reasoning was simple: "The Line Item Veto Act violates the procedural requirements ordained in Article I of the United States Constitution and impermissibly upsets the balance of powers so carefully devised by its framers. . . . The separation of powers into three coordinate branches is central to the principles on which this country was founded. The declared purpose of separating and dividing the powers of government was to 'diffuse power the better to secure liberty.' "[24] The Supreme Court upheld the ruling on June 25, 1998, by a 6 to 3 vote, arguing that the law disturbed the "finely wrought" procedure for making laws that the Founders had produced in Philadelphia. Justice John Paul Stevens wrote for the majority,

> If the Line Item Veto Act were valid, it would authorize the president to create a different law, one whose text was not voted on by either House of Congress or presented to the president for signature. Something that might be known as "Public Law 105–33 as modified by the President" may or may not be desirable, but it is surely not a document that may "become a law" pursuant to the procedures designed by the Framers of Article I, Section 7, of the Constitution.

If Congress does not like wasteful spending, it has the power to deny that spending by majority vote; if a president does not like a particular line item in a bill, he or she always has the power to veto the whole bill. "If there is to be a new procedure in which the President will play a different role in determining the final text of what may 'become a law,' " Stevens concluded, "such change must come not by legislation but through the amendment procedures set forth in Article V of the Constitution."

---

broomstick" and call it a "true son of Liberty." Adams bemoaned the narrowness of society, asking "Where is now, the progress of the human Mind?. . . . When? Where? and How? is the present Chaos to be arranged into order?" Alexander Hamilton concluded that "this American world was not made for me."

As for the author of the Declaration of Independence, Jefferson spent his last years defending his record, fighting to establish the University of Virginia in the face of intense religious opposition, and complaining about military heroes such as Andrew Jackson, who seemed to be exploiting their national popularity in pursuit of higher office. "All, all dead," Jefferson wrote of his fellow patriots in

1825, a half century after he had penned his famous words, "and ourselves left alone amidst a new generation whom we know not, and who knows not us."[25]

The Founders could not know just how well balanced their government would come to be. They could only look backward at the changes they did not like, particularly the rise of political parties. They could not predict how those parties would evolve over time, how organized interests might counterbalance one another, or how quickly the United States would become a global power. They could not know how the media might eventually become an informal fourth branch of government that would check the power of the legislature, executive, and judiciary, or how the Internet might become a new source of access for ordinary citizens. Even as they worried about the changes wrought by their majoritarian representative democracy, they could not anticipate the pluralist representative democracy that would evolve nearly two hundred years later.

What they did know was that the institutions of government would always balance one another. They may have hoped for a country led by virtuous, wise citizens, but most certainly prepared for a nation led by ambitious, self-interested representatives. As noted in Chapter 1, they hoped for the best and planned for the worst. Their government has survived to the present day precisely because it was designed to counteract ambition with ambition, maintaining a delicate balance between strength and limits on strength.

Even though the balance tips to one side or the other over time, the design has proven remarkably effective in restoring equilibrium. Congress gives the president the line item veto; the federal courts deny it. Presidents use their authority as commander in chief to order troops to some far-off land without a formal declaration of war; Congress cuts off funding and brings them home. Congress gives itself a legislative veto over the rules used by executive departments and agencies to faithfully execute the laws; the courts deny it. Even the courts can be checked if Congress and the president decide to limit their authority to decide certain kinds of cases.

The problem is that it can take decades to restore the balance, creating long periods of injustice and inequality. Slavery continued for "four score and seven years" after the founding, leading to the bloodiest war in American history; women were denied the vote for another three score, or sixty, years more, while Native Americans are still struggling to regain a measure of the economic security lost when their lands were taken. It took the better part of two hundred years for American government to finally honor Jefferson's promise of equality.

Even when the balance is restored, there is no guarantee that American government will remain balanced for long. American democracy is constantly being tested, whether by domestic unrest, political scandal, economic crisis, nuclear proliferation, terrorism, poverty, illiteracy, or accidents and events completely beyond the government's control. Some of these tests are easily met through new laws, presidential orders, or Supreme Court decisions. Others demand decades of national sacrifice and a lasting commitment to reform. Still others are simply part of the human condition and can never be resolved at all.

Such tests are the natural product of the delicate balance between strength and limits on strength. It is easy to prevent domestic unrest, for example, when government is so strong that factions can never arise; easy to prevent distant wars when government has an army so large that no nation dare challenge the United States; easy to eliminate poverty by lowering the standard of living among all Americans; easy to prevent accidents by never taking risks. Such a government might make Americans feel safer, but only at the cost of threatening the very liberty American government was founded to protect.

Maintaining the delicate balance may be the ultimate test of democracy. Americans cannot be so hungry for action that they embrace limits on their liberty, yet never so preoccupied with their liberty that they allow the United States to drift toward weakness. They cannot be so scared of unrest or disorder that, in order to prevent it, they give up the freedom the Founders worked so hard to assure.

The United States has been able to hold the balance for over two hundred years. The Founders' system of separate powers, separate interests, separate layers, and checks and balances may be frustrating sometimes—as when a lone senator stops a popular idea with a windy flourish, a district court voids a popular law with a single opinion, or a president vetoes a popular idea with a stroke of the pen. But that is precisely the way American government was designed to work. The Founders believed that occasional frustration was a small price to pay for liberty, but they also understood that liberty would hardly be possible if the nation was unable to survive.

JUST THE FACTS

terms to remember

facts and interpretations

- The American Revolution is usually discussed as a seamless web of history in which the colonies declared independence, fought a long war, and crafted a new Constitution. In fact, the first part of the revolutionary period was quite different from the middle and end. The first years involved great hopes for

68

the principles of freedom and equality, and were defined by the broad promises made in the Declaration of Independence. The middle of the Revolution involved a long war that sapped the young republic's energy. The last years of the Revolution brought a more sober assessment of the people's ability to govern themselves. Having watched their nation almost unravel under the Articles of Confederation, the delegates to the Constitutional Convention wanted a government that could first control the governed, and only then control itself.

- The greatest controversy of the Constitutional Convention centered on just how strong the new government should be. The Founders wanted their government to be strong enough to fulfill the promises made in the Preamble of the Constitution, but not so strong that it could ever become a threat to liberty. Central to establishing this delicate balance was the notion that ambition could be made to counteract ambition. Each institution of government would be given enough power to check the others. Toward these ends, the Founders eventually adopted a structure based on the Virginia Plan, which created a strong national government built around three branches: legislative (to make the laws), executive (to execute the laws), and judicial (to interpret the laws and protect individual rights). Under the "Great Compromise," the convention gave big states more power in the House of Representatives and small states more power in the Senate.

- The Constitution is still evolving two hundred years after ratification. Some of the evolution comes from the ratification of amendments, the most recent being an idea originally proposed by James Madison that was one of the two "lost" items on the Bill of Rights. Some also comes from judicial review and practice. But central to all the evolution is a constant balancing and rebalancing of power. Even as one branch pushes for greater authority, the others push back. This is the essential feature of maintaining the delicate balance.

open questions

- What kind of government would the Founders have designed if they had believed that human beings could be trusted? Would it have been faster, bigger, stronger? Or not even needed at all? What did they see in human nature that made them think they had to worry about oppression? Is there any evidence today that some Americans would use government to oppress minorities?

● The Founders created a complicated government that can be particularly frustrating when a popular idea is defeated by some obscure check or balance. To what extent does that complexity reduce public confidence in government? Do most Americans understand why the government works the way it does? Instead of pointing fingers at each other when stalemate occurs, should the nation's leaders occasionally simply say that this is the way it was meant to be?

● Thinking back to the late 1700s, would the Founders be surprised by the changes in their government over the years? What would trouble them most in the news today? What would they congratulate themselves on? Where would they say they had made a mistake?

for further study

Bowen, Catherine Drinker. *Miracle at Philadelphia: The Story of the Constitutional Convention, May to September 1787*. Boston: Little, Brown, 1966.

Burns, James MacGregor. *The American Experiment: The Vineyard of Liberty*. New York: Knopf, 1982.

Evans, Sara M. *Born for Liberty: A History of Women in America*. New York: Free Press, 1989.

Ferguson, E. James. *The American Revolution: A General History, 1763–1790*. Homewood, IL: Dorsey Press, 1974.

McDonald, Forrest. *We the People: The Economic Origins of the Constitution*. New Brunswick, NJ: Transaction Publishers, 1992.

Wood, Gordon S. *The Radicalism of the American Revolution*. New York: Vintage, 1991.

endnotes for chapter 2

1. Catherine Drinker Bowen, *Miracle at Philadelphia: The Story of the Constitutional Convention, May to September 1787* (Boston: Little, Brown, 1966), p. 4.

2. Bernard Bailyn, *The Ideological Origins of the American Revolution* (Cambridge, MA: Belknap Press of Harvard University Press, 1967), p. 160.

3. Quoted in Dante Germino, *Modern Western Political Thought: Machiavelli to Marx* (Chicago: Rand McNally, 1972), p. 127.

4. See Germino, *Modern Western Political Thought*, p. 127.

5. Douglas L. Wilson, "Thomas Jefferson and the Character Issue," *Atlantic Monthly*, November 1992, p. 72.

6. Gordon S. Wood, *The Radicalism of the American Revolution* (New York: Vintage, 1991), p. 3.

7. Wood, *The Radicalism of the American Revolution*, p. 6.

8. Pew Research Center For The People & The Press, *Deconstructing Distrust: How Americans View Government* (Washington, DC: Pew Research Center, 1998).

9. For more information about women in the revolutionary period, see Sara M. Evans, *Born for Liberty: A History of Women in America* (New York: Free Press, 1989).

10. E. James Ferguson, *The American Revolution: A General History, 1763–1790* (Homewood, IL: Dorsey Press, 1974), p. 139. For a discussion of the meaning of the Revolution for social, political, and economic life, see Wood, *The Radicalism of the American Revolution.*

11. For an easily readable account of the Constitutional Convention, see Bowen, *Miracle at Philadelphia.* For more in-depth coverage, see Max Farrand, ed., *The Records of the Federal Convention of 1787* (New Haven, CT: Yale University Press, 1966).

12. See Bowen, *Miracle at Philadelphia.*

13. James MacGregor Burns, *The American Experiment: The Vineyard of Liberty* (Knopf, 1982), p. 37.

14. Charles Beard, *An Economic Interpretation of the Constitution* (New York: Macmillan, 1913), p. 324.

15. Forrest McDonald, *We the People: The Economic Origins of the Constitution* (New Brunswick, NJ: Transaction Publishers, 1992).

16. Quoted in Wood, *The Radicalism of the American Revolution*, p. 261.

17. Wood, *The Radicalism of the American Revolution*, p. 255.

18. See Madison's *Federalist Paper No. 45,* in Roy P. Fairfield, ed., *The Federalist Papers* (Baltimore: Johns Hopkins University Press, 1981), p. 137.

19. Quoted in Howard Kurtz, "The Democrat Who Switched and Fought," *Washington Post*, June 19, 1998, p. A1.

20. Forrest McDonald, *We the People*, p. 1.

21. For a complete history of the Twenty-seventh Amendment, see Richard Bernstein, "The Sleeper Wakes: The History and Legacy of the Twenty-seventh Amendment," *Fordham Law Review*, 61, no. 3 (December 1992): 497–557.

22. *Gallup Poll Monthly*, December 1990.

23. David M. O'Brien, *Constitutional Law and Politics: Civil Rights and Civil Liberties* (New York: Norton, 1991), p. 29.

24. All quotes below are from the *New York Times*, June 26, 1998, p. A16.

25. These quotes are all drawn from Wood, *The Radicalism of the American Revolution*, pp. 367–368.

federalism

which government rules?

For most Americans, the term *federal government* is synonymous with the national government in Washington. When pollsters ask whether Americans trust the federal government to do the right thing, they assume that their respondents will automatically think about the president, Congress, federal courts, and executive bureaucracy, which is, in fact, what most respondents do. It is also how this book uses the term in later chapters. In this chapter only, the federal government in Washington will be called the *national government*.

For some Americans, however, the term *federal government* has a much more complicated definition. It refers to the unique blend of national and state governments that the Founders created under the Constitution, a blend in which the thirteen state governments were left standing as part of a larger national whole. By embracing the states as a separate layer within their new national government, albeit a layer with significant limits, while assuring that the partnership would be anything but equal, the Founders could have their constitutional cake and eat it, too. They could create the illusion of a constitution built on a state foundation, even as they rejected the Articles of Confederation as unworkable and weak. The Founders may have allowed the states to continue operating with separate legislative, executive, and judicial branches of their own, but they left no doubt whatsoever about who would be in charge. Under Article VI, which is called the **supremacy clause**, "This Constitution, and the Laws of the United States which shall be made in Pursuance thereof; and all Treaties made, or which shall be made, under the Authority of the United States, shall be the supreme Law of the Land. . . ." The states would have no power to overturn national laws.

Consider how Madison explained the new government as neither a national nor a federal government, but a combination of both, in *Federalist No. 39*. "In its foundation it is federal, not national; in the sources from which the ordinary powers of the government are drawn, it is partly federal and partly national; in the operation of these powers, it is national, not federal; in the extent of them, again, it is federal, not national; and, finally, in the authoritative model of introducing amendments, it is neither wholly federal nor wholly national."[1]

Confused? So was just about everyone else who followed the constitutional debates. That was the way supporters of the new government wanted it. As French aristocrat and author Alexis de Tocqueville mused during his visit to the United States thirty years later, "Evidently this is no longer a federal government, but an incomplete national government, which is neither exactly national nor exactly federal; but the new word which ought to express this novel thing does not yet exist."[2] The word that expresses this novel thing today is *federal*. The Founders' vision of a government not quite national and not quite federal proved strong enough to redefine the original meaning of the word.

This chapter will explore the meaning of federalism as it has evolved over time. Having agreed to create what was then a unique form of national government (majoritarian representative democracy), the Founders also endeavored to create a unique form of federal government that would blend national, state, and local strengths. The debate over federalism has always centered on just how strong a voice state and local governments would have in this experiment, and who would have the final say. At least for now, the answer is that the national government has the stronger voice and mostly the final say. But stay tuned. This debate is rarely more than a Supreme Court decision or two from a new twist. The states will never have the power to ignore or overturn national decisions on their own, but they always have the same rights as any individual citizen to petition Congress, the presidency, or the Supreme Court for redress of grievances. At least over the last decade or two, the national judicial branch has been very sympathetic to their requests.

This chapter examines the evolution of American federalism in five parts. The first section examines the Founders' basic definition of the term *federal,* asking how it came to be that the same Founders who created a strong national government could also label themselves as Federalists. The second looks at the boundaries between federal and state government set out in the Constitution. The third provides a history of the continuing debate over *state-centered federalism,* which sees the states as the more important voice, versus *nation-centered federalism,* which sees the national government as the dominant force. The fourth examines the tools of federalism today, while the fifth looks at the shape of state and local governments today.

REDEFINING FEDERALISM

The Founders would not have journeyed to Philadelphia for the Constitutional Convention if they had accepted the traditional definition of *federalism.* In 1787, a federal government had three features: (1) the states were to be equal partners in making all decisions; (2) all decisions were to be endorsed by the states; and (3) the national government was to leave most decisions to the states. As Pennsylvania delegate Gouverneur Morris explained the distinction, a *federal* government was "a mere compact resting on the good faith of the parties," while a *national* government was a "complete and *compulsive* operation" in which the national government was also the supreme government. As such, the original definition of federalism can be found in Article III of the Articles of Confederation, which proclaimed that "the said states hereby enter into a firm *league of friendship* with each other," while the original definition of a national government can be found throughout the Constitution.[3]

The Founders' preference for a national government was obvious from the very beginning of the Constitutional Convention. The Founders clearly believed that leagues of friendship left something to be desired when it came to defending the nation against foreign threats and assuring domestic tranquility. They also convinced themselves that such leagues invited tyranny. Much as traditional federalists argued that liberty was possible only in small states, Madison convinced his colleagues that liberty was more likely in large states and countries. Whereas a small state might be able to hide its oppression, a large nation could police its far corners, preventing the kind of threats to property that the Founders saw in Shays's Rebellion (see Chapter 2). It might be easy for a strong-willed majority to capture one state or two, but not thirteen states united under a vigilant national government.

As Box 3–1 shows, the states are anything but small today. There are now ten state and local governments that have budgets over $1 billion. There are also twenty-five states, one city, and one county with populations over 4 million. Although the national budget of nearly $2 trillion is slightly larger than all state and local spending combined, state and local governments employ nearly eight times as many civil servants as the national government. There are now 16 million state

BOX 3-1

The Top Ten Billion-Dollar State and Local Governments, 1998

State or Locality	Budget	Number of Residents	Number of Public Employees
1. California	$89 billion	31 million	343,000
2. New York State	$67 billion	18 million	267,000
3. New York City	$40 billion	7 million	381,000
4. Texas	$38 billion	18 million	248,000
5. Pennsylvania	$30 billion	12 million	145,000
6. Florida	$29 billion	14 million	167,000
7. Ohio	$27 billion	11 million	141,000
8. Illinois	$27 billion	12 million	132,000
9. Michigan	$26 billion	9.5 million	136,000
10. New Jersey	$24 billion	8 million	110,000

Source: *Governing's State and Local Sourcebook '98*, (Washington: DC., Governing, 1998), p. 68.

and local government employees, a number that is growing by 200,000 a year. Given that the total population of the United States in 1790 was just under 4 million, of which nearly 700,000 were slaves and more than half were women (none of whom "counted" as citizens), one can only wonder whether the Founders would consider states with fifteen or twenty times that population as safe homes for liberty.

In any case, the Founders needed at least nine states to ratify the Constitution. That did not mean support from nine state legislatures, however. Article VII of the Constitution merely required ratification by nine state conventions to be composed of the people. By ignoring state legislatures as a source of consent, while requiring the votes of only nine out of thirteen states, the Founders explicitly rejected the idea that the Constitution was some kind of compact to be ratified by all thirteen state governments, which is how the Articles of Confederation were created. This was not to be *We, the States*, but *We, the People*.[4] The new government failed all three tests of a federal government defined above: (1) the states were not equal partners; (2) the states did not endorse all decisions; and (3) the national government had the most important task of all: securing "the Blessings of Liberty to ourselves and our Posterity."

Nevertheless, good politics meant giving state conventions a reason to ratify the new government, which is precisely why the Founders agreed to include the Tenth Amendment in their Bill of Rights. Under the amendment, the states would have all powers either not delegated to the national government under the Constitution or not already prohibited to the states. Although states often point to the Tenth Amendment as proof that they have power, they would not have needed such protection had the Constitution guaranteed their independence and freedom.[5]

Good politics is also why supporters of the Constitution referred to themselves as **Federalists.** By advertising the Constitution through the *Federalist Papers*, supporters wrapped their work in the traditional term, even as they forged a unique definition that would stand the test of time. It hardly mattered whether the American people were confused by the words. What mattered most was getting the Constitution ratified.

The Case against the Constitution

Having lost the only name they thought appropriate, opponents of the new Constitution had little choice but to call themselves the **Anti-Federalists.** They argued that they were the true federalists, the honest federalists, but the Anti-Federalists were never quite able to generate much public outrage about the Constitution. They were outwritten by Hamilton, Madison, and Jay, and out-argued in their state ratification conventions.[6]

Despite their constant complaining about the "pretend Federalists" who had written the Constitution, the Anti-Federalists quickly established themselves as formidable students of the document they attacked. They started their case against the Constitution with a simple point: The document provided no guarantee that the states would remain independent and free. The states would continue to exist, but there was no grand endorsement of their independence. The Anti-Federalists were right, of course. Sometimes, what a document does not say is just as important as what it does say. Although Madison assured the readers of *Federalist No. 39* that the states would retain their sovereignty, albeit only the sovereignty not taken by the national government, the Constitution says nothing to that effect. The Founders clearly intended the national government to have the most powerful voice in deciding what the nation does.

The Anti-Federalists continued their case by making a second point: The Constitution said nothing about a *compact* between states, which meant that the states retained their independence and freedom to act in the absence of national permission. This was much more than a debating point. If the Constitution derived its authority directly from the people, the states were basically irrelevant and easily ignored. If, however, the Constitution derived its authority by a grant of power from the states and their delegates at the convention, the states retained significant freedom as *sovereign*, or independent, governments.

The Anti-Federalists did find at least some limits on the new national government in the Constitution's list of *enumerated powers* (see Chapter 2), which convinced them that the Federalists themselves had intended a more traditionally federalist government. If the Founders had wanted the legislative branch to make *all* the laws, the Anti-Federalists argued in reading a stronger role for the states between the lines, they would have said so. Instead, they gave Congress that long list of specific duties. The only problem with their wishful thinking was that the Constitution also included the *necessary and proper clause* (also discussed in Chapter 2), giving the legislative branch authority to do whatever it would take to do its job.

One argument the Anti-Federalists did not make was that the nation could somehow make the Articles of Confederation work. They were practical politicians, too, and understood that the time had come for a stronger national government. They differed with the Federalists in how strong that new government should be and whether the states had the authority to ignore, even veto, national laws if they saw fit. What if a state decided that a federal law was simply wrong? Could it take its own course? If states are free and independent, the answer is obvious: They could do what they wished.

A Political Solution

The Federalists and Anti-Federalists battled over the next three years, state by state as the Constitution moved toward ratification, arguing over the relative merits of state-centered and nation-centered federalism. At least for the future of federalism, the debate brought more heat than light to the final definitions. By confusing the debate with fuzzy language and artful labeling, the Federalists won the battle for ratification. But they also bequeathed to the future an ongoing dispute about the proper boundary between states and the national government.

The turning point in the debate actually came long before the Constitution was completed. The question of states versus nation was engaged almost immediately by the Virginia Plan, which offered the following conclusion and proposal: Resolved "that a Union of the States merely federal will not accomplish the objects proposed by the articles of Confederation, namely common defense, security of liberty and general welfare"; resolved further "that a national Government ought to be established consisting of a supreme Legislative, Executive, and Judiciary." Although the final Constitution did not contain such language, the point was made. The convention was not about rescuing the Articles of Confederation at all, but about forming a new national government as the supreme voice in the land. Even the Anti-Federalists understood that America needed something much stronger than a mere compact among the states. The debate was never about the pure federal ideal versus a national government, but about just how strong that national government would be.

Just because the Constitution was ratified, however, does not mean the battle for a stronger national government was over. Having lost their campaign against ratification, the Anti-Federalists fought the new national government at every turn, while arguing that states know best what their citizens need. Although the Anti-Federalist label had mostly disappeared by the 1820s, the notion that states were independent and free was at the heart of the Civil War forty years later. If states could not be free to practice slavery under the Constitution, the Southern states' argument ran, they would have to be free to do so under a new and independent confederacy.

Despite the Anti-Federalist claims, the Founders always believed the states would provide most of the basic services that shape daily life. If they were unwilling to guarantee the continued independence and freedom of the states, the Founders were quite willing to acknowledge their continued existence. What they wanted was a national government to worry about the whole, even as the states provided most of the government services, limited as they were at the time. The Founders hardly wanted their new national government to get into the business of hauling garbage, policing the streets, fighting fires, or teaching schoolchildren. Except for delivering mail and fighting wars, they assumed that states would do most of the basic work of government. Hence, the Constitution contains a mix of both guarantees and limitations on state power. On the one hand, all powers not given to the federal government are reserved for the states. On the other hand, all powers given to the federal government are denied to the states. As a result, states cannot enter into treaties, alliances, or confederations with other nations on their own.

As with so much of the Constitution, the precise blend of responsibilities has changed over time. States have used the Tenth Amendment as a modest check on Washington, while using occasional loopholes in national laws to create innovative programs of their own. But even as one celebrates state and local governments as what Supreme Court Justice Louis Brandeis called "laboratories of democracy," it is important to remember which comes first. After nearly two centuries of debate, the answer is almost always the national government. Although states do win their victories from time to time, the Constitution did, indeed, produce a government that is mostly national and sometimes federal.

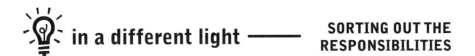

in a different light ——— SORTING OUT THE RESPONSIBILITIES

The definition of *federalism* remains almost as confusing today as it was in 1787. Americans are not always sure which level of government should do what. They certainly know that state and local government should teach children, and they clearly believe that the federal government should protect food and medicines, conserve the country's natural resources, and manage the economy to prevent recessions, but they are much less certain about who is responsible for reducing poverty, helping the elderly, reducing juvenile delinquency, and helping Americans send their children to college. Box 3–2 shows how Americans divided the responsibilities in a 1997 poll.

What seems like uncertainty on the surface may actually be quite rational thinking underneath. Americans clearly look to the national government to solve problems that cross state lines, most notably conserving natural resources, providing affordable health care, ensuring safe food and drugs, and managing the economy. In a similar way, they look to their state and local governments for help with problems closer to home, particularly setting academic standards and reducing juvenile delinquency. They are not quite sure who is responsible for helping the elderly, making college affordable, or reducing poverty, but clearly believe that individuals and community groups should take the lead on promoting greater honesty and stronger morals among people, and reducing juvenile delinquency. Although the fit is not always perfect, Americans do have some sense that problems close to home should be solved by the governments or community groups that are closest to home, too.

One thing is certain: Americans trust their state and local governments more than they trust the government in Washington. Although the Founders convinced themselves that liberty was safer in a union of states governed by a strong national

BOX 3-2

Who Should Do What

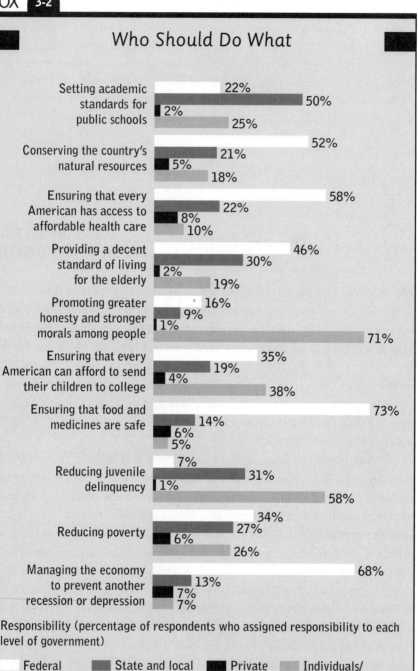

Setting academic standards for public schools
- 22%
- 50%
- 2%
- 25%

Conserving the country's natural resources
- 52%
- 21%
- 5%
- 18%

Ensuring that every American has access to affordable health care
- 58%
- 22%
- 8%
- 10%

Providing a decent standard of living for the elderly
- 46%
- 30%
- 2%
- 19%

Promoting greater honesty and stronger morals among people
- 16%
- 9%
- 1%
- 71%

Ensuring that every American can afford to send their children to college
- 35%
- 19%
- 4%
- 38%

Ensuring that food and medicines are safe
- 73%
- 14%
- 6%
- 5%

Reducing juvenile delinquency
- 7%
- 31%
- 1%
- 58%

Reducing poverty
- 34%
- 27%
- 6%
- 26%

Managing the economy to prevent another recession or depression
- 68%
- 13%
- 7%
- 7%

Responsibility (percentage of respondents who assigned responsibility to each level of government)

| Federal government | State and local government | Private industry | Individuals/ Community groups |

Source: The Pew Research Center for The People & The Press, *Deconstructing Distrust: How Americans View Government* (Washington, DC: Pew Research Center for The People & The Press, 1998), p. 82.

government, the American public today seems to have some doubts. Consider the following findings from another 1997 public opinion survey:

- Two-thirds of Americans said they are pretty interested in following local politics, compared to half who said they are generally bored by what goes on in Washington.
- Three-quarters said that, generally speaking, elected officials in Washington lose touch with the people pretty quickly.
- Two-thirds said that the federal government controls too much of their daily lives.
- Two-thirds said dealing with a federal government agency is often not worth the trouble.
- Three out of four agreed that the federal government should run *only* those things that cannot be run at the local level.

In short, Americans tend to trust the governments that they know best, which means state and local governments.[7]

It is important to note that these numbers ebb and flow over time. Back in the 1960s and 1970s, the public was less trusting toward state and local governments, in part because those governments were less professional than today, and in part because they were so reluctant to enforce the laws ending racial discrimination. Americans routinely endorsed federal intervention on poverty, discrimination, even schools because they simply did not believe states and localities would do the right thing. Thirty years later, state and local governments have regained the public's trust the old-fashioned way: they have earned it. They have become much more effective at doing their jobs and are often ahead of the national government in economic and social reform. States and localities have become the source of much of the policy innovation in the United States today and have been leaders in making their governments work better through reforms in public administration.

Most important, states administer many of the laws that Americans support. Roughly 85 percent of all environmental enforcement cases are now handled by state governments, a proportion that is likely to increase as Congress and the presidency continue to cut the number of national government employees. Americans may want a strong role for the national government in conserving natural resources, but it is state and local governments that enforce the laws, build the waste treatment plants, inspect the cars, and monitor the toxic waste dumps.[8]

THE CONSTITUTIONAL BOUNDARIES

No one can know whether the American public trusted their governments in 1787, if only because it would be over 150 years before social scientists would invent the first truly scientific public opinion surveys. Nevertheless, the odds are that the public did not trust the government in New York (not Washington yet) very much at all, which made the Founders' job of selling a new national government to the state ratifying conventions that much more difficult. At the same time, however, public demands on state governments were increasing, making the potential benefits of a national government that might quell unrest more attractive.

Constructing a Relationship

The Founders had three choices as they began debating the relationship between the new national government and the states. These three options are diagrammed in Box 3–3. First, they could have created a **unitary government,** in which there would have been essentially only one government. Although state and local governments might still exist, they would report directly to the national government, with no governors, state legislatures, county boards, mayors, city councils, or local courts to get in the way. Every policy would flow from the top to the bottom.

Second, the Founders could have created a somewhat stronger **confederation** of the states. Building on the Articles of Confederation, the national government would have remained mostly subservient to the states. Only responsibilities not reserved for the states would have been given to the national government—for example, national defense. There would have been no government for the country because, in a very real sense, there would have been no country beyond the thirteen states.

The Founders chose a third option, of course, which was a blend of modest state authority with a strong national government. Whether or not they used the term "federal" correctly in describing their choice, the Founders understood that their national government could not survive without state support. "No political dreamer was ever wild enough to think of breaking down the lines which separate the states, and of compounding the American people into one common mass," wrote Chief Justice John Marshall for the majority in *McCulloch v. Maryland,* a case that is discussed below. Without separate states, there would be no Constitution. But the Founders clearly rejected any notion that the states would somehow remain free and independent under the new government.

Central to this definition of federalism was a set of limits on just what the states could do to the nation and a set of permissions for what the nation could do to the states. Those limits have been the subject of repeated court tests over the years, forming a body of decisions that continues to shape how far those state

BOX 3-3

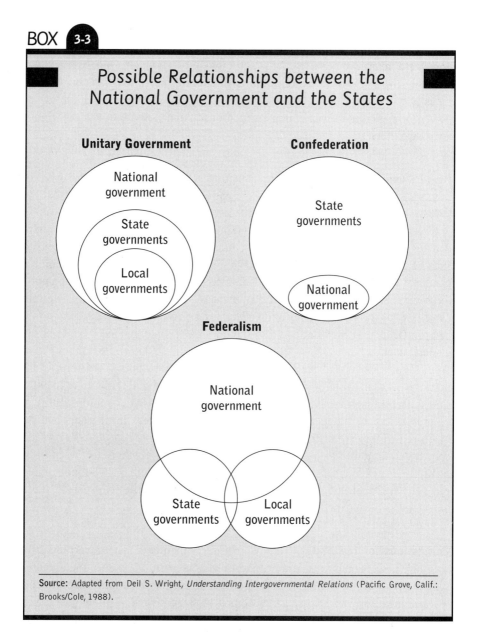

Possible Relationships between the National Government and the States

Unitary Government

National government

State governments

Local governments

Confederation

State governments

National government

Federalism

National government

State governments

Local governments

Source: Adapted from Deil S. Wright, *Understanding Intergovernmental Relations* (Pacific Grove, Calif.: Brooks/Cole, 1988).

and local circles extend into the circle marked "national government." Before turning to the major decisions, it is useful to review these limits and permissions.

Limits on the States. That the states are not independent and free is obvious in the basic text of the Constitution. Under Article I, Section 10, for example, the states are explicitly prohibited from entering into any treaties, coining money, interfering with contracts between other states and individuals, or passing any **ex post facto laws,** which declare an act criminal after it has occurred. Article I also prohibits the states from taxing imports or exports, keeping troops or ships in times of peace, or entering into any compact with another state or with a foreign power, or engaging in war unless invaded or in such "imminent Danger" that it must defend itself.

Permissions for the Nation.   The Constitution gave the new national government extraordinary authority to lead the nation. Article VI clearly states that the laws of the United States are the supreme laws of the land, while Article I, Section 8, gives Congress at least three different sources of authority over the states: Under the necessary and proper clause, it has the power to make all laws "which shall be necessary and proper" for carrying out its duties. Under the **commerce clause,** it has the power to "regulate Commerce with foreign Nations, and among the several States, and with the Indian Tribes." And under the **general welfare clause,** it has the power to "lay and collect Taxes, Duties, Imposts and Excises, to pay the Debts and provide for the common Defence and general Welfare of the United States."

All of the clauses have been used by the Supreme Court at one time or another to establish the supremacy of national law over the states, as well as to order state and local governments to implement national laws. As Hamilton argued in *Federalist No. 27*, "the legislatures, courts, and magistrates" of the states "will be incorporated into the operations of the national government as far as its just and constitutional authority extends; and will be rendered auxiliary to the enforcement of its laws."[9] The question was not whether the national government could order the states, but how far its "just and constitutional authority extends." It is a question that forms the basis of conflict to this day.

Permissions for the States.   The Constitution mentions state governments at least fifty times. States are guaranteed territorial integrity, the power to maintain a state militia (i.e., the National Guard), and authority both to ratify amendments to the Constitution and to call a new constitutional convention. If not guaranteed independence and freedom per se, states were most certainly not ignored. According to Madison, they retained "a residuary and inviolable sovereignty," which basically means they were independent and free to the extent that the Constitution did not say otherwise.

Supporters of the traditional definition of *federalism* often point to the Tenth Amendment as proof positive that all power not specifically given to the national government automatically belongs to the states. That is not the only reading of the amendment, however. When read alongside the supremacy, necessary and proper, commerce, and general welfare clauses, the Tenth Amendment appears to be more a symbolic gesture than a source of true authority.

This limited reading appears to be more accurate. The First Congress specifically rejected a proposal to add the word *expressly* to the amendment, which would have changed the wording dramatically, as follows: "The powers not *expressly* delegated to the United States by the Constitution, nor prohibited by it to the States, are reserved to the States respectively, or to the people." In rejecting the proposal, the First Congress appeared to endorse a much more limited reading of the Tenth Amendment, which is how the Supreme Court interpreted state authority until the mid-1980s, when the tide of decisions began to turn in favor of the states.

The Tenth Amendment is not entirely without force, however. It certainly underpins the Supreme Court winning streak discussed later in this chapter, and it appears to limit the authority of Congress to make all laws which shall be necessary and proper when it comes time to control the states. Nevertheless, Congress and the presidency seem gifted in finding ways to control the states with or without direct orders, particularly by dangling dollars before the states. Hence, the Tenth Amendment is best seen as a reminder of the traditional definition of *federalism* and of the politics of ratification rather than as a true guarantee of state independence and freedom.

Enforcing the Boundaries

Once the Founders redefined federalism, the national government had to enforce it. It was one thing to tell the states that the national government was in charge, and quite another to actually make it true. No case was more important to establishing the supremacy of the national voice than *McCulloch v. Maryland*, which established the dominance of national law over the states in 1819.

The facts of the case are simple. Raising money as states do, Maryland decided to place a tax on a branch of the Bank of the United States. When the tax collectors called on James McCulloch, cashier of the Baltimore branch, he refused to pay. The national courts faced two questions: (1) Because creating banks was never listed as an enumerated power of Congress, was its creation of the Bank of the United States thereby unconstitutional? and (2) Does a state have the power to tax the national government? The Supreme Court's answer to both questions was no.

McCulloch was an easy decision for the Court, at least when compared to its predecessor, *Marbury v. Madison,* which established the basic principle of judicial review in 1803 (see Chapter 2). On the question of whether the national government could create a bank, the Supreme Court turned to Article I of the Constitution: creating the bank was an appropriate expression of the legislative power "To make all Laws which shall be necessary and proper" for carrying out its duties.

Before turning to its finding, the Supreme Court felt compelled to discuss what the Founders had intended in creating their national government. It was true that the Founders had been elected by state legislatures, Marshall wrote for the Court. But that is where the Founders lived. And it was also in their several states that the Founders assembled. But, as the Supreme Court asked, "where else should they have assembled?" The fact that they came from states, Marshall argued, did not give the state the power to ignore national law. More important, the Constitution derived its authority not from the states, but from the people: "The government of the Union, then . . . is, emphatically and truly, a government of the people. In form and in substance it emanates from them. Its powers are granted by them, and are to be exercised directly on them, and for their benefit."[10]

The creation of the bank may not have been the best decision for the national economy (the bank was abolished in 1832), but it was certainly an acceptable exercise of legislative power. That is why the necessary and proper clause is also known as the *elastic clause*. As noted above and in Chapter 2, it will stretch to cover just about any exercise of power that Congress might imagine. Even though the formation of a national bank was never listed as an enumerated power of Congress, it could be considered one of the **implied powers** granted to Congress in the Constitution.

On the question of whether a state can tax the federal government, the Supreme Court turned to Article VI of the Constitution. Allowing a state to tax the federal government would make that state's law supreme over every American regardless of where they lived, thereby violating that article. Moreover, Marshall closed the opinion by saying, such action would turn the federal system upside down, putting the states in charge of the national government, not vice versa: "The difference is that which always exists, and always must exist, between the action of the whole on a part, and the action of a part on the whole—between the laws of a government declared to be supreme, and those of a government which, when in opposition to those laws, is not supreme."

The Marshall court strengthened its argument five years later in *Gibbons v. Ogden*. The case involved a steamboat operator who had a New York license to operate the only ferry on the interstate waters between New York and New Jersey. A competitor named Gibbons sued, arguing that only Congress could regulate interstate waters. The Marshall Court agreed unanimously, further strengthening the national government's power over the states.[11]

in a different light ——— A WINNING STREAK FOR THE STATES

No one argues that the states are free to ignore the national government anymore, especially not the Supreme Court. Starting with *McCulloch,* case after case has confirmed the supremacy of national laws over the states. Nevertheless, the national government is not free to order the states to do whatever it wishes. The Supreme Court has made a number of rulings in recent years that serve to remind Washington that the United States has a federal system, not a unitary government. It is all part of the constant rebalancing that occurs under the Constitution.

The current winning streak for the states began in 1975 when the Supreme Court struck down a national law extending minimum wage standards to state, county, and municipal employees. The case, *National League of Cities v. Usery*, seemed to give the states freedom to ignore at least some national laws. Writing for the 5–4 majority, Justice William Rehnquist noted that there "are attributes of sovereignty attaching to every state government which may not be impaired by Congress...."

Although this decision was reversed nearly ten years later in *Garcia v. San Antonio Metropolitan Transit Authority*,[12] the states got back on the winning track in 1992 with *New York v. United States*.[13] That decision involved enforcement of the Low-Level Radioactive Waste Policy Amendments Act of 1985, which required the states to implement national guidelines for managing radioactive waste. New York argued that the Tenth Amendment shielded the states from being used as instruments of national policy. "While Congress has substantial powers to govern the Nation directly, including areas of intimate concern to the States," the 6–3 Supreme Court majority wrote in favor of New York's case, "the Constitution has never been understood to confer upon Congress the ability to require the states to govern according to Congress' instructions...."

The states won another major victory in 1995 when the Supreme Court overturned the Gun-Free School Zones Act of 1990, which used the commerce clause as a basis for prohibiting the possession of a firearm in a school zone. Despite the compelling interest in shielding school children from gun violence, the 5–4 majority saw it as more important to protect an area in which "states historically have been sovereign."

The most recent victory for the states involved a popular national law regulating handgun purchases. The law was the direct consequence of the attempted assassination of President Ronald Reagan in 1981. Reagan's press secretary, James Brady, was struck by one of the bullets and suffered a permanent brain injury. After years of lobbying Congress for handgun control, Brady and his wife, Jane, were victorious when Congress passed the Brady Handgun Violence Prevention Act in 1993. The law required state and local chief law enforcement officers to conduct background checks on all prospective handgun buyers.

Two officers sued to overturn the law in 1996, one of whom was Sheriff Jay Printz of Ravalli County, Montana. The two officers argued that Congress had violated state sovereignty by compelling state officers to conduct the background

James Brady reads a statement in support of the handgun control act named for him. With a new Republican majority in Congress, President Clinton mounted an effort to protect the Brady law from any weakening.

checks on its behalf. In *Printz v. United States* in 1997, the Supreme Court agreed by a 5–4 majority.[14] According to Justice Antonin Scalia, "By forcing state governments to absorb the financial burden of implementing a federal regulatory program, Members of Congress can take credit for 'solving' problems without having to ask their constituents to pay for the solutions with higher federal taxes. And even when the States are not forced to absorb the costs of implementing a federal program, they are still put in the position of taking the blame for its burdensomeness and for its defects."

However politically compelling such action might be, Scalia continued, it was clearly forbidden by the division of power between state and national governments. "We held in *New York* that Congress cannot compel the States to enact or enforce a federal regulatory program," Scalia concluded in linking the Court's decision in *Printz v. United States* to its earlier decision in *New York v. United States.* "Today, we hold that Congress cannot circumvent that prohibition by conscripting the State's officers directly."

Central to the decision was the majority's definition of federalism as a system of *dual sovereignty*. In such a system, the states are independent except where the Constitution clearly says otherwise through the enumerated powers or the supremacy clause. This definition was first used in a unanimous 1990 decision giving state courts authority to prosecute certain kinds of cases under the national Racketeer Influenced and Corrupt Organizations (RICO) Act, and was further refined in a 7–2 1991 decision that upheld Missouri's right to impose a mandatory retirement age for judges despite the national Age Discrimination in Employment Act's prohibition to the contrary. "As every schoolchild learns," Justice Sandra Day O'Connor wrote in the Missouri case, "our Constitution establishes a system of dual sovereignty between the States and the Federal Government."[15] Apparently everybody knew it but two of her fellow justices, who were subsequently joined by two more justices to form a solid four-member minority block in the *Printz* case.

The *Printz* decision was not an unqualified victory for the states. The Court majority also noted that states can voluntarily enlist in any such federal regulatory program, and reminded the national government that it can always entice states to do so by offering them financial assistance. The minority also served notice that the battle over federalism was far from over. Writing for the minority, Justice John Paul Stevens argued that the *Printz* decision might actually work against state sovereignty. "By limiting the ability of the Federal Government to enlist state officials in the implementation of its programs, the Court creates incentives for the National Government to aggrandize itself. In the name of States' rights, the majority would have the Federal Government create vast national bureaucracies to implement its policies." If the states could not help the national government execute the laws, Stevens argued, the national government might become so large as to be a threat to liberty. The last thing the Founders would want is a national police force that could be used against the people.

THE HISTORY OF FEDERALISM

The history of American federalism is best viewed as a running argument about the appropriate balance between national and state power. As a general rule, the national government has grown stronger when the Democratic party has been in control and during periods of national crisis, while the states have grown stronger when the Republican party has been in charge and during periods of relative national calm.

Even the most dedicated Republican, however, could not take the nation back to the early years when the states argued that they were mostly immune to national control. It may have taken two hundred years, but Madison's definition of federalism as a blend of national and federal governments is firmly in place. It is often unclear just where the government in Washington ends and the governments of the states and localities begin. But it is clear that the national government is mostly in charge.

It is useful to describe the history of federalism in three parts, each of which may be characterized as a different kind of cake. The first era resembles a layer cake, with a relatively small national government layer perched on top of much larger state and local layers; the second resembles a marble cake, with the national, state, and local flavors mixed together from top to bottom; and the third resembles an upside-down cake, with the national government the much larger layer (at least in terms of dollars) and the state and local layers progressively smaller below. These eras are discussed in the sections that follow.

The Era of Dual Federalism

The first era in the history of federalism involved **dual federalism.** The theory underpinning this "layer-cake" era is simple: each layer has its own powers, duties, and loyalties, and never the twain shall meet. Like a layer cake, which holds its parts together with a sugar frosting, dual federalism holds the nation together through patriotism and the need for common defense. The national government does not give money to the state and local governments, and does not tell citizens who gets what, when, and how from their own state and local governments. The national government is also the smallest of the layers, holding a mere fraction of the power of state and local governments.

The layer-cake era began with ratification of the Constitution and continued off and on until the 1930s. States frequently asserted their right to be left alone, claiming that the national government could exercise only the enumerated powers of the Constitution. The first such effort came within five years of ratification of the Constitution. In 1798, the Virginia and Kentucky legislatures passed resolutions rejecting the power of the national government to enforce the Alien and Sedition Acts, which made criticism of the national government a crime. The Virginia and Kentucky Resolutions argued that the law violated the First Amendment protections of free speech and the independence of the states. The Virginia Resolution argued that the states had the "unquestionable right to judge" national laws, even to the point of refusing to obey laws that they considered violations of the Constitution. The controversy passed when Thomas Jefferson was elected president in 1801 and the Alien and Sedition Acts expired. Having secretly written the Kentucky Resolution, Jefferson had no intention of enforcing those acts.

The battle over **state-centered federalism** versus **nation-centered federalism** was far from over, however. Central to dual federalism was the notion of **states' rights**, a rallying cry for those who believed that states should have the primary role in a federal system. With the Tenth Amendment as their rallying point, advocates of states' rights often argued that the national government had no right to interfere in most state activity. In strictest terms, states' rights advocates argued that the national government could exercise only the specific powers listed in each section of the Constitution. Everything else was off limits.

The states' rights movement suffered its greatest setback in the Civil War. Southern states claimed that the national government had no business interfering in the practice of slavery, even arguing that the states were free to ignore, or nullify, national laws that they felt violated the Tenth Amendment. The Civil War, and the Thirteenth and Fourteen Amendments that immediately followed the Union victory, resolved the **nullification** debate once and for all. Slavery was abolished by the Thirteenth Amendment, while states were prohibited from depriving any persons in their jurisdictions of life, liberty, or property without "due process of law" and from denying any persons "equal protection of the laws." As discussed in Chapter 14, the Fourteenth Amendment has been a central tool for pushing civil rights downward into the states. States must abide by national law, particularly regarding the good of the United States as a whole and the protection of Americans (in this case, former slaves) as individual citizens.

The debate over nullification may have ended with Robert E. Lee's surrender at Appomattox, but dual federalism continued for another eighty years. During this period the national government had more than enough to do at a national level managing westward expansion, the Spanish-American War, and World War I without meddling in state and local affairs. When the national government did try to regulate the states, as it did in passing child labor laws in the early 1900s, the Supreme Court used the Tenth Amendment to declare the laws unconstitutional. In one famous case, the Supreme Court mistakenly rewrote the Tenth Amendment to say "the powers not *expressly* delegated to the national government are reserved" to the states and the people.[16] Such was the penetration of dual federalism into the public consciousness. Recall that the First Congress had explicitly rejected a proposal to add the word *expressly* to the amendment.

The Era of Cooperative Federalism

The second era of federalism involved **cooperative federalism.** Instead of the sharp divisions of dual federalism, cooperative federalism involves federal, state, and local governments working together to solve pressing problems: like a marble cake, in which the different flavors swirl together, it is often impossible to tell where one ends and the other begins.

The era of marble-cake federalism began with the Great Depression in the 1930s and continued through the 1960s. As the Founders knew, some threats to the nation were too big to be handled by state governments alone. The Depression was just such a problem. Started by a stock market crash in 1929 and driven forward by worldwide economic collapse, the Depression created wave upon wave of business failures, which, in turn, generated a vast population of unemployed, homeless Americans.

Arguments about whether the national government had the power to act under the Tenth Amendment hardly made sense when the entire nation was on the verge of economic and social collapse. Drawing in part on the general welfare clause, President Franklin D. Roosevelt promised the nation a "New Deal" of federal spending programs that included dozens of new programs and national agencies. Young Americans went to work building the national parks in the Civilian Conservation Corps, artists painted murals under funding from the Works Progress Administration, dams were built by the Tennessee Valley Authority, family farms were saved under the Agricultural Adjustment Act, labor unions were strengthened by the National Labor Relations Act. The national government ran some of the programs itself, but it also gave the states money to put Americans back to work. By the end of the 1930s, federal dollars accounted for one-tenth of all state spending.

This spirit of cooperation continued into the 1960s with President Lyndon Johnson's "Great Society" agenda, which was designed to end poverty and strengthen opportunities for the country's racial and ethnic minorities. The three levels of government seemed quite able to cooperate as long as big national grants to the states and localities were involved. National spending for education, interstate highways, and welfare all set new records in the 1960s, leading some politicians to wonder whether the United States had entered an era of upside-down-cake federalism—that is, with the national government almost completely covering the states and localities with money and responsibilities.

By the end of the 1960s, federal dollars accounted for one-fifth of all state spending, a figure that has remained relatively stable over the past three decades. Box 3–4 shows both the growth in national dollars (held constant for inflation) to the states and the percentage of state and local spending covered by the yearly total. Although the amount of national spending has risen steadily, state and local budgets have clearly kept pace. Almost all national funding to states and localities involves **grants-in-aid,** which tell state and local governments how dollars are to be used. Most national funding goes to states and localities in **categorical grants,** which set strict limits on what the dollars may be spent for.

While national dollars have remained relatively constant as a percentage of state and local spending, the purposes to which the spending is put have changed dramatically. In 1960, 43 cents of every national dollar granted to the states and localities was spent on transportation and highways; by 1992, that number was

BOX **3-4**

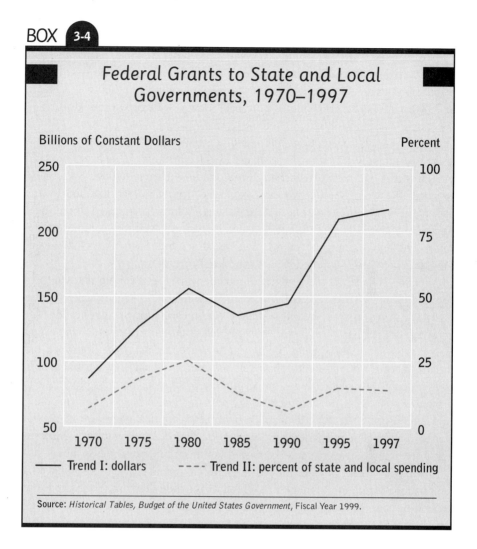

Federal Grants to State and Local Governments, 1970–1997

Billions of Constant Dollars   Percent

—— Trend I: dollars   ---- Trend II: percent of state and local spending

Source: *Historical Tables, Budget of the United States Government,* Fiscal Year 1999.

down to just 12 cents. During the same period, the amount of spending for healthcare skyrocketed from just 3 cents on the dollar to 40 cents, while spending for education more than doubled from 7 cents to 16 cents. It is not clear that, given a choice, states and localities would have approved the shift. After all, transportation and highways are politically popular. Since their choice has been between money for what the national government wants and no money at all, however, state and local governments have accepted the dollars gladly, in part because they have learned how to shift dollars from one account to another with relative ease (see the discussion of the substitution effect on pages 95 and 96).

The New Federalism

The third era of federalism involves the **new federalism,** a term President Richard Nixon coined in the early 1970s for describing his plans to shift federal responsibilities and dollars back to the states and localities. In theory, it is an era in which national responsibilities flow back down, with or without dollars, to the states.

As a Republican, Nixon believed in a smaller national government, but knew that the only way to make it smaller was to sift through the list of national programs that had been established during the New Deal and Great Society. He believed that welfare and environmental protection were best handled by the national government, in part because the states could not be trusted to set a reasonable minimum level of welfare benefits. He also believed that community development, job training programs, and social services such as mental health programs were better handled by state and local governments.

Nixon's challenge was to figure out some way to give certain national programs back to the states. After all, one of the reasons states like national programs is that Washington pays the bill for them. Nixon came up with two options for winning state support. The first involved **block grants** to the states. Nixon asked Congress to create three giant block grants—for community development, job training, and education—that states could use pretty much as they wished as long as the money was spent for the broad purposes intended. Because block grants ordinarily collapse dozens of categorical grants into single blocks, they are an expression of state-centered federalism. In contrast, categorical grants are an expression of nation-centered federalism, giving the national government significant authority to force states to spend money either in specific categories or not at all.

Nixon's second method for passing back programs to the states involved a new national funding program called **general revenue sharing.** The purpose of general revenue sharing was to give states a portion of the national tax dollars, thereby encouraging them to take more responsibility for their own programs, while reducing somewhat the amount of money the national government would have to spend on categorical grants to the states. Unlike block grants, which required the states to spend money for broad purposes such as job training or community development, revenue sharing gave the states completely unrestricted dollars. As Nixon explained in launching the program, "It is our hope to use this mechanism to so strengthen state and local governments that by the end of the coming decade, the political landscape of America will be visibly altered, and the states and cities will have a far greater share of power and responsibility for solving their own problems. The role of the Federal Government will be re-defined and re-directed toward those functions where it proves itself the only or the most suitable instrument."[17]

Begun in 1972 and ended in 1986 in an effort to reduce the national budget deficit, revenue sharing sent states and localities an average of over $6 billion a year even as the amount of money devoted to block grants continued to increase steadily. By 1995, the national government had sixteen separate block grants, totaling nearly $55 billion a year. Categorical grants had hardly disappeared, however. There were 633 grant programs for helping state and local governments in 1996. Roughly three out of every four national dollars still go to the states under categorical control.

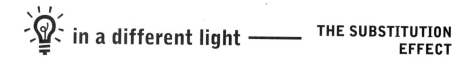

in a different light ——— THE SUBSTITUTION EFFECT

Much as state and local governments complain about the burdens of categorical grants, the reality is that states often use national grant dollars to cover costs that they were already willing to pay. Economists calls this phenomenon a *substitution effect*. Simply defined, a substitution effect occurs when a state or local government uses a national grant to free its own dollars for some other activity. Economist Arthur Okun calls this sort of situation a "leaky bucket" problem, in which some percentage of all national grants leaks out before reaching the intended target. Some of the money leaks out due to administrative costs, some to waste and inefficiency, and some to substitution effects.[18]

Without any substitution effect, a national dollar granted to the states would create exactly one dollar's worth of new activities. But with a substitution effect of, say, 60 percent, a dollar granted to the states would purchase only 40 cents' worth of new activities. Research suggests that the 60 percent figure is in fact the average. For every national dollar sent down to the states, the states appear to withdraw about 60 cents of their own funding, freeing those dollars to work elsewhere in their governments. In a sense, therefore, a grant can be seen as a kind of gift certificate. It can purchase things a government had never thought to buy, or things it was going to purchase all along.

Sewage systems provide a classic example of substitution effects. The U.S. Environmental Protection Agency has been giving grants for the better part of two decades to build better treatment facilities, and the states and localities have been happy to get the dollars. But because most states and localities have to build sewage treatment facilities anyway, the national grants create a huge substitution effect. The effect is particularly pronounced for sewer lines that run from homes and businesses to the treatment plants. Because localities would have funded those lines with or without national dollars, the substitution effect is 100 percent, meaning that the grant money replaces every last dollar that the states and localities would have spent on their own.

Sewage treatment plants like this one often involve substitution effects. Although states and lo-calities must build such facilities regardless of national funding, they often use national dollars to free up their money for other priorities.

Congress and the presidency have several options for reducing substitution. They can set tighter requirements on how grant dollars are used. They can also require that states put some of their own dollars into the grant, maintaining existing levels of state funding even when the national dollars arrive. The fact that less than half of all grants carry any of these restrictions on substitution suggests that categorical grants have become a hidden form of revenue sharing.

The Devolution Revolution

Nixon's ideas for returning power to the states are still active today. They were adopted as part of the Contract with America agenda by the new Republican House majority in 1994, where they came to be known as the "Newt Federalism" in honor of Republican House Speaker Newt Gingrich, a contemporary advocate of states' rights.[19]

Republicans were not the only ones involved in the "devolution revolution," as it was called. President Bill Clinton joined the movement in 1996 by supporting the end of the national government's Aid to Families with Dependent Children (AFDC) program. Created during the New Deal, AFDC was the central national program for delivering financial assistance to poor Americans. Administered by the states, AFDC provided benefits to 12.9 million Americans in 1996. Promising to "end welfare as we know it," Clinton endorsed the House plan to replace AFDC with a block grant, thereby giving states much greater freedom to design new welfare programs with one string attached: welfare recipients would have a five-year lifetime limit on cash benefits, and would be required to be working a minimum of twenty hours a week within two years of receiving their first check.

THE TOOLS OF FEDERALISM

Except for welfare reform, the devolution revolution was hardly a revolution at all. Even though they had promised to return authority to the states, Congress and the presidency continued to treat state and local governments as extensions of the national government. "It's much easier to devolve when somebody else is in power," said Senator Fred Thompson (R-TN) of his Republican colleagues. "When you've got the ball, the temptation is to replace those bad, old regulations with your good, new regulations, instead of sending it back to the states."[20] It is a temptation made all the greater because the two main tools of federalism—grants-in-aid and orders—are easily exploited to the national government's benefit.

Grants-in-Aid

The first tool for influencing state and local governments are grants-in-aid. When the national government pays for a specific activity such as a new highway or school lunches for poor children, it can set the terms for how states must act in spending the dollars. Recall that there are two types of grants: categorical grants and block grants. Categorical grants often carry strict rules regarding how states and localities can spend the money, while block grants give states and localities much more freedom to put the money where they think it will do the most good.

Once the national government decides to create a new grant program, it must decide how the money will be divided across the country. **Project grants** are only available for specific projects such as a new sewage treatment plant, and are usually awarded through a competition between states and localities. In contrast, **formula grants** are given to all states and localities on the basis of an agreed-upon formula that makes sure every government receives its fair share of the available national money. Most formula grants use population as the basis for allocating the dollars among the states and localities. As a general rule, the bigger the state, the bigger the amount of grant funding. Most national grants to states and localities involve formula grants.

Orders

The second tool of federalism is a direct order. Congress and the presidency have passed dozens of laws over the past few decades ordering state and local governments to behave in certain ways. Under the Marine Protection Research and Sanctuaries Act of 1977, cities are prohibited from dumping sewage sludge into the ocean. This order increases costs for New York and other coastal cities, but the national responsibility to protect the oceans exceeds the local interest in saving money.

Under the Americans with Disabilities Act of 1990, states and localities must protect the civil rights of roughly 50 million disabled Americans, which means, among other things, that they must ensure that their public buildings and services are accessible to handicapped people. This requirement imposes significant new costs on state and local governments, which must spend their own dollars to add ramps and elevators to make old office buildings wheelchair accessible, to buy new "kneel-down" buses and subway cars, and so on. Although they are free to sue the national government to declare such direct orders unconstitutional, there is little evidence that the federal courts would agree. Under the necessary and proper, commerce, and general welfare clauses, the national government appears to have ample authority to make states behave in certain ways.

Congress and the president also have the authority to preempt states from acting in certain public policies. A **preemption** expresses the national government's intent to take responsibility that might otherwise be left to the states. The First Congress issued the first preemption by passing the Copyright Act of 1790, making clear that awarding patents and copyrights would be a national, not a state, function under the commerce clause. States were forbidden to issue patents and copyrights of their own. A full preemption tells the states that the national government will fulfill all responsibilities in an area, while a **partial preemption** informs the states that the national government will set some minimum standard that all states must meet. Under a partial preemption, states are always free to exceed the national standard. The state of California does just that in requiring automobile companies to meet lower emission standards in the state than they must in the rest of the nation.

Some of the most effective orders are built around grants. Such an order is often called a **mandate.** In its simplest form, a mandate asks a state or local government to do something it otherwise would not do, either by requiring such action as a condition of receiving grant dollars or by threatening to pull funds if a state does not comply. According to Martha Derthick, early grants-in-aid, such as the Federal Highway Aid Act of 1919, had few strings attached. But over time,

> Congress slowly and steadily began treating state governments less and less like independent governments and more and more like subordinates, subject to command. As this change advanced, Congress discovered the political advantages of mandates without money—it could order other governments to do worthwhile things like give health care to pregnant women and children or educate handicapped children or treat sewage to a very high standard or guarantee transportation for the disabled while leaving them to figure out how to pay much of the costs.[21]

Such mandates without money, or unfunded mandates, as they are often labeled, take two forms. Some use **crosscutting requirements** to advance broad national goals. When a state or local government accepts a national grant for one purpose, it must agree to obey other national laws on everything from environmental protection to fair employment practices and accounting standards. Absent agreement, it cannot receive the grant. Although obeying these laws can cost money, particularly through increased employment costs, the national government rarely pays the bill, making such crosscutting requirements an unfunded mandate.

Others mandates use **crossover sanctions,** which require state and local governments to fulfill certain obligations in order to receive or retain national funding. In 1984, for example, Congress passed the National Minimum Drinking Age Act, which threatened to withhold national highway grants from states that did not raise the legal age for drinking alcohol to twenty-one years by 1986. States were free to ignore the law, but would lose precious highway funds as a result. Twenty-seven states raised their minimum drinking age as a result.

Whatever the specific device used, mandates are a source of nearly constant complaint from state and local governments. States and localities have even put together lists of the most offensive mandates. The lists rarely vary between state, county, and city governments, and cover everything from the Metric Conversion Act, which requires all national agencies to use the metric system in grants (a crosscutting requirement), to the Safe Drinking Water Act, which establishes maximum levels for contaminants in the nation's sixty thousand drinking water systems (a partial preemption), to the Endangered Species Act, which requires all national agencies to ensure that no grants jeopardize the survival of threatened and endangered species or otherwise promote the destruction of critical habitats (a crossover sanction), to the rule requiring states to use asphalt containing at least 20 percent recycled rubber from old tires (a crossover sanction).

Complaints about mandates without money eventually prompted Congress to enact the Unfunded Mandates Reform Act of 1995, which sought to raise the political costs of enacting such mandates. Under the act, Congress is required to estimate the potential cost of a mandate before enacting it into law. In theory, knowing what a mandate will cost states or localities should make Congress more sensitive to the burdens it is about to impose. In reality, Congress pays far greater attention to the size of the national budget deficit, which is why it passes unfunded mandates. Forced to choose among passing an unfunded mandate, increasing the national budget, and doing nothing at all, Congress will almost always pass an unfunded mandate. According to one estimate, one out of every four state and local government employees currently works full time for the national government under unfunded mandates.[22]

 **in a different light** ——— EARMARKING AS FEDERALISM

Members of Congress have ample reason to make sure their states and districts get their fair share from national grants-in-aid. Much as they agree that formula grants are the fairest way to make sure each state gets its rightful amount, recent years have witnessed an explosion in the number of grants set aside by members for special projects back home. These legislative *earmarks* assure that pet projects get funded.

That Congress cares about bringing home the bacon is not in dispute. As Morris Fiorina writes, "The average constituent may have some trouble translating his congressman's vote on some civil rights issue into a change in his personal welfare. But the workers hired and supplies purchased in connection with a big federal project provide benefits that are widely appreciated."[23] That is why Congress was so enthusiastic about the $217 billion transportation bill enacted in May 1998. The members certainly understood that the Building Efficient Surface Transportation and Equity Act of 1998 (BESTEA) would create jobs back home.

As the primary sponsor of the bill, twelve-term representative E. G. "Bud" Shuster (R-PA) was unapologetic about either the size of the measure, which increased federal transportation spending by nearly half, or its record-setting level of earmarks. Having warned his colleagues not to believe "this baloney that we somehow break the budget, that we somehow create a deficit," Shuster defended the $9 billion reserved for special projects earmarked by individual members of Congress. "Who knows better what is most important in their district than the Members of Congress from that district?" he asked of state officials who questioned the need for the earmarks. "I would respectfully suggest there is a bit of arrogance in those who say that somehow they know better what is important in their congressional districts than Members know. Indeed, I would suggest that if Members do not know what is really important to people in their congressional district, they are not going to be here very long."[24]

The transportation budget provides ample opportunity for congressional earmarking. In 1998, Congress passed the largest transportation budget in U.S. history.

Shuster reserved even harsher words for House colleagues who simultaneously attacked the projects even as they pushed for "multimillion dollar projects in their own congressional districts." " 'How I envy the pious," Shuster paraphrased James Michener's *Hawaii;* " 'They can be such hypocrites and never even know it.' "

Last-minute negotiations leading to final passage of the bill proved his point. The Senate, which had long protested the earmarks as wasteful spending, offered a list of 360 projects worth $2.3 billion just hours before Congress was to adjourn for a long recess. "The Senate castigates projects," Shuster said. "But when they come to conference at about 2 A.M. on the 21st day, they reach in their pocket and pull out a list."[25]

"Mr. Speaker, this is not pork," said one of Shuster's supporters in defending the bill against charges that it contained too many pet projects. "This is steak. If we want to continue to be a prime rib country, we better pass this bill quick."[26]

Members of Congress have been earmarking special projects for decades, allowing them to claim credit for national spending in their home states and districts, thereby increasing their popularity at election time. Senator Alfonse D'Amato (R-NY) was so effective in winning transportation grants for his home state during the 1990s that he became known as "Senator Pothole."

Although the Founders expected members of Congress to fight for their home districts, they might be surprised at the expanding use of earmarks today. Transportation earmarks alone have gone up from just ten projects and $262 million when Congress enacted its 1982 highway bill to 152 projects and $1.4 billion when the bill came up for its ordinary renewal in 1987, 538 projects and $6.2 billion when it came up again in 1991, and 1,850 projects and $9.3 billion in its most recent renewal in 1998.

The problem with earmarks is that individual members of Congress, not the states or localities, decide which projects should come first back home. Citizens who live in the states or congressional districts of particularly powerful members of Congress such as Shuster end up with smooth highways, state-of-the-art sewage treatment plants, and endless special projects, while citizens who live in the states or districts of junior members go to the bottom of the list. That is why states and localities often oppose earmarks. Although politics also play a role in how states spend national grants, states and localities believe they have a better idea of where the needs are than members of Congress. House members may know what is important in their own districts, but they may not know what is best for their state as a whole.

WHAT STATE AND LOCAL GOVERNMENTS DO

The focus on how the national government controls state and local government can distract from a point made early in this chapter: state and local governments have become important partners in making American government work. They may not spend as much money as the national government, but they have far more public employees and deliver some of the nation's most important services. State and local public servants teach most of the country's children, guard most of our criminals, vaccinate most of our poor children, police most of our streets, and fight almost all of our fires.

The Growth of State and Local Governments

States and localities deliver these services through a complicated web of governments. There is just one national government and only fifty state governments, but there are nearly 85,000 county, city, town, school, and special governments. The United States has over 3,000 counties and nearly 15,000 school districts.

Over the past half century, the number of school districts has actually fallen dramatically, largely due to the school consolidation movement, which encouraged small districts to combine into ever larger conglomerations. Between 1942 and 1992, the number of local school districts dropped from 108,000 to just 15,000. At the same time, the number of special districts grew from just 8,000 to nearly 32,000. A **special district** is a government body that is usually created to manage a single service, such as water treatment, a local airport, or mosquito control. The Port Authority of New York and New Jersey, the Chicago Transit Authority, and the Los Angeles County Sanitation District are all forms of special districts. Because they are usually created by state government, they are not subject to local control.

Remove school districts from the totals and add in the special districts, and the number of state and local governments has gone up from 33,000 in 1942 to roughly 70,000 today. Along the way, the number of state and local public employees skyrocketed, rising from barely 6 million in the early 1960s to 16 million today. Roughly two out of five state and local employees are school teachers, one in six are college professors and administrators, one in ten are public health professionals, one in fifteen are police officers and firefighters, and one in twenty are prison guards. Box 3–5 shows the kinds of work that state and local government employees do.

Law enforcement and schools are fueling much of the current growth. Law enforcement is growing because of get-tough crime laws. Those laws require more police to catch criminals and more prison guards to keep them incarcerated. Schools are growing because of the current baby boomlet, which has produced an increase of nearly 5 million new school-age children since the mid-1980s. Of the nearly 400,000 new teachers hired since 1986, three-quarters have been elementary school teachers.[27]

The question is whether there are just too many state and local governments today. The marvelous diversity produced by 85,000 governments is accompanied by a tangle of confusion about who is responsible for what. Is Los Angeles City or Los Angeles County government responsible for the roads? Is the Los Angeles School Board or the Los Angeles Port Authority responsible for training future workers? Because most local governments operate under state charters that give them great independence from each other, they may have little incentive to work together toward the common good. The problem is particularly severe in large metropolitan areas, where poorly funded city governments struggle to maintain enough of a tax base to provide essential services not only for their residents but also for thousands of suburban workers who commute to their jobs in the morning and leave the city behind at night.

Laboratories of Democracy

Whatever their specific authorities under the national Constitution, states look very much as if they are independent and free. Almost all have their own bill of rights, almost all of which give the state all powers not denied to it by its own

BOX 3-5

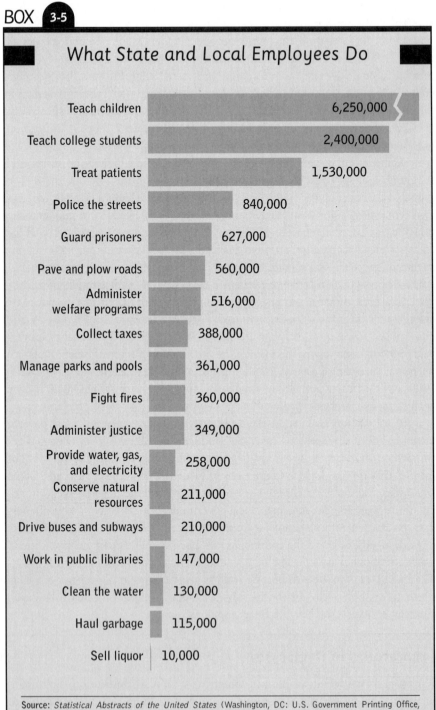

What State and Local Employees Do

Teach children	6,250,000
Teach college students	2,400,000
Treat patients	1,530,000
Police the streets	840,000
Guard prisoners	627,000
Pave and plow roads	560,000
Administer welfare programs	516,000
Collect taxes	388,000
Manage parks and pools	361,000
Fight fires	360,000
Administer justice	349,000
Provide water, gas, and electricity	258,000
Conserve natural resources	211,000
Drive buses and subways	210,000
Work in public libraries	147,000
Clean the water	130,000
Haul garbage	115,000
Sell liquor	10,000

Source: *Statistical Abstracts of the United States* (Washington, DC: U.S. Government Printing Office, 1997) p. 326.

constitution or the national government; all state constitutions provide for a legislative, executive, and judicial branch of government; almost all provide for a line item veto. All the states but one have bicameral state legislatures. (Nebraska continues to operate with the nation's only unicameral state legislature.)[28]

State and local governments may differ most from the national government in the election of executive branch officials. Thirty-six states currently elect their own secretaries of state, thirty-eight elect the state treasurer, twenty-five elect their auditor, twelve elect the agriculture secretary, and five elect the land supervisor. The pattern continues down to the local level, where some cities even elect the police chief. The result is that governors and mayors have little authority to direct the executive agencies of government. Much as one may admire the commitment to giving the people a voice in government, direct election of so many officers of government may undermine the faithful execution of the laws by making it difficult for a governor to order an agency to act. A similar pattern exists at the local level, where 98 percent of all school boards are elected independently of the rest of city government.

Despite such institutional curiosities, state and local governments have become important players in virtually every decision that gets made at the national level, including issues of free trade. Indeed, state and local governments have become aggressive advocates of national policy, and were intimately involved in the welfare reform effort discussed earlier in this chapter. They have their own trade associations to lobby Congress and the president (the National Governors Association, the National Conference of State Legislatures, the Council of State Governments, the National Association of Counties, the U.S. Conference of Mayors, the League of Cities, and the International City Managers Association); these associations have active legal staffs to challenge national laws that violate what they see as the sovereignty of the states. All but one of the "big seven," as these associations are called, are located in Washington, D.C.

More important, even as their diversity can sometimes frustrate agreement, it is a source of great national strength. As Supreme Court Justice Louis Brandeis argued, "It is one of the happy incidents of the federal system that a single courageous state may, if its citizens choose, serve as a laboratory; and try novel social and economic experiments without risk to the rest of the country."[29]

State and local governments have been more than up to the task, crafting innovative answers to some of the nation's most pressing problems and leading the way on everything from education reform, where states have pioneered the use of charter public schools, to financing health care for uninsured children. In 1997, for example, Pennsylvania won a national innovation award for its land recycling program, which redevelops abandoned and contaminated industrial sites, called "brownfields," through small grants to local governments; Boston won an award for its "Operation Cease Fire," which prevents gun violence by identifying "hot spots" and negotiating nonviolence pacts among rival youth gangs; and

Georgia won an award for its voluntary prekindergarten program, which seeks to give every four-year-old in the state a head start on school.[30]

Welfare reform is a classic example of the role of the states as laboratories of democracy. The idea for limiting the amount of time an individual would be allowed to collect welfare began in Wisconsin and spread to Michigan, Colorado, and Utah. Although the experiments were explicitly approved by the Department of Health and Human Services in Washington, the states were clearly far ahead of the national government in imagining ways to both cut welfare spending and put more Americans to work.

It is still unclear whether the national welfare reforms modeled on these state experiments will work. Welfare rolls appear to be going down in many states, while the number of former welfare recipients who have found jobs appears to be going up. The question is whether there will be enough good jobs to cover all the welfare recipients who must go to work when their eligibility expires. What is clear is that the states are trying a variety of approaches to meeting the new requirements. Some have established a "work first" policy, which requires welfare recipients to take the first job they are offered, rather than going back to school or starting a special training program. Others have increased enforcement of personal conduct rules, which require welfare recipients to show up on time for appointments or honor social contracts to spend a certain amount of time each day looking for work. Still others have loosened the restrictions on how much extra income a welfare recipient can earn before losing benefits.

MAINTAINING THE BALANCE

It is impossible to know what the Founders might think of today's multilayered federal system. Never have there been so many governments delivering so much to so many Americans through so many layers. Although the number of national government employees has fallen over the past five years, state and local government is booming. As noted above, many states and several cities are much larger today than the entire nation was in 1787.

This layering of governments protects the delicate balance in two ways. First, depending on how the Supreme Court rules from year to year, state and local governments can act as an important check on national power. It is not always clear just where the national government ends and the state and local governments begin. To the extent that states can hold their own against national mandates and grants, they prevent the national government from growing well beyond its own boundaries. The states could therefore act as a kind of fail-safe, a last protection, in the event that a majority faction captures all three branches of the national government. Conversely, to the extent that states and localities become mere extensions of the national government, they increase the threat to liberty that might arise should such a capture occur.

State and local governments may have become so dependent on national grants that they dare not challenge Washington. The more money states get from Washington, the less courageous they may be in fighting the latest crosscutting requirement, crossover sanction, or full or partial preemption. One can hardly blame states and localities for taking the money, of course, particularly given the rising number of unfunded mandates. Nor can one fault them for creating substitution effects. To paraphrase the old advertising slogan, Washington can pay the states now for unfunded mandates, or it can pay them later. But state and local governments will get paid either way.

Perhaps that is the second way the states and localities protect the delicate balance. By shifting dollars between accounts through substitution effects, they reduce their dependency on Washington, which in turn may increase their readiness to do what it takes to maintain a semblance of independence and freedom. If so, the behavior would be just one more example of how the Constitution holds the delicate balance over time. However much Washington may treat the states and localities as extensions of itself, the Constitution gives them enough leeway to maintain an independent check. Perhaps those substitution effects are not so troubling after all. Having a leaky bucket may be one small part of having a national government that is strong enough to protect the nation, yet limited enough that it never becomes a threat to liberty.

terms to remember

facts and interpretations

- The Founders changed the definition of *federalism* from being a compact among the states to being a mixed government that is mostly national and sometimes federal. The definition allowed supporters of the Constitution to label themselves as Federalists and helped win ratification of the Constitution. It is not always clear just what the Founders intended the states to be in the new government. Some, including recent majorities of the Supreme Court, believe the national government and the states were to act in a system of dual sovereignty, while others, possibly including Madison and Hamilton, appeared to view the states as a limited extension of the national government. The debate over whether or not the states are independent and free, or sovereign, continues to this day.

- The history of federalism can be described as a running debate between state-centered and nation-centered views of the relative power of the national and state governments. Although the era of layer-cake, or dual, federalism mostly ended with the New Deal in the 1930s, several recent Supreme Court decisions have rekindled the argument about whether states are independent and free of the national government. Even if states do have a claim to what the Supreme Court has called dual sovereignty, the national government remains free to offer state and local governments grants to do its bidding, which in turn can create a dependency that renders even the most sovereign state highly dependent on the national government.

- The national government has an extensive set of tools for getting state and local governments to follow its lead. If money cannot buy love, it can certainly buy attention. With national grants now providing roughly one out of every five dollars in state and local revenue, the national government has considerable say in what those governments do. Once a state or local government takes a grant, it can be obligated to follow national laws under a crosscutting requirement. And if cold cash does not create the incentive, the national government can always use one of several kinds of orders, including full and partial preemption.

- State and local governments have been growing rapidly in recent years as Americans come to expect more and more from the governments they know best. Although Americans are sometimes confused about which level of government should do what, they tend to want state and local governments to take care of the problems closest to home, and the national government to take care of the problems that either cross state boundaries or are more difficult to solve. Americans also see a significant role for individuals and community groups in addressing the nation's most pressing problems.

open questions

- What advice would you give the next Congress or president who wants to push authority back to the states? What kinds of programs are best handled at the state or local level, and when can states and localities be trusted to be left alone completely?

- Which definition of *federalism* is the most appropriate for the United States today? Have state and local governments become too dependent on Washington for money? If so, how does that dependency compromise their ability to check the national government? What would the Federalists think of the use of mandates to influence state action? What about the Anti-Federalists?

- Is the Supreme Court headed in the right direction with its recent decisions on handguns and the states? Is the pursuit of a national policy such as gun-free school zones worth an occasional blurring of the lines between state and national government? What about the effort to end age discrimination?

for further study

Altshuler, Alan A., and Robert D. Behn, *Innovation in American Government.* Washington, DC: Brookings Institution, 1997.

Conlon, Timothy. *New Federalism: Intergovernmental Reform from Nixon to Reagan.* Washington, DC: Brookings Institution, 1988.

Donahue, John D. *Disunited States: What's at Stake as Washington Fades and the States Take the Lead.* New York: Basic Books, 1997.

Fiorina, Morris. *Congress: Keystone of the Washington Establishment*, 2d ed. New Haven, CT: Yale University Press, 1989.

Nice, David C., and Patricia Fredericksen. *The Politics of Intergovernmental Relations.* Chicago: Nelson-Hall, 1994.

Okun, Arthur M. *Equality and Efficiency: The Big Trade-Off.* Washington, DC: Brookings Institution, 1975.

O'Toole, Laurence J., Jr., *American Intergovernmental Relations.* Washington, DC: CQ Press, 1993.

Tocqueville, Alexis de. *Democracy in America.* New York: Harper Perennial, 1988.

endnotes for chapter 3

1. Roy P. Fairfield, ed., *The Federalist Papers* (Baltimore: Johns Hopkins University Press, 1981), pp. 583–84.

2. Alexis de Tocqueville, *Democracy in America* (New York: Harper Perennial, 1988), p. 157.

3. These quotes are drawn from Martin Diamond, "What the Framers Meant by Federalism" reprinted in Laurence J. O'Toole, Jr., *American Intergovernmental Relations* (Washington, DC: CQ Press, 1993), pp. 39–48.

4. David O'Brien provides an excellent summary of this debate in *Constitutional Law and Politics: Struggles for Power and Governmental Accountability*, 2d ed., vol. 1 (New York: Norton, 1995).

5. See Walter Berns, "The Meaning of the Tenth Amendment," in R. A. Goldwin, ed., *A Nation of States* (Chicago: Rand-McNally, 1961).

6. For a sampling of the Anti-Federalist case, see Herbert Storing, *The Complete Anti-Federalist: Writings by the Opponents of the Constitution* (Chicago: University of Chicago Press, 1981).

7. This second Pew Research Center survey is reported in the same document as the first; see *Deconstructing Distrust: How Americans View Government* (Washington, DC: Pew Research Center for The People & The Press, 1998).

8. See Margaret Kriz, "Feuding with the Feds," *National Journal,* August 9, 1997, pp. 29–32.

9. As cited in the majority opinion in *Printz v. United States,* 117 Sup. Ct. 2365 (1997).

10. *McCulloch v. Maryland,* 4 Wheat. (17 U.S.) 316 (1819).

11. *Gibbons v. Ogden,* 9 Wheat. (22 U.S.) 1 (1824).

12. The two cases are, respectively, *National League of Cities v. Usery,* 426 U.S. 833 (1976) and *Garcia v. San Antonio Metropolitan Transit Authority,* 469 U.S. 528 (1985).

13. *New York v. United States,* 505 U.S. 144 (1992).

14. *Printz v. United States,* 117 Sup. Ct. 2365 (1997).

15. *Gregory v. Ashcroft,* 501 U.S. 452 (1991) .

16. The case was *Hammer v. Dagenhart,* 247 U.S. 241 (1918).

17. Quoted in Richard P. Nathan, "The 'Nonprofitization Movement' as a Form of Devolution," in D. Burlinggame, W. Diaz, and W. F. Ilchman, eds., *Capacity for Change: The Nonprofit World in the Age of Devolution* (Indianapolis: Indiana University Center on Philanthropy, 1996), p. 47.

18. Arthur M. Okun, *Equality and Efficiency: The Big Trade-Off* (Washington, DC: Brookings Institution, 1975), pp. 91–95.

19. See Richard P. Nathan, "Hard Road Ahead: Block Grants and the 'Devolution Revolution,' " discussion paper, Nelson Rockefeller Institute of Government, State University of New York, Albany, 1998.

20. Eliza Newlin Carney, "Power Grab," *National Journal,* April 11, 1998, pp. 27–31.

21. Martha Derthick, "New Players: The Governors and Welfare Reform," *Brookings Review* (Spring 1996), p. 44.

22. Paul C. Light, *Shrinking Government: Federal Headcounts and the Illusion of Smallness* (Washington, DC: The Brookings Institution, 1999).

23. Morris Fiorina, *Congress: Keystone of the Washington Establishment,* 2d ed. (New Haven, CT: Yale University Press, 1989), p. 40.

24. *Congressional Record,* April 1, 1998, p. H1886.

25. Quoted in Alan K. Ota, "Shuster Prepares for Onslaught against Members' Projects," *CQ,* March 21, 1998, p. 737.

26. *Congressional Record,* April 1, 1998, p. 1893.

27. See Jonathan Walters, "The Myth of the Meataxe," *Governing,* February 1998, p. 19.

28. See Ann O'M. Bowman and Richard C. Kearney, *State and Local Government,* 3rd ed. (Boston: Houghton Mifflin, 1996), for a basic introduction to these issues.

29. Quoted in O'Brien, *Constitutional Law and Politics,* p. 588. For a discussion of state and local government innovation, see Alan A. Altshuler and Robert D. Behn, *Innovation in American Government* (Washington, DC: Brookings Institution, 1997).

30. These examples are from the list of 1997 winners of the Ford Foundation's Innovation in American Government prize, which awards $100,000 to each of the ten government programs deemed most innovative.

public
opinion

the consent
of the governed

Hardly a day goes by without the release of some new public opinion poll. Americans are constantly being asked for their opinions. The polls cover every possible issue, from the sublime to the ridiculous, from people's favorite character on *Seinfeld* (Kramer was tops by nearly three to one over Jerry) to their worries about cloning (most people would just as soon not meet their clone). Pollsters are not afraid to ask Americans anything, giving us a nearly instantaneous voice on every issue, big or small, private or public.

Perhaps that is why the Founders worked so hard to insulate American government against **public opinion,** a term that describes what people think about the issues of the day. The Founders knew Americans would never lack for opinions, dividing into factions at the slightest provocation. As James Madison wrote in *Federalist No. 10,* "So strong is this propensity of mankind, to fall into mutual animosities, that where no substantial occasion presents itself, the most frivolous and fanciful distinctions have been sufficient to kindle their unfriendly passions and excite their most violent conflicts."

The Founders worried about government by the people, but that does not mean they ignored public opinion. To the contrary, they were consumed by the effort to win public support for the Constitution. As noted in Chapter 2, they wrote the *Federalist Papers* precisely to advertise the proposed constitution to a wary public, and capitulated on the Bill of Rights to gain public favor for the new government. Disappointed as they were by human nature, they worked hard to move public opinion toward their cause. With that goal in mind, they would almost certainly have viewed modern opinion polls as a potent tool for helping leaders *lead*—that is, as a way to help virtuous leaders persuade the people to give their consent to be governed.

What would have troubled the Founders is the use of public opinion polls to help leaders *follow*—that is, to determine the best course for the nation by asking the public what it wants. Indeed, it was precisely this worry that convinced them to insulate government against capture by strong-willed majorities. Hence, they created the system of separate powers, separate interests, separate layers, and checks and balances that would insulate each branch from the others. Even if a strong-willed majority somehow captured the House of Representatives, for example, it would be buffered by the Senate, the presidency, and the judiciary. Except for the election of senators by state legislatures, most of the Founders' original buffers are still in place.

The Founders would also have been troubled by the volume of public opinion that now courses through American government. Presidents, members of Congress, and the political parties have nearly instant access to every opinion poll conducted, and can easily commission their own polls if they want extra details. Presidents even have their own pollsters, who serve on the White House staff to make sure the president has up-to-the-minute access to what the people think. If a strong-willed majority exists on a public policy issue such as abortion, national health insurance, or events in Bosnia, the U.S. government's leaders are going to know about it.

It is one thing to care whether the people still support the government, and quite another to make public policy decisions based on the latest opinion poll. The former reflects a perfectly reasonable concern with the continued consent of the governed, while the latter may reflect a concern with one's own survival as a politician. The Founders did not expect government leaders to ignore the people, but neither did they expect the people to be consulted on the day-to-day operation of government. That is why the Founders did not provide a national referendum or initiative. The people would give their consent to be governed on election day, and then the governing would begin. The government had to maintain the delicate balance between caring enough about the people to gain that consent and becoming so consumed with currying favor that strong majorities would gain the upper hand in imposing their will on the rest of the nation. Because it is now possible to know what the people think within minutes of an event (through what are sometimes called "flash polls"), this delicate balance may be harder and harder to keep. At some point, the onslaught of public opinion polls may lead America's leaders to believe that short-term popularity is the only measure of their success.

Because questions about the role of public opinion appear throughout this book, this chapter will provide a much deeper definition of what public opinion is: where it comes from, what Americans know about politics, what they believe, and why they do not trust government. Before tuning to these American attitudes, it is important to know how public opinion is measured. The fact that a poll says Americans think one way or the other does not necessarily make it so. There are good polls and bad polls. Part of being an effective consumer of opinion is knowing the difference.

MEASURING AND USING PUBLIC OPINION

American government is awash in public opinion today. Starting in the 1930s, when statisticians discovered that a few hundred randomly selected Americans could accurately represent a nation of millions, the polling business has grown continuously. Hardly a day goes by without some new polling effort to find out what Americans think about politics and society. (**Polling** refers to collecting public opinion by asking a random group of individuals the same set of questions about a given topic.)

A Brief History of Polling

Polling has been part of American politics for at least two hundred years. Newspapers have been conducting polls since the early 1800s, when the *Harrisburg Pennsylvanian* and *Raleigh* (NC) *Star* began asking people what they thought about the presidential candidates. Although early polls were never used to predict the outcome of an election, they did shape how reporters covered the campaign, starting a long and often troublesome tradition of covering the horse race between candidates rather than the issues, asking who's ahead rather than what's at stake.

By the 1930s, newspapers and magazines were routinely using **straw polls** to predict the outcome of presidential elections. A straw poll is nothing more than a pretend ballot. Movie theaters coined the term as a way to sell soda. Moviegoers could vote by tossing their straws into the trash can marked for their favorite candidate. A straw poll may have been a great way to sell soft drinks, but not to measure public opinion. People who cast make-believe ballots at a movie theater do not always vote, and they most certainly do not represent the rest of the public. It was a straw poll that eventually led *Literary Digest*, the most popular news magazine of the 1930s, to confidently predict a landslide victory for Alf Landon over Franklin D. Roosevelt in the 1936 election. Just the opposite occurred, and the *Literary Digest* folded as readers turned to *Life* and *Time* instead.

The difference between a straw poll and a modern public opinion survey is simple mathematics. Using statistical theories of how a randomly selected sample of Americans could represent the public at large, a group of young pollsters actually got the 1936 election right, and began to build their reputations with further success in 1940 and 1944. The firms created by Louis Harris, Burns Roper, and George Gallup are still in business today.

The young polling industry endured its greatest test in 1948, when all the major pollsters predicted that Harry Truman would lose the presidential election to Thomas Dewey. They were so sure that Truman was out that at least one newspaper, the *Chicago Tribune,* declared Dewey the winner without waiting for the actual vote count. Pollsters had simply stopped polling weeks before the election, while voters continued switching toward Truman. "It was the first case I know of where the polls affected what they were allegedly measuring; what the polls did was make the Republicans complacent," said Burns Roper, Jr. "The unions dragged their supporters to the polls while the fat cats played golf. When we went out a few days after the election and did a poll of people who said they had voted, we had Dewey elected again. The complacent vote told us they had voted, but they hadn't."

The polling industry survived the 1948 election because it learned the right lessons from the debacle, not the least of which was to continue interviewing through the last days of a campaign. Most pollsters do not stop interviewing until twenty-four hours before the election occurs. Pollsters also discovered that the key to predicting an election is not to ask *everyone* how they are going to vote, but to ask just those people who are most likely to vote. It makes no sense to include the opinions of people who have little or no intention of actually showing up on election day. Thus, most polls during an election campaign focus on "likely voters," meaning citizens who say they intend to vote. Most polling firms have their own methods for identifying the most likely voters. Some firms interview only people who say they are following the campaign and care about who wins, while others interview only those who say they intend to vote on election day. Although polling is very much a science, there is still plenty of room for art—and the art involves, among other things, knowing whom to ask.

How Opinions Are Measured

Although polling has become more scientific over time, its purpose has never changed: to find out what the American public thinks. It is important to note, however, that public *opinions* are different from public *values*. Values are the most basic, long-term commitments people have, and are often rooted in their religious and social backgrounds: a belief in God, in the importance of hard work, in equal opportunity for all, in government by the people. Opinions flow in part from these values but are much more responsive to short-term events. Opinions are specific responses to immediate issues. Opinions change, while values are much more durable.

It is also important to note that polling is designed to measure more than just the simple number of people who favor one issue or another at a specific point in time. Polls also seek to measure four features of opinion: (1) **salience,** which measures whether Americans are following an issue at all; (2) *stability,* which measures whether the opinions are set or changing; (3) *direction,* which measures the direction in which the opinions are moving; and (4) *intensity,* which measures how strongly the opinions are held. Salience may be the most important of the four, for if Americans do not care about an issue, they can hardly hold strong opinions of any kind.

Opinions do not just exist at a given moment in time. They ebb and flow, strengthen and weaken. It is entirely possible, for example, that a small minority of Americans will feel much more intensely about abortion or school prayer than the vast majority, or that an issue just will not matter to most people. Although polls can help government understand what the public wants, they can also create the impression of a strong majority where none exists. Far too many pollsters report only the final division of opinion on a given question, ignoring questions of salience and intensity.

Before turning to how polls are used in government today, it is important to understand the basic mechanics of polling. Polling has become a science that mixes mathematics, linguistics, and statistical analysis to predict everything from the outcome of the next election to the sales potential of a new product. An accurate poll involves full disclosure, a search for truth, a random sample, a fair question, a clear connection, honest answers, careful analysis, and a final number. Each of these elements is discussed briefly in the following section.

Full Disclosure.   As the costs of conducting a public opinion survey have fallen with new technologies such as the personal computer, the number of polling organizations has expanded. Whether they do their polling primarily for business or politics, these firms are under great pressure to conduct their polls for the lowest cost. As a result, some firms may compromise their survey methodologies to save money.

Unfortunately, readers cannot know whether a particular poll is accurate unless the polling firm provides full disclosure about when, where, and how its polls are conducted. As a general rule, a reputable poll will always carry a disclosure statement revealing how many people were interviewed, when the interviews took place, what the potential for error is in the final results (see the discussion of random samples below), who paid for the survey, and how the interviews were conducted. The more information a poll carries about its survey methodology, the more confident readers can be about the results. If such a disclosure is not attached to a survey, readers are well advised to ignore the results.

A Search for Truth.   Not all polls are designed to generate truth. Some are designed to support a specific point of view, while others are used to generate mailing lists and raise money. Just because someone on the other end of the phone line says they are conducting a public opinion survey, it is not safe to conclude that they are interested only in accurate opinions. As Box 4–1 shows, there are at least five types of polls that are anything but concerned with truth.

The most troubling abuses involve advocacy polls, which seek to convince the nation that a majority favors some issue by actually manufacturing the majority, and push polls, which seek to influence elections through outright lies. In a classic example of advocacy polling, Republican pollster Frank Luntz asked the following question about public support for term limits in 1994: "Do you agree that we need term limits to replace career politicians with citizen legislators? Politics shouldn't be a lifetime job." It was a leading question that virtually assured that most Americans would favor Luntz's preferred option. Luntz then used the answers to form part of the "Contract with America" program that swept Republicans to victory in that year's congressional elections. He would have received very different answers had he asked the following: "Do you agree that we need term limits to replace experienced legislators with amateur politicians? Public service shouldn't be a part-time job."

A Random Sample.   The first challenge in public opinion polling is to round up a small number of people who represent the range of opinions of the entire population. The only way to do it is to guarantee that every person has an equal chance of being chosen to be interviewed. Using such a **random sample,** fewer than one thousand respondents can represent the entire U.S. population of 270

BOX **4-1**

Types of Problem Polls

Advocacy Polling: Designed to produce a set of results that favor a particular point of view. Questions are phrased so as to produce a specific answer.

Canvassing under the Guise of a Public Opinion Poll (Cugging): Used as a way to build a mailing list. The pollster ends the interview by asking for a mailing address.

Self-Selected Listener Opinion Polls (SLOPs): People with the money and interest call one of several 900 phone numbers to register their position on an issue.

Computerized Response Audience Polls (CRAPs): A walk-in audience registers its views on an issue or event by pressing buttons on a hand-held computer meter. Sometimes used to register reactions to a political debate or advertisement, which can be misinterpreted by the media as indicators of what a scientific sample of Americans think.

Push Polls: A phony question is used to spread a rumor about a candidate in order to "push" voters toward the other candidate or to discourage them from voting at all. Directed toward thousands of registered voters.

million. (A *respondent* is a person who agrees to be interviewed for—that is, to respond to—a public opinion survey.) Although sophisticated mathematics underpin modern sampling theory, pollster George Gallup may have described it best when he noted that an accurate blood test requires only a few drops of blood, not a gallon.[1]

Because even the most careful random sample cannot be a perfect representation of the entire population, all polling results carry a **sampling error.** Most samples produce an error of plus or minus 3 to 4 percent, with the exact degree of error determined by the actual number of people interviewed. Sampling error is usually translated into a **confidence level** that tells readers to what extent a given result can be trusted. With a sampling error of 4 percent, for example, readers can be 95 percent certain that any given question in a survey may be off by 4 percent in either direction; a candidate who is leading by a 52 to 48 margin may actually be ahead 56 to 44 or behind 48 to 52.

A Fair Question. Drawing a random sample is only the first challenge in conducting an accurate poll. The pollster also has to write a simple, clear question. As the Luntz example shows, it is possible to write a polling question that will make respondents say just about anything.

It is also possible to write a question that does little more than confuse. Consider the following Roper poll question from 1992: "As you know, the term Holocaust usually refers to the killing of millions of Jews in Nazi death camps during World War II. Does it seem possible or does it seem impossible to you that the Nazi extermination of the Jews never happened?" The question produced a deeply troubling result: a third of Americans were not sure the Holocaust had occurred, and 22 percent even said it was entirely "possible" that the Holocaust never occurred at all. How could Americans have been so unsure of history?[2]

The problem was the double negative contained in the question: Does it seem *impossible* that the extermination *never happened?* Many respondents who answered yes actually meant the exact opposite. When the question was rewritten to ask whether it seems "possible to you that the Nazi extermination of the Jews never happened, or do you feel certain that it happened?" the proportion of doubters fell to 1 percent, with another 8 percent unsure. Ask a confusing question, get a confusing answer. Ask a simple question, get a simple answer.

How questions are asked and in which order also matters. Asking someone how they intend to vote only after asking how they voted in the most recent election may bias the answer in favor of the incumbent. Asking someone how the president is doing only after asking a battery of questions about the economy may shape the entire survey.

A Clear Connection. Something curious has happened as the number of polls has increased: the number of Americans willing to answer opinion surveys has declined. Pollsters are finding it harder and harder to get the right mix of respondents to sit for an interview. As **response rates,** which measure the number of people who say yes to the request for an interview, have fallen, pollsters have been forced to think of new ways to make sure people respond. Some polling firms now pay respondents $5 to $10 for an interview, while others offer gifts. For example, the University of Michigan's Institute for Social Research (which conducts the National Election Studies that provide much of the information used in Chapters 8 and 9 of this book) offers some of its respondents a small "M Go Blue" desk clock.

Thirty years ago, most public opinion interviews were conducted in the respondent's home. Today, most interviews are conducted by telephone. The interviewer sits at a computer terminal and enters the respondent's answers to the questions. Although telephone polls are both faster and cheaper than in-person polls, they may not be as accurate. People may just not be as honest on the phone as they would be face to face, particularly when it comes to revealing sensitive information about themselves.

Honest Answers.   Once the samples are drawn and the questions asked, the challenge is to interpret results correctly. Unfortunately, many Americans read far too much into polls. They tend to believe that polls are based on actual behavior, even though respondents sometimes merely tell a pollster what they think the pollster or society wants to hear.

Take church attendance as an example. Asking people in a survey whether they went to church last week is quite different from actually watching them walk in the door. People like to tell interviewers what they think the interviewers want to hear, a phenomenon social scientists call the "social desirability bias." The Gallup poll has been reporting for years that roughly 40 percent of Americans go to church regularly, a figure that has remained steady since the 1970s. However, a recent study of how people actually spend their days showed that church attendance fell from 42 percent in 1965 to 26 percent in 1994. How to explain the difference? Instead of asking respondents whether they went to church last week, which triggers the social desirability bias, the interviewers asked people repeatedly, over several months, what they had done the previous day. Because of the long-term, "diary" format, respondents simply felt less pressure to lie.

Careful Analysis.   Once the questions are asked and the answers are collected, an accurate poll depends on careful analysis. That means using the right statistics and drawing the right conclusions. It also means telling the truth about the answers.

A recent report by Third Millennium provides an example of careless analysis. According to the organization, which says it represents young Americans, more 18–34-year-olds believe in UFOs than believe that Social Security will exist when they retire. The numbers appear to support the claim. Asked about the probabilities in a 1994 poll, over a third of the young Americans interviewed said that it is more likely that UFOs exist than that they will ever receive Social Security, compared to just a sixth who said it is more likely that they will receive Social Security than that UFOs exist. "This is an apathetic rejection of the most significant financial commitment the government has made this century," Third Millennium argued.

The only problem is that the pollster who conducted the survey never asked young Americans to make the comparison. Rather, he took two questions asked at widely separated places in the same survey and combined them to imply that young Americans had greater faith in UFOs than in Social Security. The first question came early in the survey: "Do you think Social Security will still exist by the time you retire?" The second question came at the very end of the survey, with a clear hint about the answer: "And one final question, and I ask you to take this seriously—do you think UFOs exist?" By asking the respondent to take the UFO question seriously, the pollster clearly suggested that a "no" answer might not be serious.

The only way to know for sure whether young Americans have more faith in UFOs than in Social Security would be to ask the question directly: "Which do you believe is more likely to be true: that Social Security will exist in the future or that UFOs exist today?" When that question was actually posed to young Americans in 1997, two-thirds of the respondents said it was more likely that they would get Social Security when they retire than that UFOs exist. It is one thing to say that UFOs might exist in the abstract, and quite another to say that they are more likely to exist than a government program that has already existed for over sixty years.[3]

A Final Number.   Most polls produce a single number for every question. Who is ahead in the election? Do Democrats outnumber Republicans? How many Americans approve of Congress or favor abortion rights? Is Coke better than Pepsi? But behind every such answer is a distribution of public opinion that can be focused or confused. Indeed, that single number can disguise one of three very different patterns.

First, it can disguise a **normal distribution** of opinions, meaning that the single number is at the top of a relatively smooth, flat curve of opinion, and, therefore, reflects a true midpoint of what the public truly believes. Visualize a bell-shaped curve or a single-humped camel. A single number averaged from a normal distribution is a reasonably accurate indicator of where most Americans stand. Second, it can disguise a **bimodal distribution,** meaning that the average is actually the midpoint between two very different points of view, neither of which is close to the midpoint. Visualize two bell-shaped curves side by side or a two-humped camel. Third, it can disguise a **skewed distribution,** meaning that a handful of very strong opinions on one side of an issue distorts the picture of opinion. A single number from a bimodal or skewed distribution can create the illusion of public agreement that simply does not exist.

However tempting it may be to conclude that a single number tells the whole story, smart consumers of information about public opinion know better. They want to know about the salience, stability, direction, and intensity of opinion; whether the questions were fair and the analysis honest; how many respondents answered a question with "Don't know" or "Don't care"; and whether the distribution is normal or otherwise. They also want to know who paid for the poll and why before they accept the numbers, and always pay attention to who is drawing the conclusions. They also compare and contrast findings across questions and polls.

Most importantly perhaps, smart consumers want to know how answers to one question relate to others. In early 1998, for example, conservatives were outraged that a majority of Americans seemed to believe that President Clinton was lying about his alleged sexual relationship with White House intern Monica Lewinsky (which he admitted in a nationally televised address the following August), yet still thought he was doing a good job as president. "One problem is the problem of people who say, 'I see it, I think it happened, I think he lied about it, and I don't care,'" said former Reagan administration Secretary of Education William Bennett. "That's a serious problem. That is an erosion. That is a moral decline."[4]

That was also a serious misreading of two very different questions. It was true that two-thirds of Americans said Clinton was lying. It was also true that two-thirds approved of his performance as president. But when the two questions were analyzed together, it turned out that only a third of all respondents fit Bennett's hard profile. People who thought Clinton was lying were more likely to disapprove of his job performance, while people who thought he was telling the truth were more likely to approve of his job performance. Only one half of each two-thirds overlapped.

in a different light ——— A DIFFERENT KIND OF POLL

Americans do not need to major in political science to answer an opinion poll on politics. Indeed, most polls record the answers even when respondents know absolutely nothing about the issue at hand. Would they support sending U.S. troops to keep peace in Bosnia, for example, if they knew where Bosnia is? Would they support welfare reform if they knew more about the global economy and the loss of American jobs?

One way to find out what Americans might think if they had more information is to hold a "deliberative poll," which is technically not a public opinion poll at all. Unlike a traditional poll, which lasts fifteen to twenty minutes and asks its questions regardless of what the respondent knows, a deliberative poll lasts two or three days and gives each respondent detailed information on the issues before any questions are asked.

The first national deliberative poll was held at the start of the 1996 presidential campaign, and was sponsored by the Public Broadcasting System and the University of Texas Department of Government. All told, 910 randomly selected Americans were invited to spend three days in Austin in late January. The invitation was simple. Respondents would fly to Austin on American Airlines (which donated the airfare), receive free meals and lodging, and go home with $325 in expense money. Once in Austin, they would spend their days learning about economic and foreign policy, debate their views in small groups with other respondents, listen to presentations by the Democratic and Republican presidential candidates, and come to some final agreements on what the nation should do about the issues. If every- thing worked as planned, the deliberative poll would provide a snapshot of what a random sample of Americans might think about the issues if they actually had a chance to talk with each other about the facts.

The poll's sponsors believe that is exactly what their poll did. Although only 459 respondents actually came to Austin, the poll provided a rare chance to see a truly diverse collection of Americans talking to each other: farmers talking with welfare mothers, lawyers with schoolteachers, housewives with the unemployed, young with old, rich with poor. Roughly a quarter of the attendees had never flown on an airplane.

Along with making small changes in their views of government and society, the respondents also became more trusting toward their government. The number who strongly agreed that they had opinions about politics worth listening to jumped from 41 percent before the event to 68 percent at the end, while the num- ber who said public officials care about what the people think increased from 41 percent to 51 percent. Those are big jumps, given the long-term decline in public trust documented elsewhere in this chapter.

Although the event had its flaws, not the least of which was its $4 million price tag, it did suggest that knowledge does affect public opinions. As Thomas Jef- ferson once argued: "I know of no safe depository of the ultimate powers of the so- ciety but the people themselves. . . . If we think them not enlightened enough to exercise their control with a wholesome discretion, the remedy is not to take from them but to inform their discretion by education." The deliberative poll showed one way to do so.[5]

How Public Opinion Is Used and Misused

The rising tide of opinion creates both positives and negatives for democracy. On the positive side, some Americans get a voice in politics, albeit indirectly and anonymously, that they might not otherwise have. At the same time, polls can puncture myths about what the public thinks, bringing a healthy dose of reality to the political process.

On the negative side, polls may dilute the quality of information about what the public really thinks. Opinions can be based on misinformation, samples can be flawed, and questions may be poorly worded, all leading to false interpretations of the public will. At a minimum, polls can make all opinions seem equally strong. People who feel strongly about an issue are lumped together with those whose feelings are weak. The intensity of opinions gets diluted by the inclusion of those who either do not care about an issue or know nothing about it, but must answer the question anyway.[6]

Moreover, when the polling numbers are at odds with other measures of public sentiment—for example, letters to members of Congress—the weight almost always goes to the polling numbers. As one political scientist argues, "Survey research is modeled after the methodology of the natural sciences and at least conveys an impression of technical sophistication and scientific objectivity. . . . At the same time, polls can also claim to offer a more representative view of popular sentiment than any alternative source of information."[7]

Whether the impact is positive or negative, public opinion now occupies a much more important place in American government than the Founders could ever have imagined. Not only do members of Congress and presidents anxiously await the latest figures on their public approval, but they increasingly use polls to set their agenda of issues to be addressed.

Nothing illustrates the changing role of public opinion in government better than the rise of presidential polling. Over the past thirty years, according to Lawrence Jacobs and Robert Shapiro, presidents have created a veritable warehouse of public opinion.[8] Not only does the White House track virtually every public or private poll available, but it also frequently commissions special polls of its own. As a result, presidents now know exactly what the public thinks on the issues of the day and on every conceivable issue of tomorrow.

No president did more to build that public opinion warehouse than Richard Nixon. Although his predecessors also conducted polls, Nixon focused the White House on public opinion as never before. Whereas Kennedy conducted 77 private polls during the 1960 election campaign and another 16 during his three years in office, Nixon conducted over 100 polls in the 1968 campaign and at least another 233 during his first term.[9]

The polling reflected Nixon's obsession with public approval. He was involved in all aspects of the polling, from when the surveyors would go into the field to what questions would be asked, which states would be surveyed, and how the analysis would be done. Nixon hired the first White House pollster and pioneered the use of tracking polls to monitor day-to-day shifts in his approval ratings, a practice that is now common in almost all campaigns.

The question is whether this polling makes a difference in what presidents do. Do presidents make the decisions and then measure the opinion, or do they measure the opinion first and then make the decisions? Being practical politicians, the Founders would probably understand the value of measuring the opinion as part of selling the president's program. After all, Alexander Hamilton and

Richard Nixon confers with one of his key lieutenants, Bob Haldeman. Nixon was more in-volved in the public opinion polling process than any other president, and he hired the nation's first presidential pollster.

Thomas Jefferson had both established newspapers to spread their own versions of the political truth.[10]

The Founders would be much more concerned if they found out that pub-lic opinion was somehow being used to set the president's agenda. That would mean the presidency had somehow lost its focus on the greater good—and Jacobs and Shapiro find that this is increasingly the case. Again, Nixon was the trendset-ter: "Abundant evidence suggests that when the White House faced a potentially controversial policy decision, it often tested the waters with a considerable amount of polling before making a move."[11] Nixon apparently used polls to shape decisions large and small.

Presidents still make many decisions without checking the polls, of course. Yet the presence of a large polling operation inside the White House reflects a fundamental change in how presidents decide. Having the public opinion num-bers so easily available may tempt presidents to ignore the national interest in fa-vor of short-term popularity. It is a problem in other institutions as well. Indeed, the only institution that does not do polling regularly, if at all, is the Supreme Court. But as Chapter 13 shows, there is no doubt that justices pay attention to public opinion.

 **in a different light** ——

It is not clear what the Founders might think of recent efforts to make the federal government "customer driven," or more responsive to the people it serves. All departments and agencies are currently required to identify and survey their customers, post service standards and measure actual results against them, provide customers with choices in both the sources of service and the means of delivery, and in general become "the best in the business" in exceeding customer expectations. Box 4–2 lists the service standards currently used by the Social Security Administration.

The only way to know if the agency is meeting these standards is to survey the customers, in this case the people who deal directly with the agency. In 1996, for example, 97 percent said new social security cards were mailed within five days, 94 percent said the office hours were good or very good, 85 percent said they were

BOX **4-2**

Customer Service Standards of the Social Security Administration

We will provide service through knowledgeable employees who will treat you with courtesy, dignity, and respect every time you do business with us.

We will provide you with our best estimate of the time needed to complete your request and fully explain any delays.

We will clearly explain our decisions so you can understand why and how we made them and what to do if you disagree.

We will make sure our offices are safe and pleasant and our services are accessible.

When you make an appointment, we will serve you within 10 minutes of the scheduled time. If you request a new or replacement social security card from one of our offices, we will mail it to you within five working days of our receiving all the information we need. If you have an urgent need for the social security number, we will tell you the number within one working day.

When you call our 1-800 number, you will get through to it within five minutes of your first try.

served within ten minutes of their scheduled appointments, and 83 percent of callers said they got through to the agency within five minutes.

The Founders would hardly dispute such good results. Nor would they be likely to disagree that agencies should work hard to make sure they treat citizens with dignity and respect. What they might find troublesome is the definition of citizens as customers. Such a definition gives the citizen much greater power than the Founders would have wanted. The notion that government should strive to satisfy the customer, while it may be healthy for improving public administration, violates the basic principles of the Constitution. The U.S. government was designed precisely *not* to satisfy the customers, especially if doing so meant serving members of strong-willed majorities. The only customer the Founders worried about was the common good.

More important is the fact that many government agencies have more than one customer. The Federal Aviation Administration serves the airline industry, airplane manufacturers, and passengers; the Food and Drug Administration serves the pharmaceutical industry, health care providers, and patients; the Forest Service serves loggers, recreational vehicle owners, and environmentalists; the Agriculture Department serves farmers, food processors, and consumers; and so on throughout the vast executive branch. Which of an agency's customers should come first? In the months before the 1996 ValuJet crash in Florida, which killed 109 passengers, the FAA appeared to be more interested in protecting the interests of the airline industry than passengers. It allowed ValuJet to continue operating despite serious concerns regarding the young airline's maintenance and operations.

The Founders had a different word for groups of customers with conflicting interests: *factions.* They knew that government would be under constant pressure to satisfy one group or another—the airline manufacturers or the passengers, the chemical industry or the environmentalists, those who pay the Social Security taxes or those who get the benefits. They did not believe it was government's job to satisfy these kinds of customers at all, but to serve the national interest.

THE ORIGINS OF OPINION

Public opinion is the product of learning. That learning may be incomplete or the product of great oratory and clever advertising, but it is learning nonetheless. Americans form opinions on the basis of what they know about government and politics, whom they listen to, where they get their information, which social groups they identify with, what they have thought in days and years past, and whether they care enough to form an opinion at all. "Every opinion is a marriage of information and predisposition," writes John Zaller: "information to form a mental picture of the given issue, and predisposition to motivate some conclusion about it."[12] This marriage can be called learning.

Political scientists believe this learning occurs in two stages. The first comes in childhood and adolescence as young Americans learn their first lessons about government and politics. The second happens as Americans come to identify with the social groups that help them interpret information and events.

Political Socialization

The early learning process is often called **political socialization.** Even young children form general opinions about government as they encounter police officers and firefighters, and as they celebrate civic holidays such as the Fourth of July. Although such early experiences tend to build a core of often glossy patriotic beliefs about their country, children rarely develop specific opinions about who gets what, when, and how from government until they reach adolescence.

Parents.   Children learn their first and perhaps most important lessons about politics from their parents. Parents introduce children to the basic concept of power and government. After all, parents run their own governments of a kind, setting rules, enforcing boundaries, and making choices. Although they might seek the consent of the governed, there can be little doubt that parents are in charge.

Whether a parent's use or misuse of that power affects a child's view of government later in life is in some doubt, if only because so many other factors seem to determine public opinion at any given point in time. Nevertheless, there is little question that parents play a central role in introducing children to the world of boundaries.[13] By talking about politics around the dinner table, parents also introduce children to some of the key policy issues of the day.[14] Many children can identify a parent's political views and party identification even without knowing the first thing about government and politics.

More important, perhaps, a parent's view of the outside world can shape core social values. Racism is almost always learned at home, for example, as is a basic distrust of strangers. According to a 1996 survey of Philadelphians, young Americans today are much less trusting toward strangers than any other generation. One-fifth of Philadelphians under the age of thirty said they had a lot of trust in their neighbors, compared to nearly three-fifths of Philadelphians over sixty-five. Parental warnings about not trusting strangers appear to be related to that lack of trust. Less than one-third of respondents who said their parents often warned them not to trust strangers now say that most people can be trusted, compared to almost half of those whose parents never or hardly ever warned them. Fully 43 percent of young Philadelphians reported that their parents warned them about not trusting others, compared to 34 percent of thirty- to forty-nine-year-olds and just 27 percent of those fifty and older. Parents can hardly be faulted for being cautious in what sometimes appears to be a very unsafe world; but they need to understand that such warnings may shape their child's view of others for a long time.[15]

It is important to note that much of the research on the role of parents in political socialization was conducted during the 1960s, long before the divorce rate began to climb and television viewing began to cut into family time, and long before so many parents turned away from political parties and voting themselves. It is no longer clear, therefore, what role parents play in the political socialization of children. The days when a two-parent family would sit down together at the dinner table and talk about the issues of the day appear to be long gone. Also gone, it seems, are the days when parents might consider it an obligation to teach their children about the political system more generally. With distrust toward politics at near record levels, parents might ask, "Why spoil our appetites?"

Teachers and Peers. As children get older, parents fade as agents of socialization, and teachers and friends take on a greater role. Under the standards that were adopted as part of the Goals 2000 national education reforms, schools are responsible for introducing students to a host of concepts. By the end of high school, students are supposed to know the basics about what government is and what it should do, the basic values and principles of American democracy, how the Constitution embodies the purposes and values of that democracy, the relationship of the United States to other nations, and roles of the citizen in American democracy. In short, schools are seen as a central tool for giving young Americans both the information and the motivation to become active citizens. Much of this learning is reinforced by friends.

Research suggests, however, that what students *do* in school by way of actual participation may be far more important than what they *learn* from civics courses and peers. This point was made in a famous 1963 study by Gabriel Almond and Sidney Verba, who studied civic behavior in five nations. According to their research, respondents who remembered participating in school decisions as students were much more likely to engage in politics as adults.[16]

Thirty years later, Verba participated in another study showing the importance of schools. This time, he found that involvement in student government or school clubs of any kind was a powerful predictor of future political participation. Even in high school, such organizations are "schools of democracy," as Alexis de Tocqueville described civic associations. Although civics courses are no doubt essential for providing the basic information that helps form later opinions, the most important thing a school can do in shaping future participation is to give students a chance to practice democracy. In doing so, students learn the skills that will enable them to participate in civic life as adults, while gaining confidence in their ability to make a difference.[17]

Early Events.   As children grow older, events become more important than parents and peers in shaping what they believe about government. And many events tend to take the shine off children's early patriotism. "Watch what we do," Richard Nixon once told reporters during the Watergate scandal, "not what we say." As it turns out, that is just what many Americans do.

There can be little doubt, for example, that the 1960s left an indelible mark on the children of the era. The war in Vietnam, the civil rights movement, the ur-

Robert F. Kennedy, Edward Kennedy and John F. Kennedy confer in 1959 (top), Martin Luther King in 1967 (middle), and a scene from the Vietnam War in 1965 (bottom). The assassinations of the Kennedys and Martin Luther King, and an unpopular war, all contributed to declining trust in government during the 1960s. By the early 1970s, children had stopped thinking of their presidents as benevolent and began viewing them as malevolent.

ban unrest of the mid-1960s, and the assassinations of three popular leaders—President John F. Kennedy, civil rights advocate Martin Luther King, Jr., and Senator Robert Kennedy—changed how children viewed the government and politics.

The 1963 assassination of President John Kennedy in particular had a profound effect on American children. The violent death of this popular president, who had small children himself, came at one of most stressful moments in the Cold War. The Kennedy administration had just resolved the Cuban missile crisis, which capped a terrifying confrontation with the Soviet Union. Having discovered Soviet nuclear missiles in Cuba, just 90 miles from Florida, the United States put its nuclear forces on high alert as it blockaded the tiny island nation. The thirteen-day crisis ended when the Soviets promised to dismantle the bases.

Most children heard the news of Kennedy's death from their teachers, and then went home to watch the news on television. The images were haunting—the president's limousine speeding to the hospital, First Lady Jacqueline Kennedy in a bloodstained dress, the flag-draped casket, the Kennedy children in mourning. Talking with almost 1,400 Chicago schoolchildren in the days after the assassination, political scientist Roberta Sigel found that Kennedy's death made the world seem less safe. "There was no doubt that even young children were aware that they were living in troubled times full of international conflicts and the dangers of war," Sigel wrote. "For most children it was the Kennedy warmth, not his competence, which stood out. They liked him for his liking of others, his ability to care and to respond."[18]

Kennedy's death also marked the beginning of a decade of social and political unrest. It was an era that changed how children viewed the president. Interviewing grade-school children in 1973, political scientist Christopher Arterton found that many children had come to view the president as "truly malevolent, undependable, untrustworthy, yet powerful and dangerous."[19] Only a decade earlier, roughly half of grade-school children had said the president was their favorite or almost their favorite political person; by 1973, almost two-thirds of a new group of children said the president was not one of their favorites at all.

The Role of Social Groups

Political socialization does not end with high school. People continue learning about politics from a number of agents: their coworkers, college classmates, bosses, churches, spouses, and, eventually, even their children. And they continue to respond to events. The 1960s were not just important for children, for example. Many adults changed their thinking about American government during the period, becoming much more distrusting toward the president. As Chapter 5 will argue, people also learn a great deal about politics from the media.

Much of this ongoing learning is shaped by the social groups with which individual Americans identify. Many of these groups are defined by **demographic characteristics.** Demographics are statistical measures that separate individual Americans by race, gender, age, education, income, and so forth. Although all Hispanics, wealthy people, women, or college students do not think alike, people who share the same demographic characteristics are likely to share many of the same experiences in life. Scholars know, for example, that girls and boys learn very different lessons about the world as children, as do minority children. Scholars also know that people's views of the world change as they age.

Education may be the most important demographic measure of all for understanding public opinion. It is a prime predictor of income, which is a prime predictor of an individual's **socioeconomic status,** or standing in society relative to others. Although higher education is not an absolute guarantee of future success, an individual's level of education underpins so much of later experience that it is often seen as the single most important predictor of how the person thinks about politics.

Education and income are not the only personal experiences that matter to politics, however. Religion also plays an important role in an individual's view of politics. In recent years, for example, evangelical Christians have become much more active in election campaigns at all levels of government. Many evangelicals believe that government can play an important role in strengthening the moral fiber of the country.

Other social groups affect lifelong learning, as well. Where people live, what they do for income, whether they belong to a labor union or own a small business, whether they are part of the baby boom or Generation X, whether they are veterans of war or former war protesters, even whether they are married, divorced, or remarried, all affect what they think about government and politics. And the impact of each of these and other experiences often varies depending on income, education, race, age, and gender. Put all the demographic groups together and America appears to be a very divided country indeed. Suburban, white women think very differently from young, urban union members; Western high-income veterans think very differently from Southern rural retirees.

The question is not whether some social groups affect public opinion, but which social groups affect which issues. Since people have more than one demographic characteristic, the answer may depend on the issue at stake. Race may affect certain issues, but not others; gender may affect many issues, but not all. Consider how gender, race, age, education, income, and religious preference affected views about the federal budget and approval of First Lady Hillary Rodham Clinton in 1996 (see Box 4–3).

Women were slightly more likely than men to see a balanced budget as hurting themselves or their families, and much less likely to disapprove of Hillary Clinton. These differences between men and women illustrate the **gender gap,** which emerged in the 1980s and continues to be a factor in American politics.

BOX 4-3

Attitudes on a Balanced Budget and Hillary Rodham Clinton, by Group

	Impact of Balanced Budget		View of Hillary Rodham Clinton	
	Help	Hurt/Not Affect	Favorable	Unfavorable
Gender				
Male	45%	51%	36%	61%
Female	36	58	48	48
Race				
White	41%	53%	39%	58%
Nonwhite	34	61	63	32
Black	34	62	67	27
Age				
Under 30	41%	57%	45%	51%
30–49	45	50	42	56
50–64	45	50	38	47
65 and older	24	67	43	51
Education				
Less than high school	33%	60%	46%	47%
High school graduate	41	54	41	56
Some college	42	54	41	56
College graduate	44	51	43	54
Yearly Family Income				
Less than $20,000	39%	54%	47%	48%
$20,000–$29,999	33	62	39	60
$30,000–$49,999	42	53	44	52
$50,000–$74,999	46	52	38	61
$75,000 and over	51	47	36	62
Religious Preference				
White Protestant	41%	54%	36%	60%
White Protestant evangelical	39	56	25	71
White Protestant nonevangelical	44	51	46	50
White Catholic	43	53	37	61

Source: "Balanced Budget a Public Priority, But Few See Personal Payoff," Pew Research Center for The People and The Press News Release, January 18, 1996, pp. 11–12, 16–17. The questions were: "What's your opinion . . . if the federal budget is balanced in seven years, do you think it will help you and your family financially, hurt you and your family financially, or not affect you and your family financially?" and "Would you say your overall opinion of Hillary Rodham Clinton is very favorable, mostly favorable, or very unfavorable?"

Women tend to be more liberal on social issues such as abortion rights and more likely to vote for Democratic candidates in elections. The gender gap is rooted in the early socialization experiences of girls and boys, which create lifelong differences in how males and females view government and politics, as well as the current economic experiences of men and women, which tend to lead women to support a more active role for government in reducing sexual harassment in the workplace, promoting equal pay for equal work, and providing an adequate safety net of services such as daycare and parental leave.

Nonwhites were also more likely than whites to worry about the personal impact of a balanced budget, and were even more approving of Hillary Clinton than women were. These differences also emerge from socialization and economic inequality between the races. Race is one of the most important predictors of how people vote, with the vast majority of African-Americans giving their support to Democratic candidates.

Age did not matter much to approval of Hillary Clinton, but clearly shaped views of the balanced budget. Older Americans were the group most likely to see a balanced budget as hurting them personally, in large measure because so much of the debate about spending involves Medicare, the federal government program that provides healthcare coverage to retirees. A majority of young people were also likely to conclude that a balanced budget would hurt them personally, perhaps because they believed their taxes might go up.

Both major measures of socioeconomic status—education and income—made a difference in how Americans answered the two questions. People who never completed high school were much more likely to see a balanced budget as hurting them and were somewhat more approving of the First Lady. This group of Americans certainly recognized that a tighter federal budget would mean less funding for programs to help people with lower incomes and more limited job prospects. Respondents who had lower incomes were more likely to see a balanced budget as hurting them personally than were those with higher incomes.

 **in a different light** ———— NEW DEFINITIONS OF RACE

During his rise to fame as the youngest winner of the Masters golf championship in 1997, Tiger Woods repeatedly refused to be referred to as a member of just one race. Instead, he identified himself as a "Cablinasian," his own combination of *Cau*casian, *bl*ack, American *In*dian, and *Asian*. Woods did not yet have that option in the national census, which is conducted every ten years under Article II of the Constitu-

Tiger Woods, winner of the 1997 Masters golf tournament. Woods wants to be described not as an African-American, but as a "Cablinasian," meaning a person who is part *Cau*casian, *Bl*ack, American *In*dian, and *Asian*.

tion. Prior to 2000, Americans could check only one of four boxes for race—Caucasian, African-American, Native American, or Asian.

Starting in 2000, however, Woods and millions of other multiracial Americans will be able to identify themselves more accurately. Under a federal rule adopted in 1998, they will be allowed to check off one or all of six boxes, including a new category for Native Hawaiian or other Pacific Islanders, which used to be included in "Asian."

The new rules reflect the new reality that more and more Americans are of mixed racial backgrounds. The census, which is used to allocate House seats by population, is merely acknowledging the possibility. "This is an increasingly sophisticated world we're dealing with, and simplistic, one-size-fits-all solutions, I think, are less in favor," said one federal official involved in the decision. "Life is complicated. People are complicated."[20]

The number of Americans who will check off more than one box is likely to be small—between 1 and 7 percent, according to current estimates. "Is there such a thing as a multiracial community?" asks one expert on the new census form. "Or, are there multiracial people living inside the white, Spanish, Asian and black communities? We don't know yet because we haven't been able to literally see it."

The problem is that small numbers can make a big difference when it comes to enforcing federal laws against discrimination in employment, college admissions, or voting. Does the fact that Tiger Woods considers himself to be part Caucasian mean he is no longer protected by antidiscrimination laws? Do the courts count him as part of a racial minority when it comes to ensuring that voting rights are protected? Under the 1965 Voting Rights Act, for example, states are prohibited from diminishing the voting power of any minority group when they redraw district lines following a national census. (Such action is called *retrogression*.) What happens if enough Tiger Woodses join together to reduce the minority share of a district from, say, 51 percent minority to 49 percent? Would the courts become involved?

Small numbers can also generate intense concerns within the civil rights community. "There is an unspoken fear that by giving people the option to claim multiple ancestry, you will play into a desire that people have, not so much for cultural self-determination, but for being something other than black," a civil rights advocate says. "By giving people the option, you will in fact diminish the number of people who claim to be African-American—not because the definition has changed, but because people have an option to escape. It's not that they think their lives will improve, but they'll be able to say to themselves, 'This is not me. I'm different.'"

It is also possible that allowing Tiger Woods to claim his full heritage may prompt even more young Americans to see him as a role model. And that would be a unifying force for American society, even as it would raise new questions for the courts and Congress.

THE AMERICAN ATTITUDE

In a global comparison of how people feel about politics and government, the United States emerges as both similar to and different from other democracies. There does appear to be a unique American attitude. Americans take greater pride in their country than do the citizens of any other nation, and they remain among the most enthusiastic about democracy as a form of government. According to surveys conducted across the world in the mid-1990s, 98 percent of Americans said they were proud to be citizens of the United States, a number that far outpaced the 71 percent who said they were proud to be citizens of Russia, the 62 percent who said they were proud to be citizens of Japan, and the 57 percent who were proud to be citizens of Germany.[21]

At the same time, Americans are among the least confident about their government institutions and among the most reluctant to fight for their country. According to the world surveys cited above, 77 percent of Americans said they were willing to fight for their country, compared to 96 percent of Turkish citizens, 93 percent of Chinese, 92 percent of Swedes, and 84 percent of Russians. More recent research also shows that Americans are somewhat less supportive of a strong role for government in guaranteeing every citizen food and basic shelter. Roughly 60 percent of Americans agree that government should play that role, compared to 90 percent of the citizens of France, 82 percent of the British, and 86 percent of the Spanish.[22]

Thus, if there is such a thing as a uniquely American attitude, it is great pride in the nation mixed with sharp skepticism toward government. Americans have always held what the Founders might have viewed as a healthy distrust of what government can deliver. They seem to have their own sense of the delicate balance: a government that is strong enough to create a national identity, but not so strong that it destroys individual freedom. Before turning to these views in more detail, it is important to ask whether Americans truly know enough to be considered experts on the state of their own country.

What Americans Know

The Constitution does not require Americans to know anything about govern-ment. No one has to take a test to write a letter to Congress, vote in an election, or answer a public opinion poll. No one has to pass a course on being a citizen, calling a radio talk show, or surfing the Internet. Nor do Americans have to pay for the right to give their consent to be governed. The Twenty-fourth Amend-ment, which was ratified in 1964, prohibited any such *poll tax* on the right to vote, while the 1965 Voting Rights Act prohibited literacy tests as a condition for voting. There is nothing to prevent citizens from giving their consent to be gov-erned without knowing much about politics or government. As public opinion surveys invariably show, that is exactly what many Americans do.

Take basic information about the American government, for example. Most Americans simply do not know much about either how American government works or who is in charge at any given moment. Only one-quarter of Americans know the names of their two U.S. senators. Well over half believe that foreign aid involves a greater share of the federal budget than health care for the elderly; in fact, government spending on Medicare for the elderly dwarfs foreign aid by bil-lions of dollars. (See Box 4–4 for a political pop quiz.)

Americans also show surprising gaps in their knowledge about the rules of the political game. They do know that the United States is a member of the United Nations, but cannot define the Bill of Rights; they can define a presidential veto and the length of a president's term in office, but not the length of a House term or the purpose of NATO; they know what the Constitution says about reli-gion, but not that Congress declares war. Surveying dozens of questions on what Americans know, Michael Delli Carpini and Scott Keeter conclude that "[s]imple characterizations cannot do justice to the range of political knowledge and igno-

BOX 4-4

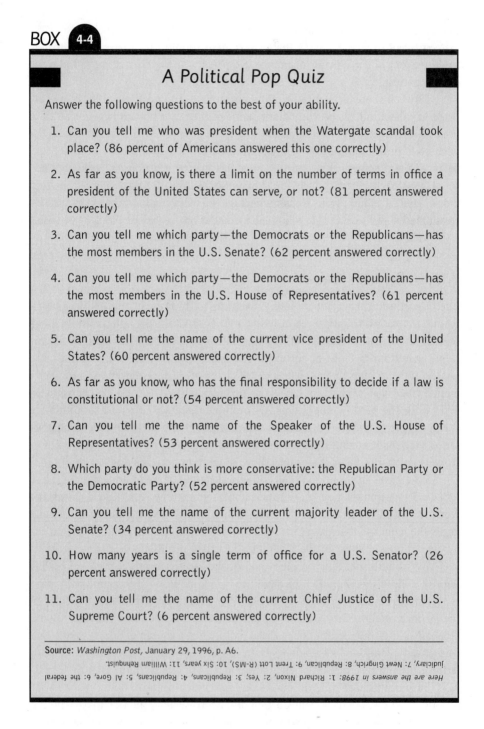

A Political Pop Quiz

Answer the following questions to the best of your ability.

1. Can you tell me who was president when the Watergate scandal took place? (86 percent of Americans answered this one correctly)

2. As far as you know, is there a limit on the number of terms in office a president of the United States can serve, or not? (81 percent answered correctly)

3. Can you tell me which party—the Democrats or the Republicans—has the most members in the U.S. Senate? (62 percent answered correctly)

4. Can you tell me which party—the Democrats or the Republicans—has the most members in the U.S. House of Representatives? (61 percent answered correctly)

5. Can you tell me the name of the current vice president of the United States? (60 percent answered correctly)

6. As far as you know, who has the final responsibility to decide if a law is constitutional or not? (54 percent answered correctly)

7. Can you tell me the name of the Speaker of the U.S. House of Representatives? (53 percent answered correctly)

8. Which party do you think is more conservative: the Republican Party or the Democratic Party? (52 percent answered correctly)

9. Can you tell me the name of the current majority leader of the U.S. Senate? (34 percent answered correctly)

10. How many years is a single term of office for a U.S. Senator? (26 percent answered correctly)

11. Can you tell me the name of the current Chief Justice of the U.S. Supreme Court? (6 percent answered correctly)

Source: *Washington Post*, January 29, 1996, p. A6.

Here are the answers in 1998: 1: Richard Nixon, 2: Yes, 3: Republicans, 4: Republicans, 5: Al Gore, 6: the federal judiciary, 7: Newt Gingrich, 8: Republican, 9: Trent Lott (R-MS), 10: Six years, 11: William Rehnquist.

rance demonstrated by the public."[23] If the schools are responsible for teaching the basics of civic life, the evidence suggests that they are mostly failing.

The lack of information is particularly sharp on some of the most important issues of the day. Of the nearly eighty questions asked over the decades about economics, only a handful were answered correctly. Most Americans cannot define monetary policy, supply side economics, fiscal policy, the prime rate, free trade, or inflation, and most cannot describe the U.S. economic system. Yet, they routinely vote for candidates on the basis of the economy's performance.

These information gaps often affect other opinions. Asked in 1974, for example, whether President Nixon should be "impeached and compelled to leave the Presidency" for his role in covering up the Watergate burglary, most Americans said no. But asked whether "there is enough evidence of possible wrongdoing in the case of President Nixon to bring him to trial before the Senate," which is the technical definition of impeachment, a majority in favor suddenly appeared. Apparently, people either did not know what impeachment was (it is merely the indictment leading to Senate trial) or did know and felt Nixon should not be convicted without a trial.[24]

Pollsters call opinions based on a lack of information **nonattitudes.** Such opinions are not opinions at all, just a passing response to a pollster's question. When asked in a 1995 survey whether the 1975 Public Affairs Act should be repealed, 24 percent of Americans said yes, 19 percent said no, and the rest had no opinion. The problem was that there was no such thing as the Public Affairs Act, meaning that 43 percent of Americans had invented opinions about something they could have known nothing about. The number of respondents ready to answer this meaningless question went ten points higher when they were told that President Clinton and the Republicans in Congress favored repeal.[25]

The problem with nonattitudes is not just in creating a flawed portrait of what Americans think, but in the real possibility that government might make a hard choice based on artificial opinions. If Congress and the president ignored Medicare in the budget debate because the public thinks it is but a small program, or decided not to commit troops to Bosnia because less than one in ten Americans know where Bosnia is, they would be making decisions on the basis of misinformation. And those decisions might turn out to be bad for the nation as a whole or for the rights of Americans as individuals.

Despite such gaps in their knowledge, Americans may know quite enough to be active participants in politics. Do citizens need to know what inflation is in order to be angry at rising prices? Do they need to be able to define supply side economics in order to worry about the federal budget deficit? And do they need to know how the American economy works in order to worry about their jobs? This is not to argue that ignorance is democratic bliss, however. Informed citizens make American government work better, if only because they are more likely to choose candidates who support their interests. Nevertheless, the nation can endure a fair amount of civic ignorance and still survive. Protecting the nation against public passions driven by civic ignorance has always been part of the delicate balance.

What Americans Believe

Much of this book deals with differences in what Americans believe, whether about the role of the media in politics or money in campaigns, the president's place in history or the size of government, the right to abortion or affirmative action. Although politics is very much about resolving disagreements, it is important to remember that Americans agree on many issues, not the least of which is their enormous pride in being Americans.[26] Consider just a few areas of widespread agreement.[27]

Celebrating Kwanzaa, a new holiday that focuses on the African heritage of African-Americans. Being an American involves much more than formal citizenship. It also involves a set of core beliefs, including individualism. Kwanza is one expression of the individualism of African-Americans.

Americans do believe in democracy, even if they are sometimes confused about the rules of the political game. Nine out of ten feel it is their duty as citizens to vote, and seven out of ten say they feel guilty when they do not vote. Of those who do vote, only a third do it out of duty, while the rest usually get a feeling of satisfaction from expressing this basic consent to be governed. Most would like to do more by way of participating, and nearly two-thirds express a great deal or a good deal of confidence in the wisdom of the American people when it comes to making political decisions.

Americans also believe in individual success. Although nine of ten Americans say society should do what is necessary to make sure that everyone has an equal chance to succeed, they also believe that individuals should rise or fall on their own. The vast majority of Americans admire people who get rich by working hard, and believe that everyone has it in their own power to succeed. They also believe that the strength of the country is based on the success of American business and a healthy market economy.

Americans also believe in a higher power. They may not go to church quite as regularly as they say, but nine out of ten believe that God exists, while eight in ten believe that everyone will be called before God on Judgment Day to answer for their sins. Most Americans also believe in the power of prayer, and say that miracles are performed by the power of God. The vast majority of Americans say that religion, whether formal or informal, plays an important role in their daily lives, and many believe that the future is very much in God's hands, not government's.

Finally, Americans believe in activist government, particularly when it comes to assuring the quality of their lives. Nine out of ten believe that the country should be active in foreign affairs (even though, paradoxically, they also think the nation should pay less attention to problems overseas and concentrate more on problems at home). A similar proportion say the federal government should spend more money to provide education and job training for American workers whose jobs have been cut, and that there should be stricter laws to protect the environment. At the same time, however, Americans worry about just how much power the federal government should have. As noted in Chapter 3, Americans trust the governments most that they know best, and show a uniquely American attitude toward keeping government in its place.

Americans do not agree on everything, of course. That is what makes them individualistic. Americans tend to divide at the points where the broad goals conflict—for example, when activism conflicts with religious beliefs on issues such as abortion, gay and lesbian rights, and pornography; when patriotism conflicts with individualism on issues such as flag burning, freedom of speech, and opposition to war; when activism conflicts with individualism on issues such as affirmative action or spending more money on the poor.

 **in a different light** ————

WHY AMERICANS DON'T TRUST GOVERNMENT

Americans may disagree on many issues, but they are almost uniformly distrusting toward government. And they have been getting more distrusting over time. By the mid-1990s, 93 percent of Americans had concluded that government wastes too much of their money; 88 percent that leaders say whatever will get them elected, but not what they are really thinking; 73 percent that politicians work for themselves and their own careers, not for the people they represent; and 70 percent that government is run for the benefit of special interests.

Even when they are given a chance to say that government often does a better job than it is given credit for, three out of four Americans refuse the opportunity. As *Washington Post* columnist E. J. Dionne, Jr., writes in his book *Why Americans Hate Politics,* "At the very moment when democracy is blossoming in Eastern Europe, it is decaying in the United States. Over the last three decades, the faith of the American people in their democratic institutions has declined, and Americans have begun to doubt their ability to improve the world through politics."[28]

Confidence in Washington to do what is right is the standard measure of trust in government. In 1958, 16 percent of the public said they could "always" trust Washington to do what was right, 57 percent said "most of the time," 23 percent said "only some of the time," and none said "never." By November 1997, just 3 percent answered "always," 36 percent said "most of the time," and the majority of Americans, 61 percent, said "only some of the time." Two percent said that the government can "never" be trusted to do what is right.[29]

The rising distrust is reflected in a host of other opinions. In the 1950s, for example, the vast majority of Americans said public officials cared about what they thought, believed that government did not waste much money, and felt government was run for the benefit of all the people.[30] By the 1990s, the numbers had changed dramatically. Americans had come to believe the worst about government.[31]

The distrust is so deep that it may be rewriting memories of a more hopeful past.[32] Even the most distrusting American can generally remember a time when he or she trusted government to do the right thing. Many older Americans think back to the 1950s, when the economy was strong and *Ozzie and Harriet* was number one on television, or the early 1960s, when President John F. Kennedy promised a New Frontier. But when asked why they have become more distrusting over time, most say that government has not changed much at all. Rather, they just know more about what really goes on than they used to.[33]

There are two main reasons for the level of distrust measured in recent surveys. One is the moral and ethical conduct, or lack thereof, of elected leaders. Two-thirds of the public gave federal officials only fair or poor marks on moral and unethical leadership. The other reason is the actual performance of government itself. Nearly three-quarters of Americans say the federal government is doing only a fair or poor job of running its programs.

There is also a generation gap in distrust. Young Americans have been far more likely than older Americans to say they distrust government because of the unethical conduct of their leaders, while older Americans were more likely than younger Americans to say they distrust government because it is not performing well. As young Americans gain more experience with government, their views may change. Leadership counts more for young Americans in part because they have had less experience with government performance. The more contact they have with huge agencies such as the Social Security Administration and the Internal Revenue Service, the more likely they are to base their level of trust on actual performance.

Recent surveys offer some hope for a rebound of trust. Although the numbers are still extremely low, they are inching upward. The bottom was reached in 1994, when just 21 percent of Americans said they trusted the government in Washington just about always or most of the time. Part of the rebound involves a good economy, which fosters hope about the future, which in turn creates more trust in government. However, American government is a long way from regaining the level of trust in government that existed in the 1950s and early 1960s. If current figures are as good as the trust in government gets when the economy is as good as it is, there may be good reason to worry about what may happen if and when the economy begins to worsen.

How Opinions Relate

Political scientists use the term **ideology** to describe how individual opinions relate to each other. Some Americans believe, for example, that government should play a strong role in solving social problems, intervening where necessary to create a better society. They believe it is the job of government to help create jobs, assure equal opportunity, clean up the environment, provide basic support for poor people, and protect the rights of people accused of crimes. Such self-described **liberals,** as they are labeled, constitute roughly one-quarter of all Americans, including just about one-quarter of college students.

Other Americans believe that government should play a sharply limited role in solving the nation's problems, letting individuals rise or fall on their own without help one way or the other. They tend to argue that it is the private sector's responsibility to create jobs, hire employees, use the environment wisely, and support the less fortunate primarily through private charities. They generally take a harder line on crime, and believe that it is the job of government to protect citizens from crime, not criminals from prosecution. These self-described **conservatives** account for just over one-third of all Americans, but only one-fifth of college students.

Still other Americans occupy the middle. These **moderates** tend to see the benefits of government intervention on some issues and of limited government on others. Moderates account for just over one-third of all Americans, but almost half of college students.

Interestingly, the mix of self-reported liberals, conservatives, and moderates in America as a whole and on college campuses has remained relatively stable over time, with an ever-so-slight shift toward conservativism in recent years. Americans seem quite content to occupy a vast middle ground that sometimes gets forgotten in the heat of national debates over abortion, budget cuts, or presidential campaigns. Box 4–5 shows the proportions of liberals, conservatives, and moderates over the past two decades. The distribution of opinion over the years has been almost perfectly normal—that is, 5 percent of all respondents in 1996 said they were either extremely liberal or conservative, another 26 percent said they were simply liberal or conservative, another 28 percent said they were slightly liberal or slightly conservative, and 36 percent placed themselves right at the center of the bell curve as moderate.

There is some debate about whether and how ideology shapes actual public opinions. Do most people say to themselves, I am a liberal; therefore, I support policy X? Or do most people mix and match issues and say to themselves, I support policy X and policy Y; therefore I am a liberal?

Some political scientists argue that most Americans are not capable of using ideology to shape other decisions. It simply takes too much discipline. The authors of one of the most famous books on voting and elections, *The American Voter,* concluded that only 15 percent of 1950s-era voters were sophisticated enough to use ideology to package their views of candidates and political parties.[34] Things had changed so little by the end of the 1980s that political scientist Eric Smith titled his investigation of public ideology *The Unchanging American Voter.*[35]

A small but growing number of political scientists believe that the American public is quite right not to think ideologically. The world is hardly a simple liberal–conservative place. Moreover, the fact that some positions on issues do not fit a particular definition of consistency or sophistication does not mean the public is incapable of thoughtful judgment.[36]

Some political scientists also argue that liberalism and conservatism provide only one dimension for understanding how opinions relate, suggesting that Americans also vary in the degree to which they favor more power to the people instead of government. Putting ideology together with support for either strong or weak government yields four different political types: true liberals (strong government + liberal), true conservatives (weak government + conservative), **populists** (more power to the people + liberal), and **libertarians** (more power to the people + conservative). Like liberals, populists favor an activist government, but one that is directed more by the people than by elites in Washington. Like conservatives, libertarians favor a weak national government, but one that minds its own business in all aspects of life, including abortion rights and school prayer.

BOX 4-5

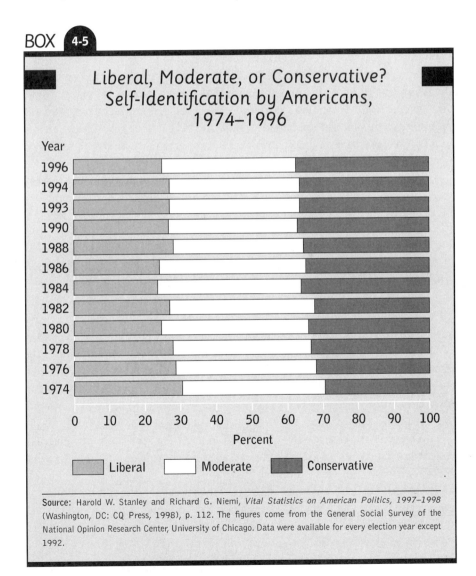

Liberal, Moderate, or Conservative? Self-Identification by Americans, 1974–1996

Source: Harold W. Stanley and Richard G. Niemi, *Vital Statistics on American Politics, 1997–1998* (Washington, DC: CQ Press, 1998), p. 112. The figures come from the General Social Survey of the National Opinion Research Center, University of Chicago. Data were available for every election year except 1992.

Most Americans turn out to be moderates on even the most divisive issues. They make tough choices about when abortion should be permitted and when it should not, when spotted owls should be protected and when lumber companies should be allowed to cut old-growth forests. Indeed, the American public may be far less volatile or unpredictable than the Founders once believed. There is ample evidence that they are quite predictable in their views. Although the public may be uninformed about the details of many policy decisions, they have a remarkable degree of common sense when given the facts.

MAINTAINING THE BALANCE

Public opinion is both a limit on government and an accelerator of action. The fact that most Americans are both skeptical toward government and moderate on the issues acts to limit government action. But the fact that most Americans are also impatient for action and poorly informed makes them easy targets for big promises. Even as large numbers of Americans believe that government creates more problems than it solves, they also seem to want more of just about every-thing that government delivers.

American government was well designed to handle just this kind of am-bivalence, however. One can even argue that the ambivalence is a product of maintaining the balance. Americans do not believe government can solve all their problems, in part because that is precisely what the Founders intended. The constitutional system makes it nearly impossible for passionate factions or clever orators to win control of all three branches long enough to impose their will on the nation, even if that means that strong majorities are frustrated by in-action.

Recent failures to enact health care reform and rein in the tobacco industry suggest that intense minorities may, indeed, have the upper hand in exploiting public skepticism to create stalemate. Americans are so poorly informed on the issues of the day and so widely convinced that government can do no right that they respond to just about any attack on Washington. Opponents merely need to invoke the three magic words of stalemate—*taxes, bureaucracy,* and *Washington*—and the public will say "stop."

The problem is that such manipulation sows the seeds of future distrust. Americans want it both ways. They want a government that delivers more of what they want by way of environmental protection, low-cost health care for the el-derly, better roads and highways, more funding for schools, and more police on the streets, but a government that does not cost too much or grow too big. In-stead of government that works better and costs less, which is the theme of Vice President Al Gore's "Reinventing Government" campaign, Americans appear to want a government that looks smaller and delivers more.[37] But when forced to choose, Americans will almost always accept stalemate over the higher taxes needed to pay for all the items on their wish list. Stalemate merely confirms what they already believe about government incompetence.

Such high levels of distrust may eventually corrode the consent of the governed. As noted earlier, Americans are hardly ready to launch a new revolution. Nor does the distrust automatically translate into lower participation in elections. Many Americans stay home on election day for other reasons: because they are basically satisfied with the way the country is going, they do not think their vote really counts, or they regard the candidates as one and the same. Nevertheless, the more skeptical Americans become toward government, the more easily they are manipulated to oppose action; the more easily they are manipulated, the less government can do; and the less government can do, the more skeptical Americans become toward government. This vicious circle could eventually lead to a complete withdrawal of the consent to be governed. And that would suggest a government seriously out of balance.

terms to remember

public opinion (p. 113)
polling (p. 114)
straw polls (p. 115)
salience (p. 116)
random sample (p. 117)
sampling error (p. 118)
confidence level (p. 118)
response rates (p. 119)
normal distribution (p. 121)
bimodal distribution (p. 121)
skewed distribution (p. 121)
political socialization (p. 128)

demographic characteristics
  (p. 132)
socioeconomic status (p. 132)
gender gap (p. 132)
nonattitudes (p. 139)
ideology (p. 143)
liberals (p. 143)
conservatives (p. 144)
moderates (p. 144)
populists (p. 145)
libertarians (p. 145)

facts and interpretations

- Public opinion is a blend of values and attitudes toward the issues of the day, and is formed through a learning process that continues throughout a lifetime. Americans are influenced by their parents, teachers, and friends, real world events, and the social groups to which they belong as adults. Demographic characteristics such as education, income, race, gender, and age are the most important determinants of what Americans think about the issues of the day.

- The Founders worried that government would be too responsive to public opinion, so they insulated all three branches in different ways from what they saw as a distinctly unvirtuous people. As the science of polling has improved, at least two of the three branches, the legislative and executive, have become much more sensitive to public opinion. Members of Congress and the president read polls constantly, sometimes to shape how they win the consent of the governed, and sometimes to determine which position to favor. The Founders might have approved of the former, but would definitely have frowned on the latter.

- Part of being an effective consumer of public opinion is knowing the strengths and weaknesses of the methodology of poll-taking. Even though the science of polling has never been stronger, pollsters can still manipulate the wording of questions and the analysis of data to produce biased results. Every poll should carry a clear statement about who sponsored the survey, who conducted it, how many people were in the random sample, when, where, and how they were interviewed, and what the sampling error and confidence levels are.

- Americans have a unique attitude toward government and politics compared to citizens of other nations. Americans are very proud to be Americans and are intensely patriotic, but they are also highly skeptical about government and maintain a fierce individualism. They want government to make sure everyone gets a fair start in life, but they also want to rise or fall on their own merits. Americans blend this skepticism toward government with moderation on the issues of the day, a combination that may make them less likely than citizens of other countries to expect government to solve their problems.

open questions

- How has socialization to politics changed over the past few decades? What changes in American society have had an impact on how children and young adults are socialized? Does the decline of the traditional two-parent family matter? What about high divorce rates, or changes in how schools operate? How does the Internet now socialize children? Do computer games have a socializing effect, too? What effect would a decline in the traditional socialization process have on the consent of the governed?

- Should citizens have some minimum amount of information in order to participate in government and politics? Would a test to screen out people who know less weaken the consent of the governed? Should government leaders give less weight to the opinions of uninformed citizens than to those of informed citizens?

- How should government use public opinion to inform its decisions? Should policymakers consult public opinion before they make a decision? And if so, to what purpose? Is it wrong for a president to have a pollster on the White House staff? Is it wrong for the Supreme Court to consider how the public might react to a particularly controversial decision?

for further study

Asher, Herbert. *Polling and the Public: What Every Citizen Should Know,* 2d ed. Washington, DC: CQ Press, 1992.

Delli Carpini, Michael X., and Scott Keeter. *What Americans Know about Politics and Why It Matters* . New Haven, CT: Yale University Press, 1996.

Dionne, E. J., Jr. *Why Americans Hate Politics.* New York: Simon and Schuster/Touchstone, 1991.

Lupia, Arthur, and Matthew D. McCubbins. *The Democratic Dilemma: Can Citizens Learn What They Need to Know?* Cambridge, Eng.: Cambridge University Press, 1998.

Page, Benjamin, and Robert Shapiro. *The Rational Public: Fifty Years of Trends in Americans' Policy Preferences.* Chicago: University of Chicago Press, 1992.

Traugott, Michael W., and Paul J. Lavrakas. *The Voter's Guide to Election Polls.* Chatham, NJ: Chatham House, 1996.

Zaller, John R. *The Nature and Origins of Mass Opinion.* Cambridge, Eng.: Cambridge University Press, 1992.

endnotes for chapter 4

1. Those who want to learn more should read Herbert Asher's *Polling and the Public: What Every Citizen Should Know,* 2d ed. (Washington, DC: CQ Press, 1992); see also Michael W. Traugott and Paul J. Lavrakas, *The Voter's Guide to Election Polls* (Chatham, NJ: Chatham House, 1996).

2. Richard Morin, "From Confusing Questions, Confusing Answers," *Washington Post National Weekly Edition,* July 18–24, 1994, p. 37.

3. See Lawrence R. Jacobs and Robert Y. Shapiro, "UFO Stories: More Social Security Bunk," *The New Republic,* August 10, 1998, p. 27.

4. See E. J. Dionne, Jr., "An Amoral Majority?" *Washington Post,* February 5, 1998, p. A17.

5. Kenneth A. Rasinski, Norman M. Bradburn, and Douglas Lauen, "An Evaluation of the 1996 National Issues Convention," December 1, 1997 (report to The Pew Charitable Trusts). For a description of the deliberative polling approach, see James S. Fishkin, *Democracy and Deliberation: New Directions for Democratic Reform* (New Haven, CT: Yale University Press, 1991).

6. See Benjamin Ginsberg, *The Captive Public: How Mass Opinion Promotes State Power* (New York: Basic Books, 1985), for a discussion of how polls may make the public complacent about government.

7. Ginsberg, *The Captive Public*, p. 61.

8. Lawrence Jacobs and Robert Shapiro, "Disorganized Democracy: The Institutionalization of Polling and Public Opinion Analysis during the Kennedy, Johnson, and Nixon Presidencies," paper presented at the annual meetings of the American Political Science Association, New York City, September 1–4, 1994, p. 3.

9. The precise number of Nixon's polls in 1968 is unknown because of continuing disputes over access to his presidential papers; however, the number of polls over the rest of the first term is exact.

10. See Mel Laracey, "The Presidential Newspaper: The Forgotten Way of Going Public," paper presented at the annual meetings of the American Political Science Association, New York City, September 1–4, 1994, p. 2.

11. Jacobs and Shapiro, "Disorganized Democracy," p. 30.

12. John R. Zaller, *The Nature and Origins of Mass Opinion* (Cambridge, Eng.: Cambridge University Press, 1992), p. 6.

13. See Robert Coles, *The Political Life of Children* (Boston: Atlantic Monthly Press, 1986).

14. See M. Kent Jennings and Richard Niemi, "Issues and Inheritance in the Formation of Party Identification," *American Journal of Political Science*, 35, no. 3 (Fall 1991), pp. 970–88.

15. The survey was conducted by the Pew Research Center for The People & The Press, *Trust and Citizen Engagement in Metropolitan Philadelphia: A Case Study* (Washington, DC: Pew Research Center, 1997); see also John Brehm and Wendy Rahn, "Individual-Level Evidence for the Causes and Consequences of Social Capital," *American Political Science Review*, 41 (1997), pp. 999–1023.

16. Gabriel A. Almond and Sidney Verba, *The Civic Culture: Political Attitudes and Democracy in Five Nations* (Princeton, NJ: Princeton University Press, 1963).

17. Sidney Verba, Kay Lehman Schlozman, and Henry E. Brady, *Voice and Equality: Civic Voluntarism in American Politics* (Cambridge, MA: Harvard University Press, 1995), p. 425.

18. Roberta Sigel, "Image of a President: Some Insights into the Political Views of School Children," *American Political Science Review*, 62, no. 2 (March 1968), p. 226.

19. Christopher Arterton, "The Impact of Watergate on Children's Attitudes toward Political Authority," *Political Science Quarterly*, 89, no. 2 (June 1974), p. 286.

20. This and the subsequent quotes come from Rochelle L. Stanfield, "Multiple Choice," *National Journal*, November 22, 1997, pp. 2352–55.

21. See Pippa Norris, ed., *Critical Citizens: Global Support for Democratic Government* (New York: Oxford University Press, forthcoming).

22. See the Pew Research Center for The People & The Press, *Deconstructing Distrust: How Americans View Government* (Washington, DC: Pew Research Center, 1997).

23. Michael X. Delli Carpini and Scott Keeter, *What Americans Know about Politics and Why It Matters* (New Haven, CT: Yale University Press, 1996), p. 71.

24. Michael Kagay with Janet Elder, "Numbers Are No Problem for Pollsters. Words Are." *New York Times*, August 9, 1992, p. D5.

25. Richard Morin, "What Informed Public Opinion," *Washington Post National Weekly Edition*, April 10–16, 1995, p. 36.

26. See Seymour Martin Lipset, *American Exceptionalism: A Double-Edged Sword* (New York: Norton, 1996).

27. The findings that follow are drawn from the Times Mirror Center for The People & The Press, *The People, the Press and Politics: The New Political Landscape* (Washington, DC, September 21, 1994).

28. E. J. Dionne, Jr., *Why Americans Hate Politics* (New York: Simon and Schuster/Touchstone, 1991), p. 9.

29. Trend summarized in *The Gallup Poll Monthly,* June 1992, p. 39; 1997 data from the Pew Research Center, *Deconstructing Distrust,* p. 64.

30. Harold W. Stanley and Richard G. Niemi, *Vital Statistics on American Politics* (Washington, DC: CQ Press, 1995), p. 157.

31. For a broader discussion of trust in government, see Stephen C. Craig, *The Malevolent Leaders: Popular Discontent in America* (Boulder, CO: Westview Press, 1993).

32. For an introduction to this "learning theory" of public opinion, see Arthur Lupia and Matthew D. McCubbins, *The Democratic Dilemma: Can Citizens Learn What They Need to Know?* (Cambridge, Eng.: Cambridge University Press, 1998).

33. For a discussion of the era, see Stephanie Coontz, *The Way We Never Were: American Families and the Nostalgia Trap* (New York: Basic Books, 1993).

34. Angus Campbell, Philip Converse, Warren Miller, and Donald Stokes, *The American Voter* (Chicago: University of Chicago Press, 1960), pp. 216–65.

35. Eric R. A. N. Smith, *The Unchanging American Voter* (Berkeley: University of California Press, 1989).

36. See Benjamin Page and Robert Shapiro, *The Rational Public: Fifty Years of Trends in Americans' Policy Preferences* (Chicago: University of Chicago Press, 1992).

37. See Paul C. Light, *Shrinking Government: Federal Headcounts and the Illusion of Smallness* (Washington, DC: The Brookings Institution, 1999).

the media

america's interpreter

As they drafted the Constitution for the new United States of America in 1787, the Founders were not quite sure just what to do about the press. The Founders clearly understood that there could no more have been an American Revolution without the press than without bullets and grape shot. They also knew that the press had been anything but free during the Revolution. Thomas Paine's famous pamphlet, *Common Sense,* may have turned the tide of public opinion toward independence in 1776, and may have sold 500,000 copies in its first year, but it had to be published secretly and anonymously to protect Paine from almost certain British prosecution.

Yet, much as they wanted a free press, most of the Founders saw nothing wrong with punishing newspapers for printing attacks on the government and other citizens. Nor did they believe the truth was a pure defense against such punishment. Whether a story was true or false, most of the Founders believed that the press should be on the government's side.

The one Founder who believed in absolute freedom of the press was James Madison. He was an unapologetic libertarian on the issue, yet he clearly understood that the press could go too far, "That this liberty is often carried to excess, that it has sometimes degenerated into licentiousness, is seen and lamented," he argued, "but the remedy has not yet been discovered. Perhaps it is an evil inseparable from the good with which it is allied; perhaps it is a shoot which cannot be stripped from the stalk without wounding vitally the plant from which it is torn."[1]

Madison lost the argument, however. Other Founders, including Thomas Jefferson, prevailed in arguing that government should have the power to restrict freedom of the press under certain conditions. Freedom of the press would be guaranteed in the First Amendment, but it would not be unfettered. The First Amendment was originally interpreted to mean only that government could not use **prior restraint,** a form of **censorship** that had been used by the British to prevent newspapers from publishing attacks on the government. Even this limited freedom was tested almost immediately with passage of the Alien and Sedition Acts in 1798, which forbade newspapers to print "any false, scandalous writing against the government of the United States." Although the acts were never enforced, the tension between freedom and restraint has not changed to this day.

What has changed is both the size and the impact of the **media,** a term that will be used throughout this chapter to refer to print (newspapers, magazines), electronic (radio and television), and cyber (Internet) sources of news and information on government and politics. Americans have never had so many sources of news and information as they have today, nor have the media ever played a more important role as in reporting events, shaping opinion, and sending messages back and forth between the government and the people. The media now act as America's interpreter. They also act as an independent check on government, whether by publishing public opinion polls on what the people think or by covering issues that government would rather ignore. And by picking and choosing among the many issues that they could cover, the media also shape what the public thinks is important. The media do not tell the people what to think, but they most certainly do tell the people what to think *about*.

This chapter examines the media's influence in more detail, starting with a history of how the media came to play such a critically important role in the democratic life of the United States. The chapter then turns to the four roles that the media play today, asking how the media can act as both a voice of the people and an instrument of government, and concludes with a discussion of the rise of a new kind of media that gives the American people greater access to information on their own terms.

One point will be clear by the end of the chapter: Information is money. As new media conglomerates trade newspapers and television stations like baseball cards, the media may be losing their courage to tell it like it is. The question is not so much whether the media are still a check on government, for politicians still quake at the rumor of an investigation by the *New York Times,* the *Washington Post, 60 Minutes,* or *Dateline*. Rather, the question is what the media are a check against. Are they checking how well government performs or which government official is having an affair with whom? Is their primary goal to educate the public or to win higher ratings?

A HISTORY OF MEDIA AND POLITICS

The role of media has remained the same throughout history: to send messages across, up, and down society, recording history and public opinion along the way. But if the basic human need to communicate has remained constant, the speed at which communication can flow has increased dramatically. Communication today is nearly instantaneous. The media have also become more aggressive in covering the news, in part because of increasing business pressures. With more and more sources of information becoming available to the public, the media have become ever more competitive in digging out the latest scandal.

An Instrument of Government

Despite the Founders' worries about occasional bad press, they mostly saw the media as a passive instrument of government. The three branches of government would make the laws, execute the laws, and interpret the laws, and the media would tell the people whatever the government wanted them to hear. The media would thus be an extension of government, printing the congressional record, publishing the laws, and promoting the greater good.

That was certainly the case in 1787. Back then, the media consisted mostly of printed communication—newspapers, occasional magazines, and pamphlets. Although town criers did their share of communicating, too, in a rather primitive version of the ten o'clock news, most information traveled on the printed page. The *Federalist Papers,* for example, were written one by one and published in several different newspapers between October 27, 1787, and August 16, 1788.

Although he is often remembered for his kite-flying skills, Benjamin Franklin invented the American press, launching his *Pennsylvania Gazette* in 1729. Having started out as a printer, Franklin had a remarkable influence on the newspaper profession, proving that newspapers could be both profitable and respectable. As America grew, so did the newspaper business. By 1750, six colonies had weekly papers; by the 1780s, all thirteen did. The first daily paper appeared in Philadelphia in 1783, a faster form of communication that spread rapidly to other large cities.

Although the Founders protected freedom of the press in the First Amendment, it is not clear just how they viewed the role of the press in their new government. On the one hand, they understood the need to protect this right. On the other hand, they certainly recognized the importance of the press in shaping public opinion, which is why Hamilton, Jay, and Madison worked so hard in writing the *Federalist Papers.*

Yet, for most of America's first one hundred years, freedom of the press largely meant publishing what government wanted the people to read. Until the mid-1800s, for example, the House and Senate did not publish their own record of their proceedings. The majority party gave this lucrative business to newspapers that provided favorable coverage. Once Congress began publishing the *Congressional Record* for itself in 1860, newspapers had more freedom to print the news as they saw fit. For the most part, however, the news that they saw fit to print was the news the government saw fit to provide.

The Muckraking Era

As the Unites States grew, so did the newspaper business. Although "penny" newspapers had been reporting local news for just a penny since the 1830s, the Civil War created an intense public demand for news and an obvious source of stories. Over the next fifty years, Americans got in the newspaper habit—the number of daily newspapers increased almost ten fold from 1850 to 1900, rising from 250 to 2,200, while the number of readers grew twenty fold from 750,000 to 15 million.

Forced to compete for subscibers and advertising revenue, newspapers invented new ways of selling papers. Some, like the *New York Times,* began covering the news more deeply, creating news bureaus in foreign capitals and Washington.

The headlines screamed war. The *New York Journal* offered a $50,000 reward for the conviction of the individuals involved in the sinking of the *U.S.S. Maine,* an amount that would equal roughly $800,000 today. The sinking may have been an accident, but ignited the Spanish-American War nonetheless.

Others began producing **yellow journalism,** consisting of highly sensational, often false, always outrageous stories that might make today's tabloid newpapers uncomfortable.

It was yellow journalism, for example, that fed the war hysteria leading to the Spanish-American War in 1898.[2] Led by William Randolph Hearst's *San Francisco Chronicle* and Joseph Pulitzer's *New York World,* papers around the country reported that Spain had sabotaged the *U.S.S. Maine,* which sank in Havana Harbor after a mysterious explosion. Although later investigations would show that the explosion could have been caused by the spontaneous combustion of coal dust on board, Americans demanded war and got it.

Not all the journalism was misleading, however. In the midst of all the excess, a special kind of reporter called a *muckraker* emerged. Muckrakers saw their job as telling the truth about the world as they saw it—whether about meat-packing plants or child labor. Mostly publishing their work in magazines, muckrakers had a dramatic impact on public opinion. Upton Sinclair's famous novel *The Jungle,* a fictionalized exposé of meatpacking plants, led directly to the creation of the Food and Drug Administration in 1907. *Cosmopolitan,* which is now a fashion and "lifestyle" magazine, was once a popular vehicle for muckraking stories on the "Treason of the Senate" and the sordid careers of leading American millionaires. This was a new role for the media: Instead of just printing what the government wanted to tell, newspapers and magazines began to show the world as it was.

Although there are certainly muckrakers in journalism today, often writing for small weekly papers in large cities, the news business is far less concerned with covering government and policy today than at any point in the last twenty years or more. As Box 5–1 shows, the percentage of stories devoted to both **straight news,** meaning strictly factual accounts of events, and traditional news, meaning analysis and in-depth coverage of straight news, have fallen, while the percentage devoted to **feature news,** meaning stories about people and celebrities, has increased dramatically. The numbers reflect a systematic sampling of stories covered by ABC, CBS, and NBC nightly news, *Time, Newsweek,* the *Washington Post,* the *New York Times,* and the *Los Angeles Times.*

BOX 5-1

Changes in Types of News Stories, 1977–1997

	1977	1997
Straight News	52%	32%
Traditional News		
Policy/Ideas	8%	8%
Political process	4	1
War and peace	2	5
Political strategy	5	4
Update/Analysis	13	7
Historical outlook	1	2
Total	33%	27%
Feature News		
Personality	4%	7%
Scandal	2	13
Quality of life	4	9
Public fear	1	2
Bizarre	0	6
Human interest	4	7
Total	15%	44%

Source: Project for Excellence in Journalism, *Changing Definitions of News: A Look at the Mainstream Press Over 20 Years* (Washington, DC: Project for Excellence in Journalism, March, 1998).

The number of entertainment stories would skyrocket if the researchers had included all the new sources of information: *Hard Copy, Inside Edition, Dateline,* and *20/20* from television; *People, Entertainment Weekly,* and *George* from the newsstand; and the *Drudge Report* from the Internet. The term **infotainment** is used to describe such news, which is designed to entertain as well as inform.

The Electronic Revolution

For the first 150 years of the republic, there was only one way to communicate with the public—through the print media. Although stories still traveled by word of mouth, the public had to wait for the morning or evening paper if they wanted the full story.

Starting in the 1920s, Americans had the option of getting their news faster on radio. This new electronic medium created a personal connection with the listener that the print media simply could not match. Instead of trusting an institution (the newspaper) for the news, Americans began trusting an individual (the announcer) for the news. Forty percent of Americans had a radio by 1930; nearly 100 percent by 1950.

Starting in the 1950s, Americans no longer even needed a reporter to interpret the news: they could hear and watch the events unfolding live and in sometimes chilling detail on television. Whereas only 9 percent of households had a television in 1950, nearly 90 percent had one a decade later. Average television viewing has increased from four hours a day in 1950 to over seven hours today. Nearly two-thirds of households were wired for cable TV by the mid-1990s, and most families had VCRs. Not surprisingly, newspaper circulation has declined significantly, from a high of 37 percent of the population in 1947 to 21 percent today.

It is useful to remember two points about the electronic revolution. First, the early years of radio and television were marked by strong network control. Although CBS was the undisputed leader in the 1950s, NBC and ABC eventually caught up, and these three networks dominated the medium for the better part of three decades. As this chapter will later show, the past decade has witnessed a steady erosion of the networks' share of the television audience.

Second, the electronic revolution introduced a remarkable range of choice into what had been a closed industry. Americans have never had greater freedom to get the news whenever and wherever they wish. "The news media are dividing into market-based niches," according to a 1998 report by the Project for Excellence in Journalism, a Washington-based effort to raise news standards, "with the result that a citizen's perception of society can vary greatly depending on the source of news." Television magazines such as *Dateline* and *20/20* have mostly abandoned covering traditional/straight news topics such as government, social welfare, education, and economics in favor of "news-you-can-use" coverage, while print magazines such as *Time* and *Newsweek* provide less straight information and more celebrity coverage.[3]

The electronic revolution continues with the rapid expansion of cable television, which gives consumers enormous choice in programming. Cable companies are now preparing to expand their offerings from seventy or so channels to hundreds, providing video on demand on a pay-per-view basis. In 1995 alone, sixty new channels were offered to the cable networks. As the choices have increased, cable viewership has exploded, drawing a large share of the audience away from the three major networks. Far from concentrating power in the hands of one company, the cable expansion has fragmented the market as never before. None of the cable channels can yet lay claim to more than 2 percent of the viewing audience.

The electronic revolution also continues with the digital spectrum, which will soon carry high-definition television (HDTV) to homes across America. The advantage is that HDTV will give viewers enormous choice over programming, including low-cost access to the Internet and brilliantly clear pictures. The drawback is that it will render the country's 222 million television sets obsolete, at a cost of roughly $200 billion.

The question here is not whether HDTV will soon replace the old analog spectrum that carries television signals today, but whether it will have an impact on American government and politics. The answer depends in part on what government asks broadcasters to provide in return for their lucrative licenses to the digital spectrum. (Government regulation of mass communication is discussed below.)

If the past is any guide to the future, Washington will stay out of the fray. The digital spectrum, which is worth billions to the broadcast industry, was given away, not auctioned off. Unlike the cellular phone and direct-broadcast satellite industry, which paid $20 billion for access to the public airwaves in 1996, broadcasters persuaded Congress to let them exchange their old analog airwaves for new digital ones. This was hardly a fair trade. By the early 2000s, the analog airwaves will be virtually worthless, particularly if Americans are forced to buy new digital televisions. But reluctance to anger the broadcast industry, which controls so much access to the people, led Congress to make the trade anyway.

The Big Business Era

Americans have more choices than ever in when and where they get the news, but they may be getting less and less variety in actual content. Much as they worried about the threat to liberty from a strong government, the Founders could never have anticipated the threat posed by the increasing concentration in control of the news media.

The New Giants.   Several large media corporations seem poised to take control of the news in a way that the Founders could not have imagined. A decade of mergers and acquisitions left the United States with six news and entertainment conglomerates as of June 1998: (1) the News Corp. (which owned Fox Broadcasting, the *Times of London, New York Post, Sydney Telegraph, TV Guide,* HarperCollins book publishers, and Star TV); (2) Time Warner (which owned Warner Brothers, Elektra Records, Time Warner Cable, *Time, People,* Little, Brown publishers, HBO, the Cable News Network, and New Line Cinema); (3) Walt Disney (which owned ABC, ESPN, Walt Disney Pictures, Touchstone, and Miramax); (4) Viacom (which owned Blockbuster video stores, Simon & Schuster, UPN, MTV, Showtime, and Paramount Pictures); (5) Sony (which owned Columbia Pictures, Loews Theaters, and Columbia and Epic records); and (6) Seagram (which owned Universal, Polygram, and Propaganda films, and MCA, Geffen, Def Jam, and Motown records).

With $24.6 billion in revenues in 1997, Time Warner was the largest of the conglomerates. Its reach into all aspects of the news was undisputed and growing, as Box 5–2 shows. Its purchase of the Turner Broadcasting System in 1997 gave Time Warner control of the Cable News Network, the TBS superstation, and Turner Network Television, not to mention the Atlanta Braves, World Championship Wrestling, and the Cartoon Network (note that Time Warner also owns Looney Tunes and Hanna-Barbera, which provide a steady stream of product). The link between CNN and *Time* creates opportunities for cross-promotion between print and television. *Time* can promote CNN stories and vice versa, thereby boosting ratings and subscriptions for both.

Time Warner and the other media giants are hardly alone in the trend toward concentration of power. Seventy-five percent of U.S. daily newspapers are now owned by media chains, with four corporations (Thompson, American, Gannett, and Donrey) now owning 21 percent of all daily papers. "Put another way," writes former *New York Times* editor Gene Roberts, "four chief executive officers control more than one-fifth of the nation's dailies."[4] Does such control shape the news? Roberts answers emphatically yes, observing: "It is seldom done by corporate directives or fiat. It rarely involves killing or slanting stories. Usually it is by the appointment of a pliable editor, by a corporate graphics conference that results in a more uniform look or by the corporate research director's interpretation of reader surveys that seek simple common-denominator solutions to complex coverage problems."

As discussed later in this chapter, the rapid expansion of the Internet as a source of news may give the public ample alternatives to big media. Moreover, big news may need big business. The days when ABC, CBS, and NBC could cover the cost of twenty-two minutes of evening news with just eight minutes of advertising revenue are long gone. Not only can conglomerates inject the dollars needed to keep the news flowing, they can provide the insurance coverage needed to run

BOX 5-2

The Time Warner Empire

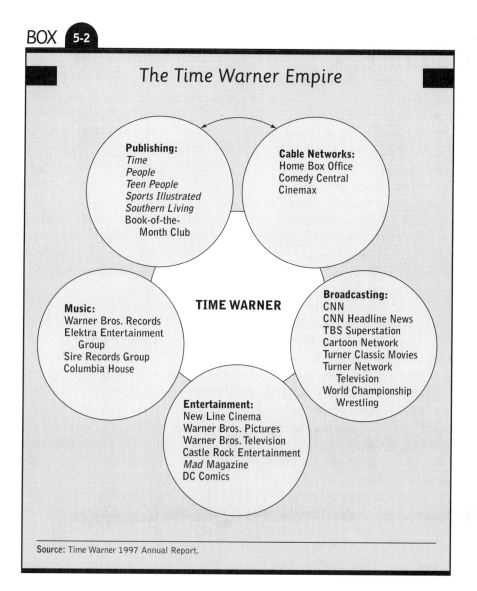

Publishing:
Time
People
Teen People
Sports Illustrated
Southern Living
Book-of-the-
    Month Club

Cable Networks:
Home Box Office
Comedy Central
Cinemax

TIME WARNER

Music:
Warner Bros. Records
Elektra Entertainment
    Group
Sire Records Group
Columbia House

Broadcasting:
CNN
CNN Headline News
TBS Superstation
Cartoon Network
Turner Classic Movies
Turner Network
    Television
World Championship
    Wrestling

Entertainment:
New Line Cinema
Warner Bros. Pictures
Warner Bros. Television
Castle Rock Entertainment
Mad Magazine
DC Comics

Source: Time Warner 1997 Annual Report.

risky stories. The days when a muckraker could take on a big business without fear of being sued are long gone. Upton Sinclair would be in court every day fighting charges of **libel,** the publication of false and defamatory statements about an individual or a company. "Who else can afford the risks or the cost of catastrophic libel insurance with its multimillion-dollar premiums and $5 million deductibles?" writes a former NBC producer. "At issue is not whether there will be a corporate parent, but the integrity and size of the corporate parent."[5]

The Dangers of Concentration.   Although it is still too early to tell how the current era of media mergers will affect news quality, there are three potential dangers in the concentration of power. First, news operations may go soft on their corporate parents. Should Americans trust *TV Guide's* program reviews now that it is part of the same company that owns the Fox television network? Should they trust *Time* now that it is owned by the same company that owns Warner Bros. Pictures and CNN? Should they assume that NBC is just as tough in its stories about General Electric's consumer products now that the network is actually owned by GE? And should they assume that MSNBC will be honest when it comes to covering Microsoft, given that Microsoft has put $500 million into that cable channel? The problem in such marriages is not in government censorship at all, but in the kind of self-censorship that comes from being owned by a powerful giant with interests to protect.

Second, news operations, under pressure to boost corporate profits, may compromise the truth to generate high ratings. The dangers were unmistakably exposed in the first collaboration between CNN and *Time* magazine, which launched a joint television magazine called *NewsStand: CNN and Time* in June 1998. The first program featured a sensational report that the U.S. military had used deadly nerve gas against American deserters in Laos during the Vietnam War. Titled "Valley of Death," the story was reported by Peter Arnett, an award-winning journalist who had earned international praise for his coverage of the Baghdad bombing at the start of the 1991 Gulf War. *Time* ran its own 2,000-word version of the story at the same time, also under Arnett's by-line.

The facts about the nerve-gas story are sketchy, and hard evidence was lacking. Although "Valley of Death" showed grainy pictures of a military raid into Laos, it turned out that many of the program's sources had doubts about what really had happened back in 1970. But doubts do not make for high ratings; a piece called "Valley of Possible Death" would not have generated much buzz. CNN and *Time* apparently succumbed to the pressure to produce generated by their parent, Time Warner. In doing so, neither exercised due diligence in checking the facts of the story. As Arnett later admitted, he "contributed not one comma" to the *Time* story, yet he allowed it to be published under his name.[6]

A third danger is that news operations may stop taking risks for fear of offending potential viewers, readers, or juries. This hazard of concentration is particularly clear in the newspaper business, where chains tend to cut costs by laying off reporters and homogenizing coverage. It is cheaper to have one Washington bureau serving ten papers than ten reporters serving one paper.

It is easy to understand why broadcast media, too, might become timid in the wake of ABC-TV's controversial 1992 *PrimeTime Live* investigation of Food Lion, a Southern grocery chain. *PrimeTime Live* sent two employees to work undercover at a Food Lion supermarket. They hid miniature cameras in their wigs to document allegations that the chain was selling spoiled meat that had been washed in bleach to kill the smell.

Food Lion eventually won a $5.5 million judgment against ABC, not because the story had been proved untrue, but because the two ABC reporters had lied to get their undercover jobs. As the jury foreman said after the verdict, "The media has a right to bring the news, but they have to watch what they do. It's like a football game. There are boundaries, and you have to make sure you don't go outside the boundaries." Although the award was later reduced to $315,000, it set a precedent for basing lawsuits on a reporter's methods, not on the accuracy of the final story.

Government Regulation of the Media

As the media became increasingly independent toward the late 1800s, the federal government became much more heavily engaged in regulating the airwaves. Congress reserved a slice of the airways for the Navy under the Wireless Ship Act of 1910, began regulating the radio industry under the Radio Act of 1927, and created the **Federal Communications Commission (FCC)** in 1933 to assure that the airwaves would be used in the public interest. In passing these laws, Congress defined the airwaves as public property, like highways or parks. To avoid congestion and promote public standards, radio stations would be given access to the airwaves only under certain conditions. Congress expanded the FCC's charter to include television in the 1940s.

It is important to note, however, that the FCC has never had the power to regulate the print media. Unlike the broadcast media, newspapers and magazines are perfectly free to editorialize for one candidate without providing space to the others, to write stories that present only one side of an issue, and to ignore pressing community concerns. The basic difference between print and electronic media, and the main reason for their different treatment by the government, is that anyone can print a newspaper if they have the money to buy printer's ink and paper, but only so many airwaves are available for broadcast use.

Over the years, the FCC has issued a number of rules that limit what the electronic media can and cannot do on the air, including using obscene language. Stations that violate the rules can be fined or can even lose their licenses (although very few have done so). Under the **equal opportunities rule,** for example, radio and television stations that sell advertising time to one political candidate or party must provide an equal amount of time to all other candidates.

Under the **reasonable access rule,** they must provide "reasonable coverage" of controversial issues within their communities, although the FCC has never quite defined just what the words *reasonable* and *controversial* mean. This rule has been expanded over the years to include political campaigns. Once a campaign begins, stations must give candidates a reasonable amount of advertising space at the lowest price possible.

Until 1987, stations also had to heed the **fairness doctrine,** which required stations "both to cover controversial issues of public importance and to broadcast opposing points of view on them." The Reagan administration repealed the fairness doctrine, arguing that it limited the free speech it was meant to protect. Instead of promoting tough coverage of controversial issues, many stations had shied away from any coverage at all, for fear that the FCC might punish them for failing to be fair.[7]

The same problem may arise under the reasonable access rule. Because they are forced to give candidates air time at the lowest possible price, stations often interpret the reasonable access rule in the most limited terms possible. Since they cannot charge the market rate, as they would for advertising slots during the Super Bowl or the final episode of *Seinfeld,* they may confine candidates' access to the least attractive slots—say, right before the 11:00 local news.

The FCC is also struggling to keep up with advancing technology, particularly surrounding the digital spectrum. In 1997, the Clinton administration appointed an advisory committee to help the FCC devise new rules for digital television, including a suggested code of conduct that would ask broadcasters to meet minimum public interest standards. The difficulty in establishing such a code is that adherence would have to be voluntary, meaning that members of the National Association of Broadcasters, a powerful lobbying group that represents the television and radio industry, could take it or leave it. The only way to guarantee some minimum level of public interest programming is to require it under law as a condition of receiving a digital license, which Congress explicitly decided not to do in 1996, when it gave the broadcasting industry the digital spectrum for free.

 **in a different light** ———— THE V-CHIP: STOP US BEFORE WE WATCH AGAIN

Americans are sharply divided about television. On the one hand, they steadfastly oppose most forms of censorship. They do not want government to tell them what to watch or when to watch it. On the other hand, they want to protect their children from violent or mature programming. That is why many applauded when President

Clinton signed the Telecommunications Act of 1996, which requires all new television sets built after the year 2000 to contain a "V-Chip" (the "V" is for violence, the "chip" is for the micro-chip that will allow parents to block certain programs).

The V-chip cannot work, however, without some kind of rating system that would trigger the block. The first attempt at delivering such a system was left to the broadcasting industry, in part because Congress worried that any government-imposed system would be challenged under the First Amendment right of free speech, although Congress gave government the authority to step in if the industry failed to act. Under public pressure from a broad coalition of children's organizations led by Vice President Al Gore's wife, Tipper Gore, and worried about possible government intervention, the industry quickly produced a six-level rating system. The rating assigned to a given program now appears for 15 seconds at the start of the program:

TV-Y means that the program is appropriate for all children.

TV-Y7 means the program is designed for children over 7 years of age.

TV-G means the program is appropriate for all ages.

TV-PG means the program contains material that parents may find unsuitable for younger children.

TV-14 means the program contains some material that many parents would find unsuitable for children under 14 years of age.

TV-MA means the program is specifically designed for adults and should not be viewed by children under 17 years of age.

The ratings system came under fire almost immediately. For starters, the television industry rates its own programs, and none of the major networks gave any of their programs the dreaded TV-MA label. Throughout all of television in 1997, there was but one TV-MA program: Comedy Central's *South Park*, an animated series about a small town populated by foul-mouthed third graders (one of whom, Kenny, gets killed in every episode), psychotic teachers, clueless parents, and corrupt politicians. Despite the rating, children under age 17 still made up one-fifth of the show's audience.

Moreover, the six-level system did not tell parents what made a given show offensive. Under still more pressure, the industry added a four-level content rating: (1) *D* means suggestive dialogue, (2) *V* means violence, (3) *S* means sex, and (4) *L* means language. According to ABC's vice president for broadcast standards, a single "damn" or "hell" will not produce an *L*, but a string of them most certainly will. A single face slapping will not earn a *V*, but a beating will. As for sex, talking about it will earn a *D*, while simulating it will draw an *S*.

Given the complexity of the ratings and the lack of any enforcement mechanism to ensure that viewers are not being misled, it should be no surprise that many parents pay no attention to the ratings. According to assorted surveys conducted over the first year the system was in place, roughly half of parents said they used the ratings, while the rest paid little or no attention at all. Moreover, neither NBC nor the Black Entertainment Television network used the content rating.

In the end, the rating system is only as effective as the parents who use it. Although the V-chip may make programming the TV easier, parents will face a staggering array of options once they start punching in the controls. To make the system work, parents will have to read the TV listings or watch the programs with their children. But if more parents had been willing to do that, there probably would have been no demand for the V-chip in the first place.

THE FOUR ROLES OF MEDIA

Public opinion and the media are inextricably linked today. How the public thinks about issues clearly influences at least some media coverage, if only because most media must turn a profit to stay in business and must therefore please the public. How the media cover issues clearly influences what the public thinks, if only because so many Americans rely on the media for basic information about the issues of the day. The media can be seen, therefore, as an interpretive institution in American government. They provide access and information in two directions: from the people to government and back.

The media thus make some of the most important decisions in American politics. Because time and space are scarce, the media must decide what gets covered and what gets ignored. As media mergers continue and competition for audience increases, the media will likely become even more aggressive in courting, some might even say exploiting, the public's interest in scandal, controversy, and personality. Whether print or electronic, magazine or e-zine, media must make money to survive. Print and electronic media can cover government and politics only if they can attract viewers and readers. The basic reason the media seem preoccupied with the unseemly side of politics—the scandals, the waste of taxpayers' money, the allegations of sexual escapades—is that controversy sells.

Nevertheless, the media will continue to have a profound impact on public opinion by playing four interpretive roles: (1) they provide raw information that the public reshapes into opinions; (2) they often set the tone of public discourse by putting a negative spin on the news; (3) they help set the agenda of issues by declaring certain issues to be of national importance; and (4) they sometimes allow themselves to be used by government to promote a specific point of view. Each role will be discussed in detail below.

The Media as Informer

The impact of the news media as a mediator between the people and government begins with information about events and people. At its most elementary level, straight news is designed to ask six basic questions: who, what, when, where, why, and how? Journalism schools still teach their students how to build news stories around an inverted pyramid that begins with a lead paragraph that gives readers the short answers to those six questions, providing details in the subsequent paragraphs.

The public clearly relies on the news for the basics of American politics (see Box 5–3). Each news source emphasizes somewhat different kinds of information. People who want news on health and medicine should turn to television and print magazines, not newspapers. The first two sources have almost twice as many stories on health and medicine as newspapers do. People who want information on government should turn to print magazines and newspapers instead of television magazines. Only 0.6 percent of 1997 television magazine stories focused on government, compared to nearly 30 percent of newspaper coverage.

Although most of the numbers in the box have not changed radically over the past few years, at least three deserve mention. First, the audience for the evening network news on ABC (anchored by Peter Jennings), CBS (Dan Rather), and NBC (Tom Brokaw) has fallen by nearly 15 percentage points since 1994, marking a continued decline in what were once the most important twenty-two minutes in the day (the other eight minutes in the half hour are advertising) for shaping what Americans think. Second, the audience for tabloid television has fallen even more, by 20 percent, marking a sobering of American views toward *Hard Copy* and *Inside Edition*. Such programs may be provocative and entertaining, but are hardly dedicated to providing the news. Finally, Howard Stern has more than doubled his impact as a source of information. Although purists would hardly call his program news either, at least one-sixth of Americans now use his program as a news source either regularly or sometimes.

Shifting Coverage.   Just because the use of sources has been relatively stable, we cannot conclude that those sources offer the same coverage. All media are devoting less and less time to straight news in general, specifically to straight news on government and politics. Consider three facts about the trends:

BOX **5-3**

Where Americans Get the News

Percent of Americans who regularly or sometimes use the following sources of information on government and politics:

Local evening news	86%
TV news magazines (*60 Minutes, 20/20,* etc.)	78
National ABC, CBS, NBC evening news	67
Cable News Network (CNN)	57
News magazines (*Time, Newsweek,* etc.)	51
FOX News Channel	47
TV "tabloid" shows (*Hard Copy, Inside Edition,* etc.)	47
CNBC	39
Political talk radio shows	35
National Public Radio	32
MSNBC	31
C-SPAN live coverage	23
Business magazines (*Fortune, Business Week,* etc.)	21
MTV	21
News Hour with Jim Lehrer (PBS's evening news)	18
Howard Stern (syndicated radio talk show)	16
Tabloid newspapers (*National Enquirer,* etc.)	15
Rush Limbaugh (syndicated radio talk show)	14
Imus in the Morning (syndicated radio talk show)	4

Source: Pew Research Center for The People & The Press, *Internet News Takes Off: Pew Research Center Biennial News Consumption Survey* (Washington, DC: Pew Research Center, June, 1998), pp.35–53.

- In 1977, three out of every five newspaper stories involved straight news. Twenty years later, the number was down to barely one out of four.

- In 1977, *Time* and *Newsweek* featured political or international figures on almost one-third of their covers and celebrities on just one-sixth. Twenty years later, the number of covers depicting political and international figures had been cut by two-thirds, to just one in ten, while the number for celebrities had jumped by half.

- In 1977, the network news devoted over 50 percent of its time to straight news of one kind or another, and just 0.5 percent to scandal. Twenty years later, the amount of straight news had fallen to barely 33 percent (or just seven minutes), while the coverage of scandal had jumped to 15 percent (or about three minutes).

The jump in scandal coverage occurred everywhere, sometimes moving directly from tabloids such as the *National Enquirer* and *Star* to the front page of the most prestigious papers. At the start of the 1992 presidential campaign, it was the *Star* that published the first allegations regarding candidate Bill Clinton's extramarital affair with Gennifer Flowers (allegations that Clinton later confirmed in his testimony regarding White House intern Monica Lewinsky), and *A Current Affair* that aired her first television interview; but it was the traditional press that gave the story national credibility by reporting on these reports. As senior *Newsweek* editor Jonathan Alter remarked after the incident, "When the *National Enquirer* sneezes, the *New York Times* catches a cold."[8]

Shifting Content.   Although the media still report straight news, they no longer cover government and politics the way they used to. From 1968 to 1996, for example, the average **sound bite**—the length of time a candidate is seen and heard in a given story—declined from 43 seconds to just 8 seconds.[9]

During the same period, there appeared to be a sharp increase in what scholars call **horse race coverage** of election campaigns, which means that the media were more interested in reporting on who was ahead or behind than on the issues. In the 1980 presidential campaign, for example, the nation's major newspapers published roughly 100 front-page stories about the results of public opinion polls; in 1992, they published 452. Although there is some evidence that horse race coverage declined in 1996, in part because there was no horse race, the polls continued to roll. Yet, even with Clinton leading by double digits from beginning to end, roughly one-third of all network news stories in the general election campaign focused on the horse race, another two-fifths on policy issues, and the final quarter on candidates' characters.

in a different light ——   WHY AMERICANS DON'T TRUST THE MEDIA

Americans view the media as both a friend and an enemy of democracy. On the one hand, they expect the media to tell it like it is. If there is corruption, the media should nail it. If there is crime, the media should show it. If the president lies, the media should reveal it. On the other hand, Americans have come to believe that the media are just as corrupt as the rest of politics.

Indeed, Americans have never trusted the media less, at least not since pollsters started tracking the question. The number of Americans who say that stories are often inaccurate increased from 37 percent in 1985 to 56 percent in 1997, while the number who rated the moral and ethical practices of journalists as excellent or good fell to just 33 percent, only slightly higher than federal government officials, and well behind state and local government officials. Two-thirds of Americans said the media unnecessarily invade people's privacy, and just one-fourth said that news organizations deal fairly with all sides of the issues.[10]

Americans have lost trust in the media for three reasons. First, Americans believe that the media often use unethical methods to get the news. Roughly half of the respondents interviewed in a 1997 survey by the Pew Research Center disapproved of running stories with unnamed sources and using hidden cameras, while two-thirds disapproved of paying informants for information and undercover investigations. Americans also believe that certain kinds of investigations should be off limits. Almost two-thirds of the Pew Research Center respondents said that press coverage of the personal and ethical behavior of political leaders has become excessive, and nearly half said that such coverage discouraged many competent people from serving in office.

This is not to argue that these Americans wanted fewer investigations. Eight in ten approved of uncovering and reporting on corruption and fraud in business, government agencies and other organizations, while six in ten wanted more, not less, investigative reporting. Rather, they want the investigations to be both fair and relevant.

Second, Americans simply do not like the news they are getting, and transfer some of their anger to the media. In 1985, for example, two out of five Americans said they enjoyed watching the news on television, while two out of five said they looked forward to reading the paper each day. By 1997, both numbers had fallen to just a quarter.

Americans were particularly offended by the news coverage of Clinton's affair with White House intern Monica Lewinsky. The coverage was unrelenting. According to one estimate, the network news devoted 1,155 minutes to the scandal from January to August, which was more than their coverage of the Asian economic crisis, nuclear testing by India and Pakistan, the United Auto Workers strike against General Motors, the Northern Ireland peace accord, the president's trip to China, the Pope's visit to Cuba, the Winter Olympics, and Viagra *combined.* And, according to the Pew Research Center, most Americans believed the coverage was often inaccurate, unfair, and overwrought.

Third, Americans have come to doubt that reporters care about ordinary Americans. As one observer argues, reporters used to be "of the people, not above the people." They were "typically underpaid, unsophisticated, chain-smoking, hard-drinking, blue-collar, salt-of-the-earth types" who "stood up for the 'little guy.'"[11]

That is clearly no longer the case. Today's reporters often travel in the same social circles as the well-to-do officials they cover. According to Hodding Carter, former press secretary to Jimmy Carter and now a senior ABC analyst, "The top journalists move in packs with the affluent and powerful in Washington. They swarm with them in the summer to every agreeable spot on the Eastern Seaboard. When any three or four of them sit down together on a television talk show, it is not difficult to remember that the least well paid of these pontificators make at least six times more each year than the average American family."[12]

In short, the public seems to believe that the media have lost touch with ordinary Americans, are rarely able to see beyond their own cynical view of the world, and express what one critic has called "a permanent sneer" toward their stories. As former *U.S. News & World Report* editor James Fallows writes, "A relentless emphasis on the cynical game of politics threatens public life itself, by implying day after day that the political sphere is nothing more than an arena in which ambitious politicians struggle for dominance, rather than a structure in which citizens can deal with worrisome collective problems."[13] At some point, the cynicism that journalists feel toward those they cover has to creep into the stories they report.

The Media as Tone Setter

Communications scholars have argued for years over whether the media actually have a distinctive influence on opinion. It is entirely possible, for example, that people pay attention to certain sources of information because they already know what they think. Perhaps people who listen to Howard Stern are not so much influenced by him as comforted or reassured.

That is precisely the conclusion of a 1960 study by Joseph Klapper that challenged the prevailing wisdom of how communications shape opinion. According to Klapper, people employ at least three defensive mechanisms to insulate themselves against great orators and clever advertising: *selective exposure*— they pay attention only to media and messages they already like; *selective perception*—they reshape information so that it fits their prevailing views; and *selective retention*—they tend to forget information and tune out people they do not like.[14] Liberals would never choose to listen to conservative pundit Rush Limbaugh, for example. But assuming they stumbled on his program in the middle of the desert with nothing else on the radio, they might make fun of everything he said, and most certainly would forget anything they found potentially persuasive as soon as possible.

Many scholars challenged Klapper's findings, arguing that he underestimated the effect of the media in setting the overall tone of public discourse. People might miss some information here and there as a result of the selective exposure, perception, or retention mentioned above, but they certainly could not miss the overall tone of coverage. Moreover, Klapper's research was completed in 1959, a year before the first televised presidential debate. That debate marked a new era in high-exposure events that unavoidably have an effect on the public.

Whatever the impact of the media in shaping specific opinions, there is no doubt that the media provide frameworks that help the public make sense of an increasingly complicated world. There is no question, for example, that the media frame stories in a way that enhances public distrust toward government and politics. In framing stories with a cynical tone, the media send a signal that Americans are right to think the worst about those who govern.

Covering Elections.   The tone of election coverage has clearly changed since the 1960s. Today, "[t]he voters begin each campaign without a firm opinion of the candidates," writes media expert Thomas Patterson, "but after months of news that tells them over and over again that their choices are no good, they believe it."[15] According to Patterson's data, campaign coverage has gotten steadily more negative over the past thirty years. In 1960, for example, "good news" stories about the candidates outnumbered "bad news" stories by roughly four to one. The ratio of good to bad news stories steadily dwindled during the Vietnam War, and continued downward during the 1970s and 1980s. By 1992, bad news stories outweighed good ones by a ratio of roughly 1.5 to 1.[16]

As Patterson also notes, once a candidate starts to sink in the polls, the media go on the attack, turning against the likely losers. In 1996, for example, Republican presidential candidate Bob Dole lagged behind Clinton in both public support and good press. Between January and March of that year, Clinton led Dole by 57 percent to 46 percent in the number of stories that said something positive about either candidate. Although Dole got a "bounce" in the month following the Republican convention, when he actually led Clinton by 9 percent in positive stories, the rest of the campaign yielded one bad story after another. During September alone, the month when so many voters decide, Clinton won the battle for favorable coverage by a margin of 54 percent to 30 percent.[17]

It is not clear whether Dole's negative coverage was due to reporter bias or to Dole's own mistakes. What is clear is that the traditional sources of news appear to be increasingly cynical toward the subjects they cover, which may ultimately help to turn the healthy skepticism that marks the American political character into a corrosive, unhealthy cynicism.

Covering the Presidency.   The tone of coverage of the presidency also appears to have changed. As soon as Clinton started his first term, the press put him on the defensive. "From up close, the Clinton White House has looked like the Not-Ready-for-Prime-Time-Players," NBC's Lisa Myers said just two days after Clinton's inauguration. "He hit the ground back-pedaling," said her print colleague Fred Barnes on "The McLaughlin Group" the next day:[18] "Incredibly inept," said Mark Shields. "Slowness and vacillation," said McLaughlin himself. "The president is stumbling," said NBC's *Meet the Press* anchor Tim Russert. "The common sense of a gnat," wrote Jack Germond and Jules Witcover. "Hope is rapidly turning to chilly uneasiness, even dismay," argued the editorial page of the *Los Angeles Times*.[19] All these comments came within a week of Clinton's inauguration, during the period ordinarily considered a honeymoon.

As with Dole during the 1996 campaign, reporters could easily claim that Clinton got his early bad press the old-fashioned way: he earned it, starting with his flip-flop on homosexuals in the military and continuing with concerns surrounding his investments in an Arkansas land deal dubbed Whitewater. In fact, it was the *New York Times,* normally considered a liberal national newspaper, that kept the pressure on the Whitewater story long after most other papers had stopped covering it. Reporters could also note that presidents always complain about the coverage they receive. As Helen Thomas, the veteran UPI reporter who has covered every president since Kennedy, explained: "No president ever liked the press, and we don't expect them to start now." Indeed, the very first president, George Washington, was the subject of nearly constant attacks from Anti-Federalist editors. Nevertheless, the public is concerned not about how tough the press is on the president, but about whether the press is fair.

The Media as Agenda Setter

Editing the news involves tough decisions about what to cover and what to ignore. After all, there are only so many pages in a paper (and only one front page) and only so many minutes in a broadcast (and only one opening image). These choices have an important bearing on what the public comes to believe are the most important issues in the country. Today's lead story might be the subject of tomorrow's legislative hearing or presidential press conference.

Once they have covered the unavoidable stories (elections, crises, and natural disasters), the media have significant discretion in setting the news agenda. These coverage decisions are made by the editors and producers who act as **gatekeepers** of information. By moving a story up or down in the news hole, a term that refers to the amount of available space or time for stories, these gatekeepers may create the impression that certain problems are more important than others. As such, the media can have a profound impact on both the *intensity* of public opinion and the perceptions of **attentive policy elites** who set the policy agenda in response. The more compelling the news story, the more likely the public is to say that a problem is very important. The more important the public says a problem is, the more likely Congress and the president are to respond.[20] And, to the extent that the effects of agenda setting show up in polls, the public can tell politicians what to act on. Much as it would offend the Founders, and much as it appears to upset the delicate balance, policy elites do pay attention to the rise and fall of issues.

These agenda-setting effects clearly vary across different kinds of media coverage. According to one analysis of the research literature, agenda setting is shaped by four factors. The first is *news play*. Stories that lead the news, whether in the first minutes of the network news or on the front page of a newspaper, are much more likely to affect public opinion than stories that come later. People pay closest attention to the lead story. The second factor is *audience interest*. Media coverage is more likely to affect public opinion among poorly informed viewers, who lack the information and predisposition to form opinions on their own, and viewers for whom a given story issue is salient. The third factor is *the nature of the issue*. Some stories, such as the Oklahoma City bombing, have nearly instant effects simply because they are unavoidable. Other stories, such as the Ethiopian famine, take months of slow coverage to take hold.[21] The fourth factor is the *intensity of coverage*. When the media concentrates its fire on a story through *pack journalism,* as it did in the Monica Lewinsky scandal, the public can hardly turn away. Much as Americans objected to the coverage, news ratings went up, not down, whenever the scandal played. Such pack journalism can produce a troubling level of standardization as reporters recycle the same story over and over. It can also produce a higher level of inaccuracy, as rumors become the basis for straight news.

The various media do not have the same degree of influence on public opinion. Under the old adage that "seeing is believing," a majority of Americans trust television news the most, with public trust in newspapers, radio, and magazines lagging far behind.[22] Although television may not be able to create the depth of understanding that the print media can, if only because most TV news stories last but a minute or two, it is able to convey the kind of searing images that stay with viewers longer.

The Media as an Instrument of Government Again

Much as reporters swear by their independence from the governments they cover, they are sometimes used by government to send selective messages. Remember, media outlets are businesses. Being first with a story, even a story planted by the government, may boost readership or viewership and, in turn, advertising revenue.

Government tries to use the media to its advantage in a variety of ways, not the least of which is shaping the news through press conferences and news releases. As the media have become accustomed to ignoring releases, government has become more skilled at manipulation. Presidents and members of Congress can always "leak," or secretly release, a piece of information, hoping that a newspaper or television network will jump on the news just because it is secret. As Box 5–4 suggests, all leaks are not created equal. Some are designed to build good will, others to float new ideas.

Leaks are only one of several ways in which government can shape the news today. Efforts by presidents and members of Congress to impose their own "spin," or interpretation, on the news have grown so visible over the years that they now have their own label: **spin control.** The White House even has a special unit, the Office of Communications, completely dedicated to shaping what the media think about the news.[23] Its goal is simple: get the president on the network news, where a picture is truly worth a thousand words. Sometimes the White House uses leaks to attract coverage; other times it prepares a **media event** designed specifically to generate coverage.

Not all spin control involves getting coverage. It can also involve efforts to kill a story or deny a rumor. The ultimate purpose of "denial spinning" is to distract the public from the story at hand by using any of several tactics: flooding the media with irrelevant information ("candor spinning"), attacking the media for having no facts ("stonewall spinning"), releasing selective information that appears relevant when it is not ("selection spinning"), or calling attention to issues by refusing to comment on them ("silent spinning"). As one media critic argues, experts assume that spin control must work, because people are always spinning; "[y]et, it makes just as much sense to assume the opposite: that the reason spin is everywhere today is that it *doesn't* work—that, because the public is getting increasingly inured to spin, spinners feel they must spin even harder, on and on, in an ever-escalating arms race."[24]

BOX 5-4

A Guide to Leaks in Government

The ego leak: Giving information primarily to satisfy a sense of self-importance: in effect, "I am important because I can give you information that is important." Popular with staff, who have fewer outlets for ego tripping. May be most frequent cause of leaking, but may not account for the major leaks.

The goodwill leak: A play for a future favor. Primary pupose is to accumulate credit with a reporter, which the leaker hopes can be spent at a later date.

The policy leak: A straightforward pitch for or against a proposal using some document or insiders' information as the lure to get more attention than might otherwise be justified. Great leaks often fit into this category.

The animus leak: Used to settle grudges. Information is disclosed to embarrass another person.

The trial-balloon leak: Used to test a proposal that is under consideration. Most likely to be sent up by opponents of an idea who hope that it will be shot down, since it is easier to generate opposition to almost anything than it is to build support.

The whistle-blower leak: Used almost exclusively by career personnel. May be the last resort of frustrated civil servants who feel they cannot correct a perceived wrong through regular government channels.

Source: Stephen Hess, "A Guide to 'Leaks' in Government," in Roger H. Davidson and Walter J. Oleszek, *Governing* (Washington, DC: CQ Press, 1992), pp. 212–13.

 **in a different light** ——— CIVIC JOURNALISM

The continued plunge in public trust in the media has led some journalists to argue for a change in how the media work. Instead of concentrating on the bad news, they believe, the media should become partners with citizens in improving communities, solving problems, even giving citizens a voice in saying which stories get covered. These advocates label their cause *civic journalism* (or, sometimes, *public journalism*). As one of the founders of the movement defines the term: "It's a set of practices in which journalists attempt to reconnect with citizens, improve public discussion and generally try to make public life go well."[25]

Civic journalism involves everything from conducting town hall meetings to producing in-depth stories on what citizens say are the most important issues in their communities. The *Portland (Maine) Press Herald* and *Minneapolis Star-Tribune* have sponsored neighborhood meetings in which citizens meet to discuss public issues. The *Daily Oklahoman* and *Boulder (Colo.) Daily Camera* have convened discussions among community leaders to create solutions to local problems. The *Wichita (Kans.) Eagle*, *Charlotte (N.C.) Observer*, and *Tallahassee (Fla.) Democrat* have all used deliberative polls of one kind or another to determine which issues they will cover in election campaigns. In all of these examples, citizens get a say in telling the media what to cover.

On the positive side, civic journalism invites citizens to participate in solving local problems and opens the press to hearing about problems from a different perspective. In 1994, for example, the *Boston Globe* launched its election coverage with a series of polls asking citizens what issues they wanted talked about in the campaign, and later matched candidate positions on those issues against citizen positions. The *Globe* also ran stories on how citizens could learn more about the issues, and even offered advice on how to get involved in the campaign.

On the negative side, some critics argue that civic journalism invites citizens too far into the newsroom. "Too much of what's called public journalism appears to be what our promotion department does," says *Washington Post* editor Leonard Downie, "only with a different kind of name and a fancy, evangelistic fervor."[26] At what point, for example, does an effort to convene community leaders to solve local problems compromise a paper's ability to cover those same leaders objectively when they go wrong? At what point does letting citizens set the election news agenda compromise a television station's judgment about the stories people need to hear?

When carried too far, civic journalism can create the same dangers as media mergers do. In North Carolina, for example, a consortium of six newspapers, seven television stations, and three radio stations agreed to let the people decide how they should cover the 1996 U.S. Senate campaign between the Republican incumbent, Jesse Helms and his Democratic challenger, Harvey Gantt. The campaign promised to be a brutal rematch between one of the most conservative members of the Senate and one of the potentially most liberal. After conducting its own opinion poll, the consortium decided to focus its coverage on crime, drugs, taxes, health care, and education, but not families (Helms was an outspoken opponent of abortion rights), foreign affairs (Helms was and still is the chairman of the Senate Foreign Relations Committee), or race (Helms is white and Gantt is African American).

The goal of the effort was noble: focus on issues that the public cares about. Unfortunately for Gantt, the issues about which the consortium decided not to carry any news were the ones that he relied on to help him win. Nor did the consortium cover allegations that the Jesse Helms Center, a foundation created to honor the three-term senator, had accepted $225,000 from the government of Taiwan, an obvious conflict of interest given the Senator's chairmanship of the Senate Foreign Relations Committee. Although Gantt had $2.5 million for advertising, he was never able to shift the media coverage to his side. And by steadfastly refusing to participate in any consortium debates, Helms was able to duck systematic coverage on even the chosen issues.

The result was some of the most timid reporting in North Carolina history and a second defeat for Gantt. "This isn't exactly a conspiracy," wrote news critic Jonathan Yardley, "but it's not a bad imitation of one. The motivations behind it seem to be at least as public-spirited as they are self-serving, but this does not make the end result any more savory. No matter how one describes what is being done, it comes down to an attempt to control the political agenda rather than to report on the candidates' activities and positions."[27] Ultimately, journalists must tell both sides of the story, not just the one the public wants to hear.

THE NEW MEDIA

Declining public trust in the networks and the national press may explain why citizens and candidates are spending more time with new media such as cable television, specialized print magazines, talk radio, and the Internet, all of which give consumers far greater control over what they see and hear. Not only do the new media provide additional places to obtain information, but government and its leaders can use the new media to reach the public with much greater ease.

Take television talk shows as an example. In 1992 the three presidential candidates—George Bush, Bill Clinton, and Ross Perot—appeared ninety-six times on talk shows: *Donahue* hosted four visits, three of which were by Clinton; CNN's *Larry King Live* and ABC's *Good Morning America* each hosted thirteen; NBC's *Today Show* hosted ten; CBS's *This Morning* hosted twenty-one.[28] None of the three ever faced the tougher questioning of *Meet the Press, 20/20,* or *60 Minutes.*

Bill Clinton was by far the most active guest of the talk shows, accounting for forty-seven, or almost half, of the ninety-six appearances. He joined the American people—or at least the ones watching morning news programs—for breakfast forty times during the campaign. Not that Clinton slighted the late-night audience, playing his saxophone on Fox's *Arsenio Hall* show. Perot was the second most frequent guest on the talk shows, with thirty-three appearances over the campaign season. Bush trailed both his rivals, with seventeen appearances.

As for hard questioners, ABC's Sam Donaldson faced Bush and Clinton once, but never Perot; *ABC Nightline* anchor Ted Koppel and *CBS Evening News* anchor Dan Rather got no interviews at all.

The Incredible Shrinking Audience

The public has few sources of absolutely pure information. Even the Internet, which is often characterized as an untamed frontier of information, is becoming increasingly crowded with carefully crafted political messages and advertising. Moreover, even the most purportedly neutral television or newspaper story almost always has a spin, whether given by reporters (who tend to be moderate to liberal), their publishers (who tend to be conservative), or the political leaders they interview.

It should also be clear that no single source of information exists that might somehow tie citizens together, at least not unless the story involves catastrophe. The entire nation tunes in to television coverage of major events such as the space shuttle *Challenger* explosion in 1986, the Los Angeles riots in 1992, and the Oklahoma City bombing in 1995, but otherwise the viewing audience is fragmented. (Fox TV's *Living Single,* for example, was the number one rated show among African American viewers in the mid-1990s, but did not even break the top one hundred for whites; NBC's *Seinfeld* was the number one show among whites during its last few years, but did not break the top one hundred for African Americans.[29])

Over the past thirty years, loyalty to any single media source has declined. Gone are the days when the big three networks could guarantee advertisers a consistent audience share. Gone, too, are the days when the *New York Times,* the *Washington Post,* and the *Wall Street Journal,* along with a handful of other national newspapers, could set the agenda for print journalism.

The trends are revealed in the numbers. The number of Americans who read any part of any newspaper—the comics, movie reviews, sports, campaign coverage—fell by nearly 25 percent between 1970 and 1995, as did the combined audiences of the three networks. All told, the networks held a 77 share of the TV audience in 1980—a *share* equaling one percent of all households watching television—but less than a 50 share by 1998.[30]

If Americans are getting more and more of their political information from television—and polls say they are—it is not from the network news. According to a 1998 survey by the Pew Research Center for The People & The Press, the number of Americans who regularly or sometimes watch the nightly network news fell from 88 percent in May 1993 to 56 percent in May 1998.[31] Many of those viewers are tuning in to CNN, where more than 57 percent of Americans regularly or sometimes went for their news in 1998. Other people's idea of a news source is *Hard Copy, The 700 Club, Oprah Winfrey, Larry King Live,* Imus, Stern, or Limbaugh. Finally, as noted below, the Internet is growing rapidly as a news source. In 1995, only 4 percent of Americans said they went on line at least once a week for news; in 1998, the number had increased fivefold to 20 percent.

Newspapers have done better than the networks at holding their audience. Although subscriptions continue to fall year by year, two-thirds of Americans reported in 1998 that they read a daily paper regularly, and nearly half said they had read one the day before. These numbers have held steady over the past few years, but the readership has changed dramatically. Only 28 percent of young Americans surveyed by the Pew Research Center said they had read a paper yesterday, compared to nearly 70 percent of older Americans. As for the national paper people read most, it was *USA Today*. Nearly three in ten Americans said they read the fast-paced paper daily, another fifth said the *Wall Street Journal,* and one-tenth said the *New York Times*.

The New Media Audience

The most important feature of the new media is choice. Consumers have a much greater say than the media might prefer in what they get and when they get it. There has been a significant increase in what might be called *raw information*— information that goes to citizens directly, without analysis or interpretation by journalists.

The new media offer more than a vast inventory of choices. They give individual Americans unparalleled access to instant information and greater control over the messages they receive, even as they give government and its leaders a greater ability to target information to specific audiences and demographic groups. Box 5–5 shows the distribution of Internet users by demographic group.

The box reveals two important trends. First, although the Internet is primarily a news source for young Americans, every age group increased its Net activity over the three years covered by the survey. Some of the gains are no doubt due to the widespread use of the Internet as a resource in the workplace. Second, the widest demographic gaps are associated with education and income, which clearly affect both the ability to purchase the needed technology for home use and access to information on how to exploit the Internet for news. The greatest gains in Internet use came in three demographic categories: people with family incomes over $50,000, college graduates, and 18–29-year-olds. The smallest gains were among people over the age of 65 and those with incomes under $20,000.

For individual citizens, the new media provide much greater access to information whenever they want it. People do not have to wait for the morning paper to find out what happened the night before: they can tune in to CNN for an instant report, or get a quick update from the Internet. They do not have to wait until the end of the week for their favorite magazine: they can almost always find

BOX 5-5

Internet Usage Expands, 1995–1998 (percentages of total U.S. population)

	1995	1998
Gender		
Men	6%	10%
Women	3	
Race		
White	4	20
African American	3	14
Hispanic	6	18
Age		
18–29	7	30
30–49	5	24
50–64	2	13
65+	1	4
Education		
College graduate	10	35
Some college	6	25
High school graduate	2	11
Less than high school graduate	1	11
Income		
Over $50,000	8	34
$30,000–$49,999	5	22
$20,000–$29,999	3	14
Under $20,000	1	8

Source: Pew Research Center for The People & The Press, *Internet News Takes Off: Pew Research Center Biennial News Consumption Survey* (Washington, DC: Pew Research Center, June, 1998), p. 8.

a cable channel that specializes in their favorite sport or hobby, and can find a Web site on just about any subject.

The new media give the consumer, not the editor or producer, the power to determine when the news comes in and what gets read and seen. The consumer, not the network, decides when the news is relevant, whether by setting the VCR to record a presidential debate, tuning in *CNN Headline News* at 2:00 A.M., or plugging in a ten-minute candidate "infomercial" that looks like real news, but is actually a paid advertisement. In a sense, each consumer can be his or her own "network program executive," choosing what to watch and when to watch it, using a handheld remote control to "zap" through programming.[32]

Even as the new media give the public more control over the news they receive, they give political candidates much greater ability to target messages to specific audiences. Candidates can reach the elderly on the QVC shopping network in the morning, news junkies on *CNN Headline News* in the afternoon, trial lawyers on Court TV after dinner, and young Americans on MTV after everyone else goes to bed, and never the audiences shall meet. Such strategies reflect the change from **broadcasting**, in which messages go out to all viewers on a single network, to **narrowcasting**, which goes out to much smaller numbers of people on highly specialized channels.

Into the Future

No one knows what the future holds for the media. New magazines and newspapers will come and go; new electronic technologies will rise and fall. For the time being, the two newest new media are talk radio and the Internet, both of which substantially increase interaction between those who talk and those who listen.

Talk Radio.   Until 1995, talk radio was the fastest-growing source of information. Between 1982 and 1992, the number of radio stations devoted entirely to talk shows tripled from two hundred to six hundred.[33]

Like most other new media, talk radio does not talk to everyone. It mainly reaches out to conservatives. President Clinton argued immediately after the Oklahoma City bombing that talk radio focuses on the extreme right, too often being used "to keep some people as paranoid as possible and the rest of us all torn up and upset with each other. They spread hate, they leave the impression, by their very words, that violence is acceptable. . . . It is time we all stood up and spoke against that kind of reckless speech and behavior." Some talk-show callers argued, for example, that the bombing was planned and executed by the government itself as a plot to generate public support for greater gun control.[34]

The evidence suggests that talk radio does, indeed, draw a somewhat narrow audience, but hardly one as extreme as Clinton described. As of 1998, talk-radio regulars were twice as likely to label themselves as Republicans and conservatives than as Democrats and liberals. They were also much more likely to be men, over thirty years old, from the West, and slightly more wealthy and educated than the population as a whole. (One reason talk radio attracts such a conservative audience is that there are few successful liberal talk shows. Rush Limbaugh still reaches 15 million listeners a week on over five hundred stations; no liberal host attracts even a million.) About 30 percent of regular listeners tune in to keep up on current issues, 20 percent to learn how other people feel, roughly 10 percent each for entertainment and as a forum for public opinion, and just 1 percent because they like the host.

Recent surveys suggest that talk radio may be starting to run out of steam. In April 1993, over half of Americans tuned in to talk radio regularly or sometimes. By 1998, the figure was down to 35 percent. Either the talk had become boring or Americans were simply sick of politics. The biggest loser was Limbaugh, whose audience share dropped from 26 percent in July 1994, to just 16 percent in 1998. The biggest winner was Howard Stern.

The World Wide Web.   Like talk radio, the Internet (and its associated on-line services) imposes very few barriers to participation. But unlike talk radio, which

Howard Stern (left) and Rush Limbaugh (right), two of America's leading radio talk-show hosts. Although once considered more of a disk jockey than talk-show host, Stern has become a best-selling author and controversial commentator on political and social issues.

often binds its listeners to a specific broadcast time, the Internet is open twenty-four hours a day. All a user needs is a personal computer and a modem to gain limitless opportunities for uninterrupted browsing. In the future, a user will probably need just a telephone or an HDTV set.

Politicians have been quick to recognize the new avenue for communicating with the public. All of the 1996 presidential candidates had their own Web sites, as do most departments and agencies of the federal government. Most members of Congress have e-mail addresses, as do the president and vice president of the United States. Want to send a message or mail to Bill Clinton? Address it to bclinton@whitehouse.gov. Want a federal government owner's manual? Get on the Web and visit www.vote-smart.org. Want to find out what is on the schedule in the House of Representatives? Visit www.house.gov—10 million Americans go to the House every month. (See Box 5–6 for a guide to the top search engines for finding information on the Internet.)

As noted earlier, it is no surprise that the most active Internet users are either college graduates with high incomes or students still in college. Internet users are also much more likely than nonusers to identify themselves as political independents and to be sharply opposed to restrictions on freedom of information. Eighty percent of Internet users believe, for example, that public school libraries should be allowed to offer any books they want, compared to just 50 percent of nonusers; 70 percent of users oppose making it illegal for a computer network to carry pornographic or adult materials, compared to 40 percent of nonusers. Although most Internet users have little sympathy for the kinds of conservative views heard on talk radio, both audiences share a common concern about big government. Among Internet users who participate in on-line discussions of politics—as opposed to those who go on line for e-mail, financial information, and games—one in five agreed that while there was no excuse for the Oklahoma City bombing, they could nevertheless understand "the frustrations and anger that may have led people to ____ it out."[35]

Given the extraordinary expansion of Internet access, it cannot be long before candidates start exploiting this electronic technology as a campaign tool. It is one thing to set up a campaign Web site that users can visit at their leisure; it is quite another to use the Internet to reach the millions of potential voters who have e-mail—but such use is clearly coming.

Whether software designers will be able to develop a "net nanny" to prevent political *spamming*, a term that refers to the Internet version of junk mail, is still in doubt. What is not in doubt is that the Internet offers the potential for a kind of two-way communication between government and the people that the Founders could not have imagined: communication that is instant in a way that even a town meeting cannot be. Something may get lost in the transmission; a cyber-community does not allow the kind of personal contact provided in a town hall meeting or a campaign rally. But with face-to-face campaigning in huge states

BOX 5-6

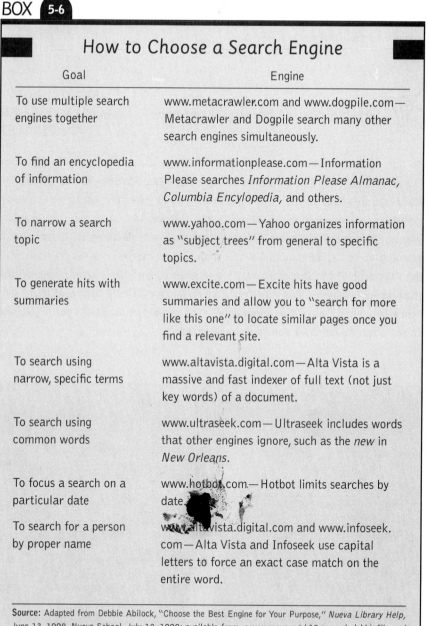

How to Choose a Search Engine

Goal	Engine
To use multiple search engines together	www.metacrawler.com and www.dogpile.com— Metacrawler and Dogpile search many other search engines simultaneously.
To find an encyclopedia of information	www.informationplease.com—Information Please searches *Information Please Almanac, Columbia Encylopedia,* and others.
To narrow a search topic	www.yahoo.com—Yahoo organizes information as "subject trees" from general to specific topics.
To generate hits with summaries	www.excite.com—Excite hits have good summaries and allow you to "search for more like this one" to locate similar pages once you find a relevant site.
To search using narrow, specific terms	www.altavista.digital.com—Alta Vista is a massive and fast indexer of full text (not just key words) of a document.
To search using common words	www.ultraseek.com—Ultraseek includes words that other engines ignore, such as the *new* in *New Orleans.*
To focus a search on a particular date	www.hotbot.com—Hotbot limits searches by date.
To search for a person by proper name	www.altavista.digital.com and www.infoseek. com—Alta Vista and Infoseek use capital letters to force an exact case match on the entire word.

Source: Adapted from Debbie Abilock, "Choose the Best Engine for Your Purpose," *Nueva Library Help,* June 13, 1998, Nueva School, July 10, 1998; available from <www.nueva.pvt.k12.ca.use/~debbie/library/research/adviceengine.html>.

such as California nearly impossible, e-mail may be the closest thing possible to a handshake. The fact that 40 percent of Californians already have e-mail makes that electronic handshake all the more likely.

in a different light ——— MATT DRUDGE— MEDIA PIONEER OR PIRATE?

No one was more important to spreading the story about Bill Clinton and Monica Lewinsky than an Internet reporter/gossip named Matt Drudge. Drudge broke the story late on a Saturday night in mid-January 1998, when he posted the following report on www.drudgereport.com: "At the last minute, at 6 P.M. on Saturday evening, *Newsweek* magazine killed a story that was destined to shake official Washington to its foundation: A White House intern carried on a sexual affair with the President of the United States!" *Newsweek* editors had, indeed, "spiked" the story about Lewinsky, worried that reporter Michael Isikoff had insufficient evidence. Drudge had no editors, and ran with the gossip the minute he got it. (No one knows where he got it—a good gossip never tells.)

Matt Drudge, Internet news source and gossip. Drudge was the first to break the story on President Clinton's sexual relationship with White House intern Monica Lewinsky.

Once posted, the story spread like wildfire. At 2:23 A.M. on Sunday morning, the Drudge report showed up in the alt.current-events.clinton.whitewater newsgroup. It moved next to the Sunday morning news programs, mentioned by conservative commentator William Kristol on *This Week with Sam and Cokie*. The Drudge report was too late for the Sunday morning papers, but did not run on Monday or Tuesday either, even as Washington went into high spin. Not until Wednesday morning did the *Washington Post* and *Los Angeles Times* run the story, giving the rumors the credibility needed to create a media feeding frenzy. "Would the story have broken if not for the Web?" asks *Slate* reporter Seth Stevenson. "Probably. Did the Web give the story additional velocity? Definitely. The ethics cops who patrol newspaper and magazine newsrooms can't control the rumors and unsubstantiated stories that people post to the Web."[36]

Whether one thinks Drudge is a scourge or a saint, he is the personification of the new freedom of Internet-based news. "Last month I had 6 million visitors," he told the National Press Club in June 1998, "and I currently have a daily average larger than the weekly newsstand sales of *Time* magazine. What's going on here? Well, clearly there is a hunger for unedited information, absent corporate considerations....We have entered an era vibrating with the din of small voices. Every citizen can be a reporter, can take on the powers that be. The difference between the Internet, television and radio, magazines, newspapers is the two-way communication. The Net gives as much voice to a 31-year-old computer geek like me as to a CEO or Speaker of the House. We all become equal."

How did Drudge get to be so powerful? He grew up in Takoma Park, Maryland, just outside Washington, D.C., skipped college, and managed the CBS gift shop in Los Angeles for seven years before starting the *Drudge Report*. Dubbed the nation's reigning mischief-maker by the *New York Times*, Drudge got his start as an electronic reporter by snooping through the trash. Here is how he explained his success to the National Press Club:

> Overhearing, listening to careful conversations, intercepting the occasional memo, I would volunteer in the mail room from time to time. I hit pay dirt when I discovered that the trash cans in the Xerox room at Television City were stuffed each morning with overnight Neilsen ratings, information gold....I was on the move— at least I thought so. But my father worried that I was in a giant stall. And in a parental panic he overcame his fear of flying and dropped in for a visit. At the end of his stay, during the drive to the airport, sensing some action was called for, he dragged me into a blown-out strip on Sunset Boulevard and found a Circuit City store. "Come on," he said desperately, "I'm getting you a computer." "Oh, yeah, and what am I going to do with that?" I laughed. As they say at CBS Studios: Cut, two months later. Having found a way to post things on the Internet, ... I moved on to

scoops from the sound stages I had heard, Jerry Seinfeld asking for a million dollars an episode, to scoop after scoop of political things I had heard from some
friends back here [in Washington]. I collected a few e-mail addresses of interest.
People had suggested that I start a mailing list, so I collected the e-mails and set
up a list called "The Drudge Report." One reader turned into five, then turned into
one hundred. And faster than you could say "I never had sex with that woman"
[Clinton's January 1998 categorical denial of the Lewinsky affair], it was one thousand, five thousand, one million. The ensuing website practically launched itself.[37]

MAINTAINING THE BALANCE

The media must maintain their own delicate balance as part of the American system of government. They must be tough enough to act as a check on government
power, but never so cynical toward government that the public withdraws its
consent to be governed. They have to tell the truth, but not exploit the public's
natural skepticism.

Americans clearly understand the balance themselves. They want the media
to be aggressive, especially when it comes time to examine the consequences of
major policy proposals such as health care reform or antitobacco legislation. And
most believe the press generally does more to keep government from doing
wrong than it does to encourage government to do right. They do not want the
press to become a passive instrument of government.

At the same time, Americans think the media are much too aggressive in
covering the personal and ethical behavior of political leaders. The public has serious questions about how the media investigate government officials. Indeed,
there is some evidence that much of President Clinton's gain in public approval
following Drudge's reports did not come from moral indifference, as some conservatives argued, but from a public backlash against the media. Substantial majorities of Americans interviewed at the time the Lewinsky scandal broke said that
the media had done only a fair or poor job in checking facts, remaining objective,
providing useful information, and giving the right amount of coverage.[38]

To the extent that the media maintain their own balance in being tough but
fair, they play a critical role as an independent check on government itself, a role
the Founders would be likely to applaud. They knew that a free press could be
aggressive, even insulting, and recognized that a free press could make mistakes
(hence, they rejected Madison's proposal to give the press complete immunity
from libeled readers). But they also knew that a free press would speak truth to
power. Even though they took a pounding from the Anti-Federalist press, they

were completely free to counterattack through their own papers. They understood that a free press would be part of the essential give and take that would simultaneously keep their government balanced and provide an outlet for public passion. Although they could hardly have anticipated the *Drudge Report*, they might well appreciate the value of having such an irreverent character keeping an eye on media and government at the same time.

JUST THE FACTS

terms to remember

prior restraint (p. 155)
censorship (p. 155)
media (p. 155)
yellow journalism (p. 158)
straight news (p. 159)
feature news (p. 159)
infotainment (p. 160)
libel (p. 163)
Federal Communications
   Commission (p. 165)
equal opportunities rule
   (p. 165)

reasonable access rule (p. 166)
fairness doctrine (p. 166)
sound bite (p. 171)
horse race coverage (p. 171)
gatekeepers (p. 176)
attentive policy elites (p. 176)
spin control (p. 177)
media event (p. 177)
civic journalism (p. 178)
broadcasting (p. 184)
narrowcasting (p. 184)

facts and interpretations

- The media have changed over the last two hundred years from being primarily a tool of government to playing four roles in government: as informer, tone-setter, agenda-setter, and a tool of government again. All four roles have an impact on the delicate balance. As informer, the media help the people shape their opinions about the issues of the day. As tone setter, the media provide frames for helping the public interpret information across stories and events. As agenda setter, the media may lead government or the people to give some issues greater attention than they deserve. And as a tool of government, the media highlights information that the government wants the public to have. To the extent that the media are overly cynical in playing these roles, the public may begin to withdraw its consent to be governed. To the extent that the media are overly timid, the public may give government too much power. Hence, to play their part in the delicate balance of American government, the media must set their own balance between toughness and timidity.

- There are several recent trends that cut both ways regarding media tone-setting and aggressiveness. Recent years have witnessed an explosion in electronic options that have given Americans more choices for getting information than ever before. Cable television is expanding rapidly, and HDTV promises a new era in communications technology. At the same time, recent years have witnessed extensive consolidation of media ownership. Mergers and acquisitions are rapidly reducing the number of newspaper firms, which may be compromising coverage. As a result, the public has more choices for information, but fewer sources of hard news. It is too early to tell whether the increasing competition will produce more sensational news, more timid news, or neither. But what is clear is that the media world is changing rapidly.

- Different media provide different types of information, with newspapers the best source for information on government and politics and television magazines the worst. In the search for higher ratings and readership, traditional media have changed both the coverage of government and politics and the content. Straight news is in sharp decline throughout the media. And the straight news that remains has a much heavier focus on scandal and sensationalism than it did just twenty years ago. No wonder pollsters find so little public interest in government and politics: Even when the public does read or view straight news on the subject, the stories are much more likely to accentuate the negative side of public officials' behavior.

- The new media offer Americans additional sources of information. As an antidote to the concentration of media power, the Internet provides unprecedented access, whether to basic information or to the latest scandal. Whether the United States is heading toward a "cyberrepublic," in which solitary Net surfers connect with other people only through chat rooms, is not yet clear. But it cannot be long before political campaigns focus on the Internet. The cost of reaching Americans through e-mail is already less than that of reaching them through traditional mail.

open questions

- To what extent are the media beginning to act as passive instruments for whatever news the government wants citizens to read and hear? With so much pure information now available, does the fact that Americans know so little about government and politics matter more than it did, say, thirty or forty years ago? What are the differences and similarities between the concentration of power in media conglomerates and the concentration of coverage in the kind of media consortium put together to help North Carolina voters in the 1996 Senate campaign?

- Does the rise of the new media, with its narrowcasting potential, increase the risk of greater divisions among Americans? Does it matter if Americans get their news from so many different sources? What are the advantages of getting the news through cyberspace? How does getting the news from newspapers and television differ?

- Do the media exploit public cynicism for profit? Or does the public fascination with scandal and sensationalism merely confirm what the Founders believed about human nature? To what extent would the Founders be surprised by what they see on the news today? Would they be offended by the coverage of the Lewinsky scandal? Or would they think such coverage helps keep government from becoming a threat to liberty?

- What does it take to be a good reporter today? Thinking back to the "Valley of Death" story, did CNN's Peter Arnett do his job well? Thinking back to Matt Drudge, did he act as a responsible journalist? Is Internet news bound by a lower standard than traditional news outlets? Should the Federal Communications Commission regulate Internet news sources more aggressively?

for further study

Abramson, Jeffrey B., F. Christopher Arterton, and Gary R. Orren. *The Electronic Commonweath: The Impact of New Media Technologies on Democratic Politics.* New York: Basic Books, 1988.

Capella, Joseph N., and Kathleen Hall Jamieson. *Spiral of Cynicism: The Press and the Public Good.* New York: Oxford University Press, 1997.

Cook, Timothy E. *Governing with the News: The News Media as a Political Institution.* Chicago: University of Chicago Press, 1998.

Davis, Richard, and Diana Owen. *New Media and American Politics.* New York: Oxford University Press, 1998.

Fallows, James. *Breaking the News: How the Media Undermine American Democracy.* New York: Vintage, 1997.

Kurtz, Howard. *Spin Cycle: Inside the Clinton Propaganda Machine.* New York: Free Press, 1998.

endnotes for chapter 5

1. James Madison, *The Writings of James Madison,* vol. 6, ed. Halliard Hunt (New York: Putnam, 1906–1910), p. 336.

2. See Edwin Emery and Michael Emery, *The Press and America: An Interpretive History of the Mass Media,* 5th ed. (Englewood Cliffs, NJ: Prentice-Hall, 1984), pp. 281–98, for a history of the period.

3. Project for Excellence in Journalism, *Changing Definitions of News: A Look at the Mainstream Press Over 20 Years* (Washington, DC: Project for Excellence in Journalism, March 1998).

4. Gene Roberts, "Corporate Journalism and Community Service," *Media Studies Journal,* Spring/Summer 1996; at <http://www.mediastudies.org/mediamergers/roberts.html>.

5. Tom Wolzien, "The Big News-Big Business Bargain," *Media Studies Journal,* Spring/Summer 1996; available from <http://www.mediastudies.org/mediamergers/wolzien.html>.

6. See April Oliver, "I Produced That Program—and Was Fired," *Washington Post,* July 12, 1998, for a discussion of how "Valley of Death" was produced and why the story about the use of nerve gas might be true after all.

7. See Jeffrey B. Abramson, F. Christopher Arterton, and Gary R. Orren, *The Electronic Commonwealth: The Impact of New Media Technologies on Democratic Politics* (New York: Basic Books, 1988), for a history of the Federal Communications Commission and efforts to regulate the media.

8. Jonathan Alter, "How Phil Donahue Came to Manage the 1992 Campaign," *Washington Monthly,* June 1992, p. 12.

9. See S. Robert Lichter and R. E. Noyes, *Good Intentions Make Bad News: Why Americans Hate Campaign Journalism* (Lanham, MD: Rowman & Littlefield, 1995), p. 246.

10. These figures are drawn from the Pew Research Center for The People & The Press, *Fewer Favor Media Scrutiny of Political Leaders* (Washington, DC: Pew Research Center, March 1997).

11. The unnamed reporter is quoted in David Shaw, "Distrustful Public Views Media as 'Them'—Not 'Us,'" *Los Angeles Times,* April 1, 1993, p. A19.

12. In Shaw, "Distrustful Public."

13. James Fallows, "Why Americans Hate the Media," *Atlantic Monthly,* February 1996, 55.

14. Joseph T. Klapper, *The Effects of Mass Communication* (New York: Free Press, 1960).

15. Thomas Patterson, *Out of Order* (New York: Knopf, 1993), p. 24.

16. Patterson, *Out of Order,* p. 20.

17. Cited in Richard M. Perloff, *Political Communication: Politics, Press, and Public in America* (Mahwah, NJ: Erlbaum, 1998), p. 313.

18. Elizabeth Kolbert, "The News Media's Rush to Judgment on Clinton," *New York Times,* January 31, 1993, p. A14.

19. Howard Kurtz, "Splitsville for Clinton and the Media?" *Washington Post National Weekly Edition,* February 8–14, 1993, p. 14.

20. For thorough discussions of the impact of the media on public opinion, see Doris A. Graber, *Mass Media and American Politics,* 2d ed. (Washington, DC: CQ Press, 1997), and Shanto Iyengar and Donald R. Kinder, *News That Matters* (Chicago: University of Chicago Press, 1989).

21. E. M. Rogers and J. Deering, "Agenda-Setting Research: Where Has It Been, Where Is It Going?" in J. Anderson, ed., *Communication Yearbook* Vol. 11 (Thousand Oaks, CA: Sage, 1988).

22. Stanley and Niemi, *Vital Statistics,* p. 68.

23. John Maltese, *Spin Control: The White House Office of Communication and the Management of Presidential News,* rev. ed. (Chapel Hill: University of North Carolina Press, 1994), pp. 238–39.

24. Malcolm Gladwell, "The Spin Myth," *New Yorker,* July 6, 1998, p. 67.

25. New York University journalism professor Jay Rosen, quoted in *APME Readership Committee,* August 1994, p. 4; the movement is supported in part by the Pew Center for Civic Journalism in Washington, D.C.

26. Tony Case, "Public Journalism Denounced," *Editor & Publisher,* November 12, 1994, p. 14.

27. Jonathan Yardley, "'Public Journalism': Bad News," *Washington Post,* September 30, 1996, p. C2.

28. Dirk Smillie, "Breakfast with Bill, George, and Ross," in The Freedom Forum Media Studies Center, *The Finish Line: Covering the Campaign's Final Days,* January 1993, p. 124.

29. Noel Holston, "TV Viewing Habits Reveal a Contrast of Black and White," *Minneapolis Star Tribune,* May 3, 1995, p. 11E.

30. Lawrie Mifflin, "Trial Gives Cable Stations Inroads on Top Networks," *New York Times,* February 20, 1995, p. C1.

31. These and other figures in this section are drawn from the Pew Research Center for The People & The Press, *Internet News Takes Off: Pew Research Center Biennial News Consumption Survey* (Washington, DC: Pew Research Center, June 1998).

32. See Abramson, F. Christopher Arterton, and Gary Orren, *The Electronic Commonwealth.*

33. Thomas Rosenstiel, "The Talk Is about New Media," *Los Angeles Times,* May 23, 1992, p. A20.

34. See Nell Henderson, "Real Right-Wing Radio," *Washington Post National Weekly Edition,* May 1–7, 1995, p. 8.

35. Times Mirror Center for The People & The Press, *Americans Going On-line . . . Explosive Growth, Uncertain Destinations* (Washington, D.C.: Times-Mirror Center, October 16, 1995).

36. Seth Stevenson, "Invisible Ink: How the Story Everyone's Talking about

Stayed out of the Papers," *Slate,* January 22, 1998; available from <www.slate.com>.

37. Address to the National Press Club, Washington, D.C., June 2, 1998.

38. According to the Pew Research Center, about half of Clinton's gain in public approval was rooted in anger toward the media; see Pew Research Center for The People & The Press, *Popular Policies and Unpopular Press Lift Clinton Ratings* (Washington, DC: Pew Research Center, February 1998).

political parties

the lost connection?

The Founders designed government with two moving parts: the people and the institutions of government. The people would elect virtuous representatives, while the institutions would protect the nation as a whole and every American as an individual. Government would be composed of these two moving parts with nothing much in between.

Over the decades, however, the space between government and the people has filled with a vast assortment of individuals and organizations who try to shape both what the people think and how government responds. Although not listed in the Constitution itself, these mediators play a key role in helping government do its work by smoothing the rough edges of public opinion while helping to form a more perfect union, establish justice, insure domestic tranquility, and so forth. The people cannot know each of the candidates for office well enough to make an informed choice on every race, nor can they hope to keep track of the thousands of proposed laws and government decisions that might make a difference in their lives. There is simply too much going on for any individual American to keep up with. Indeed, the institutions of government themselves can have trouble tracking all the activity.

This is why political parties are so important to American government. They give the people and their institutions shortcuts for understanding many of the key decisions that must be made, and they often act on the people's behalf in influencing government. A **political party** is a broad membership organization designed to win elections and influence government, in part by recruiting candidates to run for office and in part by helping citizens decide how to vote. The ultimate self-interest of parties resides in persuading government to act on behalf of their members. The fact that it represents more Americans with higher incomes means that the Republican party should (and does) favor tax cuts and lower federal spending; the fact that it represents more Americans with lower incomes means that the Democratic party should (and does) favor higher tax rates for well-to-do Americans and more federal spending for poor people.

The Founders would not be surprised that parties exist between the people and government. They saw factions, or political divisions, as both a natural product of freedom and its greatest threat. Give the people freedom, the Founders believed, and they will divide into groups competing for power over who gets what, when, and how; give them a government that caters to those divisions, and the people will not be free for long. Although the First Amendment clearly guarantees the right to petition, or lobby, government for a redress of grievances, the rest of the Constitution is designed to make such battles difficult to win.

What would be more likely to trouble the Founders is that the parties play a prominent role in making government work. As this chapter shows, parties are intimately involved in who gets what, when, and how from government, whether by recruiting candidates for office, running campaigns, organizing the institutions once their ballots are counted, or helping voters think through their choices on election day. The two national parties have their headquarters only a few steps from the Capitol and spend enormous amounts of time and energy raising money to support their candidates. They also have strong organizations inside Congress and in every state. Although parties are never mentioned in the Constitution, it is possible that government could not work without them.

The Founders might easily counter that a faction by any other name divides just the same, no matter how much it helps government perform its tasks. The more deeply both parties penetrate government, the more likely it is that one party may someday capture all three branches, using their control of Congress and the presidency to pack the judicial branch with party judges, and thereby increase the chances that a strong-willed majority will impose its will on the rest of the nation. The Founders' question would not be whether parties help government work well, but whether there might come a day when they make it work as an instrument of tyranny.

This chapter examines these and other issues surrounding the role of the parties in American politics. It starts with a brief history of the two-party system, asking why the United States has mostly had two, not three or more, political parties, and how those parties evolve over time, swallowing up smaller parties or being swallowed up themselves. The chapter then turns to the three roles that political parties play today: contesting elections, organizing government, and helping voters make choices.

A BRIEF HISTORY OF THE TWO-PARTY SYSTEM

The Founders clearly saw political parties as a threat to democracy. George Washington warned that parties were likely "to become potent engines by which cunning, ambitious and unprincipled men will be able to subvert the power of the people and to usurp themselves the reins of government." John Adams expressed "dread" at the notion that two "great parties" might emerge from the debate over ratification. And in 1789, Thomas Jefferson went so far as to say that if he "could not go to heaven but with a party," he would "not go at all."[1]

Despite their warnings, a weak version of the modern two-party system had emerged by the early 1790s. One party was led by the Federalists (originally led by Alexander Hamilton and James Madison), who supported the ratification of the Constitution, while the other was led by the Anti-Federalists (later led by Jefferson), who opposed the strong national government. The Founders fully expected these two early factions to disappear once the fate of the Constitution was resolved, but other battles soon arose. As power ebbed and flowed between the two early parties, the public became increasingly comfortable with choosing between two alternatives. In a sense, political parties became a habit. At the same time, the two parties quickly developed into efficient mechanisms both for recruiting candidates for office and for giving voters an easy way to make decisions.

Knowing that a candidate was either a Federalist or a Republican (as the Anti-Federalists came to call themselves) helped voters decide.

Why America Has a Two-Party System

Before turning to the roles and history of the American political parties, it is important to note that American government has had just four major parties over its entire two hundred years. (See Box 6–1 for a list and descriptions of the four.) The two major parties have been very effective at either defeating or absorbing the competing parties that have arisen from time to time.

Unlike many other democracies, which have multiple parties, the United States has always featured two major parties. The Founders may have sowed the seeds of the two-party system by creating the electoral college system. Recall from Chapter 2 that Americans do not vote for the president at all, but for competing slates of electors, who, in turn, vote for president as part of the electoral college.[2] Under the Constitution, the states decide how to choose their electors. Article II states, "Each State shall appoint, *in such Manner as the Legislature thereof may direct,* a Number of Electors, equal to the whole Number of Senators and Representatives to which the State may be entitled in the Congress . . . ."

Most states do so under a **winner-take-all system.** Simply defined, the candidate who gets the most votes, even if the total is not a majority of all votes cast but only a **plurality** (a larger number of votes than any other candidate), wins all the electoral votes. In 1996, for example, Bob Dole lost Florida to Bill Clinton by only 302,000 votes out of 5.3 million cast, but got none of Florida's twenty-five electoral votes. Clinton returned the favor in Texas, where he lost to Dole by just 277,000 votes out of 5.6 million cast, but got none of the state's thirty-two electoral votes. In both states, however, neither winner won a majority of the vote. Clinton won Florida with 48 percent of the vote, while Dole won Texas with 49 percent. Third-party candidate Ross Perot took enough votes in both states to assure that the winner would not have a majority. Under such a system, third parties are well advised to join with a major party to reach a winning alliance. Most Perot supporters have returned to the Republican party, from which Perot had usurped the anti-big government argument.[3]

In contrast to a **proportional voting system,** in which every party wins a share of legislative seats based on the share of votes it receives, the American system produces one winner and one winner only. All but two states (Maine and Nebraska) today assign every electoral vote to the winner, no matter how close the popular vote is. In the rest of the states, it makes sense for smaller parties to join together to fight for the biggest share of the vote possible. If you cannot beat them, as the old saying goes, join them. Because the American system is designed as a kind of tug-of-war between two sides, minor parties have to decide which end of the rope to grab, lest they be left out of the division of the spoils of victory.

BOX **6-1**

The Four Major American Political Parties

Party	Founded	Last Won Presidency	Comments
Federalists	1796	1796	Founded by Alexander Hamilton and other supporters of a strong central government; last president was John Adams.
Democrats	1800	1996	Founded by Thomas Jefferson as Republicans; became Democratic-Republicans in 1828 and Democrats in 1840.
Whigs	1834	1848	Last president was Zachary Taylor; broke apart over the issue of slavery.
Republicans	1856	1988	Founded largely by remnants of the Northern Whigs and antislavery Democrats; Abraham Lincoln was first Republican to be elected president.

Source: James M. Perry, "Win or Lose, Perot Proves One Can Run without Major Parties," *Wall Street Journal,* July 14, 1992, p. A11.

The electoral college is only one of several reasons why the United States developed a two-party system. Most elections today are contested in **single-member districts,** meaning that there can be only one winner for each election, no matter how many candidates run. Unlike **multimember districts,** in which a large group of candidates compete for several seats (for example, a school board), single-member districts create a winner-take-all mentality among candidates. Under such a system, two parties and only two parties have a chance to win.[4]

Even without these electoral pressures toward a two-party system, Americans tend to be creatures of habit. Because party loyalties are learned early in life, the fact that the first party system happened to be a two-party system matters. Had the Federalists and Anti-Federalists of the late 1700s been joined by a third party—say, the "In-Between Federalists"—the United States might be a three-party system to this day.

 **in a different light ———** **WHY THIRD PARTIES CANNOT WIN**

It is nearly impossible to create a winning third party in national politics, even when Americans insist they want one.[5] In July 1996, almost 60 percent of Americans said the nation should have a third major party. In November, exactly 10.1 percent of the electorate actually cast their votes for one.

It is difficult, although not impossible, for a third party to get on the presidential ballot in most states. Because the Constitution gives the states the authority to set the times, manner, and places for elections, a third-party campaign must first get on the ballot state by state. In California in 1996, for example, that meant convincing 89,007 registered voters to sign a ballot petition a year in advance of the election. That means, in turn, that a successful candidate must have a strong statewide organization in place long before the national candidates even show up.

Even if a third-party candidate can get on the ballot in most states, the winner-take-all nature of presidential elections makes it nearly impossible for him or her to win any electoral votes. Because a state's electoral votes go to the winning candidate alone, having the money to run national television advertisements is not enough. Candidates must have a strong presence in enough states to put together a winning total.

Even though Texas billionaire Ross Perot spent over $60 million of his own money in 1992 to create a national party from scratch, and won 20 percent of the popular vote, he failed to win a single vote in the electoral college. And lacking any semblance of state or local party organizations, he did not win a single state-level victory. He did even worse in 1996, pulling in a mere 8 percent of the popular vote and again failing to win a single electoral vote.

One of the reasons third-party candidates fare so poorly over time is that the Democratic and Republican parties often shift their political positions just enough either to recapture their wayward supporters or to create a new coalition of old and

Supporters of third-party presidential candidate Ross Perot in 1992, many of whom were getting involved in politics for the first time in their lives. Perot ran again in 1996 and lost.

new voters. After the 1968 election, for example, Republicans successfully wooed the white anti–civil rights, anticrime voters that had supported the third-party campaign of Alabama Democrat George Wallace, creating a strong Southern base that eventually helped sweep Republicans to a new majority in Congress in 1994.

Sometimes, however, the effort to absorb a third party does not work. After the 1992 election, for example, Democrats and Republicans alike went after Perot voters, both claiming to share the billionaire's commitment to a balanced budget and clean government. Both parties sent representatives to meet with Perot, too, inviting him to join their team. Their entreaties were not enough to prevent Perot from mounting another run at the presidency in 1996.

Perot was hardly the only third-party candidate out there, however. His Independence party was joined on the 1996 California ballot by the Green party, led by public-interest advocate Ralph Nader. Although Nader did not expect to win the presidency—his third party was on the ballot in less than half the states—he hoped to induce the existing parties to make a greater commitment to environmental protection. In that regard, Nader's third party was playing a time-honored role in pushing the two major parties toward change.

Traditionally, third parties have served as a wake-up call for the Democratic and Republican parties. They give voters a chance to voice their anger, but often end up strengthening the two-party system. Even the most successful third party, therefore, will not likely end up replacing one of the other two parties. Although Americans often view parties through the same lens that makes them distrust government in general, support for third parties also ebbs and flows with the nature of the times. The economy was still pulling out of a recession when more than 60 percent of Americans said the nation needed a third party in 1992 and 1994. By 1998, with the economy rebounding and Americans optimistic about the future, the number of third-party supporters declined to less than 50 percent.

Five Eras in Party History

The evolution of the two-party system was hardly smooth. There have been times when the two parties have been highly competitive: in 1800, the electoral college was deadlocked, thereby forcing the election into the House of Representatives; in 1876 and 1888, one candidate won the popular vote but lost the electoral college balloting. There have also been times when one party has been much stronger than the other: in the period 1932–1948, Democrats won five straight presidential elections. And there have been times when control has been in flux, as one party began to decline and another to rise.

Not every election involves a great battle between the two parties. Indeed, the past two hundred years have witnessed a blend of balanced two-party competition, one-party dominance, and periods of transition between the two.[6] The past forty years, for example, would be characterized as competitive: the two parties split control of government several times, with Democrats primarily in charge of Congress (at least until 1994), and Republicans primarily in charge of the presidency (at least until 1992).

The history of party competition has involved five distinct **party eras**, periods in which either one party is dominant or competition is stable, since 1800. Party eras tend to begin and end with either a whimper or a bang—that is, either one party will slowly fade from view as its followers leave, or the entire system will be rocked by some great issue that forces the two parties to reshuffle positions. (See Box 6–2 for a summary of the five party eras; a brief history follows.)

It is important to note that the five eras involved very different levels of party activity.[7] Despite the Founders' complaints about the early role of parties, the Federalist and Republican parties that evolved during the first decade hardly constituted the kind of threat to the young republic that might make a Founder prefer, like Jefferson, to go to hell.

The parties reached their peak in power during the second and third eras discussed below, during a time when the public had few sources of information on the issues of the day. Americans were so scattered across what was still a rural

BOX

The Five Party Eras

Party Era	Duration	Contestants	Developments
First	1788–1824	Federalists vs. Democratic-Republicans	Parties emerge in 1790s; one party dominant after 1800, but sharply divided internally.
Second	1828–1852	Democrats vs. Whigs	Balanced two-party competition; Democrats mostly dominant throughout period.
Third	1856–1892	Democrats vs. Republicans	Republicans dominant to 1874; balanced two-party competition until 1896; parties increasingly divided by geography (Democrats South; Republicans North).
Fourth	1896–1928	Democrats vs. Republicans	Republicans dominant except in 1912, when the party is split by a third party; parties continue to be divided by geography.
Fifth	1932–1994	Democrats vs. Republicans	Democrats dominant until 1968; Democratic New Deal coalition weakens steadily thereafter.

Source: Adapted from John Bibby, *Politics, Parties, and Elections in America* (Chicago: Nelson-Hall, 1992), p. 22.

nation that the parties served a powerful role in telling people how to vote. Moreover, as noted later in this chapter, the United States had not yet invented the secret ballot. Everyone knew how their neighbors voted, so there was enormous social pressure to join one party or the other.

The parties have been in decline ever since. Although they still play a critical role in organizing government, candidates feel quite comfortable running on their own without help from the parties. As Chapter 9 suggests, the United States is now firmly enmeshed in an era of candidate-centered campaigns. The candidate is everything, the party label mentioned only in passing.

1. The Federalists and the Democratic-Republicans (1788–1824). The first party era began when Thomas Jefferson created the first Republican party (the second one was created in 1856 and remains active today). Much as he opposed parties in principle, Jefferson created the Republican party as a counterweight to Alexander Hamilton's Federalist party, which had been formed in 1796. Although these two great leaders had worked together in founding the republic, they soon parted ways on just how strong the new government should be. Hamilton believed in a very strong national government, while Jefferson kept a more limited vision.

At some point in the early 1800s, Jefferson's opponents managed to label the party as the Democratic-Republicans in an effort to link Jefferson with democratic radicals in France. The hope was to scare his supporters into thinking that Jefferson was a tool of the French. After all, he had been ambassador to France during the Revolutionary War.

The two parties met first in the 1800 election, one of the most bitter contests in American history. Jefferson was the first of countless presidential candidates to argue for smaller government and lower taxes, suggesting that the Federalists had become the party of the rich and satisfied. Jefferson was also one of the first candidates to speak directly to the people through advertising. One of his campaign posters even reminded voters of the Revolutionary War by labeling the Federalists as Tories, or British sympathizers: "Republicans: Turn out, turn out and save your country from ruin! From an emperor—from a King—from the iron grasp of a British Tory Faction. DOWN WITH THE TORIES, DOWN WITH THE BRITISH FACTION, Before they have it in their power to enslave you, and reduce your families to distress by heavy taxation."

Energized by Jefferson's rhetoric, voters rejected John Adams and the Federalists, giving solid control to the Democratic-Republicans for the next five elections. So complete was Democratic-Republican control that James Monroe ran unopposed in 1820, winning all but one electoral college vote. During this one brief moment, known as the Era of Good Feelings, the United States actually had a one-party system in which the public had little input into selecting candidates for office. Presidential candidates were selected by an informal caucus, or committee, of congressional leaders that earned the name "King Caucus."

2. Democrats and Whigs (1828–1852).   The Era of Good Feelings ended in 1824 with a brutal campaign among five candidates, all running as Democratic-Republicans. Each one represented a different faction within a single party. The two dominant candidates were John Quincy Adams (son of the second president of the United States) and General Andrew Jackson (the hero of the War of 1812). Once again, as it had been in 1800, the contest was between a representative of the status quo (Adams) and a champion of the people (Jackson).

Just as his father had done almost thirty years earlier, Adams ran strong in the well-to-do Northeast, while a third candidate, House Speaker Henry Clay, and Jackson split the South and new states of the West, where concerns about a heavy-handed Washington, D.C., played well. Because no candidate secured a majority of electoral college votes, the election went to the House. There, Clay threw his support behind Adams, denying Jackson the presidency. Adams rewarded Clay by appointing him secretary of state (the deal immediately became known as the "Corrupt Bargain"), creating a campaign theme for Jackson's next run.

The bitter rematch between Adams and Jackson came in 1828, as the Democratic-Republican party split in two. Jackson carried the Democratic-Republican label into the election, while Adams called himself a National Republican to link himself to the strong national government advocates of the old Federalist party. Although Adams actually ran well in his Northeast base, he lost every state west and south of Maryland, including the nine new states added since 1789, five of which were slaveholding states of the South. Jackson became the first American president who was neither a Virginian nor an Adams.[8]

The next three decades were characterized by balanced two-party competition. By 1832, both major parties were choosing their candidates by national conventions, thereby laying the basis for strong state parties and local machines. By 1836, the Democratic-Republican label was gone from national politics, leaving Jackson's Democratic party on one side of the electoral system and a new party called the Whigs on the other. The Whig party was built from the same well-to-do social and economic groups that had once supported the Federalists. The name was borrowed from a British party with similar socioeconomic ties.

3. The First Republican versus Democratic Era (1856–1892).   The third party era began in 1856 as slavery forced a national crisis that would lead to civil war. Jackson's once-powerful Democratic party was doomed by its strength in both the North and South, a situation that left it unable to choose between its antislavery supporters in the North and its proslavery supporters in the South. The party decided to take no position on slavery at all, nominating a succession of weak candidates in the belief that the slavery issue would disappear.

The Whigs had no such trouble opposing slavery. Their party was so weak as it entered the 1850s that highly energized antislavery forces easily won control of the party. Just as activists often force today's Democratic and Republican parties toward strong stands, Northern antislavery Whigs seized control of the national convention in 1856, driving Southern Whigs who favored slavery out of the party.

Cut free from its Southern base, the Whig party was now free to absorb the "Free Soil" antislavery movement, which had won 10 percent of the popular vote in 1848, and to make slavery the centerpiece of the next national election. To emphasize the break, activists cast off the Whig label, calling themselves Republicans. Campaigning hard on the antislavery platform, the party emerged from the 1858 congressional elections with a dominant edge in the North. As Northern Democrats left their party to join the fight against slavery as Republicans, Southern Whigs left the new Republican party to join the fight for slavery as Democrats.

Two years later, with virtually no support left in the South, Republicans won the White House. Abraham Lincoln captured only 40 percent of the popular vote in 1860, but won enough states to secure victory in the electoral college. Following the bloody Civil War between the Blue and the Gray, America became a nation of two great parties, the Grand Old Party (G.O.P.) of the North (Republican) and one of the South (Democratic). The Democrats controlled the South all the way up to the 1960s, when their support for civil rights began to erode Southern support. The Democrats finally lost control of the South in the 1994 congressional elections.[9]

4. The Second Republican versus Democratic Era (1896–1928).

The fourth party era was forged in the economic tensions surrounding the 1896 election of Republican William McKinley. Democrats and Republicans had taken turns controlling the White House and Congress during the thirty years following the Civil War as the country struggled with an economic depression and an expanding western frontier. Democrats came to represent an angry mix of western farmers and eastern reformers; Republicans a base of financial interests and blue-collar workers scared of losing their jobs.

By 1896, the Democratic party had been captured by radical farmers, who nominated William Jennings Bryan for president. With a party agenda devoted largely to attacking big business and advocating radical reform of the U.S. currency, Bryan was outspent during the campaign by a margin of $21 to $1.[10] Although the South remained strongly Democratic, the Republicans strengthened their northern base and continued to control national politics for nearly forty years.

So great was the Republican dominance that the Democratic party was actually at risk of disappearing completely in 1912. It was rescued by Republican Theodore Roosevelt (cousin of future Democratic icon Franklin Roosevelt), who had succeeded to the presidency after McKinley's assassination in 1901 and won election in his own right in 1904. After serving nearly two terms, Roosevelt gave up the presidency in 1908, turning the office over to his handpicked Republican successor, William Howard Taft, only to reenter politics in 1912. Having lost a bitter campaign to unseat Taft as his party's presidential nominee, Roosevelt created the Bull Moose party, which ran the most successful third-party campaign in history in 1912. In doing so, however, Roosevelt so split the Republican base that Democrat Woodrow Wilson, a former college professor at Princeton University, won the presidency with just 42 percent of the vote. Democrats lost control during the economic recession that followed World War I.

Republicans were ascendant during the Roaring Twenties, a period of economic growth and scandal. The economic boom times were more than enough to ease public concerns about White House corruption. Although President Warren Harding died in office in the midst of one of the greatest scandals in U.S. history, Republicans continued undeterred until "Black Thursday," October 24, 1929, when a stock market crash plunged the nation into a fifteen-year depression. Unemployment soared, banks closed, and Republicans were chased from office in 1932.

5. The New Deal Era (1932–1994).   The fifth era began in 1932 with the landslide election of Democrat Franklin Delano Roosevelt. The Democrats were propelled into office by the widespread sense that Republican president Herbert Hoover had done little to help the millions of Americans left without work following Black Thursday.

Having promised Americans a "New Deal," Roosevelt won every state west and south of Pennsylvania, building a party base that would last for nearly four decades. Roosevelt's **New Deal coalition** was composed of workers, Southern farmers, Southern Democrats, liberals, Catholics, Jews, and African Americans, a broad assortment of "have nots" that provided the political support for one of the most ambitious legislative agendas in American history. Roosevelt's first term produced dozens of new agencies and programs, from the Civilian Conservation Corps, which put young Americans to work in the nation's forests and parks, to the Works Progress Administration, which created jobs for millions of unemployed Americans. It also produced the first federal program for insuring savings accounts, as well as the Social Security program, which provides income to America's elderly.

During its first two decades or so, the New Deal coalition was nearly unbeatable. Democrats won five presidential elections in a row, from 1932 through 1948, and controlled one or both houses of Congress for fifty-six years out of the next sixty. Yet, just as slavery unraveled the Democratic party of the 1850s, the civil rights movement that began in the 1950s divided the party again. This time, the effort to improve the lives of minorities came from the Democratic party, not the Republicans, with similar results in the South. Southern Democrats began to desert the party, moving toward the Republicans. As noted above, the 1994 congressional elections clearly marked the end of Democratic control in the South, but did not necessarily confirm the rise of a new Republican era elsewhere. The end of one era does not always mean the beginning of a new one.

Why Party Eras End

As this brief history suggests, two of the five party eras faded away with the simple passage of time: the Republican era that followed the Civil War and the New Deal era. Voters slowly shifted their loyalties in what is called a **secular realignment,** meaning a steady erosion in one party's control to the benefit of the other. The other three eras ended with what political scientists call a **critical election,** or a **realigning election.** Such an election involves a dramatic, immediate, and lasting shift, or realignment, in the underlying loyalties of voters and is usually caused by a major issue that disrupts the traditional party lines. In the 1850s, that issue was slavery; in the late 1920s, it was the Great Depression.

Options under Pressure.   The two major parties face three choices when such great divides occur: (1) they can ignore the issue, thereby taking the risk that they will fall by the wayside as new parties emerge; (2) one or both can absorb the issue into their existing platform, unless the issue is so disruptive that it cannot fit; or (3) one or both can modify or even reject their past positions to assemble a new party coalition. The most recent realigning election occurred in 1932, when Republicans decided to stand firm in the midst of the economic crisis, while Democrats absorbed the deepening public concerns into their existing platform to create a much larger party.

Although the New Deal coalition had largely disappeared by 1992, it is not clear that a new era has begun. The Democrats and Republicans are clearly battling each other for national control, but neither party has yet achieved a decisive victory. Moreover, political scientists do not agree on exactly what constitutes proof that a realignment has occurred. "Is a realignment a switch in which party is in the majority?" ask Richard Niemi and Herbert Weisberg. "Or does it only require a movement in levels of party support? Can a realignment be defined as a transition in the support coalitions for the parties? A shift in the issue bases of the party? Or a change in public policy direction following a change in party control of the presidency? Does it require changes in the political behavior of Congress and the Supreme Court? Or some combination of the above?"[11] The answer to all these questions appears to be "yes, but." Yes, a realignment involves clear evidence that the people and government have changed, but the change has to last long enough to be noticed. A realignment must involve more than the death of the dominant party. It must also involve the birth or strengthening of another party. The former development creates what can be called a **dealignment,** meaning that no party is dominant, while the latter creates the needed momentum toward a new alignment.

A Non-Realigning Election.   If one were searching for a recent realigning election, few would fill the bill better than the 1994 congressional elections. There is no question that Republicans capped a long period of growing strength with a dramatic victory. Republicans gained fifty-two seats in the House and eight in the Senate, and added eleven state governors. Not a single Republican who ran for representative, senator, or governor lost—not one. But did the election signal a dramatic shift in underlying party loyalties? Did it reflect a permanent shift in public opinion on issues such as abortion and gay rights?

The answers are mixed at best. The *Washington Post* called 1994 the year of the "Angry (White) Man." Voters who thought America's standard of living was worsening voted heavily for Republican (by 63 percent to 37 percent), as did voters who felt the economy was getting worse and voters who thought Bill Clinton was doing a poor job as president. And because voters thought things were looking more bad than good, the ballots piled up for Republicans. "No matter what you were angry about," said Andrew Kohut of the Times Mirror poll, "you voted for the Republicans. If you were angry about your standard of living declining, you voted Republican. If you were angry at Bill Clinton, you voted Republican. If you were angry at government in general, you voted Republican."[12]

Having been swept into office as the champions of change in 1992, Democrats were suddenly painted as the defenders of the status quo. Asked to explain the Republican victories in a *Time*/CNN postelection poll, roughly half of Americans put the blame on Clinton, another quarter put the blame on Democratic programs, and barely one in ten cited voter support for Republican programs. Sixty percent said the election was a repudiation of the Democrats, while just 15 percent said it was an endorsement of the Republican agenda.[13] The vast majority of Americans had either never heard of the Republicans' "Contract with America" or did not know that the phrase referred to the party's policy agenda.

What made the 1994 elections remarkable was not the size of the Republican victory, however. Turnout, party loyalty, issues, and image had been moving against the Democrats for the better part of two decades. Nor was it the gains in the South, where Republicans captured a majority of House seats and governorships for the first time in over a century (65 percent of Southern whites voted for the Republicans; 91 percent of Southern African Americans went for the Democrats).

Rather, 1994 is interesting because so many incumbents managed to win. All 177 Republican House incumbents were reelected, as were all 10 Senate Republicans. But even Democratic incumbents did well. Fourteen of 16 Senate Democrats were reelected, while only 34 of 211 House Democrats lost, yielding a reelection rate of 84 percent. Overall, 354, or over 90 percent, of the 388 House incumbents who ran in 1994 won reelection. Such reelection rates are not ordinarily the stuff of which realignments are made. Republicans captured the House largely on their strength in winning open seats.

Most analysts were cautious about labeling 1994 a realignment. "The bad news for the Republicans," Kevin Phillips wrote immediately after the election, "is that they've won their big triumph in a volatile, angry, impatient decade in which the electorate is at your throat just 12 to 18 months after they're at your feet. Public disdain for Washington and the Clinton administration has put the GOP in a position where it has to deliver—and it probably won't be able to. The era of lengthy cycles of party dominance is over."[14] People who expect a sharp realignment in a fast-moving, information-rich environment such as the modern United States may wait a very long time.

In the end, it must be said that the 1994 congressional elections, while dramatic, did not produce a deep enough change in the public's party loyalty to be classified as a realignment. Instead, the 1994 elections are best viewed as yet another confirmation that the New Deal coalition is dead. It may be that the United States has entered an era of *dealignment*, in which neither party seems able to generate the kind of lasting voter loyalty that might form the basis of a distinctive party era. Whether either major party will be able to build a new coalition that will define a sixth American party era is still in doubt. Clinton's easy reelection in 1996 suggested that Republicans are far from converting their substantial momentum into a winning coalition, in part because many Americans are still queasy about the party's social conservatism. The fact that Clinton so skillfully maneuvered his party toward the center of the ideological spectrum suggests that the existing parties are still perfectly able to absorb potential threats to the current alignment.[15]

THE THREE ROLES OF PARTIES TODAY

Political parties exist to influence what government does, whether through the recruitment of like-minded candidates or through the organization of Congress. Just as individual citizens have ideologies, so do parties have different views about how much government should be involved in the day-to-day activities of American society. They exist to translate those views into action, primarily through the exercise of three roles: (1) contesting elections, (2) organizing government, and (3) helping citizens decide how to vote.

Contesting Elections

The first role of the parties is to nominate and elect candidates for public office. They do so primarily through national, state, and local organizations called **party committees.** The party committees do much of the routine work involved in running the democratic process. They recruit candidates for office, register citizens to vote, raise money, campaign for their slates of party candidates, and get out the vote on election day. Although most candidates today keep their campaigns separate and independent of their party organizations, the party committees still host the conventions that endorse those candidates, write the **party platforms** that tell the public what the party stands for, and generally keep the party alive when it is not in power.[16]

At one time, the parties even printed their own election ballots, which listed only their own candidates for office. Until the late 1800s, when the nation switched to secret ballots listing all the candidates, citizens had to give all their votes to one party or the other. And because the party ballots were often printed in bright colors, there was rarely any doubt about voters' party loyalty as they walked to the ballot box with their decisions in hand. As noted, such public balloting increased the pressure to follow the party line.

Although the national, state, and local party committees still work closely together on national campaigns, they no longer act as a kind of political pyramid all the way from local voting precincts at the bottom to the national party committees in Washington. Rather, each tends to concentrate on its own level of government: the national committees focus on winning the presidency and seats in Congress; the state parties, on the governorship and seats in the state legislature; the local parties, on county and city posts. It is best to think of today's party system as federalist in nature—that is, as having multiple layers that often go their own ways.

The National Party Committees.   The national party committees invariably receive the greatest media attention, especially during presidential election years. Selected by the state parties, the national party committees are responsible for managing the **national party conventions** that take place every four years. The most important purpose of a national convention is to generate momentum for the party's presidential candidate. Today's primary election process virtually guarantees that a single candidate will come to the convention already having support from enough delegates to win the party's nomination on the first ballot and to get quick approval of a vice presidential nominee. Although delegates to the national convention also ratify a platform summarizing the party's views on the issues of the day, national conventions have become carefully staged events designed to give the presidential and vice presidential candidates a surge of public support that will carry into the fall's general election campaign.

Running this process takes more than party volunteers, of course. Both national party committees have permanent staffs that have grown dramatically in recent years. In the early 1970s, the Democratic and Republican National Committees had fewer than thirty employees each. By 1996, the Democratic National Committee (DNC) staff had grown to 264, while the Republican National

Presidential candidates Bob Dole (left) and Bill Clinton (right), at their respective party conventions in 1996. Both candidates were nominated on the first ballot. Today's conventions serve more as opportunities to promote the presidential candidates than as events in which delegates actually make real choices.

Committee (RNC) staff had increased to over 500.[17] These staffs are responsible for everything from planning the conventions to raising money for voter education.

Given the difference in staff size, it is no surprise that the RNC consistently raises more money, writes more letters, and runs more national advertisements than the DNC. In 1995–1996, for example, the RNC raised almost twice as much money as the DNC. This fundraising is supported by the Democratic and Republican Congressional and Senatorial Campaign Committees, which raise money on behalf of candidates for the House and Senate.

Both parties have clearly benefited from loopholes in the laws governing campaign fundraising. In 1979, the **Federal Election Commission,** which is the federal agency that administers the laws limiting how much money individuals can give to candidates and parties, decided to allow the national party committees to raise and spend unlimited amounts of money for what the FEC called "party building activities." Such activities can involve everything from voter registration drives to get-out-the-vote campaigns. Most of this unregulated, or **soft, money** is now spent on television campaigns that promote or attack candidates in broad terms. Because the advertisements do not call for the election of a candidate by name, the money involved is not subject to any limits. In 1995–1996, the RNC raised almost $160 million in soft money, while the DNC raised over $120 million. It was soft money that triggered the Senate's ongoing investigation of

Clinton/Gore fundraising practices, which allegedly included nights in the Lincoln Bedroom of the White House in return for large soft money contributions.

The State and Local Committees.   The national organizations may capture the headlines, but it is the state and local party organizations that often make or break a campaign. Indeed, for much of the nation's history, big-city **party machines** did the heavy lifting, even in presidential campaigns. A machine consisted of a party boss, thousands of party workers, and lots of cash to ensure that voters got to the polls and cast the "right" ballots.

A machine also controlled the **spoils system,** as in "To the victor belong the spoils." The spoils system was created by Andrew Jackson to make sure that the party faithful got jobs in government after the election. The party machines were undone by a series of reforms in the late 1800s, including the end of the spoils system and the use of primary elections to select candidates for state and national office.

Although the machines are mostly gone, state and local parties are far from dead. They remain closest to the grass roots, or the actual voters, and still recruit most of the candidates who run for office; Clinton, for instance, started his political career as a candidate for Arkansas attorney general. They still oversee the voter registration and get-out-the-vote efforts that can spell victory or defeat in a close campaign.[18] They will never be as powerful as they were during the machine era, but they appear to have made a remarkable comeback after decades of sleepy irrelevance.

One can even argue that the state and local parties have never been stronger. Twenty years ago, most state parties did not have headquarters, few had computers, even fewer had staff and money, and almost none had respect. Today, all have headquarters, most have computers and at least some permanent staff, and all are raising money, albeit in much smaller amounts than the national party committees. What they are getting is large amounts of the soft money raised by the national party committees. In 1995–1996, for example, the Pennsylvania Democratic party got over $6 million from the DNC, while the California Republican party received nearly $10 million from the RNC. Both national parties push dollars downward, using formulas based on past party performance. Put the money together with the headquarters, computers, and staff, and the state parties can command increasing respect from their candidates.

It is important to note, however, that state parties will never be the bosses that they once were. They are no longer in charge of the campaign process. Candidates do not have to win their party's support to run for office, nor do they need the party's help to win. Much as candidates benefit from having an effective state party operation, the days in which the state party could make or break a candidate are long gone. Lacking that kind of disciplining force, the state parties are best viewed as service bureaus that candidates are free either to rely on or to ignore.

Where the state parties do continue to play a prominent role is in selecting delegates for the national party conventions. The national committees set the number of delegates that each state may send to the national conventions on the basis of the size of the state's population (California sent 383 delegates to the Democratic National Convention in 1996, Alaska just 20) and on how well the party's nominee did in the state in the previous presidential election, while each state party decides how to select its delegates. Thirty-nine states now use some form of primary election to make the choice. Even here, however, the states are not always in charge. Having become so dependent on the national party committees for money, many state parties do whatever Washington tells them to do. Just as with federal grants to state and local government, the dollars determine who is in charge.

 **in a different light** ——— WHO GOES TO THE PARTY?

The national party committees are built from the bottom up, starting with people involved in the local party. As a result, they tend to represent those who have the greatest commitment to serve. Because that commitment often comes from ideology, party activists who eventually make it to the national party conventions may be very different from both the party's regular voters and the general population as a whole.

The differences are clear in the ideological character of the delegates to the major parties' 1996 national conventions. Delegates who made it to Chicago (Democrats) and San Diego (Republicans) not only were different from each other but were arguably out of touch with the attitudes of ordinary Americans.[19] (See Box 6–3 for comparisons of convention delegates, party regulars, and the general population.)

The differences started with basic demographics. Although women and minorities were much more likely to be Democratic convention delegates than to be Republican delegates, both party conventions had much higher proportions of college-educated, financially secure elites than their party regulars or the general population. Their delegates were also older than the general population. The reason may be that younger Americans are less willing or able to climb the ladder of meetings that lead to a national party convention.

The differences also involved political ideology. Democratic convention delegates were not only much more liberal than the population as a whole, they "out-liberaled" people who identified themselves as Democrats; Republican delegates were not only much more conservative than the rest of the population, they "out-conservatived" people who identified themselves as Republicans. Recall that most

BOX 6-3

A Comparison of Convention Delegates with the General Public, 1996

	Democratic Delegates	Democratic Party Regulars	General Public	Republican Party Regulars	Republican Delegates
Demographics					
Men	47%	37%	46%	53%	64%
Women	53	63	54	47	36
White	71	71	84	95	91
Black	17	20	11	2	3
Age					
18–29 years old	6	18	17	19	2
30–44 years old	27	29	32	33	26
45–64 years old	55	30	30	25	53
65 and older	11	23	21	22	17
Labor union member	34	13	11	7	4
College graduate	69	17	23	30	73
Family income					
under $50,000	29	78	71	60	23
$50,000–$75,000	22	10	14	19	18
over $75,000	46	8	11	17	47
Political Views					
Ideology					
very liberal	15	7	4	1	0
somewhat liberal	28	20	12	6	0
moderate	48	54	47	39	27
somewhat conservative	4	14	24	36	31
very conservative	1	3	8	17	35
Government should do more:					
to solve the nation's problems	76	53	36	20	4
to regulate the environmental and safety practices of businesses	60	66	53	37	4
to promote traditional values	27	41	42	44	56

Source: *New York Times,* August 26, 1996, p. A12.

Americans see themselves as very much in the ideological middle, which is clearly not where one needs to be to get an invitation to the party conventions.

Finally, the differences were clear on the issues of the day. Democratic convention delegates were much more likely than Republicans to favor government intervention to solve the nation's problems, while Republican delegates were much more likely to favor government intervention in promoting family values.

Democratic delegates were also much more likely than even their party regulars to favor abortion rights, a nationwide ban on assault weapons, and affirmative action programs to help women and minorities, and to oppose organized prayer in public schools. With one-third of their 1996 delegates coming from labor unions, it is not surprising that Democratic convention goers also favored international trade restrictions to protect domestic industries. In a similar vein, Republican convention delegates were much more likely than their party regulars to oppose abortion rights, an assault weapons ban, and affirmative action, and to favor public school prayer.

These differences affect the national parties in several important ways. In order to appeal to the delegates and win their party's nomination, for example, presidential candidates often have to take more extreme positions than they would otherwise favor. Republicans have to lean to the right, Democrats to the left. Ideological activists can also have a substantial role in writing the party's platform, again driving the parties toward the ideological extremes.

If a convention is visibly ideological, the party's candidate may be unable to move back toward the center during the general election campaign, in which—even if activists have determined the nomination—more moderate party regulars and independents determine the final victory. In 1992, for example, conservative delegates to the Republican National Convention in Houston forced the party so far right on issues such as school prayer and abortion rights that George Bush could not regain the center. Moderate women deserted the party, creating a large gender gap in favor of Bill Clinton. Although 1996 Republican convention goers were as ideological as their 1992 predecessors, presidential nominee Bob Dole succeeded in creating a convention that looked inclusive and open, while minimizing his commitment to the party's intensely ideological party platform. "I haven't read it yet," he said of the platform upon leaving San Diego.

Under *responsible party theory*, these platforms should form the basis for party action once the election is won. In theory, citizens would vote for the party that comes closest to sharing their views, assuming that their party will behave responsibly and enact the platform once in office. In reality, however, party platforms are rarely honored. They are more a reflection of who happens to go to the party conventions than an accurate expression of party positions on the issues of the day.

The fact that party conventions tend to overrepresent ideological extremes may reduce the general public's party loyalty. To the extent that ordinary citizens do

not see themselves reflected in the ideological views of their party, they may end up voting for third-party candidates such as Ross Perot or simply staying home on election day.

Organizing Government

The second role of the parties is to help structure the government once the campaigns are over. Being in the majority clearly matters, especially on Capitol Hill. Both the Speaker of the House and the Majority Leader of the Senate, the two key positions on Capitol Hill, are chosen from the ranks of the majority party.

The majority party also determines who gets the best offices, the largest staffs, the fastest service from the departments of government, the best seats for the president's State of the Union address, and even who gets quoted more frequently by the media.[20] Most important, members of the majority party also determine which bills get to the floor of Congress for final passage. In short, being in the majority determines who gets what, when, and how in government.

Party is not equally important to all three branches of government, however. There is no explicit role for the parties in the federal judiciary, although being involved in party politics sometimes helps in getting an appointment as a federal judge. Party is more important in the presidency, where the president is viewed as the party's most visible leader, and where being involved in party politics is often essential in getting an appointment as a presidential aide. The president also has a great say in who runs the national party committee.

Party is most important in organizing Congress, where the majority party rules. Congress relies on the majority party for everything from organizing the committees to hiring Capitol Hill police. Most important, the majority determines how many Democrats and Republicans will sit on each committee. That ratio does not have to match the actual number of seats controlled by each party. In 1995, for example, Republicans required that most committees have roughly three Republican members for every two Democrats, a 60/40 ratio, even though Republicans held only a 52–48 margin in actual seats. The powerful House Ways and Means Committee, which drafts all tax legislation, had twenty-three Republicans and just sixteen Democrats. Democrats imposed an even more lopsided ratio when they were in power before 1994.

It is important to note, however, that each party selects its own leaders and makes its own committee assignments. There are actually four party organizations in Congress (the Senate majority and minority and the House majority and minority). Meeting at the start of each two-year congressional term in secret party caucuses, party members first decide who will be their party leader. The majority party in the House appoints the Speaker, majority leader, and majority whip (who "whips up" party support on legislation), and a host of lesser posts; the minority party appoints the minority leader, minority whip, and so forth. Each of the four party organizations also appoints its own **congressional campaign committee,** which raises money for its members and candidates.

All four party organizations share the same broad goal of creating party unity on legislation. It is a goal that is often measured by asking how often party members vote together on the same bill. In the early 1970s, for example, party unity in the House and Senate averaged 60 to 65 percent—that is, Democrats voted with Democrats and Republicans with Republicans about two-thirds of the time. By the 1990s, the unity scores had increased dramatically. In 1996, for example, House Democrats voted together 84 percent of the time, while House Republicans hit 90 percent; Senate Democrats voted together 86 percent of the time, while Senate Republicans hit 91 percent. Party loyalty may be down among American voters, as this chapter discusses below, but it appears to be up among their elected representatives in Washington.

One reason for the recent level of unity is that the people who show up for the party—that is, the convention—tend to select candidates who are more liberal or conservative than the rest of the party. As a result, the number of moderates in the House and Senate appears to be falling. This means that fewer proposals are likely to earn support on both sides of the party aisle. As Democrats have become more liberal and Republicans more conservative, one would naturally expect party unity to increase. As polarization between the parties goes up, so should party unity. The problem is that the American public is not nearly so polarized. Most Americans are comfortably parked in the middle, watching their parties engage in divisive debates over seemingly trivial issues. It is little wonder, therefore, that most Americans have asked whether the parties still represent them.

Helping Voters Decide

The third role of parties is to help voters decide. Parties exist as more than formal organizations with national, state, and local headquarters. Parties also exist in citizens' minds, whether as a way to help them make choices between candidates or as a way to identify themselves with other social groups. Before asking whether and how party identification might serve as a tool for making actual voting decisions, it is useful to understand how **party identification** is measured and where Americans stand today.

Defining Identification.   There are two ways to look at party identification: direction and intensity. Direction merely indicates how many Americans call themselves Democrats, Republicans, or independents, while intensity reflects how strongly party members feel toward their choice and whether independents have any leanings toward one or the other party.

Pollsters usually combine direction and intensity into a single measure of party identification with seven categories: strong Democrats, weak Democrats, independents who lean toward the Democrats, pure independents, independents who lean toward the Republicans, weak Republicans, and strong Republicans. Strong and weak members of each party are often combined into a single category, as are the different types of independents. Almost by definition, **independents** cannot use their party identification to help them decide how to vote. (Box 6–4 shows the recent trends in the overall direction of party identification.)

On measures of direction, Democrats have clearly lost the most ground over the past half century. As the New Deal coalition began to weaken, the Democratic share of strong and weak loyalists fell from 47 percent in 1952 to 39 percent in 1996. Republicans were hardly the beneficiaries, however—another indication that the 1994 election was not a realignment. Indeed, Republicans ended up exactly where they had begun in 1952, at 28 percent. They lost ground in the wake of the Watergate scandal during the 1970s, but regained it during the Reagan years. The big gains over the years came among independents, whose share of the electorate rose from 23 percent in 1952 to 39 percent in 1992. Although the proportion of independents came down sharply in 1996 to 34 percent, the general direction in party identification has been toward a weakening of attachment.

On measures of intensity, strong identifiers in both parties have lost ground over the decades. Americans simply do not feel comfortable today declaring themselves strong Democrats or Republicans. In 1952, for example, 36 percent of the public were strong identifiers, but that proportion fell to just 24 percent in 1976. Although the number of strong identifiers did rise to 32 percent in 1996, the rebound appears to have had more to do with the strong economy than with a return of intense loyalties. Being a strong identifier today may simply not mean the same thing to respondents as it did in the 1950s. Nevertheless, strong identifiers do behave differently from the rest of the public. They are much more likely to follow government and politics in the news, pay attention to campaigns and elections, and know what their candidates believe. Not surprisingly, therefore, they are much more likely to vote.

Interestingly, pure independents (the independents who say they do not lean toward either party) are quite different from leaning independents (the ones who say they lean toward the Democratic or Republican party). The pure independents are barely attached to the political process at all. They rarely pay attention to government and politics, and are more likely than other voters to feel that politicians do not care much about their opinions. In 1952, only 6 percent of the public said they were independents. By 1996, the number had grown to 9 percent. These independents are the least likely to use issues as a basis for voting,

BOX 6-4

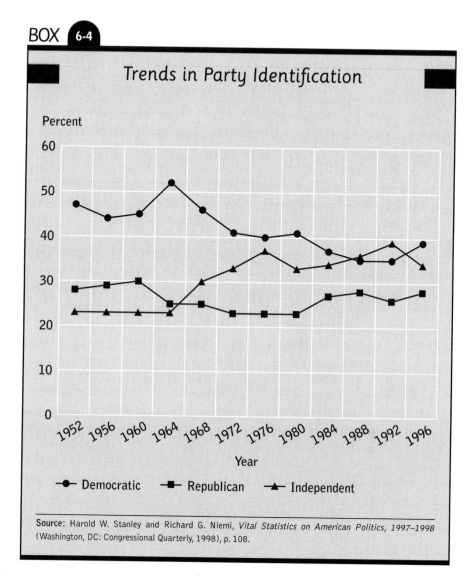

Trends in Party Identification

Percent

Source: Harold W. Stanley and Richard G. Niemi, *Vital Statistics on American Politics, 1997–1998* (Washington, DC: Congressional Quarterly, 1998), p. 108.

seeming to rely on candidate advertisements and other imagery as their primary reasons for choosing one candidate over another.

However, the independents who say they lean toward the Democratic or Republican party are actually more like strong identifiers than pure independents. They appear to be calling themselves independents either to signal their distrust of the parties or as a statement of current fashion (Americans are increasingly reluctant to label themselves at all), but still hold strong opinions on the issues. Leaners are much more interested in politics and more likely to vote than both pure independents and weak identifiers. The number of leaners has grown over the years, confirming again the erosion of party loyalty. In 1952, just 17 percent of Americans were leaners. The number peaked at 27 percent in 1992, and came down only slightly to 25 percent in 1996.

How Does Party Identification Work?   Forty years ago, party identification was believed to be the single most important factor in voting. Not only did it predict how people would vote, it also predicted how they would think. Party identification acted as a kind of funnel through which all of the issues and information would flow down to a voter's focused decision.

This view of party identification was part of what may be called the *American Voter* school of thought. The authors of *The American Voter*, all of whom were faculty members at the University of Michigan, believed that party identification determined virtually every decision a voter would make. Not all Americans would form strong loyalties, of course, and even those who did might be swayed in a moment of weakness to vote for another party. However, the authors concluded that it would take a "cataclysmic" event, a critical election of the kind experienced only three times in American history (1860, 1896, and 1932), to shatter the bond between party identification and actual votes.[21]

As party identification began to weaken in the 1960s, the *American Voter* view came under fire. By the mid-1970s, the authors of *The Changing American Voter* could argue that party loyalty was in sharp decline: "Party affiliation, once the central thread connecting the citizen and the political process, is a thread that has certainly been frayed."[22] This new school of thought found ample cause for concern about the strength of the party label. Fewer Americans were identifying with a party in the first place; fewer were using party labels as a way to sort through competing ideas and candidates; fewer had anything good to say about the parties in opinion polls; and parents were having trouble getting their children to adopt their labels.

The debate continues to rage. One recent defense of *The American Voter* was titled *The Unchanging American Voter*.[23] Much of the debate hinges on whether party loyalty is truly stable. Is it a matter of "Once a Democrat, always a Democrat"? If the answer is yes, then party loyalty will always be there when citizens need it to make a voting decision. If the answer is no, then party identification may be more a reaction to a person's most recent vote.

Recent research suggests that Americans are not as loyal as they were in the 1950s and early 1960s. Loyalty appears to increase with the economy's strength and the president's popularity—when presidents do well and the economy is healthy, their parties benefit; when the economy sinks and presidents' approval goes with it, their parties lose strength.[24] Thus, loyalty may be more a measure of what people have read last, not what their parents told them to believe about the two parties when they were being socialized to politics in childhood. Party identification may simply be more of a passing attachment than a lifelong commitment.

Who Identifies.   Although loyalty may have weakened somewhat over the years, the two parties continue to attract very different kinds of identifiers. Just as social and demographic groups help individual Americans form public opinions, they also reinforce party loyalty. To the extent that members of a labor union see mostly Democratic bumper stickers in the parking lot, or that residents of a gated community see mostly Republican lawn signs on their streets, both are reminded of the preferred party of their socioeconomic group. One way to illustrate the impact of these groups in reinforcing party identification is to ask which Americans are most likely *not* to be Democrats or Republicans. It is a question answered in Box 6–5.

Some of these differences in loyalty have been remarkably stable over the past fifty years. Republicans are still more likely to be better educated and afflu-

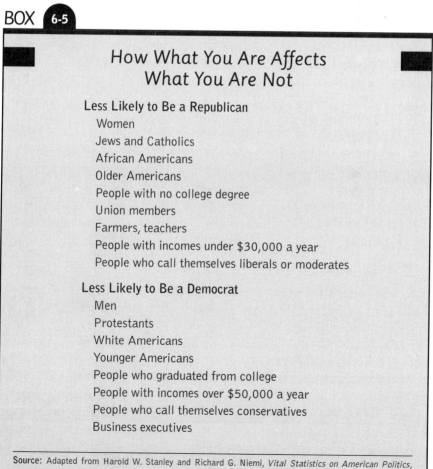

BOX 6-5

How What You Are Affects What You Are Not

Less Likely to Be a Republican
 Women
 Jews and Catholics
 African Americans
 Older Americans
 People with no college degree
 Union members
 Farmers, teachers
 People with incomes under $30,000 a year
 People who call themselves liberals or moderates

Less Likely to Be a Democrat
 Men
 Protestants
 White Americans
 Younger Americans
 People who graduated from college
 People with incomes over $50,000 a year
 People who call themselves conservatives
 Business executives

Source: Adapted from Harold W. Stanley and Richard G. Niemi, *Vital Statistics on American Politics, 1997–1998* (Washington, DC: CQ Press, 1998), p. 111.

ent; Democrats are still more likely to be African American, live in cities, and belong to labor unions.[25] Once again, the figures are less important than the general trend: the two parties still appeal to particular groups of voters.

At the same time, there has been a shift toward the Republicans among certain social groups, a shift that may have started in the late 1960s when Southern Democrats, particularly whites, began turning away from their party. By 1994, Republicans had become the preferred party for white Southerners (35 percent to 20 percent), white, non-Hispanic Catholics (47 percent to 46 percent), and white born-again Christians (38 percent to 28 percent).[26] Not only do born-again Christians now constitute almost a quarter of the U.S. adult population, but they are also much more likely to vote in elections than the traditional Democratic base. Their votes were a significant part of the Republican victory in 1994, and continue to force Republican candidates to deal with conservative social issues.

Where neither party has done particularly well of late is among younger Americans. The largest party among young Americans is no party at all. Young Americans are far more likely than older Americans to say there ought to be a third major political party. Over 60 percent of people under age thirty say yes to the idea, compared with just 36 percent of those over age sixty-five.[27] This does not mean, however, that a third party is about to spring forth around Generation X; rather, it indicates that party loyalty is less likely to influence young people's vote than some other factor.[28]

The question is what might be causing young Americans to keep their distance. It is most certainly not that the parties have somehow become irrelevant to contesting elections or organizing government; in fact, they have never been stronger, as this chapter has shown. Nor is it because there is some flashy new third-party product available to tempt voters. Third parties remain notoriously unable to hold party loyalty over time.

Rather, it may be that young Americans simply no longer have to rely on the two parties for information or influence. They can always tune in to the new media or join interest groups instead. Just as young Americans have turned away from network television and national newspapers and toward the new media, perhaps they are also turning away from the two parties and toward more specialized sources of influence.

 **in a different light** ——— **DEMOCRATIC REPUBLICANS**

Democrats have made their own gains in traditionally Republican territory. Just visit Fox Point, Wisconsin, a small town outside Milwaukee. With just seven thousand residents and carefully trimmed lawns, Fox Point is the classic bedroom sub-

urb, a haven for business executives and soccer moms. Incorporated in 1920, Fox Point gave its votes to Republicans at every turn through the 1980s. It voted for Herbert Hoover in the depths of the Great Depression of the 1930s and Barry Goldwater during the Great Society of the 1960s, and was firmly behind the Reagan Revolution of the 1980s.

But something happened in Fox Point and hundreds of other upper-income hamlets during the 1980s and 1990s: The baby boomers who grew up politically during the Vietnam War and Watergate started making money and moving in. Suddenly, voting patterns began to shift. Democrats began to take more and more votes from the Republicans. In 1996, a majority of Fox Pointers actually voted for Bill Clinton over Bob Dole. The margin was tight, only fifty-nine votes, but the message was clear: A growing number of rich Americans are voting Democratic.

The message is confirmed in a recent study of one hundred towns with per capita incomes over $30,000. In 1980, the towns gave 25 percent of their votes to Jimmy Carter, running sixteen points lower than Carter's national total of 41 percent. In 1996, those same cities gave 41 percent of their votes to Clinton, running just eight points behind Clinton's national total of 49 percent.[29] Republicans can still count on the support of most of the country's Fox Points, but income may be less of a predictor of party loyalty than it once was. "As the Republican Party's center of gravity shifts from the country club to the stock-car track," writes the *National Journal* in an analysis of recent trends, "the rich are becoming increasingly uncomfortable with the GOP." Democrats, not Republicans, are now seen in many wealthy communities as the party best able to prevent crime and protect the status quo.

Who are these Democratic Republicans? One answer is that they are the same people who went to Woodstock (the first one, in 1969), protested the Vietnam War, burned their draft cards, and now work at the highest levels of leading U.S. corporations wearing Jerry Garcia neckties, driving Volvos, and eating free-range chicken. Paul Starobin of the *National Journal* describes four types of new Democratic Republicans as follows:

- *The Boardroom Democrats*: Clinton succeeded in recruiting high-tech corporate leaders to his campaign in 1996 largely on the strength of his support for the North American Free Trade Agreement (NAFTA), which promised lower trade barriers between the United States and Mexico, and funding for an expanded Internet. Although Republicans still have a substantial edge among banking and manufacturing executives, Democrats appear to be winning the battle in Silicon Valleys all across the country.
- *Neiman-Marcus Pro-Choicers.* Baby boomers may have taken off their protest boots, but they still believe in equal opportunity and freedom of choice. The Republican hard line on both issues has driven wealthy pro-choicers into the

Democratic party. Level of education appears to be far more important on the abortion-rights issue than income. Roughly a quarter of high school graduates say that abortion should be generally available, compared to almost half of college graduates. Forced to choose between what they believe will be higher taxes and social freedom on the one hand and lower taxes and a conservative social agenda on the other, the Neiman-Marcus Pro-Choicers want the freedom.

- *Horatio Alger Ethnics.* Images of the Republican party as the protector of an older, white elite have driven some Asian Americans toward the Democratic party, particularly in places such as Fort Lee, New Jersey, where Clinton's share of the vote was 64 percent in 1996. Among ethnic voters, issues may overwhelm income as a source of party loyalty.

- *Perego Pushers.* Named after the favorite baby stroller among well-to-do Americans, this label captures the young, urban professionals ("Yuppies") who are now moving from their high-rise city apartments to the suburbs to raise their children. As with their ethnic peers, these mostly white voters are likely to favor liberal social issues with conservative economic views—exactly the platform offered by Clinton in 1996. By moving toward the center as Republicans continued to move toward the right, Clinton was able to hold his mostly liberal base, while picking up moderates who worried that Republicans intended to push their anti-abortion, antigay, pro-school-prayer agenda.

Income is still a powerful predictor of party identification, of course. People who made over $50,000 a year in 1996 were still more likely to identify with the Republican party than with the Democratic. But income is not the fixed determinant of party loyalty that it once was. Whether a corporate executive occasionally dons a Jerry Garcia tie may be just as good a predictor of party loyalty as the size of the paycheck or stock options.

Measures of Attachment.   The intensity of party identification is not the only measure of whether party still helps people decide. Political scientists ask three other questions in assessing the strength or weakness of attachment: (1) Do Americans still see significant differences between the two parties? (2) Does party identification still affect how people cast their vote for specific offices such as president or member of Congress? and (3) Does party identification affect how people vote for other offices down the ballot? At least for now, the answers suggest that parties still do influence how Americans behave.

First, Americans do continue to see significant differences between the two parties. The more differences they see, whether in the candidates, platforms, or kinds of voters each party attracts, the more likely the public is to identify with one or the other. In 1998, for example, roughly three-quarters of Americans saw at least a "fair amount" of difference between the two parties. That number has been increasing ever so slightly over the past decade or so, suggesting that the two parties are actually drawing firmer lines between themselves. Early in the 1998 congressional campaigns, the Democratic party was seen as the party most likely to bring about the kinds of changes the country needs, to be concerned with the needs of ordinary people, and to be concerned about the needs and interests of the disadvantaged. Republicans were seen as the party most concerned with the needs and interests of business and other powerful groups, which was hardly the kind of endorsement that a party might put on a bumper sticker.[30]

Second, party identification is still a strong predictor of how people will vote for presidential and House candidates. In 1996, for example, 84 percent of Democrats voted for Clinton, while 80 percent of Republicans voted for Dole. It is one thing, however, to be able to use party in predicting the vote, and quite another to assert that party is the *cause* of the vote. Here, political scientists are far less certain. It could be, for example, that party identification is merely an indication of where a person's thinking is at a given point in time—a marker or label that people use to describe their most recent opinions.

Under such circumstances, party identification would be less a cause of how people vote than a way for people to explain what they just did. According to the *American Voter* model, people would say, "I am a Democrat, therefore I will vote for Bill Clinton." More recent experience indicates that they may very well say, "I will vote for Bill Clinton, therefore I am a Democrat." Instead of being cultivated by parents as part of early political socialization, party loyalty would be much looser, easily shifted by short-term pressures and controversies. Conversely, it could be that party identification remains relatively stable and that the rise in the proportion of independents is merely a kind of political fashion. Perhaps some Americans are simply hiding their true loyalties because they think it is fashionable to do so.

Third, there appears to have been a recent rebound in the amount of **straight-ticket voting,** in which voters stick with their party all the way down the ballot, and a corresponding decrease in **split-ticket voting,** in which voters choose candidates from the different parties for various offices. The proportion of Americans who voted for the Senate candidate of one party and the House candidate of the other grew from 9 percent in the 1952 election to a high of 35 percent in the 1978 election, and has been moving back down ever since, hitting 19 percent in 1996. At the same time, the number who voted for a presidential candidate of one party and a

House candidate of the other grew from 13 percent in 1952 to a high of 30 percent in 1972, and has been backing down ever since, too, hitting 18 percent in 1996.

Neither party is doing particularly well of late at generating much passion on either side. Americans may see differences when prompted by a pollster, but they still feel mostly "blah" toward the parties. Asked what they liked or disliked about the two parties in the 1950s, most Americans had something to say. In 1952, for example, half of the public had something negative to say about one party and something positive to say about the other. They did not just like one party, they also disliked the other. Barely one in ten had nothing to say or were neutral about both parties. By the 1990s, however, the level of intensity was down. Almost one-third of the voting public felt neutral about both parties. "The major change that has taken place in the public's evaluations of the parties has been that people feel neutral rather than negative," writes political scientist Martin Wattenberg, who discovered the rising tide of neutrality, and "there seems to be little prospect for reversing the trend toward neutrality in the immediate future."[31] For a growing number of Americans, the parties are the political equivalent of Cream of Wheat. There is nothing particularly wrong with the parties, but nothing that stirs great passion either.

in a different light —— THE CONSULTANTS TAKE OVER

Recent years have witnessed a dramatic increase in the number and influence of *political consultants* in the campaign process. Consultants are now involved in virtually every aspect of campaigns, from setting general strategy to fundraising, from developing political Web sites to polling, and are taking over many of the campaign roles that were once played mainly by the parties. Consultants have become an essential part of the candidate-centered campaign, in which candidates run independently of their parties (see Chapter 9).

The seven thousand people who earn their living as political consultants fall into three tiers. At the top are *strategists,* the highly visible consultants who provide overall direction for a campaign. These are the stars of the industry—the James Carvilles and Mary Matalins who get so much press attention. In the middle are the *specialists,* the less visible consultants who provide specific services. Specialists are brought into a campaign to solve particular problems. They are the fundraisers, the petition and signature harvesters (the ones who go to the malls and sign people up, getting a dollar or two per signature), the speechwriters, television time buyers (the ones who negotiate with local television stations to get the best advertising slots at the lowest unit price), and the pollsters. At the bottom are the

James Carville, Bill Clinton's most valuable consultant. Carville, who was featured in the documentary *The War Room* and was played by Billy Bob Thornton in *Primary Colors,* made many of the decisions that helped Clinton win the Democratic nomination and the general election in 1992. He was brought back in early 1998 to help plan the president's strategy in dealing with the White House intern scandal.

vendors, who do just about anything for a price, but who do not restrict their services to politics. Vendors put together the mailing lists, the software and computer systems, the print advertisements, and the Web sites.[32]

The difference between the top and bottom of the industry involves more than just salaries—though the salaries at the top often exceed $500,000 a year. It also involves proximity to the candidate. The strategist is rarely far from the candidate, providing general advice and hiring specialists and vendors as needed. Because strategists get huge bonuses if their candidate wins, they appear to be willing to do just about anything, stopping just short of breaking the law, to get their candidate elected.

Consider the results of a 1998 survey of the profession. Asked to rate a series of practices as acceptable, questionable, or clearly unethical, consultants said candidates can do almost anything except make statements that are factually untrue. Eight of ten said that it is acceptable to focus campaigns primarily on criticizing an opponent; seven out of ten said that it is acceptable to focus primarily on a candidate's personality rather than on issues. Consultants were more reluctant about using scare tactics to attack a candidate's issue position, making statements that are factually true but taken out of context, and trying to suppress voter turnout; but none of these three practices was seen as clearly unethical. Six in ten said that taking statements out of context is questionable, but only one-quarter said that it is clearly unethical. "If it works," the consultants seemed to be saying, "do it."[33]

Yet, when asked who is to blame for public distrust of politics, most of the consultants interviewed pointed their fingers at the candidate or the press, accepting little blame themselves. For members of an industry that prides itself on knowing what people think, most consultants are surprisingly uninformed about public opinion toward modern campaigns. When Americans are asked what bothers them about campaigns, most say negative campaigning; when consultants are asked what they think bothers Americans about campaigns, most say slanted news coverage, and only one-quarter say negative campaigning.

It is no wonder that consultants would say the public is not cynical about negative campaigning: 80 percent of the consultants said they were the ones who recommend negative campaigning to their candidates. Moreover, it is not clear that consultants would change their opinions even if they talked to ordinary Americans. Two-thirds of the consultants interviewed said Americans are poorly informed about politics, and four out of ten said that they could "sell" voters a weak campaigner if they had enough money for advertising.

As for what motivates consultants, it is certainly not responsible parties. One-third say that they are in the business for the thrill of competition and another quarter say that they do it for the money. Only one-quarter say that their political beliefs are at the root of their personal commitment to the consulting industry. And as for what makes a consultant take on a particular candidate, 58 percent of consultants said that a candidate's beliefs are very important, while almost as many, 55 percent, said that the candidate's ability to pay the bills is also very important.

As consultants continue to replace party organizations as the source of campaign advice, the negatives are likely to rise. There is money to be made in those tactics. More than half of the consultants interviewed reported annual incomes of more than $150,000 per year, and one-third said they made $200,000 or more.[34]

MAINTAINING THE BALANCE

As with the media, parties must maintain their own internal balance if they are to play a positive role in the American system of government. They cannot allow themselves to be captured by extremists within their ranks, lest they use their considerable power in organizing government to help those extremists impose their will on others. Nor can they become so enamored with power that they seek dominance regardless of the costs.

Central to maintaining this balance within the parties is some minimum amount of party loyalty among the public. Unless party identifiers pay attention to what their parties do, and unless they reward their parties with at least some degree of loyalty, extremists pay no penalty for hijacking the party machinery. In this regard, party loyalty can actually be seen as a sign that Americans are willing to give their consent to be governed with the help of a two-party system.

The weakening of party identification is, therefore, more than just a troublesome problem for the parties in getting their candidates elected. It can also weaken their legitimacy in organizing government after the ballots are counted. The irony today is that the parties have never been stronger on Capitol Hill, where the majority controls everything from parking spaces to committee membership ratios, even as they seem to be losing their grip on their candidates and the public. "The two parties remind me of those old French Foreign Legion movies," says Ann Lewis, a past political director of the Democratic National Committee. "You see this fort, and it looks fine from the outside. But when you go through the gate, almost everyone inside is dead."[35]

Even as they search for balance as political organizations, parties may play an increasingly important role as a counterweight to the onslaught of lobbying by interest groups in Washington. As Chapter 7 will show, the United States is awash in powerful organizations whose primary aim is to influence government for their own self-interests. To the extent that parties exert a unifying pressure against the highly divisive efforts of interest groups, perhaps the Founders might have changed their minds about parties. Having strong parties that generate public loyalty may help maintain the delicate balance after all. Without the role of parties in contesting elections and organizing government, would government be able to work at all? The Founders did not just want a government that would protect liberty. They also wanted a government that could respond to foreign and domestic threats. The parties may contribute more toward accomplishing the latter than the Founders could have imagined.

terms to remember

facts and interpretations

- Parties have been part of the American system since the country was founded. A version of the modern two-party system was in place by 1790, with one party to defend the Constitution, the other to attack it. Although the Founders clearly opposed parties as a form of faction, the Constitution encouraged the rise of a two-party system by establishing a majoritarian, winner-take-all system of elections. If a third party cannot win on its own, which none ever has in American history, its best strategy is to try to force an existing party to accept its views on one or more issues.

- Over the years, political parties have taken on a variety of important roles in helping government do its job. They recruit candidates as part of contesting elections, organize the parties in government, and help voters decide whom to support on election day. The parties have never been stronger than they are today in organizing government, but may be losing influence in both contesting elections and shaping voter decisions. They no longer control the process by which candidates get nominated, and are increasingly relegated to a service role on behalf of any of their candidates who choose to use the party machinery. It is too early to tell whether recent increases in the amount of soft money available to the national parties will create new incentives for candidates to work more closely with their parties.

- Among individual voters, party identification is still one of the most powerful predictors of which candidates will get their support. Although the number of Americans who believe that the nation needs a third party is down somewhat since peaking in the early 1990s, there has been a weakening of party loyalty over the past four decades. The number of Americans who identify themselves as independents has gone up over the past few decades, while the number who feel passionately for or against the parties has gone down. Party identification may still be a powerful predictor of the vote, but it may be much less powerful as a determinant of the vote. Despite the general decline in party loyalty, there is some evidence that the parties may be rebounding somewhat. Straight-ticket voting is up, though not as high as 1950-era levels, while a significant majority of Americans continue to see differences between the parties.

- Despite the weakening attachment to the two parties, there is little evidence that the United States has undergone or will shortly undergo a sharp realignment. Instead, the current state of the parties is best described as a dealignment. Although some experts believe that the 1994 election was critical, the evidence suggests that Americans are reasonably comfortable with the current two-party alignment, particularly in the wake of Clinton's successful effort to move toward the center in the 1996 campaign.

open questions

- How would one recognize a realignment if it occurred? How long would it have to last? How loyal to the new majority party would citizens have to become? Thinking back to 1994 and 1996, what kinds of evidence could show that the Republicans have become the majority party? What kinds of evidence suggest that the Democrats are doing just fine?

- Why have so many Americans become less loyal to their political party? Is their reluctance just a passing fad, or does it somehow fit with other changes in politics? If Americans are not using party to help them make their voting decisions, what are they using? To what extent are candidates for office also distancing themselves from their parties?

- What are the benefits of having strong parties in Congress? If the majority party did not select the occupants of key leadership posts and committee chairs, who would? What are the alternative methods for organizing government? Does the fact that the United States has a majoritarian democracy inevitably produce parties? Would a proportional system be any better? How would such a system organize government, for example?

- How does the rise of the consulting industry affect the conduct of politics? Does the role of consultants in campaigns make citizens more or less likely to be loyal to the parties, or more or less trusting of campaigns? If consultants were to disappear tomorrow, would candidates suddenly stop using questionable campaign tactics? Although the increased reliance on soft money has generated considerable controversy and calls for reform, are there advantages to giving the parties a greater say in campaigns?

for further study

Bibby, John. *Politics, Parties, and Elections in America*. Chicago: Nelson-Hall, 1992.

Maisel, L. Sandy, ed. *The Parties Respond: Changes in American Parties and Campaigns*. Boulder, CO: Westview Press, 1998.

Reichley, A. James. *The Life of the Parties: A History of American Political Parties*. New York: Free Press, 1992.

Sabato, Larry. *The Rise of Political Consultants: New Ways of Winning Elections*. New York: Basic Books, 1981.

Sundquist, James. *Dynamics of the Party System: Alignment and Realignment of Political Parties in the United States*. Rev. ed. Washington, DC: Brookings Institution, 1983.

Wattenberg, Martin P. *The Decline of American Political Parties, 1952–1994*. Reprint ed. Cambridge, MA: Harvard University Press, 1996.

endnotes for chapter 6

1. Jefferson and Washington quoted in James Roger Sharp, *American Politics in the Early Republic: The New Nation in Crisis* (New Haven, CT: Yale University Press, 1993); Adams quoted in A. James Reichley, *The Life of the Parties: A History of American Political Parties* (New York: Free Press, 1992), p. 17.

2. Not all scholars accept this view. For an excellent critique, see James Caesar, *Presidential Selection: Theory and Development* (Princeton, NJ: Princeton University Press, 1979).

3. Reichley, *The Life of the Parties*, pp. 36–37.

4. See John Bibby, *Politics, Parties, and Elections in America* (Chicago: Nelson-Hall, 1992).

5. Times Mirror Center for The People & The Press, *The People, the Press and Politics: The New Political Landscape*, September 21, 1994, p. 58.

6. Bibby, *Politics, Parties, and Elections in America*, p. 39.

7. See Joel H. Silbey, "From 'Essential to the Existence of Our Institutions' to 'Rapacious Enemies of Honest and Responsible Government': The Rise and Fall of American Parties, 1790–2000," in L. Sandy Maisel, ed., *The Parties Respond: Changes in American Parties and Campaigns* (Boulder, CO: Westview Press, 1998).

8. Kenneth C. Davis, *Don't Know Much about History* (New York: Avon Books, 1990), p. 119.

9. For a detailed history of party change from the early 1800s to the present, see James Sundquist, *Dynamics of the Party System: Alignment and Realignment of Political Parties in the United States*, rev. ed. (Washington, DC: Brookings Institution, 1983).

10. Davis, *Don't Know Much about History*, p. 213.

11. Richard G. Niemi and Herbert F. Weisberg, *Controversies in Voting Behavior* (Washington, DC: CQ Press, 1993), p. 325.

12. Quoted in Eric Black and Steve Berg, "How Did the GOP Do It?" *Minneapolis Star-Tribune*, November 13, 1994, p. A9.

13. Richard Morin, "Myths and Messages in the Election Tea Leaves," *Washington Post National Weekly Edition*, November 21–27, 1994, p. 37.

14. Kevin Phillips, "The Voters Are Already Tapping Their Feet," *Washington Post National Weekly Edition*, November 21–27, p. 23.

15. This point is echoed in Alan J. Abramowitz and Kyle L. Saunders, "Party

Polarization and Ideological Realignment in the U.S. Electorate, 1976–1994," in Maisel, ed., *The Parties Respond*, pp. 128–43.

16. Paul Allen Beck and Frank J. Sorauf, *Party Politics in America* (New York: HarperCollins, 1992), pp. 11–12.

17. Beck and Sorauf, *Party Politics in America*, p. 105.

18. See John F. Bibby, "State Party Organizations: Coping and Adapting to Candidate-Centered Politics and Nationalization," in Maisel, ed., *The Parties Respond*, pp. 23–49.

19. *New York Times*/CBS News Poll, reprinted in *New York Times*, August 26, 1996, p. A12.

20. See Steven Smith, *The American Congress* (Boston: Houghton Mifflin, 1995), p. 162.

21. See Angus Campbell, Philip Converse, Warren Miller, and Donald Stokes, *The American Voter* (New York: Wiley, 1960).

22. Norman Nie, Sidney Verba, and John Petrocik, *The Changing American Voter* (Cambridge, MA: Harvard University Press, 1979), reprinted in Richard Niemi and Herbert Weisberg, *Classics in Voting Behavior* (Washington, DC: CQ Press, 1993), p. 244.

23. Eric R. A. N. Smith, *The Unchanging American Voter* (Berkeley: University of California Press, 1989).

24. Michael MacKuen, Robert Erikson, and James Stimson, "Macropartisanship," *American Political Science Review,* 83, no. 4 (Winter 1989): 1125–42; unless otherwise indicated, all of the statistics on party identification and behavior that follow in this chapter are from Harold W. Stanley and Richard G. Niemi, *Vital Statistics on American Politics, 1997–1998* (Washington, DC: CQ Press, 1998).

25. Times Mirror Center, *The New Political Landscape*, p. 48.

26. Times Mirror Center, *The New Political Landscape*, p. 48.

27. Times Mirror Center, *The New Political Landscape*, p. 58.

28. See MacKuen, Erikson, and Stimson, "Macropartisanship."

29. This analysis is from Paul Starobin, "Party Hoppers," *National Journal,* February 7, 1998, pp. 276–81.

30. The Pew Research Center for The People & The Press, *Democratic Congressional Chances Helped by Clinton Ratings* (Washington, DC: Pew Research Center, April 1998).

31. Martin P. Wattenberg, *The Decline of American Political Parties, 1952–1994* (Cambridge, MA: Harvard University Press, 1996), pp. 50, 72.

32. See Dennis W. Johnson, "Political Consulting: The Making of a Profession," paper prepared for the conference on "The Role of Political Consultants in Elections," Washington, DC, June 19, 1998; for an early introduction to the topic, see Larry Sabato, *The Rise of Political Consultants: New Ways of Winning Elections* (New York: Basic Books, 1981); for a recent summary of the state of the research on this topic, see the compendium of articles published in *PS: Political Science & Politics* 31 (June 1998).

33. The Pew Research Center for The People & The Press, *Don't Blame Us: The Views of Political Consultants* (Washington, DC: Pew Research Center, June 1998); the survey was conducted in association with American University's Center for Congressional and Presidential Studies, which is headed by James A. Thurber, and involved a random sample survey of two hundred consultants; available at <www.people-press.org>.

34. See James A. Thurber, Candice J. Nelson, and David A. Dulio, "The Consultants Speak: An Analysis of Campaign Professionals' Attitudes," paper prepared for the conference on "The Role of Political Consultants in Elections," Washington, DC, June 19, 1998.
35. Quoted in James Perry, "Win or Lose, Perot Proves One Can Run without Major Parties," *Wall Street Journal,* July 14, 1992, p. A1.

7

interest groups

a nation divided

The Founders not only ex-
pected Americans to divide into
factions, they guaranteed the right
to do so. Alongside its guarantees
of free religion and speech, the
First Amendment also established
the "right of the people to peaceably assemble, and to petition the
Government for a redress of grievances." The First Amendment
does not specifically mention factions, but it does permit the people to assemble in any fashion
they wish, including in associations of one kind or another. At
least for the Founders, liberty involved more than just the right to

pursue one's own happiness in solitude. It also included the right to pursue one's own happiness in association with others.

The Supreme Court endorsed this vision of association in a 1958 case involving the National Association for the Advancement of Colored People. The Alabama state attorney general had ordered the NAACP to provide a list of its members. Suspecting that the state intended to use the list to persecute its members, the NAACP refused to provide the list and was fined $100,000 by Alabama. The United States Supreme Court overturned the fine, arguing that the freedom to engage in association "for the advancement of beliefs and ideas is an inseparable aspect of the 'liberty'" assured by the First Amendment.[1]

The Supreme Court was merely seconding what French aristocrat Alexis de Tocqueville had noted in his *Democracy in America* almost 150 years earlier. "The most natural privilege of a man next to the right of acting for himself, is that of combining his exertions with those of his fellow creatures and of acting in common with them. The right of association therefore appears to be almost as inalienable in its nature as the right of personal liberty. No legislator can attack it without impairing the foundations of society."[2]

Yet, as strongly as the Founders believed in freedom of assembly, they worried about the pressures those associations might produce in the form of factions. It was one thing for an association to form to build a new school or church, but quite another for an association to come together to influence government. The first type of association is part of **civil society,** which consists of the informal associations that tie communities together without government involvement, while the second type acts as a go-between between government and the people.[3] In its simplest definition, civil society consists of everything that is neither individual nor governmental. As such, it covers everything from families to churches, and clearly includes associations and interest groups. An **association** is a formal or informal collection of individuals who come together for any purpose, be it a garden club or bowling league, while an **interest group** is an association that exists to represent a collection of individuals before government.

The Founders clearly wanted a strong civil society—families, churches, neighborhoods—and designed a government that would respect the rights of communities to solve their own problems in their own ways. They also worried about protecting and nurturing associations, in part because almost all the Founders were active members of associations themselves. Many were Freemasons, a fraternal society founded in England and imported to the colonies in 1733. (Check the back of a $1 bill for the eye in the pyramid, a Masonic symbol.)

At the same time, the Founders wanted a government that would be strong enough to prevent majorities from imposing their will on communities. After all, Shays's rebellion had involved an association of like-minded citizens who became a very real threat to both their communities and the nation. Had Shays and his friends just stayed home, their association would have been fully protected by the First Amendment. But the minute they started marching, they became subject to the full force of government. James Madison's famous line from *Federalist No. 10* is well worth repeating here: "You must first enable the government to control the governed; and in the next place, oblige it to control itself." Therein lies the delicate balance. Government cannot be so weak that associations and interest groups become a threat to society, nor can it be so strong that it becomes the threat itself. Letting associations flourish while preventing the tyranny of strong-willed majorities is a delicate balancing act, indeed.

The challenge is to maintain that balance in an era when the United States has been inundated by interest groups. Never have so many interest groups used so many tools to influence so much of what government does. Washington, D.C., is filled with lobbyists representing one organization or another; most of the nation's businesses have their own lobbyists, as do most big universities. Not everyone is represented, however. Children, the poor, and young Americans are poorly organized, if at all, and have none of the resources that enable most interest groups to succeed. They cannot mount million-dollar advertising campaigns against tobacco legislation, and cannot get most members of Congress to return their phone calls.

This chapter examines the role of interest groups in government in three sections. The first provides a history of interest groups, how they are regulated by government, and the current status of the lobbying industry. The second asks why interest groups form, how they survive over time, how groups differ from each other, and who does and does not join. The third and final section reviews how interest groups influence government, and why some groups are more successful in lobbying than others.

A BRIEF HISTORY OF INTEREST GROUPS

The United States has always been a nation of joiners. No one made the point more elegantly than Tocqueville, who attributed America's success to those associations:

> Americans of all ages, all stations in life, and all types of disposition are forever
> forming associations. There are not only commercial and industrial associations

French aristocrat Alexis de Tocqueville (1805–1859). Tocqueville remains one of the most influential thinkers about the role of voluntary associations in American democratic life.

in which all take part, but others of a thousand different types—religious, moral, serious, futile, very general and very limited, immensely large and very minute. . . . Nothing, in my view, deserves more attention than the intellectual and moral associations in America.[4]

A century and a half later, the United States is still a nation of joiners. According to the *Encyclopedia of Associations,* there were nearly 23,000 formal associations in 1998, a number that had grown by ten a week since the early 1970s. The list ran the gamut from A to Z, from the Automotive Booster Clubs International to the ZZ Top International Fan Club, and included trade and business groups, environmental and agricultural organizations, arts and culture clubs, fraternities and sororities, soccer and softball teams, and fan clubs.

How Many Interest Groups Are There?

Americans do not just join formal associations for help with their gardens or to talk about ancient rock stars, however. They also join to influence who gets what, when, and how from government. Such associations are called interest groups. The ZZ Top Fan Club would be classified as an interest group only if it suddenly decided to take a stand against music censorship and began lobbying government. The term **lobbying** refers to efforts to influence government, whether by providing information, building public support, or influencing elections.

Americans may say that Washington lobbyists wield too much power, but many of those lobbyists work for them. Roughly half of all Americans belong to an organization that lobbies government in some form or another. Even people who swear they would never join a lobbying group may be far more active than they think. For example, people who buy Girl Scout cookies make a small contribution to the organization's effort to stop government from taxing charities.[5]

Because there is no simple count of the number of U.S. interest groups, scholars must use surrogate measures of one kind or another. According to one recent survey, fifteen thousand people now earn their living as lobbyists, influencing government on behalf of interest groups. "All are advocates for some*one* or some*thing*," write the editors of the *Washington Representatives* phone book. "Together they have much to say about how this country is governed."[6] One-third of these representatives work for business groups, professional associations, and labor unions; one-fifth are lawyers who handle legal issues for those same interests; one-sixth represent special causes such as abortion rights or school prayer; another sixth work for traditional membership groups and professional associations such as the American Medical Association; one-tenth work for business corporations that keep offices in Washington; two in one hundred work in Washington research organizations called *think tanks;* and just one in one hundred works for the political parties. When the people who work for lobbyists—doing research or speechwriting or the other tasks of lobbying—are added in, the number of people who depend on the industry for their livelihoods may now be approaching 100,000 in Washington, D.C., alone, not to mention the rising number of lobbyists who work in state capitals or big cities.

It is important to note that merely counting lobbyists may underestimate the true size of the Washington lobbying industry. The exact figures are hard to pin down, in part because some lobbyists do not want to be known. "My mother has never introduced me to her friends as 'my son, the lobbyist,'" one lobbyist reports. "My son, the Washington representative, maybe. Or the legislative consultant. Or the government-relations counsel. But never as the lobbyist."[7]

The Three Waves of Interest Group Formation

Many of the nation's best-known interest groups formed during the 1960s and 1970s. Common Cause, the National Organization for Women, the Public Interest Research Group, and the American Association of Retired Persons are all less than forty years old. It would be a mistake, however, to conclude that interest groups are a recent phenomenon. They have existed since the very first Congress, expanding to their current number in three great historical waves over the past two hundred years.[8]

Tocqueville's Travels. Before turning to the three waves, it is important to note Tocqueville's influence on current thinking about associations and interest groups.

Conservatives in both political parties refer to *Democracy in America* in calling for less government and arguing that communities know best how to solve their problems. Mentoring, tutoring, and other forms of voluntary action are seen as far more effective than government programs. In a recent essay advocating a return to small towns and preindustrial America, conservative columnist Michael Barone stopped just short of arguing that Tocqueville would have been a Republican.[9]

The question is not whether Tocqueville was right about America's passion for forming associations, but whether those associations were ever truly divorced from government. Were the associations he saw filling in the gaps between government and the people, or were they also lobbying government for goods and services? The answer appears to be the latter: there was more lobbying during Tocqueville's time than he noticed.

The fact is that interest groups preceded Tocqueville's visit by almost fifty years. As veteran *Wall Street Journal* reporter Jeffrey Birnbaum reports, the lobbyists were hard at work on the very first Congress in 1789, going to the heart, or stomach, of politics: "After each legislative day, hogsheads of wine and port poured freely at sumptuous meals of mutton, pork, duck, and turkey. The dinner linens were snowy white, the cutlery was burnished and English, and the check was paid by the wealthy merchants of the day."[10] The term *lobbyist* was used as early as the 1830s to describe individuals or groups who waited outside government chambers (that is, in lobbies) to plead the case for their clients. In the late 1840s future president James Buchanan wrote to his friend (and future president) Franklin Pierce that "the host of contractors, speculators, stockjobbers, and lobby members which haunt the halls of Congress . . . are sufficient to alarm every friend of this country."[11]

Much of this growth was fueled by a uniquely governmental intervention: the U.S. postal system. By linking Americans together, the system spurred the development of larger and more formal associations, some of which would inevitably find their way to lobbying. Indeed, according to Theda Skocpol's careful history of the formation of voluntary associations over the past two hundred years, the postal system even spawned its own antipostal lobbying, including the General Union for Promoting the Observance of the Christian Sabbath, which was dedicated to stopping the transportation of mail on Sundays. As Skocpol argues, Tocqueville "may have been ideologically blind to the ways in which the early U.S. national state created a framework that encouraged widespread voluntary associations."[12]

The First Wave.   As noted above, political scientists believe that interest groups do not appear in steady numbers. Instead, they seem to multiply in relatively short bursts, followed by longer periods of stability.[13]

Political scientists generally agree that the first wave of interest group formation began in 1830 and lasted roughly forty years. The key disturbance was the general upheaval over the rapidly growing nation, which gave rise to the American Medical Association (founded in 1847), the Young Men's Christian Association (1851), the National Education Association (1857), the National Grange (which represents farmers and was founded in 1867), the Elks (1868), and the American Anti-Slavery Society (1833). Although associations had certainly existed before the 1830s, the three decades leading up to the Civil War produced a host of Bible groups, Sunday schools, missionary societies, and community associations directly concerned with the moral life of their communities and the nation. The first temperance unions formed to oppose the moral decay brought on by "intoxicating" beverages, while the YMCA and other sports clubs called on Americans to get fit in both mind and body.[14]

Many of these organizations came together to oppose slavery, creating the first national lobbying coalitions of a sort. Led by the American Anti-Slavery Society, local abolition groups created intense political pressure in the North, even persuading state legislatures to censor local newspapers that dared print any story with a hint of support for slavery. The antislavery coalition held firm even after slavery had been abolished. Even though Lincoln issued the Emancipation Proclamation freeing the slaves in 1862, the Thirteenth Amendment abolishing slavery was not made part of the Constitution until 1865, while the Fifteenth Amendment giving former slaves the right to vote was not ratified until 1870. And, as Chapter 14 shows, new forms of racial discrimination emerged almost immediately after the Civil War.

The Second Wave.   The second wave of interest group formation began in the 1880s and also lasted forty years. (Some political scientists divide this second wave in two: the 1880s and the period 1900–1920.) Forged in the Industrial Revolution, the second wave was explicitly concerned with the changes wrought by the rise of the United States as a world economic power. Some of the nation's most familiar interest groups were formed during this period: the American Red Cross (1881), the National Association of Manufacturers (1895), the National Association for the Advancement of Colored People (1909), the U.S. Chamber of Commerce (1912), the American Cancer Society (1913), and the American Farm Bureau (1919).

Almost every demographic group imaginable formed an association during this wave, and many of the associations soon turned to lobbying. Wagon drivers formed the International Brotherhood of Teamsters to fight for higher wages and better working conditions, Spanish-American War and World War I veterans formed the Veterans of Foreign Wars (VFW) and the American Legion to protect their military pensions, women formed the National American Woman Suffrage Association to press for the right to vote, mothers formed the National Congress of Mothers (later the Parent–Teacher Association) to push for better schools, and retirees got the Fraternal Order of Eagles to push for enactment of old-age pensions. Boys and girls got their own associations: the first Boy Scout troop was formed in 1910, the first Girl Scout troop in 1912. Even racists got their own organization: the Ku Klux Klan was formed in 1925.

Some of the organizations were remarkably successful in influencing government. Temperance societies won a great victory when the Eighteenth Amendment was ratified, prohibiting the manufacture or transportation of intoxicating beverages in 1919; women won an equally dramatic but far more lasting victory in winning the right to vote when the Nineteenth Amendment was ratified one year later. (The Eighteenth Amendment was repealed by the Twenty-first Amendment in 1933.) As Skocpol writes, women's groups also won a series of victories on aid to children and mothers.

> Not only would most of these policies never have been enacted without the special ability of women's federations to coordinate morally focused public campaigns across communities and states, the women's federations themselves experienced great growth and geographical expansion at the same time as their legislative crusades. They also benefited from their ability to forge partnerships with government administrators, such as those in the Children's Bureau.[15]

The Third Wave.   The third wave began in the 1960s and continues to the present, driven in part by the civil rights movement, whose success led directly to the formation of a host of public interest groups on everything from the environment to handgun control. As new laws regulating business and society were passed, corporations responded by organizing their own groups. The Business Roundtable was created as a counterforce in 1972, followed by a number of smaller, more specialized lobbies for specific industries. Political scientists generally agree that there are roughly four times as many interest groups operating in Washington today as there were when the third wave began.

There is no better example of the link between social divisions and interest groups than the women's movement. With more and more women entering the workforce during the 1960s, concern about gender discrimination grew. Although Congress protected women against employment discrimination in the Civil Rights Act of 1964, complaints about uneven enforcement led a small group of women to found the National Organization for Women (NOW) in 1966. According to Betty Friedan, author of the landmark book *The Feminine Mystique* and one of the founders of NOW, the goal of the new organization was simple: "to take action to bring women into full participation in the mainstream of American society, *now*."[16]

NOW was only the first of a long list of women's groups, from the Women's Legal Defense Fund and the National Association of Working Women in the early 1970s to the Fund for a Feminist Majority in 1987. Not all the groups were in favor of women's liberation, however. As NOW and other feminist groups launched their campaign for the Equal Rights Amendment (ERA), which would have prohibited discrimination on the basis of gender, a host of anti-ERA groups formed—STOP-ERA, Females Opposed to Equality (FOE), American Women Against the Ratification of ERA (AWARE), and Happiness of Motherhood Eternal (HOME).

As the third wave continued through the 1970s, it began to generate a different kind of interest group built around single issues such as abortion rights and the ERA. These **single-issue groups** reflect a splintering of American social groups. Single-issue groups have emerged to promote auto safety (Center for Auto Safety) and prevent drunk driving (Mothers Against Drunk Driving); to protect animals (the Fund for Animals) and reduce pesticide abuse (the National Coalition Against the Misuse of Pesticides); to reduce violence on television (Action for Children's Television); and even to improve the way members of Congress organize their offices (the Congressional Management Foundation).

The third wave also marked an unprecedented strengthening of interest group operations. Interest groups are better staffed, equipped, and funded than at any point in history, and have become more sophisticated at lobbying. One reason is the growing number of university programs that are copying George Washington University's new Certificate in Lobbying. Another is the rising level of pay. As Box 7-1 indicates, they have become lucrative places to work—at least, that is, the ones that represent businesses and other professions such as law and medicine.

Hyperpluralism—A New Wave?

It is not clear when or if the third wave of interest group formation will come to an end. What is clear is that ever smaller, more specialized organizations continue to emerge. Some political scientists have labeled this trend **hyperpluralism,** meaning a vast expansion in both the number and intensity of interest groups. Hyperpluralism involves two separate but related patterns, both of which are well described by Robert Salisbury.[17]

First, there has been a dramatic increase in what Salisbury calls narrow "self-interested groups," meaning groups that lobby government for their own financial enrichment. No issue seems to exist that is too small to warrant a separate issue group. In agriculture, for example, wheat growers, soy growers, corn growers, peanut growers, even potato growers all have their own Washington-based interest groups, as do most commodity traders, food producers, and grocery manufacturers, not to mention fast food restaurant chains.

Second, there has been a parallel increase in the number of citizens' groups that are also narrowly focused, but mostly in the public interest. The Gay and Lesbian Alliance, People for the Ethical Treatment of Animals, the Center to Pre-

BOX 7-1

Interest Group Salaries, 1996

Organization	Chief Executive's Annual Salary
Recording Industry Association of America	$1,087,846
Motion Picture Association of America	921,377
National Football League Players Association/NFL Players Inc.	894,101
Reinsurance Association of America	714,315
National Cable Television Association	675,173
Association of American Railroads	674,751
Health Insurance Association of America	666,110
Mortgage Bankers Association of America	656,693
American Council of Life Insurance	614,739
National Soft Drink Association	605,657

Source: "Executive Compensation, Washington Style," *National Journal*, April 26, 1997, p. 804.

vent Handgun Violence, and the National Network of Hispanic Women are all examples of narrowly focused citizens' groups, as are many of the single-issue groups described above.

Together, these two trends have created an interest group community that is large and small at the same time. Whereas farmers used to be represented by a single interest group such as the American Farm Bureau Federation, they now have dozens of specialized product representatives; whereas doctors used to be represented almost exclusively by the American Medical Association, they now have hundreds of organizations divided by medical specialty.

As the number of narrow groups grows, the chances that they will reach common ground on major issues such as health care reform diminish. As Chapter 15 shows, the health care debate involves hundreds of groups battling one another to influence federal policy. Instead of increasing the chances that government will work too well, which the Founders feared most, this fragmentation increases the likelihood that government will not work at all.

Government Regulation of Interest Groups

The federal government did not get into the business of regulating interest groups until the 1930s, when Congress passed three narrow statutes, all of which were reactions to lobbying scandals. One involved the shipping industry, a second focused on electric power companies, and a third focused on the activities of foreign agents. All three required lobbyists to register with government. If the hope was that registration would somehow expose lobbying activity to the sunshine of public opinion, the first two statutes clearly failed because they did not require that the registration documents be made public. If the public and media could not find out who was doing the lobbying, they could hardly track possible corruption. Although the third statute, the 1938 Foreign Agents Registration Act, had stronger registration requirements, it went largely unenforced.

Congress sought to remedy the gaps in registration with the 1946 Federal Regulation of Lobbying Act, which involved another effort to register lobbyists. Although well-meaning, the act covered only lobbyists whose *principal purpose* was to influence legislation and only activities that involved *direct communication with members of Congress*. It did not apply to the thousands of part-time lobbyists who work in law firms nor to any of the indirect techniques that are used to influence legislation today. Some experts estimate that the law covered barely a third of the lobbyists who actually worked on Capitol Hill.[18]

The Lobbying Reforms of 1995.   In an effort to address these early failures, Congress in 1995 passed two additional laws that hold greater promise for bringing the lobbying process to light.

The lack of strong registration laws does not mean that interest groups were ever free to bribe members of Congress and federal officials. Bribery has long been against the law. Until 1995, however, many interest groups engaged in a petty form of bribery by giving "gifts" to members of Congress in the form of speaking fees, Christmas fruit baskets and wine, free travel to exotic destinations, meals, and tickets to sports events. The average lobbyist could spend between $5,000 and $15,000 a year just taking members of Congress to power lunches or dinners, a time-honored Washington tradition.[19]

Under pressure from the new Republican majority, Congress ended most of these practices in 1995. Because each chamber writes its own rules, the two versions of the gift ban were slightly different. The Senate put a $50 limit on the value of all gifts, including entertainment and meals, while the House banned all gifts regardless of amount.

In theory, the gift bans were designed to end all appearances that lobbyists were buying access through gifts. However, because each ban contained its own loopholes, they may have created a whole new industry of interpretation in Washington, deciding just what constitutes a free meal. As long as food comes on a toothpick, for example, it is exempt from the ban on free meals. But once food lies on a plate or is covered by gravy, which means that it must be eaten with a fork or spoon, it becomes a meal. Breakfast is a particularly tough meal to regulate. "Coffee and doughnuts are OK," said one expert. "Croissants are probably all right. But I get a lot of questions about bagels and what you can put on them. Lox may be pushing it."[20] Actually, lobbyists found ways around the ban within days of its passage. For example, the House allows free travel and meals at "widely attended events," meaning that members now tend to eat with lobbyists at larger tables. In fact, Washington home remodelers reported a surge in business following the gift ban as lobbyists remodeled their homes to accommodate parties of more than twenty-five, the threshold for a "widely attended event."

Alongside the gift ban, Congress undertook a major reform of the 1946 registration act. Under the Lobby Disclosure Act of 1995, all lobbyists who seek to influence Congress, congressional staff, or policymaking officials of the executive branch (meaning the president, White House staff, and agency and department officials) were required to make themselves known. Only lobbyists who make less than $5,000 during a six-month period, or who spend less than $20,000 on lobbying activities, were exempted.

The Lobbying Industry

The Lobby Disclosure Act revealed a huge industry. During the first six months of 1997 alone, the lobbying industry spent more than $600 million, or $100 million a month, influencing government. At that spending rate, lobbying expenditures would hit $1.2 billion for the year. On a monthly average, lobbyists spend more than the two major political parties, three presidential candidates (Clinton, Dole, and Perot), and roughly one thousand Senate and House candidates spent to wage their campaigns for office in 1996.

The big spenders were almost all private interests, a confirmation of E. E. Schattschneider's observation that the interest group "chorus sings with a strong upper class accent."[21] The American Medical Association headed the top ten list at $8.6 million, followed by the Chamber of Commerce, Phillip Morris (tobacco), General Motors, Edison Electric Institute (an association of utility companies), Pfizer (chemicals), United Technologies Corporation (defense), AT&T, General Electric, and Citicorp. There were only two citizens groups among the top twenty spenders: the Christian Coalition at $4 million and the American Association of Retired Persons at $3.7 million. Over one hundred organizations were charter members of the million-dollar club, spending an average of $170,000 a month on lobbying. Almost all are businesses or their trade associations.

 **in a different light** ———   A WEB OF INFLUENCE

Political scientists have long known that interest groups often work together in efforts to influence government. As Chapter 15 shows, these *issue networks* come together around a specific issue such as health care reform or tobacco legislation, and break up when the goal is achieved. Issue networks are quite unlike *iron triangles,* which involve close ties among an interest group, a government agency, and a congressional committee. Whereas iron triangles are welded together in support of their goal, issue networks last only as long as needed. More like Velcro than metal, they come together and rip apart easily.

In between issue networks and iron triangles are what might be called *ideological webs,* collections of research organizations, interest groups, private donors, and selected media outlets that share a general ideological view of the world and come together to provide mutual support and encouragement. Members of such a web might oppose each other on a particular legislative goal but have a common bond created by ideological fervor.

Central to the survival of ideological webs is money. Someone has to give the dollars to fund the research and support the lobbying. The Political Club for Growth provides just that kind of support on behalf of conservative causes.[22] Created in the early 1980s to support the Reagan Revolution, the club involves fifty or so of the most committed private donors. Led by Richard Gilder, a New York investment banker, and nine other wealthy donors, the club has provided millions to support a web of conservative activities. "We're already wealthy," said Gilder of the club's motivation. "We formed the club because of what we think is good for America."

Others are dubious about the underlying motive, echoing Madison's notion that a faction is a faction is a faction. "When the network is revealed and the layers are peeled back and the connections are illustrated," says one expert in campaign finance reform, "it's much more a very sophisticated and deliberate interweaving of private and public interest. . . . If their contributions helped [Speaker of the House Newt] Gingrich engineer the revolution to create an extremely pro-business climate on Capitol Hill, then this is a wise investment for these interests."

The web supported by the Political Club for Growth involves a broad mix of players, including **GOPAC,** which is the campaign finance arm that helped elect the

Republican majority in 1994; U.S. Term Limits, a membership group that lobbies to limit the number of terms a member of Congress can serve; and the *National Review*, a leading conservative print magazine. It also includes three leading conservative research institutes, or think tanks: the Cato Institute, which takes a libertarian view of the world; the Manhattan Institute, which argues for business-oriented solutions to urban problems; and the Progress & Freedom Foundation, which provided much of the thinking behind the Republican Contract with America. (See Box 7–2 on pages 254–255 for a diagram of this web.)

Members of the club meet once a month to discuss public policy issues (with abortion and other social policy issues strictly off-limits) and to meet legislative candidates who might need a dollar or two to be competitive. The club is united by a broad concern not with conservative social causes, but with economic growth and less government—hence, its support for the Cato and Manhattan Institutes, but not the much more conservative Heritage Foundation. The club is unique in its willingness to invest in building a long-term movement that may well outlast many of today's single-issue groups. Its latest investment? The "Leave Us Alone Coalition."

WHY INTEREST GROUPS FORM, HOW THEY SURVIVE, WHERE THEY DIFFER, AND WHO DOES AND DOES NOT JOIN

Interest groups do not form by accident. Almost all are formed by entrepreneurs who create an interest group to meet some demand for action. Some entrepreneurs start the process by identifying an issue, seeking members who agree with their cause, and only then building an organization to do the lobbying. Others start by identifying a group of potential members who might join a group, building an organization, and only then identifying an issue to lobby. Still others start with a single member, usually a corporation that wants to influence government, which hires an entrepreneur to build an organization to do the lobbying.

Disturbance Theory

Building an interest group is much easier when the demand for action is high. According to **disturbance theory**, the demand for action is highest during periods of economic and social unrest—the period leading up to the Civil War, the Indus-

BOX 7-2

An Ideological Web

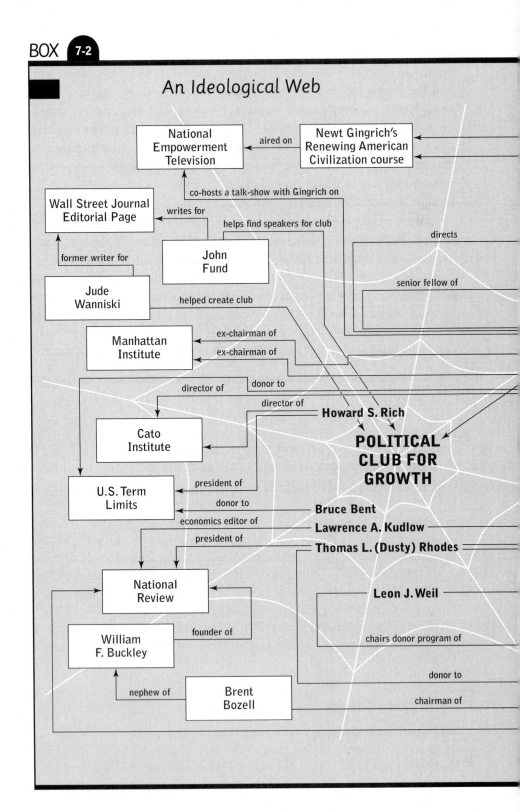

National
Empowerment
Television

← aired on — Newt Gingrich's
Renewing American
Civilization course

Wall Street Journal
Editorial Page

← writes for

co-hosts a talk-show with Gingrich on

helps find speakers for club

directs

senior fellow of

former writer for

John
Fund

Jude
Wanniski

helped create club

Manhattan
Institute

← ex-chairman of
← ex-chairman of

director of — donor to

director of — Howard S. Rich

Cato
Institute

**POLITICAL
CLUB FOR
GROWTH**

U.S. Term
Limits

← president of

← donor to — **Bruce Bent**

economics editor of — **Lawrence A. Kudlow**

president of — **Thomas L. (Dusty) Rhodes**

National
Review

Leon J. Weil

chairs donor program of

William
F. Buckley

founder of

donor to

nephew of — Brent
Bozell

chairman of

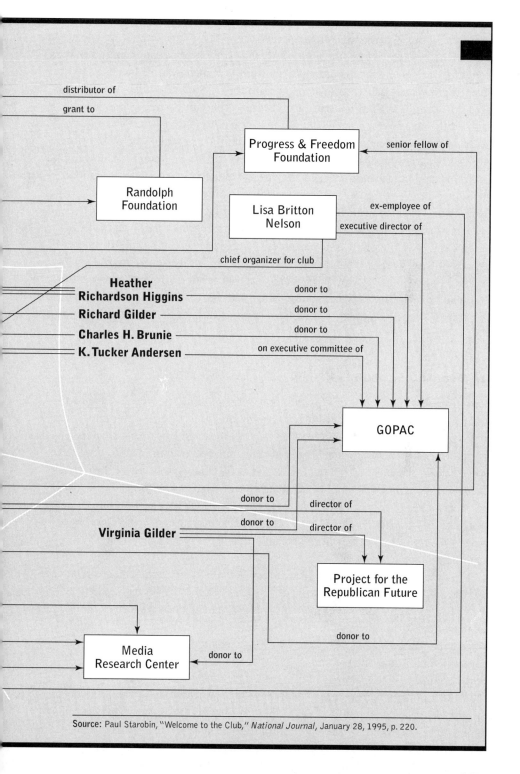

distributor of

grant to

Progress & Freedom Foundation

senior fellow of

Randolph Foundation

Lisa Britton Nelson

ex-employee of

executive director of

chief organizer for club

Heather Richardson Higgins — donor to

Richard Gilder — donor to

Charles H. Brunie — donor to

K. Tucker Andersen — on executive committee of

GOPAC

donor to

director of

donor to

director of

Virginia Gilder

Project for the Republican Future

donor to

Media Research Center

donor to

Source: Paul Starobin, "Welcome to the Club," *National Journal,* January 28, 1995, p. 220.

trial Revolution, the Great Depression, and the 1960s.[23] The angrier people are with the state of the nation, the more likely they will be to join an interest group.

Social or economic disturbances may also lead members of already existing interest groups to create their own distinct groups. The manufacturers of computers and silicon chips did not exist as a distinct economic force much before the late 1960s, and felt reasonably well represented by traditional business associations until a decade or so later. That is clearly not the case today. As the information superhighway moves from abstract fantasy to reality, computer makers, chip designers, and information specialists have created their own lobbying operations, including the American Software Association (founded in 1982), the Interactive Multimedia Association (1988), and the Computer Literacy Council (1992).

As American society becomes more complex, the number of social disturbances can only increase. That means, in turn, that the community of interest groups will inevitably expand, even as the interests represented by each new group become more narrow. The ability of big interest groups, such as the National Association of Manufacturers, to hold on to their membership may weaken, and smaller industries may become more likely to break off.

What Interest Groups Provide to Their Members

Once established, interest groups cannot survive unless they provide benefits to their members. Members join interest groups in search of one or more of four types of benefits: (1) a *material benefit* that comes back to members, such as tax breaks, higher benefit payments, government protections, even new roads; (2) a *social benefit,* which some political scientists also call a *solidary benefit,* that gives members the simple pleasure of working together; (3) a *civic benefit* that gives members a sense that they are doing something good for their community or nation; and (4) a *policy benefit,* which some political scientists call an *expressive* or *purposive benefit,* that comes from actually influencing government in a way that helps the nation as a whole.

According to political scientists Sidney Verba, Kay Lehman Schlozman, and Henry Brady, most Americans do not join interest groups for policy benefits. Rather, most people join either to obtain material benefits that come back to them as individuals or for the civic benefits that come from fulfilling their civic duty.[24] (As Chapter 8 shows, the prospect of civic and material benefits also affects other forms of political participation, including voting, giving money to campaigns, and writing letters to members of Congress.)

Recruiting new members to an interest group involves more than offering a simple list of benefits, however. As economist Mancur Olson has shown, a truly rational person would never join a group if he or she could receive the benefits

Members of the radical activist group ACT UP put pressure on the 1992 presidential candidates for action on AIDS. People join ACT UP in part to gain the material benefits that might come from more funding for research and treatment (the slogan "VOTE AS IF YOUR LIFE DEPENDS ON IT" is very much about material benefits). They can also reap social benefits by working together with others affected by the disease, civic benefits by doing something good for the nation, and policy benefits by actually influencing government decisions for those who will contract AIDS in the future.

without investing the time, effort, or expense involved in belonging to the group. Economists call this the **free rider problem.** The free rider problem can be solved only if (1) the interest group is so small that one more member would truly enhance the interest's power, (2) the benefits are reserved exclusively for the member or members, or (3) the organization can force the member to join—say, in order to get a professional credential or license.[25]

Although the rationality argument is compelling in many cases, economists may underestimate the role of altruism, or unselfishness, in explaining why people join groups. After all, some people do join groups simply because they believe in the cause. Nevertheless, the theory helps explain why interest groups try to limit **collective benefits,** which are available to everyone in society whether they are members of the interest group or not.

Some collective benefits are inevitable. All elderly people prosper when the American Association of Retired Persons (AARP) wins a Social Security benefit increase, for example; all nature lovers benefit when the Sierra Club wins greater protection for the national parks. Neither benefit can be denied to nonmembers and is thus a collective good. If such collective benefits are too great, however, every potential member will prefer to be a free rider, getting the benefits without the cost, even if such selfish behavior eventually kills the interest group itself.

Since interest groups cannot avoid collective benefits completely, they often control for the free rider problem by offering an attractive inventory of **selective benefits,** which are available only to members. The more attractive the selective benefits are, the more rational membership becomes.

Providing selective benefits is exactly how AARP got to be 33 million members strong. A yearly membership fee of just $8 entitles any American over the age of fifty to a host of discounted services: automobile and travel clubs, life and health insurance, prescription drugs by mail, magazine subscriptions, even a mutual fund. Most members join for the selective material benefits they get as individuals, not for the government influence they get as part of a collective whole.

Types of Interest Groups

Before turning to key differences between interest groups, it is important to highlight two essential points about the term *interest groups* itself. First, as noted at the beginning of this chapter, not all associations are interest groups. An association becomes an interest group only if it attempts to influence government.

Second, not all interest groups are voluntary associations. The term *interest groups* actually includes two different kinds of organizations: membership groups and nonmembership groups. Even though it is perfectly acceptable to use the term *interest group* to describe the wide range of organizations seeking to influence government, it is no longer quite as precise. Using the word *group* implies that such organizations have more than one member, when, in fact, many interest groups have just one member, a corporation.

Types of Membership Groups.   There are six kinds of membership groups.[26] The vast majority represent specific types of people, whether racial minorities (the NAACP), women (NOW), gays and lesbians, victims of handgun violence, or professionals. Even clowns have their own association, the Clowns of America.

People are not the only kind of members, however. A **federation** is a membership group that actually has other membership organizations as members. The American Federation of Labor and Congress of Industrial Organizations (AFL-CIO) is the largest federation of all, bringing together millions of workers who belong to different unions.

Other interest groups are built around large collections of individual corporations or small businesses. Such an interest group is generally labeled a **peak business association.** The National Federation of Independent Businesses represents millions of small businesses around the country, and became a key player in killing the Clinton administration's health care reform plan in 1994.

When an interest group's member companies, whether big or small, happen to come from a single industry—say, steel or computers—it is called a **trade association.** Some are "Goliaths," such as the National Association of Home Builders, which is composed of more than 100,000 contractors; others are tiny, including the Bow Tie Manufacturers Association.

When an interest group is built around members of a specific profession, it is called a **professional association.** There are hundreds of professional associations in health care, for example, including the American Academy of Family Physicians, American Academy of Ophthalmology, American Nurses Association, American Dental Association, American Optometric Association, and American Chiropractic Association. The hyperpluralism discussed above is driven in part by the recent expansion in such associations.

Finally, when an organization is built around people who come together to support a specific cause, it is usually labeled a **public interest group.** People who care about the environment might join the 650,000-member Sierra Club or the 5.6 million-member National Wildlife Federation; people who believe in an unfettered right to bear arms might join the 2.6 million-member National Rifle Association; people who support campaign finance reform might join the 270,000-member Common Cause or one of the state Public Interest Research Groups (PIRGs) set up by consumer advocate Ralph Nader in the 1970s; people who oppose abortion might join one of the three thousand local chapters of the National Right to Life Committee; those who support the right to abortion might join the 450,000-member National Abortion Rights Action League; those who worry about clean food might join the Pure Food Campaign, which claims celebrity chefs Wolfgang Puck, Julia Child, and Alice Waters as members.[27] As this list suggests, public interest groups range from liberal to conservative.

Nonmembership Groups. Membership groups are not the only organizations that try to influence government, however. The 1970s and 1980s witnessed an explosion in the number of interest groups with just one member. Corporations are perfect examples of nonmembership groups. Almost all of the *Fortune 500* companies have their own Washington lobbyists, and many of the top hundred have their own offices.

Consider the defense industry, which earns billions from the federal government making everything from tanks to toilet seats. The nation's top twenty-five private contractors spent over $38 million making their positions known to Congress in the first half of 1997. General Motors led the group at $5.2 million in lobbying expenditures, followed by United Technologies at $4.2 million, General Electric at $4.1 million, Northrop Grumman at $3.6 million, and Boeing at $2.9 million.

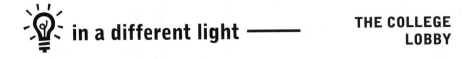 **in a different light** —————— THE COLLEGE LOBBY

American colleges and universities have never been more active in lobbying Congress for a larger share of the federal budget than they are today. Many have their own lobbyists in Washington, and almost all are members of interest groups such as the American Council on Education, the American Association of Universities, and the National Association of Independent Colleges and Universities that lobby on their behalf. The notion that "higher education couldn't organize its way out of a paper bag," as House Budget Committee chairman John Kasich (R-OH) once said, is no longer true.[28]

Few firms have done better at recruiting colleges and universities as clients than Cassidy and Associates, a Washington lobbying firm that earns hundreds of thousands of dollars in fees from schools ranging from Miami-Dade Community College to Golden Gate University to Northwestern University. And Cassidy is just one college lobbyist.

Colleges and universities are willing to spend that kind of money on lobbying for a reason, of course: each year, Congress spends billions of dollars on colleges and universities, whether in the form of student aid or special projects that are earmarked for specific universities. In 1998, for example, Congress set aside $495 million for specific projects around the country. California colleges and universities brought home the biggest share in 1998, winning nearly $60 million in earmarks, with Pennsylvania, Hawaii, Florida, New Mexico, and West Virginia following at or near $20 million. Only Rhode Island got nothing.

The fact that California did so well is hardly surprising. The state has a large concentration of colleges and universities, and also has a huge delegation of well-placed members of Congress to help it make its case. The question is how Hawaii, New Mexico, and West Virginia did so well. The answers are Daniel Inouye (D-HI), Pete Dominici (R-NM), and Robert Byrd (D-WV), all of whom sit on the Senate Appropriations Committee and work tirelessly to make sure their home states benefit in the competition for federal dollars. Two of Byrd's home state colleges were particularly lucky; Wheeling Jesuit University received nearly $10 million in earmarks for its National Technology Transfer Center, and Shepherdstown College got $3.22 million from the Department of Housing and Urban Development to enlarge its Scarborough Library.

Two problems with such earmarks are hardly restricted to colleges. (Recall the discussion of earmarking for state and local government from Chapter 3.) First, earmarks generally reduce the amounts of money available under both competitive and formula grant programs. For example, Congress's setting aside $495 million for university earmarks meant that other programs took at least some cuts. Although Congress increased the overall amount of money available under the Housing and Urban Development program that helped Shepherdstown, boosting the president's request from $50 million all the way to $138 million, it then earmarked roughly $100 million of the total, thereby cutting the competitive program by $12 million.

Second, as colleges and universities battle over the earmarks, broader higher education may get lost in the shuffle. Concerns about potential cuts in student support prompted the National Association of Independent Colleges and Universities and the American Council on Education to create the Alliance to Save Student Aid in 1995. Instead of lobbying on behalf of single colleges and universities, the alliance mobilized college students to demand an increase in federal funding for higher education in general. It set up toll-free telephone numbers that students could use to call their members of Congress and bought rush-hour radio commercials in the districts of key legislators. The effort appeared to work. When Congress finally passed its 1996 budget, student aid was left almost intact.[29]

Who Does and Does Not Join

People with social and economic resources are not the only Americans with a stake in what government does, of course, but they are the most likely to join an interest group. They have the economic incentive to join, the dollars to do so, and the skills to make contact. They also have the education to know why lobbying might matter. Finally, as James Q. Wilson argues, they may have the luxury to think about the longer term, investing in an interest group today in the full awareness that lobbying may take years to produce tangible legislative results.[30]

Box 7–3 shows the differences between people who join a political organization and people who do not. As the box reveals, people with incomes over $75,000 are three times more likely to join an interest group than people with incomes below $15,000, while whites are significantly more likely to join than are African Americans and Latinos. People who receive welfare benefits from govern-

BOX **7-3**

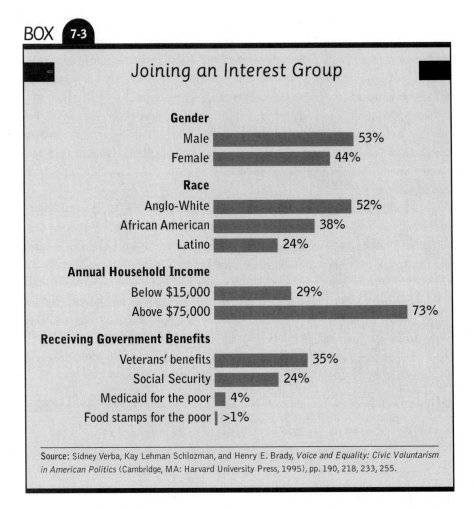

Joining an Interest Group

Gender
Male — 53%
Female — 44%

Race
Anglo-White — 52%
African American — 38%
Latino — 24%

Annual Household Income
Below $15,000 — 29%
Above $75,000 — 73%

Receiving Government Benefits
Veterans' benefits — 35%
Social Security — 24%
Medicaid for the poor — 4%
Food stamps for the poor — >1%

Source: Sidney Verba, Kay Lehman Schlozman, and Henry E. Brady, *Voice and Equality: Civic Voluntarism in American Politics* (Cambridge, MA: Harvard University Press, 1995), pp. 190, 218, 233, 255.

ment are the least likely of all Americans to join an interest group, as are people who are having trouble making ends meet. They either do not have the time and money to join or believe that joining would get them into trouble with government or be a waste of time.

Interestingly, Americans who receive government benefits on the basis of need are far less likely to join an interest group than those who get government benefits on the basis of service in the armed forces or from Social Security. Paradoxically, the more people seem to need special help from government, the less likely they are to join an interest group to get it.

This does not mean poor Americans have no representation in Washington. They are often represented through charitable groups such as the Children's Defense League, the Salvation Army, and the American Public Welfare Association, all of which lobby government in one way or another. And they have begun to form their own groups, such as the National Welfare Rights Organization. Nevertheless, when it comes time to make budget cuts or to make another run at welfare reform, those least likely to be involved in the process are the people most likely to be affected by it.

in a different light ——— WASHINGTON'S MOST POWERFUL INTEREST GROUPS

Fortune magazine conducted a remarkable opinion survey in 1997. The respondents were not ordinary Americans, and the questions did not deal with the issues of the day. Rather, the survey was of nearly two thousand Washington insiders, and the questions were about which interest groups had the greatest influence. Box 7-4 lists the 25 interest groups that ranked highest on *Fortune's* list.

    Fortune's "Power 25" list is notable both for who is on it and for who is not. Missing from the list are some of America's most active public interest groups: the Sierra Club, Common Cause, the Children's Defense Fund, the Natural Resources Defense Council. So are the tax reformers, most notably Americans for Tax Reform. As *Fortune* notes, fully half of the top ten groups (numbers 1, 4, 6, 7, and 10) are broad membership groups with active, intense memberships, and one other group (number 25) is the largest U.S. labor union.

    According to survey respondents, there are four simple sources of influence: (1) delivering the straight facts to lawmakers, (2) having active allies on Capitol Hill, (3) being able to mobilize members for letter-writing and phone-call campaigns, and (4) being able to get along with politicians and their staffs. According to the survey respondents, four tactics do not work: (1) providing volunteers during an election year (candidates can recruit their own), (2) buying media to promote the general cause, (3) buying media to attack a member of Congress for his or her stand, and (4) retaining high-priced lobbyists in Washington.

    There is only one problem with the *Fortune* list: asking members of Congress and other recipients of lobbying pressure to reveal what works and what does not is rather like asking a fox how best to build a chicken coop. Chapter 4's discussion of public opinion noted that members of Congress have ample reason *not* to tell a pollster just which tricks work best for winning a legislative campaign. To the contrary,

BOX 7-4

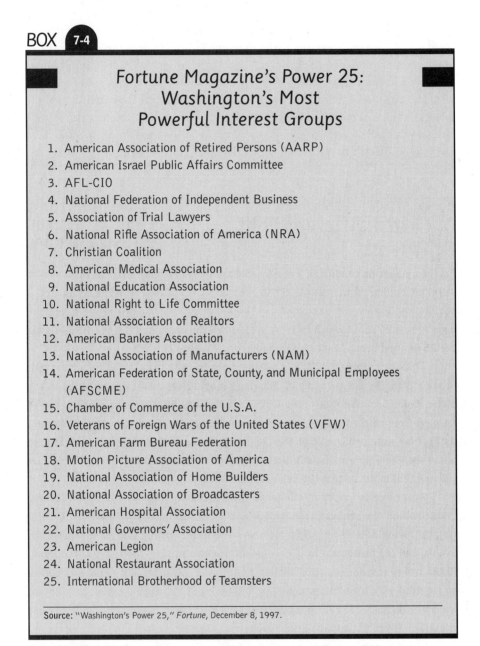

Fortune Magazine's Power 25: Washington's Most Powerful Interest Groups

1. American Association of Retired Persons (AARP)
2. American Israel Public Affairs Committee
3. AFL-CIO
4. National Federation of Independent Business
5. Association of Trial Lawyers
6. National Rifle Association of America (NRA)
7. Christian Coalition
8. American Medical Association
9. National Education Association
10. National Right to Life Committee
11. National Association of Realtors
12. American Bankers Association
13. National Association of Manufacturers (NAM)
14. American Federation of State, County, and Municipal Employees (AFSCME)
15. Chamber of Commerce of the U.S.A.
16. Veterans of Foreign Wars of the United States (VFW)
17. American Farm Bureau Federation
18. Motion Picture Association of America
19. National Association of Home Builders
20. National Association of Broadcasters
21. American Hospital Association
22. National Governors' Association
23. American Legion
24. National Restaurant Association
25. International Brotherhood of Teamsters

Source: "Washington's Power 25," *Fortune*, December 8, 1997.

they have every incentive to tell pollsters that what works is for interest groups to be straightforward and nice. They also have every reason to assure pollsters that spending lots of money on issue-oriented ads against a member does not work. That is how incumbents stay incumbents.

INFLUENCING GOVERNMENT

Lobbying is a sophisticated business, with legions of well-dressed Washington lawyers plying their trade in the corridors of power on Capitol Hill and the White House. Successful lobbying today depends on far more than just showing up at a senator's or House member's office to make the case on behalf of the elderly or a local college. It also involves a host of efforts, small and large, to focus legislative attention on a specific issue, none of which will matter to the final outcome if the interest group does not have the two basic elements of success: (1) resources and (2) influence. Each of these aspects of successful lobbying will be discussed below.

Resources

An interest group's influence depends on several broad measures of strength, including size, intensity, and money. First, there is clearly power in size. In theory, or so the largest interests argue, size translates into votes on election day. Many divide their membership lists by congressional district, all the better to show Congress just what might be at stake on a given issue in a future election. Many also publish box scores of key legislative votes to remind Congress that someone is watching.

It is AARP's 33 million members, for example, that give its lobbyists such influence in the halls of Congress. AARP's new Washington headquarters employs a full-time lobbying staff of eighteen, and generates so much incoming and outgoing mail that it has earned its own zip code. AARP also has 251,000 legislative volunteers across the country ready to organize a letter-writing campaign on the latest Social Security or Medicare crisis.[31]

However, large groups may be sluggish when it comes time to compromise on major legislation. It is like turning an aircraft carrier in rough seas. Being a very big ship creates certain advantages—not the least of which is the fear it strikes into the enemy—but it also limits mobility.

Second, there is power in intensity. Size is useless if members are not fully committed to the cause. Groups that are small but intense may be much more successful than ones that are large but ambivalent. Large groups may have difficulty reaching agreement on what they want, and may be unable to rally their members around controversial positions.[32] To keep members happy, they often adopt the least controversial positions, and may have problems deciding to act at all.

Third, there is power in money. Whether raised through dues, magazine subscriptions (the Consumers Union, for example, publishes *Consumer Reports*), or grants from private foundations and government, money pays for the essentials of organizational survival: staff, rent, lobbyists, advertising, printing, postage, heat, and light. Half of AARP's $300 million yearly budget comes from

President Clinton addresses the American Association of Retired Persons. Its more than 33 million members give AARP significant influence on the federal government's aging policy.

its membership dues, the other half from member fees for the discounted services mentioned earlier.

Influence

Gone are the days when a hogshead of wine was enough to secure the support of a member of Congress. According to a survey of Washington representatives by political scientist Ronald Hrebenar, interest groups do many things to lobby government. Some they do regularly (alerting clients about issues); others they do sparingly (filing an **amicus brief,** which is from the term *amicus curiae,* meaning friend of the court, to make their position on a case known to the Court); still others they do just once every few years (providing money to campaigns). (See Box 7–5 for Hrebenar's list of activities.)

All these activities are designed for just one purpose, however: *to apply an interest group's resources to a specific position on who gets what, when, and how from government.* Members of Congress can hardly help an interest group if they do

BOX 7-5

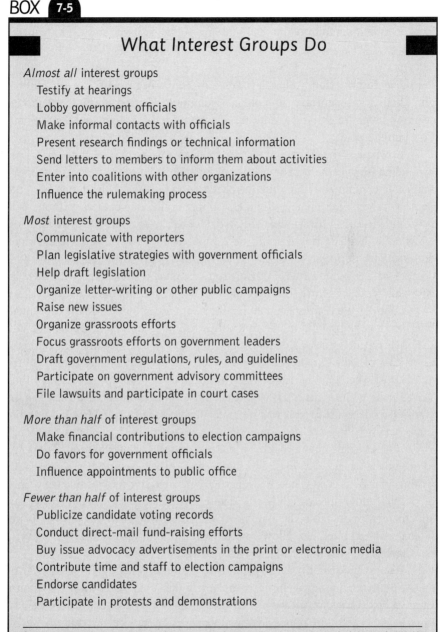

What Interest Groups Do

Almost all interest groups
    Testify at hearings
    Lobby government officials
    Make informal contacts with officials
    Present research findings or technical information
    Send letters to members to inform them about activities
    Enter into coalitions with other organizations
    Influence the rulemaking process

Most interest groups
    Communicate with reporters
    Plan legislative strategies with government officials
    Help draft legislation
    Organize letter-writing or other public campaigns
    Raise new issues
    Organize grassroots efforts
    Focus grassroots efforts on government leaders
    Draft government regulations, rules, and guidelines
    Participate on government advisory committees
    File lawsuits and participate in court cases

More than half of interest groups
    Make financial contributions to election campaigns
    Do favors for government officials
    Influence appointments to public office

Fewer than half of interest groups
    Publicize candidate voting records
    Conduct direct-mail fund-raising efforts
    Buy issue advocacy advertisements in the print or electronic media
    Contribute time and staff to election campaigns
    Endorse candidates
    Participate in protests and demonstrations

Source: Adapted from Ronald J. Hrebenar, *Interest Group Politics in America,* 3rd ed. (Armonk, NY: M. E. Sharpe, 1998), p. 154.

not know what the interest group wants. Although all the activities involve an effort to focus government attention, the list can be collapsed into three basic activities: (1) providing information, (2) building public support, and (3) influencing elections.

Providing Information.   Most legislative decisions begin with simple information about a problem and its potential solutions. That is why interest groups spend so much time trying to educate Congress, the presidency, and the Supreme Court on the issues.

Nowhere is the effort to inform more aggressive than on Capitol Hill. Lobbyists often supply the first draft of a bill, provide most of the witnesses that testify before committees, and write the background papers that find their way into floor speeches by members. Congress simply could not operate without help from lobbyists. Democrats were shocked, *shocked,* in early 1995 to see business lobbyists sitting side by side with new Republican House committee chairmen drafting bills, scripting legislative hearings, and planning ways to undo four decades of Democratic rule. Democrats had similar relationships with their favorite lobbyists, of course, but were more skilled at keeping the contacts discreet.

Lobbyists do not restrict their focus to Congress, however. Many use amicus briefs to provide background arguments to the courts on key cases. Not all amicus briefs are on the same side, of course. In 1984, for example, the U.S. Supreme Court case of *Sony Corporation of America v. Universal City Studios* turned on the question of whether Americans were free to tape television programs with their VCRs. In all, 140 amicus briefs were filed, most from corporations involved in the high-stakes decision (which was ultimately decided in favor of free taping), but some were from free-speech groups such as the American Civil Liberties Union.[33]

Amicus briefs offer a relatively low-cost option for interest groups to weigh in on judicial issues. While filing a suit is both expensive and time-consuming, writing an amicus brief is not. It is a particularly attractive tool for relatively small or poorly funded interest groups to demonstrate their commitment to an issue and thereby to increase the likelihood that they will grow bigger and better funded. Amicus briefs also allow interest groups to introduce new arguments that may have been ignored at earlier stages of a case.

Interest groups also participate in the formal rulemaking process used by federal departments and agencies to implement the laws. Under the 1946 Administrative Procedure Act, all proposed rules must be made public before they go into effect. During this "notice and comment" period, any citizen can provide his or her views of the proposed rule. This process was explicitly designed to create greater public participation in how government executes the laws, but has clearly favored certain kinds of lobbyists over the years. Not surprisingly (given the earlier discussions of the role of money and skills in who joins interest groups), the available evidence suggests that businesses are by far the most active participants. In a detailed study of recent efforts to tighten automobile emission standards, reduce hazardous waste, and limit acid rain, Marissa Martino Golden finds that businesses accounted for 80 percent of all comments received. Labor unions, professional associations, and individual citizens accounted for exactly *zero* comments on these key rules, while public interest groups accounted for barely 1 or 2 percent.[34]

Why are business groups so active in the rulemaking process? First, they have the dollars to monitor the process so that they know just when the notice and comment process will begin. Second, they have the dollars to pay someone to write the comments and they know where to send them. Unlike public interest groups, which must decide where to allocate their scarce organizational dollars, business groups can cover all the odds, thereby increasing the chances that they will either win their point or stalemate the system.

Finally, interest groups seek the appointment of sympathetic officials to top government jobs. Every new presidential administration must fill roughly six hundred top jobs, including cabinet secretaries, agency administrators, and a host of lesser positions. By lobbying for the appointment of friends and colleagues to those posts, interest groups increase the chances that their phone calls will be returned. And by giving jobs to government officials when they leave office, interest groups increase their stature and influence with whoever comes behind. Although laws against bribery and corruption prohibit interest groups from offering a current government official a job in return for a favorable policy decision, interest groups are free to hire a former government official to twist the arms of his or her old friends. It was precisely to close this *revolving door* that the Ethics in Government Act was enacted in 1978, requiring executive branch officials to wait a year before lobbying their former departments and agencies.

Building Public Support. As noted in Chapter 4, Washington, D.C., likes nothing better than a good public opinion poll. Members of Congress and presidents clearly pay attention to what the people think, if not to make final decisions, then at the very least to help set the agenda of issues they will address. That is why interest groups spend so much energy building and showing public support for their issues.

If an interest group is large enough, of course, the action of its own members is often enough to get attention. Letter-writing campaigns, telegrams, telephone trees, petitions, and marches are all time-honored methods for demonstrating member interest. Merely producing a million form letters is far less effective than generating highly personalized, handwritten requests. The latter are seen as true grassroots public demand, while the former are often dismissed by Congress as manufactured, or what some members call "astroturf," support. The more personal and individual the letter, the more likely Washington is to take it seriously.

As members of Congress have become more sophisticated at detecting manufactured campaigns, interest groups and consulting firms have become more sophisticated at disguising them. Some use computer programs that change a word or two in every letter, make typographical errors, and produce actual signatures. Others send their members long-distance phone cards with just enough time to make a personal call. Still others will even pay consulting firms to troll a state or congressional district for potential supporters. Working from lists of registered voters, these firms call thousands of citizens a night in search of the handful who might be willing to send a telegram, write a letter, or call their member of Congress to demand action. Anyone who wants to call their member is merely patched through to Capitol Hill at no cost. Such action is still astroturf, but it feels to Congress like real grassroots.

For smaller interest groups or on highly controversial issues in which more than one interest group might be involved, a mail campaign may not be enough. Many interest groups have started to use paid advertising to persuade the American public to support their cause, hoping that public opinion polls will create momentum behind their preferred option. This *issue advocacy advertising,* as it is labeled, was particularly visible during the 1993–1994 debate over health care reform. Americans were treated to a media barrage, including advertisements featuring "Harry and Louise," a sympathetic couple (portrayed by actors) who wondered what government involvement might do to their health care.

Issue advocacy is defined as a communication to the public whose primary purpose is to promote a set of ideas or policies. Such advocacy is clearly protected by the Constitution and honors a long tradition of public advocacy that dates back to the *Federalist Papers* and Thomas Paine's anonymous pamphlets. In recent years, however, issue advocacy has begun to seep over into the campaign season, becoming a potent and largely unregulated form of campaign advertising. Whereas candidates and parties are governed by tight federal rules on how they raise and spend money for what the Supreme Court calls "express advocacy" regarding the election or defeat of a candidate, issue advocacy is completely unregulated. As long as an issue advertisement does not include what experts call the Supreme Court's "magic words"—"vote for," "vote against," "cast your ballot for," or "support candidate X"—it is not subject to any government regulation. (Box 7–6 provides examples from three recent issue advocacy campaigns.)

According to one recent estimate, the 1996 election involved roughly $150 million in issue advocacy advertisements, many of which came inches from the line that would have made them express advocacy.[35] In the 1996 congressional election in Montana, for example, a conservative issue group called Citizens for Reform ran an advertisement attacking Democratic House candidate Bill Yellowtail. "Who is Bill Yellowtail?" the ad asked. "He preaches family values, but he

BOX 7-6

Issue Advocacy Advertisements

"ILLINOIS"

Announcer: "Some things are wrong. They've always been wrong. And no matter how many politicians say they're right, they're still hateful and wrong. Stand up for the right values. Call Representative Richard Durbin today. Ask him why he voted against the Flag Protection Amendment. Against the values we hold dear. The Constitutional Amendment to safeguard our flag, because America's values are worth protecting."

Sponsor: Citizens Flag Alliance, founded by the American Legion in 1994 to lobby Congress in support of a constitutional amendment to protect the flag.

"CHILDREN"

Announcer: "Smoking cigarettes kills. Every day 3,000 kids start smoking. The addiction will kill one out of three. The FDA wants to stop the tobacco companies from targeting our children. But last year your Congressman— Gary Franks—who's taken over $49,000 from big tobacco companies— lobbied the FDA to back off. He's put the interests of big tobacco before our children. Tell Congressman Franks to stop protecting big tobacco companies and start protecting our children."

Sponsor: Tobacco Accountability Project, a coalition of consumer and health advocacy groups supporting stricter federal regulations to prevent teen smoking, is affiliated with Ralph Nader's Public Citizen.

"PEGGY"

Peggy: "My name is Peggy Phillips. I was clinically dead twice. I had no pulse. And no blood flow to my brain. It was cardiac arrest. Doctors implanted a medical device that can shock my heart to keep me alive. My implant's special battery needs changing from time to time. But unfortunately, it may no longer be made because of the threat of frivolous product liability lawsuits. Congress passed product liability reform legislation. Mr. President, won't you please sign this bill? I might not be lucky the third time around."

Sponsor: Citizens for a Sound Economy, founded in 1984, a grassroots advocacy organization active in debates on regulatory reform, tax policy, free trade, and the size of government.

Source: Deborah Beck, Paul Taylor, Jeffrey Stanger, and Douglas Rivlin, *Issue Advocacy Advertising during the 1996 Campaign* (Philadelphia: Annenberg Public Policy Center, 1997).

took a swing at his wife. And Yellowtail's explanation? He 'only slapped her.' But her nose was broken."

Although the ad never said, "Vote against Bill Yellowtail," its purpose was unmistakable. But because it did not include any of the "magic words," it was defined as issue advocacy. As a result, Citizens for Reform was not required to follow any of the rules that governed Yellowtail as he struggled unsuccessfully to refute the charges, which eventually were proved to be true.

Influencing Elections.   Once an interest group convinces a member of Congress or a president to support its cause, nothing could be worse than to lose that supporter in the next election. That is why many interest groups endorse candidates for office, and why they often encourage members to participate in party politics. The 16 million members of U.S. labor unions, for example, constitute a highly motivated resource for the Democratic party, whether as voters or as party workers.

Keeping supporters in office is why interest groups also create **political action committees (PACs).** A PAC is a legally distinct organization that raises and spends money on election campaigns, whether by giving money directly to candidates and political parties or by spending money indirectly for campaign activities such as advertising and get-out-the-vote efforts.

The first PACs were created in 1973 under sweeping campaign finance reform legislation. Because this legislation altered the campaign finance system across the board, it is discussed in more detail in Chapter 9. For the time being, it is useful to note that interest groups are prohibited from making contributions to candidates through any other device but PACs, and are limited in how much they can give to any one candidate in any one election campaign, primary or general.

There is no question that PACs have become significant players in election campaigns. The number of PACs has grown from 722 in 1975 to over 4,000 by 1996, while the amount of money raised by PACs rose from $54 million in 1975 to $437 million by 1996.[36] Even as the numbers increased, the mix of interests remained relatively stable. (See Box 7–7 for the mix of PACs.)

There are two other points to remember about the mix of PACs. First, corporations account for the largest percentage of PACs and give the greatest amounts of money. In 1996, for example, corporate PACs gave roughly $78 million to candidates, while trade, membership, and health groups (which include substantial numbers of corporations among their members) came in second with nearly $60 million, and labor came in third with just under $48 million. Nonconnected groups, a term that includes public interest groups, came in a distant fourth at just $24 million. Again, the interest group chorus sings with that particular upper-income voice.

Second, the number of nonconnected groups has grown the fastest over the years. However, not all public interest groups have PACs. Many prefer to earn their influence the old-fashioned way, by providing information and building public support. AARP does not have a PAC, for example, nor does the National

BOX 7-7

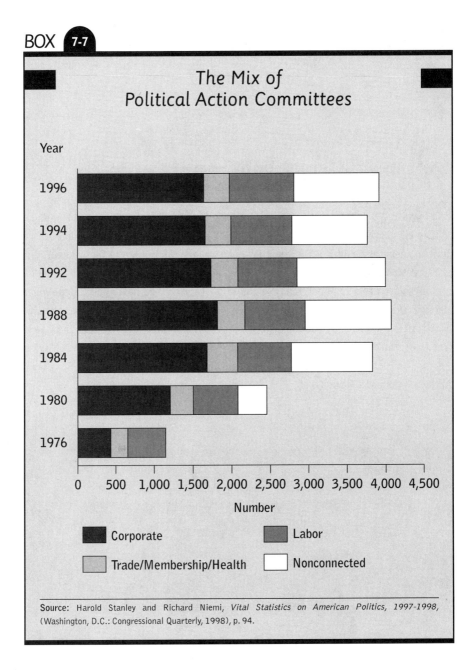

The Mix of Political Action Committees

Year

Source: Harold Stanley and Richard Niemi, *Vital Statistics on American Politics, 1997-1998*, (Washington, D.C.: Congressional Quarterly, 1998), p. 94.

Wildlife Federation, the Children's Defense League, Mothers Against Drunk Driving, or Common Cause.

Just because PACs spend large amounts of money, there is no guarantee that they can dictate how Congress votes. PACs tend to give their money to incumbents who already support their position, making it difficult to determine which came first: the PAC money or the member's favorable position.[37] Moreover, PAC money constitutes a relatively small share of campaign funding from year to year, barely topping a tenth of all dollars spent in 1996.

in a different light ———   LOBBYING'S
DREAM TEAM

The largest U.S. lobbying firm, Verner, Liipfert, Bernhard, McPherson, and Hand, got a little bit bigger in 1997 when it hired 1996 Republican presidential candidate Bob Dole as a senior partner. With 108 clients and nearly $9 million in fees collected in the first six months of 1997 alone, the firm seemed quite capable of covering Dole's annual salary of $600,000. Even though Verner, Liipfert had never had a Republican partner, Dole brought the firm what most of the lobbying powerhouses want: the ability to work both sides of the aisle. Clients such as Ameritech, Fruit of the Loom, Shell Oil, Northwest Airlines, the National Football League, the National Hockey League, and RJR Nabisco have no loyalties when it comes to Capitol Hill. They want lobbyists that win. Period.

In 1997, the lobbying firm of Verner, Liipfert, Bernhard, McPherson, and Hand hired 1996 Republican presidential candidate Bob Dole as senior partner. Dole (left) joined former 1988 vice presidential candidate Lloyd Bentsen and two other Democrats—former Texas governor Ann Richards (center) and former Senate majority leader George Mitchell (right)—in the firm's foursome of lobbying "rock stars."

Dole was hardly the only "rock star," as such visible lobbyists are called at Verner, Liipfert. He joined a veritable "who's who" of Democratic stars: former Texas governor Ann Richards, former Senate majority leader George Mitchell, and former Clinton Treasury secretary, Texas senator, and 1988 Democratic vice presidential candidate Lloyd Bentsen. Richards brought in several clients right off the bat, including Lockheed Martin, the giant defense contractor, while Mitchell brought in Disney and the top five tobacco companies. The fact that his former party colleagues on Capitol Hill were at the forefront of efforts to regulate tobacco did not deter Mitchell. (Verner, Liipfert was not the only lobbying firm with tobacco money, however. The companies had a habit of retaining several firms at the same time, all the better to make sure their voice was heard as Congress turned to legislation.)

Verner, Liipfert had clearly adopted one of the most traditional lobbying strategies of all: Hire the most senior, respected former politicians in Washington and put them to work opening doors on Capitol Hill. Bob Dole most certainly did not intend to twist arms for his clients. But what Dole, Richards, Mitchell, and Bentsen could do was raise the odds that their former colleagues would return the firm's phone calls.

Verner, Liipfert has more than just its rock stars on its side in making the case for its clients, however. It is also one of many law and lobbying firms that make campaign contributions to members of Congress. In 1996, for example, law and lobbying firms gave $51 million to political campaigns, making them the second largest industry giver behind banks and real estate firms, which are counted as one industry. Of the $51 million total, $440,000 came from Verner, Liipfert. (The big giver in the industry was the Trial Lawyers Association, which accounted for nearly $2.5 million.) Of Verner, Liipfert's $440,000, roughly 60 percent went to Democrats, a proportion that actually went up once Bob Dole joined the firm. During the first six months of 1998, for example, Verner, Liipfert gave nearly $200,000 to congressional candidates, 63 percent of which went to Democrats.[38]

It makes perfect sense for Verner, Liipfert to make campaign contributions, of course. A little campaign money is as much a way of creating good will as a call from Bob Dole. This does not mean that the Verner, Liipfert money buys legislative votes for its clients, however. The firm's $10,000 contribution to Sen. Ron Wyden (D-OR) or $7,500 to Sen. Paul Coverdell (R-GA) is not going to buy a contract for Lockheed Martin or special protection for Disney.

Rather, the contributions are merely one more device for focusing congressional attention on what Verner, Liipfert and its partners think is important. Because members of Congress have so little free time in the day, they must decide whose call to take, which issue analysis to read, and which constituents to see. Bob Dole may not be known well enough in his home town of Russell, Kansas to get a check cashed, which was the punch line from his Super Bowl Visa commercial, but he is certainly well known enough on Capitol Hill to get a return phone call. A small campaign contribution here and there is not going to buy a vote, but it may well increase the likelihood that Bob Dole gets the first return phone call, or that Verner, Liipfert's analysis gets the first read, in what is always a busy day on Capitol Hill.

MAINTAINING THE BALANCE

The state of interest groups today confirms the Founders' worst fears about human nature. The number of groups is rising, their focus is narrowing, and their willingness to work together in long-term coalitions is nonexistent. As a result, Washington often seems unable to make a move without some interest group finding a way to stall progress. Designed to prevent a majority faction from ever imposing its will on others, the Founders' government often seems tied down by a thousand Lilliputian ropes.

The frustration comes to a head when major issues such as health care reform arise. Besieged by hundreds of interest groups and thousands of well-paid lobbyists, government seems unable to make a move. With dozens of checks and balances to exploit, and the latest public opinion polls at the ready, even the tiniest interest group seems capable of grinding the whole system to a halt. Americans can only throw their hands up in disbelief as the "special interests" prove once again that they have the money and influence to prevent even modest reforms from passing. The status quo rules again.

There are only two problems with this portrait. First, as later chapters will show, American government *is* able to act, just not as quickly as the public or the media might like. It is not easy to pass a major bill such as health care or welfare reform, particularly given the hyperpluralism that reigns in Washington, but major legislation does pass from time to time. Laws pass even under conditions that seem utterly hostile—for example, when the president is from one party and the congressional majority is from the other, which was precisely the situation when the welfare reform legislation of 1996 was passed.

Second, those assorted checks and balances and separations of power were designed precisely to allow intense minorities to stop the system cold. The fact that the Bow Tie Manufacturers Association might be able to stop the necktie industry from enacting a ban on bow ties is just the way the Founders wanted it.

One cannot know, of course, whether the Founders would have reduced the checks and balances a bit if they had foreseen hyperpluralism. After all, the

Constitution was not designed only to prevent strong majorities from imposing their will on the rest of the nation. It was also designed to protect the nation from foreign and domestic threats. The notion that a single interest group might use an advertising campaign to paralyze Congress could only strike the Founders as the height of folly. Manipulating the public to manipulate Congress? The Founders might well wonder whether the delicate balance had been completely lost, pushed so far toward stalemate that the nation could not defend itself. Although they were most certainly defenders of the status quo and worried about giving the people too much power, they did not want government to be so feeble and indecisive that it could not rise to meet the demands of the future.

terms to remember

civil society (p. 241)
association (p. 241)
interest group (p. 241)
lobbying (p. 243)
single-issue groups (p. 248)
hyperpluralism (p. 248)
issue networks (p. 252)
iron triangles (p. 252)
ideological webs (p. 252)
disturbance theory (p. 253)
free rider problem (p. 257)

collective benefits (p. 257)
selective benefits (p. 258)
federation (p. 258)
peak business association
   (p. 259)
trade association (p. 259)
professional association (p. 259)
public interest group (p. 259)
amicus brief (p. 266)
political action committee
   (PAC) (p. 272)

facts and interpretations

- The United States has always been a nation of joiners, with associations of one kind or another an essential part of civil society. Interest groups are just one of many kinds of associations people can join. What makes interest groups different from other kinds of organizations is the effort to influence who gets what, when, and how from government. The term *interest group* includes traditional membership-based interest groups, as well as a new breed of nonmembership organizations such as individual corporations and colleges and universities. The past half century has witnessed an explosion in both the number of groups and the narrowness of their causes. The result may be that government is less able to come to agreement than the Founders could ever have imagined.

- Interest groups form during social or economic disturbances, and exist to provide one or more of four basic benefits: (1) material, (2) social, (3) civic, or (4) policy. Most interest groups provide material benefits to their members, while preventing the free rider problem of collective benefits by offering selective benefits available to their members and their members only. In doing so, they may isolate themselves and their members from the rest of society, thereby further reducing the odds of finding common ground on the divisive issues of the day.

- Interest groups seek to influence, or lobby, government in three ways: (1) providing information, (2) building public support, and (3) influencing elections. Their success in doing so depends on their size, intensity, and financial resources. As the interest group community has grown, the tools of influence have become more sophisticated, and now include a range of approaches for manufacturing public support. The problem is that members of Congress may have an increasingly difficult time telling the real public concerns from the manufactured ones.

- Over half of all interest groups give money to campaigns through political action committees, or PACs, thereby creating the appearance that legislative votes are bought and sold. The largest amounts of money come from corporate PACs, with nonconnected (or public interest group) PACs giving the least. Whatever their interest, however, most PACs tend to give most of their money to incumbents. There can be little doubt that the interest group community overrepresents Americans with the resources and skills to join, which appears to increase the odds that well-to-do Americans could impose their will on the rest of society.

- The past thirty years have produced a remarkable increase in the number of interest groups, creating concerns about whether government can still do its job. As this hyperpluralism accelerates, every interest group seems to be able to win some battle somewhere in the Founders' government of separate powers, interests and layers, and checks and balances. Ironically, the Founders might view a strong two-party system as a way of counterbalancing the rising number of narrowly focused interest groups.

open questions

- Are there too many interest groups today? Does the increasing number confirm the tendency of human beings to divide into factions? What are the parallels between the rising number of groups and the new media? Is the United States becoming a nation of mostly separate peoples, using highly specialized sources to get their news and joining highly specialized interest groups to represent their views? If so, have the chances that Americans will agree on much of anything gotten better or worse?

- If Americans are so critical of special interests, why are they so active as members? Are they being overly critical, or is something else happening here? Is it possible, for example, that individual Americans think very highly of the groups they join, but less so of the corporate lobbyists or others associated with the kinds of conflict of interest involved in the gift ban? Why would an older American join AARP? Why does AARP set the cost of joining so low?

- How does the rise of interest groups fit with the decline of party loyalty? Are the two related, and if so, how? Would the United States be better off abandoning the two-party system and opting for parties built around interest groups (recall that Ralph Nader ran for president as the candidate of the environmentalist Green party in 1996)? How do interest groups weaken party loyalty? And how do they weaken civil society? Do they pull Americans toward national associations and away from their own neighbors?

for further study

Berger, Peter L., and Richard John Neuhaus. *To Empower People: From State to Civil Society.* Washington, DC: American Enterprise Institute, 1996.

Birnbaum, Jeffrey. *The Lobbyists: How Influence Peddlers Work Their Way in Washington.* New York: Times Books, 1993.

Cigler, Alan, and Burdett Loomis, eds. *Interest Group Politics,* 4th ed. Washington, DC: CQ Press, 1994.

Hrebenar, Ronald J. *Interest Group Politics in America,* 3rd ed. Armonk, NY: M. E. Sharpe, 1998.

Salisbury, Robert H. *Interest and Institutions: Substance and Structure in American Politics.* Pittsburgh: University of Pittsburgh Press, 1992.

Schattschneider, E. E. *The Semi-Sovereign People.* New York: Holt, Rinehart and Winston, 1960.

endnotes for chapter 7

1. *National Association for the Advancement of Colored People v. Alabama,* 357 U.S. 449, 78 Sup. Ct. 1163 (1958).

2. Alexis de Tocqueville, *Democracy in America,* ed. J. P. Mayer, trans. George Lawrence (Garden City, NY: Harper Perennial, 1988), p. 196.

3. There is a dense and growing literature on the elements of civil society today. For a sampling, see Benjamin R. Barber, *Jihad v. McWorld: How the Planet Is Both Falling Apart and Coming Together and What This Means for Democracy* (New York: Times Books, 1995); Harry C. Boyte, *Common-Wealth: A Return to Citizen Politics* (New York: Free Press, 1989); Amitai Etzioni, *The Spirit of Community: The Reinvention of American Society* (New York: Simon & Schuster, 1993); and Peter L. Berger and Richard John Neuhaus, *To Empower People: From State to Civil Society* (Washington, DC: American Enterprise Institute, 1996).

4. Tocqueville, pp. 513–17.

5. David Segal, "Main Street America Has Advocates Aplenty," *Washington Post,* July 10, 1995, p. A6.

6. *The Washington Representatives* (Washington DC: Columbia Books, 1992), p. 2.

7. Jeffrey Birnbaum, *The Lobbyists: How Influence Peddlers Work Their Way in Washington* (New York: Times Books, 1993), p. 7.

8. See David Truman, *The Governmental Process* (New York: Knopf, 1971), and James Q. Wilson, *Political Organizations* (New York: Basic Books, 1975).

9. Michael Barone, "Returning to Tocqueville: Are 19th Century Values Making a Comeback in America?" *Washington Post Weekly Edition,* January 15–21, 1996, p. 23; see Theda Skocpol, "The Tocqueville Problem: Civic Engagement in American Democracy," presidential address for the annual meeting of the Social Science History Association, New Orleans, October 10–13, 1996.

10. Birnbaum, *The Lobbyists,* p. 8.

11. Birnbaum, *The Lobbyists,* p. 9.

12. Skocpol, "The Tocqueville Problem," p. 33.

13. See Ronald J. Hrebenar, *Interest Group Politics in America,* 3rd ed. (Armonk, NY: M. E. Sharpe, 1998), for an introduction to interest groups in general and the specific topic of their growth.

14. For an introduction to this history, see Gerald Gamm and Robert D. Putnam, "Association-Building in America, 1850–1920," paper presented at the 1996 annual meeting of the Social Science History Association, New Orleans, October 10–13, 1996.

15. See Skocpol, "The Tocqueville Problem"; see also her book, *Protecting Soldiers and Mothers: The Political Origins of Social Policy in the United States* (Cambridge, MA: Harvard University Press, 1995).

16. Quoted in Ethel Klein, *Gender Politics: From Consciousness to Mass Politics* (Cambridge, MA: Harvard University Press, 1984), p. 23.

17. Robert H. Salisbury, *Interest and Institutions: Substance and Structure in American Politics* (Pittsburgh: University of Pittsburgh Press, 1992).

18. See Hrebenar, *Interest Group Politics in America*, p. 277.

19. See Peter H. Stone, "Lobbyists on a Leash," *The National Journal*, February 3, 1996, p. 245.

20. Eric Schmitt, "Order for Lobbyists: Hold the Gravy," *New York Times*, February 11, 1996, p. 30.

21. E. E. Schattschneider, *The Semi-Sovereign People* (New York: Holt, Rinehart and Winston, 1960), p. 35.

22. Paul Starobin, "Welcome to the Club," *National Journal*, January 28, 1995, p. 219.

23. See Robert Salisbury, "An Exchange Theory of Interest Groups," *Midwest Journal of Political Science*, 13, no. 1 (February 1969), pp. 1–32.

24. Sidney Verba, Kay Lehman Schlozman, and Henry E. Brady, *Voice and Equality: Civic Voluntarism in American Politics* (Cambridge, MA: Harvard University Press, 1995), p. 122.

25. Mancur Olson, *The Logic of Collective Action* (Cambridge, MA: Harvard University Press, 1965), pp. 64–65.

26. Kay Schlozman and John Tierney, *Organized Interests in American Democracy* (New York: Harper & Row, 1986), p. 41.

27. See Marian Burros, "Chefs' Environmental Politics Is Making the Kitchen Hotter," *New York Times*, September 30, 1992, p. B1.

28. This quote and the figures provided below are from Colleen Cordes, "The Academic Pork Barrel Begins to Fill Up Again," *Chronicle of Higher Education*, June 19, 1998, p. A30; see also James D. Savage, *Funding Science in America: Congress, Universities, and the Politics of the Academic Pork Barrel* (New York: Cambridge University Press, forthcoming), and Constance E. Cook, *Higher Education: How Colleges and Universities Influence Federal Policy* (Nashville, TN: Vanderbilt University Press, 1998).

29. See Douglas Lederman, "A Scholar Examines a Higher-Education Lobby," *Chronicle of Higher Education*, July 10, 1998, p. A25.

30. James Q. Wilson, *Political Organizations*, reprint ed. (Princeton, NJ: Princeton University Press, 1995).

31. These figures are drawn from Ron Suskind, "Whose Side Are They On, Anyway?" *SmartMoney*, February 1993, p. 98.

32. See Olson, *The Logic of Collective Action*, pp. 9–36, for a discussion of the problems of large groups.

33. See Henry J. Abraham, *The Judicial Process*, 6th ed. (New York: Oxford University Press, 1993), p. 239.

34. Marissa Martino Golden, "Interest Groups in the Rule-Making Process: Who Participates? Whose Voices Get Heard?" *Journal of Public Administration Research and Theory*, 8 (Spring 1998), pp. 2245–70.

35. Deborah Beck, Paul Taylor, Jeffrey Stanger, and Douglas Rivlin, *Issue Advocacy Advertising during the 1996 Campaign* (Philadelphia: Annenberg Public Policy Center, 1997).

36. Harold W. Stanley and Richard G. Niemi, *Vital Statistics on American Politics* (Washington, DC: CQ Press, 1998), pp. 94–95.

37. These numbers come from Frank Sorauf, *Inside Campaign Finance: Myths and Realities* (New Haven, CT: Yale University Press, 1992), p. 71.

38. These figures are from the Center for Responsive Politics database on campaign donors, which can be found at <www.crp.org>.

participation and voting

the democratic habit

Just as the United States has always been a nation of joiners, it has also always been a nation of political participators. "No sooner do you set foot upon American ground than you are stunned by a kind of tumult," Alexis de Tocqueville wrote upon his return to France after his visit to a young America 150 years ago. "[A] confused clamor rises on every side, a thousand voices are heard at once. . . . To take a hand in the government of society and to talk about it is [the] biggest concern and, so to say, the only pleasure [an American] knows."[1] Participation is one part of what Tocqueville labeled "the habits of the democratic heart."

Tocqueville would still hear the clamor of participation today, whether in million-man marches on Washington or in local battles for increased school funding. Citizens still write to their president and members of Congress, still vote in elections, still work together as volunteers to address public problems in their own communities, and in general still create a kind of tumult with their activity.

Participation is hardly even across society, however. Some Americans do not participate because they simply lack the resources or civic skills to be effective; others refuse to participate because they simply do not trust politics; still others have become "checkbook activists," in which their sole activity is writing a check to a candidate or interest group. As this chapter shows, property owners (meaning well-to-do, highly educated Americans) are still the most likely to engage in politics, still the most likely to give time and money to campaigns, and still the most likely to use the levers of politics. To the extent that they saw property ownership as a source of civic virtue, which is what Thomas Jefferson and others clearly believed, the Founders might be pleased with the lack of participation by America's economic "have-nots."

Moreover, the Founders might well caution modern Americans that there is such a thing as too much participation, particularly if government becomes so consumed with satisfying the public that it loses the delicate balance. There cannot be so much petitioning by interest groups, for example, that Congress and the president have no time to confront foreign and domestic threats, nor can petitioning be so intense that the branches cannot make a decision without risking the ire of the people. The people must give their consent to be governed, not their consent on every last decision.

The rest of this chapter explores these problems of participation in more detail, first by looking at the options for participating in general, then at voting specifically. Many of the reasons Americans may be checking out of the political process involve declining resources and skills for participating. Every act of participation costs something in time and energy. Even the least expensive act of all, voting, takes more than a moment's notice.

Throughout this chapter, it is essential to remember one point: Participation in American politics is a voluntary choice. As such, it reflects a deliberate decision to act. Staying home does not always indicate a lack of consent to be governed—to the contrary, it can mean a nonvoter is perfectly happy with the way things are. But as fewer and fewer Americans exercise their voluntary freedom to act, government may have less active consent, which can undermine the delicate balance when it comes time to do something unpopular, such as draft young people for war or impose higher taxes.

HOW AMERICANS CAN PARTICIPATE

Participating in politics is very much an act of consent to be governed. By showing up to vote, citizens not only endorse a specific candidate but also endorse representative democracy. By writing a letter to their representatives, they not only convey a specific message but also acknowledge the legitimacy of those leaders in deciding who gets what, when, and how from government. And by volunteering to help others in their communities, they not only improve their communities but also express their commitment to the common good.

By any measure, Americans are still giving their consent to be governed. Roughly 80 percent of Americans engage in some form of political participation every year, from volunteering with their neighbors to address some community problem such as crime or traffic to showing up for jury duty, signing a petition, working in a campaign, talking about politics with their friends or family, voting in an election, or watching the evening news.[2]

Lost in these numbers, however, are very real differences among Americans in the extent to which they participate. Not all Americans can afford to give money to campaigns and not all can find the time to register to vote. And because politics is run by those who show up, these differences affect who gets what, when, and how from government. Before these differences are discussed, it is first important to inventory the options for participating and understand more about why Americans participate at all.

With over a half million elected officials to contact, over 85,000 units of government (national, state, and local) to petition, nearly 18 million public employees to talk to, and thousands upon thousands of membership groups to join, Americans have a nearly infinite list of opportunities for engagement.

Although the options are many, political scientists often winnow the list down to eight basic acts that almost all Americans can do:

1. voting;
2. working as a volunteer for a candidate running for office;
3. giving money to a campaign;
4. communicating with government by mail or in person;
5. taking part in a protest, march, or demonstration;
6. working with others to address community problems;

7. joining a local governmental board such as the school board or city council; and

8. joining or giving money to an interest group.[3]

The average American participates in two of these eight acts per year. (Count your own level of participation by checking off the questions in Box 8–1.) There is an option for just about every American, from the most extroverted to the most introverted, from the richest to the poorest. The acts differ in the degrees to which they are private, interactive, frequent, conventional, expensive, and send a clear message to government about what citizens want. In many ways, American participation is like a shopping mall. There are anchor stores (voting) in democracy, and boutiques (letters to Congress). How and where Americans decide to "shop" depends in large measure on which of the following choices they make.

Public or Private? Some Americans like to participate in private, others in public. Nothing is more visible, for example, than serving on a school board. The decisions are often highly controversial, particularly when it comes time to raise taxes or cut programs. Nothing is less visible, perhaps, than volunteering with others to solve some community problem. Millions of Americans do so every day, with no acknowledgment asked and none given.

Voting is both the least and most visible act of all. *How* a person votes is completely invisible—that is, after all, the point of a secret ballot. But *whether* a person votes is a very public act. Showing up at the polling booth is an admittedly old-fashioned way of showing consent to be governed. As this chapter suggests later, the movement toward voting by mail reduces the visibility of voting, perhaps weakening the act as a shared expression of consent.

Separate or Together? Some Americans like to participate by themselves—for example, by writing a solitary e-mail or letter to Congress. Others like to participate in union with others—for example, by joining a protest march, chat group, or community cleanup campaign.

Recent years have witnessed a dramatic increase in the number of Americans who are ready to volunteer in one-on-one settings, whether helping young Americans learn to read, mentoring troubled youths, delivering clothing to the poor, or serving soup in shelters for the homeless. This kind of volunteering can be described as highly individualized—the relationship is between the volunteer and the child or the hungry family.

Even as the amount of such individualized volunteering is going up each year, the amount of collective volunteering appears to be going down. Americans are spending less time working together to solve the local problems that might be

BOX 8-1

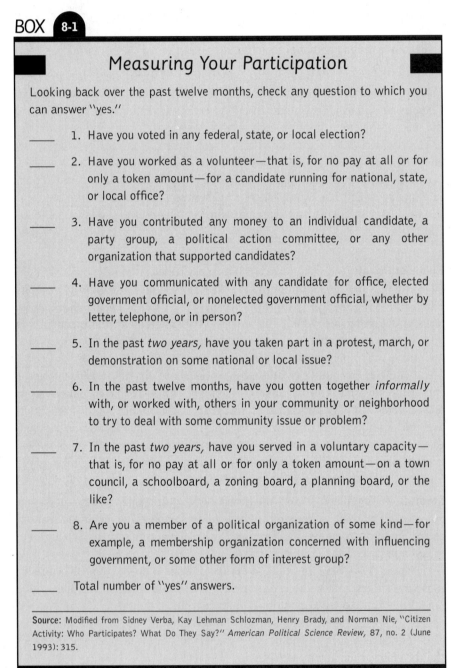

Measuring Your Participation

Looking back over the past twelve months, check any question to which you can answer "yes."

____ 1. Have you voted in any federal, state, or local election?

____ 2. Have you worked as a volunteer—that is, for no pay at all or for only a token amount—for a candidate running for national, state, or local office?

____ 3. Have you contributed any money to an individual candidate, a party group, a political action committee, or any other organization that supported candidates?

____ 4. Have you communicated with any candidate for office, elected government official, or nonelected government official, whether by letter, telephone, or in person?

____ 5. In the past *two years,* have you taken part in a protest, march, or demonstration on some national or local issue?

____ 6. In the past twelve months, have you gotten together *informally* with, or worked with, others in your community or neighborhood to try to deal with some community issue or problem?

____ 7. In the past *two years,* have you served in a voluntary capacity— that is, for no pay at all or for only a token amount—on a town council, a schoolboard, a zoning board, a planning board, or the like?

____ 8. Are you a member of a political organization of some kind—for example, a membership organization concerned with influencing government, or some other form of interest group?

____ Total number of "yes" answers.

Source: Modified from Sidney Verba, Kay Lehman Schlozman, Henry Brady, and Norman Nie, "Citizen Activity: Who Participates? What Do They Say?" *American Political Science Review,* 87, no. 2 (June 1993): 315.

causing illiteracy, juvenile delinquency, poverty, and homelessness. Many Americans, particularly young Americans, have become so distrusting toward politics that they will volunteer only where they can instantly see the results of their work.

Occasional or Frequent?   Some options for participating occur only on occasion, while others permit nearly infinite activism. Voting is clearly fixed by law and practice. Elections take place only on occasion, and every voter has just one vote (unless, of course, one wants to risk going to jail for voter fraud). In a similar vein, serving on local government boards is limited by the number of openings and the election process itself.

The rest of the options for participating are unlimited. Americans can e-mail Congress and the president until their computer keyboards wear out and can contribute money to politics until they hit the federal limits, at which point they can start giving soft money to the parties or completely hidden money to purchase issue advocacy (see Chapter 7). And the more frequently Americans participate in these activities, the more influence they can have. The more money a citizen gives to campaigns, the more campaigns will court that citizen; the more visible a citizen becomes in local politics, the more responsive government is likely to be. Although the relationship between activity and influence is not perfect, citizens rarely gain influence by staying at home.

Conventional or Unconventional?   Americans do not believe all forms of participation are civically acceptable, a judgment that is usually based on whether a given act fits with what the nation defines as being good citizenship. Not surprisingly, voting is seen as the most **conventional participation,** or civically acceptable act. Americans are so certain that it is their civic duty to vote that they feel guilty when they do not do so.

What Americans do not like are protests of one kind or another, which are considered **unconventional participation,** or civically unacceptable acts. Only 15 percent approve of consumer boycotts, and just 11 percent approve of lawful demonstrations and marches, both of which are guaranteed under the right to peaceable assembly in the First Amendment, and both of which contributed to the founding of the nation two hundred years ago. They are even less supportive of breaking the law to advance a cause: just 1 percent approve of blocking traffic, painting slogans on walls, engaging in personal violence, and damaging property.[4]

Giving money to politics, at least in large amounts, may be about to become unconventional, if not outright illegal. Even large contributors are having second thoughts about the amounts they give. According to a 1998 survey of 1,100 donors who gave $200 or more to congressional candidates in the most recent election, one-half agreed both that contributors regularly pressure elected officials for favors and that money is the single most important factor in elections. Although four-

Conventional and unconventional participation. Voting (top) is considered a civic duty, while protesting (bottom) is considered less acceptable.

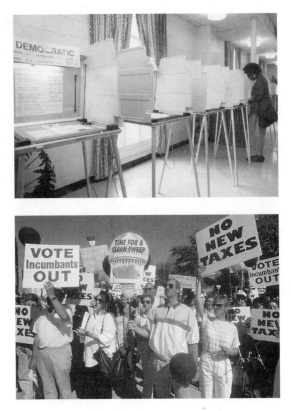

fifths believed that contributing is a legitimate form of participation, almost as many said the campaign finance system needs to be changed. If not quite embarrassed by their behavior, they were not particularly proud of it, either.[5]

Inexpensive or Expensive?   Every option for participating in politics carries a cost, whether in time, information, or money. Americans cannot give money to a campaign, for example, without having money to give, nor can they give time to an organization if they have no time to give. And, if they do not have information, they cannot decide where their time and money should go.

Although voting is sometimes characterized as a no-cost option, there is a price of admission. In most states, citizens cannot vote unless they are registered, which requires at least some effort to figure out where and how to register, and even more effort to actually go through the act of registering itself. Voters also have to know when the election will take place, which means paying at least some attention to the news, and where to vote, which usually means at least a quick glance at the inside pages of a newspaper or election guide.

Once election day arrives, voters have to find the time and energy to actually go to the polling place. If **voter turnout,** which is the number of registered voters who actually vote, is high, they might have to wait in line to be checked off the registration list, then wait in line to pick up their ballot, then wait in line for the next open voting booth, and only then cast their ballots.

Just getting past the mechanics is tough enough for many Americans. However, if they wish to make their choices on the basis of something other than party identification or whether the candidate has a familiar last name, voters must do more: They must spend at least some time before the election listening to advertisements, reading newspaper and magazine articles about the candidates, watching debates, and paying attention. Being informed is not "cheap" in either time or energy, particularly in the United States, where elections are frequent, party differences are sometimes minimal, and voting registration laws differ state by state. No single act takes more than a few minutes, but together the acts add up.

Clear or Ambiguous?   Every option for participating conveys some sense of what a citizen wants in return—for example, lower taxes, safer streets, or some personal benefit. It is just that some of the information conveyed is clear, and some is foggy.

Voting in a presidential election is the least effective way for individual citizens to tell government what they want. Voters only get to say "aye" or "nay" to each candidate, meaning that the winning candidate is free to interpret the election results as a mandate for implementing a wide range of ideas. Voting in state and local elections is not much better as a communication channel, unless, of course, those elections allow citizens to vote on an initiative or referendum.

In contrast, contacting government directly provides the clearest form of participation of all. Letter writers can tell their representatives exactly what they want, when they want it, and what they will do if they do not get it. They can pinpoint specific decisions they care about, and offer sharp opinions about their preferences. Unlike interest groups, which vary greatly in the clarity of their message depending in part on their size, the solitary letter writer can say whatever she or he thinks.

Giving money to a campaign falls in between voting and contacting government as a way to send a message. On the one hand, people who give small amounts of money to a campaign have little or no opportunity to convey a message of any kind. The best they can hope for is a computer-generated note of appreciation. The small contributions of $100 here and there will be forgotten soon after the election is over, if not before, while the $3 check-off on income tax returns that gives every American the chance to contribute to presidential campaigns will never be noted.

On the other hand, people who give very large contributions almost always get a chance to send a clear message about what they want. Asked by a Senate

BOX 8-2

Choices in Participation

Political Act	Public vs. Private	Separate vs. Together	Occasional vs. Frequent
Voting	Public and private	Separate	Occasional
Volunteering in a campaign	Public	Together	Can be either
Giving money to a campaign	Public	Separate	Depends
Contacting government	Public	Separate	Can be frequent
Protesting	Public	Together	Can be either
Working with others	Public	Together	Can be either
Joining a board	Public	Together	Frequent
Joining an interest group	Depends	Depends on the kind of group	Can be either

committee why he had given $300,000 in soft money to the Democratic Committee in 1996, one contributor candidly acknowledged that he wanted to buy a private meeting with the president to lobby for an oil pipeline project that needed U.S. government approval. Asked if he was frustrated that his contribution had only bought an invitation to a White House coffee and no action, he answered, "I think next time I'll give $600,000." As Senator Carl Levin (D-MI) remarked, "I think you were hustling, I think you were being hustled at the same time. And that's the culture. That's the bad news. The good news is you didn't get your one-on-one meeting with the President, and his policy was not changed, if there is any good news in this story. But the bad news is that you hustled for a lot of money that you thought would get you access, and that, in fact, did contribute in getting you access."[6]

Conventional vs. Unconventional	Inexpensive vs. Expensive	Clear vs. Ambiguous
Conventional	Inexpensive	Ambiguous
Conventional	Expensive	Clear
Depends on amount	Expensive	Depends on amount
Conventional	Expensive	Clear
Unconventional	Expensive	Clear
Conventional	Expensive	Ambiguous
Conventional	Expensive	Clear
Conventional	Depends	Clear

Box 8–2 provides a comparison of the different options for participation. Choosing a specific option depends very much on what Americans want by way of access and what they have by way of resources.

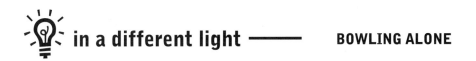

in a different light ——— BOWLING ALONE

Few political scientists are more identified with concern about declines in public participation than Harvard University's Robert Putnam, who wrote a paper in 1994 titled "Bowling Alone: Democracy in America at the End of the Twentieth Century."[7]

The paper earned him a discussion with President Clinton and a feature story in *People* magazine.

Putnam made three broad arguments about the state of civic engagement in the United States. First, he argued that civic participation has declined over the past two decades. Since 1973, the number of Americans who had attended a political rally or speech in the previous year had fallen by over 30 percent, the number who had attended a public meeting on town or school affairs had fallen by almost 40 percent, and the number who had worked for their political party had fallen by almost 50 percent.

Second, Putnam argued that Americans have been pulling away from the traditional civic organizations that once held the nation together. Membership in the Boy Scouts dropped 26 percent between 1970 and 1993, in the League of Women Voters by 42 percent, and in the Red Cross by 62 percent. Membership in men's clubs such as the Elks, Lions, and Moose also dropped.

Putnam's most whimsical evidence of the decline in civic engagement was bowling. "More Americans are bowling today than ever before," Putnam wrote, "but *league* bowling has plummeted in the last ten to fifteen years. Between 1980 and 1993 the total number of bowlers in America increased by 10 percent, while league bowling decreased by 49 percent. . . . The rise of solo bowling threatens the livelihood of bowling proprietors because league bowlers consume three times as much beer and pizza as solo bowlers, and the money in bowling is in the beer and pizza, not the balls and shoes."

Third, Putnam argued that Americans have become less trusting not only of government and politics, but also of each other. The number of Americans who say that most people can be trusted fell from 58 percent in 1960 to 34 percent in 1994. A majority of Americans now believe most people will take advantage of others if given the chance. If they do not trust their neighbors, perhaps it is no surprise that Americans do not trust their government.

Not everyone agrees with Putnam's assessment, however.[8] Research shows that certain kinds of participation are actually going up, not down. PTA membership has increased over the past two decades as the 75 million baby boomers born between 1946 and 1964 have focused on raising their children. Soccer leagues and softball leagues are also way up.

Americans also are giving more money to charity and reporting increased volunteering, including a dramatic surge in crime watch patrols. And, as the old civic organizations decline, Americans are building a new generation of organizations such as COOL (Campus Outreach Opportunity League) and Habitat for Humanity instead of joining, say, the League of Women Voters or the Elks Club.

All the same, given the nation's need, Americans may not be participating enough. America needs more than just an offset to league bowling. It needs a substantial boost in activism if it is to care for an aging society and reduce drug abuse, crime, and urban decay. Participation is no less important today than it was when Tocqueville visited the nation 150 years ago.

THE DECISION TO PARTICIPATE

Americans may have ample options for participation, but many simply do not engage. Political scientists believe there are three reasons why Americans do not participate: because they can't; because they don't want to; or because nobody asked. "They can't" means they simply do not have the essential resources to participate—the money to contribute, the time to learn, the skills to use the time and money effectively. "They don't want to" means they either are just not interested or do not believe that their participation will make a difference. "Nobody asked" means that they are so isolated from the rest of society that they never get called. Political scientists know, for example, that the best way to get young Americans to participate is simply to ask. But with more and more Americans bowling alone, the asking may never occur.[9]

Before these and other explanations of nonparticipation are discussed, it is important to understand a bit more about what Americans seek to gain from participating in politics.

The Benefits of Participation

The choice of one option for participating over another depends on the benefits each option provides. Americans seek the same benefits from participating in politics as they seek in joining interest groups: (1) a *material benefit* that comes back to individual citizens, such as tax cuts, higher benefit payments, better streets, or new schools; (2) a *social benefit* that comes from the simple pleasure of working together; (3) a *civic benefit* that comes from fulfilling one's duties as a citizen; and (4) a *policy benefit* that comes from actually influencing government in a way that helps the community or nation as a whole.

The degree to which a given option provides any of these benefits depends largely on the publicness, frequency, collectiveness, conventionality, cost, and sharpness of the message, as discussed above. Just as not all stores offer the same products, not all participation options offer the same levels or kinds of benefit.[10]

Start with voting, which remains the anchor of American political participation. Because voting does not allow individual citizens to tell the federal government what they want (note again that the Founders did not allow the referendum or initiative), it is an exceptionally poor vehicle for providing material benefits. And because voting is so infrequent and is done in private, it is also a poor source of social benefits. Casting one vote every year or two is hardly the way to convey a sharp message, especially since elected officials have no way to know exactly how an individual voted, or why.

Working in campaigns and volunteering in the community are not particularly potent sources of material benefits, either. It is hard to see how working on a Habitat for Humanity house would redound to the volunteer's favor at the Internal Revenue Service, or how licking envelopes for a candidate would help with a government contract. Like voting, both activities offer enormous civic benefits, giving participants a sense that they are doing something good for their society. Unlike voting, both activities offer high social benefits. There is nothing quite so rewarding as working with others in building a house for a deserving family or serving a bowl of hot soup to a homeless person, nothing quite so energizing as working together for a candidate in whom one believes.

Communicating with government offers a broader mix of benefits, depending on the nature of the contact. Some people who write to their leaders do so in search of material benefit for themselves by asking for government help, whether in finding a missing Social Security check or pushing an application to West Point. Members of Congress have staffers called **congressional case workers** to handle just such requests. Other people write in search of policy benefits by taking a position on some pending legislative decision. Still others simply think that writing their members of Congress is the right thing to do as a citizen. What communicating with government cannot provide is much of a social benefit. It is more a private experience.

Protesting is the form of participation that provides the greatest social benefits to those who march. Participants may not remember exactly what was said by the speakers, but they will long remember the sense of solidarity that came from linking arms for a cause. Indeed, there is some evidence that indicates people who participated in the antiwar marches of the late 1960s and early 1970s were marked for life. They tend to remember the marches vividly and have been more active in politics ever since.[11] The same holds for many of the individuals involved in the civil rights marches of the 1950s and early 1960s. People who heard the Rev. Martin Luther King, Jr. speak of his dream of racial equality in 1963 will never forget the experience.

Finally, contributing money offers different benefits depending on the size of the check and where it goes. People who give to individual candidates in small amounts (as noted in Chapter 6, the federal government limits the amount that a citizen can give to any one candidate in any single election campaign) appear to do so for the civic benefits. In contrast, people who give money to an issue orga-

A 1963 civil rights march on Washington, D.C. The civil rights movement was guided by a commitment to nonviolent action, and included many peaceful protests.

nization appear to do so for policy benefits, putting their dollars where their policy beliefs are, whereas people who give money to a political action committee appear to do so for the material benefits that will eventually come back to them as individuals.

How Much Do Americans Participate?

Given the variety of reasons for participating, it should not come as a surprise that not all Americans participate in every act. Not all Americans want or need material benefits; not all seek social or civic rewards. Political scientists Sidney Verba, Kay Schlozman, and Henry Brady found that of the eight options in Box 8–3, voting was the most popular form of participation.

Americans put their political activities together in many ways. Indeed, political scientists often describe six types of participators. Roughly 20 percent of Americans are *inactives* who do not participate at all: they do not vote, write or phone, and certainly do not join. Another 20 percent are *voting specialists* who vote and do nothing else. Roughly 5 percent are *parochial participants* who communicate with public officials on their own behalf only, and otherwise stay out of politics completely. Another 20 percent are *communalists* who get involved in

BOX **8-3**

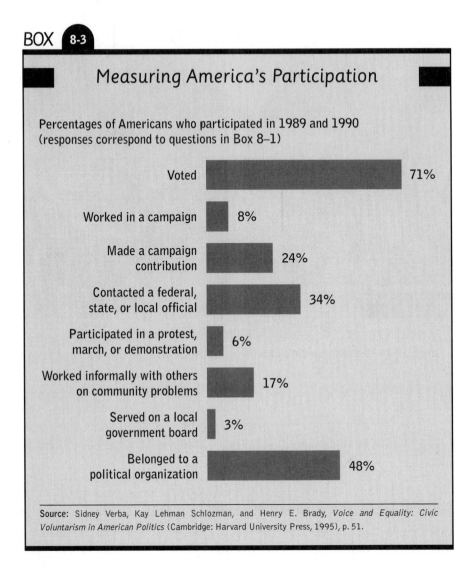

Measuring America's Participation

Percentages of Americans who participated in 1989 and 1990
(responses correspond to questions in Box 8–1)

Voted	71%
Worked in a campaign	8%
Made a campaign contribution	24%
Contacted a federal, state, or local official	34%
Participated in a protest, march, or demonstration	6%
Worked informally with others on community problems	17%
Served on a local government board	3%
Belonged to a political organization	48%

Source: Sidney Verba, Kay Lehman Schlozman, and Henry E. Brady, *Voice and Equality: Civic Voluntarism in American Politics* (Cambridge: Harvard University Press, 1995), p. 51.

public life to improve their communities, usually vote, but otherwise stay out of politics. Another 15 percent are *campaigners* who get involved in campaigns, but otherwise stay away from volunteering. Another 10 percent are *complete activists* who do it all: write, call, attend, vote, campaign, and contribute. A final 10 percent do not fit any category.

Regardless of which option for participating is chosen, the central question is whether the level of participation, and the consent that goes with it, is up or down. There are three ways to answer: (1) by comparing the United States to the rest of the world, (2) by comparing the past with the present, and (3) by comparing the young with the old. All three comparisons suggest that Americans are still giving their consent to be governed, albeit in changing numbers.

The United States versus the World.   Start by looking abroad, where other democracies outpace America in several important measures of political participation. The United States trails most other Western democracies in voter turnout, for example. Between 1980 and 1989, Belgians (94 percent), Austrians (92), Australians (90), Swedes (88), Germans (87), Italians (84), Israelis (79), Greeks (78), Britons (74), Irish (73), Canadians (72), and Japanese (68) all turned out to vote at higher rates than Americans (53 percent). Indeed, the United States trails all established democracies but one: Switzerland (49 percent).[12]

This does not mean that Americans are behind in all areas of participation, however. America tends to lead the free world in campaign volunteering, contact with government, and community work and is near the top in the number of citizens who attend political meetings.[13] Even if America could do better in getting voters to the polls, which is not clear, it has become an international leader in getting its people to spend time helping others.

The Past versus the Present.   Continue the comparison by looking back over time. The evidence from the past three decades suggests that Americans are becoming more active in some areas and less active in others. Participation in elections is off sharply since the 1950s and 1960s, whether measured by voting in national or local elections. Participation in efforts to influence other people's election decisions also appears to be off, as is working in campaigns and for the local political party.

One area in which the numbers have gone up is giving money to campaigns. The numbers are also up in contacting government. The number of letters, calls, faxes, and e-mail messages sent to Congress and the White House has exploded over the past two decades, in part because interest groups have become much more skilled at generating public demands for action. Looking back to the 1960s for comparison, the number of Americans who get in touch with local officials in any given year has increased by over 70 percent, while the number who communicate with state or federal officials has doubled.

The Young versus the Old.   Young Americans clearly spend less time in conventional participation than older Americans. They are less likely to vote (in part because they move so often that they do not know where or when to register) and are far less likely to attend hearings, write letters, or donate money to political

BOX 8-4

Participation by Age

Activity	Age 18–24	25–29	30–34	35–49	50–64	65+
Wrote letter to elected official	23%	27%	32%	41%	42%	40%
Wrote letter to the editor	14	14	16	15	15	10
Signed or circulated a petition	52	51	58	62	52	34
Attended a public hearing	26	27	30	42	41	28
Boycotted a company	26	27	30	29	16	9
Took part in a public demonstration	20	12	13	9	5	2
Attended a political meeting or rally	20	20	22	30	31	22
Donated tax dollars to a compaign fund	18	21	23	28	30	23

Source: Times Mirror Center for The People & The Press, "The People, the Press, and Politics, Campaign '92: 'The Generations Divide,' " July 8, 1992, p. 44.

campaigns (in part because they have less money to give). See Box 8–4 for a summary of the relationship between age and participation.

There are two theories about why young people participate less. One is that young people are less likely to see the benefits of participation until they get older. Under this **life-cycle theory of participation**, young people will become more and more active as they settle down, get married, have children, and start worrying about paying a mortgage, making ends meet, and planning for retirement. As they age through the life cycle, they begin to see the benefit of participating in politics. If this theory is true, there is little to fear in the current levels of participation. Today's young Americans will eventually catch up to their older siblings and their parents.

There may be a second reason why young people participate less. Under the **generational theory of participation,** people born into the same generation (for example, the baby boom or Generation X) learn the same lessons about the costs and benefits of participation. What matters is not age, but the events that shape a generation's attachment to the political process early in life. Once alienated from politics, always alienated from politics.

It is not clear which theory holds for today's young Americans. From a life-cycle view, younger Americans are likely to see more reasons to participate if and when they put down roots in communities. From a generational view, however, they may always feel less confident that government can be trusted, being marked for life by having grown up in a period of great distrust.

Not all the figures show that young Americans are completely disengaged from politics. They are just as likely as middle-aged and older Americans to sign petitions and attend political rallies, and much more likely to engage in unconventional forms of participation, most notably demonstrations and protests.[14]

in a different light ——— ROCK THE NATION!

College freshmen had a record-setting year in 1996–1997. On the one hand, they had a banner year for community engagement. According to annual surveys conducted by the University of California at Los Angeles, almost half of the class of 2000 spent at least some time tutoring, mentoring, or volunteering, a thirty-year record. Nearly one in three said that becoming a community leader is a very important or essential life goal.

On the other hand, they set new lows for paying attention to politics, tuning out the 1996 presidential campaign in record numbers. Barely 30 percent said that keeping up to date with political affairs was a very important or essential life goal, down from an all-time high of nearly 60 percent in 1966.

These are not just life-cycle effects. Other surveys suggest that young Americans appear to have divided their world into two continents, one composed of nonpolitical community activities such as tutoring and mentoring, the other consisting of traditional political activities such as voting, letter writing, and grassroots organizing. The two continents are separated by a gulf of political distrust and disgust. Young Americans are simultaneously the most willing of any generation in recent history to say that volunteering is the best way to make a difference in one's own community, and the least likely to think that voting can make a difference in what government does.

If young Americans are to reconnect to politics, they must build a bridge from their enormous commitment to community volunteering to more traditional political participation. Imagine what young Americans could do if they put the same energy they currently devote to tutoring and mentoring into grassroots organizing and voter registration.

Rock the Vote, a national organization that started out combating music censorship, believes that community problem solving can become that bridge from tutoring and mentoring to political action. Alongside teaching children to read and feeding the homeless, Rock the Vote is asking young Americans to help solve the problems that lead to illiteracy and homelessness in the first place. Using public service announcements on MTV, VH1, and FM radio stations across the country, its new advertising campaign, which is called Rock the Nation, features young Americans who are making a difference by joining together to solve community problems, whether by building a skateboard park in Santa Monica, creating a citywide network of after-school centers in New York, or monitoring a pollution prevention program in Baton Rouge.

Rock the Vote, a national organization committed to voter registration, launched the Rock the Nation advertising campaign in the summer of 1998. The campaign is designed to show young Americans that they can make a difference in their communities.

Rock the Nation also invites young Americans to embrace the Declaration of INTERdependence, which was signed by thirteen delegates from around the nation on July 2, 1998, in Philadelphia.

We are the Youth of America.

We are young adults. We are students, professionals, athletes, workers and homemakers. We are thinkers, hopers, dreamers and achievers. We are all unique, but we have one thing in common: we depend on each other to make the changes that will improve our society.

We will drive change. We believe that if we want to improve our nation and our world, we cannot wait for change, WE must do it—each of us, all of us. We cannot hope that others will protect us or fix things for us. We cannot assume that everything will be OK.

We must fix things ourselves—from the ground up.

We hereby pledge to involve ourselves at the community level and solve problems one step at a time. We will commit our time and reaffirm our desire to make our communities better for us and for those who come after us. We will fight apathy and conquer indifference. We will INTERdependently overcome these foes and build the road to a better tomorrow.

We will strive to improve our communities and our country.

We will make a difference.

WE WILL BE THE DIFFERENCE.

We will Rock the Nation—One Community at a Time.

The reason young Americans do not participate much in politics is not that they can't. Rather, they don't because they don't want to and have not been asked to. Rock the Nation is designed to reverse both of those situations.

Why Do Some Americans Participate More Than Others?

Americans give many reasons for not participating. Nearly 40 percent of political inactives say they do not have enough time to participate, and almost as many argue that they should take care of themselves and their families before worrying about the community or nation. Nearly 20 percent say the important things in their lives have nothing to do with politics, and almost as many say they never thought of being involved, politics is uninteresting or boring, politics cannot help with their personal or family problems, politics is too complicated, and one individual cannot have an impact.[15]

These explanations are closely related to the two most important causes of low participation: *lack of resources* and *lack of civic skills*. Together, these causes help explain who has the strongest voice in influencing who gets what, when, and how from government.

Lack of Resources.   Participating in American politics takes more than a simple desire to do so. As noted, even voting, which may be the easiest way to participate in American politics short of answering a public opinion poll or listening to talk radio, takes some minimum amount of effort.

Thus, the role of resources in political participation is clear: resources pay the costs of participation outlined above. And the two key resources are education and income. (Recall from Chapter 4 that education and income are the major indicators of an individual's socioeconomic status.) Education gives people the skills and confidence to be effective; income gives them a greater stake in getting involved, as well as the ability to purchase time (through babysitters, housekeepers, etc.) to engage in more expensive activities. As Box 8–5 shows, the relationship between resources and participation are borne out in the list of eight options noted earlier in this chapter. People with more money are much more likely to participate than are those with less.[16]

The role of resources is particularly clear in campaign contributions. People who gave more than $200 to one or more congressional candidates in 1996 were clearly different from the average American. Twenty percent of donors had family incomes over $500,000 a year; only 5 percent had incomes below $49,999. More than 80 percent had college degrees and 40 percent had postgraduate degrees (most frequently a law degree or an MBA, Master of Business Administration). Not surprisingly, most had high-status occupations, frequently in business or law.[17]

So looking back at this chapter's earlier discussion of why people do or do not participate, people with money *can* give contributions, *want to* give money because they feel it matters to elections (recall that half believe dollars are the single most important factor in elections), and are most certainly *asked* to give. Indeed, four-fifths of 1996 donors surveyed said that elected officials regularly pressure them for contributions.

Lack of Civic Skills.   Regardless of their socioeconomic level, Americans need certain skills to participate. Making a campaign contribution involves more than just having money. A citizen must know where to send the check, to whom it

BOX **8-5**

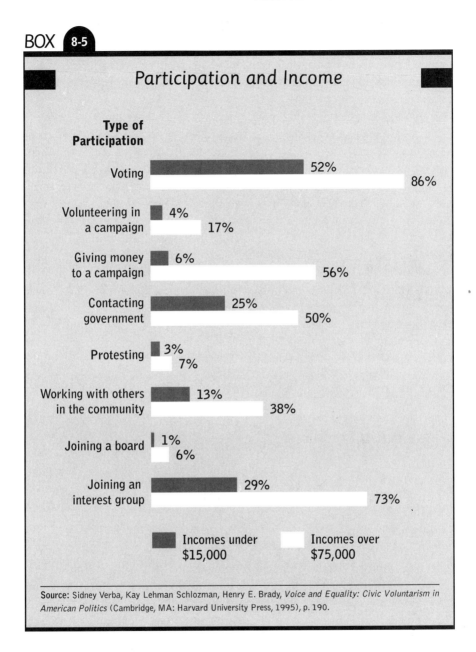

Participation and Income

Type of Participation

Voting
52%
86%

Volunteering in a campaign
4%
17%

Giving money to a campaign
6%
56%

Contacting government
25%
50%

Protesting
3%
7%

Working with others in the community
13%
38%

Joining a board
1%
6%

Joining an interest group
29%
73%

Incomes under $15,000   Incomes over $75,000

Source: Sidney Verba, Kay Lehman Schlozman, Henry E. Brady, *Voice and Equality: Civic Voluntarism in American Politics* (Cambridge, MA: Harvard University Press, 1995), p. 190.

should be sent, and how to satisfy the laws on how much they can give. Nor is it enough to want to volunteer for a campaign. A citizen must know something about how a campaign works, how to interact with others, and where to make the connection.

Luckily, civic skills are taught in many places. Many Americans start learning how to participate early, whether in classrooms or on student councils. Young Americans can learn a great deal about how to participate from religious education programs, Boy and Girl Scouts, sports leagues, and a host of other nonpolitical activities.

Once again, people with more education and higher incomes are more likely to have the practical experience that produces civic skills. People with family incomes of more than $75,000 a year are more than twice as likely to learn civic skills on the job than those with incomes under $20,000, whether by leading business meetings (which helps them learn how to chair political organizations), writing effective letters (which helps them learn how to communicate with government), or speaking before small and large groups (which helps them run for office and speak at schoolboard meetings). They are also twice as likely to learn civic skills in nonpolitical organizations, such as clubs and alumni groups.[18]

Civic skills are related to greater **political efficacy,** which is simply an individual's sense that he or she can influence government. The more practice people have in participating, the more likely they are to say that government officials care about what they think. In turn, the more people say that government officials care about what they think, the more likely they are to actually participate in politics. Because income and education affect skills, and skills affect efficacy, it should come as no surprise that people with higher socioeconomic status feel the most confident, or efficacious, about participating in politics.

Whose Voices Are Missing?

The combined impact of resources and civic skills creates a twofold bias in participation. The first bias is that government tends to hear most often from people who are already doing quite well. People who receive government benefits based on their lack of income are far less likely to participate than people who receive government benefits based on their age or prior military service.

Again, think back to the eight basic political activities noted earlier: voting, campaign work, contributing money, communicating with government, protesting, volunteering in the community, belonging to a government board, and joining an interest group. People who get veterans' benefits, student loans, Medicare (government health insurance for the elderly), or Social Security are much more likely to engage in those activities than are people who get welfare, Medicaid (government health insurance for poor people), housing support, or food stamps.[19]

The question is why people who are doing well would participate more than people who are in trouble. One answer is that the people doing well can buy the time and information needed to participate. They also have the resources to contribute to campaigns and the education to target their contacts most effectively. At the same time, poor people do not have equal access to the resources and skills to participate. They may need the attention more—people who delay getting medical care and paying the rent to put food on the table would seem to have a good claim on government attention—but may not know whom to contact, let alone how to be heard. Rightly or wrongly, some might also be worried that contacting government will jeopardize their benefits.

The second bias based on differences in resources and civic skills is that government tends to hear different messages from different people. When lower-income Americans get in touch with government, they tend to focus on their own needs—such as a lost Social Security check, ways of making their housing better, help for a small business, or efforts to make the streets safer; in short, all issues of material need. By comparison, when upper-income Americans communicate with government, they tend to focus on broader policy concerns, such as a clean environment and equality. Because lower-income Americans participate less to begin with, the result may be that their messages get lost in the process, are easily dismissed as self-centered, or, worse yet, are ignored in the flood of more elegant messages from those with greater resources and skills.[20]

These biases are only likely to increase with growing attention to e-mail and other interactive participation. As noted in Chapter 5, poor Americans, older Americans, and Americans with only a high school education or less are far less likely to use the Internet than are young Americans, well-to-do Americans, and Americans with some college experience.

VOTING: THE TEST OF DEMOCRACY

Voting deserves special attention in a book about American government. Not only is it the most common form of participation, it was also the Founders' preferred tool for giving consent. Although contacting government is certainly covered in the Bill of Rights—through the First Amendment's right to petition government, for example—it is voting that provides the central test of a citizenry's commitment to democracy.

Voter Turnout

Voting may be cherished as essential to the Founders' democracy, but it has been declining over time. Turnout in national elections has fallen from a high of over 80 percent in the late 1800s to barely 50 percent today, while voting in local elections has dropped even further.

Comparisons over such a long time are risky, however, if only because daily life has changed so much over the years. It is not clear, for example, whether the voters of 1876, who set the all-time turnout record of 82 percent, set a record worth admiring—in large part because it involved denying the vote to women and keeping African Americans away from the polls. Turnout is not a pure measure of consent. It can reflect only how many *eligible* voters actually show up. Restricting eligibility to upper-income Americans will make turnout jump dramatically. Expanding it to include citizens of every kind will naturally cause turnout to fall. High turnout may look good on paper, but not if it comes at the price of exclusion.

So noted, there is still cause for concern in the recent trends. Voting clearly dipped during the early 1900s, rose a bit during the 1930s to 1960s, then dipped again sharply during the 1970s and 1980s. In 1960, 62.8 percent of eligible voters turned out to cast votes in the presidential election; by 1988, the proportion had dropped to 50.2 percent. Although it rebounded to 55.2 percent in 1992, it resumed its long decline in 1996, falling below 50 percent for the first time since 1924. With incumbent president Bill Clinton far ahead throughout the 1996 campaign, some Americans may have concluded that their votes did not matter.

The fact is that 1992 was a nearly perfect election for getting people out to vote. The United States had an older, better-educated, and more skilled voting population than before; the presidential candidates represented very different views of the future; the campaign was close; media attention was intense; the presidential debates were engaging; the rest of the campaign had a high number of close races for the House, Senate, and state governorships; and many states had made it easier for their citizens to register and vote. Yet despite all that, the election produced only a 55 percent turnout.[21] This may mean that 55 percent is about as high as turnout will ever get with today's electorate.

Those who do not vote may be sending one of two messages. Either they are perfectly happy no matter who gets elected, expressing their general satisfaction with government and its leaders by not voting, or they are extremely unhappy with the choice of candidates, withholding their votes as a sign of absolute dissatisfaction.

Which message is the electorate sending? Most Americans (84 percent) say that voting in all elections is a very effective or fairly effective way of trying to influence the way the government is run and which laws are passed, and even more (93 percent) say they have a duty to vote. As noted earlier, large numbers (70 percent) even feel guilty when they stay at home.[22] This deep sense of civic duty can be viewed as a form of consent to be governed. It does not matter if the people do not vote, or so the notion goes, as long as they feel they should vote.

Moreover, it is not clear that voting is always worth the time. Some political scientists argue that it is perfectly rational not to vote if the benefits of the election do not outweigh the cost of voting. It takes time to register, time to follow the campaigns closely enough to know something about the choices, time to get to the polling place. American elections are always held on Tuesdays, right in the middle of the workweek. That means taking time before or after work, a particularly high cost for single parents.[23]

Nonvoting may also be a referendum on the candidates and a voter's own self-confidence. Asked why they stay home from elections, nearly two-thirds of nonvoters say they do not know enough about the candidates to vote and sometimes just do not like any of the candidates. Roughly one-third of nonvoters say that it does not matter very much who gets elected, and one-fourth say they just do not want to involve themselves in politics. Only one-fourth say it is difficult to get to the polls to vote, and just one-tenth say it is too complicated to register.[24]

in a different light —— VOTERS AND NONVOTERS

Although nonvoting may raise concerns about the consent of the governed, people who stay home on election day would have voted pretty much the same as those who did turn out. As voting expert Ruy Teixeira asks, "What if they gave an election and everybody came? Would it make a difference? The answer, it turns out, is not much."[25] Getting more people out on election day would mostly increase the margin of victory for the winner.[26]

Yet, much as they might agree on their choice of candidates, voters and nonvoters are anything but identical. The two groups clearly differ by population characteristics. In 1996, for example, voters tended to be married, over age forty-five, college educated, less mobile, and white, with age being the most important predictor. All other things being equal, Americans under the age of thirty are half as likely to vote as Americans over the age of sixty.[27]

Not surprisingly, voters and nonvoters sharply disagree over the value of voting as a civic act. Nonvoters are much less likely than voters to say that voting is either a civic duty or a way to stay connected to their community. They also are less likely to believe that voting is a way to change the government or let people in power know what they think. In the 1998 California primary election, a hotly contested election that involved record-setting spending by three visible Democratic candidates for governor and a record-setting lack of turnout, the number one reason nonvoters said they stayed home was that voting just does not change the way things are.[28] It is important to note, however, that distrust of government is *not* a cause of nonvoting. Voters share with nonvoters a lack of confidence that the government in Washington will do the right thing.

Thus, nonvoting matters not because a candidate would have done better if more people had turned out, but because the winning candidate specifically, and government generally, may not have the consent of the governed. To the extent that people stay home because they are content, the consent endures. But to the extent that people stay home because they are frustrated or angry, the declining turnout is troublesome, indeed.

The Mechanics of Voting

What makes voting so powerful as a tool of consent is that it is the great equalizer. It may be a relatively limited form of participation when compared to contacting government or joining an interest group, but everyone over the age of eighteen (except for convicted felons) has the right to do it.

They also have the right to keep their votes secret. Recall from Chapter 6 that the political parties once printed all the ballots, each party listing only its own candidates. "Party hawkers" would stand outside the polling place promoting their party's ballot to voters. Because each party's ballot came in a different color and on different-sized paper, and because voters dropped their ballots in voting boxes out in the open, rather than in closed booths, it was easy to spot who was voting for whom.[29] And because voters could deposit one ballot and one ballot only, it was nearly impossible to split one's ticket between parties.

The movement toward secret ballots began in 1888 when Massachusetts printed the first **Australian ballot.** An Australian ballot is printed by government, lists all the candidates, and is cast in secret—for example, in a voting booth. In less than eight years, 90 percent of the states had followed suit.[30] Voter turnout began to decrease almost immediately. Some political scientists argue that the high turnouts of the late 1800s were primarily a result of corruption—that is, the parties were not only printing and promoting their own ballots, but were actually dropping ballots in the voting box for citizens who did not show.

For the most part, voting is much simpler today. Only United States citizens over the age of eighteen can vote, and most prospective voters must register with states, usually through their county registrar. Assuming they have passed these two simple tests of citizenship and registration, they show up at their designated polling place on election day and cast their secret ballot.

The fact that voting is a simple process does not mean it is entirely without restrictions. Consider five questions about the mechanics of voting: (1) Who sets the rules? (2) Who has the right to vote? (3) Where do the votes count? (4) What appears on the ballot? and (5) How many votes does it take to win?

Who Sets the Rules?   States have the greatest say over the basic rules of voting. Under Article I, Section 4, of the Constitution, "The Times, Places and Manner of holding Elections for Senators and Representatives, shall be prescribed in each State by the Legislature thereof; but the Congress may at any time by Law make or alter such Regulations, except as to the Places of choosing Senators." Under this provision, states decide who gets to register to vote, when elections occur, and even how many votes it takes to win a given contest. Almost all states currently have winner-take-all, plurality-rules election systems—that is, the candidate who wins the most votes wins the election.

The Constitution does not give states complete control, however. Article I also gives Congress the right to determine how its own members are selected, and Article II makes clear that Congress may determine the time when members of the Electoral College are chosen, which was set as the first Tuesday in November. Congress also decides when the president is inaugurated, which was first set at March 4, then moved up to noon on January 20 under the Twentieth Amendment (ratified in 1933).

Article I also gives Congress enormous influence over how states behave. In 1971, for example, Congress decided to allow eighteen- to twenty-year-olds to vote in *national* elections. The only problem was that most states had long ago set the minimum voting age at twenty-one. Faced with the administrative cost of issuing two separate ballots, one for eighteen- to twenty-year-olds listing just the national contests and another for everyone twenty-one and over listing national, state, and local contests, states quickly adopted the federal standard. (A similar strategy led to major voting reforms under the Voting Rights Act of 1965, which banned a number of discriminatory practices used by states to deny the vote to minorities. Both strategies are examples of crosscutting requirements, as discussed in Chapter 3.)

Still other rules are set jointly under constitutional amendments. The Fifteenth Amendment, ratified in 1870, gave the right to vote to all races; the Seventeenth Amendment, ratified in 1913, allowed for the direct election of senators (the Constitution had originally required that senators be elected by state legislatures); the Nineteenth Amendment, ratified in 1920, gave the right to vote to women; the Twenty-fourth Amendment, ratified in 1964, prohibited use of a poll tax in national elections; and the Twenty-sixth Amendment, ratified in 1971, changed the minimum voting age to eighteen.

Over the years, differences in federal and state laws have created a complex set of rules governing elections. Some rules are common across the country: people over eighteen are allowed to vote, and national general elections are held the first Tuesday after the first Monday in November. Other rules vary: some states elect their governors and legislators in odd years, some in even; some states use primaries to select candidates, others use caucuses, or conventions, of party delegates, and still others use both.

Who Has the Right to Vote?   As noted, the Constitution is quite clear on just who is eligible to vote. Beyond age and citizenship, however, states still have considerable say in who gets to vote by setting the basic rules of *voter registration*. Voter registration was originally designed to prevent election fraud by requiring voters to prove their eligibility by showing up some days in advance to prove their residency, citizenship, and age.

Although former slaves won the right to vote under the Fifteenth Amendment, many Southern states refused to accept them as equal citizens until the 1960s. Instead, they invented a variety of devices to raise the cost of voting for African Americans. Some states imposed a poll tax on voters, requiring citizens to pay a fee to vote in a given election, while others created literacy tests, requiring citizens to prove their knowledge or moral character before being allowed to vote. In Mississippi, for example, citizens had to be able to "read and write any section of the constitution of this state and give a reasonable interpretation thereof to the country registar" before voting, while Louisiana required citizens to both "understand the duties and obligations of citizens under a republican form of government" and provide two other voters as references. Because African Americans were less likely to have the money or education to pay the tax and pass the test, these devices reduced their turnout in elections.

The South may have invented the tests to discriminate against former slaves, but other states quickly learned how to use the barriers to prevent other "undesirables" from voting. All such tests were outlawed by the Voting Rights Act of 1965, including Idaho's test of moral character that barred prostitutes, people who "habitually resort to any house of prostitution or of ill fame," gays and lesbians, and advocates of bigamy and polygamy from voting.[31]

Many states continue to ease the burdens of voting. Minnesota, Maine, and Wisconsin, for example, allow voters to register on the same day and in the same place as they vote. Voters in those three states must merely show some form of identification—a driver's license, a utility bill—to prove they live where they say.[32] Uniquely, North Dakota does not require registration at all.

Some states keep their citizens on the registration rolls even if they do not vote in election after election. In contrast to states that automatically cancel a registration if a voter fails to vote in just one general election (Arizona, Hawaii, and Nevada) or two (Colorado, Delaware, Kansas, New Hampshire, Rhode Island, and Virginia), at least nine states never purge, or clean, their rolls of nonvoters. Such states clearly make voting much easier.[33]

Finally, most states now allow volunteers to register voters on the state's behalf. Instead of requiring people to register only at the county seat, most allow volunteer deputy registrars, as they are called, to go where the voters are, which means setting up registration booths on college campuses, in housing projects, at shopping malls, and just about anywhere else potential voters can be found.

Where Do the Votes Count?   The House of Representatives has not always had 435 members, nor the Senate 100. The growth of the Senate was driven by each decision to admit a new state to the Union. The Senate added two members with each new state, reaching 100 with the admission of Hawaii and Alaska in the late 1950s.

The growth of the House was driven by a more complicated formula that mixed population, as measured every ten years by the census, and politics. From 1790 to 1830, Congress had one member for every 30,000 citizens, growing from 196 to 242 members. If the same number, or apportionment of seats to citizens, applied today, Congress would have over 7,500 members! Congress raised the number of citizens per member of Congress to 70,680 in 1840, then decided in 1850 that it would merely set the number of seats in advance and divide it into the total population determined in the census (conducted under constitutional order in the first year of every decade). By 1910, Congress had reached 435 seats, and decided to stop growing.[34] From then on, the population size of the districts, not Congress, would have to grow. By 1990, each member of Congress had an average of 570,000 constituents.

The problem with drawing the district lines is that the population does not grow at the same rate in every state. Some states are expanding rapidly, while others are shrinking. In the last reapportionment, California (plus seven), Texas (plus three), and Florida (plus four) all gained congressional seats in 1990, while New York (minus three), Michigan (minus two), and New Jersey (minus one) all lost seats. Montana also lost one, leaving that state with more senators (two) than House members (one).

Changes in total population mean that every state, except those with only one representative in the House (Alaska, Delaware, Montana, North Dakota, South Dakota, Vermont, and Wyoming), must redraw its districts every ten years. Congress may determine how many members it has, but the states say which people vote in what district—that is, the states apportion the population into House districts. Since state legislatures and governors have the ultimate authority to draw the lines (subject to federal court review in cases where voting rights might be affected) there is considerable room to shape and reshape district lines to benefit one party or the other.[35]

Drawing Lines.   Efforts to draw favorable lines have existed since 1812, when Massachusetts governor Elbridge Gerry and his party machine redistricted the state into a patchwork of oddly shaped districts, one of which looked like a salamander. To this day, such efforts are labeled **gerrymandering** (*Gerry* plus *salamander*).[36]

During the early 1990s, apportionment was used to increase the likelihood that districts would elect more minority members of Congress. The goals of redistricting may have changed—from favoring one party over another to ensuring greater minority representation—but the result still looks the same: voting districts that make little geographic sense.

These **majority-minority districts** were the product of the 1982 amendments to the 1965 Voting Rights Act. Under the 1982 amendments, states were allowed to draw district lines to prevent minority votes from being "diluted" by large white populations. Working with the new population figures from the 1990 census, several Southern states used race-based redistricting to create more than a dozen majority-minority districts. The most dramatic result was North Carolina's Twelfth District, a long, thin district that once ran 160 miles along Interstate 85 from Gastonia to Durham, including Charlotte, Greensboro, and Winston-Salem. It was one of two North Carolina districts drawn to pool African American votes. (See Box 8–6 for a map of North Carolina's Twelfth District.)

Given North Carolina's 78 percent white and 20 percent African American population, defenders claim that such districts are the only way to enhance African American representation. Kenneth Spaulding, a Durham lawyer who was one of four African Americans who had repeatedly lost to whites in the old Second Congressional District, said, "How a district looks, I'm not concerned about. I'm concerned about how a congressional delegation looks. What everyone seems to be missing is any mention of the history of an all white male congressional delegation. "[37]

Other states also created majority-minority districts, including Georgia's Eleventh, Louisiana's Fourth, and Texas's Eighteenth, Twenty-ninth, and Thirtieth. Voting rights experts suggest that racial redistricting may have accounted for the election of thirteen additional African Americans and six Hispanics in 1992 alone.[38]

Majority-minority districts are highly controversial. As noted in Chapter 6, African Americans are very likely to vote Democratic. Because majority-minority districts concentrate a party's strength in particular districts, their existence may increase the likelihood that Republicans will win elsewhere. Moreover, given its enormous impact on who votes where, majority-minority redistricting prompted a number of lawsuits alleging reverse discrimination. Whites who objected to becoming the minority in some racially gerrymandered districts sued in federal court to have many of the new districts declared unconstitutional.

A Constitutional Challenge.   The challenges produced a mix of results in the lower courts. Louisiana's Fourth District, all three Texas districts, and Georgia's Eleventh District were all declared unconstitutional by the lower courts, but

BOX **8-6**

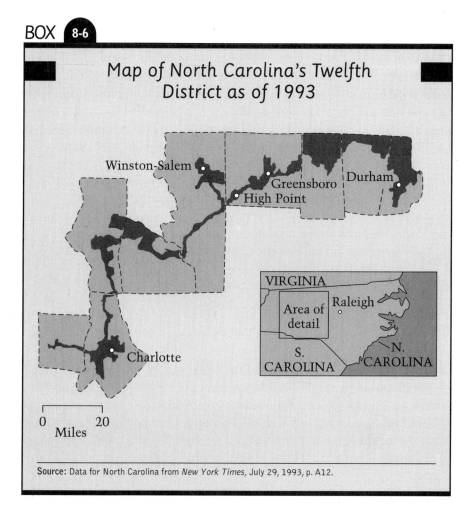

Map of North Carolina's Twelfth District as of 1993

Winston-Salem

Greensboro · Durham

· High Point

VIRGINIA

Area of detail · Raleigh

S. CAROLINA · N. CAROLINA

· Charlotte

0   20
Miles

Source: Data for North Carolina from *New York Times*, July 29, 1993, p. A12.

North Carolina's Twelfth was not. The Supreme Court reconciled the differences in three decisions. The first came in 1993 with *Shaw v. Reno;* the next in 1995 with *Miller v. Johnson,* and the most recent in 1996 with *Shaw v. Hunt.*

Ruth Shaw was a voter in North Carolina's Twelfth Congressional District; Janet Reno was the attorney general of the United States responsible for approving the redistricting plan that had created that district. Shaw and several other white citizens sued Reno (and the federal government she represented) to overturn the district on the grounds that it was so extremely irregular in shape that it could only be viewed as an effort to segregate races for voting, thereby violating the Fourteenth Amendment's **equal protection clause**—which says that no state can deny any person equal protection of the laws—by creating reverse discrimination against whites.

After a federal district court rejected the argument, Shaw appealed. Although the Supreme Court did not declare the North Carolina district unconstitutional at the time, it did send the case back to the lower court for another review on a 5–4 vote. The majority opinion was written by Justice Sandra Day O'Connor:

> Racial classifications of any sort pose the risk of lasting harm to our society. They reinforce the belief, held by too many for too much of our history, that individuals should be judged by the color of their skin. Racial classifications with respect to voting carry particular dangers. Racial gerrymandering, even for remedial purposes, may balkanize us into competing racial factions; it threatens to carry us further from the goal of a political system in which race no longer matters—a goal that the Fourteenth and Fifteenth Amendments embody, and to which the Nation continues to aspire. It is for these reasons that race-based districting by our state legislatures demands close judicial scrutiny.[39]

In 1995, while the North Carolina case was still moving forward in the lower courts, the Supreme Court took the next logical step on the issue in *Miller v. Johnson,* ruling that Georgia's Eleventh Congressional District was unconstitutional.[40] The 5–4 majority argued that using race as the predominant factor in drawing a new district line is almost always going to be unconstitutional, carrying forward O'Connor's argument from *Shaw v. Reno.* Within hours of announcing the decision, the Supreme Court accepted two more redistricting cases, one from Texas and the old one from North Carolina. In *Shaw v. Hunt* in 1996, the Supreme Court finally overturned North Carolina's Twelfth District and three other districts.[41]

What Appears on the Ballot?   Almost all elections involve a choice among candidates. Candidates vary by the *level of office* involved (federal, state, and local), as well as by the *stage of the campaign* (primary and general). General elections have the highest voter turnout, particularly when they fall in a presidential year—they create the greatest public interest. Primary elections have the lowest turnout, particularly when they fall in odd years or involve local offices only—they generate only passing interest.

Some voters also get to vote about policy issues. Twenty-five states have the **referendum,** which (as Chapter 1 explained) allows the legislature to put bills on the ballot for public decision; twenty-three states have the **initiative,** which (as also discussed in Chapter 1) allows citizens to put legislation on the ballot through petitions signed by roughly 5 to 10 percent of eligible voters; and fifteen states have the **recall,** which allows voters to remove elected officials from office

A protest in 1994 against California's Proposition 187, an initiative that proposed to ban public assistance for illegal immigrants and their children. The proposition passed, but was immediately declared an unconstitutional denial of equal protection by the federal courts.

in special elections, again through petitions. Finally, all states except Delaware require voters to ratify changes to their constitutions.[42]

Whatever the Founders might have thought of these opportunities for direct
democracy, there has been a dramatic increase in the number of ballot initiatives
over the past decade. Roughly 50 percent of the nearly two thousand initiatives
considered in U.S. history have been on the ballot in the last fifty years, with
nearly 25 percent in just the last decade, and almost 10 percent in 1994 alone.

Ballot initiatives now run the gamut of topics: crime, gambling, taxes, term
limits for elected officials, and bans on gay and lesbian rights. Efforts to limit tax
increases are almost always on the ballot somewhere, as are efforts to reduce
crime. Term-limit initiatives have been a more recent wave, spurred by distrust of
government. Since 1990, twenty-two mostly western states have passed some
form of term limits on members of Congress; all these measures were rendered
unconstitutional in 1995 when the Supreme Court concluded that limiting the
number of terms members can serve would constitute a new qualification for
holding national office. Because the Founders had decided that age and citizenship would be the only qualifications for office, the only way to impose such a

new qualification would be through a constitutional amendment. Voters in nine states responded to the Supreme Court decision by passing initiatives in 1996 that ask congressional candidates to pledge their support for term limits. Supporters and opponents were to be listed as such on the actual ballot, giving voters an obvious opportunity to use the information to punish or reward candidates.

Term limits were not the only initiatives on the 1996 ballot. In what was a record-setting year, citizens were asked to vote on over ninety initiatives, including affirmative action in California, riverboat gambling in Ohio, conservation and protection of the Everglades in Florida, legalization of marijuana for medical use in Arizona and California, limits on clear-cutting of forest land in Maine, and bear hunting in Idaho. (See Box 8–7 for a sampling of the 1996 initiatives.) As Chapter 9 shows, the number of initiatives kept climbing in 1998. California, for example, considered a variety of initiatives in its June 1998 primary, including one to ban labor unions from using member dues for campaign contributions, which failed on a close vote.

Because initiatives are often controversial, they can increase voter turnout. However, because they do so by stimulating popular passions, they may fuel the factionalism that so worried the Founders. California's Proposition 209, which was designed to abolish affirmative action programs in state and local government, including the state's higher education system, provoked intense opposition across racial lines in 1996 and passed with 54 percent of the vote.

Direct democracy is a growing business. Private firms can be hired to do virtually everything needed to pass an initiative, from "harvesting " the citizen signatures needed to put an idea on the ballot to the advertising and direct mail needed to get it passed. Signature harvesters—students, part-timers, and homeless people—are paid anywhere from 35 cents per valid signature in California to $6 a signature in Nevada.[43] Costs depend on how early or late the harvesting begins (late = more expensive), how popular or unpopular the cause (unpopular = more expensive), and how difficult the initiative is to explain to potential petitioners (more complex = more expensive).

How Many Votes Does It Take to Win?   As noted above, almost all elections are won or lost on the basis of total votes. Although several states require runoff elections when the top candidate does not win a majority of all votes cast, most states merely require the winner to have a **plurality**—that is, to have the largest number of votes, even if that number is not an absolute majority.

Only two offices at the national level are elected on the basis of anything but the number of popular votes: president and vice president. Recall from Chapter 2 that they are elected by members of the *electoral college,* a curious invention of the Founders designed both to cool the passions of the public and to ensure that the president was the leader not just of the American people but also of the separate states.

BOX 8-7

The Voters Speak, 1996

Affirmative action: California voters amended the state's constitution to abolish affirmative action in state and local government, including employment, education, and contracting.

Campaign finance: Maine voters agreed to provide state funding for candidates who voluntarily accept spending limits in their races for statewide office. California voters approved restrictions on campaign contributions.

Environment: Florida voters rejected a 1 cent per pound tax on raw sugar grown in the Everglades as a device for funding conservation of the endangered wetlands, but passed two other measures to protect the area.

Gambling: Voters in five states rejected measures that would have permitted gaming casinos or other gambling. Michigan voters approved gambling casinos with the condition that all tax revenues from the gambling be used for crime prevention, economic development, and public education.

Hunting: Voters in three states voted to restrict the use of hounds, traps, or bait in hunting. Idaho voters prohibited the use of dogs or bait to hunt black bears; Massachusetts voters prohibited the use of steel-jaw leg traps to hunt bears.

Crime: Arizona voters approved an initiative that will try juveniles, fifteen years old and older, as adults for armed robbery, murder, or rape.

Family values: Colorado voters rejected a constitutional amendment declaring that parents have the "inalienable right" to control "the upbringing, values, and discipline of their children."

Marijuana use: Arizona and California voters approved the use of marijuana for medicinal purposes.

Term limits: Voters in nine states approved measures that require candidates to pledge their support for term limits or risk being listed on the ballot as having refused.

Victims' rights: Voters in eight states approved initiatives on behalf of crime victims.

Taxes: Colorado voters approved a measure that eliminates tax exemptions on property used for religious purposes, profit-making schools, and certain other charitable purposes.

Because the Constitution sets the number of electors by adding Senate and House seats, it clearly encourages presidential candidates to concentrate their energies on winning the big states. Why bother with the relatively few votes to be had in Delaware, South Dakota, or Idaho? And because the system awards final votes on a winner-take-all basis, it also almost always inflates the margin of victory for the winner. In 1980, for example, Ronald Reagan won just 51 percent of the popular vote, but took 91 percent of the electoral college; in 1992, Bill Clinton won just 43 percent of the popular vote, but 69 percent of the electoral vote. Even though Clinton did much better in 1996, winning 49.2 percent of the popular vote, he still pulled down just 70 percent of the electoral vote.

As a result, the winner-take-all system creates the very real possibility that a president can be elected without having won the popular vote. It is simple mathematics: If a candidate can win New York (33 electoral college votes) and Pennsylvania (23) in the northeast; take Ohio (21), Michigan (18), and Illinois (22), in the Midwest; go south to pick up Texas (32), Florida (25), North Carolina (14), and Georgia (13); then head west for California (54) and Washington (11); and throw in just one small state such as Hawaii (4) along the way, that candidate can become president of the United States after winning just twelve of fifty states.

Fear of such a skewed election has prompted calls for abolishing the electoral college in favor of using a simple national vote. Candidates would mount a national campaign, instead of fifty separate state campaigns. Under the notion that "if it ain't broke, don't fix it," however, it is unlikely that the nation would approve such a reform until the worst case actually occurs. After all, the last time a candidate won the election but lost the electoral college was in 1888, when Grover Cleveland won the popular vote by 48.6 percent to 47.8 percent, but lost the electoral vote to Benjamin Harrison by 168 to 233—not even close.

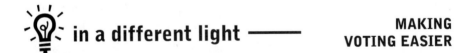

in a different light —— MAKING VOTING EASIER

Efforts to make voting easier peaked in the 1960s and early 1970s with passage of the Voting Rights Act and ratification of the Twenty-sixth Amendment. However, the 1990s have produced two efforts to encourage greater electoral participation, both of which may make voting easier.

The first is a nationwide effort designed to give citizens more opportunities to register. Under the 1993 National Voter Registration Act, which is often called the *motor voter law*, states must allow citizens to register whenever they get other state and local services such as a driver's license (hence the term *motor voter*) or a welfare check.

A voter registration effort at the University of California, Santa Barbara. Allowing deputy registrars to register voters is one way to lower the barriers to voting. Allowing citizens to register when they get other government services such as a driver's license and allowing them to vote by mail are two others.

According to early estimates, nearly 40 million new voters had registered under the law by 1998. Although most of the new voters registered at driver's license bureaus, 10 to 20 percent signed up at public welfare agencies. By reducing the costs of registering for these poor Americans, the motor voter law helps reduce some of the bias in the current registration system. Contrary to early expectations that most of these new voters would register as Democrats, neither party has benefited from the easier registration. Democrats accounted for roughly half of the new registrations in 1995–1996, which is just about where the party was in the public as a whole, while Republicans captured about one-third, which is just about where it was in the public as a whole. The rest of the registrations were for independents.

If there is a problem with the motor voter law, it is for young people. Most Americans get their first driver's license at age sixteen, but cannot register to vote until eighteen. Because most states do not require a license renewal for six years, young people do not get the benefit of the motor voter law until after their first election, at the very earliest. That is why Florida is considering allowing students to register to vote when they register for college classes. The proposal, called "Register Once," was developed by the Florida Student Association, an interest group that lobbies on behalf of students at state universities and community colleges.[44]

The second effort to encourage greater participation is designed to reduce the personal costs of voting by allowing citizens to vote by mail. Oregon tried the idea in a special U.S. Senate election in early 1996. The state sent every registered voter a ballot and prepaid return envelope twenty-one days before election day. Voting simply meant marking the secret ballot and dropping it in the mail. In all, 66 percent of registered voters returned their ballots, producing a much higher turnout than would have occurred otherwise. At the same time, the state saved $1 million by not having to open polling places on election day.

Oregon's vote-by-mail experiment produced both positives and negatives for participation. On the positive side, it sharply lowered the cost of participating. Voters did not have to find babysitters or take time off from work, nor did they have to find the polling place. And turnout increased. On the negative side, vote-by-mail may have altered the conduct of the election campaign. Because most voters sent in their ballots within five days of receiving them, there was no final election day. As one observer argued, vote-by-mail made "the process the equivalent of picking an NBA champion the week before the finals begin."[45] Vote-by-mail may also increase the chances of fraud by leaving so many ballots in circulation for so long. More troubling, perhaps, is vote-by-mail's elimination of all chances that citizens will run into each other in this most central act of democracy, furthering the "bowling alone" problem discussed earlier in this chapter.

MAINTAINING THE BALANCE

The United States may still be a nation of participators, but there are warning signs on the horizon. The clamor of a thousand public voices that greeted Tocqueville 150 years ago may soon become the eerie quiet of a thousand individual letters and e-mails dropping silently on congressional desks and appearing on computer screens. Although the *amount* of participation may be relatively steady and high, the *quality* of participation is clearly changing.

Two changes in American participation may be threatening the delicate balance. First, there are substantial pockets of intense apathy. Many Americans simply do not have the resources or skills to participate at all. Even as the United States struggles to lower the barriers to voting, voter turnout continues to decline.

Already, less than half of registered voters participate in the country's most visible election, for president. The question is whether government is perilously close to losing the consent of the governed, not because Americans are angry, but because they just do not care. Lacking at least some minimum level of interest, can government be confident in imposing the burdens necessary to defend the nation against foreign and domestic threats?

Second, American participation seems to be shifting from visible, public activities to much more private, one-on-one engagement. The same forces that lead people to stay at home on election day may also lead them to avoid their neighbors on the street, and ignore community problems such as drugs and crime. Although there is still plenty of debate about whether, in fact, Americans are bowling alone, the rising tide of narrow interest groups and declining party loyalty support the notion that politics is becoming a spectator sport. Such a lonely nation can easily transform a government designed to be just strong enough into one that does not have the consent to govern at all.

American government depends on having enough participation to give consent, but not so much as to paralyze action. Unfortunately, the current trends suggest that American government is farther from the former and closer to the latter. Fewer and fewer Americans seem willing to give their consent, while highly specialized participation through interest groups is increasing. The result may become a government that has neither the consent of the governed nor the capacity to act—and that would be a government desperately out of balance.

terms to remember

conventional participation
(p. 289)
unconventional participation
(p. 289)
voter turnout (p. 291)
congressional case workers
(p. 296)
life-cycle theory of participation (p. 300)
generational theory of participation (p. 301)
political efficacy (p. 306)

Australian ballot (p. 310)
gerrymandering (p. 314)
majority-minority districts
(p. 314)
equal protection clause
(p. 315)
referendum (p. 316)
initiative (p. 316)
recall (p. 316)
plurality (p. 318)
motor voter law (p. 320)

facts and interpretations

- Americans have a veritable shopping mall of options for participating in politics. Some are public, others private; some involve collective action, others individual; some involve sharp
messages, others blunt. The United States may trail the rest of
the world in voter turnout, but leads in virtually every other
category, including communicating with government. America's commitment to individualism means that its people engage in participation that fits their personal goals, be they
material, social, civic, or policy.

- There are vast pockets of nonparticipation in American society, largely based on socioeconomic factors that limit the resources and civic skills for participation. Poor Americans do not have the dollars to contribute to campaigns, while the less educated may have trouble following politics or knowing how to register to vote. The result is that participation is skewed toward the well-to-do and better educated. Those groups are much more likely to engage in contributing money to campaigns, writing letters, and running for office. The only place where they do not have absolute dominance is in protests and demonstrations. There, young Americans hold the lead.

- Voting is the test of democracy, the Founders' preferred tool for Americans to use in giving their consent to be governed. Turnout in elections continues downward from its all-time high in the mid–1870s, giving rise to questions about whether Americans are withdrawing their consent. The easiest way to raise turnout would be to restrict eligibility, but the United States has chosen a different, more hopeful course: raising turnout by lowering barriers to voting. Even with new laws to make registration easier, turnout in the 1996 presidential election dropped below 50 percent, and shows no signs of rebounding soon. Although the election campaign could have been more exciting, Americans who did not vote mostly agreed that voting does not make a difference in what the government does. Their votes might not have made a difference in the outcome, but would have brought a very different set of attitudes to the election.

- The United States continues to struggle with how to divide itself into congressional districts. With the 2000 census just around the corner, the question is how to ensure that every American has an equal voice. Under the 1965 Voting Rights Act, Congress allowed states to redraw district lines to favor the creation of majority-minority districts. The goal was perfectly reasonable: to increase the odds that more minorities would be elected to Congress, thereby perhaps increasing the participation of a historically underparticipating segment of the population. The Supreme Court disagreed, arguing that such districts create more division than consent.

open questions

- Should America worry about political participation? What messages do people who do not participate send their government? Does the fact that so many Americans stay at home on election day weaken the legitimacy of government?

- What might the Founders think about the balance of participation in America today? Would they worry about the amount of money being contributed to politics? Would they like the current levels of letter writing and other direct contact with government? What would they say about the socioeconomic status of the top campaign contributors?

- Should the United States work harder to increase voter turnout? What are the positives in efforts to improve voter turnout by making voter registration easier? Even if Americans still do not vote, is it important for government to keep trying to encourage them to vote? What about efforts to encourage greater participation by redrawing district lines to favor people who historically do not participate, such as young people or the poor?

- How politically active is your campus? How much are you participating in politics these days? And how much of your participation is alone rather than with others? What might explain the sharp increase in the number of Americans making contact with government in private? Does that increase relate to the decline in voting? What could you do to participate more with others, and what kind of resources and civic skills would you need to do so? Does your college or university offer any help in getting those resources and learning those skills? If not, should it?

for further study

Berry, Jeffrey M., Kent E. Portney, and Ken Thompson. *The Rebirth of Urban Democracy.* Washington, DC: Brookings Institution, 1993.

Butler, David, and Bruce Cain. *Congressional Redistricting: Comparative and Theoretical Perspectives.* New York: Macmillan, 1992.

Magleby, David. *Direct Legislation: Voting on Ballot Propositions in the United States.* Baltimore: Johns Hopkins University Press, 1984.

Verba, Sidney, Kay Lehman Schlozman, and Henry Brady. *Voice and Equality: Civic Voluntarism in American Politics.* Cambridge, MA: Harvard University Press, 1995.

Wolfinger, Raymond, and Steven Rosenstone. *Who Votes?* New Haven; CT: Yale University Press, 1980.

endnotes for chapter 8

1. Alexis de Tocqueville, *Democracy in America,* ed. J. P. Mayer, trans. George Lawrence (Garden City, NY: Harper Perennial, 1988), pp. 242–43.
2. The 80 percent figure is drawn from the discussion later in this chapter about the six types of political participants. Only 20 percent of the American public can be labeled as absolutely inactive in politics.
3. This list is drawn from Sidney Verba, Kay Lehman Schlozman, and Henry Brady, *Voice and Equality: Civic Voluntarism in American Politics* (Cambridge, MA: Harvard University Press, 1995).
4. Samuel Barnes and Max Kasse, eds., *Political Action: Mass Participation in Five Western Democracies* (Beverly Hills, CA: Sage, 1979), p. 545.
5. John Green, Paul Herrnson, Lynda Powell, and Clyde Wilcox, *Individual Congressional Campaign Contributors: Wealthy, Conservative—and Reform Minded,* release by authors, June 9, 1998.
6. The exchange occurred on September 17, 1997, before the U.S. Senate Governmental Affairs Committee.
7. "Bowling Alone: Democracy in America at the End of the Twentieth Century," paper prepared for delivery at the Nobel Symposium "Democracy's Victory and Crisis," Uppsala, Sweden, August 27–29, 1994; the paper was published as "Bowling Alone: America's Declining Social Capital," *Journal of Democracy,* 6, 1 (January 1995): 65–78; a more recent statement on the issue is Robert D. Putnam and Steven Yonish, "New Evidence on Trends in American Social Capital and Civic Engagement: Are We Really 'Bowling Alone?'" preliminary draft, January 4, 1998.
8. For dissenting views of the state of civic life in the United States, see Nicholas Lemann, "Kicking in Groups," *Atlantic,* April 1996, pp. 22–26; Frank Riessman and Erik Banks, "The Mismeasure of Civil Society," *Social Policy,* Spring 1996, pp. 2–5; and Katha Pollitt, "For Whom the Ball Rolls," *The Nation,* April 16, 1996, pp. 9–11; see also the defense of Putnam in response to Pollitt's scathing editorial from Benjamin Barber, *The Nation,* July 1, 1996, pp. 2, 24; for a broad, perhaps less politicized assessment see the entire fall 1997, issue of *The Brookings Review,* which was edited by E. J. Dionne and includes articles by Alan Wolfe, Jean Elshstain, Theda Skocpol, and William Galston, among others.
9. Kay Lehman Schlozman, Sidney Verba, Henry Brady, and Jennifer Erkuwater, *Why Can't They Be Like We Were? Understanding the Generation Gap in Participation,* unpublished paper, June 1998.
10. The following discussion draws heavily on data presented by Verba, Schlozman, and Brady, *Voice and Equality,* p. 115.
11. See M. Kent Jennings and Richard G. Niemi, *Generations and Politics: A Panel Study of Young Adults and Their Parents* (Princeton, NJ: Princeton University Press, 1981).
12. Ruy Teixeira, *The Disappearing American Voter* (Washington, DC: Brookings Institution, 1992), p. 8.
13. Verba, Schlozman, and Brady, *Voice and Equality,* p. 70.

14. Times Mirror Center for The People & The Press, *The People, The Press and Politics, Campaign '92: The Generations Divide,* July 8, 1992, p. 44.

15. Verba, Schlozman, and Brady, *Voice and Equality,* p. 129.

16. Verba, Schlozman, and Brady, *Voice and Equality,* p. 190.

17. Green et al., *Individual Campaign Contributors.*

18. Verba, Schlozman, and Brady, *Voice and Equality,* p. 319.

19. Sidney Verba, Kay Lehman Schlozman, Henry Brady, and Norman Nie, "Citizen Activity: Who Participates? What Do They Say? " *American Political Science Review,* 87, no. 2 (June 1993): 305.

20. Verba et al., "Citizen Activity," p. 312.

21. See Ruy Teixeira, "Turnout in the 1992 Election," *Brookings Review,* Spring 1993, p. 47.

22. Times Mirror Center, *Campaign '92,* p. 40.

23. Anthony Downs, *An Economic Theory of Democracy* (New York: Harper & Row, 1957).

24. Times Mirror Center, *Campaign '92,* p. 42.

25. Teixeira, *The Disappearing American Voter,* p. 95.

26. See Teixeira's analysis in *The Disappearing American Voter,* pp. 95–97.

27. The Melman Group and Wirthlin Worldwide, "Analysis of a Survey on Non-Voting," memo to the League of Women Voters, May 29, 1996.

28. Pew Research Center for The People & The Press, *Voters Not So Angry, Not So Interested* (Washington, DC: Pew Research Center, June 1998).

29. See Jerrold G. Rusk, "The Effect of the Australian Ballot Reform on Split Ticket Voting: 1876–1908," in Richard G. Niemi and Herbert F. Weisberg, *Classics in Voting Behavior* (Washington, DC: CQ Press, 1993), p. 313.

30. Rusk, "Australian Ballot Reform," p. 313.

31. The tests are listed in *Congressional Quarterly Almanac* (Washington, DC: CQ Press, 1965), p. 539.

32. Teixeira, *The Disappearing American Voter,* p. 108; see also Raymond Wolfinger and Steven Rosenstone, *Who Votes?* (New Haven, CT: Yale University Press, 1980).

33. Harold W. Stanley and Richard G. Niemi, *Vital Statistics on American Politics* (Washington, DC: CQ Press, 1994), pp. 37–39.

34. This history can be found in David Butler and Bruce Cain, *Congressional Redistricting: Comparative and Theoretical Perspectives* (New York: Macmillan, 1992), p. 19.

35. See Richard Miniter, "The Computer That Defeated a Congressman," *Washington Post National Weekly Edition,* September 28–October 4, 1992, p. 24.

36. Butler and Cain, *Congressional Redistricting,* p. 17.

37. Quoted in Ronald Smothers, "Fair Play or Racial Gerrymandering," *New York Times,* April 16, 1993, p. B9.

38. See Smothers, "Fair Play," p. B9.

39. *Shaw v. Reno,* 61 U.S.L.W. 4818 (1993).

40. *Miller v. Johnson,* 63 U.S.L.W. 4726 (1995).

41. *Shaw v. Hunt,* Sup. Ct. Docket No. 94–923.

42. For a history of the initiative and the referendum, see David Magleby, *Direct Legislation: Voting on Ballot Propositions in the United States* (Baltimore: Johns Hopkins University Press, 1984).

43. James Sterba, "Politicians at All Levels Seek Expert Advice, Fueling an Industry," *Wall Street Journal,* September 1, 1992, p. A1.

44. See "Florida May Take Motor Voter Step Further," special to the *New York Times,* February 25, 1996, p. 39; for a systematic analysis of the Oregon vote-by-mail initiative, see Michael W. Traugott, "An Evaluation of Voting-by-Mail in Oregon," prepared for the Workshop on Voting-by-Mail, Washington, DC, August 27, 1997.

45. Norman Ornstein, "A Vote Cheapened," *Washington Post,* February 8, 1996, p. A19.

campaigns and elections

the feast of democracy

Election campaigns are the feast of democracy. They are the only times the Founders truly wanted the people and their representatives to "dine" together. For their part, voters consume vast quantities of information about candidates, issues, and the state of the nation, picking through the offerings in search of a decision about how to vote. And for their part, candidates consume vast quantities of information about what voters think, building a menu of ideas that might motivate more of their supporters to go to the polls than their opponent's, which is, after all, the ultimate goal of a campaign.

This feast of information and ideas may be the single most important event in American democratic life, a rare opportunity for Americans to give their consent to be governed and simultaneously hold their representatives accountable for what they have or have not done since the last election. There is good evidence that Americans take the opportunity seriously. Even when they think a campaign is dull and boring, which is how half the public described the presidential campaign in 1996, the vast majority of Americans still pay a lot of or some attention to the ebb and flow of the campaign. Most Americans watch the televised debates, talk now and then with their friends and neighbors, and make at least some effort to keep up, even if they do not intend to vote.

Nevertheless, the Founders might be worried about how long and expensive election campaigns have become, and how heavily candidates have come to depend on political consultants and television. They might be disturbed to discover how much time candidates for office spend raising money, and would likely wonder why campaigns have to be so long. They might also be puzzled at how much candidate image appears to matter to the final vote. In short, although they would agree that campaigns are still a feast of democracy, they might wonder why so much junk food gets served.

This is not to say that the Founders would disapprove of campaigning per se. The Founders were practical politicians who knew that candidates had to campaign to get elected. When George Washington first ran for office in 1757, for example, he is said to have provided the "customary means of winning votes": 28 gallons of rum, 50 gallons of rum punch, 34 gallons of wine, 46 gallons of beer, and 2 gallons of cider royal. Given that there were only 319 voters in his district, Washington spent 2 quarts per vote.[1]

Rather, what would trouble the Founders is how winning elections has become less a test of a candidate's virtue than a test of a candidate's ability to craft a clever message and effective negative advertisements. They might even ask whether a George Washington could get elected today, or whether he would be painted as too old and stuffy, or whether an investigative reporter might find some scandal in that long winter at Valley Forge (why didn't he win the Revolutionary War in less time?).

To the extent that modern campaigns decay into an unrelenting barrage of promises and a constant battering of attack advertisements, they may actually undermine the delicate balance the Founders worked so hard to create. By overpromising, candidates encourage citizens to expect more from government than it could ever provide, drawing the people into the public policy process in a way that limits government's ability to make the tough choices needed to protect the nation. By engaging in constant attacks on their opponents, candidates also encourage citizens to devalue elections. The less they respect the election process, the more they may withdraw their consent to be governed.

Campaigns do not have to be nice to be honorable, of course. Candidates ought to fight hard. They ought to feel free to point out their opponents' weaknesses. But it is one thing to offer such comparative information, which voters find both useful and redeeming, and quite another to focus almost entirely on the weaknesses. A good campaign consists of hard argument, tough comparison, and a basic respect for the democratic process—in short, good manners, good food, and a hungry audience. Candidates should want to win, but recent campaigns may have produced a level of negativism that reduces the public's confidence in the very offices that are up for election. In that regard, campaigns can undermine government's ultimate ability to act.

As this chapter shows, modern campaigns are anything but simple affairs. There are complex rules governing elections, complex organizations for conducting campaigns, and complex strategies for persuading voters. Yet, as this chapter also shows, the final decision that each voter makes may be anything but complex. In the end, most voters cast their ballots for the candidate they like the best, or the one they dislike the least.

HARD RULES, TOUGH CHOICES

Running for political office is one of the most challenging tasks in America. It means intense public scrutiny, a nearly constant search for campaign money, and moments of great drama. It is not a decision to be taken lightly, for it involves hard rules and tough choices.

Choosing Nominees

The Constitution provides few details on who gets to run for national office. Although Articles I and II set simple qualifications such as age and citizenship for those who hold national office, the Constitution leaves the rest of the decisions to the states. The result is a patchwork of rules across the nation.

Recognizing these differences, reaching office almost always involves winning at least two separate campaigns: one for a party's **nomination** and one for the **general election.** The first campaign is to get on the general election ballot; the second is to win the office itself.

Under Article I, Section 4, states have considerable influence over how nomination contests are decided, often using one system for selecting Senate and House nominees and a second, different system for choosing the national party delegates who select the presidential nominees. States also have considerable influence over how general elections are conducted, and sometimes set the dates for state elections in odd-numbered years to keep national politics out of the debate. Many states also give their localities similar freedom to set election dates.

Choosing Congressional and State Nominees. The most frequently used method for selecting congressional and state nominees is by **primary election,** in which voters decide who gets to run as a party's nominee. Most primary elections take place several months before the general election, which determines who gets to hold the office. All fifty states use some kind of primary election either as the sole method for selecting nominees (thirty-seven states) or as part of a more complicated nomination process that involves local and/or state party conventions (the thirteen other states).

All states give the people a say somewhere in the process, but they vary greatly in defining who gets to vote in a primary. The vast majority of states use a **closed primary,** in which only party members are allowed to cast ballots in their party's primary. These states require voters to declare their party preference when they register to vote. Republicans are allowed to vote only in Republican primaries, Democrats only in Democratic primaries. Some states allow independents to choose one or the other primary on election day; others prohibit independents from participating in primaries altogether.

A much smaller number of states use an **open primary,** in which voters are allowed to cast ballots in any party primary they wish. But once a voter decides on a party primary in which to participate, that voter must stay in that party's ballot. Because voters are not required to declare their party preference until they arrive to vote, Republicans and Democrats are free to cross over and vote in the other party's primary, while independents are free to vote in whichever primary they wish. Such crossover voting is more likely if one party has a particularly exciting contest.

An even smaller number of states use a **blanket primary,** in which voters receive a ballot listing all candidates of both parties and are free to move back and forth across party lines all the way down the ballot. "In a Different Light" on page 336 describes how California adopted a blanket primary in 1996 and used it for the first time in June 1998.

Of the three types, closed primaries do the most to strengthen the role of the parties in choosing nominees. Because independents and voters from the opposition party cannot cross over to vote in a closed primary, candidates must appeal to their party's faithful if they are to win. In contrast, open and blanket primaries do little to help the parties.

Choosing Presidential Nominees.   States are also responsible for selecting delegates to the national party conventions.[2] Although each state party must follow whatever rules might be set by its national committee—the national Democratic party requires, for example, that all state delegations consist of equal numbers of men and women—state governments set the broad rules that govern the selection of delegates for both parties.

As with congressional and state offices, most of the states use a primary system for selecting presidential delegates, and most of those use a closed primary, in which only party voters are allowed to choose among competing candidates. (A small number of states use a delegate selection primary, in which party voters are allowed to vote only for the names of delegates who are pledged to particular candidates. As with the electoral college, voters get to cast ballots only for the delegates, who then get to vote for the candidate.) By tradition, New Hampshire holds the first presidential primary in February of every fourth year.

Although the number of primaries continues to grow, a quarter of the states still use a **caucus system,** in which delegates are selected through a series of party meetings that usually begin at the local level (*caucus* simply means convention). In contrast to a primary, which involves a brief moment of participation, local caucuses are intense face-to-face events, often running late into the night as friends and neighbors talk about the future of their party. By tradition, Iowa hosts the first major party caucus, also in February of every presidential election year.

Because the purpose of primaries and caucuses is to select delegates to the national conventions, the states must decide how to allocate seats to each candidate. Under national Democratic party rules, all states must allocate their Democratic delegates using a **proportional voting system,** in which delegates are divided up according to the final votes in the primary or caucus. A candidate who won 40 percent of the final vote would get 40 percent of the delegates. Roughly half of all Republican primaries are winner-take-all, in which the top vote-getter wins all the delegates.

Because the Democratic party has more minority members to begin with and has rules encouraging the selection of minority and women delegates, its delegates are likely to be more diverse than Republican party conventiongoers. In 1996, for example, about half the Democratic delegates were women, while 17 percent were African Americans. In contrast, barely 33 percent of Republican delegates were women, while only 3 percent were African Americans. What both sets of delegates shared was inexperience. Roughly 60 percent of the delegates were attending their first national convention, suggesting a possible renewal of the future leadership base in both parties.

Democratic candidate Bill Clinton talks with the voters on the eve of the New Hampshire presidential primary in 1992.

The past fifty years have witnessed two important changes in the presidential nomination process. First, the number of convention delegates selected through primaries has steadily increased, rising from roughly 40 percent of all delegates in the early 1900s to over 80 percent today. Primaries were adopted as a way to give citizens a greater role in the selection process, and they have certainly done so. More than 25 million Americans participated in the 1996 Democratic and Republican primaries.

Second, the number of early primaries and caucuses has steadily increased. It used to be that only small states liked to go early, on the theory that they got greater influence by helping sort out the early candidates, while larger states liked to go late, on the theory that they would get attention through sheer size. New Hampshire and Iowa came first, California last. In 1972, for example, only 7 percent of all Democratic delegates were selected prior to March, with almost 25 percent selected in June.

In 1998, however, California moved its primary to the first Tuesday in March in an effort to compete with the growing number of smaller states going earlier. "March Madness" is no longer just a term for the NCAA national basket-ball tournament. Roughly two-thirds of the 2000 presidential delegates will be chosen during March, a compression of the nominating process that was caused by what experts call front-loading. Front-loading clearly reduces the time candidates can spend in a given state and tends to favor candidates who have more money for paid advertising.

in a different light —— CALIFORNIA'S BLANKET PRIMARY

California voters have been in the mood for reform in the 1990s, passing three different initiatives designed to clean up state politics. One put a sharp limit on campaign contributions, a second created term limits on members of Congress, and a third created a blanket primary. Although the first two were ruled unconstitutional, one as a violation of free speech (see the discussion of *Buckley v. Valeo* below) and the second as an unconstitutional addition to the Article I list of qualifications for office, the blanket primary was used for the first time in June 1998. It may turn out to be an idea whose time has come for many states.

The basic argument in favor of a blanket primary is simple. Instead of restricting voters to one party or the other through a closed or open primary, the blanket primary invites all voters, regardless of party affiliation, to declare their favorites, office by office. If they favor one of the Democratic candidates for governor, they are free to vote in the Democratic gubernatorial primary; if they favor one of the Republicans for their local House district, they are free to switch and vote in the Republican House primary. In effect, a blanket primary creates a separate primary for every office on the ballot. By allowing voters to move back and forth with ease, supporters hoped to increase interest among citizens with weak or nonexistent party loyalties, inviting California's 1.5 million independents back into primary politics.

The blanket primary is not without controversy, however. The California Democratic party challenged the primary in court, arguing that it violated the First Amendment freedom of association by denying party members the right to choose the party's own nominees. The party also argued that the blanket primary would increase the amount of "raiding" organized by opposing campaigns. In theory, an incumbent running unopposed on one side of the ballot could organize his or her supporters to vote for the weakest challenger on the other side, thereby assuring reelection. Although the case was still pending in June 1998, the District Court refused to prevent the primary from being held.

Preliminary evidence suggests that there was little raiding during the June primary and at least some increase in turnout. Overall turnout for the primary was 42 percent, which was well ahead of the 34 percent in the last nonpresidential primary in 1994. Because the state had just cleared its voter registration rolls of people who had moved or failed to vote, however, it is not clear that the increase was really the product of popular interest. With nearly 1.1 million names removed from the registration rolls, turnout—as a proportion of eligible voters—was bound to increase.

Nevertheless, the anecdotal evidence supports at least some of the claims regarding increased participation by independents. In Orange County, for example, turnout among independents increased from 25,000 voters in 1994 to 51,500 in 1998. Those are real votes, not just illusions created by changes in the voter registration rolls.

The problem with the blanket primary may be exactly as the Democratic party feared: A blanket primary weakens the incentives for citizens to identify with one party or the other. Although the increase in participation is desirable, the potential for weakening the party's control over the choice of its own nominees may actually strengthen the role of political consultants in determining who gets to run, while creating substantial opportunities for mischief making by clever incumbents.

Raising Money

Money pays for just about everything a campaign does, from building an organization to hiring a consultant and persuading voters. It even pays for raising more money. "There are two things that are important in politics," said Mark Hanna, the father of modern campaigning, in 1895. "The first is money and I can't remember what the second one is."[3]

Most candidates for federal office will attest that raising money is the most difficult thing they do. Calling strangers to ask for money is hard enough, but calling hundreds of strangers a day is even tougher. Candidates call it "trolling for dollars." "I felt like a total whore, running after rich people begging with your tin cup," said Colorado Democrat Patricia Schroeder, who ran briefly for the Democratic presidential nomination in 1988.[4] (The special problem of presidential financing will be covered at the end of this section.)

Campaigns clearly cost more today than they did even twenty years ago. That much is obvious from the figures. In 1972, according to campaign finance expert Frank Sorauf, all congressional candidates put together spent barely $77 million. By 1986, the total topped $450 million. Even adjusted for inflation, the increase was over 100 percent.[5] By 1996, the total had reached $850 million.

The conventional wisdom is that an effective House campaign today needs to raise roughly $600,000 to be competitive: $150,000 for two broad mailings to every home in the district; $100,000 to produce and run three television commercials and six radio spots; and another $350,000 for consultants, polling, office rental, and travel. Given the fact that the average congressional campaign actually averaged barely half of the ideal in 1994, Sorauf suggests that "one can make a plausible argument that candidates spend too little, not too much, in congressional campaigns."[6] In 1996, the average winning House campaign cost $673,000, while the average winning Senate campaign came in at $4.7 million.[7]

Like most averages, these disguise enormous variation. Congressional campaigns in large states such as California are "media intense," with heavy television advertising and direct mail, and can cost millions to win; campaigns in small states such as South Dakota, with ample amounts of "free media" coverage, remain within reach of a challenger with but a few hundred thousand dollars. Speaker of the House Newt Gingrich (R-GA) ran the most expensive House campaign in 1996, spending $5.6 million to defeat a well-financed challenger who argued that the Speaker had lost touch with the people, while Representative Mark Sanford (R-SC) ran the least expensive, spending just $66,071. The most expensive Senate campaign involved Jesse Helms (R-NC), who spent $14.5 million to win his second contest against Harvey Gantt, while the least expensive involved Michael Enzi (R-WY), who spent just $953,000 to win a second term.

This does not mean that campaigns in small and mid-size states always come cheap. The state spending record was held for almost a decade by North Carolina, where Helms and Governor Jim Hunt spent a combined $26.5 million in 1984. It was broken ten years later when Michael Huffington and Dianne Feinstein spent $43 million in the 1994 Senate campaign. As if to prove that Senate campaigns are not the only costly races, California broke its own record in the 1998 Democratic gubernatorial primary, where Northwest Airlines executive Al Checchi, Jane Harman, and Gray Davis together spent more than $70 million to earn the right to face Republican candidate Dan Lungren in the fall gubernatorial election.

Raising money also has an impact on the democratic process. At the very minimum, fund-raising takes time away from other activities. Assume that a congressional candidate has to call fifty potential donors a day to find ten who are willing to contribute; also assume the candidate has to spend five minutes on each call making the pitch and closing the deal, including asking the donor to get

California Senate candidates Dianne Feinstein and Michael Huffington appear on *Larry King Live* in October 1994, in a rare opportunity for free media in the most expensive Senate campaign of the year. Together, the two candidates spent $43 million, or $100,000 a day, during the campaign, most of it going for paid media. Feinstein won.

the check in the mail right away.[8] That comes to 250 minutes a day, or four solid hours that could be used for something else.

Time is hardly the only casualty of expensive campaigns, however. A candidate's ability to raise money becomes a key qualification for running, displacing what might be more important qualifications for serving—for example, leadership ability, civic-mindedness, intelligence, and experience. Moreover, good candidates may decide they would rather not run than spend four hours a day raising money, leaving the candidacies to those whose major attribute is either the ability to dial for dollars or the willingness to spend huge amounts of their own money.[9] The result may be a Congress of either the very wealthy, who are willing and able to spend great quantities of their own money to win a seat, or great fund-raisers, who can pry $1,000 out of even the most reluctant contributor but have very little else to offer in terms of skills.

Government Regulation of Campaign Spending. Until the 1970s, raising campaign money was a relatively simple enterprise. Candidates got most of their money from two sources: individual contributors and people who wanted jobs in government (before 1884, almost all federal jobs were given on the basis of *patronage,* or political connections). The number of fund-raising calls a candidate

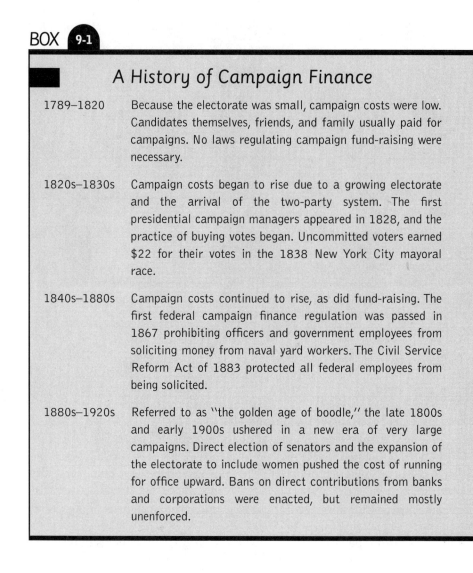

BOX 9-1

A History of Campaign Finance

1789–1820	Because the electorate was small, campaign costs were low. Candidates themselves, friends, and family usually paid for campaigns. No laws regulating campaign fund-raising were necessary.
1820s–1830s	Campaign costs began to rise due to a growing electorate and the arrival of the two-party system. The first presidential campaign managers appeared in 1828, and the practice of buying votes began. Uncommitted voters earned $22 for their votes in the 1838 New York City mayoral race.
1840s–1880s	Campaign costs continued to rise, as did fund-raising. The first federal campaign finance regulation was passed in 1867 prohibiting officers and government employees from soliciting money from naval yard workers. The Civil Service Reform Act of 1883 protected all federal employees from being solicited.
1880s–1920s	Referred to as "the golden age of boodle," the late 1800s and early 1900s ushered in a new era of very large campaigns. Direct election of senators and the expansion of the electorate to include women pushed the cost of running for office upward. Bans on direct contributions from banks and corporations were enacted, but remained mostly unenforced.

had to make was small, the size of the individual contributions very large. (See Box 9–1 for a brief history of campaign fund-raising.)

The 1896 election ushered in the modern era of large individual contributions from the country's wealthiest citizens and corporations. This dependence on large contributions, and the sense that elections were being bought and sold, eventually prompted three waves of campaign finance reform. The first came in the early 1900s, when Congress banned all direct campaign contributions by banks and corporations. The second wave, in the early 1940s, banned contribu-

1930s–1940s   More elections, including the advent of primaries, as well as a growing electorate, and greater government involvement in the economy combined to increase costs. Labor unions became significant contributors to Democratic candidates. Franklin Delano Roosevelt raised more than $500,000 from the Congress of Industrial Organizations for the 1936 election. The CIO formed the first political action committee in 1944 to circumvent contribution limits passed in 1940 and 1943.

1950s–1970s   With growth in the electorate starting to slow, television took over as the leading cause of increasing campaign costs. The 1972 election produced a long list of illegal contributions, including a $200,000 contribution delivered in cash to the Committee to Reelect the President (Nixon). The Watergate scandal revealed further abuses of power, leading to a broad reform effort.

1980s–1990s   Campaign costs have continued upward, driven by the rising number of candidate-centered campaigns, in which candidates run without strong ties to their party. Money is much easier to track under the Watergate-era legislation. States have led the effort to control campaign spending.

Source: Adapted from Center for Responsive Politics, *A Brief History of Money in Politics* (Washington, D.C.: Center for Responsible Politics, 1995).

tions by labor unions. All three groups now make their contributions through political action committees. (See Chapter 7 for a basic introduction to PACs.)

As the cost of presidential campaigns rose, momentum for a third wave of reform grew, culminating in the early 1970s with passage of three separate election campaign acts. The first was the *Federal Election Campaign Act of 1971*, which established full disclosure of congressional and presidential campaign contributions and spending. The second was the *Revenue Act of 1971*, which created a checkoff on the tax form that allows taxpayers to contribute to the presidential campaign fund. The third was the *Federal Election Campaign Act of 1974,* which placed limits on how much individuals and political committees (parties and PACs) could contribute to a single campaign. The 1974 act also created the Federal Election Commission, which monitors campaign spending.

Together, the 1974 act and its later amendments created three different systems of campaign finance law. One covers candidates for the two houses of Congress and stipulates that they receive no public funding. A second covers candidates in the presidential primaries who receive matching dollars. A third covers candidates in the presidential general election who receive full public funding.[10]

The result is an intricate and often puzzling set of rules governing campaign finance. It affects individual givers, congressional candidates, and presidential candidates. (The rules for campaign contributions are summarized in Box 9–2).

Because congressional and presidential campaigns are covered by different rules, they are treated separately here. Before turning to each, it is useful to note that the 1974 law succeeded in reducing contributions from wealthy individuals and corporations. Neither can give more than $25,000 a year total to federal candidates, party committees, or PACs. There are only two exceptions. First, large contributors are free to spend as much as they want on behalf of, but independently of, a given candidate. In 1976, the Supreme Court declared such **independent spending** to be a form of free speech and therefore not subject to limits.[11] Second, large

BOX **9-2**

Rules Governing Campaign Contributions

	A Person May Give	A PAC May Give	A Party May Give
Each federal candidate per election	$ 1,000	$ 5,000	$ 1,000
Each national party committee per year	20,000	15,000	20,000
Each PAC per year	5,000	5,000	5,000
Limit on total contributions per year	$25,000	Unlimited	Unlimited

contributors are free to give as much as they want to the national party committees for party building and get-out-the-vote campaigns. Such contributions are called **soft money** because their amount is not restricted by hard limits.

Congressional Campaign Money. Raising money is particularly important for congressional campaigns, where there are four, and only four, sources of money for congressional candidates: (1) individual donors, (2) the political parties, (3) political action committees (PACs), and (4) the candidates themselves. Of the $850 million raised for the 1996 congressional campaigns, individual donors gave over half the dollars and PACs nearly a quarter. Loans and contributions from candidates to themselves accounted for another sixth, with the rest of the money coming from the parties and other loans.

The easiest way to raise money is to give it to yourself—that is, to be rich enough to back your own campaign, which is what Al Checchi did in spending $40 million on his losing bid for the California Democratic gubernatorial nomination in 1998. The First Amendment protects free speech, and giving money to one's own campaign has been defined by the Supreme Court as a form of free speech. (As noted later in this chapter, presidential candidates who accept public financing also accept voluntary limits on the amount of their own money they can put into their campaigns. Because congressional candidates receive no public financing, they face no such limits.)

Although individual donors and the candidates themselves are obviously major sources of congressional financing, PACs have received the greatest attention in recent years, in part because their numbers have grown so quickly from just a few hundred in the early 1970s to roughly four thousand today), and in part because they give so much of their money to incumbents. In 1995–1996, for example, PACs gave roughly 70 cents out of every dollar to incumbents.

The numbers on PAC giving in the 1990s confirm two trends. First, business and trade associations connected with business are the big givers, accounting for nearly 65 cents of every dollar given in PAC money, while labor accounts for just 25 cents, and issue groups for the rest. (Box 9–3 lists the most generous PAC spenders in 1996 by industry, along with the top giver in each industry.)

Second, PACs are hardly risk takers in spending their money. They tend to give their dollars to winners, which mostly means giving to incumbent members of Congress. In 1995–1996, for example, PACs gave nearly $120 million to House incumbents and only $22 million to challengers, yielding a 6:1 ratio. In the Senate, where elections are more hotly contested, PACs gave nearly $30 million to incumbents and $7.5 million to challengers, for a 4:1 ratio.

This does not mean PAC money always goes to incumbents. Business money started moving away from Democratic incumbents and toward Republican challengers late in the 1994 congressional campaigns, when it started to look

BOX 9-3

The Most Generous PACS in the 1996 Elections

Industry	Amount Contributed
Finance, insurance, and real estate	$86.1 million
Lawyers and lobbyists	51.7 million
Labor	49.3 million
Miscellaneous business	48.6 million
Health	41.8 million
Agriculture	29.5 million
Ideological/Single-Issue	29.3 million
Communications/Electronics	23.7 million
Transportation	22.5 million
Energy and natural resources	22.1 million
Construction	19.3 million
Defense	9.7 million

like Republicans just might do the impossible and take control of the House. Once the election was over, the trend reverted to form—only now the Republicans, not the Democrats, were the beneficiaries. In the first three months of 1993, with Democrats controlling both houses of Congress, AT&T had given 64 percent of its PAC money to Democrats; in the first three months of 1995, with Republicans now in charge, AT&T gave 79 percent of its dollars to Republicans.[12] The only thing that had changed was the incumbent majority party.

Presidential Campaign Money.   Presidential campaigns are unlike any other campaigns in the United States. First, they last much longer than any other cam-

Largest Donor in Industry	Amount Contributed
National Association of Realtors	$2.1 million
Association of Trial Lawyers of America	2.3 million
Teamsters Union	2.7 million
National Beer Wholesalers Association	1.3 million
American Medical Association	2.5 million
Philip Morris	1.0 million
National Rifle Association	1.6 million
AT&T	1.5 million
National Auto Dealers Association	2.3 million
Action Committee for Rural Electric	0.7 million
National Association of Home Builders	1.5 million
Lockheed Martin	1.3 million

Source: Center for Responsive Politics, *The Big Picture: Money Follows Power Shift on Capitol Hill* (Washington, D.C.: Center for Responsive Politics, 1997), pp. 35, 39–84.

paigns. Presidential campaigns start well before Iowa and New Hampshire in February. Candidates must be up and raising money at least six months earlier if they are to survive the early nomination tests, and many run informally for several years before, taking repeated trips to Iowa and New Hampshire to test the presidential waters.

Second, they are tightly compressed. In 1992, for example, the candidates had 113 days between the first Iowa caucus and the critical California primary in June. Because of front-loading in 1996, these events were separated by just forty-three days; roughly three-quarters of all delegates to the national party conventions were selected between the Iowa caucuses on February 12 and the California primary on March 26. If the candidates do not have their financing on hand to start rolling in early February, they will never find the time to raise it later.

Once past the conventions, presidential campaigns become even more intense. Although successful candidates need not compete in all fifty states, the District of Columbia, Puerto Rico, and the American territories to win, they must contest the major sources of electoral votes. Even states that are almost automatic for one or the other party—Texas was nearly guaranteed to George Bush in 1992—cannot be neglected, lest the opposing candidate make an unexpectedly strong showing.

Third—and not surprisingly, given their length and intensity, and the number of states involved—presidential campaigns are extraordinarily expensive. Twenty million dollars was considered the minimum needed for a Republican to be competitive in the 1996 nomination campaigns, an amount that had to be raised in $1,000 or $5,000 contributions. For a little-known candidate such as former Tennessee Republican governor Lamar Alexander, who started his campaign in January 1995, the $20 million target meant raising $77,000 every business day of the campaign.[13]

Fourth, presidential campaigns are funded mostly with public money raised through the $3 checkoff on the income tax form. As noted earlier, the money comes in two installments: the first involves matching money for the nomination campaign; the second involves full public funding for the general election campaign.

The public funding is part of a quid pro quo, or promise, candidates make: In return for public funding, they agree not to use more than $50,000 of their own money in the campaign season. If they do not agree to the personal limit, they do not get the public funds. In 1996, for example, Steve Forbes refused the public funds, spending $37 million of his own money in his bid for the Republican nomination. Undeterred by his failure, Forbes seems ready to sink even more money into the 2000 campaign.

During the nomination season, the first payment of public funds is available only to candidates who raise $5,000 in at least twenty states in contributions of no more than $250. Once a candidate meets this test, he or she gets dollar-for-dollar matching up to a preset spending ceiling. In 1992, for example, candidate George Bush received almost $11 million in matching dollars for his nomination campaign, far outdistancing his nearest Republican rival, former Nixon speechwriter Patrick Buchanan, at $5.2 million. With $12 million, Democratic candidate Bill Clinton also bettered his party rivals, leading former California Governor Jerry Brown at $4.1 million and former U.S. Senator Paul Tsongas at just under $3 million.[14]

Once past the nomination, all the money is public, provided the candidate accepts voluntary limits on personal spending. In 1996, for example, the two major-party candidates divided $120 million for the campaign. Even though the two party candidates are spending public money, private money is not banned from presidential campaigns. As noted earlier, organizations and individuals are free to spend as much money as they want independently of the two presidential campaigns. Such money can finance get-out-the-vote efforts, direct mail to potential voters, and even extensive television advertising.

in a different light —— SOFT MONEY AND BUNDLING

Despite the 1974 Federal Election Campaign Act, large contributions still flow into federal campaigns. Money in campaigns is very much like mercury—push it here and it goes there; push there and it goes here. Even the tightest campaign finance law leaves gaps into which the money can flow.

During the 1980s, parties and candidates developed two new techniques for exploiting those loopholes. The first involves soft money gifts to the national parties. As noted in Chapter 6, individuals and corporations may contribute unlimited amounts of money to the parties as long as the money goes into administrative accounts for party-building activities, such as voter registration drives and get-out-the-vote campaigns. Just what constitutes a legitimate party-building activity is very much open to interpretation, however. Both parties used soft money in 1996 to promote voter turnout by attacking the other party. Indeed, Clinton campaign advisers were unapologetic about the role of early soft money ads in building an unassailable lead.

As large contributors discovered the loophole, the money started to flow. Between 1991 and 1994, the Republican National Committee raised $95 million in soft money, or roughly one-fifth of its total budget; the Democratic National Committee raised $75 million, or one-sixth of its budget. Among the soft money pioneers were Hard Rock Cafe co-owner Peter Morton, who gave $100,000 to the Democrats; Wall Street investment banker and future Clinton secretary of the treasury Robert Rubin, who gave $275,000 to the Democrats; and Dwayne Andreas and his Archer Daniels Midland Company (a huge agricultural conglomerate), who gave $227,500 to the Republicans.

By 1995–1996, soft money was no longer the province of well-heeled individuals. Having learned how to exploit the loopholes, both parties (and their presidential candidates) went into high gear. The Clinton administration hosted hundreds of White House coffees to thank big givers, and reserved the Lincoln Bedroom for overnight stays by particularly important donors. When the numbers were added up,

President Clinton greets former
Texas Governor Ann Richards at
an EMILY's List event in 1995.
EMILY's List gives its bundled
dollars only to women candidates
and usually early in a campaign.
The acronym EMILY stands for
Early Money Is Like Yeast.

the two parties had banked over $260 million in soft money, triple the amount they
had raised in the 1991–1992 period. The biggest giver was tobacco giant Philip
Morris at $3 million, just ahead of Seagram & Sons and RJR Nabisco. The Walt Dis-
ney Company came in fourth at $1.3 million.

    The two parties have clearly been strengthened by soft money, which has
given them added leverage with members of Congress and state officials in enforcing party discipline. That is likely a good thing, particularly as a counterweight to
the growing number of interest groups. However, soft money may deepen the widespread public belief that government is run for the special interests.

    It can hardly strengthen trust, for example, when the two national party com-
mittees create special clubs for donors who give $100,000 or more in soft funding;
the Republicans call them members of "Team 100," while the Democrats call their
$100,000 givers "Trustees" and their $200,000 givers "Managing Trustees." A

$100,000 contributor in 1996 got two meals with President Clinton, two meals with Vice President Al Gore, a slot on a foreign trade mission with Democratic National Committee leaders, and a host of smaller benefits, including a party staffer assigned to address the contributor's "personal requests."[15]

The second technique for raising more money outside the constraints of campaign finance laws is known as *bundling.* Bundling involves nothing more than collecting large numbers of individual checks and turning them over to a candidate or candidates. Each check is made out to the candidate, not to the person or organization doing the bundling. Technically, the bundler is not making a contribution at all.

EMILY's List (*E*arly *M*oney *I*s *L*ike *Y*east) is currently one of the most effective bundling operations. Established to help women candidates get desperately needed early funding for their campaigns, EMILY's List proved so successful that it became one of the largest sources of money for House and Senate candidates in 1993–1994 at $7.5 million, making it the second largest spender of all.[16] Technically, however, EMILY's List did not give any money at all. It merely transferred bundles and bundles of individual checks.

Soft money and bundling are perfectly legal techniques for raising needed campaign cash, and clearly help candidates mount credible campaigns. But the techniques may be hurting public confidence nonetheless. Whether right or wrong, the vast majority of Americans believe that campaign contributions buy special access. Because soft money and bundling produce some of the largest contributions of all, they contribute to the public's belief that elections have become auctions to the highest bidder.

CAMPAIGNING 101

Campaigning for office is a grueling prospect. It means spending night after night on the road, separated from family and friends, cocooned in aircraft and cheap hotels, raising dollars every spare minute, working crowds, and keeping a constant smile. It is also where winners and losers are made. Citizens have an uncanny ability to detect candidates who hate campaigns.

Campaigns do not start out in high gear, of course. They start with a series of decisions that gradually escalate into a winning or losing effort. As the following pages argue, the candidates must first decide to run, then build a campaign organization and devise a winning strategy. Then and only then can they start sending messages to voters through paid and earned media.

Deciding to Run

The most important decision candidates make is whether to enter the campaign in the first place. Candidates need what some call a "fire in the belly" to survive the grueling process, particularly once they enter national politics. In 1996, for example, General Colin Powell decided early on that he simply did not have the ambition needed to mount a serious campaign for the Republican presidential nomination—at least "not yet."

Most candidates for office are motivated by a commitment to public service. They believe they can accomplish something worthwhile, most believe in the democratic process, and most have a strong sense of purpose. "Who sent us the political leaders we have?" asks journalist Alan Ehrenhalt in his book *The United States of Ambition.* "There is a simple answer to that question. They sent themselves. And they got where they are through a combination of ambition, talent, and the willingness to devote whatever time was necessary to seek and hold office."[17]

Nevertheless, there is some evidence that the kinds of candidates who decide to run today are different from those who ran in earlier times. Because campaigns are longer, the sacrifices demanded of family are greater and the demands for fund-raising skills are much more intense. Physical endurance is clearly more important today than ever before, as is an ability to communicate through television. A commitment to public service is still essential but is clearly no longer enough. Candidates must also have well-developed campaigning skills. And

Ret. Gen. Colin Powell says "no" to a presidential bid in 1996 as his wife looks on. In announcing his decision not to run, Powell said that a campaign requires "a calling I do not yet hear."

those skills may have little to do with the abilities needed for actually governing once in office.

Building an Organization

Putting together an effective campaign starts with the basics: an organization. At the very minimum, a campaign must have a legally established organization to receive and spend campaign contributions. But the organization is also the home for a host of other essential activities.

The key question in building an organization is whether the campaign organization is going to do everything for itself or let the national, state, or local party committee do some of the work. In a **party-centered campaign,** the candidate runs as a representative of the party. All messages focus on reminding voters of their party identification, all fund-raising and polling come from the party organization, and the hard work of getting voters to the polls is done by the party field staff, which operates through state and local committees. What matters is not so much whether the candidate wins, but how strongly the candidate is tied to the party, for the party organization will endure long after the election is over.

In contrast, a **candidate-centered campaign** is of the candidate, for the candidate, and by the candidate. The focus is on whatever it takes to get the candidate elected. If that means abandoning all ties to the party, so be it. All messages focus on electing the candidate, all fund-raising and polling come from the candidate's own organization, and the get-out-the-vote effort is handled by the candidate's own field staff. The candidate-centered organization is a temporary shelter for dozens of specialized staff members, who may be out of a job as soon as the last ballot is counted.[18] (Box 9–4 shows the organization chart for today's candidate-centered presidential campaign.)

Most of the outsider jobs were once done by the party. In today's candidate-centered campaign, they are performed by consultants and specialists of one kind or another. The most visible outsider post belongs to the lead campaign consultant, the individual most responsible for developing the broad campaign strategy. Unlike the campaign manager, who handles the day-to-day details of *how* the campaign runs, the consultant helps make broad decisions about *what* the campaign does and brings a pure focus on doing whatever it takes to win.

Creating a candidate-centered campaign makes perfect sense, given the decline of party loyalty and the rise of the new media. Candidates no longer need to rely on the parties or traditional media to get their message out. Indeed, many candidates see the party label as a liability. Running against Washington is also "in," even for long-time Washington insiders. It is no small trick to portray oneself as an agent of change after serving in Congress for twenty years, but incumbents do it all the time. Once back in office, these members may have much less incentive to work together to make government run.

BOX **9-4**

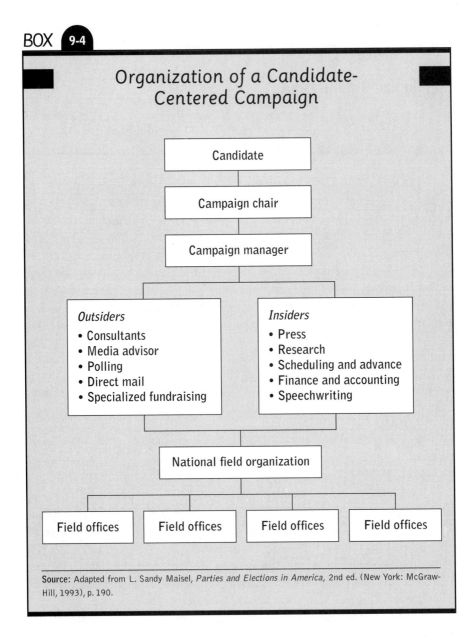

Organization of a Candidate-Centered Campaign

Candidate

Campaign chair

Campaign manager

Outsiders
- Consultants
- Media advisor
- Polling
- Direct mail
- Specialized fundraising

Insiders
- Press
- Research
- Scheduling and advance
- Finance and accounting
- Speechwriting

National field organization

Field offices | Field offices | Field offices | Field offices

Source: Adapted from L. Sandy Maisel, *Parties and Elections in America,* 2nd ed. (New York: McGraw-Hill, 1993), p. 190.

Hiring a Consultant

Hiring a lead political consultant may be the single most important decision a national campaign makes. Just as hiring an architect is essential for building a home, so, too, is hiring a consultant for creating an effective campaign. The architect (consultant) draws the blueprints, and often hires the specialists. The general contractor (campaign manager) makes sure every nail goes in on time, but the architect often tells the contractor where each nail should go. As noted in Chapter 6, consultants will do just about anything a campaign needs. One consulting firm advertised that "We know how to handle indictments, arrests, or a candidate that simply falls down stairs a lot."[19]

The growth of the consulting industry is unmistakably tied to the decline of the parties, although it is not quite clear which came first. Whatever the order of events, candidates have come to rely less and less on the parties to organize their campaigns, instead importing expertise in the form of political consultants. According to Roger Stone, a top Republican consultant, "What has happened is that in many ways, the political consultants have replaced political parties and the party leaders." His Democratic counterpart, Robert Squier, agrees, observing that in the 1950s:

> there was an accidental timing of technologies. There was the mass production of the automobile, the television set, and the creation of the suburbs. People drove out from under the existing political systems, which really existed only in the cities. . . . Suddenly there were no block captains, people had to make decisions for themselves. It basically knocked whatever strength there was out of our party system.[20]

The consulting industry also grew because there was money to be made. There were 500,000 offices up for election in 1996. Although most did not involve much campaign spending, the totals add up. A few thousand here for a campaign for county commissioner, a few hundred thousand there for a U.S. House seat, and suddenly campaigns are a $3 *billion* biannual industry.[21] No wonder people are getting into the business. Recall that most national consultants make more than $150,000 a year. Moreover, there are virtually no start-up costs for a consulting firm—no licenses to get, no fancy equipment to buy.

This single-minded commitment to winning can weaken democracy, however. Consultants have a big stake in making sure that those in power stay in power. Incumbents always make good clients, in part because they raise and spend more money and in part because they have a high chance of winning and thereby improving a consultant's won–lost record. They are also *known* clients who return a consultant's phone calls.

Devising a Strategy

Having decided to run, built a campaign staff, and hired a consultant, a candidate must develop and execute a credible strategy for winning. A campaign strategy maps out which issues to highlight, what messages to emphasize, and where the most supportive voters can be found. Its purpose is to match what the candidate says and does with the prevailing mood of the electorate.

A winning strategy need not be complex. In 1992, for example, Bill Clinton won the presidency with a one-sentence strategy printed on a huge sign at campaign headquarters: "It's the Economy, Stupid!" Every campaign stop, every message, and every advertisement reminded voters of the poor economic performance under incumbent president George Bush.

Because no candidate is perfect, a campaign strategy also addresses the candidate's strengths and weaknesses, playing up the things voters might like and playing down the things voters might dislike. As Chapter 10 shows, incumbent members of Congress have a host of advantages over challengers, not the least of which are that they have already won at least one election and they have a certain level of name recognition. They also do many of the things that voters like, including casework on behalf of individual constituents.

Incumbents also have remarkable access to campaign funding. In 1994, for example, incumbents had, on average, a 5:1 advantage over their challengers and an 8:1 advantage in cash on hand going into the final weeks of the election.[22] The fact is that most contributors like to bet on a winner. The average Democratic House incumbent spent nearly $600,000 in the 1994 campaign, compared to just $230,000 for the Republican challenger; the average Republican House incumbent spent nearly $450,000, against just $150,000 for the challenger. In contrast, Democratic and Republican challengers for open seats spent roughly $550,000 each.[23]

The most important step in creating a campaign strategy is to take stock of these strengths and weaknesses. Take the presidency as an example. Some historians even argue that incumbent presidents can tell if they are going to win reelection by asking thirteen key true-or-false questions at the start of the campaign. When the answer to six or more of these questions is "false," the challenger will win. (See Box 9–5 for the thirteen questions, also called keys.)

The thirteen keys worked well for predicting the 1996 election. Incumbent president Clinton's Democratic party entered the campaign in deep trouble. Republicans won fifty-two seats in the House, eight in the Senate, and the first congressional majority in over forty years. Not a single Republican incumbent who ran for reelection in the House or Senate lost—give Clinton his first "false"; his party was clearly in decline.

At the same time, Clinton had no opposition in winning his party's nomination—give him his first "true"—and was running for reelection—another "true," which conferred all the benefits of being presidential (the seal of office, the military pomp and circumstance, the chance to sign popular legislation such as an increase in the minimum wage). Although Ross Perot ran again for the presidency, he was left out of the presidential debates and was never considered a serious candidate—another "true" for Clinton.

The economy was not in a recession in 1996—another "true" for Clinton—and had improved significantly since 1992, with the stock market setting an all-time record just before the election—yet another "true." On national policy,

BOX **9-5**

The Thirteen Keys to Predicting a Presidential Election

True/False: The sitting president's party has more seats in the House of Representatives today than it had four years ago.

True/False: There is no serious contest for the nomination of the sitting president's party.

True/False: The president is running for reelection.

True/False: There is no significant third-party or independent candidate such as Ross Perot.

True/False: The economy is not in a recession during the presidential campaign.

True/False: The economy has been as strong or stronger during the sitting, or incumbent, president's term of office as it was before.

True/False: The sitting president has been able to make major changes in national policy such as national health insurance.

True/False: There has been no sustained social unrest during the sitting president's term such as the 1965 race riots (the 1991 Los Angeles riots would not count since they did not spread and were quickly contained).

True/False: There has been no major scandal such as Watergate or Whitewater.

True/False: There has been no major failure in foreign or military affairs such as the Vietnam War.

True/False: There has been a major success in foreign or military affairs such as the Persian Gulf War or the Haiti invasion.

True/False: The sitting party's candidate is a charismatic leader or a national hero such as retired General Colin Powell.

True/False: The challenger is a *not* a charismatic leader or a national hero.

Source: Allan Lichtman and Ken DeCell, *The 13 Keys to the Presidency* (Lanham, Md.: Madison Books, 1990), p. 7.

Clinton had a mixed record. His national health insurance plan never came to a formal vote in either chamber of Congress, but a number of lesser initiatives such as family leave passed—his second "false."

Moving down the keys, there was no civil unrest during the administration (a "true"), no major failure in foreign or military affairs ("true"), and a major foreign policy success in restoring democratic rule to Haiti ("true"). Although the administration was tainted by a series of scandals (a third "false"), the lapses did not seem to matter in the 1996 election because Clinton was so charismatic (another "true") and because his opponent, Bob Dole, was not (another "true"). According to the thirteen keys, then, Clinton was destined to win, with ten "trues" to just three "falses."

It is not yet clear how the thirteen keys will work out in the 2000 campaign. The economy has been strong, but Clinton has been besieged by another scandal (a first "false"). Although Vice President Gore is the front-runner, Clinton will not be running (a second "false"). There has been no major foreign policy failure, but no major foreign policy success, either (a third "false"). If Gore is nominated, the Democrats will *not* have a charismatic nominee (a fourth "false"), and he is likely to get the nomination only after a serious primary contest (a fifth "false"). Republicans could pick up the sixth and final required "false" by nominating a charismatic candidate of their own.

Sending the Message

The ultimate purpose of a campaign is simple: get more supporters to the polls than opponents. That means reinforcing the things voters already like about the candidate, while emphasizing the things voters dislike about the opponent; it also means minimizing the things voters dislike about the candidate, and making them question the things they like about the opponent.

These likes and dislikes can involve the candidate's party, issue positions, or image as a leader. As noted later in this chapter, voters appear to make their decision by adding up their likes and dislikes and voting for the candidate who comes out on top. Becoming the most liked candidate is always the preferred strategy, but being the least disliked candidate will do also.

The media play a central role in shaping these likes and dislikes, with television the undisputed key. Nearly two-thirds of Americans say they often do not become aware of political candidates until they see the candidate's advertising on television; more than half say they get some sense of what candidates are like through their commercials; and three-quarters say they like to have a picture of a candidate in their minds when they go to vote.[24] Not surprisingly, therefore, getting the candidate on television is usually the centerpiece of a campaign strategy, whether through **paid media,** such as advertising, or **free media,** such as news programs and talk shows.

Paid Media.   Television advertising is viewed as the most effective form of paid media. It is also by far the most expensive. According to media analysts Stephen Bates and Edwin Diamond, authors of *The Spot: The Issue of Political Advertising on Television,* "a dollar spent on TV advertising may reach as many voters as $3 worth of newspaper ads or $50 worth of direct mail. Banning spots would probably *increase* campaign spending, by diverting candidates to less efficient forms of communication."[25] The greatest cost in a media campaign is not in making the advertisement itself, but in buying the television or radio time. (Box 9–6 shows the ways that Clinton and Dole spent their dollars in 1996, as well as the sources of that money.)

Media campaign planners must decide whether to go with positive or negative advertisements. Positive ads are designed to increase voter "likes" about a candidate, while negative, or "attack" ads are designed to increase voter "dislikes" about the opponent. (See Box 9–7 for examples of positive and attack advertisements from the 1996 Republican primary campaign.)

The problem with positive ads is that the public tends to believe the worst about their candidates. "In August, we spent about $1.2 million running positive ads, basically detailing her accomplishments as a senator—getting guns out of schools, the assault weapons ban, and so on," said Dianne Feinstein's campaign director about the heated 1994 California race for the U.S. Senate. "But the public's cynicism about politics and politicians is such that whatever you assert positively about your candidate, it is almost impossible to get beyond the cynicism. The reaction is, 'Who can believe anything that a politician says about themselves?'"[26]

The problem with negative ads is that they can backfire on the candidate who sponsors them. Much as Americans watch and remember negative ads, they consistently say they want candidates to stick to the issues. Nevertheless, voters seem to believe attacks more than positives, and they learn from comparisons. Candidates may hate negative ads, said Senator William Cohen (R-ME), but "what they hate worse is losing."[27]

Free Media.   Campaigns also seek free coverage whenever they can get it, whether from newspapers, radio stations, or television. (Recall Chapter 5's discussion of the role of talk shows in the 1992 campaign.) Free coverage is important not only in reinforcing campaign messages, but also in conferring legitimacy on a candidate's message. The local news anchor is often one of the most trusted figures in a community.

Like so many other aspects of modern campaigns, getting free television coverage is becoming a sophisticated business. Major campaigns today routinely feed local television stations prepackaged video news releases and candidate "actualities" that provide brief *sound bites*—short, highly quotable segments from a speech or news conference that are specifically designed to grab public attention—for convenient unedited use on the evening news. Campaigns are also

BOX **9-6**

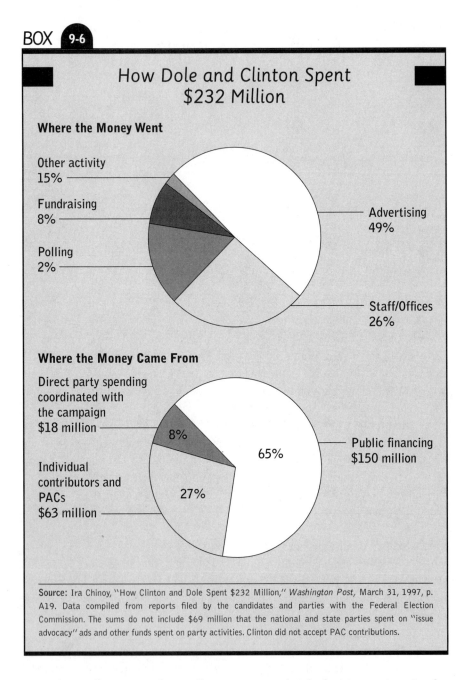

How Dole and Clinton Spent $232 Million

Where the Money Went

Other activity
15%

Fundraising
8%

Polling
2%

Advertising
49%

Staff/Offices
26%

Where the Money Came From

Direct party spending coordinated with the campaign $18 million — 8%

Individual contributors and PACs $63 million — 27%

65%

Public financing $150 million

Source: Ira Chinoy, "How Clinton and Dole Spent $232 Million," *Washington Post,* March 31, 1997, p. A19. Data compiled from reports filed by the candidates and parties with the Federal Election Commission. The sums do not include $69 million that the national and state parties spent on "issue advocacy" ads and other funds spent on party activities. Clinton did not accept PAC contributions.

more than willing to pay for satellite time to give local television stations "exclusive, live" interviews with the candidate.

These techniques are catching on, in part because local news budgets are too tight to cover national campaigns directly. The local station looks as if it has landed

BOX 9-7

Going Positive/Going Negative

Going Positive	Going Negative
TYPE: Sainthood Spot	TYPE: Frontal Assault
PURCHASER: Pat Buchanan	PURCHASER: Bob Dole
LENGTH: 30 seconds	LENGTH: 30 seconds
IMAGES: Old photos of President Richard Nixon boarding a helicopter, President Reagan speaking to a crowd, the space shuttle *Challenger* explosion, a battle scene from the Vietnam War.	IMAGES: Pictures of opponent Steve Forbes, the White House, World War II troops, militant Muslims, and gravestones at the Arlington National Cemetery
BACKGROUND NOISE: Patriotic music	BACKGROUND NOISE: Eerie, windy music
KEY NARRATIVE: "The convictions I learned from my parents, work, family, faith, character, have served me well. I've never been afraid to speak my mind. I will never be afraid to lead."	KEY NARRATIVE: "A look at his past indicates he is largely untested in making big decisions."
LASTING POINT: Pat Buchanan will not compromise.	LASTING POINT: Forbes cannot be trusted with the job of being president.
HIDDEN POINT: Front-runner Bob Dole will compromise.	HIDDEN POINT: Front-runner Bob Dole can be trusted.
MISSING INFORMATION: Pat Buchanan has never held elected office, and never served in Vietnam.	MISSING INFORMATION: Bob Dole appears nowhere in the ad even though his campaign paid for it.

an exclusive interview with a presidential candidate, when, in fact, hundreds of stations have received the same material. The only difference is that each local anchor "dubs" or "voices over" the interview questions. The number of local stations using such video news releases increased fourfold between 1988 and 1992.[28]

The blurring of the lines between free and paid advertising may help explain the growing public distrust toward the media. People may not know that the live interview with the candidate is being bought by the campaign, but may suspect something sinister is going on nonetheless.

As campaigns have become more sophisticated in using the media, the media have come under greater pressure to be more careful about how they cover campaigns. CBS News adopted a rule in 1992 requiring that in all campaign stories broadcast, candidate sound bites be at least thirty seconds long (they have been averaging less than ten seconds in recent years). Many newspapers now run "truth in advertising" stories questioning false or misleading campaign ads and dissecting specific campaign messages for accuracy and fairness.

Whether such efforts will improve the quality of advertising and reporting is not known. After all, even the most misleading spot can have a devastating impact the one time it is aired, often because it can generate free news coverage of its own. As for efforts to show more of what the candidate says, CBS's thirty-second rule had two immediate effects: either reporters paraphrased candidate positions instead of quoting them directly, or the candidates were never shown at all.

☀ in a different light ——— DOES NEGATIVE ADVERTISING WORK?

Negative advertising has been part of campaigning for office since the beginning of the republic. According to one historian, Abraham Lincoln was called almost every name in the book in his two runs for the presidency: "Ape, Buffoon, Coward, Drunkard, Execrable, Fiend, Ghoul, Hopeless, Ignoramus, Jokester (in the face of war tragedies), Knave, Lunatic, Murderer, Negro, Outlaw, Perjurer, Robber, Savage, Traitor, Usurper, Vulgar, Weakling."[29]

History noted, there has been a recent increase in both the number and intensity of negative advertisements. Fully half of all political advertisements emphasize the weaknesses of opponents rather than the strengths of the sponsoring candidate.[30] The "infection" of hard ads is not restricted to politics, however. Over half of today's consumer product ads are negative, too.

The reason candidates "go negative," as some scholars label it, is that they are absolutely convinced that negative advertising is essential to victory. "Everyone wants to say that stuff doesn't work," says Republican attack expert Eddie Mahe, "but the fact is that everywhere in the country I've gone on the attack, I've made progress." "People say they hate negative advertising," says his Democratic colleague, Jill Buckley. "But it works. They hate it and remember it at the same time. The problem with positive is that you have to run it again and again and again to make it stick. With negative, the poll numbers will move in three or four days."[31]

Despite nearly uniform enthusiasm among campaign consultants, the hard evidence suggests that negative advertising is vastly oversold. Consider three questions about whether and how negative advertising works.[32]

1. *Are negative advertisements easier to remember than positive advertisements?* The best answer is that negative advertisements are neither more nor less memorable than any other advertisements. Some studies suggest that negative advertisements do "stick" better than positives, but other equally rigorous studies suggest just the opposite.

2. *Do negative advertisements work?* The usual goal of a negative advertising spot is to move voters away from the opponent. That is what consultants mean when they say negative ads move the electorate one way or the other. Rigorous research suggests a more nuanced answer. There are groups of voters that do move away from an opponent in response to a negative advertisement, others that become even more convinced of the opponent's virtue, and still others who turn on the sponsor. Steven Ansolabehere and Shanto Iyengar even found party differences in the impact of negative advertisements. Such paid media can actually hurt the sponsoring candidate among Democrats, perhaps because Democrats want to believe more in government's ability to do good, but negative ads appear to help the sponsoring candidate among independents and Republicans, perhaps because these voters are predisposed to think the worst about government.

3. *Do negative advertisements hurt democracy?* Recent research suggests two equally troubling answers. First, negative advertising appears to polarize the electorate into angry camps. "On election day," write Ansolabehere and Iyengar, "the electorate speaks with a highly partisan vote, for that is the mindset reinforced by the candidates' campaign messages."[33] Negative advertising may not change many votes, but it certainly makes both sides angrier.

Second, negative advertising may weaken the public's willingness to participate. Ansolabehere and Iyengar estimate that the negative advertising in the 1992 Senate campaigns may have led over 6 million eligible Americans to stay home, and another 1 million voters to skip the Senate election on their ballots.[34] Hence, even as the motor voter law and vote-by-mail make voting *easier,* negative advertising may make voting *less inviting.*

This is not to argue that negative advertising should be banned. Candidates are entitled to the same protection of free speech that the rest of Americans enjoy. Moreover, certain kinds of negative advertising can be helpful to voters, particularly the "compare-and-contrast" ads that show the two candidates and their issue positions side by side. The problem appears to be the growing tide of "frontal assault" spots—that is, spots that are designed solely to weaken a given candidate's support without giving voters any alternative. Such spots may help the sponsoring candidates win, but may weaken public confidence in elections along the way.

HOW VOTERS DECIDE

Deciding how to vote is easy. Most voters come to the polling place having thought a bit about all their likes and dislikes about the leading candidates and the two parties—likes and dislikes that come from advertisements, images, issues voters care about, candidate debates, and so on. Weighing the likes and dislikes equally, voters cast their ballots for the candidate with the greatest net number of likes. If no candidate has an advantage, and a given voter has a party identification, he or she typically votes with the party. If the voter has no party identification, he or she may vote on the basis of some particular like or dislike (a fleeting memory from a campaign debate, a momentary image of a negative advertisement).[35]

All in all, it is a simple process that raises two questions about how voters decide. First, do campaigns matter to the typical voter's list of likes and dislikes? Second, how do voters come to have likes and dislikes in the first place?

Do Campaigns Matter?

Given all the hard work that goes into running for office, candidates and their supporters have to believe that campaigns matter. Otherwise, why should they abandon all semblance of a normal life for the rigors of the campaign trail? The fact is, however, that most campaigns do not change the outcome of elections. As in a chess match, candidates will almost certainly lose if they do not move. But even the most brilliant campaign cannot win the election if the candidate starts the game with a weaker position—say, a struggling economy, a declining party, or an angry electorate.

Nevertheless, belief in the power of campaigning is hard to shake. According to Bill Clinton's chief 1992 political consultants, James Carville and Paul Begala, having a good campaign staff is definitely not the reason most candidates for any office win. "Bill Clinton could have taken his staff and defeated George Bush's, or he could have taken Mr. Bush's staff and beat his own. The single best strategic decision we made as political consultants was to go to work for Bill Clinton in the first place."[36] But what Carville and Begala fail to note is that Clinton could not have taken Bush's record as the incumbent and won. As the thirteen keys discussed earlier suggest, Bush's fate was sealed long before the first television advertisement ran.

Consider the presidential debates as one test of whether campaigns matter. The first challenge is to get Americans to watch. Although debates historically attract large audiences, the 1996 debates were among the least watched in history, largely because most Americans saw little drama in the campaign. The second challenge is to change votes, something debates have rarely been able to do.[37] *Washington Post* pollster Richard Morin writes:

> Like so many things in the campaign, they entertain and occasionally inform.
> They solidify existing preferences, making people feel good about their choices,

Clinton and Dole meet in a town hall debate during the 1996 presidential campaign. The town hall format gave Clinton a clear advantage as he roamed about the stage, while Dole stayed pinned to his podium. Although Clinton won the debate, there is little evidence that the debate made a difference in the final outcome.

and give more reasons not to vote for the other guy. They mark a milestone in the campaign season, and represent the only opportunity to see both candidates together. But they don't push around a lot of votes.[38]

The reason debates do not move more votes is that a high percentage of voters make up their minds long before the presidential debates even take place. In 1996, for example, roughly three out of five voters said they had made their decision either before the campaign even began (39 percent) or during the primaries (13 percent) and conventions (8 percent). The rest made their decisions in September (12 percent), during the debates (3 percent), in the last week (6 percent), the last weekend (5 percent), and on election day (6 percent).

Clinton could not have won the presidency without a campaign, of course. In 1992, he needed to remind independent and Republican voters why they were mad at George Bush, and offer them a credible reason for voting Democratic. Hence, the campaign slogan "It's the Economy, Stupid!" In 1996, he needed to remind independent and Republican voters why they were so happy with the economy, and who had brought them the good news. In both campaigns, Clinton also needed to remind Democratic voters to get to the polls to do what was already on their minds—that is, vote for a Democratic candidate.

Campaigns do more than simply reinforce preexisting likes and dislikes, however. They often add new issues to the contest, and they clearly have some impact on which issues voters think are most important.[39] These **priming effects,** which lead voters to pay attention to some issues more than others, are particularly powerful when the economy is poor.[40] Because voters have a great material stake in whether the economy is doing well or poorly, campaigns can heighten their readiness to vote their pocketbooks. In bad economic times, such priming invariably helps the challenger; in good times, it almost always helps the incumbent. Moreover, media coverage and advertising often create new likes and dislikes, as they did in 1992, when Clinton's draft record and rumored marital infidelity became part of his credibility problem.

Finally, even if all but a handful of voters have made up their minds long before the election is held, campaigns clearly shape what that handful thinks. Elections are often won and lost at the margins—that is, among voters who add a few percent one way or the other to the total. Woe be to the candidate for any office who assumes that an election cannot be lost, particularly in a winner-take-all system that awards nothing for coming close.[41]

Indeed, history is replete with the names of candidates who lost despite a favorable climate. In 1948, for example, Republican presidential candidate Thomas Dewey was so confident of victory that he slowed down his campaign in the week before the election. The *Chicago Daily Tribune* was so confident,

Victorious Democratic presidential candidate Harry Truman holds an early edition of the *Chicago Daily Tribune* headline heralding his defeat. Pollsters had stopped tracking voter sentiment in the last two weeks of the campaign, assuming that Republican Thomas Dewey would be easily elected.

too, that it set its "Dewey Defeats Truman" headline before the results were in. The only problem, of course, was that Truman continued campaigning and won by 5 percent of the popular vote. If equal efforts cancel out, unequal efforts matter. That is why incumbents do so well—they have higher name recognition and much more money than most of their challengers. Even so, a few always lose.

Whether a campaign shifts votes from one side to the other is not the only measure of whether campaigns matter, however. Campaigns also matter to basic public support for the American system of government. Campaigns can make the public proud or disgusted, energized or apathetic. As such, campaigns offer an opportunity to confirm the consent of the governed. To the extent that Americans emerge from the campaign feeling disgusted and apathetic, government may be less able to act, thereby undermining the delicate balance embedded in the Constitution.

How Voters Make the Final Choice

Once the curtain closes behind a voter, the final decision gets made on the basis of three sources of likes and dislikes: party loyalty, policy issues, and candidate images.

Party Loyalty.   In the 1950s and early 1960s, party loyalty was considered to be the single most important factor in how people voted. The authors of *The American Voter* talked of a "funnel of causality" that shaped everything a potential voter saw and heard. At the wide end of the funnel were all the long-term factors that influence party identification: childhood socialization, past votes, income, education, race, and ideology. At the narrow end were all the short-term factors unique to a particular election: the condition of the economy, the candidates, debates, campaign advertising, and so forth. As the funnel narrowed over the life of a campaign, party identification helped voters make sense of all the information and events. Democrats would interpret everything they heard as proof that a Democrat should win; Republicans would interpret everything as proof that a Republican was best. The short-term forces had to be very powerful, therefore, to break the force of party identification in determining the vote.[42]

For many Americans today, party loyalty no longer resides at the open end of the funnel. In fact, it may actually have moved past those short-term forces to the very narrowest point in the funnel. For these voters, party loyalty is less a predictor of how they will vote than a simple way to remember what they did in the most recent election.

There is no question that party loyalty still carries great influence over voting decisions, particularly among older Americans with lifelong ties to a party. However, the decline of party loyalty increases the number of Americans who make their decisions later in the campaign, making their choices less predictable and much more responsive to what candidates say and do.

Policy Issues.   In a perfectly informed electorate, candidates would carefully outline their positions on the issues, voters would be highly informed about where the candidates stood, and elections would be determined by **issue voting.** Voters would start each campaign with their own list of "most important problems" facing the country. The candidates would then provide voters with their detailed policy positions on each of the top issues. The voters would measure their distance from the candidates, and give their vote to the one who came closest to their views. Everything would be perfectly rational.

But the electorate is not perfect. Most voters do not meet the requirements for truly rational voting.[43] Voters might not know their own self-interest, and might not follow the campaigns closely enough to know where the candidates stand; indeed, candidates might not provide the information needed to allow voters to measure distances.[44]

Yet a kind of issue voting can occur under less exacting circumstances. What if voters only have to take stock of how they think the country is doing, or whether they feel that change is needed, or even whether they feel better off today than they did four years ago? That would be a less elegant form of issue voting—no careful assessments of position papers and candidate speeches here—but it would be issue voting of a sort.

This kind of general referendum on the past may be the closest most Americans can get to the issue-voting ideal. Instead of thinking about the future and all the promises candidates are making, perhaps they are quite rational to think back over the past year or two and ask how they are doing. If they are doing well, they vote for the incumbent party. If they are doing poorly, they vote for change. "Citizens are not fools . . . ," political scientist Morris Fiorina notes in his theory of **retrospective voting**. "They need *not* know the precise economic or foreign policies of the incumbent administration in order to see or feel the *results* of those policies. And is it not reasonable to base voting decisions on results as well as on intentions?"[45]

If party loyalty continues to weaken, this kind of simple retrospective voting may take on an even larger role in explaining voting decisions. Indeed, Ronald Reagan built much of his 1980 campaign around the simplest retrospective theme by asking voters whether they were better off in 1980 than they had been in 1976, and using something he called a "misery index" to prove that inflation, income, and unemployment were all worse after four years of Jimmy Carter than before. It was a theme Bill Clinton picked up in 1992, asking voters whether their economic lives were any better after twelve years of Ronald Reagan and George Bush than before. In a similar vein, Bob Dole urged voters to ask whether their economic lives were any better after four years of Bill Clinton than before. Apparently, the answer was mostly yes.

Candidate Image.   The Founders clearly wanted voters to judge the candidates' fitness for office. Since they opposed political parties, and did not believe candidates should make promises about the future course of the nation, the Founders hoped voters would choose their candidates on the basis of virtue and ability to lead the nation.

Image still matters to campaigns at all levels. It is the only factor for voters who have no party identification and no knowledge of the issues. Moreover, today's candidate-centered campaigns tend to focus on giving voters evidence that a candidate has the ability to lead. Voters look for *human qualities,* such as compassion for others, sincerity, and high ethical standards; *political qualities,* such as experience in Washington, party loyalty, and political savvy; and *leadership qualities,*

BOX 9-8

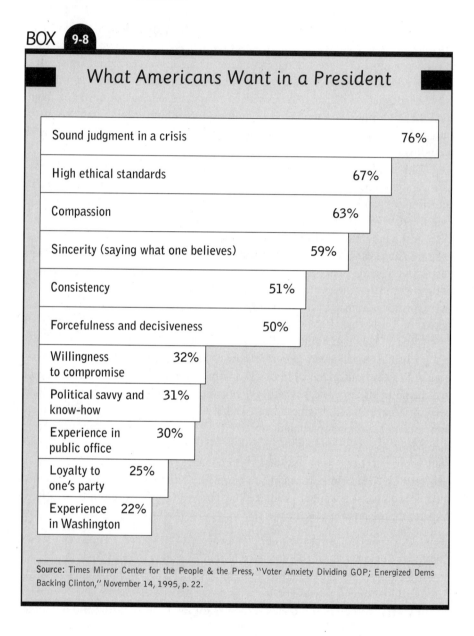

What Americans Want in a President

Sound judgment in a crisis	76%
High ethical standards	67%
Compassion	63%
Sincerity (saying what one believes)	59%
Consistency	51%
Forcefulness and decisiveness	50%
Willingness to compromise	32%
Political savvy and know-how	31%
Experience in public office	30%
Loyalty to one's party	25%
Experience in Washington	22%

Source: Times Mirror Center for the People & the Press, "Voter Anxiety Dividing GOP; Energized Dems Backing Clinton," November 14, 1995, p. 22.

such as consistency, forcefulness, and sound judgment in crisis. Together, these qualities create a general sense of a candidate's competence. (See Box 9–8 for what Americans said they wanted in a president at the start of the 1996 campaign.)

Voters do see differences between candidates in terms of these qualities. In 1992, for example, Bill Clinton was seen as relatively weak on human qualities.

Although voters thought he was in touch with ordinary people, they had lingering doubts about his moral character and his overall courage, in part because of negative advertisements reminding them of his draft record. At the same time, Clinton was seen as very strong on decision-making qualities. Although voters thought he waffled too much on the issues and wondered whether he had enough experience as the governor of a small Southern state to be president, they had no doubt about his intelligence. More important, they thought he was in much closer touch with ordinary people, and believed he had the capacity to inspire the nation, qualities they saw lacking in George Bush.

There is some evidence that voter confidence in the candidates has been falling in recent years.[46] Just as Americans think little of politicians in general, they think little of candidates specifically. Part of the explanation rests with attack ads. Candidates who are ahead know that going negative is a way to keep the other candidate down; candidates in trouble know that one way to get back in a race is to sling as much mud as necessary to increase their opponent's negative ratings.

However, something deeper may be going on than just a deluge of negative advertising. Political campaigns may be increasingly attracting individuals who are just not very likable. The kinds of skills that make for a *successful* candidate—the ability to raise money, the willingness to go negative, the focused ambition to stay on the road month after month, and the readiness to sacrifice one's friends and family—may not make for a very *likable* candidate.

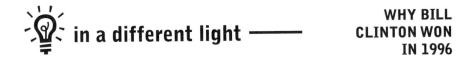 **in a different light** —— WHY BILL CLINTON WON IN 1996

The 1996 election is perhaps best described as uneventful. Despite tight races here and there, the overall outcome was never in doubt. Republicans gained a bit in the Senate and lost a bit in the House, but still maintained a majority in both chambers of Congress; Bill Clinton ended up getting reelected with just 49 percent of the popular vote, up from 43 percent four years before, and 379 electoral votes, up just six.

After a long, expensive, and, some would argue, nasty campaign, many Americans remained bored by it all. Turnout sagged to just 49 percent, setting a seventy-year low. Whether by intent or accident, voters endorsed divided government for a second straight election, giving Democrats control of the presidency for another four years (the first time a Democrat had won a second term since Franklin Roosevelt) and Republicans control of the Congress for another two years (the first time a Republican majority was continued since 1930).

BOX 9-9

Dividing the Electorate, 1996

Group	All Voters	Bill Clinton	Bob Dole	Ross Perot
Gender				
Male	48%	43%	44%	10%
Female	52	54	38	7
Race				
White	83%	43%	46%	9%
African American	10	84	12	4
Hispanic	5	72	21	6
Asian	1	43	48	8
Other	1	64	21	9
Age				
18 to 29	17%	53%	34%	10%
30 to 44	33	48	41	9
45 to 59	26	48	41	9
60 or over	24	48	44	7
Education				
No high school	6%	59%	28%	11%
High school graduate	24	51	35	13
Some college	27	48	40	10
College graduate	26	44	46	8
Post-graduate	17	52	40	5

All three factors that shape the simple act of voting—party, issues, and image—came into play in giving Democrats and Republicans alike cause to claim victory. On party, Democrats and Republicans both did reasonably well in holding their loyalists at the top of the ticket. Eighty-four percent of Democratic voters cast their ballots for Clinton; 80 percent of Republican voters went for Dole; and independents split their vote total 43 percent for Clinton, 35 percent for Dole, and 17 percent for Perot.[47]

Group	All Voters	Bill Clinton	Bob Dole	Ross Perot
Family Income				
Less than $15,000	11%	59%	28%	11%
$15,000 to $30,000	23	53	36	9
$30,000 to $49,000	27	48	40	10
$50,000 to $74,999	21	47	45	7
$75,000 to $100,000	9	44	48	7
$100,000 and up	9	38	54	6
Religion				
Protestant	38%	41%	50%	8%
Catholic	29	53	37	9
Other Christian	16	45	41	12
Jewish	3	78	16	3
No religion	7	59	23	13
Party Identification				
Democrat	39%	84%	10%	5%
Republican	35%	13	80	6
Independent	26	43	35	17
Political Ideology				
Liberal	20%	78%	11%	7%
Moderate	47	57	33	9
Conservative	33	20	71	8

Source: Courtesy of CNN/TIME All Politics and Voter News Service.

Clinton and Dole also did well among their parties core demographic groups. (See Box 9–9 for a summary of how different groups of voters split in the 1996 election.) Clinton ran strongest among women (who created a large "gender gap" between Clinton and Dole), as well as among African Americans and Hispanics, younger and older Americans, those with less education, Catholics and Jews, and lower-income groups. Dole ran strongest among men, whites, the middle-aged, college graduates, Protestants, and upper-income groups. Perot did not do particularly well in any demographic group, and did not even win a majority of those who had voted for him in 1992—a plurality went for Dole.

Of the groups, women gave Clinton his margin of victory. Clinton ran well among working women, who gave him a 57 percent endorsement, as well as home-makers, who gave him 49 percent. Clinton also did well among "soccer moms," the relatively well-to-do suburban women who received so much attention during the campaign.[48]

On issues, Americans were clearly more satisfied with the economy in 1996 than they had been when George Bush was defeated for reelection in 1992. A major-ity said the country was headed in the right direction, and almost three-quarters of that group voted for Clinton. To the extent that the election was a referendum on Clinton's policy leadership, the outcome was an endorsement, albeit a lukewarm one. Clinton also did well on education, where those who cited the issue as a top concern went 78 percent for the president and only 16 percent for his challenger. The issue was particularly important to young female college graduates and singles.

On image, Clinton fared much worse than he might have hoped. Fifty-four percent of voters said Clinton was neither honest nor trustworthy, and 60 percent said he was not telling the truth about the Whitewater scandal. Yet, in spite of Dole's nearly constant attack on Clinton's character during the final weeks of the campaign, only one out of five voters said honesty was the top factor in their vote. (Not surprisingly, the vast majority of those voters went for Dole.)

Consider two possible reasons why the character issue did not stick. First, Americans may have devalued the presidency itself. They may not have thought Bill Clinton was honest or trustworthy in general, but most certainly believed he was honest and trustworthy *enough* to be president of the United States. Second, voters liked Clinton as a person more than Dole. Asked in June 1996 to imagine going into business with either Clinton or Dole, most Americans thought Dole would devote more time and energy to making the business a success, and most wanted Dole to keep the books, but it was Clinton whom they most wanted out there selling the product. Asked to imagine giving their car keys to Clinton or Dole, roughly equal numbers thought the two candidates would know where to drive to, but it was Clin-ton with whom they said they would most enjoy the ride.[49]

Two questions emerge from this analysis of party, issues, and image. First, did the campaign matter to the final outcome? The answer is mixed. As noted earlier in this chapter, Clinton entered 1996 as an incumbent president with a strong econ-omy. The polls showed him with a commanding lead from March 1996 all the way to election day, suggesting the great difficulty Dole confronted in unseating a reason-ably popular president with a mostly satisfied public.

Second, did the election give either party a mandate to govern? The answer is no. With voter turnout at a modern low and distrust edging higher with the huge amounts of soft money and independent expenditures coursing through the campaigns, neither party could claim much of an endorsement for action.

The 1998 Congressional Elections

There are two ways to interpret the 1998 congressional elections. On the surface, nothing much changed on November 4 of that year. The Republicans lost five seats in the House of Representatives, held their 55–45 edge in the Sentate, and lost one of their 34 governorships. Newt Gingrich was still Speaker on November 5 and Trent Lott was still Senate Majority Leader.

Despite occasional surprises, including the election of former professional wrestler Jesse "the Body" Ventura as governor or Minnesota, the election left the battle lines pretty much where they had been since the Republicans recaptured Congress in 1994. Only six of the 401 House members who ran for reelection were defeated, a 98 percent survival rate that showed the continued power of money. The candidate who spent the most money won in 95 percent of the House and Senate campaigns, and that candidate was almost always an incumbent.

Beneath the surface, however, the election was a dramatic defeat for the Republican party, which had expected to gain two to three dozen seats in the House, five or six in the Senate, and two or three governorships. They also expected to hold their Senate seats in New York and North Carolina, and the governorship in California, but they lost all of these important offices.

The Republicans certainly had the money to fulfill these expectations, outspending Democrats by $110 million across the nation. They also had history on their side. The president's party almost always loses seats in the midterm election, particularly in the sixth year of an administration. With Democrats paralyzed by the scandal surrounding President Clinton's relationship with White House intern Monica Lewinsky, House Speaker Newt Gingrich persuaded his fellow Republicans to make the election a referendum on the president's morality. The strategy failed, for two reasons.

First, most voters were far more interested in education, the economy, Social Security, and taxes than the sex scandal. Only one of five voters said they had come to the polls in part to express their outrage about the Clinton/Lewinsky affair, and only one in twenty said that it was the most important issue in deciding how they voted. Roughly three out of five voters said that they disapproved of the way Republicans in Congress had handled the scandal and did not want Clinton to be impeached.

Voters hardly approved of the president's behavior, however. Election day surveys showed that a slight majority of voters approved of the way Clinton was handling his job *as president,* but held a very unfavorable opinion of him *as a person.* If the president was looking for salvation in the balloting, he did not find it. But if the Republicans were looking for an endorsement of impeachment, they did not get what they wanted, either. Voters mostly wanted the nation to continue on pretty much the same path.

The second explanation for the Republicans' disappointment was that Democrats won the battle for turnout, especially among women and African American voters. Democratic strategists had originally worried that the Clinton scandal would depress turnout—that is, that their voters would be so angry or disgusted by the president's behavior that they would just stay home, thereby giving Republicans an advantage in turnout. Republicans bet on that theory, using much of their advantage in campaign funding to run ads asking whether voters wanted to reward the president for his behavior or trust Republicans to "do the right thing" when it came to impeachment. The Republican strategy began to fail as voters began focusing on the issues that mattered most around their kitchen tables. Although Republicans won the vast majority of voters who saw moral and ethical standards as their top issues, Democrats won among voters concerned about education, the economy, and Social Security.

The campaign involved more than just elective office, of course. Nationwide, there were 240 measures on the 1998 ballot, including three to permit the medical use of marijuana (it passed in all three states), one in favor of assisted suicide (it failed), one to allow gambling on riverboats that float in artificial moats (it passed), two on campaign finance reform (both passed), and measures on everything from abolishing South Carolina's 103-year-old ban on interracial marriages (it passed) to ending affirmative action in Washington state (it passed) and allowing topless lawn mowing in Newport, Maine (it passed).

Although the election did little to change the balance of party power in Washington, it had an immediate impact on Congress. Facing an open revolt by Republican House members disappointed by the election results, Gingrich resigned as Speaker only three days after the election. The ensuing battle over the future of the party is likely to continue through the 2000 election.

MAINTAINING THE BALANCE

Election campaigns are the most important moments in American democratic life. They give citizens an opportunity to select or reject their representatives and give candidates the strongest incentive to listen to what the people want. There is no better time for parties to strengthen their membership, nor any better moment for the media to provide the kind of information that citizens need to exercise their right to vote. Campaigns can bring out the very best in American democratic life, offering citizens and candidates alike the opportunity to earn one another's respect.

Campaigns thus provide the essential elements needed for a delicate balance. To the extent that candidates are honest with the public and the public is realistic with the candidates, campaigns can provide the consent to be governed. To the extent, however, that candidates overpromise and the public overdemands, campaigns can leave government confused and uncertain.

Recent years have witnessed a number of changes that threaten the status of campaigns as proud moments in democratic life. Consultants occupy a much more prominent role in shaping candidate-centered campaigns, big campaign donors have become even more visible due to the soft money loophole, the media continue to be preoccupied with covering campaigns as if they were horse races, and candidates run increasingly on image. Winning has become everything, even when the tactics used undermine public confidence in the offices the candidates seek. In media-driven states such as California, New York, and Texas, campaigns are increasingly a feast in which candidates spend half their time in television studios making commercials and the other half meeting with big donors, while ordinary citizens are left on the outside, as if peering through the window of an exclusive restaurant.

The result is that Americans come away from elections giving just about everyone poor grades. In 1996, for example, barely 40 percent of citizens gave themselves an A or B grade, with the average a C+. They were even tougher on the press (C), pollsters (C+), campaign consultants (C), the Republican party (C), and talk show hosts (C). They were hardly easier on the winner: Clinton received a B– while his party earned a C+. All the grades were down from 1992 and 1988.[50]

There is a tiny glimmer of good news in such grades, however. Citizens are not quite ready to flunk the campaign process, and they are clearly aware that they are part of the problem. Nevertheless, election campaigns could be so much better, so much more satisfying. Campaigns do not have to be polite in order to nourish democratic life, but neither should they be so caustic that citizens back away from them in disgust.

terms to remember

nomination (p. 332)
general election (p. 333)
primary election (p. 333)
closed primary (p. 333)
open primary (p. 333)
blanket primary (p. 333)
caucus system (p. 334)
proportional voting system
  (p. 334)
independent spending (p. 342)
soft money (p. 343)

bundling (p. 349)
party-centered campaign
  (p. 351)
candidate-centered campaign
  (p. 351)
paid media (p. 356)
free media (p. 356)
priming effects (p. 364)
issue voting (p. 366)
retrospective voting (p. 367)

facts and interpretations

- Recent decades have witnessed an increase in candidate-centered campaigns and a parallel decline in party-centered campaigns. The focus of a candidate-centered campaign is to get the candidate elected at all costs, even if that means abandoning party labels altogether. Because officials elected through candidate-centered campaigns owe no allegiance to their party, such campaigns may weaken government's ability to act once the election is over.

- Money has become increasingly important to campaigns for office. Although raising money has always been part of politics, the amounts needed to wage a competitive campaign have increased over the past half century, as have the rules governing what candidates and contributors can and cannot do. The ultimate cost of raising money may be the time lost for performing other campaign duties, such as talking with voters or reflecting on issues. The ability to raise money may also become a primary qualification for running.

- It is not clear that campaigns do much to change voter decisions about the candidates. Voters enter campaigns with predispositions to like or dislike the candidates, and usually vote on the basis of how those likes and dislikes add up. Therefore, most campaigns are designed to reinforce what voters already believe going into the election. However, campaigns often do add new issues to the contest, while media coverage and advertisements often create new likes and dislikes. Whether a campaign actually matters to the final outcome may be less important than whether it contributes to an overall sense of pride in the American system of government.

open questions

- What are the elements of a "good campaign" in a healthy democracy? How would one know a good campaign if it occurred—through turnout, citizen trust in government, a close election, a unanimous choice? What would make for a bad campaign? What do you think the current balance between good and bad is, and what can the nation do to assure more good campaigns and fewer bad ones?

- How would you raise money for a campaign if you were the candidate or campaign manager? What kinds of promises would you be tempted to make to contributors in return for their support? Can a $1,000 contribution from an individual affect what a member of Congress or president does in office? Can a $5,000 contribution from a PAC? Does soft money or bundling change how money influences politics?

- How should voters make their final decisions? Should Americans rely on their party identification? What about the large number who use a candidate's image as their criterion? Is issue voting the ideal way to decide? And, if so, are Americans really capable of the kind of issue voting they seem to admire most? (Recall from Chapter 4 how little Americans know about the issues.) What might the Founders think about issue voting? Would they support retrospective voting?

- Would you ever run for office? Why or why not? Are the best people running for office these days? And are the skills needed to win a long campaign the same ones needed to govern wisely once in office?

for further study

Ansolabehere, Stephen, and Shanto Iyengar. *Going Negative: How Political Advertisements Shrink and Polarize the Electorate.* New York: Free Press, 1996.

Center for Responsive Politics. *A Brief History of Money in Politics.* Washington, DC: Center for Responsive Politics, 1995.

Ehrenhalt, Alan. *The United States of Ambition: Politicians, Power, and the Pursuit of Office.* New York: Times Books, 1992.

Flanigan, William, and Nancy Zingale. *Political Behavior of the American Electorate.* Washington, DC: CQ Press, 1994.

Sorauf, Frank. *Inside Campaign Finance: Myths and Realities.* New Haven, CT: Yale University Press, 1992.

Wattenburg, Martin. *The Rise of Candidate-Centered Politics: Presidential Elections of the 1980s.* Cambridge, MA: Harvard University Press, 1990.

endnotes for chapter 9

1. See George Thayer, *Who Shakes the Money Tree? American Campaign Financing Practices from 1789 to the Present* (New York: Simon & Schuster, 1973), p. 25.

2. See Stephen J. Wayne, *The Road to the White House, 1996: The Politics of Presidential Elections* (New York: St. Martin's Press, 1997), p. 100, for a discussion of how the national parties influence state nomination procedures.

3. Quoted in Center for Responsive Politics, *A Brief History of Money in Politics* (Washington, DC: Center for Responsive Politics, 1995), p. 3.
4. Quoted in Richard Berke, "To Campaign (v): To Beg, to Borrow, to Endure," *New York Times,* February 5, 1995, p. D6.
5. Frank J. Sorauf, *Money in American Elections* (New York: HarperCollins, 1988), p. 1.
6. Frank Sorauf, *Inside Campaign Finance: Myths and Realities* (New Haven, CT: Yale University Press, 1992), p. 189.
7. These and other campaign finance figures in this section of the chapter come from several sources, including the Center for Responsive Politics <www.crp.org> and Harold W. Stanley and Richard C. Niemi, *Vital Statistics on American Politics, 1997–1998* (Washington, DC: CQ Press, 1998).
8. For a story on calling for cash, see Richard Berke, "Before Asking for Votes, Candidates Ask for Cash," *New York Times,* April 10, 1994, p. A1.
9. Sorauf, *Inside Campaign Finance,* p. 188.
10. Sorauf, *Money in American Elections,* p. 6.
11. The case was *Buckley v. Valeo,* 424 U.S. 1 (1976).
12. Jonathan Salant and David Cloud, "To the '94 Election Victors Go the Fundraising Spoils," *Congressional Quarterly,* April 15, 1995, p. 1057.
13. Jason DeParle, "The First Primary," *New York Times Magazine,* April 16, 1995, p. 30.
14. See Anthony Corrado, *Paying for Presidents: Public Financing in National Elections* (New York: Twentieth Century Fund Press, 1993).
15. See Charles Lewis, *The Buying of the President* (New York: Avon, 1996), p. 29.
16. Harold W. Stanley and Richard G. Niemi, *Vital Statistics on American Politics* (Washington, DC: CQ Press, 1998), p. 101.
17. Alan Ehrenhalt, *The United States of Ambition: Politicians, Power, and the Pursuit of Office* (New York: Times Books, 1992), p. 19.
18. For background on the candidate-centered campaign, see Stephen Salmore and Barbara Salmore, *Candidates, Parties, and Campaigns: Electoral Politics in America* (Washington, DC: CQ Press, 1985), p. 17; see also Martin Wattenburg, *The Rise of Candidate-Centered Politics: Presidential Elections of the 1980s* (Cambridge, MA: Harvard University Press, 1990).
19. James Sterba, "Democracy Inc.: Politicians at All Levels Seek Expert Advice, Fueling an Industry," *Wall Street Journal,* September 21, 1992, p. A1.
20. Quoted in Thomas Edsall, "Taking the Money and Helping Others Run," *Washington Post National Weekly Edition,* December 13–19, 1993, p. 11.
21. These figures are drawn from Sterba, "Democracy Inc."
22. Stephen Labaton, "On the Money Trail, Most 'Insiders' Had the Advantage," *New York Times,* November 9, 1994, p. B1.
23. Federal Election Commission, "1994 Congressional Spending Sets Record," news release, December 22, 1994.
24. Times Mirror Center for The People & The Press, *The People, The Press, and Politics, Campaign '92: The Generations Divide,* July 8, 1992, p. 51.
25. Stephen Bates and Edwin Diamond, "Damned Spots," *The New Republic,* September 7 and 14, 1992, p. 14.

26. Robin Toner, "Bitter Tone of the '94 Campaign Elicits Worry on Public Debate," *New York Times,* November 13, 1994, p. A14.

27. Toner, "Bitter Tone," p. A14.

28. John Pavlik and Mark Thalhimer, "From Wausau to Wichita: Covering the Campaign Via Satellite," *Covering the Presidential Primaries* (New York: Freedom Forum Media Studies Center, 1992), p. 36.

29. See Bruce Felknor, *Dirty Politics* (New York: Norton, 1966), p. 27.

30. See Stephen Ansolabehere and Shanto Iyengar, *Going Negative: How Political Advertisements Shrink and Polarize the Electorate* (New York: Free Press, 1996), p. 90.

31. Both quotes are from Andrew Rosenthal, "A Battle of the Negatives," *New York Times,* October 31, 1992, p. A7.

32. Richard A. Lau and Lee Sigelman, "The Effectiveness of Negative Political Advertising: A Literature Review," paper prepared for the Conference on Political Advertising in Election Campaigns, American University, Washington, D.C., April 17, 1998.

33. Ansolabehere and Iyengar, *Going Negative,* p. 96.

34. Ansolabehere and Iyengar, *Going Negative,* p. 112.

35. Modified from Stanley Kelley, Jr., and Thad Mirer, "The Simple Act of Voting," *American Political Science Review,* 68, no. 2 (June 1974): 572–91.

36. James Carville and Paul Begala, "It's the Candidate, Stupid!" *New York Times,* December 4, 1992, p. A15.

37. Richard Berke, "Debating the Debates: John Q. Public Defeats Reporters," *New York Times,* October 9, 1996, p. A13.

38. Richard Morin, "The Effects of Debates Are Debatable," *Washington Post National Weekly Edition,* September 28–October 4, 1992, p. 37.

39. For a discussion of how campaigns affect elections, see Marion R. Just, Ann N. Crigler, Dean E. Alger, Timothy E. Cook, Montague Kern, and Darrell M. West, *Crosstalk: Citizens, Candidates, and the Media in a Presidential Campaign* (Chicago: University of Chicago Press, 1996).

40. Larry M. Bartels, "How Campaigns Matter," draft paper, June, 1997.

41. William Flanigan and Nancy Zingale, *Political Behavior of the American Electorate,* (Washington, DC: CQ Press, 1994), pp. 162–63.

42. Angus Campbell, Philip Converse, Warren Miller, and Donald Stokes, *The American Voter* (New York: John Wiley and Sons, 1960), pp. 24–32.

43. Flanigan and Zingale, *Political Behavior of the American Electorate,* p. 180.

44. See Benjamin Page and Robert Shapiro, *The Rational Public: Fifty Years of Trends in Americans' Policy Preferences* (Chicago: University of Chicago Press, 1992), p. 387, for a counterargument; they suggest that voters do not need large amounts of information to make rational choices.

45. Morris Fiorina, *Retrospective Voting in American National Elections* (New Haven, CT: Yale University Press, 1981), p. 5.

46. Flanigan and Zingale, *Political Behavior,* pp. 171–72.

47. These figures come from the presidential exit poll posted on the Internet by Allpolitics <www.allpolitics.com>, a news service of CNN and *Time,* November 7, 1996, located at <atl.exit.poll/index2.html>.

48. See Gerald Seib, "Women's Vote Proved to Be Key in Clinton's Victory over Dole," *Wall Street Journal,* November 7, 1996, p. A11.

49. These figures are drawn from "Revealing Opinions on the Presidential Contest," *The American Enterprise,* 7, no. 6 (November/December 1996): 101.
50. The Pew Research Center for The People & The Press, *Campaign '96 Gets Lower Grades from Voters* (Washington, DC: Pew Research Center, November 1996).

congress

to make the laws

Congress was created to perform two jobs: make the laws and represent the people. The first task is defined in the very first sentence of Article I in the Constitution, which vests all lawmaking powers in a Congress of the United States. The second task is confirmed through the use of elections to select senators and representatives.

The two jobs can be perfectly compatible, particularly when threats to the nation affect every citizen regardless of where they live. That is why votes to declare war are so often unanimous. There was only one vote against declaring World War II, and that was from a member of the House who simply believed that no such votes should be unanimous.

The two jobs can also be in great conflict, particularly when members of Congress become so consumed with holding office that they will do whatever the people want. Although they most certainly expected members of Congress to fight hard for their home districts and states, the Founders also hoped that members would be able to see and work for the broader public good. Pay too much attention to what the people want and Congress becomes incapable of making the hard choices needed to defend the nation from foreign and domestic threats; pay too little attention and Congress will lose the consent of the governed.

Maintaining this balance was essential to the Founders. They saw Congress, not the presidency, as the most dangerous branch. It was to be the most powerful, yet the most likely to be captured by popular passion. They wanted the House of Representatives to be close to the people. That is why they gave the House the power to raise revenue: precisely to assure that there would be no taxation without representation, a rallying cry of the Revolution. At the same time, however, they were particularly worried that the House might become too "hot" for reasoned judgment.

The question confronting the Constitutional Convention, therefore, was how to prevent Congress from abusing its power while protecting the young nation. It is always useful to remember James Madison's simple answer from *Federalist No. 51*: "In framing a government which is to be administered by men over men, the great difficulty lies in this: you must first enable the government to control the governed; and in the next place oblige it to control itself."[1] As noted in Chapter 2, a central answer was to divide Congress into two chambers, giving each enough power to check the other and enough reason to do so.

The Founders were quite right to believe that members of Congress might worry about what the people think. That is part of running for reelection. They were also right to think that the legislative branch might develop considerable sympathy toward what the people want. Members of Congress are much more likely than executive branch officials to have confidence in the people. Asked in 1998 how much trust and confidence they had in the wisdom of the American people when it comes to making choices on election day, two-thirds of the members of Congress said "A great deal," compared to just one-third of presidential appointees and senior civil servants. They were also twice as likely to say that Americans know enough about the issues to form wise opinions about what should be done.[2] Where one stands on the wisdom of the public clearly depends on where one sits.

It is far from clear, however, that the Founders were right about the dangers of Congress. As this chapter shows, Congress is a highly complicated institution with hundreds of access points where interest groups, presidents, and even individual citizens can stop action. It is no wonder that so many legislative proposals die without a hearing. Indeed, the odds against action are so staggeringly high that the Founders might ask whether Congress has become too great an obstacle to action. Although they would certainly want intense minorities to have the opportunity to slow the process down, they might also wonder whether Congress retains the ability to address foreign and domestic threats.

This chapter examines just how Congress works to simultaneously make the laws and represent the public, and whether doing the second job somehow weakens Congress's ability to do the first.

The first section asks what the Founders imagined in creating this branch of government. The second section examines the realities today, looking at the internal structure of the institution and the reasons for its changing complexity. The final section examines the process for making the laws.

THE IMAGINED CONGRESS

The Founders went to Philadelphia with plenty of legislative experience. Some had served in the Continental Congress, which was a single-chambered, unicameral legislature. Others served in the Confederation Congress established under the Articles of Confederation, which was also unicameral. Still others had served in their state congresses, most of which were two-chambered, bicameral legislatures. As a result, they knew what they were doing in creating Congress.

The Constitutional Convention also served as an introduction to how the Founders hoped the future Congress would act. With fifty-five delegates, it was as large as the Continental Congress (which had fifty-six delegates), and operated under a series of careful legislative rules that covered everything from who could speak to how votes were to be taken.[3] Similar rules govern the House and Senate to this day.

The Founders also established **norms,** or informal rules governing behavior. Delegates were to address each other with respect, never descending into personal attack. They were to defer to the Committee on Detail that did the hard work of refining the various planks of the Virginia Plan that had been adopted early in the convention. And they were to remember always the broad national interest, even as they represented their individual states—a point reinforced when the convention unanimously selected George Washington, who was already recognized as a national leader, as its chair on its first day in session. Similar norms have held throughout most of history, but are clearly changing today.

A Divided Branch

There was never any doubt among the Founders about which branch would be first in the Constitution. It was to be Congress, for lawmaking was to be the essential activity. That is where Congress was on the third day of the Constitutional Convention when the Founders made the decision to create a national government consisting of "a supreme legislature, judiciary and executive." And that is where Congress was when the convention adjourned three months later.

Although they never discussed their reasons for putting Congress first, the Founders clearly considered Congress to be closest to the people. Neither the presidency nor the judiciary was directly accountable to the public. As South Carolina Representative John Calhoun observed in 1817, "This, then, is the essence of our liberty; Congress is responsible to the people immediately, and the other branches of Government are responsible to it."[4]

This is not to say that all the details involved in creating Congress were agreed upon easily. It took nearly three months for the Constitutional Convention to resolve all the disagreements over how members should be elected.

Immediately after deciding to create a supreme legislature, the Founders divided Congress into two bodies, the House of Representatives and the Senate. Having given Congress the job of making the laws, the Founders immediately created one of the single most important obstacles to doing so. As Madison noted, they enabled government to control the governed, then obliged it to control itself.

The Founders obliged Congress to do so through a number of devices, from different terms to different constituencies, but none was more important than dividing the Congress into two chambers. Worried about the tendency for the legislative branch to dominate government, they made the two chambers "as little connected with each other as the nature of their common functions and their common dependence on the society will admit."[5]

The Founders were absolutely clear about having a bicameral Congress. Indeed, bicameralism is the most distinctive organizational feature of the U.S. Congress. Each chamber has its own place to meet in separate wings of the Capitol Building; each has offices for its members on separate ends of North and South Capitol Street; each has its own committee structure, its own rules for considering legislation, and its own record of proceedings (even though the record is published jointly as *The Congressional Record*); and each sets the rules governing its own members (recall from Chapter 7 that the ban on gifts from lobbyists applies differently in each chamber).[6]

It is hardly surprising that the Founders split the legislature. Bicameral legislatures had been standard practice in most of the colonies. Moreover, a split

Congress was seen as essential to a government that would prevent strong-willed majorities from oppressing individual Americans.[7] Having a two-house legislature was merely one more way to assure that government would be just strong enough to act, but not so strong as to threaten liberty. As Madison put it, "In order to control the legislative authority, you must divide it."[8]

The Duties of Congress

Article I of the Constitution begins quite simply: "All legislative Powers herein granted shall be vested in a Congress of the United States, which shall consist of a Senate and House of Representatives." In theory, that single statement gives all lawmaking power to Congress. Almost everything Congress does by way of its internal structure and operations is intimately connected to this one duty.

As if to emphasize the point, the Founders gave the longest list of enumerated powers to Congress. Because it was closest to the people, Congress would have the first say about taxes and finances—that is, the power to raise and spend taxes. It would also have the power to organize government by creating the departments and agencies of the executive branch, as well as the entire federal court system (which it used to create the first federal courts in 1789). It would be responsible for protecting the nation against foreign threats by declaring war, raising armies, building navies, and ratifying treaties negotiated by the president, as well as for protecting against domestic threats by regulating commerce and immigration, providing for the creation of state militias to maintain the peace, and controlling the power to borrow and coin money. Finally, Congress would be responsible, in part, for holding the nation together by establishing post offices and building roads. (To this day, the interstate highways are federal, while all other roads are state or local. The interstate highway system binds the nation together as no state or local road can.)

Just in case the list was not enough to allow Congress to do the job, the Founders added the *elastic clause,* allowing Congress to "make all Laws which shall be necessary and proper for carrying into Execution the foregoing Powers, and all other Powers vested by this Constitution in the Government of the United States, or in any Department or Officer thereof." Congress also had complete authority to set its own rules for its proceedings (see Article I, Section 5, of the Constitution).

Yet even as they gave Congress these duties, the Founders fueled future conflict by creating a list of specific powers for each chamber. The House, and only the House, would be given the authority to originate all tax bills, reassuring large states that small states would not be able to impose an unfair share of the burden on their bigger neighbors.

The Senate, and only the Senate, would have the authority to ratify treaties (by a two-thirds vote of all senators who are present and voting) and presidential appointments (by a simple majority) to executive offices and the courts. Recall from Chapter 2 that senators were originally selected at arm's length from the public, by the state legislatures, thereby supposedly assuring a greater wisdom in making these difficult decisions.

Finally, the Founders divided the power to impeach the president. The House would be responsible for drafting the *articles of impeachment* needed to call a Senate trial, while the Senate would make the final decision to acquit or convict the president for high crimes and misdemeanors. Although a simple majority of the House would be sufficient to pass the articles of impeachment, a two-thirds majority of the Senate would be needed for conviction. Box 10–1 shows the formal process used to impeach a president.

Prior to 1998, when Congress began considering the possibility of impeaching President Clinton for covering up his sexual affair with White House intern Monica Lewinsky, there had been only three attempts to impeach a president. The first involved charges of corruption and misconduct against John Tyler, which were never forwarded by the House to the Senate. The second involved similiar charges of misconduct against Andrew Johnson, which were forwarded to the Senate by the House, but rejected by the Senate by a margin of just one vote. The third involved charges of abuse of power against Richard Nixon, which would have probably led to impeachment had Nixon not resigned before the House voted on the articles of impeachment.

All in all, the Founders had divided enough of the power to make governing just a bit more difficult. By requiring that all bills for raising revenue come from the House, the Founders assured virtually ceaseless conflict. The Senate may be the incubator of great policy ideas, for example, but the House has considerable say over where the money to implement great policy ideas comes from. By giving the Senate the power to ratify treaties and the authority to confirm all presidential appointees, the Founders added more reason for conflict. The House may decide where the money comes from, but the Senate has a great deal of say over who gets to spend it.

Qualifications for Office

The Founders set different minimums for serving in the House and Senate. House members have to be at least twenty-five years old, while senators have to be at least thirty; House members have to be U.S. citizens for at least seven years; senators for at least nine. Other than age and citizenship, there are no other qualifications for office. (See Box 10–2 for a comparison of the backgrounds of members in the First Congress versus the 105th Congress two hundred years later.)

It is no secret why the Founders set the age limits: they simply did not trust young people. As Virginia delegate George Mason argued, age was a way of "measur-

BOX 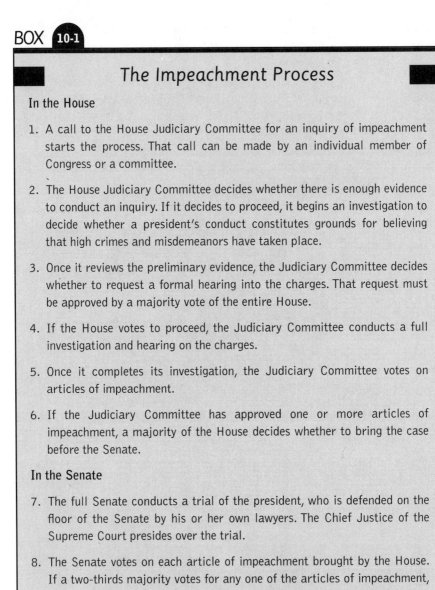 10-1

The Impeachment Process

In the House

1. A call to the House Judiciary Committee for an inquiry of impeachment starts the process. That call can be made by an individual member of Congress or a committee.

2. The House Judiciary Committee decides whether there is enough evidence to conduct an inquiry. If it decides to proceed, it begins an investigation to decide whether a president's conduct constitutes grounds for believing that high crimes and misdemeanors have taken place.

3. Once it reviews the preliminary evidence, the Judiciary Committee decides whether to request a formal hearing into the charges. That request must be approved by a majority vote of the entire House.

4. If the House votes to proceed, the Judiciary Committee conducts a full investigation and hearing on the charges.

5. Once it completes its investigation, the Judiciary Committee votes on articles of impeachment.

6. If the Judiciary Committee has approved one or more articles of impeachment, a majority of the House decides whether to bring the case before the Senate.

In the Senate

7. The full Senate conducts a trial of the president, who is defended on the floor of the Senate by his or her own lawyers. The Chief Justice of the Supreme Court presides over the trial.

8. The Senate votes on each article of impeachment brought by the House. If a two-thirds majority votes for any one of the articles of impeachment, the president is removed from office and replaced by the vice president.

ing the deficiency of young politicians," particularly since "political opinions at the age of 21 were too crude & erroneous to merit an influence on public measures."[9]

As for the different requirements for the House and Senate, part of the justification flowed from the Senate's treaty-making power (the Founders wanted even more wisdom), and part flowed from images of the House as the less predictable

BOX **10-2**

Congress, Then and Now

	First Congress		105th Congress	
	House	Senate	House	Senate
Size	65	26	435	100
Average Age	44	46	52	58
Sex				
Male	100%	100%	88%	91%
Female	0	0	12	9
Race				
White	100%	100%	87%	96%
Black	0	0	8	1
Hispanic	0	0	4	0
Asian American	0	0	1	2
Native American	0	0	0	1
Lawyers	38%	38%	40%	56%
Advanced Degrees	0%	0%	65%	70%

Source: Data on the First Congress from "Congress: The First and the 100th," *New York Times,* January 5, 1987, p. A14; data on the 105th Congress from "The 105th Congress: A Study in Sameness," *New York Times,* January 19, 1997, p. E5.

chamber. The Founders may have called the House the "first branch," but they still worried about the impact of direct election. By setting the Senate's requirements higher and giving its members a six-year term, the Founders hoped the Senate would be the more enlightened body. Concerned about the "fickleness and passion" of the House of Representatives, Madison in particular saw the Senate as "a necessary fence against this danger."[10] One hundred years later, a Princeton professor named Woodrow Wilson endorsed the notion as follows:

> It is indispensable that besides the House of Representatives which runs on all fours with popular sentiment, we should have a body like the Senate which may refuse to run with it at all when it seems to be wrong—a body which has time and security enough to keep its head, if only now and then and but for a little while, till other people have had time to think.[11]

It is important to note that the Founders explicitly rejected any limits on the number of terms a House member or senator could serve. Having seen how term limits had worked under the Articles of Confederation, which prohibited anyone from being a member of Congress for more than three years out of six, they rejected the concept unanimously and without debate.[12] It was not that term limits had been a failure under the Articles. To the contrary, they had worked precisely as intended in forcing several talented members out of office, leaving the Continental Congress less effective and souring the Founders on the idea.

Fueled by public distrust toward Congress, the idea returned with a vengeance nearly two hundred years later. By 1995, half of the states had adopted term limits for House members and senators, most of which involved twelve years of service total (six House terms or two Senate terms). Thus, when the Supreme Court was asked to rule on the constitutionality of term limits in 1995, it concluded that the Founders' voice still held force today. The states argued that they could impose term limits under their power to set the manner, places, and times of elections, but a 5–4 majority of the Court ruled otherwise. Writing for the majority, Justice John Paul Stevens made the case overturning Arkansas's three-term limit on House members and two-term limit on senators as follows:

> The Framers decided that the qualifications for service in the Congress of the United States be fixed in the Constitution and be uniform throughout the Nation. That decision reflects the Framers' understanding that Members of Congress are chosen by separate constituencies, but that they become, when elected, servants of the people of the United States. They are not merely delegates appointed by separate, sovereign states; they occupy offices that are integral and essential components of a single National Government. In the absence of a properly passed constitutional amendment, allowing individual States to craft their own qualifications for Congress would thus erode the structure envisioned by the Framers, a structure that was designed, in the words of the Preamble to our Constitution, to form a more perfect Union.[13]

Under the ruling, all other state term limits on federal officers were rendered unconstitutional.

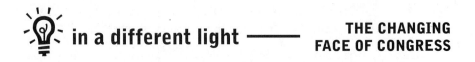 **in a different light** ——— **THE CHANGING FACE OF CONGRESS**

Although race, gender, and wealth were not used as qualifications for office, the Founders clearly expected Congress to be a white, male, mostly propertied institution. After all, women and slaves could not vote.

The changing face of Congress. A portrait of the Senate in 1850 (top) and a picture of the new members of the House in 1996 (bottom).

The Founders would be surprised at the face of Congress today. Recent Congresses have had record numbers of women and minorities, including the first African American woman ever elected to the Senate, Carol Moseley-Braun (D-IL), and the first Native American, Ben Nighthorse Campbell (R-CO). The 104th Congress in 1995–1996 had the largest number of African American and Hispanic members of the House in history, while the 105th in 1997–1998 had the largest number of women members in both the House and Senate. Where minorities seem unable to gain ground is in the Senate, where the number has been stuck at four or less for almost three decades.

The changing face of Congress reflects more than just the changing demographics of society. It also reflects the growing effectiveness of women and minority candidates. Running as the ultimate outsiders, for example, women candidates offered an option to voters who saw Congress as out of touch with ordinary Americans. Voters also judged women to be more honest than men by 5 to 10 percentage points, more caring by 5 points, and less tied to special interests.[14]

The changing face of Congress also reflects the rising number of majority-minority districts. Of the sixteen African Americans newly elected to Congress in 1992, all but three came from the new districts forged after the 1990 census. There were similar gains for Hispanic Americans in Texas and California. Most of the gains have held in spite of the Supreme Court's decisions in *Shaw v. Reno, Miller v. Johnson*, and *Shaw v. Hunt*. (Recall the discussion of majority-minority districts in Chapter 8.)

The face of Congress may be changing, but its pocketbook definitely is not. Almost one-third of the senators who served in the 104th Congress were millionaires, and lawyers remain vastly overrepresented compared to other occupations. Moreover, old customs die hard. Even with the Democratic senator from Washington, Patty Murray, sitting on his Appropriations Committee, chairman Robert Byrd still referred to the members as "Gentlemen."[15] However, with new sources of campaign funds for women and minority candidates and a growing list of election wins by these candidates, the Senate and House are likely to continue changing.

Having more women and minorities in Congress is already changing both the agenda and style of the institution. Women legislators are more likely than men to oppose limits on access to abortion and the construction of nuclear power plants, for example. They are also more likely to support equal rights for women and are generally more liberal on economic and social issues.

Women and minority legislators can also bring a new point of view to Congress. Consider how first-year senator Moseley-Braun changed the Senate's position on the great seal of the United Daughters of the Confederacy. The seal depicted a Confederate flag, the same flag that the South had flown in the fight for slavery. Under an ancient statute that required periodic government approval, the Senate had initially approved the seal by a vote of 52 to 48.

It was not until Moseley-Braun took the floor that the Senate began to understand just how offensive the seal was to African Americans. "On this issue there can be no consensus," Moseley-Braun reminded her colleagues in a passionate floor statement. "It is an outrage. It is an insult. It is absolutely unacceptable to me and to millions of Americans, black or white, that we would put the imprimatur of the United States Senate on a symbol of this kind of idea."

Moseley-Braun then moved that the Senate overturn its earlier decision. Twenty-seven senators changed their votes, rejecting the seal by a vote of 79 to 11. "We must get racism behind us. We must move forward," explained Senator Campbell as he changed his vote. "We must realize we live in America today." Even Alabama Democrat Howell Heflin changed his mind, saying his grandfathers, both of whom served in the Civil War, "might be spinning in their graves" because of his flip-flop, but he would change his vote nonetheless.[16]

THE REAL CONGRESS

Time has not stood still on Capitol Hill. As with so much that happens in legislative life, the devil is not in the broad outline but in the details. Over the years, Congress has grown larger, more complicated, and more divided over the issues of the day.

Before discussing the institutional Congress today, it is important to recognize that the future complexity was apparent in the First Congress that convened in 1789. The Founders did not believe Congress would convene and somehow produce legislation by magic. Just as they had used rules and committees to force decisions in the Constitutional Convention, the Founders expected the First Congress to use structure and rules in making laws.

The Evolving Congress

The first task of the First Congress was to organize itself to do business. After all, the Constitution had merely specified that each house was to set its own rules, keep its own journal of proceedings, and meet at least once a year. (Note that Congresses are numbered in two-year terms; the First Congress was elected in 1788 even as the Constitution was still being ratified, and served until 1791, when the Second Congress, which was elected in 1790, came into office. Hence, the 106th Congress came into office in 1999, precisely 210 years after the First Congress.)

Everything else had to be invented from scratch—the leadership, the committees, and the rules. And that is exactly what the fifty-nine members of the first House and the twenty-two members of the first Senate did. (Note that the Senate had only twenty-two members because North Carolina and Rhode Island had not yet ratified the Constitution and had not selected members.)

Almost all the first members of Congress had served in their state legislatures, one-half in either the Continental or Confederation Congresses, and one-fourth in the Constitutional Convention itself. These were legislative experts who drew on their prior experience in federal or state government, as well as lessons from the British Parliament, which had (and still has) a House of Commons (akin to the U.S. House) and the House of Lords (akin to the U.S. Senate).

Because of its size, the first House needed to quickly create a basic structure and rules. Members acted immediately to select a **Speaker of the House** to keep individual members from tying up the body by talking too much or introducing too many bills. The Speaker was also given authority to appoint members of the temporary committees that came and went with specific bills, an approach that resembled use of the Committee of Detail to flesh out the fine points of the Constitution. The First Congress acted unanimously in choosing James Madison as its first Speaker.

The House membership had nearly tripled in size by 1810. And as it grew, so did the House structure and rules. After relying on hundreds of ad hoc committees in its first six years, the House had created four permanent, **standing committees** by 1795, and had added another six by 1810. The powerful House Ways and Means Committee was formed in 1802, and remains to this day the first stop for all tax proposals in Congress.[17]

The political parties also began playing a more significant role in organizing both the House and the Senate during this period. "The existence of the two parties in Congress is apparent," wrote Senator John Taylor of Virginia in 1794. "The fact is disclosed almost upon every important question. Whether the subject be foreign or domestic—relative to war or peace, navigation or commerce—the magnetism of opposite views draws them wide as the poles asunder."[18] By 1800, the Speaker of the House had become the top job for the majority party, and officers were in place for the minority.

Because of its small size, the Senate adopted a structure and rules much more slowly than did the House. The Senate had fewer than fifty-nine members (the size of the first House) until 1848 when Wisconsin entered the Union; by that time, the House had grown to 237 strong. Moreover, the Founders had taken it upon themselves to establish the Senate's leadership structure by creating a president of the Senate (who would always be the vice president of the United States) and a president pro tempore (or temporary president) who would lead the chamber in the vice president's absence (which is almost always). They had also resolved the greatest procedural problem the Senate could ever face: the president of the Senate would cast the deciding vote whenever there was a tie among the Senate's always even-numbered membership.

Nothing in these differences would be likely to surprise the Founders. They clearly expected the Senate to be led by a "cooler" kind of representative. In contrast to the passionate House, the Senate would be a bastion of decorum and civility. Even when the Senate did adopt rules, they were less about how to pass a bill and much more about how individual senators should treat each other. One of the rules adopted in the first Senate prohibited senators from reading newspapers during debates; another prevented members from speaking twice in any one debate on the same day.

As for establishing permanent committees, the Senate had little need for such structure early on. Its first committees were ad hoc and dissolved as soon as a legislative issue was resolved. When the Senate finally began creating permanent committees in the early 1800s, it did so more to accommodate the growing activity in the House than to control its own members. (As Chapter 8 explained, the House membership was capped at 435 in 1910 when Congress passed a reapportionment act ordering the states to stop drawing new districts, a perfectly legal act of Congress allowed under Article I, Section 4, of the Constitution. The Senate kept growing by twos as each new state was added, most recently Alaska and Hawaii during the 1950s.)

The Institutional Congress

Today's House and Senate can be as different from each other as they are from the presidency and the Supreme Court. The Senate prides itself on being an incubator of ideas, a place in which individual members can take the floor on behalf of an oppressed minority and hold it forever; the House prides itself on being the voice of the people, a place in which, as former House Speaker Thomas "Tip" O'Neill once remarked, "all politics is local." (See Box 10–3 for a list of the key differences.)

The two chambers are no more complex, however, than the society they have come to represent and the government they must oversee. It was far easier to control the 59 House members and 22 Senators who represented only white male property owners in 1789 than it is to control the 435 House members and 100 Senators who represent the diverse United States of today; far easier to write legislation for the tiny government in 1789 than for the $1.5 trillion government today. In the 1790s, a handful of permanent committees could handle the entire task of making the laws and checking government. As this chapter discusses below, today's Congress has more than two hundred committees and subcommittees of one kind or another.

Key Differences between the House and Senate

Size

The House has 435 members; the number from each state varies by population.

The Senate has 100 members, two from each state.

Terms

House members serve for two years.

Senators serve for six years.

Elections

House members are elected by districts; all come up for election every two years.

Senators serve their entire state; one-third of the Senate comes up for election every two years; the two senators from the same state do not come up for election at the same time.

Rules

The House has 700 pages of rules governing itself.

The Senate has 100 pages of rules governing itself.

Leadership

The House has more layers of leadership, and more leaders at each layer.

The Senate has fewer layers of leadership, and fewer leaders at each layer.

Legislative Passage

The House operates under a simple majority rule: Bills come to the floor for final passage under a strict "rule," or ticket, that sets limits on debate and amending activity.

The Senate operates mostly under unanimous consent: Bills usually come to the floor with the consent of every member; final passage is also by simple majority rule.

Role of Individual Members

Individual House members have little power to influence legislation.

Individual Senators have great power to influence legislation, including the ability to hold the floor indefinitely.

Despite the many differences between the House and the Senate, being in the same business produces important similarities. Both chambers have leadership, committees, and staff, albeit in rather different numbers. Understanding how the two chambers are organized is essential in learning how a bill becomes a law.

Leadership. Every organization needs leaders, if only to gavel a meeting to order. In Congress, that leadership is picked by the two parties at the start of every two-year period. Only party members may participate in the election of the party leaders of the House and Senate.

Once selected, everything the party leaders do is aimed at getting the 218 votes in the House and 51 in the Senate that are needed to pass most legislative proposals, or **bills,** and thus enact them into law. "The only thing that counts is 218 votes," House Minority Leader Richard Gephardt (D-MO) once explained. "Nothing else is real."[19] En route to a majority, however, the parties do everything from selecting administrative employees (including, for example, members of the Capitol Hill police) to scheduling floor business, influencing members, and working with the president to shape legislation.

Members do not get to be party leaders unless they have a certain level of **seniority,** or length of service in the chamber. But seniority is not the only criterion for selecting leaders. If it were, South Carolina Republican Senator Strom Thurmond, and not Kansas Senator Bob Dole, would have been the Senate majority leader in 1995. After all, Thurmond was first elected to the Senate in 1956, twelve years before Dole. What made the difference for Dole in 1995 was his reputation for getting things done and his connections within the Republican party.

Because it is easier to lead 100 senators than 435 House members, it is best to think of four parties in Congress: two in the Senate (majority, minority), and two in the House (majority, minority). Together, these four parties determine virtually everything that happens in making the laws and representing the public.

In the House, the majority party meets to select the Speaker and the holders of its two top party jobs: (1) the **majority leader,** who acts as a kind of deputy Speaker, and (2) the majority **whip,** who is responsible for whipping up party support on the floor. At almost the same time, the minority party selects the holders of its two top jobs: (1) **minority leader,** and (2) minority whip. If the minority party recaptures the majority, its minority leader or whip almost always becomes Speaker. Each party also selects its own **committee on committees,** which is responsible for filling its party's committee and subcommittee slots.

The speakership of the House may be the single most important position in the entire Congress, for it concentrates power in one individual far beyond any other post in either chamber. The Speaker schedules all legislation, presides over debates, chairs the committee that decides who sits on all committees, decides which committees will consider what legislation, and, as the chief administrative officer of the House, even determines which members get the best offices. These

House Speaker Newt Gingrich. When his party recaptured the House in 1994 after forty years in the minority, Gingrich became one of the most visible leaders in America. His popularity fell in 1996 as Americans began to believe that the Republican "Contact with America" had gone too far in cutting domestic programs.

powers help explain why Newt Gingrich became instantly visible after being elected the new Speaker of the House in 1995, and why he became so controversial as his Republican majority shut down government twice later in the year.

Gingrich had risen to power in part because he controlled what political scientists call a **leadership PAC**, which is a political action committee controlled by a leader of Congress. Unlike traditional PACs, which give their money mostly to incumbents, Gingrich's GOPAC (Grand Old Party) gave millions to Republican challengers in the 1994 congressional election, thereby increasing the odds that Republicans would recapture the House, while making Gingrich the prohibitive favorite to be elected Speaker.[20] GOPAC continued to support Republicans even after Gingrich became Speaker. Headed by a hand-picked Gingrich ally, GOPAC gave $4.5 million to Republicans in 1996. The largest Democratic leadership PAC that year was the Effective Government Committee, which gave $1.1 million to candidates on behalf of Minority Leader Gephardt. The biggest Senate leadership PAC trails far behind, testifying to the ability of senators to raise plenty of money on their own.[21]

Party leadership is much less important in the smaller, more intimate Senate. Despite its mention in the Constitution, president pro tempore of the Senate

BOX **10-4**

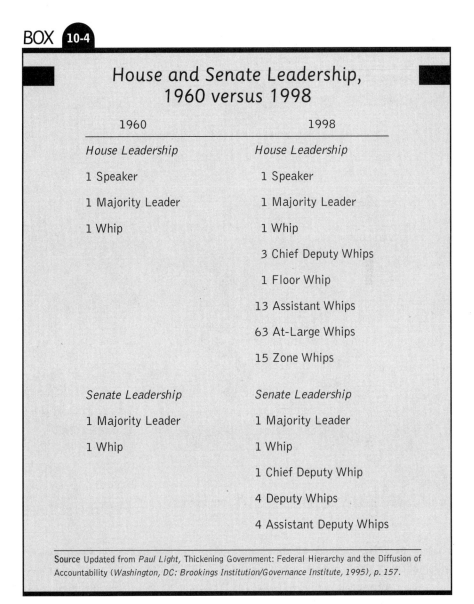

House and Senate Leadership, 1960 versus 1998

1960	1998
House Leadership	*House Leadership*
1 Speaker	1 Speaker
1 Majority Leader	1 Majority Leader
1 Whip	1 Whip
	3 Chief Deputy Whips
	1 Floor Whip
	13 Assistant Whips
	63 At-Large Whips
	15 Zone Whips
Senate Leadership	*Senate Leadership*
1 Majority Leader	1 Majority Leader
1 Whip	1 Whip
	1 Chief Deputy Whip
	4 Deputy Whips
	4 Assistant Deputy Whips

Source Updated from *Paul Light,* Thickening Government: Federal Hierarchy and the Diffusion of Accountability (*Washington, DC: Brookings Institution/Governance Institute, 1995*), p. 157.

is largely a ceremonial position. Instead, the majority leader occupies the single most powerful position in the Senate, followed by the minority leader. If not as important as the Speaker of the House, the Senate majority leader is often the most visible political leader in the country after the president. It is often the leader of the opposition party in the Senate who gives the response to the president's State of the Union address, for example.

Compared to the House, however, the Senate party leadership has relatively little power. The majority leader cannot strip a member of a committee assignment, force a bill from the calendar, or make a committee act. "Many times I've wished I could simply impose my will and do what I want done without the need to consult and explain," said Senate Majority Leader George Mitchell in 1991. Instead, Mitchell had to build "the best-developed patience muscle in America."[22] Because rules are much weaker in the Senate, the majority leader is often at the mercy of strong-willed colleagues. "All of us are entrepreneurs," said one senator. "The leadership has no handle on us. They can't really do anything for us or to us."[23]

Despite these differences in power, the two chambers have both produced increasingly complex leadership structures. There are now more layers of party leaders in each chamber, and more leaders at each layer. (See Box 10–4 for a comparison of the majority party leadership in 1960 and 1998.)

One reason the congressional party leadership structure has grown more complex is that members have so many demands on their time, which, in turn, makes the job of the House and Senate whips so important. The job of the whip is simple: get party members to support the party position on legislative votes. As former congressional staffer Christopher Matthews notes, "The job of party whip in the Senate resembles that of a shop steward on the factory floor. This person looks out for the members' endlessly developing problems and interests. If they need to have the schedule changed because of an important event back home, it is the whip's job to see whether something can be done."[24] As one senator once remarked about his whip's function, "If you took out a pencil, he'd sharpen it."[25]

in a different light ——— SENATE PECULIARITIES

There is no better example of the peculiarities of Senate rules than the *filibuster*, which allows a single Senator to talk a bill to death. Under Senate rules, any member who rises to speak is allowed to talk as long as he or she wishes. Although most senators courteously abide by whatever time limits their colleagues set for a given debate, they are always free to keep talking until at least 60 senators vote to stop the filibuster by invoking *cloture*. Because such "supermajorities" are difficult to create, Richard Fenno argues that every senator has "an atomic bomb that can blow up the place."[26]

Filibusters were never part of the constitutional design, however. They emerged through practice as the Senate developed its own rules governing behavior. The first filibuster occurred in 1841 as part of sweeping debates over slavery and the role of national government in economic affairs. It was not until 1917 that the Senate finally created a rule for invoking cloture.

It used to be, for example, that filibusters were physically exhausting events—rent a copy of the movie *Mr. Smith Goes to Washington* for the classic Hollywood rendition of the filibuster as a marathon. Strom Thurmond still holds the individual endurance record, talking for 24 hours and 18 minutes straight in killing a 1957 civil rights bill.

Today's filibusters are less stressful physically but do carry occasional moments of drama. For example, in 1988, Senate Majority Leader Robert Byrd (D-WV) kept the Senate in session for three days straight in an effort to break a Republican filibuster against a Democratic campaign finance reform bill. Republicans were so angry at the pressure that they finally stopped coming to the chamber in protest. Byrd, in turn, ordered the Senate's sergeant-at-arms to arrest the absent Republicans and bring them to the Senate floor, a power that had not been used for forty years. Former Senator Robert Packwood (R-OR) resisted arrest, so to speak, and had to be physically carried to the Senate floor at 1:19 A.M. Despite Byrd's efforts, the Democrats could not break the filibuster. After losing the eighth cloture vote to limit debate, Byrd was forced to withdraw the bill from Senate consideration.

Except for such rare examples, filibusters are not dramatic events. By the 1970s, according to journalist Hendrik Hertzberg, "the production was automated. It is no longer actually necessary to conduct a filibuster; it suffices merely to announce one, and the Senate moves on to other business until the required sixty votes can be assembled or the targeted bill dies. No muss, no fuss, no embarrassing Cleghorns in string ties reading excerpts from the telephone directory far into the night."[27]

In part because filibusters have become easier, their use has grown. There were no filibusters during the 1700s, sixteen in the 1800s, sixty-six from 1900 to 1950, twenty in the 1960s, fifty-two in the 1970s, eighty in the 1980s, and, if current trends hold, there will be more than two hundred in the 1990s.

Filibusters are not the only peculiarity of the Senate, however. Individual senators are free to place a *legislative hold* on a bill, which usually involves nothing more than a phone call to a senator's party leader. A legislative hold merely expresses a senator's personal objection to a given proposal, which in turn signals a problem for scheduling. Since much of the Senate's business is conducted by unanimous consent—all senators must agree to allow a bill to come to a vote—a single senator's objection can doom a proposal. The only way to challenge a legislative hold is to force a formal vote to proceed, a rare occurrence in the more courteous Senate. All holds are secret unless the individual member chooses to reveal his or her action.

These delaying tactics can seem undemocratic, particularly when a majority of senators want action. But by allowing a single senator to delay or kill a bill, the filibuster and its cousins give minorities an extra source of protection. The problem is that they are being used on a host of less-than-significant issues. "The threat of a filibuster is now a regular event in the Senate, weekly at least, sometimes daily," argued an exasperated Senate Majority Leader George Mitchell in his last term in office. "It is invoked by minorities of as few as one or two Senators and for reasons as trivial as a Senator's travel schedule."[28]

Committees. Congressional committees exist to fulfill both jobs of Congress. First, committees are a key tool for making the laws. They hold the legislative hearings that define the problems, draft the bills that provide the solutions, lead the fights for final passage, and make sure the executive branch is faithfully executing the laws.

Second, committees provide important opportunities for members to speak on behalf of their **constituents,** that is, the people who live and vote in their district or state. Members of Congress from farm states tend to gravitate toward the agriculture committees, members from high-tech districts toward energy and commerce committees.

Like the leadership and staff of Congress, the committee structure has become ever more complex over time. Starting from just four standing committees in the 1790s, the number and jurisdiction of committees have expanded steadily thereafter. By the 1940s, committees had become so numerous that Congress undertook a sweeping reorganization designed both to reduce the total number and to strengthen the power of committee chairs. The 1970s brought another effort to make the committee structure more rational, as did the first days of the 104th Congress under the new Republican House majority in 1995, when three full committees and over thirty subcommittees were abolished.

Most committees today have subcommittees to deal with specific areas of legislation. The Senate Commerce, Science, and Transportation Committee, for example, has subcommittees on aviation, communications, consumer affairs, oceans and fisheries, space, and surface transportation/merchant marine. The House and Senate appropriations committees, which allocate money to federal programs, each have thirteen subcommittees, one for each of the thirteen major spending bills that must be enacted every year.

Compared to the 1800s, the number of committees and subcommittees today is staggering: two hundred for Congress as a whole. However, the complexity is not so much in the number of committees and subcommittees as in the number of assignments each member receives. The average House member now sits on five committees and subcommittees, roughly the same level as in the 1950s, while the average senator sits on eleven, up from seven in the 1950s.

Types of Committees.   Not all congressional committees have equal authority or permanence. *Standing committees* and their *subcommittees* are permanent and are the sources of most bills. *Select* and *special committees* reflect temporary priorities of Congress and rarely author legislation. *Joint committees* have members from both bodies and exist either to study some issue of interest to the entire Congress or to oversee congressional support agencies such as the Library of Congress and the U.S. Government Printing Office.

Of the various types of committees, standing committees and subcommittees are clearly the most important arenas for making laws and representing constituents, and fall into four different types: authorizing, appropriations, rules (only in the House), and revenue. (See Box 10–5 for a list of the standing House and Senate committees in 1998.)

- *Authorizing committees* pass the basic laws that tell government what to do. The House and Senate education and labor committees, for example, are responsible for setting the basic rules of the Pell Grant student loan program—who can apply, how much they can get, where the loans come from,

The Senate Armed Services Committee holds a hearing on gays in the military in the wake of President Clinton's "don't ask/don't tell" policy. Clinton's policy allowed gays to serve in the military provided they keep their sexual orientation a secret.

BOX 10-5

Standing Committees of the 105th Congress, 1997–1998

House	Senate
Agriculture	Agriculture, Nutrition, and Forestry
Appropriations	Appropriations
Banking and Financial Services	Armed Services
Budget	Banking, Housing, and Urban Affairs
Commerce	Budget
Education and the Workforce	Commerce, Science, and Transportation
Government Reform and Oversight	Energy and Natural Resources
House Oversight	Environment and Public Works
International Relations	Finance
Judiciary	Foreign Relations
National Security	Governmental Affairs
Resources	Indian Affairs
Rules	Judiciary
Science	Labor and Human Resources
Small Business	Rules and Administration
Standards of Official Conduct	Small Business
Transportation and Infrastructure	Veterans Affairs
Veterans Affairs	
Ways and Means	

and how defaults are handled. In 1997–1998, there were fifteen authorizing committees in the House and thirteen in the Senate.

Authorizing committees do more than author legislation, however. They also conduct *oversight hearings* on the current operation of government.

Some of the hearings are designed to ask whether programs are working well; others to ferret out fraud, waste, or abuse in an agency of government; still others to conduct investigations of some major scandal. The amount of oversight is clearly increasing. Political scientist Joel Aberbach found, for example, that just 8 percent of all legislative hearings focused on oversight in 1961 compared to over 25 percent just two decades later.[29]

- *Appropriations committees* determine just how much money government gets to spend for each program—for example, how much money students will actually get in Pell Grants. There is just one appropriations committee in each chamber. Because money talks, the appropriations committees have great power to undo or limit decisions by the authorizing committees. The education and labor committees authorized Pell Grants to rise as high as $3,700 a year in 1992, but the appropriations committees provided enough money for grants of only $2,300.

  Thirteen appropriations bills must be enacted each year to keep government open; hence there are thirteen appropriations subcommittees in each chamber. Each one is responsible for determining the annual funding for a specific department and/or function of government.

- *Rules* and *administration committees* determine the basic operations of the two houses—for example, how many staffers individual members get. The House Rules Committee is an extraordinarily powerful committee. It has special responsibility for giving each bill a rule, or ticket, to the floor of the House, and determines what, if any, amendments to a bill will be permitted. Under an *open rule,* any amendment can be considered; under a *closed rule,* only amendments that the Rules Committee approves can be considered.

- *Revenue* and *budget committees* deal with raising the money that appropriating committees spend, while setting the broad targets that shape the federal budget. The House Ways and Means Committee is arguably the single most powerful committee in the U.S. Congress, for it is both an authorizing committee responsible for making basic decisions on the huge Social Security and Medicare programs and a revenue committee responsible for setting basic tax policy. It is the committee responsible for the fulfillment of the constitutional requirement that all revenue bills originate in the House.

Getting Assigned.   Winning a good committee assignment is one of the most important campaigns a new member of Congress mounts. A good assignment can make or break the next election, allowing the new member to claim great influence over issues that matter in his or her home district; a bad assignment can allow the challenger to point out how little influence the member has.

New members work hard to make their preferences for committee assignments known. As newly elected Representative Sam Coppersmith (D-AZ) said of the few seats open in 1995 on the most desirable committees, "There would be a certain poetic justice if they just threw three juicy steaks into a room full of sixty-five hungry dogs and see which three dogs come out with the steaks. It would be an amazing labor-saving device."[30]

All the decisions on appointments to House and Senate committees are made by the parties. Although the majority party sets the ratio of majority to minority seats on each committee, it has no say about whom the minority party appoints to its slots. Each party in each chamber appoints its own committee on committees, which, in turn, appoints all committee members. As a general rule, all reelected members can keep their old assignments. If they decide to change committees, however, they must get approval from the committee on committees, which almost always honors such requests.

Each committee on committees has a somewhat different set of rules for keeping the process fair. New House Democrats who are assigned to an "exclusive," or especially powerful, committee, such as Appropriations, Ways and Means, or Rules, usually do not get another standing committee assignment; no member gets a second "major" committee assignment until all other members have a major assignment of their own; and new members who are likely to face a particularly tough first reelection campaign may get an extra boost where possible.

Informal Committees.   Alongside the formal committees and subcommittees, members of Congress often serve on informal committees. There are two types of informal committees: conference committees and caucuses.

Conference committees are anything but lasting. They come together for a brief moment in legislative time to accomplish one goal: find agreement when the House and Senate pass different versions of a proposed law. What the Founders had set asunder through separate powers and interests, conference committees put together to make sure government is strong enough to act. Created in the First Congress, they are an example of how practice changes the constitutional design.[31]

"When I came to Congress I had no comprehension of the importance of conference committees which actually write legislation," a member said. "We all know that important laws are drafted there, but I don't think one person in a million has any appreciation of their importance and the process by which they work."[32]

Conference committees derive their power from striking the final agreement on a bill between the House and Senate. Conference committee members are appointed by the party leadership of both chambers, but each chamber has just one vote to cast on behalf of the bill. The goal is simple: instead of passing a bill back and forth between chambers until one or the other backs down, conference committees take the House and Senate versions of a bill and, if successful, *report,* or send back, a single compromise version.

Technically, the compromise does not have to resemble either version of the original bill, a political reality that once prompted President Ronald Reagan to note, "You know, if an orange and an apple went into conference consultations, it might come out a pear."[33] If a conference committee cannot reach a 2–0 vote, the original bills cannot advance—unless, of course, one chamber backs down and passes the other's version.

In contrast to conference committees, **caucuses** do not have a legislative role at all. They are best defined as informal committees that individual members join to promote their legislative interests. Members can join any caucus they wish, provided that they meet the caucus's own criteria. It would hardly make sense for a member to join the Steel Caucus, for example, if he or she did not represent a district with a steel industry.

The very first caucuses were formed around the rooming houses where most members stayed during the brief sessions of their part-time First Congress. What makes the current list of caucuses different is their number (130), diversity (more of just about every interest is represented among the caucuses), character (many have paid staff, dues-paying members, and offices), and ability to monitor legislative actions that affect their interests.[34] There are caucuses for House members only, for Senators only, and for members of both chambers together. By the 1990s, according to one count, House members actually served on more informal caucuses than on committees and subcommittees.[35]

The growing diversity of the caucuses parallels that of the rest of society. They include the Black Caucus, Hispanic Caucus, Women's Issues Caucus, Rural Health Caucus, Children's Caucus, Cuba Freedom Caucus, Pro-Life Caucus, Homelessness Task Force, Urban Caucus, and Ethiopian Jewry Caucus. The diversity also parallels the fragmentation of interest groups discussed earlier in this book, with caucuses on nearly every business and public interest issue—from the B-2 stealth bomber, steel, beef, bearings, high tech, computers, mushrooms, mining, gas, sweeteners, wine, footwear, and soybeans to animal welfare, the Chesapeake Bay, clean water, drug enforcement, adoption, the arts, energy, military reform, AIDS, and antiterrorism. There are also friends of the Caribbean Basin, of the Animals, of Human Rights Monitors, and of Ireland.

Although the Republican majority cut funding for the caucuses in 1995, it appears that many will survive by raising outside money from lobbyists. Such fundraising merely confirms the link between the caucuses and the interest groups they often serve.

Congressional Staff.   The institutional Congress also includes the thousands of staffers who make sure the members and committees are well equipped to do their two jobs of legislation and representation. It is the staff who write most of the bills, draft most of the questions that get asked at hearings, produce the legislative reports that support final action, and generate much of the flowery language used on the floor. They also write most of the letters back home to the district and work closely with the executive branch on behalf of constituents.

Congressional committees and member offices are best seen as small businesses in which often anonymous employees do the basic work of producing the final product under the company's label. As such, consider three different kinds of staff that help Congress work: personal, committee, and support agency.

The first kind of staff involve the *personal aides* that surround individual members. The hierarchy of the average office is simple: legislative correspondents at the bottom answer the letters; legislative assistants in the middle handle the constituent needs; legislative directors just below the top keep track of the key bills; and the administrative assistant or chief of staff at the top makes sure that the member is kept informed.

In the 1930s, there were fewer than 1,500 House and Senate personal staffers *total;* today, there are well over 11,000.[36] The average House office is between fifteen and twenty staffers strong; the average Senate office is over forty staffers. The cost of running Congress has increased accordingly. It cost $343 million to pay the salaries of members and staff in 1970, $1.2 billion in 1980, and $2.8 billion in 1992—a sevenfold increase over just twenty years.[37]

The proportion of personal staff that works in the home district or state has increased as well. Roughly half of House and one-third of Senate staffers are now located back home.[38] These staffers maintain a constant election presence and provide immediate access whenever "some poor, aggrieved constituent becomes enmeshed in the tentacles of an evil bureaucracy and calls upon Congressman St. George to do battle with the dragon," as political scientist Morris Fiorina describes it.[39]

The second kind of staff members are the *committee and subcommittee professionals* that support the lawmaking process. Divided into majority and minority staffs, they schedule the hearings, conduct the investigations, mark up the bills, and write the legislative reports.

Here, too, the hierarchy is simple: interns and staff assistants at the bottom do the routine work; professional staff handle the specific bills and hearings; the committee clerk keeps track of the schedule; legislative counsels make sure the language of each bill is clear; and the staff director makes sure the committee chair is kept informed. The majority staff is always larger than the minority, and has the offices with windows.

Committee and subcommittee staffs have also grown over the years. It was not until the 1940s that Congress had any permanent committee staff at all; today, there are over 2,500. Although the new Republican House majority cut committee and subcommittee staffs by nearly one thousand in 1995, most of the cuts came on the minority side of the aisle.

The third kind of staffers work for the three legislative *support agencies* that Congress has created to provide basic research and information on key issues: (1) the General Accounting Office (GAO), which oversees executive agencies and audits the performance of specific programs; (2) the Congressional

Research Service of the Library of Congress, which does basic research on policy issues; and (3) the Congressional Budget Office (CBO), which was established in 1974 to give Congress its own source of information on the federal budget and spending. Together, over ten thousand people work in these three agencies.

Why the Institutional Structure Matters

Each piece of the institutional Congress can be seen as an access point for influence. Party leaders, committees and subcommittees, conference committees and caucuses, and congressional staff all have at least some power to slow down the legislative process. If an interest group does not like the answer it gets from a House subcommittee, it can approach a Senate subcommittee. If it does not like the proposed schedule for the Senate floor debate, it can approach an individual senator for a hold. If it does not like the proposed rule for a House bill, it can lobby the minority whip. The list of access points is nearly endless.

It is not clear which came first: the access points or the explosion in the number of narrowly focused interest groups. The two clearly feed on each other. The greater the number of access points, the greater the ability of a new interest group to claim early success in lobbying Congress. What is clear, however, is that the multitude of access points increases the odds against action, because a bill must survive many challenges to become a law.

How Congress Has Changed

Much of this complexity reflects the increasing length of congressional careers. Gone are the days when members of Congress came to Washington for a term or two and then went home.[40] During the first one hundred years or so, being a member of Congress was definitely a part-time job. Members came to Washington for a few terms, averaged less than five years of continuous service, and quickly returned to their careers. Congressional pay was low, and Washington was still a long carriage ride from home.

A Professional Congress.   The pattern began to change in the late 1800s. Congress started to meet more frequently, pay increased, and being a member of Congress became increasingly attractive.[41] In the 1850s, roughly one-half of all House members retired or were defeated at each election; by 1900, the number was down to roughly one-quarter.

Turnover remains low to this day. Even in the 1994 congressional elections, when Republicans won the House majority for the first time in forty years, 90 percent of House members who ran for reelection won. The Republicans took control of the House by winning a remarkable share of the open seats created by

Democratic retirements, by defeating just enough incumbent Democrats, and by reelecting all but one of their own party members.

By the 1950s, being a member of Congress had become a lifelong profession and a full-time job. Members came to Washington to stay, and began to exploit the natural advantages that come with running for reelection as an **incumbent,** or sitting member, of Congress: name recognition, service to constituents, the lion's share of PAC money, and nearly unlimited free mailings back home. In 1954, for example, members of Congress sent 44 million pieces of mail back home. By 1992, the number had increased tenfold to nearly 460 million.[42]

The workday also got longer. By 1998, the vast majority of members reported that they worked more than 70 hours a week, dividing their time among committee and subcommittee hearings, floor debates, meetings with constituents and interest groups, and raising money for the next election. Members do not seem to think the job is too tough: 358 members ran for reelection in 1996, a number down from the 402 in 1988 but average for the last fifty years. Nor has job satisfaction declined: 96 percent of members reported that they were very or mostly satisfied with their jobs in 1998, and only 15 percent said the job had gotten less satisfying since they first entered Congress. There appears to be little softening of interest in holding these jobs, despite the high levels of public distrust in Congress as an institution discussed in Chapter 4.[43]

Having professional members of Congress clearly affects how Congress operates. Members think about their constituents constantly and worry about how to keep their jobs. As one political scientist argues, congressional elections are "unsafe at any margin."[44] If the incumbent Speaker of the House can be defeated, as Democratic Speaker Thomas Foley (D-WA) was in 1994, any member can be defeated.

It just makes sense, therefore, for even the most junior member to establish visibility back home as quickly as possible. If that means getting to the floor as quickly as possible at the start of a career, even if it means trampling on seniority and apprenticeship, so be it. Today's new member of Congress cannot wait to be seen *and* heard.

The result is a Congress filled with legislative entrepreneurs—that is, members who may care more for their reelection and policy goals than for the overall institution itself. Just as premed students cannot afford to fail introductory biology and prelaw students cannot afford to fail constitutional law, members of Congress who want to stay in the profession cannot afford to fail an election. That means having more opportunities to serve constituents, which, in turn, means having more committee slots to chair and more staff to develop legislation and help constituents. As noted in Chapter 9, it also means candidate-centered campaigns: Members cannot risk their jobs in a party-centered effort. In turn, the changing electoral needs of individual members put ever greater pressure on the leadership of Congress as it seeks enough consensus among members to forge legislation.

Norms of Conduct.   As members of Congress became attached to their careers, they began to abandon many of the norms that once guided their behavior.[45] The old norms were simple. Members were supposed to specialize in a small number of issues (the norm of specialization); defer to their elders (the norm of seniority); never criticize anyone personally (the norm of courtesy); and wait their turn (the norm of apprenticeship). As longtime House Speaker Sam Rayburn once said, new members were to go along in order to get along, and to be seen and not heard.

These norms began to die with a surge of younger liberal Democrats elected in the late 1950s. These first-term members of Congress were no longer willing to wait their turn. The norm of apprenticeship steadily declined throughout the 1960s as new members became much more visible participants in the lawmaking process. So, too, did the norm of specialization recede, as even the most junior members gained enough staff to be able to weigh in on just about any issue at just about any point in the legislative process. And, as apprenticeship and specialization fell, so, too, did the norm of seniority. By the 1970s, the old norms, except for the norm of courtesy, no longer dictated how Congress ran.

As a result, today's member of Congress is much more independent and entrepreneurial than at any other time in history. As Burdett Loomis writes in his book *The New American Politician:* "Beginning with the class of '74, a new generation of leaders rushed to the fore of American politics and brought with them a new way of doing business. . . . They have established an issue-oriented, publicity-conscious style that differs dramatically from that produced within the seniority-dominated Congress of the 1950s."[46] With many members driven to obtain publicity, Congress has no time for the old norms of specialization, courtesy, seniority, and apprenticeship. Members must take care of themselves first.

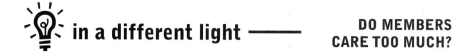

in a different light ——— DO MEMBERS CARE TOO MUCH?

Taking care of the folks back home is one of the best ways a member can increase the odds of winning reelection. That is why many members travel home every weekend to talk about the issues, why they send out bales of newsletters and press releases touting their successes, why they work to solve constituent problems with government, and why they struggle to ensure that the home district gets its share of federal spending.

The reason they offer this level of service is obvious: Members must be reelected if they are to maintain their careers. Woe be to the member blinded by the bright lights of Washington. As Richard Fenno observes,

Representatives and prospective Representatives think about their constituencies because they seek support in their constituencies. They want to be nominated and elected, and then renominated and reelected. For most members of Congress most of the time, this electoral goal is primary. It is the prerequisite for a congressional career and, hence, for the pursuit of other member goals. And the electoral goal is achieved— first and last—not in Washington but at home.[47]

Each member of Congress even has what Fenno calls a unique *home style*— that is, a way of simultaneously developing trust with his or her constituents and explaining votes in Congress. That home style usually includes some way of advertising their successes, claiming credit for the good things happening back home, and creating a sense that they are still connected to the district. But if that home style does not include helping constituents solve problems, which is called *casework*, that member will not be a member of Congress for long. Home style and casework help explain why Americans trust their own members of Congress, but not the institution as a whole.[48]

It is to build trust that the average House member answers 10,000 letters a year, sends a quarterly newsletter to each of the 200,000 to 250,000 homes in the district, and handles 10,000 constituent requests for help a year. Such casework might involve help with a late Social Security check, a passport problem, a question about welfare, or a nomination to the military academies (which can be made only by members of Congress).

At some point, this concern for the folks back home may distract members from the national good. Instead of being *trustees* of the people, as English philosopher Edmund Burke (1729–1797) described legislators who vote for the greater good even when their constituents are opposed, members of Congress may become *delegates* who do only what the constituents want. That is exactly what the Founders worried about, and it is something many members readily acknowledge. "We're too much in touch," said Senator Warren Rudman (R-NH) before retiring in 1993. "People here are traumatized by the polls, by the focus groups, by all of that." His colleague Richard Lugar (R-IN) calls Congress a "hyper weather vane," blowing one way and the other with the latest wind of opinion.[49]

Unfortunately, the more closely members stay in touch with the district, the less likely they may be to cast tough votes for the national interest. They may end up giving the district the final say, asking themselves not what the people *need*, but what the people *want*. Had the Founders known that members would work so hard to serve the people, they might well have reconsidered their stand against term limits, forcing members to leave before they became too comfortable in their jobs.

FORGING LEGISLATION

The odds against a bill becoming a law are great. Congress may be spending more time in session and casting more votes than ever, but it is producing fewer laws. Almost twice as many bills were introduced in the late 1940s than in the mid-1990s, and more than four times as many actually passed in the 1940s than in the 1990s.

One of the reasons it is so hard to pass a bill is that the process provides ample chances for defeat. A bill must win many small contests on the way to final passage.[50] There are four steps from beginning to end: (1) crafting a bill, which involves setting a goal and writing a proposed law; (2) surviving committee, which involves holding a hearing and marking up the bill; (3) passing the floor, which means getting on the legislative calendar, passing once in each chamber, surviving a conference to iron out any differences between the House and Senate versions, and passing once again in each chamber; and (4) winning the president's signature. Each one constitutes a potential barrier to becoming a law. (See Box 10–6 for the standard chart on how a bill becomes a law.)

Crafting a Bill

The legislative process starts with an idea for a bill, an idea that may come from a constituent, an interest group, or the media. Whatever the source, members of Congress are constantly looking for ways to express their concerns about the issues of the day. The average member introduces roughly fifteen bills a year.

Setting a Goal.   Members of Congress care about legislation because they are motivated by one or more of four basic goals. The first goal is *reelection*. The longer members stay in office, the more influence they have over legislation. And the more influence they have over the legislation, the more likely they can help their constituents back home.

The second goal of members of Congress is *good policy*. Contrary to public opinion about the role of special interests, most members of Congress do care about the national interest. As Democratic representative Tim Penny of Minnesota said of his decision to run for Congress, "I was young and idealistic, and I went into politics at a relatively early age. I was enough of a true believer that I ran for office. I wanted to be part of it. I wanted to show people that government can work and that partisanship doesn't have to be the dominant force in politics, that interest groups don't have to be a deciding factor on every vote."[51]

The third goal is *higher office*. House members may develop ideas that generate statewide results in the effort to establish credibility for a future run at the Senate or governor's office; senators may push ideas that establish credibility for a

BOX 10-6

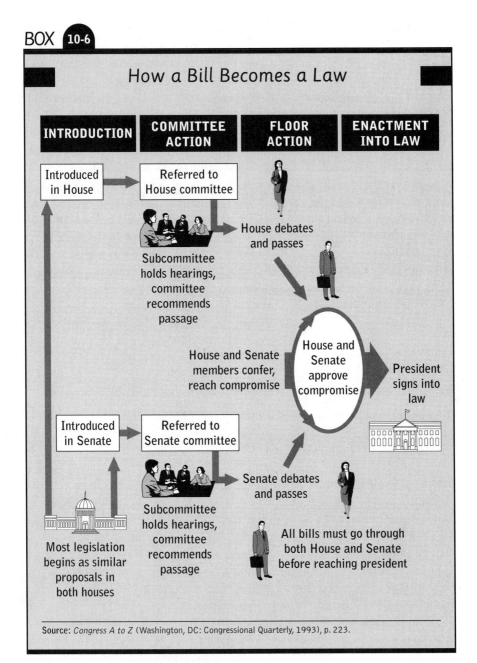

How a Bill Becomes a Law

| INTRODUCTION | COMMITTEE ACTION | FLOOR ACTION | ENACTMENT INTO LAW |

Introduced in House → Referred to House committee

Subcommittee holds hearings, committee recommends passage

House debates and passes

House and Senate members confer, reach compromise

House and Senate approve compromise

President signs into law

Introduced in Senate → Referred to Senate committee

Subcommittee holds hearings, committee recommends passage

Senate debates and passes

Most legislation begins as similar proposals in both houses

All bills must go through both House and Senate before reaching president

Source: *Congress A to Z* (Washington, DC: Congressional Quarterly, 1993), p. 223.

future run at the White House. In 1998, at least a dozen House members ran for higher office: eight ran for the Senate, while five ran for governor.

The fourth goal is *personal impact.* "Politicians are human beings," said Massachusetts representative Joe Kennedy II. "When there is a degree of very personal pain that one feels toward an issue—it might be gun control [Kennedy's father, Bobby Kennedy, was assassinated with a handgun] or my uncle's interest in fighting cancer [Senator Ted Kennedy's son had bone cancer]—the commitment level is higher and your willingness to compromise is lower."[52]

Many bills involve a blend of all four goals. In 1998, for example, Republicans and Democrats alike endorsed the general goal of legislating a "Patient's Bill of Rights" for Americans covered by Health Maintenance Organizations. Each party lined up with its own version of the bill: The Democrats wanted to give patients the right to sue their HMO's for denying care, while Republicans wanted to give Americans greater freedom to build tax-exempt medical savings accounts to cover the cost of care. Although individual members of Congress sought a blend of goals in the legislation, the effort looked more like election-year politics than a true search for good policy. With the American Medical Association opposed to the Democratic bill, and organized labor against the Republican bill, the bill became an opportunity to voice traditional Democratic and Republican themes at the start of what was a dull election season.

Writing a Bill.   Under a House–Senate rule passed in 1871, every bill begins with the same title, "A BILL for the establishment. . . ." and the same first sentence, "Be it enacted by the Senate and House of Representatives of the United States of America in Congress assembled, That, . . ." Once past this enactment clause, as it is called, all bills instruct government to do something, whether to launch a new program, spend a certain amount of money, or stop a program.

Once a bill is finished, House members introduce it for consideration by placing a copy in the mahogany box (called the *hopper*) on a desk at the front of the House chamber, while senators can either hand the bill to the clerk of the Senate or rise from the floor to introduce the bill in a speech. A bill that comes from the House is always designated *H.R.* followed by its number, and a bill from the Senate is always designated *S.* followed by its number. The number is given at the top of the first page, followed by the date, the chief sponsor, and any cosponsors. In theory, the longer the list of cosponsors, the greater the chance of passage. Unless the member has a special request for a number—in each session of Congress, S. 1 and H.R. 1 are reserved for the majority party's top priorities—the bill is simply given the next available number in line.

It is important to remember that all bills that do not pass die at the end of each two-year period. They can always be reintroduced, but nothing carries over from one Congress to the next.

It is also important to note that a bill does not have to pass as a separate proposal to become a law. Many bills are swallowed up in *omnibus* legislation that can cover hundreds of separate topics, while others are appended to legislation as amendments. An appropriations bill that attracts a great number of amendments is often called a "Christmas tree" bill in honor of its many legislative ornaments. It was to reduce the number of such ornaments that Congress gave the president the line item veto in 1996. (Recall from Chapter 3 that the Supreme Court declared the line item veto unconstitutional in *New York v. United States* two years later.)

Clearing Committee

Once a bill is introduced in either chamber, it is "read" into the record as a formal proposal and referred by the House Parliamentarian to the appropriate committee—tax bills to Ways and Means or Finance, farm bills to Agriculture, technology bills to Science, Space, and Technology, small business to Small Business, and so forth.

The Referral Decision.   Although most bills are referred to a single committee, particularly complex bills may be referred to multiple committees at the same time. President Bill Clinton's 1993 proposal for national health insurance went to sixteen House and Senate committees simultaneously. In the House, for example, Ways and Means, Banking, Budget, Energy and Commerce, Government Operations, Judiciary, Small Business, Science, Space, and Technology, and Veterans' Affairs all received jurisdiction over some aspect of the 1,364 page bill.

Once received by a committee, a bill often gets further referred to a subcommittee. Whether in the full committee or a subcommittee, a serious bill usually receives a hearing in which witnesses speak to its pros and cons. (Some bills simply die in committee at the end of a session without a hearing or any action beyond the referral.) This committee or subcommittee hearing is part of the **legislative record** that the executive agencies and courts use later to interpret what Congress wants, and it is usually carefully scripted so that witnesses speak to particularly important questions that might influence future implementation.

Markup.   Once a committee or subcommittee decides to pass the bill, it holds a *markup* to clean up and/or amend its version of the bill. The term *markup* refers to the pencil marks that members make on the final version of the bill.

At the end of the markup, the bill must be passed by the committee or subcommittee and forwarded to the next step in the process. If it is passed by a subcommittee, for example, it is forwarded to the full committee; if it is passed by a full committee, it is forwarded to the full chamber.

Passing the Floor

Once reported to the full chamber, a bill will either be scheduled for floor action or dropped entirely. Whether a bill gets scheduled for floor debate on the legislative calender depends on what the leadership wants and the amount of time left in the session. The busiest time of the year is right before the end of a session, usually in late September or early October. (See Box 10–7 for a list of the bills up for consideration during the week of July 20, 1998, a week that included debates on a number of the thirteen annual appropriations bills required to keep government open. The Senate was considering two bills that had already passed the House—a bill retains the number given it by the chamber that passes it first.)

Getting on the Calendar. Given the different sizes of the two chambers, it should not be surprising that the House and Senate floors work differently. No bill gets to the floor of the House without a rule, or ticket, which can be granted only by the Rules Committee. The rule tells the House when the legislation will be allowed to come up and what amendments are to be in order, or permitted, for consideration. Once the House leadership decides to act, there are few surprises.[53]

The Senate, in contrast, is far less predictable. Senators have far greater freedom to call a bill up for consideration, and have nearly unlimited authority to propose amendments to any bill. As already noted, they also have nearly unlimited opportunity to talk, and sometimes use that freedom to talk a bill to death.

In general, the Senate legislative calendar is set by the majority and minority leaders, who work together to find an agreeable time for specific bills. The schedule is then presented to the full Senate for unanimous consent—a request that all senators agree in advance on how a bill will be debated. Almost all bills passed are so noncontroversial that unanimous consent is easy. If, however, a bill is so controversial that unanimous consent is impossible to achieve, it can be brought up for action with a simple majority vote.

These differences in floor procedure can make the House and Senate look very different: one is efficient, one not; one a well-oiled legislative machine, the other a wandering conversation. May 7, 1994, is as good an example of how the two chambers work as any, a day *New York Times* reporter David Rosenbaum summarized in a piece titled "A Day in the House Equals a Week in the Senate":

> On Thursday, the House had two and a half hours of crisp debate on whether to ban semiautomatic assault weapons. Almost every seat was filled. Most representatives spoke for a minute or two. No one spoke for more than five.
>
> Then, before 5 P.M., they voted. The excitement built as the running tally was registered on the electronic scoreboard overhead. After 15 minutes, the opponents of the ban were ahead, 214 to 213. Then a Congressman switched, and the proponents were ahead. Two more voted yes. One voted no. And that was

BOX **10-7**

A Sampling from the Legislative Calendar, Week of July 30, 1998

In the Senate

S. 2260: An original bill making appropriations for the Departments of Commerce, Justice, and State, the Judiciary, and related agencies for the fiscal year ending September 30, 1999.

S. 2307: An original bill making appropriations for the Department of Transportation for the fiscal year ending September 30, 1999.

H.R. 1151: A bill to amend the Federal Credit Union Act.

H.R. 4112: A bill making appropriations for the Legislative Branch for the fiscal year ending September 30, 1999.

In the House

S. 1260: A bill to amend the Securities Act of 1933 and the Securities Exchange Act of 1934.

S. 2316: A bill to require the Secretary of Energy to submit to Congress a plan to ensure the treatment and recycling of depleted uranium hexafluoride.

H.R. 6: A bill to extend the authorization of programs under the Higher Education Act of 1965.

H.R. 1122: A bill to amend title 18, United States Code, to ban partial birth abortions.

H.R. 2183: A bill to amend the Federal Election Campaign Act of 1971 to reform the financing of campaigns for election to federal office.

it. The bill was approved by the narrowest of margins, 216 to 214, and the House went on to other matters.[54]

Over in the Senate, Rosenbaum reported, most of the day was spent on delaying action. Technically, the Senate can remain in session only if a majority of members are present, and any member can request a quorum call just to make sure. Then "from 7 P.M. to 10 P.M. the Senate was paralyzed," wrote Rosenbaum. "Several Senators were at a black tie dinner for the Prime Minister of Malaysia.

H.R. 3616: A bill to authorize appropriations for military activities of the Department of Defense for the fiscal year ending September 30, 1999.

H.R. 4059: A bill making appropriations for military construction, family housing, and base realignment and closure for the Department of Defense for the fiscal year ending September 30, 1999.

H.R. 4193: An original bill making appropriations for the Department of the Interior for the fiscal year ending September 30, 1999.

H.R. 4194: An original bill making appropriations for the Department of Veterans Affairs and Housing and Urban Development for the fiscal year ending September 30, 1999.

H.R. 4250: A bill to provide new patient protections under group health plans.

H.R. 4276: A bill making appropriations for the Departments of Commerce, Justice, and State, the Judiciary and related agencies for the fiscal year ending September 30, 1999.

H.J.Res. 121: A joint resolution disapproving the extension of non-discriminatory treatment (most-favored-nation treatment) to the products of the People's Republic of China.

H.Res. 504: A resolution providing for consideration of the bill (H.R. 4193) making appropriations for the Department of the Interior for the fiscal year ending September 30, 1999.

Nothing could be done without them. . . . It is routine for the Senate to interrupt its work for the convenience of one or two members."[55]

Passage.   After all the hard work that goes into getting a bill on the calender, voting for passage is easy. House members vote electronically by inserting a magnetic card and their personal code number into one of the many automatic voting machines on the floor; senators must still cast their votes in person as their names are read in alphabetical order by the clerk. An amendment to the Constitution requires a two-thirds vote for passage, but almost all other legislation needs only a simple majority for passage.

Members cast their votes on the basis of at least four different influences. The first is *constituency interest*. Members clearly worry how a given vote will affect their standing back home, and sometimes poll their constituents on particularly difficult votes.

The second is *ideology*. Just as the public splits among liberal, moderate, and conservative, so do members of Congress. In 1997, for example, Barbara Boxer (D-CA) and Paul Wellstone (D-MN) shared the title of most liberal member of the Senate, while John Ashcroft (R-MO), Sam Brownback (R-KS), Phil Gramm (R-TX), and Tim Hutchinson (R-KS) shared honors as the most conservative members of the Senate. Over in the House, Henry Waxman (D-CA), Lynn Woolsey (D-CA), and Xavier Beccera (D-CA) were the most liberal members of the House, while Bill Paxon (R-NY), Bob Riley (R-AL), Pete Sessions (R-TX), and Gerald Solomon (R-NY) were the most conservative. The geographic patterns are clear down both lists: Seven of the top twenty liberals in the House came from California, while most of the Senate's most conservative members came from the Midwest and South.[56]

The third influence is *party*. As noted earlier in this chapter, both parties have strong whip systems for counting votes and lobbying their own members to remain loyal. Party unity on the floor is less a function of effective whips than a response to electoral fortunes. From 1937 all the way through the 1980s, conservative Southern Democrats formed a broad conservative coalition with Republicans, giving Ronald Reagan the votes needed to pass his budget and tax cuts in 1981, for example. As Republicans gained strength in the South, those Democrats began to retire and lose elections. By 1994, the South was Republican and the conservative coalition was mostly a memory. The result has been a purification of both parties, with Democrats now more likely to be liberal, Republicans more likely to be conservative, and few members in the moderate center.

The party differences set a modern record following the Republican victory in 1994. In 1995, a majority of House Democrats voted against a majority of House Republicans a record 73.2 percent of the time, while a majority of Senate Democrats voted against a majority of Senate Republicans 68.8 percent of the time. The tension ran particularly high in the House, where the new Republican majority pushed one party vote after another in the first one hundred days of the session. All told, seventy-nine of the first one hundred votes taken in the 104th House were along party lines.[57]

Although ideology and party are closely related, some Republicans are more liberal than some Democrats, and vice versa. In 1996, for example, New England Republican senators John Chafee and Jim Jeffords were consistently more liberal on matters of social and foreign policy than Southern Democrats Ernest Hollings,

Bob Graham, and Wendell Ford. In the House, Maryland Republican Constance Morella was more liberal than Texas Democrat Ralph Hall.

The final influence is *the president* of the United States. Presidents take positions on many issues up for a final vote, and those positions do matter to how members of Congress vote, particularly if those members belong to the president's own party. Obviously, presidents do worse when their party is in the minority, as Bill Clinton did in 1995 in facing the new Republican majority. Clinton took a position on 123 votes and won on just 36 percent, a record low for a third year of a presidency. By comparison, Dwight Eisenhower won 75 percent of his votes, Richard Nixon 75 percent, and George Bush 54 percent, even though all three were also working with a minority party.[58] One reason for Clinton's difficulty was the ideological fervor of new House Republican majorities in both chambers.

Surviving Conference.   If both chambers have passed the same version of the same bill, the bill goes on to the president for signature. But if they have passed different versions of the same bill, they must agree on a final compromise. Under the Founders' original design, the chambers would pass a bill back and forth until one finally accepted the other's version.

Starting with the First Congress, however, the two chambers began using conference committees as a shortcut. As noted in the discussion of informal committees, the party leadership of each chamber appoints its own slate of conferees, who are usually drawn from the majority and minority membership of the originating committees. It does not matter how many conferees get appointed, for each chamber in the conference committee has just one vote. If the House and Senate sides cannot agree, the bill dies. If the conference committee agrees on a final version, it produces a conference report that describes the bill. Once both chambers pass the final agreement, which is usually automatic given the hard work involved, the bill is ready to move on for the president's signature.

The President's Signature

Once a final bill is passed by both chambers, it is enrolled, or printed, on parchment paper and hand carried by congressional messenger to the White House for the president's signature that will make it a public law. Presidents do not have to sign the bill, of course. As Chapter 11 explains, there are several ways to kill a bill in the White House, the most familiar being to *veto* the bill by returning it to Congress unsigned. Congress can override, or overturn, a veto by passing the bill a third time by a two-thirds vote in each chamber, a nearly impossible task. From 1993 to 1996, for example, Clinton vetoed 17 bills, of which just one was overridden into law.

Obviously, the vast majority of enrolled bills do not get vetoed. Once signed into law, an enrolled bill is forwarded to the Archivist of the United States, where it is assigned a public law number that begins with the number of the Congress in which it passed—hence, laws passed in the 105th Congress, 1997–1998, are numbered 105-1, 105-2, and so on. The law then becomes part of the federal statute books that tell the American people who gets what, when, and how from government.

Given the complexity of the legislative process described earlier, it seems fair to ask how any bill can pass. The answer is that important legislation passes even under the most difficult circumstances. The president and Congress are able to work together whether they are divided by party or not. Republican presidents do get legislation out of Democratic Congresses, and vice versa.[59]

In fact, some of the most important laws in recent history were passed during periods of divided party control—that is, when Congress and the presidency were controlled by different parties. The twentieth century's first civil rights act was passed in 1957, for example, when each end of Pennsylvania Avenue was controlled by a different party. Although such periods rarely produce as much legislation as periods of unified control, Americans need not fear that the nation will completely collapse when different parties occupy these two branches of government.

The fact is that forging legislation has always been a messy business. There are as many exceptions to the rules, it sometimes seems, as there are rules. When Congress wants to act, it can mostly find a way to do so; when it wants to stall, its options for doing so are nearly endless.[60]

 **in a different light** ——— **A TALE OF TWO CONGRESSES**

The 104th Congress, which convened in 1995, was easily the most controversial Congress in a half century. With a new Republican majority in control of both houses for the first time in four decades and a beleaguered Democrat in the White House, Congress was as sharply divided as it has been since *Congressional Quarterly* first started tracking congressional performance in the 1940s. As noted earlier, President Clinton lost 64 percent of the congressional votes on which he took a position, a modern record in presidential frustration.

At the same time, a majority of one party in Congress voted against a majority of the other nearly three-quarters of the time, another modern record. Although Congress took more votes on legislation than at any time in American history, 1995 produced fewer new laws than any year since the early 1930s.[61] The party divisions also showed up in how members talked to each other on the floor, with the old norm of courtesy clearly disintegrating. The number of times a member said another member was lying increased fourfold from 1993 to 1995, while the number of times a member asked the House to rule another member out of order or to remove another member's words from the record also skyrocketed. All in all, it was a divisive, uncivil session, which resulted in two shutdowns of government and enormous public frustration.[62]

Yet, even though 1995 was a year of great activity as well as great conflict, it yielded very little product. Despite spending 168 days and 1,525 hours in session, and despite working nearly 9 hours a day on average, Congress passed just 88 public laws, the lowest first-session total in recent history. Although 1996 brought more agreement, the 104th Congress's two-year total of 333 laws passed and signed was also the lowest in recent history.

The Constitution, however, worked in 1995 exactly as designed. Clinton did poorly precisely because the people changed their minds about which party should be in control of Congress; Congress did poorly precisely because the House and Senate often disagreed on who should get what, when, and how from government; Congress took so many votes precisely because it took its job seriously. Lost in all the press coverage about partisan conflict and the failure to pass legislation is the real story: American government was actually a spectacular success in 1995, precisely because it did *not* produce huge volumes of legislation. The American public was protected from great swings in the laws by a system that sets very high barriers against quick action.

Despite a nearly identical party majority and the same leadership, the Congress that convened in 1997 was dramatically different. The 105th Congress was not only much more civil, it was also much more productive. It spent less time in session (132 days and barely 1,000 hours), worked just over 7 hours a day on average, yet produced 140 laws by the end of the year. It passed landmark legislation to balance the federal budget by the year 2002, gave families a $500-per-child tax credit, created a new program to provide nearly $20 billion in medical insurance for children of poor families, passed all thirteen appropriations bills on time (no government shutdowns), made it easier for Americans to adopt abused and neglected children, passed a sweeping reform of the federal drug-approval process to speed new drugs and medical devices to market, and ratified the world Chemical Weapons Convention, which outlawed chemical and biological weapons. In short, 1997 produced an impressive record of defending the nation against foreign and domestic threats.

The Constitution worked exactly as intended in 1997, too. Where members of Congress could agree on modest ideas, the Constitution allowed the process to continue. Despite all the congressional back-patting about the balanced budget, for example, the final bill was mostly an acknowledgment of the economic realities. In-deed, had Congress *not* passed the agreement, the federal government would have had its first surplus a few months earlier than it actually did. The booming economy meant that more people were working (meaning less welfare and unemployment payments) and paying taxes (meaning more revenue). Nevertheless, Congress did make a series of important budget decisions, shifting dollars across accounts, help-ing poor children, funding tax credits, building more highways, and promising to somehow save Social Security; but the agreement was less controversial or sweep-ing than members and the president claimed. Although Congress can act quickly when intense threats arise, it is more accustomed to reaching modest agreements that move the country forward in small steps. And that is precisely what the Founders intended.

MAINTAINING THE BALANCE

Many of the changes chronicled in this chapter suggest that Congress is getting closer to the people than it used to be. Indeed, it is reasonable to think of most members of Congress as corporations, complete with their own product lines (legislation and positions), marketing engines (mail, campaign spending), and or-ganizational support (personal, committee, and support agency staffs). These leg-islative enterprises exist to advance a member's market share (reelection margin, amount of campaign support), to shut out possible competitors, and to move the member higher up the corporate ladder (to more prestigious committees, leader-ship posts, or even the presidency).

A major difference between the corporate world and Congress, however, is that corporations are prohibited by law from monopolizing a market. Incumbent members of Congress face no such constraints. Because they get most of the cam-paign financing and most of the name recognition back home, incumbents get most of the electoral breaks.

Members of Congress do not behave as if they have a lock on reelection, how-ever. To the contrary, they act as if they are constantly in danger of losing, which mo-tivates them even further toward doing whatever it takes to win. If that means becoming a simple delegate of the people, casting legislative votes to curry favor back home, fighting for the lion's share of federal dollars and programs, so be it.

The dangers of the single-minded focus on reelection lie not in the threat to liberty, but in the inability to act. As members become enterprises unto themselves, they may see less and less reason to come together as trustees of the people. Driven by their own ambitions, they may lose sight of the greater good, ignoring foreign and domestic threats. Although it is not always clear just what constitutes such a threat, Congress appears less able to come to judgment today than it was even twenty years ago. If so, that represents a clear erosion in the delicate balance the Founders worked so hard to create.

JUST THE FACTS

terms to remember

facts and interpretations

- The Founders did not want Congress to be an efficient institution, and divided power precisely to create obstacles to quick action. Although Congress often frustrates the public by not acting, the Founders wanted the legislative process to be difficult. In 1995, that process created one of the least productive Congresses in modern history. There are times when the Founders would see such lack of action as a success. They wanted Congress to be strong enough to meet foreign and domestic threats, but not so strong that it would move with the whims of a deeply divided public. There are also times when the Founders might argue that the odds against action have grown too high.

- Congress has become a complicated institution, with layer upon layer of leadership, committees and subcommittees, and staff. The result is an extraordinary number of access points where a single interest group can stop action. The increase in such access points is both a cause and a consequence of the increase in narrowly focused interest groups that now operate on behalf of smaller and smaller numbers of Americans. Although the congressional parties have grown stronger during the same period, in part because of leadership PACs and soft money to the national party committees, it is not clear that they have been able to offset the rise in interest group pressure.

- For the first 150 years of Congress, members came for short stays and then went home to resume their former careers. Since the late 1800s, being a member of Congress has become a long-term career. Most members come to Washington to stay as long as possible. One reason members are able to stay longer is that they have enormous advantages as incumbent, or sitting, members, which they exploit to discourage strong challengers from even daring to enter a race.

- The legislative process starts with an idea for change. Having that idea can involve the goal of reelection, a desire for good policy, a hope for higher office, or a personal issue that a member carries into office. Although reelection is obviously at or near the top of the list of goals that members bring into office—not getting reelected is the surest way of losing influence over legislation—it is important to remember that members care about more than just the next campaign. Nevertheless, reelection remains a primary explanation for the decline of the institutional Congress's traditional norms such as seniority and apprenticeship. Members simply cannot wait to make their mark.

open questions

- Should Congress be more efficient than it is? What might be done to make it faster and more effective in passing legislation? Would it be good to eliminate some of the rules that get in the way of action, including the Senate filibuster? If so, what might happen to the country?

- How much do you trust your own member of Congress? Do you recall having received any mail over the years? Whom would you call if your student loan was delayed? Whom would you call if your passport got lost? Does all the constituent casework provided by Congress help the country or hurt it? Should

Congress simply tell everyone to get in line with the rest of the country, or continue to help anyone who figures out how to call? Thinking back to Chapter 8, who uses Congress to solve such problems? Who has to stand at the back of the line?

- Should Congress pass a constitutional amendment imposing term limits on its members? What might happen as a result? Would congressional staff get more or less power? Would the public get better or poorer representation? How might the Founders reframe the issue if they had a chance to do so?

- Who would make the best president in 2001: a House member or a Senator? Given the role of the government in protecting the nation as a whole and Americans as individual citizens, which chamber does a better job of each? Is the country better off because more senators get to be president?

- Which role is more appropriate for a member of Congress today: delegate or trustee? Which role is actually taken more often? Are there some public policy issues for which being a delegate is perfectly reasonable? Some for which being a trustee is the only acceptable approach?

for further study

Aberbach, Joel. *Keeping a Watchful Eye: The Politics of Congressional Oversight.* Washington, DC: Brookings Institution, 1990.

Congressional Quarterly. *Origins and Development of Congress.* Washington, DC: CQ Press, 1982.

Davidson, Roger, and Walter Oleszek. *Congress and Its Members,* 4th ed. Washington, DC: CQ Press, 1994.

Fenno, Richard. *Home Style: House Members in Their Districts.* Boston: Little, Brown, 1978.

Kaminer, Wendy. "Crashing the Locker Room," *Atlantic Monthly,* July 1992.

Loomis, Burdett A. *The Contemporary Congress,* 2nd ed. New York: St. Martin's Press, 1998.

Matthews, Christopher. *Hardball: How Politics Is Played by One Who Played the Game.* New York: Harper and Row, 1988.

Schneier, Edward V., and Bertram Gross, *Legislative Strategy: Shaping Public Policy.* New York: St. Martin's Press, 1993.

endnotes for chapter 10

1. Roy P. Fairfield, ed., *The Federalist Papers* (Baltimore: Johns Hopkins University Press, 1981), p. 160.
2. See Alexis Simendinger, "Of the People, for the People," *National Journal,* April 18, 1998, for a report on the survey.

3. See Max Farrand, ed., *The Records of the Federal Convention of 1787*, vol. I (New Haven, CT: Yale University Press, 1966).

4. Quoted in Charles O. Jones, *The United States Congress: People, Place, and Policy* (Homewood, IL: The Dorsey Press, 1982), p. 6.

5. Fairfield, *The Federalist Papers*, p. 160.

6. See Roger Davidson and Walter Oleszek, *Congress and Its Members*, 4th ed. (Washington, DC: CQ Press, 1994), p. 24.

7. Richard Fenno, *The United States Senate: A Bicameral Perspective* (Washington, DC: American Enterprise Institute, 1982), p. 1.

8. James Madison, *Notes of Debates in the Federal Convention of 1787* (New York: Norton, 1969), p. 127.

9. Max Farrand, *The Records of the Federal Convention of 1787*, vol. I, p. 375.

10. Charles Warren, *The Making of the Constitution* (Boston: Little, Brown, 1928), p. 195.

11. Woodrow Wilson, *Congressional Government* (1885, reprinted Cleveland: Meridian, 1956), p. 154.

12. Congressional Quarterly, *Origins and Development of Congress* (Washington, DC: CQ Press, 1982), pp. 53–54.

13. *U.S. Term Limits v. Thornton*, 63 U.S.L.W. 4430 (1995).

14. For an overview of why it is so difficult to elect women to Congress, see Wendy Kaminer, "Crashing the Locker Room," *Atlantic Monthly*, July 1992, pp. 59–70.

15. In Kaminer, "Crashing the Locker Room," p. 65.

16. Adam Clymer, "A Daughter of Slavery Makes the Senate Listen," *New York Times*, July 23, 1993, p. A10.

17. Congressional Quarterly, *Origins and Development of Congress*, p. 107.

18. Congressional Quarterly, *Origins and Development of Congress*, p. 205.

19. Quoted in Davidson and Oleszek, *Congress and Its Members*, p. 167.

20. See Burdett A. Loomis, *The Contemporary Congress*, 2d ed. (New York: St. Martin's Press, 1998), pp.75–76.

21. See Leslie Wayne, "Congress Uses Leadership PACs to Wield Power," *New York Times*, March 13, 1997, p. B10.

22. Quoted in Davidson and Olezsek, *Congress and Its Members*, p. 167.

23. Quoted in Davidson and Oleszek, *Congress and Its Members*, p. 177.

24. Christopher Matthews, *Hardball: How Politics Is Played by One Who Played the Game* (New York: Harper & Row, 1988), p. 54.

25. Quoted in Matthews, *Hardball*, p. 54.

26. Quoted in Adam Clymer, "In House and Senate, Two Kinds of G.O.P.," *New York Times*, November 15, 1994, p. A12.

27. Hendrik Hertzberg, "Catch-XXII," *The New Yorker*, August 25, 1994, pp. 9–10.

28. Quoted in Davidson and Oleszek, *Congress and Its Members*, p. 348.

29. Joel Aberbach, *Keeping a Watchful Eye: The Politics of Congressional Oversight* (Washington, DC: Brookings Institution, 1990), p. 33. Aberbach's data exclude hearings by Appropriations, Administration, and Rules, but do include Budget and the revenue committees.

30. Clifford Krauss, "Vying for Committees, Freshmen Mimic Elders," *New York Times*, November 30, 1992, p. A9.

31. Lawrence Longley and Walter Oleszek, *Bicameral Politics: Conference Committee in Congress* (New Haven, CT: Yale University Press, 1989), p. 30.

32. Quoted in Longley and Oleszek, *Bicameral Politics*, p. 3.

33. Quoted in Longley and Oleszek, *Bicameral Politics*, p. 1.

34. See Davidson and Oleszek, *Congress and Its Members*, p. 310.

35. Davidson and Oleszek, *Congress and Its Members,* p. 307.

36. The House and Senate figures are both from Stanley and Niemi, *Vital Statistics,* p. 217.

37. Carla Fried, "How Congress Perks Up Its Pay," *Money,* August 1992, p. 132.

38. Norman Ornstein, Thomas Mann, and Michael Malbin, *Vital Statistics on Congress 1995–1996* (Washington, DC: Congressional Quarterly, 1996), pp. 135–36.

39. Morris Fiorina, *Congress: Keystone of the Washington Establishment,* 2nd ed. (New Haven, CT: Yale University Press, 1989), p. 42.

40. For a history of the first Congresses, see James Sterling Young, *The Washington Community, 1800–1828* (New York: Columbia University Press, 1966).

41. Davidson and Oleszek, *Congress and Its Members,* p. 30.

42. Ornstein, Mann, and Malbin, *Vital Statistics,* p. 170.

43. Pew Research Center for The People & The Press, *Washington Leaders Wary of Public Opinion* (Washington, DC: Pew Research Center, April 1998), p. 30.

44. Thomas Mann, *Unsafe at Any Margin: Interpreting Congressional Elections* (Washington, DC: American Enterprise Institute, 1978).

45. Herbert Asher, "The Learning of Legislative Norms," *American Political Science Review,* vol. 67, no. 2 (June 1973) pp. 499–513.

46. Burdett Loomis, *The New American Politician: Ambition, Entrepreneurship, and the Changing Face of Political Life* (New York: Basic Books, 1988), p. 28.

47. Richard Fenno, *Home Style: House Members in Their Districts* (Boston: Little, Brown, 1978), p. 31.

48. Davidson and Oleszek, *Congress and Its Members,* p. 444.

49. Helen Dewar, "The Trees Get in the Way of the Forest," *Washington Post National Weekly Edition,* June 15–21, 1992, p. 13.

50. There are dozens of wonderful case studies of how a bill becomes a law. For a sampling, see Gary C. Bryner, *Blue Skies, Green Politics: The Clean Air Act of 1990* (Washington, DC: Congressional Quarterly, 1993); Janet M. Martin, *Lessons from the Hill: The Legislative Journey of an Education Program* (New York: St. Martin's Press, 1994); and Steven Waldman, *The Bill: How the Adventures of Clinton's National Service Bill Reveal What Is Corrupt, Comic, Cynical—and Noble—About Washington* (New York: Viking, 1995).

51. Quoted in Lloyd Grove, "How a Bright Penny Just 'Wore Down,'" *Washington Post National Weekly Edition,* August 30–September 5, 1993, p. 12.

52. Quoted in Clifford Krauss, "How Personal Tragedy Can Shape Public Policy," *New York Times,* May 16, 1993, p. A16.

53. Steven Smith, *Call to Order: Floor Politics in the House and Senate* (Washington, DC: Brookings Institution, 1989), p. 253.

54. David Rosenbaum, "A Day in the House Equals a Week in the Senate," *New York Times,* May 8, 1994, p. A6.

55. Rosenbaum, "A Day in the House Equals a Week in the Senate," p. A6.

56. Richard Cohen, "Business as Usual," *National Journal,* March 7, 1998, p. 7.

57. Dan Carney, "As Hostilities Rage on the Hill, Partisan-Vote Rate Soars," *Congressional Quarterly,* January 27, 1996, p. 199.

58. Jon Healy, "Clinton Success Rate Declined to a Record Low in 1995," *Congressional Quarterly,* January 27, 1996, p. 193.

59. David Mayhew, *Divided We Govern* (New Haven, CT: Yale University Press, 1991).

60. See Edward V. Schneier and Bertram Gross, *Legislative Strategy: Shaping Public Policy* (New York: St. Martin's Press, 1993), for a review of the legislative process; see also Steven S. Smith, *The American Congress* (Boston: Houghton-Mifflin, 1993), for an introduction to Congress more generally.

61. These results are from Jeffrey Katz, "A Record-Setting Year," *Congressional Quarterly,* January 27, 1996, p. 195.

62. Kathleen Hall Jamieson, *Civility in the House of Representatives,* background report prepared for the Bipartisan Congressional Retreat (Philadelphia: The Annenberg Public Policy Center, 1997).

chapter 11

the presidency

mission impossible

The Founders created the presidency to do three jobs: faithfully execute the laws, represent the nation as a whole, and check Congress from becoming too powerful. The Founders never saw the presidency as the all-powerful center of government, but they did believe America needed a strong executive if the young nation was to survive.

Unlike Congress, where the Founders decided to divide power in order to control it, they decided to unify power in a single president as a way to ensure that government would be strong enough to act. The Founders came to believe that only a single person could act with the "energy, dispatch, and responsibility" needed in an emergency, said Pennsylvania's James Wilson.[1]

That is not where the Founders started, however. They spent far more time talking about Congress, and actually had agreed on a relatively weak executive until rather late in the Constitutional Convention. By the end of the summer, however, advocates of "energy in the executive" had worn down the opposition, in part because many of the Founders had come to worry about how to control the Congress they had created.

No one was more important to the campaign for a strong executive than New York delegate and future *Federalist Paper* author Alexander Hamilton, who worked to strengthen the presidency at every turn. Hamilton made the case for a strong executive in *Federalist Paper No. 70:* "A feeble Executive implies a feeble execution of the government. A feeble execution is but another phrase for bad execution; and a government ill executed, whatever it may be in theory, must be in practice a bad government."[2] (Hamilton's version of a strong president is often labeled the Hamiltonian model.)

Indeed, the presidency was so much stronger, as compared to original expectations, that some opponents argued that the Constitution had created an American king. Hamilton rebutted the charges in *Federalist Paper No. 69,* emphasizing that the president was to be elected into office, not born, and would serve for four years, not life. Moreover, even though the president would have the power to faithfully execute the laws, veto legislation, wage war, run the government, and make treaties, all these powers would be checked by Congress.

Therein lies the delicate balance. The president must be able to speak for the nation as a whole, command the military during times of calm and crisis, and faithfully execute the laws, yet never use those powers to create an American monarchy. Much as they hoped that the president would rise above petty politics and factions, a hope easily reinforced by their belief that George Washington would be the first president, the Founders also planned for the worst. The president would never have complete authority to impose the will of the majority on the nation. Even as commander in chief, the president would have to go to Congress to find the money to raise an army and build a navy.

This chapter examines the founding of the presidency in more detail, and asks how the presidency works today. The first section discusses the presidency imagined by the Founders as a single, independent executive, reviewing the duties and qualifications of the office. The second section asks how the real presidency has evolved over time, examining the precedents set by George Washington, the institutional structure and operation of the presidency today, and the American public's often unrealistic expectations of the office and its occupant. The third section examines the role of the president in setting the legislative agenda, with a particular focus on the ways in which presidents are constrained by the ebb and flow of political resources. The final section of the chapter asks how the tactics of presidential leadership have changed, emphasizing the new tendency of presidents to go directly to the public for support of their programs.

THE IMAGINED PRESIDENCY

Just as the Founders had plenty of experience with legislatures, they also had plenty of experience with executives. On the one hand, they had all experienced the great tyranny inflicted by the all-powerful British king, and most certainly did not want a similar concentration of unlimited authority in the American presidency. On the other hand, most of the Founders came from states with weak governors, and all had witnessed the paralyzing weakness of the executive that had been created under the Articles of Confederation. Most governors were appointed by their state legislatures for single terms lasting but a year, obviously making the governors enormously dependent on keeping the legislatures happy. And the president created under the Articles was nothing more than a presiding officer of Congress.

The lone exception to this history of weak executives was the governor of New York, a single executive elected directly by the people for a three-year term. Unlike the governors of other states, who could serve only one term, the governor of New York could serve as long as the public voted for reelection. It was in New York that Alexander Hamilton learned his lessons about the value of a strong executive. And, as noted, it was Hamilton who became the greatest champion of a strong presidency.

Hamilton's vision of a strong executive clearly shaped the final outcome at the Constitutional Convention. Almost every decision strengthened the office as a counterweight to Congress, most important among them the creation of a single executive selected by the people (albeit only through the electoral college), not by Congress itself. They also gave the presidency just enough power to create a central focus on protecting the nation as a whole. These decisions are discussed below.

A Single Executive

It is safe to argue that the Founders' single most important decision about the presidency was also their first. Meeting on June 1, 1787, the Constitutional Convention decided that there would be a single executive. The proposal for "a single vigorous executive" came from Pennsylvania's James Wilson. Even though nine of the thirteen states already had a single executive, Wilson's proposal was met by intense opposition from delegates who wanted a plural executive—that is, a kind of presidential clerkship in which three individuals would share the job of running the government.

Despite worries that a single president might become what Virginia's Edmund Randolph called the "fetus of monarchy," the Founders eventually concluded that the new government needed energy in the executive. They were willing to increase the risk of tyranny in return for some efficiency. As much as the delegates feared an American version of the English king, they feared foreign and domestic threats more. They also knew that a weak version of the single executive had failed under the Articles of Confederation, and believed that a plural executive would be more of the same.

The delegates eventually voted seven states to three in favor of a single executive, with the Founders' hoped-for first president, George Washington, voting "aye." The fact that Washington was the president-apparent made it easier for many delegates to vote for a single executive.

An Independent Executive

Having decided on a single executive, the Founders had to decide just how independent that executive would be, which, in turn, meant finding an appropriate method of selection or election. The Founders also had to decide how presidents would leave office.

Entering Office. The convention was initially divided on how the president would be selected. A small number of delegates favored direct election by the people, which Pennsylvania's James Wilson thought would ensure that the president was completely independent of Congress. Despite his earlier persuasiveness on the single executive, the convention never seriously considered Wilson's proposal for direct election. As Virginia's George Mason said, it would be as unnatural to refer the choice of the president to the people as it would be to ask a blind man to separate the colors of the rainbow.

An equally small number favored selection by Congress, tying the president more closely to the legislative branch. Those delegates also supported a single seven-year term to keep the president from bribing Congress to ensure reelection.

Yet by making the successful candidate dependent on Congress, these proposals would have sharply weakened the presidency as a check against congressional tyranny.

Selection by Congress fared well over the summer, and was actually adopted at several points. The problem was the single, seven-year term: A good president would be out after one term, and a bad president would never feel the heat of a reelection battle. In the end, the convention rallied around the cumbersome electoral college, in which voters cast their ballots for competing slates of electors, who, in turn, cast their electoral votes for president. It might be called a form of indirect direct election. They also opted for a four-year "renewable" term—that is, the president would be able to serve as long as the public wanted.

Building a Ticket.   The final constitutional outline was hardly perfect, however. Along the way to a single executive, the Founders also created a remarkable electoral arrangement: the candidate who received the most electoral college votes would become president, while the candidate who came in second would become vice president. In short, the runner-up only received the vice presidency by failing to win the presidency.

Since the Founders imagined a country without political parties, this runner-up rule made perfect sense. Surely great candidates would be able to work together after the election. But imagine if this runner-up rule had been in place in 1996. America would have inaugurated Democratic president Bill Clinton and Republican vice president Robert Dole, a rather unworkable combination given their sharp disagreements over national and international issues.

It did not take long for the Founders to experience the problem for themselves. The 1796 election produced Federalist president John Adams and Democratic-Republican vice president Thomas Jefferson. Because the two disagreed so sharply about the future of the country, Jefferson was rendered virtually irrelevant to government. Indeed, speaking of Jefferson during the 1796 campaign, Adams said, "I am almost tempted to wish he may be chosen Vice-President. . . . For there, if he could do no good, he could do no harm." Adams got his wish and Jefferson was banished to serve his term in complete isolation from his president. A similar fate might have befallen Dole had he become vice president under Clinton.

Having created an awkward pairing in 1796, the runner-up rule created a constitutional crisis in 1800. The election could not have been more important, for it occurred during a time of rising public anger about the nation's direction. Two Democratic-Republicans, Thomas Jefferson and Aaron Burr, emerged from the 1800 election with exactly seventy-three electoral votes each, while Federalist John Adams received just sixty-three. Under the Constitution, a tie vote of the electoral college forces the election of the president into the House of Representatives. It took thirty-six House ballots before Jefferson was elected. His vice president was none other than Aaron Burr, the candidate whom he had just defeated.

It was in response to these two early elections that the states ratified the Twelfth Amendment in 1804. Under the amendment, electors were required to cast separate votes for the offices of president and vice president, thereby creating the incentive for presidential and vice presidential candidates to run together as a **presidential ticket.**

Leaving Office. Having decided how a president would enter office, the Founders also decided how a president would leave. Short of defeat, death, resignation, or retirement, the only other way out was through impeachment for treason, bribery, or other high crimes and misdemeanors. Recall from Chapter 2 that the House votes the articles of **impeachment,** which list the charges against the president, and the Senate votes to impeach, or convict, the president.

Over the years, constitutional amendments have added two other ways for presidents to leave office. The Twenty-second Amendment (ratified in 1951) prohibited presidents from being elected to office more than twice, while the Twenty-fifth Amendment (ratified in 1967) established a process for removing the president for disability. The Twenty-second Amendment was enacted in a backlash against Franklin D. Roosevelt, whose four consecutive terms violated the two-term tradition established by George Washington. The Twenty-fifth Amendment was adopted because medical technology had created the very real possibility that a severely disabled president might survive a stroke or assassination attempt, but be unable to discharge the powers and duties of the office. (See Box 11–1 for the options for departure today.)

The vast majority of the forty-two presidents of the United States have left office because of defeat or death, or after serving two full terms. Of the past eleven presidents, two died in office, three lost their bids for reelection, one chose not to run, one resigned, and one left after serving two full terms. With two years left in his term as of this writing, President Clinton's fate is not yet known. Under the 1978 Ethics in Government Act, which was passed to curb the abuses that led to Richard Nixon's resignation, the Justice Department has the power to ask the federal courts for the appointment of an **independent counsel** to investigate the president and other senior members of the administration.

There have been eighteen independent counsels appointed under the statute, including one to investigate allegations that a member of Jimmy Carter's personal staff had used cocaine in 1978 (the charges were false), another to explore charges that the Reagan administration had used funds from illegal arms sales to Iran to help the Nicaraguan anticommunist rebels in the mid-1980s (the charges were mostly true), and still another to review allegations that Clinton's secretary of agriculture had accepted $35,000 in gifts and Super Bowl tickets from the agriculture companies his department regulated (the charges were true).

It was the Ethics in Government Act that led to the 1994 appointment of Kenneth Starr to investigate allegations that Bill and Hillary Clinton had violated

BOX 11-1

Seven Ways to Leave the Presidency

There are seven ways for someone who has been elected president of the United States to leave office.

1. The president can lose a bid for reelection (Ford, Carter, and Bush).

2. The president can choose not to run for a second term (Johnson).

3. The president can serve out the two full terms permitted under the Twenty-second Amendment and leave undefeated (Truman, Eisenhower, and Reagan).

4. The president can die in office (Roosevelt, Kennedy).

5. The president can resign (Nixon), automatically elevating the vice president to be president.

6. The president can be declared either temporarily or permanently unable to discharge the powers and duties of the office under the Twenty-fifth Amendment, which was ratified in 1967. No president has yet to leave office under this amendment.

7. The president can be impeached and convicted by Congress for what the Constitution calls "Treason, Bribery, or other high Crimes and Misdemeanors." Impeachment requires a majority vote by the House upholding the charges made against the president. The Senate then must hold a trial and can only convict the president by a two-thirds vote. Andrew Johnson is the only president ever to be impeached. He survived conviction by one vote. However, Nixon resigned to avoid impeachment and a likely conviction for his involvement in the Watergate scandal.

the law in a failed 1980s Arkansas land deal called Whitewater. Having found no hard evidence of wrongdoing in Whitewater, Starr expanded his investigation in early 1998 to include allegations that Bill Clinton had lied under oath regarding a sexual affair with White House intern Monica Lewinsky. After denying the affair for seven months, in August Clinton finally acknowledged having an "inappropriate relationship" with Lewinsky.

Clinton's apology did not end the Starr investigation, however. The alleged crime was not the inappropriate relationship, but rather lying under oath. Under

Independent Counsel Kenneth Starr (left) was appointed under the 1978 Ethics in Government Act to investigate allegations surrounding Bill and Hillary Clinton's involvement in the Whitewater development in Arkansas. His investigation expanded early in 1998 to include charges that the president had lied under oath regarding a sexual relationship with White House intern Monica Lewinsky. (Below) Capitol police officers unload copies of Starr's report and boxes of supporting evidence, which were delivered to the House in September 1998.

the Ethics in Government Act, Starr was required to report his findings to Congress, which he did on September 10. Congress published his full report on the Internet the very next day. Filled with details on Clinton's sexual relationship with Lewinsky, the report argued that Clinton's behavior constituted grounds for possible impeachment. The House of Representatives voted to begin an impeachment investigation as this book went to press, meaning that the process of impeachment, discussed in Chapter 10, had begun.

The Duties of the Presidency

Article II of the Constitution begins even more simply than Article I: "The executive Power shall be vested in a President of the United States of America." The problem comes in trying to define just what "the executive power" means. Some scholars argue, for example, that the executive power covers just about everything not listed under Congress. Compare the first sentence of Article II with the first sentence of Article I: "All legislative Powers *herein granted* shall be vested in a Congress of the United States." By not using the same "herein granted" language in Article II, perhaps the Founders meant the presidency to rely more on implied, rather than express, powers. The Founders were hardly sloppy writers and might have meant something by the difference in wording.

At the same time, the Founders also gave the presidency a list of enumerated powers, thereby suggesting that the president be bounded by specifics. The president's powers fall into two broad categories, one dealing with what appear to be mostly exclusive powers to run the executive branch and the other dealing with shared powers on making the laws. After examining these two sets of duties, this section briefly discusses how Congress and the presidency continue to share power today.

Executive Powers.   Unlike the long list of duties for Congress, the Constitution provides only the briefest sketch of executive powers.[3] Leaving some of the duties unspecified helped the Founders accept the notion of a strong executive. This is not to argue that the presidency was left powerless. Although thin on detail, Article II did speak to foreign threats and the day-to-day operations of government, establishing the president's authority to play three central roles in the new government: (1) commander in chief, (2) negotiator in chief, and (3) administrator in chief.

Commander in Chief.   The president's first duty is to be commander in chief of the army and navy. It is a fundamental expression of the president's role in protecting the nation as a whole. The Founders always saw the president as the commander in chief, but were divided over which branch would make war.[4] Under the Virginia Plan, the Founders had initially agreed that Congress would make war, raise armies, build and equip fleets, enforce treaties, and suppress and repel invasions.

By the end of the Constitutional Convention, however, the list of congressional responsibilities in war had been shortened, and the term "make war" had been changed to "declare war." In making the change, the Founders agreed that it would be Congress's responsibility to initiate war and the president's to repel invasions and protect citizens. But the specifics were not carried forward into the Constitution itself. President Clinton used this power in ordering troops to invade Haiti in 1994, arguing that the continued suppression of democracy threatened the United States.

Negotiator in Chief.   By enumerating the power to make treaties, Article II also makes the president negotiator in chief. (It is a power reinforced elsewhere in Article II in the power to appoint U.S. ambassadors and receive ambassadors from other countries.)

Once again, the Founders appeared to change their minds over time. As late as August 1787, the Founders assumed that the Senate, not the president, would have the treaty-making power. By the end of the month, however, the Founders had shifted this power back to the president, giving the Senate a secondary role by requiring a two-thirds vote of consent. Along the way, the Founders defeated a motion by James Madison that would have given the Senate its own treaty-making power separate from the presidency. Presidents eventually expanded the treaty power through the use of **executive agreements,** which are simple agreements between the heads of countries. Not quite treaties, these agreements can cover a range of issues, from student and cultural exchanges to commitments on international trade.

Administrator in Chief.   By enumerating the president's authority to appoint the officers of government (for example, the heads of departments, ambassadors, U.S. marshals) and compel their opinions in writing, Article II clearly makes the president administrator in chief. Although this might seem to be the least controversial of the president's enumerated powers, it provoked enormous debate at the convention. The Founders worried about favoritism in the appointment process and struggled with ways to ensure that only the very best people would be asked to serve. At one point, for example, the Founders wanted the Senate to appoint ambassadors; at another, they wanted Congress as a whole to appoint the secretary of the treasury.

In the end, the Founders gave the president the appointment power, provided that the Senate would confirm all individual nominees through simple majority votes. It is important to note, however, that Congress, not the president, is responsible for creating all appointive positions through its lawmaking power. Congress creates the departments and agencies, judgeships, and ambassadorial slots by law, while the president makes the final appointments with the Senate's confirmation. It is a sharing of power that guarantees no one branch will ever be in complete control.

Beyond giving the president the enumerated roles of commander, negotiator, and administrator in chief, the Founders also provided a broad implied power in the **take care clause,** which was discussed in Chapter 2. Located near the end of Article II is the simple statement that the president "shall take Care that the Laws be faithfully executed." Short though it may be, this clause gives the president ultimate authority to implement the laws. This power is particularly important if Congress is fuzzy about what it wants. And since fuzzy language is sometimes the best way to get a bill passed, the president ends up with broad authority to execute the legislation once it is signed.

Kenneth Starr invoked the take care clause in making the case for impeachment against Bill Clinton. According to Starr's 1998 report to Congress, the president had "engaged in a pattern of conduct that was inconsistent with his constitutional duty to faithfully execute the laws." In lying under oath, Starr argued, Clinton had violated the most central duty of any elected or appointed official: to uphold the Constitution of the United States. Although Clinton argued that he had been "legally accurate" when questioned about his relationship with Lewinsky, the vast majority of Americans concluded that he had not been telling "the truth, the whole truth, and nothing but the truth" under oath, leading growing numbers to call for his resignation, if not outright impeachment.

Lawmaking Powers.   The president's legislative powers reflect the Founders' concern with protecting the nation as a whole and checking Congress. Although Congress is responsible for *making* the laws, presidents have a substantial role in *shaping* the laws, whether through direct lobbying by the White House or efforts to mobilize public opinion and interest groups. As this chapter discusses later, presidents have a particularly important role in setting the agenda of issues that Congress will address. This agenda-setting role is part of the president's duty to represent the nation as a whole, and is contained in the Article II requirement that the president "from time to time give to the Congress Information of the State of the Union, and recommend to their Consideration such Measures as he shall judge necessary."

The state of the union is an example of how the presidency and Congress share the power to make the laws. Over the years, the phrase "from time to time" has come to mean "annually," while the phrase "information on the State of the Union" has come to be known as the **State of the Union address.** Until the early 1900s, the address was not an address at all, but an annual message delivered to Congress on paper. Today, the address is delivered orally before a joint session of both chambers and is carried live on the major television networks and many cable channels.

It is important to note that not all of the president's legislative powers are found in Article II. Under Article I, the president has the power to veto legislation passed by Congress. Under the veto power, the president has ten days (not counting Sundays) from the time a bill reaches the White House to make one of three choices: (1) sign the bill into law, (2) veto the bill by returning it to Congress with a list of objections, or (3) do absolutely nothing, letting the ten-day clock expire. If the ten-day clock runs out while Congress is still in session, the bill automatically becomes a law. If, however, the clock runs out after Congress has formally adjourned to go home (as opposed to just taking a short *recess,* or break), the bill is automatically killed under a **pocket veto.**

The process is not necessarily over with the formal veto, however. Except for pocket vetoes, which occur after members have gone home at the end of a session and therefore do not allow for any further action, Congress has the option to override a veto, provided it can muster a two-thirds vote in each house. The bill then becomes law over the president's veto. Thus does the president have a check on Congress, and Congress a check on the president.

The Ebb and Flow of Shared Power.   The presidency and Congress share many of the essential powers for governing the nation. Neither can quite paralyze the other, but neither has absolute power to act on its own. Congress and the

President Ronald Reagan delivers his 1982 State of the Union address to a joint session of Congress. Behind him are Vice President George Bush (left) and House Speaker Thomas P. "Tip" O'Neill (right).

presidency are, as political scientist Richard Neustadt once observed, separate institutions sharing power.[5]

Not surprisingly, the two institutions are constantly competing against each other for visibility and power. From the 1870s through the early 1900s, for example, Congress was the dominant institution, easily eclipsing the presidency in national visibility and impact. The Speaker of the House, not the president, was regarded as the most important political leader during the era.

After President Franklin D. Roosevelt recaptured the upper hand for the presidency in the 1930s, Congress passed two laws in the 1970s seeking to regain its place in declaring war and making the laws.[6] The first of these laws involved an effort to restrain the president's warmaking power. Under the 1973 **War Powers Resolution,** which was passed into law over President Richard Nixon's veto, presidents are required to consult with Congress whenever there is a chance that U.S. troops will be involved in hostilities. The law also requires the president to report to Congress within forty-eight hours of sending those troops into harm's way, and must withdraw those troops if Congress does not declare war within sixty days.

Although the law sounds tough in theory, it has been routinely ignored in practice. Presidents have argued that the War Powers Resolution is an unconstitutional infringement on their authority as commander in chief. Moreover, Congress has always had the power to bring an end to any troop deployment by cutting off funds through the appropriations process. That it has never done so suggests the great difficulty in stopping a war once fighting begins. No one wants to be accused of undermining the morale or support of troops in battle.

The second law involved an effort to strengthen congressional influence over the federal budget. Under the **Budget and Impoundment Control Act** of 1974, which Nixon signed just four weeks before resigning from office, Congress made three major changes in how the budget process works: (1) it sharply limited the president's authority to *impound,* or refuse to spend, legally appropriated funding; (2) it created its own independent source of budget information in the form of the Congressional Budget Office; and (3) it established a new budget process designed to help the many committees and subcommittees that are involved in raising and spending money keep track of the bottom line.

With the passage of this law, Congress was much more successful in swinging the pendulum of power back toward the legislative branch. Although congressional committees and subcommittees still have trouble keeping their eyes on the bottom line—witness the effort to control wasteful spending through the Line Item Veto Act—Congress is doing a better job of informing itself on key budget issues, and presidents no longer have unlimited freedom to impound funds.

Qualifications for Office

Just as the Founders set minimum qualifications for serving in Congress, they also established minimums for the presidency. However, the Founders came to the discussion of qualifications for the presidency late in the convention.

During the first part of the summer of 1787, the Founders had generally assumed that Congress would be choosing the president, making a discussion about qualifications mostly irrelevant. Congress would not select a president who did not meet the minimums for service in the House or Senate. In addition, by assuming that George Washington would be the first president, the Founders established a rather impressive standard against which to measure future presidential candidates.

Establishing minimum qualifications became much more important once the Founders gave the public a voice in choosing the president, however. Even once removed from direct election by the electoral college, the public would still have a say about who would serve as president. Therefore, to further protect the government from basic human nature, the Founders created three qualifications for serving as president. The president had to be: (1) over thirty-five years old; (2) a natural-born citizen, as opposed to an immigrant who becomes a citizen by applying to the U.S. government for naturalization; and (3) a resident of the United States for at least fourteen years. These qualifications were the stiffest of any in the three branches of government.

The citizenship and residency requirements reflected a variety of concerns. The Founders worried that the public might drift toward a popular foreign war hero such as Prussian general Baron Frederick von Steuben, drawn to such leaders out of a longing for "the good old days" of a foreign monarchy. The citizenship requirement also ended rumors that the Founders were somehow plotting to import a European monarch to take the presidency—Prince Henry of Prussia and Frederick, Duke of York, who was King George III's second son, were supposedly on the list. The residency requirement was designed to keep British sympathizers out of the new government. Colonists who had fled to England during the Revolutionary War would be ineligible for election.

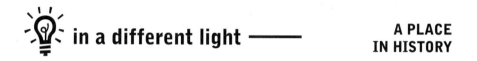

-ٌ۞- in a different light ——   **A PLACE IN HISTORY**

Presidents have the same goals as members of Congress: reelection (every first-term president wants to win a second term), good policy (every president enters office with at least some commitments to broad policy achievements), and personal

concerns (Lyndon Johnson's experiences as a schoolteacher shaped his commit-ment to federal funding for education). Because presidents cannot run for reelec-tion past a second term, however, and because there is no higher office than the presidency itself (although President William Howard Taft later became the Chief Justice of the Supreme Court), they also care about their place in history.[7]

According to rankings by America's leading historians, winning a place in his-tory involves a mix of strength, crisis management, legislative accomplishment, po-litical skills, and character. The list of great presidents is the same year after year: Abraham Lincoln, Franklin Roosevelt, George Washington, Theodore Roosevelt, Thomas Jefferson, Andrew Jackson, Woodrow Wilson, Harry Truman, Dwight Eisen-hower, and William McKinley.[8]

It is useful to note that nine of the ten were involved in America's great wars—Lincoln, McKinley, Wilson, Franklin Roosevelt, and Truman were all presi-dents during wartime, Washington was a Revolutionary War hero, Jackson was a hero in the War of 1812, Theodore Roosevelt was a hero in the Spanish-American War, and Eisenhower was the commander of Allied forces in World War II. It is also important to note that all were involved in managing the great domestic crises of their times—the Revolutionary War, the 1800 election, the Civil War, the Industrial Revolution, the Great Depression, and the technological revolution following World War II. Finally, it is important to note that all were involved in expanding the role of government: Jefferson engineered the purchase of the Louisiana Territory, which more than doubled the size of the United States, while Theodore Roosevelt helped the United States become an international power.[9]

The list of failed presidents rarely changes, either: William Henry Harrison, Warren G. Harding, James Buchanan, Franklin Pierce, Richard Nixon, James A. Garfield, Andrew Johnson, Millard Fillmore, and Ulysses S. Grant. Some earned their position through scandal: Nixon had Watergate, Harding had the Tea Pot Dome oil-leasing scandal. Others just happened to serve during the wrong era—for example, during the decades of congressional dominance in the late 1800s. Still others had the misfortune to follow great presidents: Andrew Johnson followed Lincoln. And obviously, being a war hero is not enough by itself to guarantee greatness; other-wise, Grant might be near the top.

It is not yet clear where the most recent presidents will end up. Jimmy Carter, Ronald Reagan, and George Bush are generally placed in the middle of the rankings, while Bill Clinton's affair with Monica Lewinsky seems destined to push him to the bottom of the ratings.

Ratings can change with time, however. Harry Truman was very poorly rated in the first two decades following his presidency, often dismissed as having been too much of a common man to be placed at the top of the charts. Truman has aged well,

President Richard Nixon waves goodbye to his White House staff after resigning in disgrace from the presidency. Secret tape recordings of key White House meetings in which Nixon discussed a cover-up of the Watergate scandal ultimately proved his downfall. The tape recording system was originally installed to help Nixon keep accurate records for his memoirs.

though, and is now routinely ranked near the top. Nevertheless, as Vice President Walter Mondale once said, political reputation is like cement: "You can stir it and stir it for a while, but pretty soon it becomes harder to stir and then it's set."[10]

Such ratings are not without controversy. Because historians who do the ratings have tended to be more liberal than conservative, the ratings may reflect a preference for activist presidents. A recent survey of conservative historians confirms the hunch. Conservative academics rate Franklin Roosevelt not as a great president, but as a near-great one; they rate Kennedy not as a near-great, but a near failure; and they rate Reagan not as below average, but as a near-great.[11] Greatness is very much in the ideological eye of the beholder.

Whatever his place as a great or near-great, Roosevelt is described by liberal and conservative historians alike as the first modern president. By creating the Executive Office of the President, which is the nerve center of the executive branch, and increasing the staff support available to the president, Roosevelt was able to enhance the supervisory power that Washington had originally established in the 1790s. Although conservative historians do not always like the way he used that power to expand the federal bureaucracy, they agree with liberals that Roosevelt left an indelible mark on the presidency itself.

Over his nearly four full terms in office, Roosevelt also set a precedent for aggressive government involvement in the economy. Roosevelt's first one hundred days in office in 1933 produced a staggering inventory of federal intervention in fighting the Great Depression, and much of his New Deal agenda for helping working and poor Americans is still on the statute books today, most notably Social Security for the aged, making the federal government an unmistakable presence in

American life. Moreover, as noted in Chapter 3, Roosevelt expanded the role of the federal government in cooperating with state and local government, launching the era of cooperative, or marble-cake, federalism.

The problem with lists of great presidents is that sitting presidents can take them too seriously. The secret tape recordings that led to Nixon's resignation had been made to help him write a more accurate biography of his time in office, which he hoped would lead to a high rating among historians. The best way to earn a place in history is to focus on solving problems and representing the nation in the present. History may deal a harsh judgment to presidents who devote too much attention to their personal futures, yet worrying about their place in history is one way for presidents to remind themselves that satisfying public demands in the present is not the only path to success.

THE REAL PRESIDENCY

Time has not stood still at 1600 Pennsylvania Avenue any more than it has on Capitol Hill. The presidency has grown bigger, more complicated, and infinitely more visible than the Founders could have imagined. Presidents also spend more time rallying the public to their causes and "spinning" the news in their favor.

Nevertheless, today's presidency reflects precedents set in the very first presidency of George Washington. The Founders could not have anticipated the kinds of foreign and domestic threats that now preoccupy the office—from international terrorism to the war on crime, from global competition to nuclear waste—but they would recognize the importance of the president in representing the nation as a whole.

The First Presidency

As with the First Congress, America's first presidency set important precedents for the future. It established a precedent on just how the president would be addressed in public. Vice President John Adams argued that the president should be called "His Highness the President of the United States and protector of Their Liberties," a title the popularly elected House immediately rejected. The president of the United States would be called "the President of the United States."[12]

George Washington in a painting by George Hicks. Washington set precedents for conducting the presidency that stand to this day.

Much more important was the fact that the first presidency established George Washington as the model against which to measure future presidents. And Washington, for his part, helped establish the legitimacy and basic authority of the office. He negotiated the new government's first treaty, appointed its first judges and department heads, received its first foreign ambassadors, vetoed its first legislation, and signed its first laws.

Washington also established a host of lesser precedents for running the presidency that still hold today. He started by assembling the first White House staff. It was hardly large, composed of just two clerks, but it was an office nonetheless. (Washington never used federal dollars to cover his office budget; he paid for staff and expenses out of his own pocket. Today's president could not afford such generosity: the budget for the White House staff, including travel expenses, mail, and security, runs almost $200 million a year.)

Washington also appointed the first department secretaries. His choices for the top jobs were impeccable: Thomas Jefferson became secretary of state and Alexander Hamilton secretary of the treasury. With James Madison as the floor leader of the House, Washington was able to develop a smooth liaison with Congress, establishing precedents for communication between the two branches that continue to this day.

Washington may have set his most important precedent in establishing the president's *sole* authority for supervising the executive branch. He was absolutely clear about the division of executive and legislative powers. Congress could appropriate money, confirm appointees, conduct oversight hearings, and always change the laws, but it could not run the departments. That was the president's job.

Congress did not give up control easily. In creating the Treasury Department, for example, Congress required the new secretary to report to both branches simultaneously, a requirement that stands in law to this day but is ignored in practice. Congress also tried to limit Washington's power to fire his own political appointees. Because Congress was responsible for confirming presidential appointees, the argument went, it only stood to reason that Congress would be responsible for removing appointees. Washington argued just the opposite. Confirming appointees was an appropriate check on executive power, but removing appointees was an essential tool for supervising the daily work of the departments. Nevertheless, legislation requiring prior congressional approval of all firings nearly passed the first Senate, and was defeated only when Vice President John Adams cast the tiebreaking vote.

The war over the presidential removal power was not over. Congress tried again to limit it in 1868, this time under the Tenure of Office Act, which required the president to submit all removals to the Senate for approval. This time, however, the battle occurred with a far less popular president, Andrew Johnson, in the White House. It was Johnson's decision to fire his secretary of war that led the House to pass a bill of impeachment indicting the president for high crimes and misdemeanors. Although Johnson was eventually acquitted after a six-week trial in the Senate, the struggle over executive power remains near the surface to this day. Congress routinely requires, for example, that federal departments keep offices open in the districts of particularly powerful senators and House members.

Washington's final contribution to the evolution of the presidency came in his decision to retire after two terms. His decision was motivated in part by the continuing worries about an American king. Although he would have been easily reelected to a third term, Washington believed that two terms were enough and returned to his Mount Vernon estate in 1796.

The Institutional Presidency

The structure that helps presidents do their jobs is referred to as the **institutional presidency.** Like Congress, the presidency has its own leadership, its own organizations for making decisions, and its own staff to provide advice and to faithfully execute its decisions.

Leadership. The leadership of the presidency is both simple and complex. It is simple because there is only one leader who counts—the president. It is complicated because that leader has so many sources of advice on what to do.

The **Executive Office of the President (EOP)** is where presidents get most of their advice. As noted earlier, Franklin Roosevelt created the EOP to give presidents more tools to supervise a fast-growing government. The term "Executive Office of the President" refers to the small number of offices that serve the president directly, not to the executive branch as a whole, which contains all the departments and agencies that execute the laws. As such, the Executive Office of the President is part of the executive branch, but not vice versa.

The EOP brought the Bureau of the Budget (now called the Office of Management and Budget) directly under the president's control. It provided a home for future growth of the president's staff, which rose from roughly 700 at the height of World War II in the mid–1940s to nearly 1,600 today. As the EOP grew, it became a key source of presidential control over the rest of government. As Box 11–2 shows, it also became a rather complicated organization.

If the EOP is the nerve center of the presidency, the president is the nerve center of the EOP. Although the offices contained within the EOP are set by law, presidents have great latitude to organize the flow of advice to fit their personal styles. Over the past three decades, presidents have used three very different models for running the EOP: competitive, collegial, and hierarchical.

Among modern presidents, Franklin Roosevelt and Lyndon Johnson both used the *competitive approach,* a "survival of the fittest" situation in which the president allows aides to fight each other for access to the Oval Office. Johnson frequently gave different staffers the same assignment, hoping that the competition would produce a better final decision.

In contrast, John Kennedy, Jimmy Carter, and Bill Clinton all used the *collegial approach,* in which presidents encourage aides to work together toward a common position. It is a much friendlier way to work than the competitive approach, but may have the serious drawback of producing what some social psychologists call *groupthink.* Groupthink is simply a term that describes the tendency of small groups to stifle dissent in the search for happier common ground.[13]

It was groupthink, for example, that led the Kennedy administration to launch the Bay of Pigs invasion in 1961, a disastrous effort to unseat Cuba's communist government. Looking back on the decision, Kennedy realized that few of his advisers had actually supported the invasion, but wanted so badly to agree that dissenters did not speak up in opposition. Kennedy worked to prevent groupthink two and a half years later in the Cuban missile crisis. Having discovered secret Soviet nuclear missile bases on Cuban soil in 1962, Kennedy made sure dissenters were given an opportunity to speak as the thirteen days of intense debate continued. In the end, Kennedy and his aides decided to impose

BOX 11-2

Executive Office of the President, 1939 and 1997

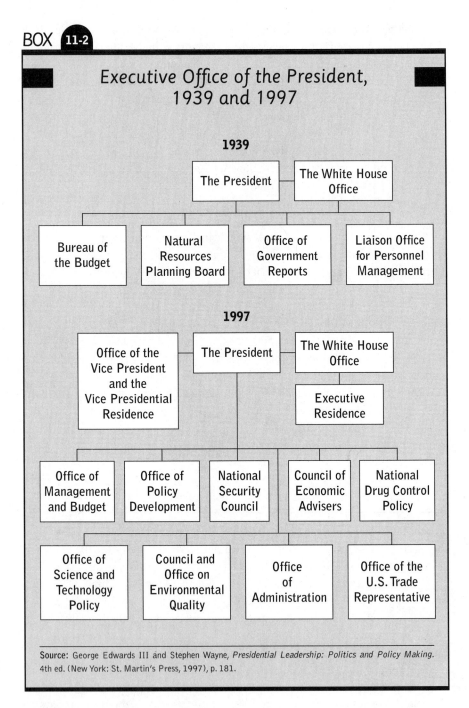

1939

| The President | The White House Office |

| Bureau of the Budget | Natural Resources Planning Board | Office of Government Reports | Liaison Office for Personnel Management |

1997

| Office of the Vice President and the Vice Presidential Residence | The President | The White House Office |
| | | Executive Residence |

| Office of Management and Budget | Office of Policy Development | National Security Council | Council of Economic Advisers | National Drug Control Policy |

| Office of Science and Technology Policy | Council and Office on Environmental Quality | Office of Administration | Office of the U.S. Trade Representative |

Source: George Edwards III and Stephen Wayne, *Presidential Leadership: Politics and Policy Making.* 4th ed. (New York: St. Martin's Press, 1997), p. 181.

Franklin D. Roosevelt (seated) meets with his Cabinet and several members of Congress. Roosevelt favored the competitive approach to running the White House.

a naval blockade of Cuba that eventually led the Soviets to withdraw their missiles.[14]

Finally, Dwight Eisenhower, Richard Nixon, Ronald Reagan, and George Bush all used the *hierarchical model,* in which presidents establish tight control over who does what in making decisions. A hierarchy is a form of organization that looks very much like a pyramid—one leader at the top, two right underneath, three or more right underneath those two, and so on down the organization. The chief advantage of a hierarchy is in reducing the number of people the leader has to deal with—the tighter the hierarchy, the fewer the contacts. Most hierarchies depend on a "gatekeeper" near the very top, usually the **chief of staff,** to enforce tight control over access to the leaders.

Advisory Offices. Just as committees in Congress exist to make the laws, the EOP's political and policy offices exist to shape presidential decisions. Staffed by people chosen for their loyalty, these offices act as agents on the president's behalf. Unlike Congress, in which committees have substantial power to shape final

Jimmy Carter and his advisers in 1977. Carter favored the collegial approach to running the White House. In the foreground left is Vice President Walter Mondale, who set important precedents in making the vice president a key member of the president's inner circle.

decisions, the president's advisory offices are just that: advisory. The final decision is always the president's.[15]

Political Offices.   Political offices are designed to help the president both run for reelection and represent the public. Almost all the president's political advice comes from the White House Office: the Congressional Relations Office handles the president's legislative agenda and lobbies for passage on Capitol Hill; the president's attorney provides legal advice on executive authority and is closely involved in the choice of presidential appointees to department and agency positions; the Public Liaison Office keeps in touch with key constituencies that are important to the president's reelection; the Intergovernmental Affairs Office keeps in touch with state and local governments; and the Office of Communications coordinates media strategy and includes the press secretary's office.

The Office of Public Affairs is the newest of the advisory units, created by Ronald Reagan as a trusted source of support on winning reelection. This office reflects the nearly constant campaigning that now goes on in the presidency. Bill Clinton, for example, began airing reelection advertisements well over a year before the 1996 campaign. The Public Affairs Office merely confirms in organizational terms what presidents and their staffs have long known: the only way to be a truly successful first-term president is to win a second term. As noted, reelection is never far from the mind of today's first-term president.[16]

Policy Offices.   Policy offices are designed to give substance to the president's foreign and domestic agendas. Like congressional authorizing committees, policy offices collect information and write legislation. What they do not do, of course, is hold public hearings and markups, or pass bills. They must rely on the president to forward their ideas to Congress. They also have substantial influence when it comes time for the president to sign or veto a law. The president's policy offices fall into three broad categories: (1) those that deal with the economy and budget, (2) those that deal with domestic issues such as transportation, education, and energy, and (3) those that deal with foreign policy and national defense.

Economic policy is shaped by four key EOP offices: the *Office of Management and Budget (OMB),* which is responsible for monitoring all federal spending; the three-member *Council of Economic Advisers,* which keeps track of current economic trends; the *Office of the U.S. Trade Representative,* which handles international trade issues; and the *National Economic Council,* which was created by Clinton in 1993 to bring together economic advice from across government. Of the four offices, OMB is by far the largest. Preparing the president's budget, while keeping track of a nearly $2 trillion federal budget, takes a staff of almost five hundred.

Making domestic policy involves a mix of several EOP offices: a very small *Domestic Policy Council* staff, which has traditionally handled social policy such as health care and welfare reform; the tiny *Office of Environmental Policy,* which provides coordination among the many federal agencies involved in protecting the environment; the *Office of National Drug Control Policy,* which was designed to coordinate the war on drugs and is headed by the nation's "drug czar"; and again OMB, which has a stake in most domestic policy decisions through the federal budget.

In contrast to both economic and domestic policy, which involve a mix of different offices, foreign policy is supposed to be shaped by a single unit, the *National Security Council* (NSC). Created by law in 1947, the council consists of the president, the vice president, the secretaries of defense, state, and treasury, the U.S. ambassador to the United Nations, and three White House aides: the chief of staff, the national security assistant, and the economic policy assistant.[17]

Advisers.   There are three levels of presidential staff. In order of their closeness to the president, they are (1) the inner circle of intimate advisers; (2) the White House staff, which exists solely to serve the president; and (3) the cabinet, composed of the heads of the fourteen executive departments of the federal bureaucracy—thirteen department secretaries and one attorney general, who heads the Department of Justice.

The Inner Circle. The term **inner circle** refers to the president's most loyal and trusted advisers. Sometimes called the "kitchen cabinet" because of its informality, the inner circle is usually engaged in every key decision. Members of the inner circle can include particularly loyal heads of departments, White House staffers, even personal friends who have special White House passes. Whoever they are, they have at least one factor in common: they are intensely loyal to the president. Bill Clinton's 1998 inner circle included the chief of staff (Erskine Bowles), the First Lady (Hillary Rodham Clinton), and Vice President Al Gore, plus one or two other trusted advisers, depending on the issue.

For the most part, members of the inner circle have immediate access to the president and can be called on at a moment's notice. A map of office assignments in the West Wing of the White House is a good indicator of whether someone is in the inner circle. Typically, the closer an adviser sits to the president, the more power that person has. As Vice President Walter Mondale once remarked, being in the Old Executive Office Building just across the alley from the West Wing is like being in Baltimore. The best space is just down the hall from the Oval Office,

President Clinton with two members of his inner circle in January 1998: White House Chief of Staff Erskine Bowles (left) and Vice President Al Gore (center). Presidents ultimately rely on a very small number of aides for advice, including their chiefs of staff, spouses, and in recent years, vice presidents.

where the president works. That is where the chief of staff, national security adviser, vice president, press secretary, and communications director all work. (See Box 11–3 for a map of the office assignments in the West Wing of the White House in 1995.)

One job that now appears to be a fixed ticket to the inner circle is the vice presidency. It was not always that way. After all, the job was once described by Vice President John Nance Garner, who served under Franklin Roosevelt, as not being worth a bucket of warm spit. As the very first vice president, John Adams, once wrote, "My country in its wisdom has contrived for me the most insignificant office that ever the invention of man contrived or his imagination conceived; . . . I can do neither good nor evil."[18]

Through most of American history, vice presidents have been a necessary nuisance. After all, they had but one real job beyond casting tiebreaking votes in the Senate: to take the president's place in the case of death or resignation. To this day, vice presidential nominees are usually chosen for geographic or ideological balance (northerners tend to choose southerners, liberals tend to choose conservatives), even though they might add only a percentage point or two, at best, to their ticket's total votes. Moreover, the vice president can create enormous embarrassment for the president, as Dan Quayle did with his insistence that *potato* was spelled *potatoe*. It was one of several gaffes that prompted Bush to consider dropping Quayle from the ticket in 1992.

Nevertheless, the vice presidency had changed by the 1980s. Vice presidents now have their own aircraft (Air Force Two) instead of the windowless cargo plane that once carried Spiro Agnew, Nixon's first vice president, on his foreign travels. They also have their own song ("Hail Columbia"), seal of office (thanks to Ford's vice president, Nelson Rockefeller, who paid for the design out of his own pocket), an office in the West Wing of the White House just down the hall from the president, access to all the paper flowing into and out of the Oval Office, regular private meetings with the president, and a growing staff of nearly one hundred.

Being vice president has turned into a very good political job, indeed, and is now the most frequent launching pad for future presidents. Four of the past eight presidents had been vice presidents (Johnson, Nixon, Ford, and Bush), three had been governors (Carter, Reagan, and Clinton) and only one had been a senator (Kennedy). Although being vice president is no guarantee of nomination, let alone an inaugural, it does position a politician as a nearly automatic front-runner. Having stood in the limelight, though always a bit in the president's shadow, vice presidents are immediately credible as presidential timber. They are also able to do the kind of political favors that future nominating convention delegates are likely to remember, whether getting a picture with the president or securing funding for a new highway bridge for a congressional district.

The White House Staff.   The president relies on sixty or so advisers to help manage the day-to-day details of the presidency. These advisers are all hand-

BOX 11-3

A Map to the Stars, 1995

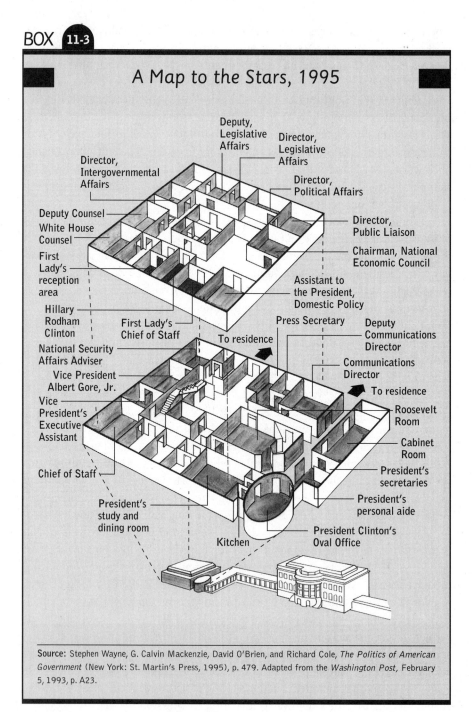

Source: Stephen Wayne, G. Calvin Mackenzie, David O'Brien, and Richard Cole, *The Politics of American Government* (New York: St. Martin's Press, 1995), p. 479. Adapted from the *Washington Post*, February 5, 1993, p. A23.

picked by the president for their loyalty and are referred to as the **White House staff.**

Most of these advisers have offices in the Old Executive Office Building. Once used to house all the federal departments in the early 1800s, the Old Executive Office Building now holds only presidential and vice presidential staff. These staffers must be available to brief the president on a moment's notice, and often serve as a buffer between the president and the heads of the departments and agencies.

The White House staff is supported by nearly 350 permanent employees, including clerical staff, communication aides (the president is kept in constant contact with the Departments of State and Defense in case of an international crisis), schedulers, event planners, and even a webmaster to maintain the White House home page (www.whitehouse.gov).

In theory, the White House staff exists for one purpose only: to advise the president. Yet a presidential adviser cannot help revelling in the reflected power of the presidency. As Reagan speechwriter John Podhoretz remembers, the top of the line is having a White House West Wing office and parking space:

> Political staffers who have made it to the West Wing have achieved a rare condition of the soul: They do not wish to be anybody else, do not wish to be anywhere else. This is as good as it gets for people in politics who do not have it in them to run for public office themselves. Real proximity to real power produces a special high, one made up of equal parts self-congratulation (I have finally made it) and anxiety (They'll figure out I'm really an incompetent nobody and come and take it all away). If parasites could fear, this is what their fear would be: expulsion from the host.[19]

Gone are the days, however, when presidential staffers were invisible to the public. Some White House staffers are as visible as the president. Some even cultivate political careers of their own: Republican presidential hopeful Patrick Buchanan began his career as speechwriter to Vice President Spiro Agnew.

The Cabinet.   The **cabinet** is composed of the 14 secretaries who head the federal departments, all of whom are appointed by the president and confirmed by the Senate. It also includes any other senior officials that the president wishes to invite.

The term *cabinet* itself was first used by the press in 1793 when George Washington called the first meeting of the "Heads of the Great Departments" as a source of advice on the issues of the day.[20] Although cabinet secretaries are appointed by the president, their loyalties are not always with the White House. Many enter office with strong constituencies of their own, and some become strong advocates for their departments in the annual budget process. Rare indeed is the cabinet secretary ready to support deep cuts in his or her department's budget, regardless of what the president might want.

There are currently fourteen cabinet departments, up from just two at the end of Washington's first term and ten in 1960. Not all cabinet departments are created equal. As Chapter 12 shows, the departments vary by staff size (the Department of Defense has nearly a million employees, while the Department of Education has barely five thousand) and budget (the Department of Health and Human Services has a budget of well over $200 billion, while the Department of State barely hits $10 billion).

They also vary in their influence with the White House. Presidents tend to pay the greatest attention to the oldest and most visible of the departments: Defense, Justice, State, and Treasury. These four departments are often called the *inner cabinet* because they are so important to the president's foreign and domestic success. The economy (Treasury), crime (Justice), and international affairs (State and Defense) are rarely far from the top of the president's agenda of policy concerns. Presidents almost always appoint very close allies to head the inner cabinet, even if those allies do not always have the best credentials for the jobs.

The other departments are generally called the *outer cabinet,* largely because they are more distant from the day-to-day worries that occupy the president and White House staff. The Department of Veterans Affairs, for example, is rarely in the headlines, even though its 250,000 full- and part-time employees make it the second largest department in the federal bureaucracy.

in a different light ——— THE FIRST LADY AS FIRST ADVISER

The president's inner circle has always included the First Lady to some extent. In recent decades, however, the First Lady has steadily become much more visible as a policy adviser to the president, in part because the media have become so aggressive in covering the White House. And no First Lady has been more visible than Hillary Rodham Clinton. Hillary Clinton is not listed on any White House organization chart, but is clearly first among presidential advisers on almost every policy issue.

Her strong policy role has come as no surprise to those who have followed Bill Clinton's career. The couple worked so closely together in the Arkansas governor's office that the two became known as "Billary." James Carville, Clinton's campaign consultant, described her influence in very clear terms: "If the person that has the last word at night is the same person who has the first word in the morning, they're going to be important. You throw in an IQ of a g'zillion and a backbone of steel, and it's a pretty safe assumption to say this is a person of considerable influence."[21]

Other First Ladies have also played important roles in the presidency. Woodrow Wilson's wife, Edith, is said to have actually run the presidency after Wilson suffered a stroke in his last year in office. Eleanor Roosevelt was highly public and influential in her husband's presidency from 1933 to 1945. Lady Bird Johnson became a champion of beautifying the nation's highways and cities. Betty Ford and Rosalynn Carter both supported the Equal Rights Amendment. Carter also sat in on cabinet meetings and represented the president in foreign countries, which led some observers to criticize the extent of her power in the White House.

What made Hillary Clinton different early in her husband's administration was her highly visible policy role. She headed the president's health care reform task force and emerged as a key player on a host of other issues. She clearly had the experience and the credentials for the job: she graduated first in her Yale Law School class, just ahead of the future president, and was headed for a career in law and public service long before Bill Clinton came along.

The only ones not ready for Hillary Clinton's hoped-for role were the American people. Many of them simply do not want any First Lady, however competent, to be a strong policy adviser. They want the First Lady to be a gracious and elegant hostess and even a strong advocate for issues such as highway beautification, children, and the arts. But when it comes to taking strong positions on an issue such as

Eleanor Roosevelt (left) and Hillary Rodham Clinton (right) were two of the most influential First Ladies in history.

abortion or health care, some Americans believe the First Lady is better off being seen and not heard. They view the First Lady as something of a national treasure, somehow above the messy business of real politics. Many came to admire Mrs. Clinton for standing by the president during the Lewinsky investigation.

Hillary Clinton will not be the last First Lady to enter office with substantial credentials of her own. Indeed, Elizabeth Dole promised to return to her job as president of the American Red Cross regardless of whether her husband was elected president in 1996. Moreover, it cannot be much longer before the country finds itself with its first First Gentleman.

Expectations of the Presidency

The presidency has become larger and more complicated over the past half century, for many reasons. Much of the growth involves the decline of the parties, the rise of candidate-centered campaigns, and parallel changes in Congress. Presidents now oversee activites inside the White House—for example, polling and campaign planning—that once were either unnecessary or were the responsibility of the national party committees. Winning reelection, not to mention passing the president's legislative program, means that the White House must often operate like a public relations firm. And, as the president's agenda has grown, so has the firm.

The presidency also grew because the American people have come to hold impossibly high expectations of what the president should do. These expectations became so high in the 1950s and 1960s that political scientists began to write of a "cult of the Presidency."[22] The cult celebrated the presidency as the only hope for defending the United States in an increasingly complex world. True believers in the cult hardly talked of Congress at all.

Evidence of the cult could be found in a host of places, from surveys of children showing that the president was uniformly liked and trusted to college textbooks heralding the president as the engine of freedom. William Young's 1964 *Essentials of American Government* described the president as "without question, the most powerful elected executive in the world. . . . And his power and responsibility are increasing."[23] Four years earlier, Clinton Rossiter's introductory text on the presidency described the office in even more glowing terms: "He is . . . a kind of magnificent lion who can roam widely and do great deeds so long as he does not try to break loose from his broad reservation." Rossiter continued, "He reigns, but he also rules; he symbolizes the people, but he also runs their government."[24]

It is no surprise that the cult blossomed when it did. Soviet nuclear missiles had been deployed in communist Cuba just ninety miles off the Florida coast, the Vietnam War was escalating, and the Berlin Wall dividing East and West Germany had just been built. Americans desperately wanted to believe that somebody was in charge.

The cult of the presidency began to collapse in the early 1970s when it confronted the realities of Vietnam and Watergate. The president was not all-knowing after all, nor was the office necessarily the source of democratic integrity. The United States lost its first war, sacrificing 53,000 young men and women in the cause, and Nixon became the first president to resign, sacrificing the trust of a generation in the process.

Even some of the cult's strongest leaders began to doubt their vision of the presidency, perhaps no one more so than historian Arthur M. Schlesinger, Jr. Having written admiringly of Kennedy's strong presidency in his 1966 best-seller *A Thousand Days,* Schlesinger attacked the Nixon administration in *The Imperial Presidency,* another best-seller, just seven years later: "In the last years presidential primacy, so indispensable to the political order, has turned into presidential supremacy. The constitutional presidency—as events so apparently disparate as the [Vietnam] War and the Watergate affair showed—has become the imperial presidency and threatens to be the revolutionary presidency."[25]

The cult allowed the people's confidence in *individual presidents* such as Roosevelt and Kennedy to increase their enthusiasm for a more powerful *institution of the presidency.* The two are not the same thing. The Founders were acutely aware of this fact as they tried to structure the office of the presidency. Being president is a temporary job. What permanence there is lies in the institution of the presidency, which continues on as a collection of powers, duties, hopes, and expectations regardless of which individual happens to be president.

The presidency was most certainly not the sole engine of American government. It was to be just one of three parts of a government that would maintain the delicate balance. As Charles Jones argues, there are very real dangers in exaggerating the importance of presidential leadership: "The natural inclination is to make the president responsible for policies and political events that no one can claim a legitimate right to control. Presidents are well advised to resist this invitation to assume a position of power as though it conveyed authority. Rather they need to identify and define their political capital, and must do so repeatedly in a search for the limits of their influence."[26]

Even though the cult of the presidency is now just about about dead, Americans still say they want a strong leader as president. Recall that half of Americans say they want a president who is forceful and decisive, and three-quarters want a president with sound judgment in a crisis.

There are two problems with high expectations of the presidency: first, as already suggested, the presidency has never had the kind of absolute power needed to meet the public's hopes; and second, the presidency may be even less able today than ever before to convert its limited powers into action. Being president is a mission impossible, and Americans seem to know it. When asked "just for fun" at the end of a 1993 *Washington Post*/ABC News poll, "Would you rather serve one term as president or one week in jail?" about half of the respondents opted for a week in the jailhouse rather than four years in the White House.[27]

THE PRESIDENT'S AGENDA

Presidents are obviously much more than faithful executors of the laws passed by Congress. They have long had a substantial, if not always dominant, role in shaping what Congress does. Their primary vehicle for doing so is the **president's agenda,** which is an informal list of their top legislative priorities. Whether through the State of the Union address or through countless other messages and signals, presidents make clear what they think Congress should do.[28]

It is one thing to proclaim a presidential priority, however, and quite another to actually influence congressional action. As Neustadt argued in *Presidential Power*, the president's constitutional powers guarantee very little by way of actual influence. According to Neustadt, a president's constitutional powers add up to little more than a job as America's most distinguished office clerk. It is a president's ability to persuade others that spells the difference between being a clerk and being a national leader.[29] Lyndon Johnson may have said it all in a single sentence: "You can tell a man to go to hell, but you can't make him go."[30] The power to persuade rests in the resources a president brings to office and the skills that he or she uses in making the most of those resources.

Presidential Resources

There are two kinds of resources that shape both the size of a president's agenda and its ultimate impact on Congress. The first involves the political resources that lead Congress to support the president, while the second involves the decision-making resources that help presidents decide what they want.

Political Capital.   **Political capital** is a mixture of public approval and party seats in Congress. As Democratic Vice President Walter Mondale once explained the concept, "A president, in my opinion, starts out with a bank full of goodwill and slowly checks are drawn on that, and it's very rare that it's replenished. It's a one-time deposit."[31] Some presidents start their terms with more capital than others. Lyndon Johnson started his first full term in 1964 with a deep reservoir of capital. Having become president following Kennedy's assassination, he won the 1964 election by a landslide, while building the largest House majority in the past fifty years.

In contrast, Gerald Ford entered office with little political capital at all. He did not become president because of a stunning electoral victory, but because of two resignations. The first came in 1973 when Spiro Agnew resigned from the vice presidency following his indictment for tax evasion. In the first use of the Twenty-fifth Amendment since its ratification in 1967, Nixon appointed the mild-mannered Ford to fill out Agnew's term. Eighteen months later Nixon resigned from the presidency following the court-ordered release of the secret White House tape recordings. As if to confirm Ford's precarious political support, his Republican party lost 43 seats to the Democrats only two months after his swearing-in, resulting in the smallest congressional minority for a sitting president in this century.

Political capital helps create a *mandate* for governing. The term refers to the president's ability to claim broad public support for specific policy initiatives. In 1993, for example, Clinton claimed a mandate for national health insurance, arguing that the issue was at the core of much of his public support. The claim would have been more plausible, however, had Clinton won with a popular vote larger than 43 percent.

Decision-Making Resources. Presidents can hardly claim mandates or invest their political capital if they do not have the time, energy, and information to actually set the agenda. The first two of these internal resources, time and energy, run out over the course of the term and are difficult to replace. Unlike members of Congress, presidents have only so much time to make their mark. Since they can only serve for two consecutive terms, and since they are lame ducks by the end of the sixth year, they must make every day count. As Johnson said at the start of his first full term in 1965, "I keep hitting hard because I know this honeymoon won't last. Every day I lose a little more political capital. That's why we have to keep at it, never letting up. One day soon, I don't know when, the critics and the snipers will move in and we will be at stalemate. We have to get all we can now, before the roof comes down."[32]

In a similar vein, presidents and their staffs have only so much energy to give. As Gerald Ford remarked, "It's a hard job being President. . . . Anybody who walks in there thinking he can punch a time clock at 9 in the morning and leave at 5 has got another thought coming. We do not elect Presidents who want that kind of a life." While 300-pound William Howard Taft could nap three hours each afternoon in 1910, today's president can ill afford to rest. Nor can the president's staff. Johnson apparently considered it something close to treason for a staff member to spend Sundays with his or her family.[33]

Clinton delivers his State of the Union addresses in 1993 (left) and 1998 (right). Clinton clearly aged during his first five years in office. One reason can be spotted in the upper right area of each of these photographs. In 1993, the Speaker of the House was a Democrat, Tom Foley; in 1998, the Speaker was a Republican, Newt Gingrich.

Even as presidents lose time and energy, they tend to gain information. They learn more about their jobs and the issues, and almost always leave office smarter than when they entered. In a sense, the presidency is the nation's most intense American government course. One way presidents can increase their learning is to take "prerequisites" before entering office—that is, by holding other executive offices, such as the vice presidency or a governorship, that are similar to the presidency or by studying issues as a senator or member of the House that are central to the president's constitutional duties.

Presidential Skills

After all is said and done, a president's political capital determines whether Congress will support his or her agenda. In an era of high party unity, the number of party seats is central to a president's ultimate success. A president who enters office with low public approval and a congressional minority will always be less persuasive than one who enters with high approval and a majority.

The question is not whether political capital is the sine qua non of influence, which it most certainly is, but whether presidents can do anything to increase the "buying power" of the capital they have. Do all presidents with low public approval and a party minority suffer the same fate? Do all with high approval and strong majorities achieve the same victories? The answer to both questions is no. Presidents can stretch their political capital if they have the legislative skills to do so.[34]

No skill is more important for converting scarce political capital into legislative success than the ability to focus public and congressional attention on the president's top priorities. This **focusing skill** consists of two specific tactics: timing and lobbying. The first part of focusing is timing, which involves a president's ability to set the legislative agenda early in the term, while avoiding unnecessary delays caused by overloading in key congressional committees and unproductive controversy.[35]

The second part of focusing is lobbying. The president must make his or her priorities known and keep the pressure on. As Lyndon Johnson argued, "Merely placing a bill before Congress is not enough. Without constant attention from the administration, most legislation moves through the congressional process at the speed of a glacier."[36] Presidents can offer a number of rewards for their allies on Capitol Hill, not the least of which are invitations to elegant events called state dinners and special White House tours for a favored member's constituents. More tangibly, presidents still have a great say about where their party invests its campaign money, and a presidential visit back home can spell the difference between a candidate's victory and defeat in the next election.

Whatever the tactic, the purpose of focusing is to let the public and Congress know what the president wants, to make sure the list of priorities is not too long, and to keep the pressure on. Presidents who focus attention can make their political capital go farther.

Policy-Making Cycles

The pressure to move quickly is shaped by two cycles. The first is called the **cycle of decreasing influence**: Presidents tend to lose public and congressional support over time. The second is called the **cycle of increasing effectiveness**: Presidents almost always get better at their jobs over time.

The cycle of decreasing influence reflects the erosion of political capital over time. At least since 1960, presidential approval tends to be at its highest at or near the start of the first term, falling more or less steadily over the next two years, rebounding in the fourth year with the presidential campaign, and, if the president is reelected, falling again from the fifth year on.[37]

The fact that a president's approval is higher at the beginning of the term and lower at the end does not mean it can never go up in between. When drawn on a chart, the general decline is often interrupted by occasional jumps in approval. Presidents almost always get a boost from American military action abroad, even if the action fails. Kennedy got a 5 percent boost in public approval following the failed Bay of Pigs invasion.

The public tends to "rally 'round the flag" during foreign crises. These **rally points** are particularly strong when military action, such as an invasion or bombing, is both short and successful. Gerald Ford's approval rating jumped 11 percent after he sent special troops to rescue the crew of a merchant ship called the *Mayaguez,* which had been seized by the Cambodian government; George Bush's jumped nearly as much when he ordered U.S. troops into Panama to capture dictator Manuel Noriega. (See Box 11–4 for a sampling of rally points over the past forty years. The chart also includes two failed rally points. The Christmas bombing of North Vietnam came at the very end of a highly unpopular war, while the Baghdad bombing reminded Americans that Iraqi dictator Saddam Hussein was still in power despite the 1992 Gulf War victory.)

Not all rally points involve foreign crises. Clinton's approval rose after the Oklahoma City bombing in 1995, in large part because Americans turned to him for leadership in the crisis. Presidential approval can also rise during periods of great national pride. Reagan's public approval (and reelection chances) jumped during the 1984 Olympic Games as the United States won one gold medal after another, in part because the Soviet Union and its Eastern European allies boycotted the event.

The problem with rally points is that they evaporate rather quickly once the crisis eases. Bush's public approval hit 89 percent at the height of the Gulf War in 1991, only to plummet to barely 30 percent eighteen months later. The Gulf War turned out to be rather like a television miniseries that slowly faded from memory as the season wore on. Moreover, as Box 11–4 shows, not all rallies are positive.

Alongside the decline in public approval, presidents almost always lose seats in Congress in the midterm elections. Indeed, there have been only two elections since 1862 in which the president's party has gained seats in the House. The worst of the recent defeats came in 1994, when Clinton's Democrats lost fifty-two seats, eclipsing the 1974 election that followed the Watergate scandal, when Republicans lost forty-eight seats. Much as members of Congress try to make campaigns about local issues, the midterm elections have traditionally been an opportunity for the public to hold a referendum on the president. Because presidents rarely accomplish all that they promise, the losses are inevitable.

Even as presidents tend to lose influence over time, they begin to benefit from the cycle of increasing effectiveness. They steadily become better at their jobs. Just as students in an American government course should know more at the end than at the beginning, presidents know more in the fourth year of their term than in the first. This cycle means that presidents should become more effective at spending their political capital over time. They may have less capital to work with, but should be able to make the most of what they have.

BOX 11-4

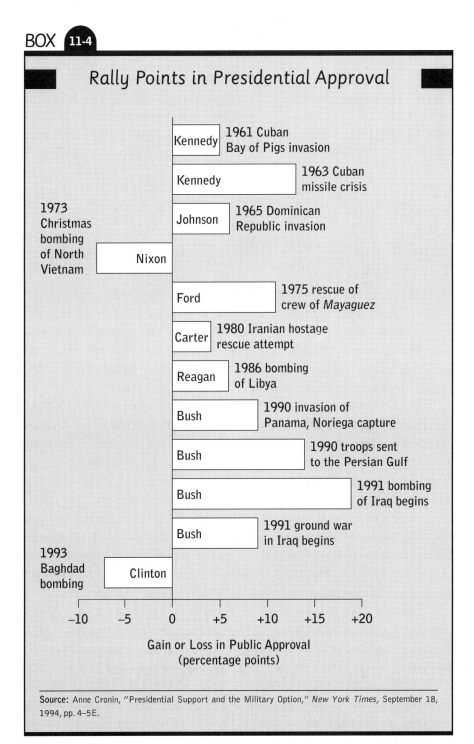

Rally Points in Presidential Approval

Kennedy — 1961 Cuban Bay of Pigs invasion

Kennedy — 1963 Cuban missile crisis

Johnson — 1965 Dominican Republic invasion

1973 Christmas bombing of North Vietnam — Nixon

Ford — 1975 rescue of crew of *Mayaguez*

Carter — 1980 Iranian hostage rescue attempt

Reagan — 1986 bombing of Libya

Bush — 1990 invasion of Panama, Noriega capture

Bush — 1990 troops sent to the Persian Gulf

Bush — 1991 bombing of Iraq begins

Bush — 1991 ground war in Iraq begins

1993 Baghdad bombing — Clinton

−10   −5   0   +5   +10   +15   +20

Gain or Loss in Public Approval
(percentage points)

Source: Anne Cronin, "Presidential Support and the Military Option," *New York Times*, September 18, 1994, pp. 4–5E.

Thus, Bill Clinton was a much better president at the end of 1996 than at the beginning of 1993. He had learned painful lessons about how Congress worked, and reshuffled his White House staff to bring in much greater experience. Out went his old Arkansas friend Thomas "Mac" McLarty as chief of staff; in came former long-time House member Leon Panetta. Out went many of the twenty-somethings who came into the White House directly from working on their first presidential campaign; in came old hands such as former Jimmy Carter legal adviser Lloyd Cutler.

 **in a different light** ———— **A NO-WIN PRESIDENCY?**

Put together, the two cycles of policy making create a dilemma for a new administration: presidents are most influential when they are least knowledgeable, most knowledgeable when they are least powerful. In a sense, they are in a "no-win" situation. If they move too quickly, they make mistakes; if they move too slowly, they lose momentum. As Clinton adviser George Stephanopoulos argued, "We're always stuck in the small crawl space between 'must win' and 'can't lose.'"[38]

Because presidents are rarely willing to admit they do not know enough about their jobs to make policy decisions and because they face enormous pressure to take advantage of their popularity while they still have it, they tend to pay much more attention to the cycle of decreasing influence. As a result, presidents are tempted to follow five rules at the start of the term: move it or lose it, learning must wait, take the first alternative, avoid details, and reelection comes first.

Move it or lose it. If presidents hope to use what little honeymoon time they have, they must set their agenda early and repeat it often. Because this agenda-setting process determines what issues will be at the top of the president's list of concerns, it is the key first step of the policy-making process. If the agenda is not set quickly, Congress will turn its attention to its own list of priorities.

Learning must wait. Presidents do not have time to learn during their first year in office. If they do not know the issues coming into office, they just have to take the staff's word about them. Again, the risk is major policy mistakes. Knowing that the clock was ticking, Clinton pushed his highly complicated national health insurance proposal onto the agenda barely six months into his first term, and was criticized even then for being late. With the proposal in tatters by the end of the year, Clinton's advisers privately admitted they should have spent more time working through the details.

Take the first alternative. If presidents have no time to think through innovations, they are pressed to take whatever programs are lying around at the start of the term and call them their own. Thus, much of what presidents propose is merely repackaging of ideas already floating around in Congress. Going with the available ideas is a safe way to get success, but hardly fits a candidate who comes into office promising great change.

Avoid details. The fast-moving president has little time for digging into the details of legislation. The result, again, can be hastily drafted bills that may collapse under close public scrutiny. Yet presidents who stop to read the details either slow the process down or burn out. The less reading the president does, the better.

Reelection comes first. As presidents survey the territory after their first inauguration, most are struck by the remarkably short amount of time they truly have. The first year is for setting the agenda and appointing the key staff and department officers, the second for helping out with a tough midterm election, the third and fourth for campaigning for reelection. And even if they win a second term, presidents have at best a year to a year and a half before the media and Congress start talking about the next presidential election. As such, presidents are "lame ducks," or powerless, by the end of their sixth year in office.[39]

THE PRESIDENT AND THE PUBLIC

Given the role of public approval in shaping their agendas, which in turn have such a significant impact on their reelection and place in history, it would be surprising if presidents did not invent new ways of boosting their standing with the American people. As noted in Chapter 4, they have become consumed with tracking public opinion, creating what Larry Jacobs and Robert Shapiro describe as a veritable warehouse of public opinion inside the White House.[40] They have also become experts at two new tactics of generating public support: the first is the tendency to "go public" on issues that once would have been negotiated with Congress, while the second is the new capacity to "spin" the news to the president's advantage.

Going Public

One of the reasons presidents spend so much time these days measuring public opinion is that they are much more willing to "go public" about their contests with Congress. One way to build a fire on Capitol Hill in favor of the president's program is to light a match in the congressional districts. Going public simply means that the president, instead of the individual members of Congress, is doing the talking in the congressional districts.

Presidents have been communicating with the public from the very beginning of the republic, when presidents even created their own newspapers to communicate their policies. What is different today is that presidents are communicating much more often and for a very different purpose: to focus public pressure on Congress.[41]

There is no question that recent presidents are going public more frequently. They are making more prime-time television appearances, giving more speeches, and spending more time out of the White House. According to Samuel Kernell, the number of major and minor presidential addresses has grown from just a dozen or so in the first three years of the Hoover administration (1929–1931) to well over a hundred in the first three years of the Bush presidency almost sixty years later. The greatest growth came in the number of minor addresses before specialized audiences—trade associations, college graduations, advocacy groups.

According to Kernell, the number of public appearances has also jumped significantly. Whereas Herbert Hoover made barely two dozen appearances in his first two years, George Bush made over 150. Travel outside Washington is also up. During his first three years, Hoover was barely out of town for one week total; Bush, in contrast, spent nearly ten weeks out of Washington, including frequent trips to foreign countries.[42] One reason for the increase in travel involves declining trust in government—presidents cannot afford to be seen as Washington insiders and sometimes travel just to get media exposure outside the Beltway, the interstate highway that surrounds the capital city. The paradox is that knowledge of Washington is essential if a president is going to get anything done. Thus, the most popular president is likely to be an insider who looks and acts like an outsider.

The advantage of going public is simple: The president controls the setting and the content, deciding who gets to attend and what he or she will say. Given this desire for greater control, it is not surprising that presidents have cut back on their press conferences. Whereas Franklin Roosevelt held almost seven press conferences a month during his twelve years in office, Reagan, Bush, and Clinton (at least through 1994) averaged barely one per month.[43]

The reason for the sharp decline in the number of presidential press conferences may be simple. Presidents have much greater control over the news if they, not reporters, set the agenda. And the rise of new media such as CNN, C-SPAN, and MTV gives them outlets beyond the traditional television networks and newspapers. They would much rather meet with the local press outside Washington than inside, much rather give exclusive interviews than face a roomful of unpredictable reporters, and much rather use live satellite feeds to remote stations to get their message across than deal with the *Washington Post, New York Times,* or *Wall Street Journal.*

Going public clearly fits with changes in the electoral process. Presidents now have the staff, the technology, and the public opinion research to tell them how to target the message and the nearly instant media access to go public easily. And, as elections have become more image-oriented and candidate-centered, presidents have the incentive to use these tools to operate a permanent White House campaign. Unable to count on their party to deliver the voters, presidents go public because it is one of the few strategies that promise success. Presidents are still welcome to bargain and persuade, to focus congressional attention and twist arms, but members of Congress may pay attention only when pressure is coming from the voters back home.

Spin Control

Even as they go directly to the people, presidents have become increasingly effective at managing the news. As noted in Chapter 5, they even have a White House Office of Communication to oversee the **spin control,** which is a term that came into popular use during the Reagan administration. Spin control involves a number of tactics that are designed to get the media to cover an event or story in the most favorable light. When done well, the media do not even know they are being spun.

Once again, Roosevelt was the first modern president, giving "fireside chats" on the radio to keep the public informed during the Depression and World War II. He also invented the modern press conference, inviting reporters to ask him questions in an essentially unrehearsed setting. Every president since has followed the practice, though some to a much greater degree than others. Compared to Roosevelt's average of seven press conferences a *month,* Nixon barely held seven press conferences a *year.* Nixon was extraordinarily uncomfortable in front of reporters, and kept his contact with them to a minimum.

Clinton was also reluctant to meet the press, preferring to go directly to the public through events and town hall meetings. During the early months of the Lewinsky scandal, Clinton remained mostly silent on the specifics, letting lieutenants such as James Carville fire back on his behalf. "What I do is just launch another attack," said Carville when asked how he deals with criticism of the president. "Just pull out your launch codes. Put the key in, type out your launch codes, and let her rip."[44]

Clinton's strategy clearly made sense, given the changes in the media described in Chapter 5. Presidents can no longer command instant access to the press and, much as they spin, can no longer determine either the placement or tone of a story. In the White House press operation of today, political reporter Michael Kelley argues, "the day is composed, not of hours or minutes, but of news cycles. In each cycle, senior White House officials speaking on background define the line of the day. This line is echoed and amplified outside the Beltway, to real people, who live out there, by the President's surrogates, whose appearances create actualities (on radio) and talking heads (on television)."[45]

 **in a different light** ——— A GREAT STATE OF THE UNION

Bill Clinton gave one of the greatest State of the Union messages in American history in 1998. It was moving, uplifting, and closely watched. It was also unlike almost every other State of the Union speech in history. "If you imagine political rhetoric as a big broad river like the Mississippi," says former Reagan speechwriter Peggy Noonan, "an inaugural address is a big sleek sloop, a real dream boat." But a State of the Union "is a big, old gray tugboat weighed down with cargo. You stop and look at it as it goes by, and sometimes you're marvelously impressed that it didn't sink."[46]

The difference for Clinton was in the swirl of events leading up to the address. Coming on the heels of the first news reports on the Monica Lewinsky story, Americans tuned in to see whether the president would crack, what he might say about the allegations that he had had an affair with a White House intern, and listen to his plans for the coming year.

Clinton never said a word about Lewinsky, but Americans still liked what they heard. Before the speech, only 35 percent of Americans told the Gallup Poll that Clinton was setting a good or very good moral example for the country; after the speech, the number jumped to 49 percent; before, only 33 percent were very confident in Clinton's ability to do his job; after, the figure was 48 percent. In all, 84 percent of the Gallup respondents rated the speech as positive, with over half calling it very positive. Back-to-back surveys by The Pew Research Center for The People & The Press also showed that Clinton's job approval went up 10 percentage points following the speech, with one-third of the gain entirely due to favorable impressions of his performance and another one-third due to a backlash against what some Americans thought was unfair media coverage of what they still believed was an alleged affair.[47]

How could one speech do so much for a beleaguered president? The answer is twofold. First, Clinton greatly exceeded all expectations in his performance. He was sharp, empathetic, calm, and bipartisan. If the Lewinsky investigation was on his

BOX 11-5

The State of the Union, 1993 vs. 1998

	1993	1998
Jobless rate	7.3%	4.7%
Poverty rate	14.8%	13.7%
Median income	$16,665	$17,587
Consumer confidence (1985 = 100)	76.7	134.5
Conventional mortgage rate	8.0%	7.03%
Budget deficit	$290 billion	$22 billion
Welfare recipients	14.1 million	10.2 million
Violent crime rate (per 100,000 people)	757.5	634.1
Satisfied with nation's direction	29%	50%
Inflation rate	2.9%	1.7%
Dow Jones average	3,242	7,794
Minimum hourly wage	$4.25	$5.15

Source: Mark Murray, "States of the Union: Then and Now," *National Journal*, January 24, 1998, p. 154.

mind, he never showed it. Second, and much more important, the state of the union was great. The best way to deliver a strong State of the Union address is to have a strong state of the union to celebrate. If the state of the union has gotten better during the president's term, all the better. As Box 11–5 shows, the economy was running strong, wages were up, crime was down, and welfare rolls were falling. The country clearly had reason to give Clinton credit for the good times, which he gladly claimed.

MAINTAINING THE BALANCE

As with Congress, most of the changes chronicled in this chapter suggest that the presidency is getting closer to the people, whether in measuring what the people think or in shaping what news they will read; whether in going directly to the public to sell the president's agenda or in exploiting what little remains of the cult of the presidency to enhance their influence. As the presidency has become better at going public and spinning the news, it may become much more of a voice for the people than the Founders could have imagined.

Interestingly, however, there is little evidence that recent presidents have used this new-found closeness to launch grand new initiatives. With only occasional exceptions such as Reagan's 1981 budget and tax cuts, which were approved by Congress, Bush's North Atlantic Free Trade Agreement, which was eventually ratified by the Senate, and Clinton's national health insurance plan, which never came to a final vote, the president's agenda has been steadily shrinking over the past ten years.

The problem could be that the era of limited government brought on by tight federal budgets and the Republican revolution has reduced the marketability of all but the most mundane reforms. It could also be that public approval and party seats in Congress simply do not produce the same opportunities as they did twenty years ago. It could even be that Washington has simply run out of big ideas. But whatever the cause, Reagan, Bush, and Clinton had fewer big ideas than Kennedy, Johnson, and Nixon before them. If American government is out of balance because presidents are getting too close to the people, it is most certainly not on behalf of major public policy initiatives of the kind Roosevelt pursued in the New Deal.

So what is the president's purpose in reaching out to the people? The answer appears to be the search for reelection and public approval. Facing a divided Congress; a sharper, more focused interest group community; a vast array of new media; and a factional public, the presidency had to change, too. The campaign for the presidency could no longer so easily stop on election day. Instead, it has to continue nearly every day of the first term as presidents fight to get their positions heard and their reelection assured. Instead of campaigning for the right to govern, presidents increasingly govern as an act of campaigning, constantly seeking opportunities to convince the public that they selected the right person for the job, and ultimately becoming delegates rather than trustees of the people.[48]

This might be the appropriate strategy for dealing with the changing political landscape, but it is unlikely to ensure an appropriate balance when it comes time for a president to ask the American people to sacrifice for the greater good. To the contrary, it may be a recipe for creating a different kind of cult of the presidency, one based not in high expectations for leadership, but in intense interest in what the public wants. The president becomes "empath in chief," expected to feel the public's pain, soothe the public's divisions, and create a politics of warmth and love. Such a cult might be fine for periods of calm, but might create a real threat to the nation during periods of sacrifice. Empathy is more than enough perhaps when the economy is growing and old enemies such as the Soviet Union have faded away. The question is how to defend the nation when times are tough, new adversaries are looming, and the public must accept a measure of pain for the sake of the greater good. That is when the new cult of the presidency comes into sharp conflict with the Founders' vision, and when the delicate balance is most at risk.

JUST THE FACTS

terms to remember

presidential ticket (p. 437)
impeachment (p. 437)
independent counsel (p. 437)
executive agreements
(p. 441)
State of the Union address
(p. 442)
pocket veto (p. 443)
War Powers Resolution
(p. 444)
Budget and Impoundment
Control Act (p. 444)
institutional presidency
(p. 450)
Executive Office of the President (EOP) (p. 451)

chief of staff (p. 453)
inner circle (p. 456)
White House staff (p. 459)
cabinet (p. 459)
president's agenda (p. 464)
political capital (p. 464)
focusing skill (p. 467)
cycle of decreasing influence
(p. 467)
cycle of increasing effectiveness (p. 467)
rally points (p. 468)
spin control (p. 473)

facts and interpretations

- The Founders designed the presidency to do three jobs: faithfully execute the laws, represent the nation as a whole, and check Congress from becoming too powerful. They also expected the president to be strong enough to protect the nation from foreign and domestic threats, yet never become an American king. It was and still is a difficult balancing act, particularly in periods of high public expectations of presidential action.

- Since the Founders originally saw a strong presidency as essential for checking the power of an even stronger Congress, they gave the president an impressive list of duties, including commander in chief, negotiator in chief, and administrator in chief. They also gave the president significant authority to set the agenda by requiring an annual report on the state of the union. Presidents have used the state of the union requirement, the veto authority, and the take-care clause as opportunities to press their own agenda on Congress. Their ability to influence Congress depends on both resources and skills. Presidents cannot create congressional majorities where none exist, but they can use their lobbying power to make sure that every last seat they do have on their side stays there.

- As with Congress, the presidency has become a more complicated institution over time. The White House is composed of several layers of senior advisers, with multiple sources of advice on the issues of the day. Presidents have so much help today that it is reasonable to divide their advisers into the inner circle, the more general White House staff, and the inner and outer cabinets. They also have substantial political support inside the White House, including their own pollsters and "spin doctors." The result is that presidents have never been more capable of reaching out to the public directly, whether through town halls, travel, or e-mail. This outreach capacity has made the president more responsive to public opinion than the Founders could have imagined.

- Given other changes in American government described elsewhere in this book, presidents are under extraordinary pressure to set their policy agendas early and repeat them often. The problem with this "move it or lose it" strategy is that presidents know the least about their jobs at the beginning of their terms. Although having been a governor may help a new president learn the administrative ropes and having been a senator or member of the House may help a new president work their congressional levers, there is truly no job like being president of the United States. Therefore, presidents are more likely to have the decision-making resources and skills to make good decisions later in their terms than earlier. At least in recent administrations, presidents have generally decided that the learning must wait. They move their agendas early, even when they know that what they are proposing may not be exactly the right thing to do.

open questions

- Is being president really such a hard job? One that would be worse than going to jail, as some poll respondents seemed to believe? What are the checks on presidential power that make the job so difficult? And what, if anything, can a president do to be more effective in office? Thinking back to the discussion of how Americans choose presidents, are voters asking the right questions and casting their votes for the right reasons? Could George Washington get elected president today?

- Do Americans expect too much from the presidency today? Do they understand how limited the duties of the presidency are? Would it make sense for presidents to make an effort to explain their jobs better to the public? Can any president succeed, given the complexity of the job and the competing cycles that appear to govern the term? Would it make sense today to institute the plural executive that the Founders once considered?

- Does the president get too much advice? To what extent do all the people who serve the president build up the public's hope that the president will solve all their problems? Is it a good thing that presidents now have their own pollsters on staff? That they have so much capacity to go public?

- What is the state of the union in your home town? How are changes in how the economy works affecting your own decisions about which courses to take and where you want to focus in your own college career? Do you expect the state of the union to get better or worse in the next five to ten years? What one issue do you think should be at the top of the president's legislative agenda? Is it there? If not, why not? If so, do you think Congress will act on it?

for further study

Hart, John. *The Presidential Branch from Washington to Clinton.* Chatham, NJ: Chatham House, 1994.

Light, Paul C. *The President's Agenda: Domestic Policy Choice from Kennedy to Clinton,* 3rd ed. Baltimore: Johns Hopkins University Press, 1998.

Milkis, Sidney, and Michael Nelson. *The American Presidency: Origins and Development, 1776–1990.* Washington, DC: Congressional Quarterly Press, 1990.

Neustadt, Richard E. *Presidential Power,* 2d ed. New York: Basic Books, 1990.

Sundquist, James. *The Decline and Resurgence of Congress,* Washingon, DC: Brookings Institution, 1981.

Walcott, Charles E., and Karen M. Hult. *Governing the White House: From Hoover through LBJ.* Lawrence: University of Kansas Press, 1995.

endnotes for chapter 11

1. These and other quotes about the history of the presidency can be found in Sidney Milkis and Michael Nelson, *The American Presidency: Origins and Development, 1776–1990* (Washington DC: CQ Press, 1990).
2. Roy P. Fairfield, ed., *The Federalist Papers* (Baltimore: Johns Hopkins University Press, 1981), p. 198.
3. Richard Pious, *The American Presidency* (New York: Basic Books, 1978), p. 29.
4. This history of presidential powers draws heavily on Milkis and Nelson, *The American Presidency.*
5. Richard E. Neustadt, *Presidential Power,* 2d ed. (New York: Basic Books, 1990).
6. James Sundquist, *The Decline and Resurgence of Congress* (Washington, DC: Brookings Institution, 1981).
7. See Bruce Miroff, "The Presidency and the Public: Leadership as a Spectacle," in M. Nelson, ed., *The Presidency and the Political System* (Washington, DC: CQ Press, 1988).
8. See Stephen J. Wayne, "Great Expectations: What People Want from Presidents," in Thomas Cronin, ed., *Rethinking the Presidency* (Boston: Little, Brown, 1982).
9. For a discussion of different kinds of modern presidents, see Fred I. Greenstein, ed., *Leadership in the Modern Presidency* (Cambridge, MA: Harvard University Press, 1988).
10. Personal conversation with the author, 1993.
11. For a different set of rankings, see James Piereson, "Historians and the Reagan Legacy," *The Weekly Standard,* September 29, 1997, pp. 22–24.
12. For a recent biography of Washington, see Richard Brookhiser, *Founding Father: Rediscovering George Washington* (New York: Free Press, 1996).
13. See Irving Janis, *Groupthink* (Boston: Houghton Mifflin, 1982).
14. See Graham Allison, *Essence of Decision: Explaining the Cuban Missile Crisis* (Boston: Little, Brown, 1971).
15. For a history of many of these offices, see Charles E. Walcott and Karen M. Hult, *Governing the White House: From Hoover through LBJ* (Lawrence: University of Kansas Press, 1995).
16. See John A. Maltese, *Spin Control: The White House Office of Communications and the Management of Presidential News,* 2d ed. (Chapel Hill: University of North Carolina Press, 1994).
17. John Hart, *The Presidential Branch from Washington to Clinton* (Chatham, NJ: Chatham House, 1994), p. 68.
18. Quoted in Paul C. Light, *Vice Presidential Power: Advice and Influence in the White House* (Baltimore: Johns Hopkins University Press, 1984), p. 12.

19. John Podhoretz, "Little Shop of Horrors," *The Washingtonian*, November 1993, p. 52.

20. Milkis and Nelson, *The American Presidency*, p. 74.

21. Maureen Dowd, "Hillary Clinton's Debut Dashes Doubts on Clout," *New York Times*, February 8, 1993, p. A10.

22. See Thomas Cronin, *The State of the Presidency* (Boston: Little, Brown, 1980).

23. William Young, *Essentials of American Government*, 9th ed. (New York: Appleton-Century-Crofts, 1964), p. 251.

24. Clinton Rossiter, *The American Presidency*, rev. ed. (New York: New American Library, 1960), pp. 250, 84, 68–69, 17; in Cronin, *The State of the Presidency*, pp. 28–29.

25. Arthur M. Schlesinger Jr., *The Imperial Presidency* (New York: Popular Library, 1973), p. 10.

26. Charles O. Jones, *The Presidency in a Separated System* (Washington, DC: Brookings Institution, 1994), p. 281.

27. Richard Morin, "Vox Populi," *Washington Post National Weekly Edition*, July 5–11, 1993, p. 37.

28. See Paul C. Light, *The President's Agenda: Domestic Policy Choice from Kennedy to Clinton*, 3rd ed. (Baltimore: Johns Hopkins University Press, 1998), for a discussion of the agenda-setting process.

29. The phrase "power to persuade" is from Neustadt, *Presidential Power*, p. 7.

30. Lyndon Johnson, *The Vantage Point: Perspectives on the Presidency, 1963–1969* (New York: Holt, Rinehart and Winston, 1971), p. 461.

31. Quoted in Light, *The President's Agenda*, p. 13.

32. Quoted in Jack Valenti, *A Very Human President* (New York: Norton, 1975), p. 144.

33. Doris Kearns, *Lyndon Johnson and the American Dream* (New York: Harper & Row, 1976), p. 252.

34. See George Edwards, *Presidential Influence in Congress* (San Francisco: W. H. Freeman, 1980), p. 202.

35. See Paul Light, "The Focusing Skill and Presidential Influence in Congress," in C. Deering, *Congressional Politics* (Homewood, IL: Dorsey Press, 1989), p. 256.

36. Johnson, *The Vantage Point*, p. 448.

37. Howard W. Stanley and Richard G. Niemi, *Vital Statistics on American Politics* (Washington, DC: CQ Press, 1995), p. 261.

38. Quoted by Elizabeth Drew, *On the Edge: The Clinton Presidency* (New York: Touchstone, 1994), p. 345.

39. This list is modified from Light, *The President's Agenda*, pp. 217–22.

40. Lawrence Jacobs and Robert Shapiro, "Disorganized Democracy: The Institutionalization of Polling and Public Opinion Analysis during the Kennedy, Johnson, and Nixon Presidencies," paper presented at the annual meeting of the American Political Science Association, New York, September 1–4, 1994, p. 3.

41. See Jeffrey Tulis, *The Rhetorical Presidency* (Princeton, NJ: Princeton University Press, 1987).

42. Samuel Kernell, *Going Public* (Washington, DC: CQ Press, 1993), pp. 92, 102.

43. Stanley and Niemi, *Vital Statistics*, p. 53.

44. Quoted in James Bennet and Adam Nagourney, "White House's Familiar Battle Plan: Keep Silent, Strike Often and Soldier On," *New York Times,* January 30, 1998, p. A13.

45. Quoted in John Maltese, *Spin Control: The White House Office of Communication and the Management of Presidential News,* rev. ed. (Chapel Hill: University of North Carolina Press, 1994), p. 50.

46. Quoted in Alison Mitchell, "State of the Speech: Reading between the Lines," *New York Times,* February 2, 1997, p. E5.

47. The Gallup poll was conducted with CNN and *USA Today,* and was released on January 27, while the Pew Research Center for The People & The Press poll was released on February 8.

48. See Charles O. Jones, *Passages to the Presidency: From Campaigning to Governing* (Washington, DC: Brookings Institution, 1998), for a discussion of these trends.

the federal bureaucracy

the faithful branch

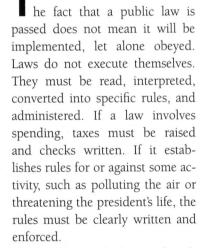

The fact that a public law is passed does not mean it will be implemented, let alone obeyed. Laws do not execute themselves. They must be read, interpreted, converted into specific rules, and administered. If a law involves spending, taxes must be raised and checks written. If it establishes rules for or against some activity, such as polluting the air or threatening the president's life, the rules must be clearly written and enforced.

Executing the laws is the job of the **federal bureaucracy**, a term that political scientists use to describe the executive branch's four-teen departments, eleven independent regulatory commissions, sixty agencies, three to four dozen government corporations, and almost 2 million full-time employees that deliver on the promises others make. The federal bureaucracy does not exist to make the laws, but to administer them.

Faithful execution of the laws is crucial to the delicate balance. Whatever Congress and the president decide to do, or not do, about an issue, they must have confidence that the executive branch will do what it is told. The Founders most certainly did not want the ex-ecutive branch to be incompetent. As Alexander Hamilton wrote in *Federalist Paper No. 70:* "A feeble Executive implies a feeble execution of the government. A feeble execution is but another phrase for bad execution; and a government ill executed, whatever it may be in the-ory, must be in practice a bad government."[1] Although Hamilton be-lieved that a strong president was the best way to prevent a government ill executed, all the Founders supported effective public administration. As noted in Chapter 2, they may have expected, even hoped, that Congress and the president would have sharp disagree-ments over public policies, but were unwavering in their belief that all the laws had to be faithfully administered. The people could hardly have confidence in their representative democracy if federal bureaucrats could pick and choose which laws to implement.

Unfortunately, there may now be so many laws on the statute books that the federal bureaucracy has no other choice but to ignore some and execute others. Part of the problem is that Congress and the president almost never repeal the old laws before passing new ones. It is usually up to those faceless bureaucrats or the federal courts to figure out which laws apply under what circumstances. Part of the problem is that the number of federal employees has actually decreased over the past few decades, even as the federal budget has continued to grow. As this chapter shows, there are fewer federal em-ployees today than there were in 1960. Even if they wanted to exe-cute all the laws, there are simply not enough federal employees to do so. If Congress and the president will not tell them exactly which laws come first, it is again up to the bureaucrats or courts to decide. And part of the problem is that Congress is often deliberately vague about what it wants the federal bureaucracy to do. Although a little ambiguity can go a long way to winning passage of a law, it makes implementation much more difficult, again forcing the bureaucracy or the courts to resolve the confusion.[2]

When the federal bureaucracy decides which laws to execute, it becomes much more than the faithful branch the Founders created. In effect, it becomes Congress, the presidency, and the courts all rolled into one. To the extent the bureaucracy decides which laws come first, it performs a legislative function. To the extent it decides which laws to ignore, it performs both a judicial and a legislative function. And to the extent it decides who should do what, it performs a presidential function. By adding more laws even as they cut the federal bureaucracy, Congress and the president may be asking the bureaucracy to do much more than execute the laws. They may be asking it to make the laws by default.

This chapter provides an introduction to the federal bureaucracy at three levels. First, it looks back to the Founders' imagined bureaucracy, asking just what the Founders had in mind as they mostly ignored the bureaucracy in their constitutional debates. Second, it examines the real federal bureaucracy, showing how Congress and the presidency shaped the first bureaucracy in the 1790s, and how that bureaucracy continues to evolve to this day. This second section also asks just how big the federal bureaucracy actually is, concluding that it is both big and small at the same time. Third, the chapter provides an inventory of how Congress and the presidency control the federal bureaucracy.

THE IMAGINED BUREAUCRACY

The Founders never used the word *bureaucracy* to describe the executive branch. The term was invented by sociologists in the late 1800s to describe what sociologist Max Weber called the most perfect form of organization known to humankind. The Founders may not have known about the word *bureaucracy,* but they most certainly knew something about administering programs. George Washington had run the Continental Army, and many of his colleagues at the Constitutional Convention had run banks, businesses, and farms. None of them would have been in Philadelphia had they not been at least moderately successful at running organizations of one kind or another.

Perhaps that is why they did not spend much time worrying about the administrative structure of government. They knew that the new executive branch would have departments and officers (otherwise, why give the president the power to require the written opinions of the officers of government?), and believed that the administrative apparatus would constitute what the Founders called "a complicated piece of machinery."

But they had more important things to do in Philadelphia than design the departments and agencies of government. That could be left to the first Congress and the first president. On the one hand, they saw the day-to-day operation of government to be far less controversial than the balance of power among the three branches. On the other hand, they expected the new government bureaucracy to be small. The new government would hardly have the money to pay off its Revolutionary War debt, let alone hire large numbers of employees.

Moreover, there is at least some evidence that the Founders simply expected Congress to establish the same departments that had existed under the Articles of Confederation, which is precisely what Congress did in creating the Departments of State, War, and Treasury in 1789.[3] There is also some evidence that the Founders expected good administration to flow naturally from the same virtue and wisdom that they hoped would characterize America's first elected leaders.

Whatever the reason, the federal bureaucracy remains the Constitution's undefined branch, but one with great duties nonetheless. Before turning to those duties, it is useful to consider two key decisions that reveal at least some of the Founders' intentions as to who was to run the future bureaucracy.

The Undefined Branch

The federal bureaucracy may have been mostly undefined by the Constitutional Convention, but the Founders did make two decisions that continue to shape the bureaucracy today. Both decisions reinforced the president's responsibility for executing the laws.

First, the Founders clearly decided not to allow members of the House and Senate to hold executive branch positions. They drew a sharp line on the issue in Article I, Section 6, of the Constitution: "No Senator or Representative shall, during the Time for which he was elected, be appointed to any civil Office under the Authority of the United States, which shall have been created, or the Emoluments whereof shall have been increased during such time, and no Person holding any Office under the United States, shall be a Member of either House during his Continuance in Office." The provision prevented members of Congress from creating jobs for themselves in the executive branch, a common form of corruption in England prior to the Revolutionary War.[4] The Founders also worried that simultaneous service in both branches would weaken the separation of powers.

Second, the Founders decided not to give Congress the power to appoint the treasurer of the United States (now called the secretary of the treasury). For much of the summer of 1787, appointing the treasurer was first on the list of the legislature's enumerated powers, reflecting the convention's concern about the financial stability of the new nation. It was not until the third-to-last working day of the convention that the Founders deleted the provision in an effort to reaffirm the president's authority to supervise the officers of government.

Despite their limited debate, the Founders clearly wanted public administration to be efficient. One way to have a government strong enough to protect the nation as a whole and American citizens as individuals was to make sure that the departments and agencies worked well. The Founders obviously had a high tolerance for frustration in the making of public policy, where they wanted ambition to counteract ambition. But they had no such plans for what would become the federal bureaucracy. Once the laws were written, they were intended to be executed faithfully and efficiently.

The Duties of Bureaucracy

By not naming any of the executive departments in the Constitution, the Founders left the future of the bureaucracy up to Congress and the presidency. Congress would authorize the departments and agencies of government, determine which presidential appointments would be subject to Senate confirmation, and appropriate the money to act. Only then could the president order those departments and agencies to work. Thus, the duties of the federal bureaucracy are not to be found in the Constitution but in the individual laws that describe who gets what, when, and how from government—laws that also say just where in government a program will be run.

As the laws have accumulated over the years, the federal bureaucracy has become a vast enterprise. It runs the national parks and national forests, tracks hurricanes, and helps small businesses get started. It operates the air traffic control system, oversees the stock markets, collects the national census every ten years, and issues crop forecasts. It enforces laws for cleaning up the air and water, investigates and prosecutes a host of federal crimes such as kidnaping and counterfeiting, and provides the first line of defense against the Ebola virus and HIV. It helps prevent accidents on the job, protects workers and citizens from toxic chemicals, runs a national railroad, and writes checks to millions of Americans, including 35 million Social Security recipients.

Even though it is sometimes less efficient than the private sector, the bureaucracy's responsibilities are almost always greater. Federal Express may be faster in delivering overnight packages in part because it does not have to deliver everywhere, a requirement only the U.S. Postal Service must meet. Congress often sets other requirements that make bureaucracy less efficient than it might otherwise be, not the least of which is that government must be fair in its decisions about whom it helps.

By leaving the duties of bureaucracy to the future, the Founders ensured that Congress and the presidency would create the bureaucracy one department and agency at a time. The result is that the bureaucracy often looks hopelessly confused. The Department of Agriculture runs the national forests, but the Department of the Interior runs the national parks; the Department of Health and Human Services runs Temporary Assistance to Needy Families, the federal block grant that replaced Aid to Families with Dependent Children (AFDC) in 1996, but the Department of Agriculture runs Food Stamps (a program that gives those same families coupons to buy food). By 1995, the federal bureaucracy had 163 separate job training programs located in 55 different departments or agencies,

90 early-childhood programs located in 31 places (the Department of Health and Human Services ran 28, the Department of Education ran 34), and 35 food safety laws administered in 12 different agencies.[5]

in a different light ——— MAKING BUREAUCRACY RESPONSIVE

People have been complaining about big government ever since the dawn of time. As one Roman officer complained after visiting Egypt in 288 B.C., so many local officials had "invented titles for themselves, such as comptroller, secretary, or superintendent" that they were swallowing up all the profits from the Roman conquest. The only option was to cut the bureaucracy. "It has therefore become necessary for me to send you instructions to arrange a single superintendent of good standing to be chosen for each estate on the responsibility of the local municipal council, and to abolish all remaining offices, though the superintendent elected shall have power to choose two, or at most three, assistants."[6]

Imagine what that Roman officer might say upon meeting the federal bureaucracy in Washington today. Two thousand years after Rome conquered Egypt, and two hundred years after the Constitutional Convention conquered the Articles of Confederation, the federal bureaucracy is anything but small. It is a $1.5 trillion, 2 million employee business, with branches in every state of the union. It owns trillions of acres of land—parks, military bases, and forests—and occupies more square feet of office space than any single corporation in the world. As for those who criticize the "bureaucrats in Washington," only one out of ten federal employees actually work in the nation's capital; the rest work in regional and local offices all across the nation, from a few thousand in South Dakota to over 250,000 in California.

The federal bureaucracy may have grown so large and complex over the decades that it has lost touch with the public. With employees spread out in thousands of offices across the country, the federal bureaucracy may be so big that no one, least of all members of the public, can truly know everything it is doing. Moreover, as the sole provider of essential services such as national defense, it will stay in business whether citizens like what it does or not.

Reformers argue that there are two ways to make the federal bureaucracy more responsive to the public. The first is to expose the bureaucracy to market pressure by converting some of its service agencies into private businesses (a process known as *privatization*) or by having the bureaucracy compete with private businesses to deliver the same services. In theory, the marketplace should make the federal bureaucracy more sensitive to its customers, the citizens of the United States. Although the idea has worked at the local level of government, where cities have privatized everything from garbage collection to city jails, some federal services simply cannot be privatized. It is difficult to imagine the chaos that would be created by having a private army, air force, and navy, for example.

A second way to make the federal bureaucracy more responsive to the public is to make it look more like the public. By creating a *representative bureaucracy,* at least in terms of race and gender, the federal government would increase its chances of having some connection to the people it serves.

There is no question that the face of the federal bureaucracy has changed over the past two decades. There have never been more women and minorities in federal jobs. Women accounted for 43 percent of all federal jobs in 1990, while minorities constituted over 27 percent of the federal workforce.[7] Both numbers had gone up slightly by 1998.

Even though the number of women and minorities in the federal workforce had increased by 1990, there are two other problems with creating a representative bureaucracy. First, women and minorities are not equally represented across all departments and agencies. Women and minorities tend to concentrate in departments

Minorities hold 27 percent of all federal jobs, but only a very small percentage of the very top posts. Here, a federal worker checks newly printed U.S. currency for the U.S. Mint.

with strong social service missions such as Education, Health and Human Services, Housing and Urban Development, and Veterans Affairs (which runs the VA hospital system, with its mostly female nursing corps), all of which have more than 50 percent women. Military and technical departments such as Defense, Energy, NASA, and Transportation have far fewer women. Health and Human Services has 65 percent women, while Transportation has just 25 percent; 50 percent of the Department of Education's employees are minorities, compared to just 16 percent of Agriculture's.

Second, women and minorities are not represented at all levels of the federal system. Women held roughly 35 percent of all professional and administrative jobs in 1990, where the higher-paying management posts are, but 70 percent of the lower-paying technical and clerical positions. Minorities were also heavily represented in the lower-paying jobs. Together, women and minorities held almost half the jobs at the bottom level of the federal pay system in 1990, and just 10 percent of the posts at the top.[8] Thus, if the federal bureaucracy is to become more representative of the public it serves, it has a long way to go.

THE REAL BUREAUCRACY

There is no question that the federal bureaucracy is larger than the Founders could have ever imagined. The federal bureaucracy has grown from a handful of clerks to a complicated network of public and private employees who work to administer the laws. The Founders might be surprised to find, for example, that not all federal jobs are done by federal employees.[9] In all, there may be as many as four private employees under contract to the federal government for every one public employee on the federal payroll. Private contractors build the airplanes and ships for the Department of Defense, program the computers for the Commerce and Treasury Departments, run welfare programs for the Department of Health and Human Services, prepare the space shuttle for NASA, and build nuclear warheads for the Department of Energy. The Founders might also be surprised to discover just how active the federal government is in American life. Hardly a minute goes by when Americans do not have direct or indirect contact with government, most of it for the good.

This is not to say that the Founders would recoil at the size and scope of today's federal bureaucracy. They knew society would become more complex, and fully expected Congress to write laws on a host of emerging issues. Nor is it to say that the Founders would think government is too big. They might note that many organizations in American society have gotten bigger over time, including state and local bureaucracies and private companies.

The First Bureaucracy

The first bureaucracy was anything but large. As public administration scholar Leonard White once wrote, the entire federal bureaucracy of 1790 consisted of nothing more than a "foreign office with John Jay and a couple of clerks to deal with correspondence from John Adams in London and Thomas Jefferson in Paris; . . . a Treasury Board with an empty treasury; . . . a 'Secretary at War' with an authorized army of 840 men; . . . [and] a dozen clerks whose pay was in arrears."[10]

Creating the first departments was not without controversy, however. Congress not only wanted to restrict the president's removal power for all officers, it also continued the Constitutional Convention debate over who should run the Department of the Treasury. Having lost the power to appoint the secretary in the last days of the convention, the first Senate pressed to have the new department headed by a board rather than a single secretary, and briefly succeeded in requiring the secretary to submit all plans for implementing certain financial plans to Congress for approval. The Senate's proposals would have sharply limited the president's authority to execute the laws and were eventually defeated on close votes.

Once past the legislative disputes, the first departments came on line rather smoothly. Washington made three excellent first appointments: Thomas Jefferson at the Department of State, Alexander Hamilton at the Department of the Treasury, and Henry Knox at the War Department. All three were easily confirmed and quickly went about the business of running their departments. At roughly the same time, Congress also created the Post Office Department and allowed for the appointment of a U.S. attorney general.

Even though the federal bureaucracy was but the tiniest fraction of its current size, it was not long before the country was demanding smaller government. Jefferson made smaller government a centerpiece of his first inaugural address in 1801, promising "a wise and frugal government, which shall restrain men from injuring one another, shall leave them otherwise free to regulate their own pursuits of industry and improvement, and shall not take from the mouth of labor what it has earned." Jefferson wanted a government that worked better and cost less, one that taxed lightly, paid its debts on time and in full, and sought "economy in the public expense."

Ultimately, Jefferson's promise to reduce government far outweighed his actual success. Despite tax cuts and a reduction in the size of the armed forces, Jefferson's Louisiana Purchase doubled the size of the nation, requiring a rapid expansion of the General Land Office, which was responsible for granting deeds to western land. Most of the deeds were handled by career government employees, who stayed in office regardless of who was president. Many of them took bribes to set aside the best parcels of land.

Corruption in the General Land Office fueled the western anger that swept Andrew Jackson—and the two-party system—into office in 1828. As noted in Chapter 6, Jackson decided that the way to stop corruption was to fill *all* government jobs with presidential appointees who would be fired at the start of a term and replaced by individuals loyal to the incoming president and his political party. Jackson called this system "rotation in office," meaning that no one would stay in a public job long enough to be corrupted. Most political scientists call it the "spoils system," as in "To the victor belong the spoils." If someone wanted a job in the federal government, whether delivering the mail or registering deeds, first they would have to join the party.[11]

Although the spoils system quickly became corrupt itself (it was not long before party workers began selling government jobs), Jackson saw the change as a way to return power to the people. "They regarded their administrative handiwork, not as an attempt at modernization, but as the restoration of something old and respectable," political scientist Matthew Crenson wrote in quoting Jackson. "They aimed to purify the federal establishment of all its newfangled complexity, to restore 'the government to its original simplicity in the exercise of all its functions.'"[12]

Jackson did not stop reforming government with the employment system, however. He also reorganized the federal departments to make them more efficient, created accounting systems to track spending, and established codes of ethics to regulate the behavior of government workers. In a sense, he was the first president to worry seriously about making government work better. (See Box 12–1 for a sampling from the code of ethics at the Post Office Department in Jackson's time.)

The United States emerged from Jackson's presidency with the outlines of today's federal bureaucracy. The federal bureaucracy had grown from a few thousand employees to over thirty thousand, and was well on its way to becoming a major presence in Americans' daily lives.

The Institutional Bureaucracy

Paging through the *U.S. Government Manual,* a reference book that provides brief descriptions of every department and agency in government, is like conducting an archaeological dig. Because the federal bureaucracy was created one unit at a time over a period of two hundred years, no two agencies are quite alike. Some, such as the Department of Defense, are collections of huge agencies in their own right. The Defense Department contains the Departments of the Army, Navy, and Air Force, each with its own separate duties (as if to confirm how Congress sometimes divides responsibilities, the Army has its own air corps, and the Navy has its own army, the Marines). Others, such as the Department of Education, are tiny

BOX 12-1

Rules for Government Conduct in 1830

Every clerk will be in his room, ready to communicate business, at nine o'clock A.M., and will apply himself with diligence to the public service until three o'clock P.M. . . .

Newspapers or books must not be read in the office unless connected directly with the business at hand, nor must conversation be held with visitors or loungers except upon business which they may have with the office. . . .

The acceptance of any present or gratuity by any clerk from any person who has business with the office, or suffering any such acceptance by any member of his family, will subject any clerk to instant removal. . . .

Strict economy will be required in the use of the public stationery or other property. No clerk will take paper, quills, or anything else belonging to the government for the use of himself, family, or friends.

Source: Matthew Crenson, *The Federal Machine: Beginnings of Bureaucracy in Jacksonian America* (Baltimore: Johns Hopkins University Press, 1976), pp. 76–78.

by comparison, with but a handful of employees and a relatively limited set of duties. Nevertheless, all departments and agencies share at least three basic features: leadership, an organization chart, and employees.

Leadership.   Every department and agency of the federal bureaucracy is headed by a **presidential appointee,** who is either subject to confirmation by the Senate or appointed on the sole authority of the president. As political officers, presidential appointees serve at the pleasure of the president and generally leave their posts at the end of that president's term in office.

In turn, presidential appointees work closely with **senior executives,** who serve at the very top of the career federal workforce. As career professionals, senior executives continue in their jobs regardless of who is in the White House, and are selected on the basis of merit, not political connections. Presidents have very little say about who gets chosen as a career executive.

Together, these two types of executives—political and career—constitute the leadership of the federal bureaucracy. All told, there are ten thousand executives: three thousand political and seven thousand career. Of the three thousand political, roughly six hundred are subject to Senate confirmation, while the rest are appointed solely by the president. The number has grown dramatically over the past three decades as the federal government has "thickened" with more layers of leadership and more leaders at each layer.[13] (See Box 12–2 for a list of the job titles open for appointees and senior career officials.)

Whereas President John F. Kennedy selected 10 department secretaries in 1960, President Bill Clinton picked 14 in 1992; Kennedy 6 deputy secretaries, Clinton 21; Kennedy 14 under secretaries, Clinton 32; Kennedy 81 assistant secretaries, Clinton 212; Kennedy 77 deputy assistant secretaries, Clinton 507; Kennedy 52 deputy administrators, Clinton 190. Adding up all the layers, the total number of senior executives and presidential appointees grew from 451 in 1960 to 2,393 in 1992, a 430 percent increase.

The cost of this thickening is not in the salaries of all the managers. Adding more layers to the federal hierarchy is not particularly expensive—federal salary costs are a very small part of the overall budget. Rather, thickening contributes to a weakening of accountability between the top and bottom of government. Presidents and their political appointees may be unable to see the bottom of government, which can increase the freedom of faceless bureaucrats to enforce or not enforce the laws as they see fit.

Organizations.   Public administration scholars use four terms to classify the organizations of government: (1) departments, (2) independent regulatory commissions, (3) independent agencies, and (4) government corporations. Originally, these terms were used to describe different sizes and missions of organizations. Departments were to be the largest organizations of all, agencies the smallest, independent regulatory commissions free of political control, and government corporations the most businesslike—hence the term *corporations*. Over time, however, some of the distinctions have blurred. The Department of Education, a department with less than five thousand employees, is smaller than many independent agencies, while the Social Security Administration, an independent agency with sixty-five thousand employees, dwarfs all but the largest of departments. (See Box 12–3 for the federal government's organization.)

Departments.   Cabinet **departments** are the most visible organizations in the federal bureaucracy. Today's fourteen departments of government employ more than 70 percent of all federal civil servants and spend 93 percent of all federal dollars. Thirteen of the departments are headed by secretaries, while the fourteenth, Justice, is headed by the attorney general.

The largest department by far is the Department of Defense, followed by Veterans Affairs, Treasury (which contains the Internal Revenue Service and its vast collection of local field offices), Justice (which contains the Federal Bureau of Investigation), and Health and Human Services (which operates Medicare and most federal welfare programs). The smallest department is the Department of

Federal Job Titles Open for Occupancy by Presidential Appointees and Senior Executives, 1998

Secretary
Chief of Staff to the Secretary
Deputy Chief of Staff to the Secretary

Deputy Secretary
Chief of Staff to the Deputy Secretary
Deputy Deputy Secretary
Principal Associate Deputy Secretary
Associate Deputy Secretary
Deputy Associate Deputy Secretary
Assistant Deputy Secretary

Under Secretary
Chief of Staff to the Under Secretary
Principal Deputy Under Secretary
Deputy Under Secretary
Principal Associate Deputy Under Secretary
Associate Deputy Under Secretary
Principal Assistant Deputy Under Secretary
Assistant Deputy Under Secretary
Associate Under Secretary
Assistant Under Secretary

Assistant Secretary*
Chief of Staff to the Assistant Secretary
Principal Deputy Assistant Secretary
Associate Principal Deputy Assistant Secretary
Deputy Assistant Secretary

Principal Deputy Deputy Assistant Secretary
Deputy Deputy Assistant Secretary
Associate Deputy Assistant Secretary
Assistant Deputy Assistant Secretary
Principal Associate Assistant Secretary
Associate Assistant Secretary
Chief of Staff to the Associate Assistant Secretary
Deputy Associate Assistant Secretary
Assistant Assistant Secretary
Chief of Staff to the Assistant Assistant Secretary
Deputy Assistant Assistant Secretary

Administrator
Chief of Staff to the Administrator
Assistant Chief of Staff to the Administrator
Principal Deputy Administrator
Deputy Administrator
Associate Deputy Administrator
Deputy Associate Deputy Administrator
Assistant Deputy Administrator
Deputy Assistant Deputy Administrator
Associate Administrator
Chief of Staff to the Associate Administrator
Deputy Associate Administrator
Assistant Administrator
Chief of Staff to the Assistant Administrator
Deputy Assistant Administrator
Associate Assistant Administrator

---

*The Assistant Secretary title covers all Executive Level IV titles, including Commissioner, Director, Administrator, Inspector General, General Counsel, and Chief Financial Officer.

Source: Paul C. Light, *Federal Headcounts and the Illusion of Smallness* (Washington, DC: Brookings Institution, 1999).

BOX 12-3

Organization Chart of Government

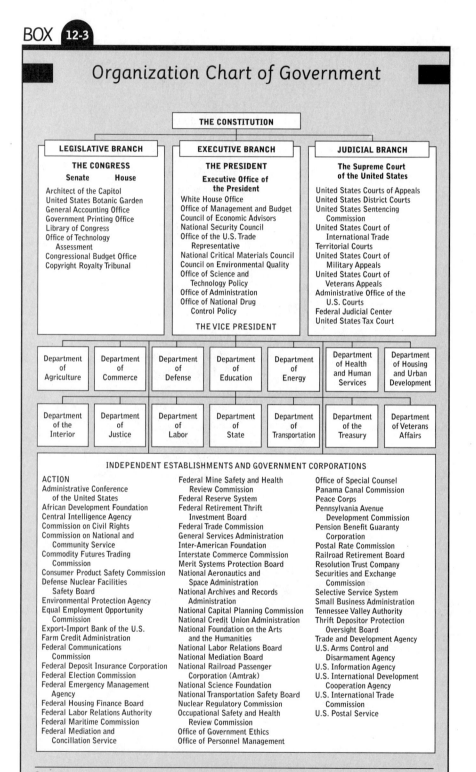

THE CONSTITUTION

LEGISLATIVE BRANCH

THE CONGRESS

Senate   House

Architect of the Capitol
United States Botanic Garden
General Accounting Office
Government Printing Office
Library of Congress
Office of Technology
  Assessment
Congressional Budget Office
Copyright Royalty Tribunal

EXECUTIVE BRANCH

THE PRESIDENT

Executive Office of the President

White House Office
Office of Management and Budget
Council of Economic Advisors
National Security Council
Office of the U.S. Trade
  Representative
National Critical Materials Council
Council on Environmental Quality
Office of Science and
  Technology Policy
Office of Administration
Office of National Drug
  Control Policy

THE VICE PRESIDENT

JUDICIAL BRANCH

The Supreme Court of the United States

United States Courts of Appeals
United States District Courts
United States Sentencing
  Commission
United States Court of
  International Trade
Territorial Courts
United States Court of
  Military Appeals
United States Court of
  Veterans Appeals
Administrative Office of the
  U.S. Courts
Federal Judicial Center
United States Tax Court

Department of Agriculture | Department of Commerce | Department of Defense | Department of Education | Department of Energy | Department of Health and Human Services | Department of Housing and Urban Development

Department of the Interior | Department of Justice | Department of Labor | Department of State | Department of Transportation | Department of the Treasury | Department of Veterans Affairs

---

INDEPENDENT ESTABLISHMENTS AND GOVERNMENT CORPORATIONS

ACTION
Administrative Conference
  of the United States
African Development Foundation
Central Intelligence Agency
Commission on Civil Rights
Commission on National and
  Community Service
Commodity Futures Trading
  Commission
Consumer Product Safety Commission
Defense Nuclear Facilities
  Safety Board
Environmental Protection Agency
Equal Employment Opportunity
  Commission
Export-Import Bank of the U.S.
Farm Credit Administration
Federal Communications
  Commission
Federal Deposit Insurance Corporation
Federal Election Commission
Federal Emergency Management
  Agency
Federal Housing Finance Board
Federal Labor Relations Authority
Federal Maritime Commission
Federal Mediation and
  Conciliation Service

Federal Mine Safety and Health
  Review Commission
Federal Reserve System
Federal Retirement Thrift
  Investment Board
Federal Trade Commission
General Services Administration
Inter-American Foundation
Interstate Commerce Commission
Merit Systems Protection Board
National Aeronautics and
  Space Administration
National Archives and Records
  Administration
National Capital Planning Commission
National Credit Union Administration
National Foundation on the Arts
  and the Humanities
National Labor Relations Board
National Mediation Board
National Railroad Passenger
  Corporation (Amtrak)
National Science Foundation
National Transportation Safety Board
Nuclear Regulatory Commission
Occupational Safety and Health
  Review Commission
Office of Government Ethics
Office of Personnel Management

Office of Special Counsel
Panama Canal Commission
Peace Corps
Pennsylvania Avenue
  Development Commission
Pension Benefit Guaranty
  Corporation
Postal Rate Commission
Railroad Retirement Board
Resolution Trust Company
Securities and Exchange
  Commission
Selective Service System
Small Business Administration
Tennessee Valley Authority
Thrift Depositor Protection
  Oversight Board
Trade and Development Agency
U.S. Arms Control and
  Disarmament Agency
U.S. Information Agency
U.S. International Development
  Cooperation Agency
U.S. International Trade
  Commission
U.S. Postal Service

Source: U.S. Department of Commerce, *Statistical Abstract of the United States* (Washington, DC: U.S. Government Printing Office, 1994), p. 326.

Education, which was created in 1979. It was originally part of what was then the Department of Health, Education, and Welfare, but was split into a separate department as a way to show government support for the nation's teachers.

The greatest expansion in the number of departments occurred between 1945 and 1990: Health, Education, and Welfare (HEW) was created in 1953; Housing and Urban Development (HUD) in 1965; Transportation in 1966; Energy in 1977; and Veterans Affairs (VA) in 1989. In addition, HEW was divided in two in 1979 to create two new departments, Health and Human Services and Education.

These fourteen departments represent two very different approaches to department building. One approach is to use a department to conglomerate, or bring a number of related programs under one broad umbrella. The Department of Transportation was created by combining a number of smaller, independent agencies, including the National Highway Administration, the Federal Aviation Administration, and the Federal Railroad Administration. The Departments of Agriculture, Commerce, and Defense also reflect a conglomerate approach.

The other approach is to use a department to give added visibility to a popular issue such as education, housing, or energy, or to a large group of Americans such as the elderly or laborers. These departments are not conglomerates at all, but highly specialized voices for a specific group of Americans. Not surprisingly, these departments are often closely tied to interest groups. In 1988, for example, veterans' groups successfully pushed Congress to change the Veterans Administration from an independent agency to a cabinet department, Veterans Affairs, as a way to show support for the nation's 10 million military veterans.

Independent Regulatory Commissions.   Size and age are not the only ways to compare units within the federal bureaucracy. Power, or impact on daily life, is also important. Indeed, when Americans complain about bureaucracy being on their backs, they are often talking about the federal bureaucracy's **independent regulatory commissions.**

Yet that is exactly why Congress and the president created the federal government's independent regulatory commissions. All were designed to "get on the backs" of people and corporations, whether to protect consumers (the Consumer Product Safety Commission), regulate stock markets (the Securities and Exchange Commission), oversee federal election laws (the Federal Election Commission), monitor television and radio (the Federal Communications Commission), regulate business (the Federal Trade Commission), control the supply of money (the Federal Reserve Board), or watch over nuclear power plants (Nuclear Regulatory Commission).

The commissions may be small in budget and employees (just $70 million and 1,200 employees for all the independent commissions combined), but their influence over American life is large. Indeed, according to some experts, the chairman of the Federal Reserve Board may be the second most influential person in the nation, second only to the president.[14]

The key difference between commissions and other departments and agencies is the president's appointment power. All independent regulatory commissions are governed by boards or commissions that cannot be removed by the president or Congress without cause, which is defined by law to mean "inefficiency, neglect of duty, or malfeasance in office."

This is not to say that the president and Congress have no authority whatsoever over these agencies. The president appoints board members to vacancies, with Senate confirmation, and Congress has a say over budgets. But once the appointments are made and confirmed, board members are independent.

Independent Agencies.   The word *independent* means at least two things in the federal bureaucracy. When it is linked to the words *regulatory commission,* it means an agency that is independent of presidential control. When it is linked to *agency* or *administration,* a much looser term is created that merely means "standing alone." Whereas independent regulatory commissions do not report to the president, **independent agencies** do.

As a general rule, independent agencies are small federal bureaucracies that serve specific groups of Americans or work on specific problems. Becoming an agency is often the first step toward becoming a department. As noted above, the Department of Veterans Affairs is basically the same organization that once existed as the Veterans Administration. The Department of Transportation was created as an umbrella for the old Federal Aviation Administration, the Federal Railroad Administration, and the Federal Highway Administration.

Independent agencies are usually headed by an administrator, which is the second most senior title in the federal bureaucracy behind secretary/attorney general. There are roughly sixty such agencies today, including the Environmental Protection Agency (EPA), the Central Intelligence Agency (CIA), the National Aeronautics and Space Administration (NASA), the Federal Emergency Management Agency (FEMA), the General Services Administration (GSA), and the Small Business Administration (SBA).

As noted earlier, independent agencies do not have to be small. NASA, for example, has an annual budget of over $11 billion and a workforce of over twenty-three thousand employees, not to mention all the private contractors who help put the space shuttle into orbit. Indeed, NASA's budget puts it ahead of four cabinet departments (Justice, Interior, State, and Commerce).

Moreover, independent agencies can be more important to the president than some cabinet departments. There are times, for example, when the director of the CIA or the administrator of EPA gets a higher place on the president's agenda than the secretary of HUD or Agriculture. And both usually have a seat at the cabinet's conference table. Although being a cabinet secretary certainly conveys some visibility, it is no guarantee of attention from the president or Congress.

It is useful to note that independent agencies are not the only government organizations that call themselves agencies. There are a number of highly visible agencies that actually exist within departments, including the Forest Service (located in the Agriculture Department), the National Park Service (located in the Department of the Interior), the Occupational Safety and Health Administration (located in the Labor Department), and the Census Bureau (in the Commerce Department). What makes these agencies different from the independent agencies described above is that they do not report to the president directly, but through a cabinet secretary.

Government Corporations.   Perhaps the least understood organizations in the federal bureaucracy, **government corporations** are designed to act more like businesses than like traditional government departments and agencies. They are generally given more freedom from the assorted rules that control what agencies do by way of hiring and firing employees, purchasing goods and services, and accounting for spending. And they are most certainly encouraged to make money.[15]

Yet no two government corporations are quite alike. The term is so loosely used that no one knows exactly how many corporations the federal bureaucracy has. What experts do know is that the number is between thirty-one and forty-seven, including the Corporation for Public Broadcasting (which runs PBS television), the U.S. Postal Service, the Tennessee Valley Authority (TVA), the National Railroad Passenger Association (better known as Amtrak), and Americorps (which runs the national service program created by the Clinton administration), along with a host of financial enterprises that make loans of one kind or another. Once again, the fact that these organizations are not departments does not mean they are small or insignificant. The U.S. Postal Service employs almost 800,000 people, making it the second largest organization in the federal bureaucracy.

Employees.   The federal bureaucracy currently employs roughly 1.8 million civil servants, or government employees. (This number does not include those who serve in the armed forces or U.S. Postal Service workers, who are covered by a different personnel system.) Members of the **civil service** are selected on the basis of merit, or qualification for the job, and continue to serve regardless of who is president. To protect against political interference in the execution of the laws, the civil service system is designed so that firing employees is difficult.

The civil service was created in 1883 to address corruption in the spoils system. Recall that Andrew Jackson had created a system in which federal jobs were filled on the basis of political connections. In essence, all federal positions were political. Job seekers had to either know someone or pay someone to get a job. Actual ability to do the work had almost nothing to do with obtaining an appointment. Also recall that the spoils system gave the president's party complete control over almost every government job, from cabinet secretaries all the way down to post office clerks. This political job system became known as *patronage*—patronize, or support, the president's party, and get a job in government.

It was a disappointed job seeker who started the federal bureaucracy down the road toward today's civil service system. Unfortunately for President James Garfield, that job seeker happened to be both disappointed and a good shot. Garfield's assassination prompted Congress to pass the Pendleton Act of 1883, which began a sixty-year effort to cover all federal jobs under the merit principle. The merit principle simply means that jobs are awarded on the basis of ability to do the work, not political connections.

Continuing concerns about merit led Congress to pass "An Act to Prevent Pernicious Political Activities" in 1939 precisely to remove any hint that political loyalties might influence public employees. The act, usually called the Hatch Act in honor of its sponsor, Senator Carl Hatch (D-GA), flatly prohibited career civil servants from taking part in any form of political activity, all the way from running for office down to wearing a campaign button. Employees were free to vote, but any other overt acts were off limits.

Congress repealed the Hatch Act in 1994, giving federal employees the same rights to participate in public life as other Americans. The final vote was anything but unanimous, however. Democrats favored the measure because federal employees tend to favor Democratic candidates; Republicans opposed the measure for the same reason. As such, repeal of the Hatch Act rekindled a long-standing debate about whether Republicans can trust federal employees to faithfully execute the laws when Republicans happen to be in charge of government.

 **in a different light** —— ARE GOVERNMENT ORGANIZATIONS IMMORTAL?

One reason bureaucracy may seem too big and expensive to the average citizen is that bureaucratic organizations so rarely disappear. The Federal Helium Reserve is one example. Using underground caves in Texas to store the volatile lighter-than-air gas, the reserve was created in the 1920s to assure a steady supply of helium for the nation's fleet of blimps. Although the armed services had long ago replaced blimps with airplanes and helicopters and although private sources of helium existed for industrial uses, the reserve stayed in business until 1995.

The Federal Helium Reserve is hardly the only agency to linger on long after its mission was over. Indeed, as political scientist Herbert Kaufman discovered in writing his book *Are Government Organizations Immortal?*, many agencies that long ago lost their reason for being are still alive, in large part because they fight so hard to keep going.[16] "They are not helpless, passive pawns in the game of politics as it affects their lives;" wrote Kaufman, "they are active, energetic, persistent participants."[17]

Presidents quickly find that even the weakest agency has enormous resources available to fight an attack, not the least of which are the presidential appointees who head the agency. "Once aroused, they have a large arsenal of weapons to employ in their agencies' defense," Kaufman wrote about the heads of imperiled agencies. "They cultivate their allies and the mass media. Covertly and openly, they attack and try to embarrass their adversaries. They strike bargains to appease the foes they cannot overcome. If this sounds like warfare, it is—at least a type of warfare, a struggle for organizational existence."[18]

Although not every agency will live forever, Kaufman's research shows that most agencies can expect to live a very long time. Of 175 agencies that had existed in 1923, Kaufman found that 148, or 85 percent, were still alive fifty years later.

Some survivors were barely alive when Kaufman conducted his research, while others had been demoted to a less visible position in the executive branch. Nevertheless, according to Kaufman, "the chances that an organization in the 1923 sample would not only be alive in 1973 but in virtually the same status were quite good; 109 of the original 175 (over 62 percent, or better than three out of five) were in this situation."[19]

Moreover, even as large numbers of old agencies were surviving the test of time, an even larger number of agencies were being born. During the fifty years of Kaufman's study, the federal bureaucracy celebrated the births of 246 new units, an average of five per year. Given these birth and survival rates, it is no surprise that the number of federal agencies would grow dramatically over the decades, creating new access points for interest groups, new opportunities for congressional credit claiming, and new jobs for federal employees.

The birth and survival rates also raise troubling questions about the ultimate size of the federal bureaucracy. If current trends hold, for example, the next century will witness the creation of over five hundred new units. These new units will likely have important new duties, but there may be some limit to how many organizations the president can supervise without losing all hope of democratic accountability.

How Big Is the Federal Bureaucracy?

Unlike the Founders, Americans have plenty to say about the federal bureaucracy. By the mid-1990s, roughly 70 percent of Americans said that almost anything run by the federal bureaucracy is bound to be inefficient and wasteful,[20] that the federal bureaucracy controlled too much of their daily lives and was much too large and powerful, that dealing with a federal agency was often not worth the trouble, and that big bureaucracy in general had become the biggest threat to the country's future.[21] Little wonder that public administration scholar Charles Goodsell describes bureaucracy as a great "hate object."[22]

Yet Americans want more of virtually everything the federal bureaucracy delivers—from new roads to student loans, from cleaner air to safe food and drugs. Americans will probably never come to love the Internal Revenue Service agent who collects their taxes, but most report high levels of satisfaction whenever they meet the federal bureaucracy face to face. And they appear to want more of virtually everything government does, even if it costs money. Ask Americans if they support a constitutional amendment requiring the federal government to balance its budget, and overwhelming numbers of them will say yes. Ask them if they support the amendment if it means cutting popular programs such as Social Security, and almost half will change their minds and vote no.[23] Americans want a government that costs less, yet delivers more of everything.

One of the reasons Americans are so confused about the federal bureaucracy is that it is both big and small at the same time. It is most certainly not the largest government bureaucracy in the world, for example. The budgets of all

Food Stamps are part of a welfare program that helps poor people. Americans vastly overestimate how much money the federal government spends on welfare. They also overestimate the number of minorities on welfare. The majority of welfare recipients are white.

American governments (federal, state, and local) add up to a total equal to just over 35 percent of gross domestic product (GDP), which is a measure of total economic activity. That is less than Sweden, Denmark, Belgium, France, Norway, and Italy, each of which spends over 50 percent of its GDP on government; less than West Germany, Canada, and Britain, each of which spends over 40 percent; and only slightly above Japan (33 percent).[24]

At the same time, the federal bureaucracy contains some of the biggest "companies" in the United States. The Department of Defense employs more people than Sears, IBM, and the Ford Motor Company combined, while the Department of Health and Human Services spends more money in a year than General Motors, Exxon, and General Electric earn combined. The Department of the Treasury alone pushes more money out each year than IBM takes in.[25]

Beyond comparing the federal bureaucracy to other nations and companies, there are two other ways to evaluate how big the federal government is. One is to ask whether the government is growing, which can create the perception that it is somehow getting too big. The other is to ask where government is spending its money, which can create the perception that it is not addressing the right priorities or is headed in the wrong direction.

Counting Heads.   Compared to the 1940s, the federal bureaucracy is not growing very fast at all. Indeed, the total number of federal employees just about stopped growing in the 1950s. The number has grown by a few hundred thousand here and there over the years, but it is barely larger than it was when Republicans held Congress and the White House in the early 1950s. Further, it is scheduled to lose almost 275,000 employees by 1999, dropping below 2 million civilian employees for the first time in three decades. (See Box 12–4 for a chart on the growth in federal employment and budget.)

State and local government is where bureaucracy is growing the fastest. In the 1940s, the total of state and local employees was roughly 3 million—teachers, police and firefighters, hospital workers, and prison guards (most of America's 1 million prisoners are in state and local jails). By 1998, there were over 16 million state and local employees, a growth rate of almost 500 percent. The total number of state employees grew by almost 900 percent; county employees by almost 700 percent, school district employees by 400 percent, and city employees by 300 percent. As noted in Chapter 3, state and local employees deliver most of the services that keep the country moving, from cleaning the streets to teaching the children.

The specific numbers are far less important than the trend: the number of state and local employees has been growing steadily since the 1940s, while the federal workforce has remained roughly level since the early 1950s. Indeed, compared to total U.S. population, the federal bureaucracy has actually gotten much

BOX 12-4

Growth Trends in the Size of the Federal Bureaucracy

Year	Employment (in thousands)	Budget (in billions of 1987 dollars)	Budget as a Percent of GDP
1940	699	$ 96.8	9.9%
1945*	3,370	812.6	43.7
1950	1,439	241.4	16.0
1955	1,860	380.0	17.8
1960	1,808	392.1	18.3
1965	1,901	446.1	17.6
1970	2,203	596.1	19.9
1975	2,149	698.5	22.0
1980	2,161	832.1	22.3
1985	2,252	1,001.4	23.9
1990	2,250	1,110.4	22.9
1995	2,018	1,168.1	21.9
1998	1,830	1,206.2	21.2

*The figures for 1945 were high because of World War II; fighting a world war is an extraordinarily expensive proposition.

Source: United States Office of Management and Budget, *Budget of the U.S. Government, Fiscal Year 1998, Historical Tables* (Washington, DC: U.S. Government Printing Office, 1998); 1998 figures are estimated.

smaller. In 1950, for example, there was one federal employee for every fifty Americans; by 1990, there was one for every eighty. In contrast, there was one state or local employee for every forty Americans in 1950; by 1990, there was one for every sixteen.

Changes in how the federal bureaucracy delivers programs may have been responsible for much of the growth in state and local employment, however. One way the federal bureaucracy has managed to stay slim is by pushing much of the administrative load downward.[26]

Counting Dollars.   The federal government is hardly about to shrink into nothingness. The number of employees may be down, but the budget is way up. The increase is particularly striking looking back to the 1930s. Viewed as a percentage of GDP, the federal budget has more than doubled since then. Since 1975, however, overall federal spending in dollars has almost doubled, rising fastest during the Reagan administration. (Refer to Box 12–4 for the trends in spending.)

More important, a considerable share of the federal budget goes not to new programs but to **uncontrollable spending**—defined as programs (1) that Congress and the president have been unwilling to cut and (2) that rise in cost nearly automatically. Although candidates for federal office often promise they will go to Washington and balance the budget, the share of the federal pie they can cut in any given year is quite small (see Box 12–5 for the figures). Even programs such as defense, which is technically subject to yearly control, may be almost impossible to cut without controversy, leaving even less room for reducing the budget.

The largest share of uncontrollable spending comes from Social Security and Medicare, which are guaranteed to any American who has paid taxes into the program for enough years. The aging of the American population means that more older people than ever will qualify for Social Security and Medicare—hence, uncontrollable spending will most certainly rise over the next two decades.

Another, much smaller share of the uncontrollable budget involves welfare for the poor, which is linked to economic performance. More unemployment, for example, means more federal unemployment insurance; more poverty means more food stamps, job training, Temporary Assistance to Needy Families, and other income support programs. It is important to note, however, that welfare for the poor is not the only welfare in the federal budget. American business receives a substantial amount of welfare, too. (See Box 12–6 for a sampling of "corporate welfare" programs.)

What makes these uncontrollable programs similar is that they guarantee benefits to anyone eligible; hence, these programs are often called **entitlements.** All told, these automatic programs cost the federal government $858 billion in 1997–1998, accounting for over half of the federal government's $1.6 trillion budget.

The uncontrollable budget is not growing just because more people are eligible for entitlements, however. Many of these entitlements are subject to **indexing**—that is, they grow automatically with inflation, regardless of how the economy is doing. Indexing affects a growing list of federal programs, again leaving Congress and the president with little control over year-to-year increases. The

BOX **12-5**

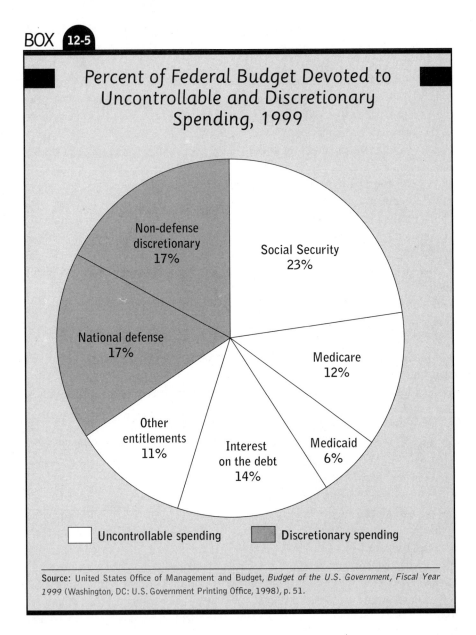

Percent of Federal Budget Devoted to Uncontrollable and Discretionary Spending, 1999

Non-defense discretionary 17%

Social Security 23%

National defense 17%

Medicare 12%

Other entitlements 11%

Interest on the debt 14%

Medicaid 6%

☐ Uncontrollable spending   ▨ Discretionary spending

Source: United States Office of Management and Budget, *Budget of the U.S. Government, Fiscal Year 1999* (Washington, DC: U.S. Government Printing Office, 1998), p. 51.

number of programs indexed to automatic cost of living adjustments, or COLAs, grew from seventeen in 1966 to almost one hundred by 1998.[27]

Ironically, Congress originally started indexing programs as a way to stop itself from spending even more. The Social Security program was indexed to rise with inflation in the early 1970s mostly to stop Congress from giving huge in-

BOX **12-6**

A Sampling of Corporate Welfare Programs in the Federal Budget

American drug manufacturers do not have to pay taxes on their operations in Puerto Rico and other U.S. territories. Cost: $4 billion a year in lost tax revenue.

Airlines and owners of private planes do not pay for the costs of running the Federal Aviation Administration, including air traffic control, even though they make substantial profits from using the system. Cost: $2 billion a year.

The Agriculture Department, which runs the U.S. forest system, builds roads primarily to help private logging companies remove timber from the forests. Cost: $150 million a year.

The federal government artificially raises the cost of sugar to help the domestic sugar industry. Cost to consumers: $300 million a year in higher sugar prices.

Mining companies are allowed to extract minerals from U.S. government lands free of charge. Cost: $200 million a year in lost revenues.

Source: Kirk Victor, "Takin' on the Bacon," *National Journal,* May 16, 1995, p. 1084.

creases in benefits during election years, and a host of other programs were soon indexed, too.

Together, entitlements and indexing have moved a steadily increasing share of the federal budget out of the hands of elected officials and subjected it to unforeseen events. In the early 1960s, uncontrollable spending accounted for less than thirty cents of every federal dollar spent. There was no Medicare program back then, no automatic COLA for Social Security, no automatic increase for veterans' benefits. By 1998, in part because of changes in these three programs, the number had increased to sixty-six cents. Politicians who want to balance the federal budget have a much smaller piece of the pie with which to work. Most of the pie is already divvied up.

The fastest-growing category of uncontrollable spending is neither an entitlement nor an indexed program, however. It is interest on the federal debt. Just like individual citizens, the federal bureaucracy must pay for the money it borrows. People who buy U.S. Treasury bonds, which cover the federal debt, must be paid interest. In the early 1960s, interest on the debt weighed in at $7 billion, or less than 7 percent of the entire federal budget. By 1998, interest was up to almost $244 billion a year, or 14 percent of the budget.[28] Much of the increase came in the 1980s, when federal taxes went down and defense spending went up. The shortfall was covered by borrowing, and the interest on that debt has to be paid.

Whether uncontrollable or not, at least this spending is visible to the public. A large part of the budget is invisible to most Americans. By allowing taxpayers to deduct certain items from their annual income tax, the federal bureaucracy loses revenue, thereby "spending" money it would otherwise have had. These **tax expenditures,** as economists label this little-noticed spending, are just as important a tool of public policy as direct expenditures. In 1998 alone, tax expenditures accounted for almost $500 billion in income taxes *not* paid, which, with $1.6 trillion in direct spending, made the total federal budget $2.1 trillion. The tax expenditures included deductions for home mortgage interest ($75 billion), state and local taxes ($33 billion), charitable contributions ($25 billion), and employer contributions to employee pension funds ($72 billion).[29]

The Shadow of Government

The fact that the number of federal employees has fallen over the past five years does not mean that the federal workforce is actually smaller. The people who work for federal departments and agencies under contracts and grants may not get their checks directly from Uncle Sam, but they deliver services for the federal government nonetheless. This **shadow government**, as it is called, consists of nearly 13 million nonfederal employees who make their living doing jobs for the federal government, including 2.5 million who work for colleges and universities (including some of the readers of this book, no doubt) under research grants from the National Science Foundation, the National Institutes of Health, and a host of other federal agencies that cover the costs of basic research, and 4 million who work for state and local governments under the mandates discussed in Chapter 3.[30]

Well over half the shadow government consists of Americans who work for private firms that supply goods or services to the federal government under contracts. The number includes over 1.5 million Americans who build things for government, whether tanks, ships, and airplanes for the Department of Defense, computers for the Department of Transportation, or furniture for the General Services Administration. The number also includes nearly 4 million Americans who provide services for the federal government, whether programming computers for the Social Security Administration, running nuclear weapons plants for the Department of Energy, or operating prisons for the Department of Justice.

Roughly one out of every six Americans currently works for a private firm that receives federal contracts. Roughly two-thirds of those contracts came from the Department of Defense, which accounted for over $120 billion in 1997, and roughly two-thirds of those defense dollars went to just five firms: Lockheed-Martin (airplanes), McDonnell Douglas (airplanes), Northrup Grumann (airplanes), General Motors (tanks and trucks), and Raytheon (weapons systems).

At some point, the government may become so dependent on contractors to fullfill its promises that it has no choice but to spend the money, even if it no longer sees a need for the goods or services. In this regard, outgoing president Dwight Eisenhower's 1961 farewell address is as relevant today as when it was delivered. "This conjunction of an immense military establishment and a large arms industry," as Eisenhower described the **military-industrial complex,** "is new in the American experience. The total influence—economic, political, even spiritual—is felt in every city, every State house, every office of the Federal Government. We recognize the imperative need for this development. Yet we must not fail to comprehend its grave implications. Our toil, resources and livelihood are all involved. So is the very structure of our society."

Eisenhower was particularly worried that government contracts would hurt America's colleges and universities:

> Today, the solitary inventor, tinkering in his shop, has been overshadowed by task forces of scientists in laboratories and testing fields. In the same fashion, the free university, historically the fountainhead of free ideas and scientific discovery, has experienced a revolution in the conduct of research. Partly because of the huge costs involved, a government contract becomes virtually a substitute for intellectual curiosity. For every old black board there are now hundreds of electronic computers. The prospect of domination of the nation's scholars by Federal employment, project allocations, and the power of money is ever present—and is gravely to be regarded. Yet, in holding scientific research and discovery in respect as we should, we must also be alert to the equal and opposite danger that public policy could itself become the captive of a scientific-technological elite.[31]

Although the military-industrial complex has shrunk since the end of the Cold War, defense contractors continue to lobby government to spend more on tanks, ships, and airplanes. Defense contractors gave over $15 million to congressional candidates in 1996, for example, and spent over $38 million lobbying Congress in the first six months of 1997 alone.

At the same time, the effort to keep total federal employment as small as possible is pushing more and more federal jobs into the private sector. The last person an astronaut sees before lifting off into orbit is an employee of Rockwell, Inc., not NASA, while the first person a frightened community meets after a toxic waste spill works for ICF-Kaiser, Inc., not the Environmental Protection Agency. Congress and the president seem to want a government that only looks smaller, but delivers more.

in a different light —— THE BUREAUCRACY'S PERFORMANCE GAP

A 1997 survey of Americans' trust in government yielded good news and bad for the federal bureaucracy. The good news was that Americans were mostly favorable toward federal employees and their departments and agencies. Roughly 70 percent of the respondents interviewed by The Pew Research Center for The People & The Press had a favorable opinion of government workers in general, and of civil servants in particular. When asked whom they trusted more to do the right thing—politicians who lead the federal government or the civil service employees who run departments and agencies—the civil servants won hands down, by nearly five to one.

Moreover, most Americans had good things to say about the departments and agencies that deliver the goods. As Box 12–7 shows, they rated most federal departments and agencies well above mediocre. The much maligned U.S. Postal Service came in at the top of the favorability ratings at 89 percent, prompting the Postmaster General to run nationwide ads congratulating his workforce on its performance. The National Park Service came in second at 85 percent, the Centers for Disease Control at 79 percent, Defense at 76 percent, and the Food and Drug Administration at 75 percent.

Compared to ratings taken at the height of the Reagan war on waste in 1987, all but four of the nineteen agencies rated in the Pew survey moved up. Defense was the biggest gainer of all, rising 19 points over the ten years. Much of the gain reflected renewed public confidence following a series of military victories during the late 1980s and early 1990s, most notably the 100-hour Gulf War.

The bad news revealed by the survey is that most Americans do not believe the federal government is doing a very good job on the issues they care about most. Contradictory though it may sound, Americans love their bureaucracies even as they doubt government's ability to produce results.

Asked how well the federal government is running its programs, only one-fourth of Americans said excellent or good, one-half said only fair, and one-fifth said poor. Asked whether criticism of government performance is justified, most said it was. Only one-quarter said that government in general was doing an excellent or good job of running its programs; the rest rated performance as only fair or poor.

BOX 12-7

Ratings of Selected Federal Departments and Agencies (percentage of respondents who gave a favorable rating)

Agency	1987	1997
Postal Service	76%	89%
Park Service	80	85
Centers for Disease Control	—	79
Department of Defense	57	76
Food and Drug Administration	74	75
National Aeronautics and Space Administration	66	73
Federal Aviation Administration	53	70
Environmental Protection Agency	62	69
Department of Agriculture	60	68
Federal Bureau of Investigation	78	67
Social Security Administration	—	62
Department of Education	60	61
Department of Veterans Affairs/Veterans Administration	68*	59
Department of Commerce	57	58
Department of Justice	53	56
Federal Trade Commission	56	63
Department of Housing and Urban Development	49	51
Central Intelligence Agency	52	51
Internal Revenue Service	49	38

*The Department of Veterans Affairs was created in 1988.

Source: The Pew Research Center for The People & The Press, *Deconstructing Distrust: How Americans View Government* (Washington, DC: Pew Research Center, 1998), p. 16.

BOX **12-8**

Performance and Blame

	Evaluation of Government Performance		Explanation for Fair or Poor Performance	
	Excellent or Good	Only Fair or Poor	Government's Fault	Issue too Difficult
Ensuring safe food and drugs	58%	41%	46%	49%
Conserving natural resources	34	64	51	44
Providing for the elderly	26	72	49	44
Setting academic standards	23	74	49	44
Ensuring affordable health care	18	80	45	49
Ensuring everyone can afford college	18	79	37	56
Reducing poverty	14	84	33	61
Reducing juvenile delinquency	11	85	25	69

Source: The Pew Research Center for The People & The Press, *Deconstructing Distrust: How Americans View Government* (Washington, DC: Pew Research Center, 1998), p. 33.

Finally, asked to consider everything they get from the federal government, over half said they were paying more than their fair share in taxes.

Americans were mostly underwhelmed with the federal government's actual performance in eight key areas tested by the Pew Research Center. As Box 12–8 shows, only one of these eight issues, ensuring that food and medicines are safe, earned a majority of "excellent/good" responses. The other seven fell well short, with the government's efforts at reducing poverty and juvenile delinquency earning less than 15 percent each.

Respondents split the blame when asked why the federal government was doing only a fair or poor job on most of the issues. Roughly half said the lackluster performance was government's fault, while the other half said the issue was just too difficult or too complicated to solve. There were three areas where a majority of respondents said good performance was beyond government's reach: ensuring an affordable college education, reducing poverty, and reducing juvenile delinquency. Juvenile delinquency was seen as the most difficult issue of all. Although only 11 percent of the Pew respondents said government was doing an excellent or good job on the issue, almost 70 percent of the critics said the issue was simply too difficult to solve.

Alongside these doubts about government performance, respondents also seemed to believe that government at all levels has the wrong priorities. Three-quarters said the government should give a high priority to ensuring access to affordable health care, for example, but only 15 percent said government had actually done so; 72 percent said the government should give a high priority to providing the elderly a decent standard of living, but only 17 percent said government had done so; and 72 percent said the government should give a high priority to conserving natural resources, but only 24 percent said the government had done so.

It is performance, not the priority gap, that has the most impact on public trust in government. Statistically, the performance ratings are almost seven times more powerful in explaining the distrust than dissatisfaction with government's priorities. Americans can disagree on the priorities, it seems, but not on the need for government to perform well on whatever priorities it sets. Performance does count.

Given the relatively low ratings of performance discussed above, it is not surprising that the public's confidence in Washington's ability to do the right thing all or most of the time was just 38 percent in 1997, up from a modern low of just 21 percent in 1992 but far from the modern high of 76 percent in 1964. If this is as good as confidence gets at the end of five years of exceptional economic performance, what will happen to that confidence once the good times pass?

CONTROLLING THE BUREAUCRACY

Every president enters office promising to make the federal bureaucracy work better. Indeed, Jimmy Carter, Ronald Reagan, and Bill Clinton all made bureaucratic reform a central part of their presidential campaigns. Carter promised to create a government as good as the American people; Reagan promised a war on waste; Clinton promised to reinvent government.

Yet almost all presidents leave office frustrated by their lack of success. As political scientist James Q. Wilson states, "Almost every president in modern times has admitted to his advisors, if he has not shouted from the rooftops, that he rued the day a 'disappointed office seeker' killed President Garfield, thereby energizing the civil-service reform movement. Presidents see much of the bureaucracy as their natural enemy and always are searching for ways to bring it to heel."[32]

Presidents are not the only ones who want to control the bureaucracy. Congress, too, clearly worries about making bureaucracy work better. Together, the two branches have four basic tools of control: (1) laws and executive orders, (2) the budget, (3) presidential appointees, and (4) oversight by Congress and presidential agencies.

Laws and Executive Orders

The first way to control bureaucracy is to tell it precisely what to do through laws of one kind or another. Congress and the president have passed dozens of statutes to do just that over the years. All told, at least 141 major management bills have been passed since 1946.[33] These bills have tried just about every approach known for improving the federal bureaucracy.

In addition to laws, presidents can control the federal bureaucracy through **executive orders.** An executive order carries the same force as a federal law except that it can apply only to the executive branch and its employees. Although an order can always be repealed by a future president, it does give the president an important tool for making immediate changes in bureaucracy. Harry Truman used an executive order to integrate the armed services in the late 1940s; prior to his order, African American and white soldiers were kept separate.[34]

Executive orders can also give the president an opportunity to send important messages to the bureaucracy and the nation. On his first day in office, Clinton issued four executive orders: (1) lifting the restrictions on abortion counseling at federally financed clinics, restoring the right to perform abortions at American military hospitals overseas, and allowing the use of fetal tissue in federally sponsored research; (2) ending restrictions on American financial aid to United Nations family planning and population control programs; (3) imposing new ethics guidelines that barred senior government officials from lobbying the federal agency in which they work for five years after leaving the federal bureaucracy; and (4) abolishing a Bush administration program that gave businesses a way to obtain exemptions from federal regulations. He also used an executive order several weeks later to lift the ban on gays and lesbians in the military.

The Federal Budget

The federal budget is generally viewed as the most powerful tool presidents have for controlling the bureaucracy. In an era of nearly constant budget cutting, money talks and the bureaucracy listens. The process for setting budget priorities is controlled from the Office of Management and Budget (OMB), which is headed by a highly trusted presidential aide, and involves an eighteen-month process of negotiation between the bureaucracy and the White House.

The first nine months of the process occur in the presidency. It starts in March, when OMB prepares its general forecast of future revenues and spending, continues through the spring as OMB asks departments and agencies for their plans, and comes to a head in the summer, when OMB provides the general estimates that guide the budget. These estimates form the basis for a series of hearings for each department and agency. Although each unit gets to defend its estimates and make its case for any increases, it is not clear whether the hearings make any difference whatsoever in the final decisions OMB makes in early fall.

Once the departments and agencies get their final budget "marks," or specific targets, they redo their estimates and resubmit their budget requests. They can appeal any cuts to the president, but they almost always lose. The final budget requests are merged into a massive document that becomes the draft *Budget of the United States* for the fiscal year, which starts on October 1 and ends the following September 30. (The fiscal year, which is merely a term that covers the twelve months of actual spending, is numbered by the year in which it ends—thus, fiscal year 1998 ended on September 30, 1998.) By law, the president is required to submit a budget plan to Congress at the beginning of each calendar year.

The budget process does not end with the presentation of the president's budget plan. The nine-month congressional phase of the process begins in February, when the Congressional Budget Office (CBO) offers its analysis of the president's budget, and continues when the House and Senate Budget Committees hold hearings. It moves forward in March with the **budget resolution**, which sets broad revenue and spending targets. The resolution also contains "reconciliation instructions" designed to force Congress to raise revenues or cut spending to make the budget totals add up to the targets.

In theory, the budget process should keep the authorization, appropriations, and revenue committees from overspending or undertaxing. Indeed, the desire for greater coordination is exactly why Congress designed a new budget process in 1974. Before the Budget and Impoundment Control Act, there had

A budget stalemate between Congress and the president in 1995 caused the closing of the federal government, including all national parks.

been no coordination across the assorted committees that influence what the federal bureaucracy spends. Under the new budget process, or so its authors hoped, the entire Congress would be working toward the same targets, creating a greater likelihood that authorizing and appropriations committees would not spend more money than the revenue committees would raise.

In reality, the process has rarely worked as intended. The appropriations process is almost never completed early enough in the legislative year to come under the discipline of reconciliation. In most years, the thirteen appropriations bills required to keep government running are not completed until the very last days of the session, if then.

Congress has tried other ways to close the gap between spending and revenues, most recently enacting the Gramm-Rudman-Hollings budget process in 1985, so named for its three authors, Phil Gramm (R-TX), Warren Rudman

(R-NH), and Ernest Hollings (D-SC), which promised automatic cuts if Congress did not meet unbendable targets for cutting the deficit. But the "unbendable" targets always seem to get bent. Even a balanced budget amendment to the Constitution would not necessarily discipline the system. Most of the proposals for an amendment still give Congress and the president just enough room to continue the deficit spending if the economy turns sour.

Presidents won a small and ultimately fleeting measure of increased influence over the budget in 1996, when the new Republican congressional majority passed the line item veto. Unlike the constitutional veto, which requires the president to either sign or veto a bill in its entirety, the new veto gave the president limited authority to strike specific spending categories from appropriation bills. Recall from Chapter 2 that the Supreme Court declared the line item veto unconstitutional in 1998, arguing that Congress had delegated its legislative power to the president in clear violation of Article I.

Presidential Appointees

Presidential appointees are more than just the leaders of bureaucracy. They are also key controllers of what agencies do. They push the president's orders downward into the federal bureaucracy, oversee the execution of the laws, and represent their departments and agencies on Capitol Hill.

Presidents usually start looking for these appointees long before the election occurs, and may even promise some of the key jobs in exchange for political support. Once the president is in office, the search process is led by the White House, where almost every appointee must be cleared, or approved, by the senior staff. Job seekers can expect to be asked their party identification and how they voted in the election, and are given extra points if they worked in or gave money to the campaign.

There is no guarantee, however, that presidential appointees will do exactly what the president wants. Some appointees represent strong interest groups (farmers, veterans, teachers, oil companies, big business) whose priorities are different from the president's; others are quickly "captured," as the White House calls it, by their departments, becoming strong advocates for whatever the department wants; and still others, to get a job, simply mislead the president as to what they believe.

As a result, presidents have become increasingly cautious about whom they appoint to the top jobs. It would not be appropriate to ask Supreme Court nominees for advance commitments on rulings regarding abortion and other issues that might come before the Court, but presidents are free to impose such "litmus tests" of loyalty on their own appointees. Richard Nixon and Ronald

Reagan, for example, both tried to put their own ideological stamp on the bureaucracy, and no one was to be appointed who did not pass muster as a true conservative.[35]

Beyond appointing their own people to key administration posts, presidents can also try to isolate or remove career civil servants who get in the way. The Nixon administration, for example, used at least four strategies for moving what it saw as disloyal career officers out of the way. These unethical strategies were uncovered during the congressional investigations of the Watergate scandal.[36]

The first strategy was to remove the offending employee from government completely, whether through what the Nixon staff called the *frontal assault* ("You simply call an individual in and tell him he is no longer wanted," a secret White House handbook recommended), the *transfer technique* ("By carefully researching the background of the proposed employee-victim, one can always establish that geographical part of the country and/or organizational unit to which the employee would rather resign than obey and accept transfer orders"), or the *special assignment technique (the traveling salesman)* ("especially useful for the family man and those who do not enjoy traveling").

The second strategy was to build a wall of loyalists around the offending executive. By creating new layers of management both above and below the problem officer, "You have thus layered into the organization into key positions your own people, still isolating your roadblocks into powerless makeshift positions. In all likelihood they will probably end up resigning out of disgust or boredom."[37]

The third strategy was to strip an agency of its duties, rendering the unit unable to do much of anything considered offensive. The Nixon team argued that the technique was expensive (creating a new agency is no small cost), but was essential for isolating and bypassing "an entire organization [that becomes] so hopeless that there is an immediate desire to deal with nobody in the organization at all."[38]

The final strategy, called "wholesale isolation and disposition of undesirable employee-victims," was to draw disloyal employees to a glamorous new unit. Once safely transferred into the new unit, these employees would find that they had jobs of no real consequence. This technique was "designed to provide a single barrel into which you can dump a large number of widely located bad apples."[39]

Today's presidents do not have to use such extreme and clearly unethical tactics. The Senior Executive Service (SES), for example, was created in 1978 precisely to give presidents more freedom to move career executives from post to post. The Reagan administration used this and other tools to control the bureaucracy in a host of controversial areas: the Environmental Protection Agency reduced its hazardous waste inspections; the Food and Drug Administration reduced its seizures of unsafe products; the Office of Surface Mining reduced its efforts to stop "outlaw" mining companies from damaging the earth.[40]

Oversight

Congress and the president spend a great deal of energy monitoring the federal bureaucracy. The hope is that **oversight,** or the process of monitoring day-to-day activities, will somehow encourage agencies to perform better or, at the very least, deter them from worse performance.

Presidents have a number of tools for keeping a watchful eye: presidential appointees, the White House staff, even blue-ribbon commissions. However, they tend to use OMB for most routine oversight. Departments and agencies must get OMB approval before sending any testimony to Congress, collecting any survey information from the public, or imposing any new paperwork burdens on the private sector. They must also get OMB approval before sending any legislation to Congress. Under this **central clearance** system, OMB forwards legislation to Congress under three categories: "in accordance" with the president's program (reserved for the president's top priorities), "consistent with" the president's program (indicating the president's second-tier priorities), or "no objection." If the president has an objection, OMB simply does not forward the legislation to Congress. OMB also conducts oversight as it assembles the president's budget plan.

Congress also has a number of tools for oversight, not the least of which are the individual members of Congress themselves, who are free to ask agencies for detailed information on just about any issue. Members and committees are also free to ask the General Accounting Office to conduct a study or investigation of a particular program. The agency also undertakes oversight work on its own. Under the direction of the comptroller general, the GAO and its five thousand employees produce hundreds of reports each year, on everything from how new weapons systems operate to the effectiveness of environmental protection. The comptroller general is appointed by the president but serves for a fixed term of fifteen years to protect the agency from political interference.

Congress uses these and other sources of information as a basis for committee and subcommittee hearings on specific agencies or programs. Today, Congress holds more oversight hearings than ever before. In the 1960s, for example, both chambers held a total of 157 days of oversight hearings; by the early 1980s, the number had more than tripled, to 587 days. The greatest increase occurred in the 1970s, fueled in part by the increasing number of legislative staff and in part by the growing independence of individual members.[41]

Together, Congress and the president conduct two basic types of oversight. One is what can be called "police patrol" oversight, in which the two branches watch the bureaucracy through a routine pattern. They read key reports, watch the budget, and generally pay attention to how the departments and agencies are running. If they happen to see a "crime" in progress, all the better. But the general goal of the patrol is to deter problems before they arise. The other can be called "fire alarm" oversight, in which the two branches wait for citizens, interest groups, or the press to find a major problem and pull the alarm. The media play a particularly important role in such oversight, often uncovering a scandal before a routine "police patrol" can spot it.[42]

 **in a different light** ——— REINVENTING GOVERNMENT

Although every administration since 1932 has campaigned for better government, none of the efforts was more visible than the "reinventing government" campaign launched in 1993. Led by Vice President Al Gore, the effort promised a new era of high performance. "Washington is filled with organizations designed for an environment that no longer exists," Gore's first report to the president stated, "bureaucracies so big and wasteful they can no longer serve the American people."[43]

Gore proposed four ways to make the federal bureaucracy work better. First, he wanted the federal bureaucracy to cut most red tape and rules by half. His notion was that federal employees spend far too much time filling out paperwork, and not enough time doing their jobs: the Defense Department spends more money on monitoring employee travel than on the travel itself. (For an example of a needlessly complex rule, see Box 12–9.)

Second, Gore wanted departments and agencies to establish customer service standards against which to measure their performance. The Social Security Administration, for example, promised to answer its 800-number telephone lines faster; the Internal Revenue Service promised to be more courteous to taxpayers. Gore's hope was that federal bureaucrats would start thinking of citizens as customers, just as private companies do.

Third, Gore wanted the federal bureaucracy to give its frontline employees more freedom to solve customer problems. (Frontline employees are the ones who actually deliver the basic services of government: the air traffic controllers, VA hospital nurses, forest rangers, Social Security claims representatives.) Gore argued that the bureaucracy's midlevel managers were spending too much time getting in the way and proposed a deep cut in the number of midlevel jobs.

Finally, Gore wanted the federal bureaucracy to spend less money on wasteful

BOX 12-9

Making Brownies at the Department of Defense

Excerpts from the 22-page Defense Department rule governing fudge brownies:

The texture of the brownie shall be firm but not hard.

Pour batter into a pan at a rate that will yield uncoated brownies which, when cut such as to meet the dimension requirements specified in regulation 3.4(f), will weigh approximately 35 grams each.

The dimensions of the coated brownie shall not exceed $3\frac{1}{2}$ inches by $2\frac{1}{2}$ inches by $\frac{5}{8}$ inch.

Shelled walnut pieces shall be of the small piece size classification, shall be of a light color, and shall be U.S. No. 1 of the U.S. Standards for Shelled English Walnuts. A minimum of 90 percent, by weight, of the pieces shall pass through a $\frac{4}{16}$-inch-diameter round-hole screen and not more than 1 percent, by weight, shall pass through a $\frac{2}{16}$-inch-diameter round-hole screen.

Source: John Kohut, *Stupid Government Tricks* (New York: Plume, 1995), pp. 4–6.

programs. He proposed over $100 billion in budget cuts, including a reduction of nearly 275,000 federal jobs and cuts in dozens of popular programs.

Gore campaigned hard for implementation of his agenda for reinventing government. He even appeared on David Letterman's TV show to break a government-issue ashtray as an example of a silly federal rule. Although Congress did adopt the federal job cut and made important changes in how departments and agencies bought products such as office supplies and computers, it was much less favorable toward giving federal employees more freedom to do their jobs. Congress worried that such freedom would make the bureaucracy even less accountable to the people and rejected many of Gore's recommendations for cutting popular programs.

The key problem in reinventing government is that Congress and the president often disagree about how to make bureaucracy better. Presidents tend to want more freedom to direct the bureaucracy, while Congress tends to want tighter rules. Both might agree that agencies should become more customer friendly, but may disagree sharply on just who the customers are and which ones come first. Because

Vice President Al Gore appears on *The Late Show with David Letterman* to promote his campaign for reinventing government. Gore smashed a government ashtray to illustrate the needless rules required to purchase government supplies. Under federal rules, an ashtray must shatter into a fixed number of pieces when smashed with a hammer and chisel.

Congress relies on the bureaucracy to do casework for constituents, it is extremely sensitive about any changes that might weaken its place as the government's most important customer.

MAINTAINING THE BALANCE

There are two ways in which the federal bureaucracy can undermine the delicate balance between a government strong enough to protect the nation and one not so strong as to threaten liberty. First, the bureaucracy can become so large and cumbersome that it cannot act quickly even when Congress and the president give it an unambiguous order. Although federal employment has remained just about steady since the 1950s, the bureaucracy's budget has increased dramatically. By using private contractors, grantees, and state and local governments to accomplish much of its work, the federal bureaucracy has become a large enterprise indeed. It may look smaller, but it delivers much more today than it did even two decades ago.

Second, the bureaucracy can also become so overburdened with new laws and ambiguous tasks that federal bureaucrats must decide which laws to enforce and which ones to ignore. Given a vague law to execute, the federal bureaucracy may have little choice but to invent its own interpretations of just what Congress and the president actually intended.

Concerns about both of these threats to the delicate balance have led to a number of reforms over the years, including representative bureaucracy and Gore's reinventing government campaign. Such efforts certainly reduce the chances that bureaucracy will become a threat to liberty, but they ultimately depend on a civil service that has the talent and commitment to faithfully execute the laws. And that means making sure that government continues to employ its share of America's best and brightest young people.

Recent surveys suggest that young Americans are less and less interested in working for government. Although nearly 70 percent of the 18–29 year olds interviewed in the 1997 survey of trust in government discussed earlier in this chapter said government is a good place for somebody else to start their career, only 27 percent said that government was a good place for them.[44] America's best and brightest simply do not believe that government in general, and the federal bureaucracy in particular, can provide the kind of careers they want.

The lack of interest is not about pay, which ranks low on the list of goals most young Americans bring to a career. Rather, it is mostly an issue of challenging work, the chance to rise on one's own merit, and the ability to make a difference in the world. Whether the federal bureaucracy is able to maintain the delicate balance may well depend on its ability to get more young Americans to consider government service as a career.

JUST THE FACTS

terms to remember

facts and interpretations

- The federal bureaucracy has become a complicated piece of machinery. It consists of dozens of departments and agencies, roughly 2 million full- and part-time employees, and almost 13 million contractors, grantees, and state and local employees who provide goods or deliver services on behalf of the federal government. Whether it is too big, however, depends very much on how one asks the question. In terms of gross domestic product, for example, our federal government is one of the smallest governments in the world. In terms of federal spending, it is one of the largest.

- The federal bureaucracy consists of a number of interlocking parts that sometimes mesh together efficiently and sometimes weaken performance. There have never been more layers of managers in the federal government, and never more managers at each layer. This thickening reduces a president's ability to see the bottom of agencies where services get delivered, and thereby increases the ability of individual federal employees to make decisions that enhance the faithful execution of the laws. To the extent that federal employees make the decisions about which laws to implement, they take on a lawmaking role that the Founders clearly reserved for Congress.

- The president and Congress both have tools for controlling the excesses of bureaucracy. They can tell the bureaucracy what to do through laws and executive orders, limit what it can do through the federal budget, order it to act through presidential appointees, and hold it accountable through congressional oversight. The problem is that the federal bureaucracy may have gotten so big that none of those tools is sufficient.

- Bureaucracy has always been unpopular. Americans do not trust the federal bureaucracy and believe it causes more problems than it solves. They also worry that it is getting so big as to become a threat to liberty. Nevertheless, Americans tend to applaud the bureaucrats who help them in their daily lives and who want government to do more to create a clean environment, help the elderly, provide for health care, and cure social ills such as juvenile delinquency and poverty. They seem to want a government that looks smaller in the total number of employees, but delivers more services.

open questions

- Is there any way to increase the public's confidence in bureaucracy? Cut more government jobs? Make it easier to fire government employees? Would it help to have more federal agencies think of Americans as customers? What might the Founders think of calling citizens customers? Would they want government officers thinking about how to satisfy the customer?

- Is there any reason to believe that the federal bureaucracy is too small or that it spends too little money? Do America's political leaders spend too much time criticizing big government, particularly given that people hate bureaucracy but love their bureaucrats? Which is better, a big shadow government composed of private contractors or a big federal workforce? What are some of the reasons government should ask the private sector to deliver some of its services? What are the risks of concentrating power in a handful of big contractors such as Lockheed-Martin or Boeing?

- Does knowing that the federal government spends over $200 billion a year paying interest on its debt increase support for cutting the federal deficit? Thinking back to Chapter 4 on public opinion, do most Americans know where their tax money goes? Would they be more likely to support a balanced budget amendment to the Constitution if they knew more about where the dollars go?

- Would you ever consider a job in government as a place to start your career? What do you think are the good things about working for government? What are the bad things? Would you prefer a job working for federal, state, or local government? What about a job working for government at a private firm?

for further study

Goodsell, Charles. *The Case for Bureaucracy: A Public Administration Polemic,* 3rd ed. Chatham, NJ: Chatham House, 1993.

Gore, Al. *From Red Tape to Results: Creating a Government That Works Better and Costs Less.* Report of the National Performance Review. Washington, DC: U.S. Government Printing Office, 1993.

Kettl, Donald F. *Sharing Power: Public Governance and Private Markets.* Washington, DC: Brookings Institution, 1993.

Rohr, John A. *To Run a Constitution: The Legitimacy of the Administrative State.* Lawrence: University Press of Kansas, 1986.

Wilson, James Q. *Bureaucracy: What Government Agencies Do and Why They Do It.* New York: Basic Books, 1989.

endnotes for chapter 12

1. Roy P. Fairfield, ed., *The Federalist Papers* (Baltimore: Johns Hopkins University Press, 1981), p. 198.
2. See Robert A. Katzmann, *Courts and Congress* (Washington, DC: Brookings Institution, 1997), for an analysis of how the courts often have to resolve disputes between laws.
3. See Stanley Elkins and Eric McKitrick, *The Age of Federalism* (New York: Oxford University Press, 1993), pp. 50–51.
4. See John A. Rohr, *To Run a Constitution: The Legitimacy of the Administrative State* (Lawrence: University of Kansas Press, 1986).
5. See General Accounting Office, "Government Reorganization: Issues and Principles," Statement of Charles Bowsher, Comptroller General of the United States (Washington, DC: U.S. General Accounting Office, May 17, 1995); go to the General Accounting Office Web site at <www.gao.gov> for a list of more recent reports on how government is working.
6. Marshall Dimock, *Administrative Vitality: The Conflict with Bureaucracy* (New York: Harper and Brothers, 1959), p. 116.
7. General Accounting Office, "The Changing Workforce: Demographic Issues Facing the Federal Government" (Washington, DC: U.S. General Accounting Office, March 1992).
8. General Accounting Office, "The Changing Workforce."
9. See Donald F. Kettl, *Sharing Power: Public Governance and Private Markets* (Washington, DC: Brookings Institution, 1993).
10. Leonard White, *The Federalists* (New York: Macmillan, 1956), p. 1.
11. Matthew Crenson, *The Federal Machine: Beginnings of Bureaucracy in Jacksonian America* (Baltimore: Johns Hopkins University Press, 1976), p. 3.
12. Crenson, *The Federal Machine,* p. 66.
13. See Paul Light, *Thickening Government: Federal Hierarchy and the Diffusion of Accountability* (Washington, DC: Brookings Institution/Governance Institute, 1995).
14. Donald Kettl, *Leadership at the Fed* (New Haven, CT: Yale University Press, 1986), p. 1.
15. James Fesler and Donald Kettl, *The Politics of the Administrative Process* (Chatham, NJ: Chatham House Publishers), 1991, p. 68.
16. Herbert Kaufman, *Are Government Organizations Immortal?* (Washington, DC: Brookings, 1976).
17. Kaufman, *Are Government Organizations Immortal?,* p. 9.
18. Kaufman, *Are Government Organizations Immortal?,* p. 10.
19. Kaufman, *Are Government Organizations Immortal?,* p. 34.
20. Times Mirror Center for the People & the Press, *The People, Press & Politics: The New Political Landscape* (Times Mirror Center, September 21, 1994), p. 24.
21. Times Mirror Center for the People & the Press, *The People, Press & Politics,* p. 24.
22. Charles Goodsell, *The Case for Bureaucracy: A Public Administration Polemic,* 2d ed. (Chatham, NJ: Chatham House, 1985), p. 11; see also

Linda Bennett and Stephen Bennett, *Living with Leviathan: Americans Coming to Terms with Big Government* (Lawrence: University of Kansas Press, 1990).

23. David Rosenbaum, "In Loss, Republicans Find Seeds of Victory," *New York Times,* March 5, 1995, p. E16.

24. Figures from Fesler and Kettl, *The Politics of the Administrative Process,* p. 2.

25. Fesler and Kettl, *The Politics of the Administrative Process,* p. 6.

26. John DiIulio and Donald F. Kettl, *Fine Print: The Contract with America, Devolution, and the Administrative Realities of American Federalism* (Washington, DC: Brookings Institution Center for Public Management, March 1, 1995), p. 16.

27. Kent Weaver, *Automatic Government: The Politics of Indexation* (Washington, DC: Brookings Institution, 1988), p. 1.

28. Harold W. Stanley and Richard G. Niemi, *Vital Statistics on American Politics* (Washington, DC: CQ Press, 1995), p. 425.

29. For a discussion of the politics of tax expenditures, see Michael Wines, "Taxpayers Are Angry. They're Expensive, Too," *New York Times,* November 20, 1994, p. E5.

30. See Paul C. Light, *Shrinking Government: Federal Headcounts and the Illusion of Smallness* (Washington, DC: Brookings Institution, 1999).

31. Dwight D. Eisenhower, Farewell Address, January 17, 1961, *Public Papers of the Presidents of the United Staes,* vol. 47 (Washington, DC: Government Printing Office, 1961), p. 192.

32. James Q. Wilson, *Bureaucracy: What Government Agencies Do and Why They Do It* (New York: Basic Books, 1989), p. 257.

33. These figures are from Paul Light, *The Tides of Reform: Federal Management Reform and the Confusion of Accountability, 1946–1994* (New Haven, CT: Yale University Press, 1997).

34. See Paul Light, *The President's Agenda: Domestic Policy Choice from Kennedy to Clinton,* 3rd ed. (Baltimore: Johns Hopkins University Press, 1998), p. 117.

35. Wilson, *Bureaucracy,* p. 261.

36. U.S. Senate, Select Committee on Presidential Campaign Activities, *Use of Incumbency-Responsiveness Program,* 93rd Cong. 2nd sess., vol. 19 (Washington, DC: U.S. Government Printing Office, 1974), pp. 8907 ff.

37. *Use of Incumbency-Responsiveness Program,* pp. 9009–11.

38. *Use of Incumbency-Responsiveness Program,* p. 9012.

39. *Use of Incumbency-Responsiveness Program,* p. 9014.

40. B. Dan Wood and Richard Waterman, "The Dynamics of Political Control of the Bureaucracy," *American Political Science Review,* 85, no. 3 (September 1991), pp. 801–28.

41. See Steven Smith, *The American Congress* (Boston: Houghton Mifflin, 1995), pp. 217–18; see also Joel Aberbach, *Keeping a Watchful Eye: The Politics of Congressional Oversight* (Washington, DC: Brookings Institution, 1990).

42. See Matthew McCubbins and Thomas Schwartz, "Congressional Oversight Overlooked: Police Patrols versus Fire Alarms," *American Journal of Political Science,* 2, no. 1 (February 1984), pp. 165–79.

43. Al Gore, *From Red Tape to Results: Creating a Government That Works Better and Costs Less*, Report of the National Performance Review (Washington, DC: U.S. Government Printing Office, 1993), p. 3; go to the Gore Web site at <www.npr.gov> for an update on what is happening with reinventing government today.

44. The Pew Research Center for The People & The Press, *Deconstructing Distrust: How Americans View Government* (Washington, DC: Pew Research Center, 1998).

the federal judiciary

the final check

Once a law is finally implemented by the federal bureaucracy, it must still be enforced and interpreted. The Constitution gives both jobs to the **federal judiciary,** or court system. By enforcing the laws that Congress and the president enact, the judiciary assures that Americans conform with the decisions of Congress and the presidency. By interpreting the laws, the judiciary ensures that those decisions are constitutional—that is, that neither Congress nor the presidency has exceeded its authority. And by giving individual citizens a final check against government and their fellow citizens alike, the judiciary acts to protect civil liberties and civil rights. In doing all these jobs, the federal judiciary must simultaneously protect the nation as a whole and Americans as individual citizens.

Because of its role as a final check against strong-willed majorities, the federal judiciary is heavily insulated against both public opinion and Congress. Toward protecting the courts against public passions, the Founders rejected the direct election of federal judges, which had been the case in many colonial courts and remains the case to this day in many states and localities. Instead, the Founders decided that federal judges would be nominated by the president and confirmed by the Senate, with no role for the House.

Toward protecting the courts from Congress, the Founders rejected any limits on judicial terms. Federal judges would be allowed to serve during good behavior, which ordinarily means for life. Absent terms of office, judges do not have to be reappointed and thus are insulated from the presidency and the Senate. The Founders decided that Congress would never be allowed to cut a judge's pay after that judge was nominated and confirmed, thereby removing financial pressure as a source of possible interference in the judiciary's independence.

These decisions were essential for protecting the branch that the Founders saw as the least likely ever to threaten liberty. As Alexander Hamilton wrote, "The Executive not only dispenses the honors, but holds the sword of the community. The legislature not only commands the purse, but prescribes the rules by which the duties and rights of every citizen are to be regulated. The judiciary, on the contrary, has no influence over either the sword or the purse."[1] To play its role as a check against the other two branches, the judiciary had to be insulated from both the sword and the purse—hence the open-ended terms of office and the protection against cuts in pay.

Lacking the sword or the purse, the judiciary has only one tool for doing its job: its judgment. The federal judiciary has no army or police force to enforce its will, no credible threat that it can use to make the people obey. It can order the federal government or individual citizens to act, but it has no real means of extracting obedience. To a much greater extent than Congress or the presidency, the judiciary must rely on the consent of the governed to accept its decisions on their merits.[2]

The challenge is to maintain this consent while tackling the tough issues that the United States faces. There are times when the federal judiciary must reject what the public wants, striking down laws that most Americans support or protecting individuals that most Americans cannot abide. To play its role in maintaining the delicate balance, the federal judiciary must be ready to accept intense public outrage.

This chapter examines the job of the federal judiciary in detail. The first section asks what the Founders intended as they designed the third branch of government, looking specifically at the duties of the judiciary and qualifications for appointment. The second section examines the real judiciary today, looking at the first federal courts created in 1789, then turning to the modern institutional judiciary and the process for finding and appointing federal judges. The third section takes a close look at how the Supreme Court works.

THE IMAGINED JUDICIARY

The Founders arrived at the Constitutional Convention in Philadelphia with substantial legal experience. Thirty-one of the fifty-five delegates were lawyers, including James Madison and Alexander Hamilton, and many had experience in the state and local courts of the prerevolutionary days. Almost all knew something about the complicated British court system, which had nearly one hundred different kinds of courts, including some that dealt only with the English royalty.

As they had done with Congress and the presidency, the Founders drew on their experience to design the new federal judiciary, simultaneously simplifying the complicated British system, while accepting its tradition of two kinds of law. One set of laws comes from Congress and the president and is labeled **statutory law**. A *statute* is a more formal term for a law passed by a legislature and signed by an executive. Federal statutes can be found in the *U.S. Code*, which catalogues every public law currently in effect. A second set of laws come from the judiciary, whether through interpretations of statutory law or from the accumulated body of previous judicial opinions. These judge-made laws reside in the decisions themselves, not in formal statutes, and are labeled **common law.**

Whether based in statute or judicial practice, laws convey the rules that govern society. *Civil law* governs relationships between individuals as private citizens, as well as relationships between individuals and government; *criminal law* governs the behavior of individuals as members of society; *administrative law* addresses the actions of the bureaucracy as it executes the laws; and *constitutional law* involves questions surrounding interpretations of the Constitution.

The Basic Framework

Whether because of their training as lawyers or through their personal contact with the law as property owners, bankers, or merchants, the Founders had reached a number of decisions about the future of the federal judiciary long before the Constitutional Convention began. They certainly had a sense of how the judiciary should look and act, and clearly they accepted the principles of English common law, most importantly the notion of **stare decisis.** Under this principle, which means "let the decision stand," every judicial decision made today must be linked to one made previously. Judges are thereby bound by **precedents**—the decisions made in previous cases—which ensure that most legal disputes have predictable outcomes. Judges make law by making decisions, which, in turn, establish precedents that bind future judges to the past.

In 1992, for example, the Supreme Court upheld the right to abortion established under *Roe v. Wade,* in part because the justices felt that a "terrible price would be paid for overruling" the 1973 decision. As the majority wrote, "A decision to overrule *Roe*'s essential holding under the existing circumstances would address error, if error there was, at the cost of both profound and unnecessary damage to the Court's legitimacy, and to the Nation's commitment to the rule of law. It is therefore imperative to adhere to the essence of *Roe*'s original decision, and we do so today."[3]

This acceptance of *stare decisis* and other principles of English common law was nearly inevitable. As one historian puts it, English common law was as central to day-to-day life as the English language itself.[4] Although the American public had no love of lawyers, particularly since many had been British sympathizers during the war, common law was essential to the new nation's survival. It was the way the colonies had governed society and was the backbone of the economy.

Given this experience, the Founders naturally assumed there would be at least two kinds of courts, trial and appellate, each with a separate jurisdiction that would determine which cases it could resolve. As courts of original jurisdiction, **trial courts** would hear all cases for the first time and make the first decision resolving blame or innocence. Appeals from the trial courts would be heard by **appellate courts**, which would make their decisions not on the facts of the original case (for example, who did what to whom?), but on the legality of the trial (for example, was the trial court fair?). Both trial and appellate courts existed in the colonies before the war and in the states after the war. It was no surprise, therefore, that the Founders imagined such a structure for the new judiciary, creating the Supreme Court as the highest appellate court of all while leaving the rest of the federal judiciary to Congress and the presidency.

Finally, the Founders assumed that there would be separate systems of federal, state, and local courts. Just as the colonies had been divided by state and local courts, and the government as a whole had been divided into a federal system, the Founders imagined a federal judiciary that would allow several layers of courts.

The Third Branch

In contrast to the Founders' summer-long debate over the legislative branch, their invention of the judiciary was easy. As Hamilton later explained in *The Federalist Papers,* the judiciary would be least able to "annoy or injure" the basic rights of the Constitution, and could "take no active resolution whatever. It may truly be said to have neither FORCE nor WILL, but merely judgment. . . ."[5]

This is not to say that the Founders were in complete agreement on the precise outlines of the judicial branch. Advocates of a limited national government wanted just one federal court—the Supreme Court—as the court of last resort (or final appeal) for appeals upward from the states, while advocates of a stronger national government argued that state courts could not be trusted to faithfully administer national laws.

The dispute was settled by compromise. Article III begins quite simply by vesting the judicial power of the United States in a supreme court "and in such inferior Courts as the Congress may from time to time ordain and establish." It would be up to the First Congress to decide just how many lower courts would be needed, how they would operate, and where they would be located.

Because the Founders knew that laws would be made at each layer of government—federal, state, and local—they decided to make clear that the laws and treaties of the federal government would come first as "the supreme Law of the Land." As noted in Chapter 2, the *supremacy clause* establishes federal laws as the strongest laws of all. When federal and state laws conflict, the federal law generally wins, unless the federal law is clearly exercising a power reserved for the states.

The Duties of the Federal Judiciary

Article III is the briefest of the three articles establishing the institutions of government, yet, brief as it is, it divides into two sections, one giving the judicial power to the courts and the other outlining judicial limitations.

Judicial Power.   Article III never defines the judicial power, however. There is no enumerated powers, no list of implied authorities. As Hamilton argued, the courts are to protect the Constitution against the "ill humors" that create "dangerous innovations in government and serious oppressions of the minor party in the community."[6] Although Article III leaves judicial power undefined, it provides a short list of the controversies reserved for judicial action:

- Controversies to which the United States shall be a Party;
- Controversies between two or more States;
- Controversies between a State and Citizens of another State;
- Controversies between Citizens of different States; and
- Controversies between Citizens of the same State claiming Lands under Grants of different States, and between a State, or the Citizens thereof, and foreign States, Citizens or Subjects.

Even this brief list was immediately changed under the Eleventh Amendment, ratified in 1795, which prohibits the federal courts from hearing cases in which a state is sued by a citizen of another state.

The debate over Article III did have its moments of controversy, most importantly over whether the federal judiciary would be allowed to enforce and interpret the Constitution itself. Once again, the fight was between those who favored giving the states greater power and those who favored a strong national government. Those in favor of a stronger state role wanted to restrict federal jurisdiction to cases arising under the laws passed by Congress and signed by the president.

Article III leaves no doubt about who won the argument: the judicial power extends not just to all national laws but to "all Cases . . . arising under this Constitution, the Laws of the United States, and Treaties made." The Founders ensured that the federal judiciary would be allowed to resolve conflicts over the Constitution itself. It is not clear, however, just how far the Founders wanted the federal judiciary to go in resolving such conflicts. Some, including Hamilton, believed that the judiciary would have the duty to "declare all acts contrary to the manifest tenor of the Constitution void."[7] Although the Supreme Court waited over a decade to use this power of **judicial review,** these Founders believed that the judiciary needed the power to grind government to a full and complete halt.

Other Founders were less sure about giving the judiciary such a significant power, and the issue was never completely resolved in the Constitutional Convention. Unlike the power of the purse or the power of appointments, which are both mentioned explicitly, the power of judicial review is neither defined nor mentioned in the Constitution.[8]

It was left to Chief Justice John Marshall to make the first assertion of judicial review in the 1803 case *Marbury v. Madison*. Recall from Chapter 2 that Marbury had been offered a federal judgeship in late 1800 by President John Adams, but his papers of commission had not been delivered before the new president, Thomas Jefferson, was inaugurated. Since the two presidents were members of different parties, it is hardly surprising that Jefferson would order his secretary of state, James Madison, not to deliver the late papers. As allowed under the Judiciary Act of 1789, Marbury went directly to the Supreme Court with his complaint, asking the Court to issue a *writ of mandamus* directing government officials (in this case, Secretary of State Madison) to act (deliver the papers). In filing his case first with the Supreme Court, Marbury called on the Court to exercise original, not appellate, jurisdiction.

In *Marbury v. Madison,* Marshall reasoned that the Constitution had been quite specific in limiting the Supreme Court's original jurisdiction only to cases affecting ambassadors, foreign ministers, and states. In all other cases, the Founders clearly stated that the Supreme Court would only have appellate jurisdiction. Thus, when Congress added writs of mandamus to the Supreme Court's original

John Marshall in a painting by James R. Lambdin. Marshall wrote the opinion in *Marbury v. Madison* that established the power of judicial review.

jurisdiction under Section 13 of the 1789 Judiciary Act, it did so against the clear intent of the Founders. The expansion was, therefore, unconstitutional and held no effect. Since the Supreme Court had no power to issue a writ of mandamus as a court of original jurisdiction in Marbury's case, he never got his papers. At the same time, the Supreme Court got the essential power to review and declare acts of Congress unconstitutional. By the early 1900s, the Supreme Court had overturned 141 other acts of Congress, plus 919 state laws and 105 local laws.[9]

Judicial Limitations.   Even as the Founders insulated the judiciary against Congress and the presidency, they gave the two branches several limited checks on the judiciary. As noted, they gave Congress the power to create the inferior federal courts in the first place. They also allowed Congress to restrict the judiciary's appellate jurisdiction. Although presidents would have the power to appoint appellate judges, the Senate retained the power to confirm those appointees, while Congress as a whole retained the power to limit the judicial agenda.

Stronger checks were hardly necessary given the judiciary's natural weakness. Federal courts are often described as passive, not active, institutions—that is, they can only make decisions on cases that are brought before them. Unlike members of Congress or presidents, judges cannot "invent" policy out of thin air. They must first have a "case or controversy," as former Chief Justice Earl Warren once observed, and that case must raise a **justiciable issue**—that is, it must involve a real dispute that the federal courts, and only the federal courts, can resolve. The courts do not waste their time on hypothetical issues or on cases where one side is unwilling to fight.

As a result, any case before the federal judiciary must pass at least three tests: (1) it must have **adverseness,** that is, a real dispute and not some hypothetical issue invented just to get an advisory opinion from a court; (2) the parties involved must have **standing to sue,** that is, the individuals who bring the case must be truly injured; and (3) it must be **ripe for decision,** that is, it cannot come too early in the process or come so late that it is **moot,** meaning the issues in the case have already been answered elsewhere.[10] The Supreme Court adds a fourth criterion to the list in setting its agenda: the case must involve a controversy worth deciding.

Qualifications for Appointment

Unlike Congress and the presidency, the Constitution sets absolutely no minimums for serving on the Supreme Court; nor did the First Congress when it created the federal lower courts. Since judges were to be appointed by the president with the advice and consent of the Senate (as a check against political favoritism by the president), perhaps the Founders simply assumed that judges would be at least as old as the president and appointed on merit.

In addition, the Founders clearly assumed that federal judges would be persons of great integrity, though the Constitution does not set any particular requirements. As Hamilton explained, the judiciary would attract good judges because "there can be but a few men in the society who will have sufficient skill in the laws to qualify them for the stations of judges. And making the proper deductions for the ordinary depravity of human nature, the number must be still smaller of those who unite the requisite integrity with the requisite knowledge."[11] Hamilton was the consummate elitist: Few would want to be judges, in his view, and fewer still would fit his qualifications.

Judges are not immune from congressional review. Once in office, they can be removed by impeachment and conviction for the same treason, bribery, and other high crimes and misdemeanors that allow impeachment of all officers of the United States government under Article II. It is a device used only in extreme cases. In the entire history of the courts, only forty-five judges have been impeached by the House, of whom only nine faced Senate trials and only four were convicted.

Although impeachment is more than a hollow threat, it is not the primary source for ensuring "good behavior" on the part of federal judges. More than most elected politicians, judges behave in the national interest because that is simply the right thing to do. They pay attention to what their colleagues on the bench think, and they worry about their reputation in the legal community. They also care about their place in history—that is, where they will rank among others who have come before and who will serve after.[12]

in a different light ——

THE CHANGING FACE OF THE JUDICIARY

The very devices that insulate the judiciary from public pressure can create an anti-democratic bias. Whereas many states and localities allow for the direct election of judges, the federal judiciary remains conspicuously above the political fray. Thus, the question is how the judiciary can know enough about the ordinary lives of Americans to keep its perspective.

The Supreme Court in 1997. From left, are Associate Justices Clarence Thomas, Antonin Scalia, Sandra Day O'Connor, Anthony M. Kennedy, David H. Souter, Stephen Breyer, John Paul Stevens, Chief Justice William H. Rehnquist, and Associate Justice Ruth Bader Ginsberg. O'Connor was the first woman ever appointed to the Supreme Court; Ginsberg was the second. Thomas was the second African American appointed to the Supreme Court.

U.S. District Court Judge Sonia Sotomayor. Raised in the housing projects of the Bronx, graduate of Princeton and Yale, Judge Sotomayor was nominated to be a U.S. Circuit Court Judge in 1997. Senate Republicans blocked her advancement in part to stop what conservative talk show host Rush Limbaugh called her "rocket ship" ride to the Supreme Court. She was finally confirmed just before Congress adjourned in October 1998.

As with the federal bureaucracy, one answer is to have a representative judiciary, which simply means to assure that, demographically speaking, the face of the judiciary is not very different from the face of the public. The first courts made no such effort, of course. The only Americans who got to be judges were those who had earlier gotten to be lawyers. And the only Americans who got to be lawyers were white, male property owners.

Over the past thirty years, however, the face of the federal judiciary has changed. The Founders would be surprised to find that there are now two women (Sandra Day O'Connor and Ruth Bader Ginsburg) and an African American (Clarence Thomas) on the Supreme Court, and to learn that the lower courts—a term used to cover both the appellate and district courts—have also become less white and less male. As the first African American on the Supreme Court, Thurgood Marshall remarked during the bicentennial of the Constitution, the Founders "could not have imagined, nor would they have accepted, that the document they were drafting would one day be construed by a Supreme Court to which had been appointed a woman and the descendant of an African slave."[13]

No president has placed a higher premium on making the judiciary resemble the general population than Bill Clinton. Only fifteen of Clinton's first forty-eight judicial nominees were white males, compared to thirty out of Jimmy Carter's first thirty-four, forty-one out of Ronald Reagan's first forty-five, and seventeen out of

BOX 13-1

Diversity on the District and Appellate Courts (percentage of appointees by gender and race or ethnicity)

Appointing President (number of appointees)	Johnson (162)	Nixon (224)	Ford (64)
Gender of Appointees			
Male	98.1%	99.5%	98.4%
Female	1.8	0.5	1.5
Ethnicity or Race of Appointees			
White	93.8	95.9	90.6
African American	4.3	2.6	4.6
Hispanic American	1.8	0.8	1.5
Asian American	0.0	0.4	3.1
Native American	0.0	0.0	0.0

George Bush's first twenty-three. Thus, the federal judiciary is becoming more representative of the public it serves. (See Box 13–1 for the racial and gender composition of court appointees by the last seven presidents.)

However, merely appointing more women and minority judges does not assure that the courts will suddenly become more closely connected to ordinary Americans. After all, the only Americans who get to be judges today are still lawyers. There may be more women and minority candidates, but it still takes a college degree, three years of law school, and a bar exam to get a ticket to the federal bench. And usually it takes much more. Most federal judges have had substantial legal experience with the nation's top law firms, which means they have acquired substantial personal wealth. Thus, even though the demographic face of the judiciary appears to be changing, the socioeconomic face remains virtually unchanged

Carter (258)	Reagan (368)	Bush (185)	Clinton (198)
84.4%	92.3%	80.5%	69.7%
15.4	7.6	19.4	30.3
78.6	93.4	89.1	72.2
14.3	1.9	6.4	18.6
6.2	4.0	4.3	7.1
0.7	0.5	0.0	1.5
0.0	0.0	0.0	0.6

Sources: David M. O'Brien, "Clinton's Legal Policy and the Courts: Rising from Disarray or Turning Around and Around," in Colin Campbell and Bert A. Rockman, eds., *The Clinton Presidency: First Appraisals* (Chatham, NJ: Chatham House, 1996), p. 137; and Harold W. Stanley and Richard G. Niemi, *Vital Statistics on American Politics, 1997–1998* (Washington, DC: CQ Press, 1998), pp. 272–73.

from two hundred years ago. The average net worth of Clinton's 1996 judicial appointees was just over $1 million; the net worth of his 1997 appointees was $1.8 million.

Despite the recent effort to increase the racial diversity of the federal judiciary, the Supreme Court has yet to seat its first Hispanic American justice. The problem is not a lack of motivation: both parties recognize that appointing the first Hispanic justice would be politically popular in states such as Florida, Texas, and California, where high numbers of Hispanic voters are up for grabs. Rather, the problem has been the lack of a visible appeals court judge who has the considerable experience needed to withstand the Senate confirmation process.

Worries about the seasoning of liberal New York District Court Judge Sonia Sotomayor for a possible appointment to the Supreme Court led Senate Republicans to block her appointment to the Court of Appeals in 1998. "Basically, we think that putting her on the appeals court puts her in the batter's box to be nominated to the Supreme Court," said one senior Republican aide of the delays. "If Clinton nominated her it would put several of our senators in a real difficult position."[14] Translated, this means that they would have to either reject her nomination on ideological grounds, thereby facing the wrath of Hispanic and women voters, or support her nomination, thereby facing the wrath of conservative interest groups such as the Christian Coalition, which would be sure to oppose her elevation. Sotomayor's nomination was finally approved by the Senate in early October under pressure from national Hispanic groups.

THE REAL JUDICIARY

Today's federal judiciary bears a close resemblance to what the Founders imagined. Although the Founders might be pleasantly surprised that the Supreme Court finally got its own building in 1935—designed as a replica of an ancient Greek temple, with the words "Equal Justice Under Law" carved above its massive bronze doors—they would not be surprised by what happens inside. Unlike Congress and the presidency, which have been profoundly altered by television, the Supreme Court—indeed, all federal courts—still operates pretty much as it always has, mostly as a consequence of the common law tradition.

What has changed, however, is the workload. The federal judiciary is handling more cases than ever, and the Supreme Court is becoming tougher about the cases it chooses to hear. And even though the Supreme Court has not grown dramatically in the number of justices, the rest of the federal court system has continued to expand as new laws require more judges. A rapidly changing society has meant more disputes, and more laws have meant more conflicts suitable for courts. And if television has not penetrated the workings of the federal judiciary, as it has done in many state and local courts, it certainly has raised the visibility of what the courts do.

Before turning to the structure of the modern judiciary and questions about what judges do, it is useful to examine the rise of the first courts. Recall that the Founders left the structure of the lower courts entirely to Congress and the president. They also left the internal workings of the Supreme Court to the future. Although Article III established one Supreme Court, it did not specify how many justices would sit on this highest "bench" of all.

The First Courts

Today's federal judiciary was outlined in the very first act passed by the First Congress. Numbered as the first bill considered by the first Senate (S. 1), the Judiciary Act of 1789 laid out a three-tiered system composed of a *Supreme Court* with a chief justice and five associate justices, three *courts of appeal* with two Supreme Court justices "riding" the circuit with a single district court judge, and thirteen *district courts,* each with a single district court judge. This three-tiered court system exists to this day, supplemented by a number of *specialty courts* that handle the special needs of veterans, taxpayers, and others.

Although Congress struggled with many of the same questions raised in the Constitutional Convention, practical politics decided the shape of the judiciary. Figuring out how to pay for the new system clearly affected the final bill, leading to a much simpler system than had existed under the British.[15]

The Supreme Court was placed at the *top* of the newly created system, the district courts at the *bottom,* one for each state, and the courts of appeal in the *middle.* (As this chapter notes below, Congress finally created a separate appeals court system with its own judges in 1891.) The courts of appeal originally were called circuit courts for the circuit, or map of towns, that the three judges would follow to hear cases. Given the abysmal transportation system of the late 1700s, it was much easier for the judge to go to the case than for the case to go the judge. (See Box 13–2 for the basic structure of the federal judiciary today. Appeals of decisions by specialty courts and independent regulatory commissions usually go directly to the U.S. Courts of Appeal.)

The first courts were far less visible than either the First Congress or Washington's presidency. The first Supreme Court was headed by John Jay, the least-known author of *The Federalist Papers.* The first term, or year, of the Jay Supreme Court was barely noticed. As one modern historian described it: "The first President immediately on taking office settled down to the pressing business of being President. The first Congress enacted the first laws. The first Supreme Court adjourned."[16]

Only four of the six members could make it to Philadelphia for the term, and the term itself lasted only ten days. Lacking cases to decide, the Court had little to do but select a clerk, choose a seal, and give several lawyers permission to present cases at some undefined point in the future. As the final court of appeal, the Supreme Court had to wait for cases to work their way up from the bottom.

The Institutional Judiciary

Today's judiciary remains far less visible than Congress or the presidency. Most Americans know little about the operation of the federal judiciary, let alone the division of responsibilities among federal, state, and local courts. Most hear about the judiciary at one of two levels: either in connection with highly visible local

BOX 13-2

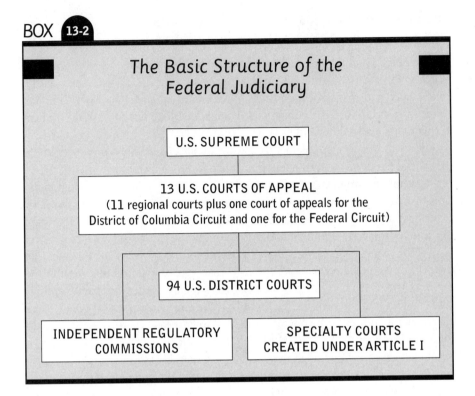

The Basic Structure of the Federal Judiciary

U.S. SUPREME COURT

13 U.S. COURTS OF APPEAL
(11 regional courts plus one court of appeals for the
District of Columbia Circuit and one for the Federal Circuit)

94 U.S. DISTRICT COURTS

INDEPENDENT REGULATORY COMMISSIONS

SPECIALTY COURTS CREATED UNDER ARTICLE I

criminal cases such as the O. J. Simpson murder trial or when the Supreme Court makes a well-publicized decision on an issue such as flag burning or abortion.

Nevertheless, as Chapter 14 shows, the federal judiciary plays a prominent role in American life. Name an issue and the federal courts have likely had some say about it. The courts have done their share of lawmaking over the decades, often moving far ahead of Congress and the presidency in addressing the controversial issues of the day. Freed from public pressure, they broke the "color" barrier in the public schools, drew the lines between church and state on religion, took a stand on abortion, and continue to struggle with the rights of criminals. Much of what the courts do is highly unpopular, but most Americans agree that the courts have shown great courage over the years.

Unlike Congress and the presidency, which are highly complicated institutions, the federal judiciary is actually quite simple. It consists of two components: judges and the courts in which they work. Although the federal judiciary does have a small staff of law clerks and administrators, these employees play a far less important role than do congressional and presidential staffs.

Judgeships.   The federal judiciary is headed by more than eight hundred federal judgeships that are filled by individual judges. As of 1993, there were 9 judges on the Supreme Court (one chief justice and eight associates), 167 on the courts of appeal, and 649 on the district courts.

The job of every judge is the same: to render justice. But how a judge does so depends very much on the kind of court involved. A trial court judge renders justice largely by being a referee between the plaintiff and the defendant. The plaintiff is the party who alleges that a wrong has been committed, while the defendant is the party who allegedly committed that wrong. In criminal cases, the government represents the public as a whole by acting as the prosecution. In the American legal system, every defendant is to be considered innocent until proven guilty beyond a reasonable doubt.

In contrast, appellate judges render justice by reviewing the decisions of trial courts. Their job is to ask whether the plaintiff and defendant received a fair trial, evidence was presented correctly, and punishment, if any, was appropriate to the act. They can void a trial court decision on several grounds, from violations of procedural fairness to breaches of constitutional protection.

Every judge, whether trial or appellate, has a somewhat different court-room presence. Some are strict disciplinarians who enforce every rule to the letter; others are willing to grant greater latitude in the give-and-take of a trial. Although they are all bound by the same law, every judge has enough discretion, whether in admitting evidence or conducting the trial, to shape the outcome. As a result, judging is much more an art than a science. As this section argues below, Congress has occasionally tried to limit discretion, particularly by restricting the judiciary's authority to impose sentences. In theory, judges are supposed to make the punishment fit the crime. But under legislation passed in the 1980s, punishments for certain kinds of crimes are preset by Congress.

Courts.   Judges do their work in courts, which are nothing more than devices for handling cases. The federal judicial system is relatively simple, consisting of district courts, courts of appeal, and the Supreme Court created under Article III, and an assortment of specialty courts created by Congress under Article I.[17] Article III courts are generally called **constitutional courts**, while Article I courts are generally called **legislative courts.**

Level One: District Courts.   District courts handle the largest number of cases and originate the vast majority of the cases that reach the Supreme Court for final appeal. District courts have original jurisdiction over all crimes against the United States; all civil cases arising under the Constitution; federal laws, or treaties; and cases involving citizens of different states.[18] There is at least one district court in every state.

As the number of laws has grown and the number of states has increased, the number of district courts also increased. Congress created thirteen districts under the 1789 Judiciary Act and provided funds for just thirteen district court judges in 1789. By 1996, the number was up to 94 districts and nearly 650 judges. The growth was clearly a response to the number of cases pending before the district courts. (See Box 13–3 for the trends in workload.)

Level Two: Courts of Appeal.   The modern appellate court system was created in 1891, when Congress established nine separate courts of appeal with funds for a total of twenty judges. Prior to 1891, individual justices of the Supreme Court rode different circuits as the first layer of appellate review. As the district courts have expanded, so have the courts of appeals. There are now 13 courts and 167 judges.

Courts of appeal conduct no trials and are only allowed to make decisions on facts in the existing record. The number of judges in a given circuit depends on the workload, with the smallest circuit having four judges and the largest twenty-eight. Most decisions are made by panels of three judges, who review the

BOX 13-3

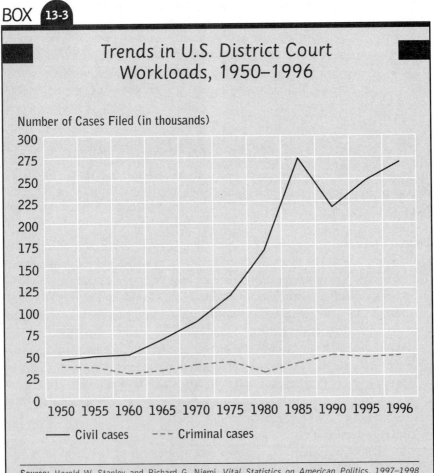

Trends in U.S. District Court Workloads, 1950–1996

Number of Cases Filed (in thousands)

—— Civil cases   - - - Criminal cases

Source: Harold W. Stanley and Richard G. Niemi, *Vital Statistics on American Politics, 1997–1998* (Washington, DC: CQ Press, 1998), p. 280.

given district court record to assure that the original decision was fair. Each court of appeals has a chief judge to handle the administrative workload and assign cases to panels. On particularly important cases, the chief judge may decide to create a panel composed of the entire membership, which is called hearing a case *en banc,* as a collective body.

As with the district courts, there has been a dramatic increase in the court of appeals workload. In 1915, there were less than 1,500 cases filed for appeal; by 1996, the number had grown to nearly 52,000. Unlike the district courts, the courts of appeals are under no obligation to act quickly. Because the Supreme Court cannot reach down to the district court level to select cases it wants to hear, it must wait for the courts of appeals to act, thereby giving this intermediate layer of appeal enormous responsibility for both the timing and content of the Supreme Court's agenda.

It is important to note that district and appeals courts are not the only Article III constitutional courts that Congress has created over the years. The U.S. Customs Court was created to handle disputes arising over the appraisals of imported goods by the Customs Service. Judges on such constitutional courts serve for life, and can be removed only through impeachment.

Level Three: The Supreme Court.   It is tempting to describe the Supreme Court as the highest point on a single, sleek pyramid of justice that rises from the district courts on up. In fact, the Supreme Court is more accurately described as the highest peak on what one pair of legal scholars describe as "an eroded mountain range."[19] Depending upon where a case begins its climb, it may or may not reach the Supreme Court.

Compared to Congress and the presidency, the Supreme Court has changed the least since 1789. There are nine Supreme Court justices today (eight associate justices and one chief justice), compared to six in 1789, and oral argument proceeds in much the same way as it did two hundred years ago. The Supreme Court is still sharply limited in what cases it can hear because, as noted earlier, it can only react to cases brought before it.

Today's Supreme Court is a much more active institution than it once was. It fashions its docket, or agenda, of cases from a much larger number of appeals than ever before. Whereas the average district court judge hears 40 cases per year, and the average court of appeals judge hears 30, the nine Supreme Court justices together hear 100 to 120. Not surprisingly, the Supreme Court has added more staff to keep up. In 1930, there were just fifty staff positions to help the justices dispose of their cases. By 1993, there were nearly 350.

Legislative Courts.   Under Article I, Congress has the power to create "tribunals," or courts, to do special jobs. Judges on legislative courts serve for specific terms of office, not life, and can be reappointed only through the normal confirmation process. Two examples of legislative courts are the U.S. Tax Court, which resolves disputes between taxpayers and the Internal Revenue Service, thereby helping Congress exercise its authority to impose and collect taxes; and the Court of Veterans Appeals, which reviews benefit decisions made by the Department of Veterans Affairs, thereby helping Congress exercise its authority to provide for the general welfare. Both courts handle cases that would not ordinarily appear before the constitutional courts.

A Brief Note on State Courts. The federal judiciary is not the only judiciary in the United States. Under America's federalist system, state courts were guaranteed a continued role in providing justice. Just as the state and local bureaucracies are much larger than the federal, so are state and local courts larger than the federal. Indeed, the real explosion in workload has been in the states. As Federal Appeals Court Judge Frank Coffin notes, "It is in state courts that by far most of the nation's litigation is decided; the huge size of the state court component of our dual system is seldom appreciated."[20]

Coffin estimates that state trial courts handle nearly 32 million cases a year, accounting for 99 percent of all cases heard by federal and state courts combined, an estimate that would swell if he counted courts of limited jurisdiction (juvenile courts, domestic relations, wills), where 18,000 judges handle over 73 million cases a year. There are now 23 state courts for every one federal trial court; 14 state judges for every one federal; 113 state cases for every one federal.[21]

In general, most civil and criminal law is handled by the state courts (murder, drug selling, and burglary, for example, are almost always state offenses). Federal courts also handle civil and criminal law, but of a different kind (counterfeiting is a classic federal offense; states cannot coin their own money). Civil cases make up the bulk of the state court workload, accounting for nearly 85 percent of the caseload in 1996. Almost all state court decisions on these cases are final, with no room for appeal upward into the federal system.

There are times, however, when federal law provides alternative paths to justice. The 1992 Rodney King case is one example. King was the African American motorist who was beaten by four white Los Angeles police officers who alleged that he resisted arrest following a speeding violation. Although a passerby's videotape showed that King was on the ground during the beating, a California jury acquitted all four officers of criminal assault charges under state law. The acquittals sparked the Los Angeles riots, and led the federal government to charge the four officers with having violated King's civil rights. Although the officers could not be tried twice for the same offense—the Constitution protects citizens against double jeopardy—they could be tried by the federal courts for a different offense. Using the same videotape, federal prosecutors were able to convince a federal jury that the officers had used excessive and unnecessary force with the intent of denying King's civil rights. The two officers served two years in federal prison.

The federal courts can also hear appeals from state and local courts involving violations of constitutional law. For example, sometimes when the death penalty is imposed in criminal cases by state courts, it is contested in federal courts as a cruel and unusual punishment prohibited under the Eighth Amendment.

A passerby videotaped Rodney King being beaten by police in Los Angeles after being stopped for a traffic violation (top). He is shown being released three days later from jail (bottom). The four officers who were tried on charges of assault were found not guilty by a California court. The acquittals sparked rioting in Los Angeles. Two of the four acquitted officers were later found guilty in a federal court of violating King's civil rights.

The Growing Judicial Workload

The judicial workload is tied to demographic, social, and economic changes in society. More people means more relationships; changing families, increasing divisions between the rich and poor, and the changing economy all contribute to more stress in those relationships; more stress creates pressure for more laws and regulations to govern behavior; more laws and regulations generate greater efforts at enforcement; and the results end up in the courts' workload. As Federal Appeals Court Judge Stephen Reinhardt writes, "There are more and more people in this country, and Congress passes more and more laws affecting the quality of life. Thirty years ago, we had no environmental laws, no Civil Rights Act of 1964, no right to challenge many forms of arbitrary action. The 1960s changed all that. There is no going back."[22]

The workload also reflects both the public's fear of crime and law enforcement's increased activity. Violent crime (murder, rape, robbery, and aggravated assault) increased nearly five times between 1960 and 1991, from 161 to 758 crimes per 100,000 Americans; property crime (burglary, larceny, and car theft) jumped more than three times between 1960 and 1991, from 1,887 to nearly 6,000 crimes per 100,000.[23] The crime rate clearly declined during the early and mid-1990s, in part because of tougher law enforcement in major cities such as New York and Los Angeles and in part because of economic growth. By 1995, for example, violent crime had declined to 685 per 100,000, while property crime had fallen to 5,278 per 100,000. All of the numbers were still well above their historical lows, however, and were still climbing among certain demographic groups.

As crime rates increased, the federal government wrote tougher and tougher laws, applying the death penalty to a number of additional offenses and requiring judges to impose tougher sentences for certain kinds of offenses. Whether these tougher laws actually deter crime is in some dispute, but there is no question that they increase the judicial workload. (See "Three Strikes and You're Out," below.)

The judicial workload also reflects Americans' tendency to sue, a tendency that may be linked to the rising number of lawyers. In 1850, there was one lawyer for every 1,000 Americans; today, there is one for every 350 or so.[24] As the number of lawyers has grown, so has their search for business. The more Americans bump into each other, both figuratively and literally (two-thirds of state and local court cases deal with traffic violations or accidents), the more they decide to sue.

The courts have struggled to keep up. Despite the 1974 Speedy Trial Act, which requires that all federal criminal trials begin within 100 days, the average delay increased from just under 120 days in 1980 to nearly 210 days by 1996.[25] Merely adding more judges is not necessarily the solution to the problem. As the number of judges has increased, so has the amount of administrative work involved in actually deciding cases. And as the administrative backlogs have increased, so have the delays in coming to decisions. The result is a steady increase in the backlog of civil and criminal cases.

 **in a different light** ——— **THREE STRIKES AND YOU'RE OUT**

As Americans have grown increasingly worried about crime, Congress, state legislatures, and voters have pushed for harsher sentences for a host of crimes. Many of these sentences are mandatory, meaning that a judge must impose a certain penalty if a given defendant is convicted of a particular crime. New York state law, for example, requires a mandatory minimum sentence of fifteen years to life for anyone involved in the sale of two or more ounces of cocaine, whether that sale was the offender's first or hundredth.

One of the most popular forms of mandatory sentencing is called "three strikes and you're out." Under such laws, anyone convicted of a third serious crime, such as murder or drug trafficking, is sentenced to life in prison without the chance of early release through parole. In 1993, voters in Washington state approved an initiative establishing the nation's first "three-strikes-and-you're-out" legislation. In 1994, thirteen other states followed suit, as did the federal government. Almost 80 percent of Americans favor laws imposing such tough mandatory sentences, even if doing so means that state and federal taxes must go up to pay for new prisons.[26]

Such laws have had at least two results that affect the judicial system. The first is an apparent decline in the number of plea bargains in criminal cases. Under such agreements, government reduces the charges against a defendant in return for a guilty plea. The defendant gets less jail time, government saves trial costs, and the judicial workload stays down.

Defendants are clearly less willing to plea bargain when a guilty plea constitutes the third strike against them, especially if the mandatory sentence for a third strike is life in prison. The stiffer the mandatory sentence, the more likely it becomes that the defendant will take his or her chances in court. Before its "three-strikes" law took effect, 90 percent of California's more serious crimes were plea bargained. By March 1995, only 14 percent of "second-strike" cases and 6 percent of "third-strike" cases were being plea bargained, meaning the rest of the cases were awaiting trial.[27] With higher penalties at stake, many of the cases that do go to trial will be appealed, meaning a bigger workload higher up in the judicial system.

The second result of mandatory sentencing laws is a growing number of Americans in jail. At the end of 1994, the U.S. prison population exceeded 1 million inmates for the first time in history. Prison construction is one of the fastest-growing items on state and local budgets, having grown from $6 billion a year in 1980 to well over $30 billion today.

Judges are particularly concerned about the rise in mandatory sentences, largely because such laws reduce their ability to fit the punishment to the circumstances of a particular crime. "Mandatory minimums are frequently the result of floor amendments to demonstrate emphatically that legislators want to get tough on crime," said Supreme Court Chief Justice William Rehnquist in 1993. "It seems to me that one of the best arguments against any more mandatory minimums, and perhaps against some of those that we already have, is that they frustrate the careful calibration of sentences, from one end of the spectrum to the other. . . ."[28] Because mandatory sentences are particularly popular in the war on drugs, a first-time cocaine dealer can get fifteen years without parole, while a first-time rapist can get parole and serve much less time in prison.

Nevertheless, there is some evidence that mandatory sentencing laws may reduce crime. Having repeat offenders in jail means they are not on the streets. One recent study suggested that California's three-strikes law will reduce violent crimes by as much as one-third. Whether spending $20 billion to build the twenty-six new prisons needed to house California's third-strike criminals for life is the only way to get the cut in crime is not quite so clear. As one expert argues, "If you want to deter crime, you have to increase the certainty of punishment, not the severity." In other words, catching more criminals is likely to be more effective in reducing crime than putting a relatively small number of repeat offenders in prison for life.[29]

Appointing Judges

As the number of judgeships has grown with the workload, so, too, has the pressure to find talented people to fill judgeships. Federal court appointments are governed by the same language that applies to all presidential appointments. Under Article II, the president nominates all judges by and with the advice and consent of the Senate. Because most federal judges serve for life, a president can continue to influence the courts long after leaving office.

George Washington established the two basic criteria for the selection process. He tried to make sure, first, that his appointees would be political and ideological allies (all of Washington's judgeships went to Federalists) and, second, that every state would be represented on some court somewhere. Thus, from the very beginning, the courts were instruments of practical politics. (Jimmy Carter added a third test for judicial nominations: racial and gender diversity. It was a test dropped under Reagan and Bush and revived under Clinton.)

Both of Washington's precedents still hold today. Presidents nominate judges who are most likely to agree with them on the key issues before the courts. Democrats nominate Democrats; Republicans nominate Republicans. (See Box 13–4 for the figures over the past fifty years.) In a similar vein, presidents routinely rely on the senators in a given state to provide recommendations for federal judges, thereby meeting Washington's second criterion, state representation. (See Box 13–5 for the steps involved in becoming a Supreme Court Justice.)

Presidents who hope to change how the federal courts decide by making ideological appointments are often disappointed, especially at the Supreme Court level. President Dwight Eisenhower appointed Chief Justice Earl Warren expecting conservative leadership only to watch as Warren led off the civil rights revolu-

BOX **13-4**

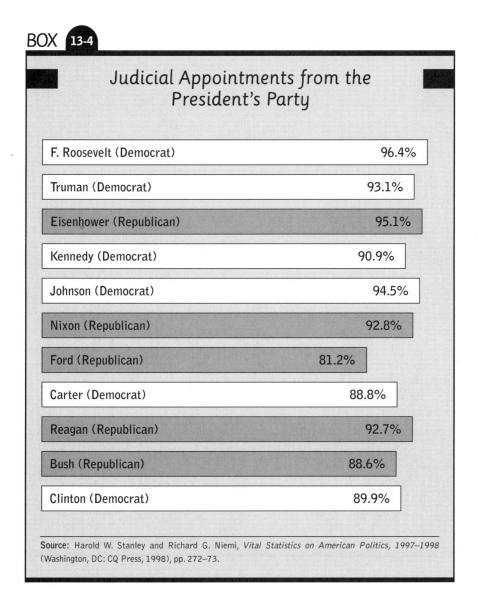

Judicial Appointments from the President's Party

F. Roosevelt (Democrat)	96.4%
Truman (Democrat)	93.1%
Eisenhower (Republican)	95.1%
Kennedy (Democrat)	90.9%
Johnson (Democrat)	94.5%
Nixon (Republican)	92.8%
Ford (Republican)	81.2%
Carter (Democrat)	88.8%
Reagan (Republican)	92.7%
Bush (Republican)	88.6%
Clinton (Democrat)	89.9%

Source: Harold W. Stanley and Richard G. Niemi, *Vital Statistics on American Politics, 1997–1998* (Washington, DC: CQ Press, 1998), pp. 272–73.

tion with *Brown v. Board of Education,* which ended racial segregation of public schools. Eisenhower later called his appointment of Warren "the biggest damn-fool mistake" he had ever made.[30]

Harry Truman felt the same way about his appointment of former Attorney General Tom Clark. Having been nominated to the Supreme Court as a friend of the president's, Clark went against Truman in a key case involving the president's war power, even though he had sided with Truman on the same issue as attorney

BOX 13-5

Steps in Becoming a Supreme Court Justice

1. *Find the Candidate.* Most presidents have delegated that responsibility to someone in their administration, most likely in the attorney general's office. Recommendations might be solicited from White House staff, Congress, governors, bar associations, sitting and retired justices, and personal sources.

2. *Make a Short List.* The president makes a first cut of candidates based on the political impact of their appointment and their fitness to serve. Those that are found acceptable are placed on a short list.

3. *Investigate the Candidates.* Each candidate on the short list is thoroughly investigated by the Federal Bureau of Investigation and formally reviewed by the American Bar Association, which rates candidates either Well Qualified, Qualified, or Not Qualified.

4. *Choose the Nominee.* Weighing a host of political and ideological factors, as well as the chances for Senate confirmation, the president formally nominates a candidate for Senate confirmation.

5. *Hold a Hearing.* The nominee meets informally with members of the Senate Judiciary Committee; the committee holds a formal hearing, takes a vote, and passes the nomination onward to the full Senate.

6. *Confirm the Nominee.* The full Senate approves or rejects the nomination by a simple majority vote. Twenty-nine nominees have been rejected or withdrawn since 1790; only twelve of the twenty-nine actually came to the Senate floor for a final vote.

general. "Whenever you put a man on the Supreme Court he ceases to be your friend," Truman later reflected. "I'm sure of that. Tom Clark was my biggest mistake. No question about it. . . . I don't know what got into me. He was no damn good as Attorney General, and on the Supreme Court . . . it doesn't seem possible, but he's even been worse. He hasn't made one right decision that I can think of."[31]

Presidents also worry about the Senate, where confirmation of their judicial appointees is anything but certain. Although all of George Washington's Supreme Court appointments were quickly confirmed, no precedent was established: 28 of the next 142 were rejected, the most recent defeat coming in 1987 with Reagan's nomination of Robert Bork. Bork was defeated as the result of a campaign launched by abortion-rights groups who feared that he would become the swing vote in reversing *Roe v. Wade*.

Supreme Court nominations have always been controversial to one degree or another; John Tyler, who served as president for one term from 1841 to 1845, lost five nominees. The difference between then and now is that judicial nominations were once handled almost completely out of public view. For many years, Supreme Court nominees did not even appear before the Senate Judiciary Committee for hearings. As a result, senators could support or oppose a president's choice with little fear of consequences for their reelection. The public either did not follow the process or did not care.

Those days of nearly invisible review are long gone, in large part because interest groups in Washington have come to see the appointment of federal judges as a key opportunity to shape what government does. Pro-choice and women's rights groups mounted a successful national campaign against the Bork nomination, and nearly succeeded in stopping the nomination of Clarence Thomas, who was accused of sexual harassment.[32] Bork was so angered by the process that he raised $1.4 million and formed his own group of conservative activists to stop the appointment of what he labeled "activist liberal judges." The result of this increasing political tension may be an increasing number of vacancies, which is discussed in "A Crisis in the Courts?" below.

 **in a different light ———**   **A CRISIS IN THE COURTS?**

As the head of the federal judiciary, Chief Justice William Rehnquist issued a shocking end-of-the-year warning in 1997: One out of every ten federal judgeships was vacant, he noted, and unless something was done soon to fill them, the quality of American justice would surely erode. Rehnquist offered a simple opinion: "Judicial vacancies can contribute to a backlog of cases, undue delays in civil cases, and stopgap measures to shift personnel where they are most needed. Vacancies cannot remain at such high levels indefinitely without eroding the quality of justice that traditionally has been associated with the federal judiciary." He also offered an equally simple solution: "The Senate is surely under no obligation to confirm any particular nominee, but after the necessary inquiry it should vote him up or vote him down. In the latter case, the president can then send up another nominee."[33]

There is no doubt that the Senate played a prominent role in the delays. Convinced that Clinton's nominees were too liberal, and perhaps a bit frustrated with his continued high public approval, Senate conservatives began delaying the president's judicial nominees through holds and seemingly endless investigations. (Recall from Chapter 10 that a hold is one way a senator can kill a bill; it is also an easy way to delay a nomination.) Senate inaction accounted for roughly two-thirds of the 80-plus vacancies at the end of 1997. The Senate confirmed only 17 judges in 1996 and another 36 in 1997, significantly fewer than the 101 it confirmed in 1994.

Republicans used a variety of reasons to waylay individual appointments. They refused to either confirm or reject University of California law professor William Fletcher largely because he was active in Democratic party politics, lawyer Margaret Morrow because she questioned California's use of the referendum process to deny welfare to illegal immigrants, and state-level judge Judith McConnell because she granted a sixteen-year-old boy's custody request to live with his father's gay partner in the wake of his father's death, even though his mother had been declared unfit. Common to all the cases, according to Senate Judiciary Chairman Orrin Hatch (R-UT), was judicial activism, which is discussed later in this chapter. "There are many parties who have a role in these problems," Hatch told the Associated Press. "The No. 1 problem happens to be activist judges who continue to find laws that aren't there and expand the law beyond the intent of Congress."[34]

The Clinton administration played a role in the vacancies, too. The presidential appointments process was notoriously slow in producing names, in part because the president was so eager to find more women and minorities to nominate to the judiciary and in part because the White House was simply disorganized. The Senate could hardly vote on nominations that the president had not yet made, which is a situation that accounted for one-third of the 1997 vacancies.

Whatever the causes of the delays, the effects were ominous. "From 1979 to 1996, the average time taken to fill [U.S. district and appeals court] vacancies was 464 days," writes David Meador. "To my knowledge, there is no other nation on earth, high or low, developed or undeveloped, that has such a situation. This borders on a national disgrace in my view. In England, a vacancy on the bench is filled within a week or two. On the continent of Europe, vacancies are usually filled within a month or less."[35] Consider the impact of vacancies in the U.S. District Court that handles cases in northern New York state. With two of its five judgeships vacant, the average caseload had increased from roughly 700 cases per judge to 1,100, producing one of the biggest backlogs in the nation. A stunning percentage of cases are now over three years old. It hardly matters who is at fault. Three years is a long time to wait for justice.

THE SUPREME COURT AT WORK

Although the Supreme Court is only one part of a much larger judicial system, it would be a mistake to underestimate its impact on American life. Its total number of cases may be small, but they are the most important cases heard and decided. Not only is the Supreme Court the final word in specific cases, it has the ultimate power to overturn acts of Congress, state laws, local ordinances, and even its own past decisions.

This power means that even the most insignificant Supreme Court decision can create a ripple effect across the nation. Declaring one state's law unconstitutional usually means that all similar state laws are unconstitutional; requiring one school or university to open its doors to women usually means that all similar schools must do so; requiring that one prisoner be given decent cell space usually means decent cell space for all prisoners.

That power, and its increasing use in recent years, also means that the Supreme Court has become a much more significant check on Congress and the presidency. Whether the Founders intended the federal judiciary to become such a dominant player is a question best left to constitutional scholars.

Making Opinions

The Supreme Court is nothing if not predictable. It starts each of its yearly terms on the first Monday in October and usually finishes by the end of June. Each week from the start of the term through April, the justices follow the same schedule: oral arguments for three or four hours each Monday, Tuesday, and Wednesday; private conferences attended by all nine justices each Friday. The justices spend the rest of the time working on opinions, most of which are released in the spring and summer.

Because so much is at stake when the Supreme Court decides, its process deserves special attention. The process involves four steps: (1) receiving the request for appeal, (2) deciding which requests to accept, (3) hearing the case, and (4) making the decision and writing the opinion.

Receiving the Request for Appeal.   Besides its very limited original jurisdiction, the Supreme Court can only make decisions on requests for appeal from below. Almost all such requests come to the Supreme Court docket, or agenda, from either a state supreme court or a federal court. (See Box 13–6 for diagrams of the two paths upward.)

Reaching the Supreme Court is no small feat. In the state courts, most cases must rise through three levels before making their way to the Supreme Court:

BOX 13-6

How a Case Reaches the Supreme Court

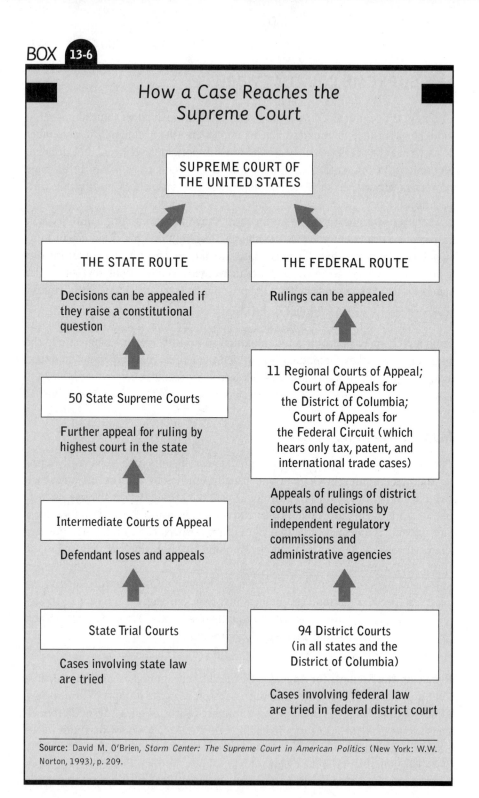

SUPREME COURT OF THE UNITED STATES

THE STATE ROUTE

Decisions can be appealed if they raise a constitutional question

50 State Supreme Courts

Further appeal for ruling by highest court in the state

Intermediate Courts of Appeal

Defendant loses and appeals

State Trial Courts

Cases involving state law are tried

THE FEDERAL ROUTE

Rulings can be appealed

11 Regional Courts of Appeal; Court of Appeals for the District of Columbia; Court of Appeals for the Federal Circuit (which hears only tax, patent, and international trade cases)

Appeals of rulings of district courts and decisions by independent regulatory commissions and administrative agencies

94 District Courts (in all states and the District of Columbia)

Cases involving federal law are tried in federal district court

Source: David M. O'Brien, *Storm Center: The Supreme Court in American Politics* (New York: W.W. Norton, 1993), p. 209.

Level 1. A case starts out in any one of several courts with original jurisdiction: a state or local administrative agency might say an adult bookstore cannot open near a church or preschool; a specialized court might take a baby away from his or her adoptive parents in favor of a long-lost grandparent; a municipal court might order all Amish to put reflective safety triangles on their horse-drawn carriages, even though such "decorations" violate their religion; or a superior court might convict a murderer on the basis of a DNA blood test.

Level 2. Once decided, the case can go up on appeal to a state court of appeal, which can consider state constitutional questions governing any decision and often must review any appeal of a superior court conviction.

Level 3. Once decided again, the case can go up for one last appeal to the state supreme court, which makes the absolute final decision in all but the cases permitted to go into the federal system under the Constitution.

When a case involves a constitutional question (such as freedom of speech for an adult bookstore, freedom of religion for the Amish, or due process for a murderer), it is a likely controversy for the Supreme Court. Roughly one in five Supreme Court requests come up from the state supreme courts; almost all the rest come up from the federal courts of appeals (cases from federal agencies can get to the Supreme Court more directly under certain circumstances).

In the federal courts, the same pattern holds, but for just two levels:

Level 1. Once again, the case starts out in a court of original jurisdiction: the Federal Communications Commission (which is a regulatory agency) might deny a radio license to a religious broadcaster; the Department of Commerce (an administrative agency) might fire a federal employee; or a district court might convict someone of violating a federal law (recall that of the four police officers involved in the Rodney King beating who were first acquitted in a state court, two were later convicted on a different charge in a federal court).

Level 2. Once again, the case moves up to a court of appeals. Anyone who loses a case in a district court has a right to appeal upward for review. However, as noted earlier, the appeal can address only the fairness of the process, not the facts of the case. As a result, most district court decisions are not appealed.

Whatever the route, nearly every case comes to the Supreme Court docket under a petition for a **writ of certiorari,** a Latin term meaning "made more certain" or "better informed." The petition asks the Supreme Court to order a lower court to produce the record of the case—*writ* is merely a term meaning "order."

Petitions for certiorari, or "cert.," do not have to be neat or even written by lawyers to be granted. Indeed, it was a handwritten petition on yellow legal paper from Florida state prisoner Clarence Gideon that led the Court to hear *Gideon v. Wainwright,* a landmark 1963 case that established the right to a court-appointed attorney for all poor persons accused of felonies.[36] When the Supreme Court is willing to hear a case after considering a petition for writ of certiorari, it grants cert.; when it chooses not to hear the case, it denies cert.[37]

The Supreme Court will not hear just any case. Under its own rules, it will grant cert. only in one or more of the following situations: (1) when a federal court of appeals has rendered a decision that conflicts with the decision of another federal court of appeals on the same matter; (2) when a federal court of appeals has rendered a decision that conflicts with that of a state supreme court; (3) when a federal court of appeals has departed from the accepted and usual course of judicial proceedings; (4) when a state supreme court has decided a federal question that conflicts with a ruling by another state supreme court or the federal courts; or (5) when a state or federal court of appeals has decided an important question of federal law that should have been settled by the U.S. Supreme Court.[38]

Deciding Which Requests to Accept. As these five tests suggest, the Supreme Court does not take ordinary cases. As Justice Felix Frankfurter once stated, "Importance of the outcome merely to the parties is not enough."[39] The Supreme Court reserves its limited time and energy for the kinds of controversies described just above. Lower courts and lawyers should be able to interpret past decisions well enough to determine what the law means. Thus, the Supreme Court's power *not to decide* can be as important as many of its formal decisions.

The Supreme Court decides not to decide by denying certiorari without explanation in 85 to 90 percent of the requests. "I would guess that somewhere between one and two thousand of the petitions for certiorari filed with the Court each year are patently without merit," writes Chief Justice William Rehnquist; "even with the wide philosophical differences among the various members of the Court, no one of the nine would have the least interest in granting them."[40]

The justices grant certiorari through a rather informal process of assigning, reading, and debating potential cases. If even one justice thinks a petition is worth discussing, it is put on the agenda for the regular weekly conference of all the justices. About one-quarter of all requests are discussed at one point or another. The justices use a **Rule of Four** to make the decisions on granting certiorari—four justices must agree to grant the request.

As the number of requests for Supreme Court action have increased, the percentage of petitions granted has gone down. A Supreme Court of nine members had to pare back. In the 1920s, roughly 20 percent of all petitions for certiorari were granted; by 1992, the rate was down to just 3 percent. The absolute number of requests granted fell, too: the Supreme Court granted just 105 writs of certiorari in 1995, down from a high of 299 in 1971.[41]

Even after cert. has been granted, a case can still be pulled from the schedule by the plaintiff. In November 1997, for example, plaintiffs in the case of *Piscataway Board of Education v. Sharon Taxman* withdrew their complaint only weeks before the Supreme Court was to hear oral argument. The case had originally been filed by Taxman, a white schoolteacher who had been laid off from her job so that an African American teacher could stay. Because the two schoolteachers had started their teaching careers in Piscataway, New Jersey, on the same day, and had very similar qualifications, Taxman argued that she had been fired solely on the basis of race. The lower courts agreed, awarding her $433,500 in back pay and penalties. Although Taxman had already been rehired by the time the case was resolved, the school board did not want to pay the money and appealed, turning the case from *Taxman v. Piscataway* into *Piscataway v. Taxman*.

The problem with the case was that it appeared to invite the Supreme Court to make a sweeping decision against programs that give minorities preferences in getting and holding jobs. For civil rights groups such as the National Association for the Advancement of Colored People, the case was "too perfect," meaning that the Supreme Court would have little trouble reaching a unanimous or near-unanimous decision to strike down the use of race by employers to make hiring and firing decisions. Worried that the Supreme Court would do just that, civil rights groups banded together and raised the money to pay most of Taxman's $433,500 settlement. Once Piscataway agreed to pay the $433,500, the case was deemed moot and removed from the calendar. The battle over racial preferences would have to be fought again elsewhere, perhaps on a case that was somewhat less perfect.[42]

Hearing the Case. For the vast majority of plaintiffs, being granted cert. is a cause for celebration. It means that they will be allowed to present their case to the highest court in the land, appearing before the nine justices to make their oral arguments in the ornate chambers of the U.S. Supreme Court. (See Box 13–7 for a list of the major decisions made during the 1997–1998 term.)

The oral argument usually occurs three months after cert. is granted. At a precisely appointed time, nine justices take their places on the bench (the chief justice in the middle, the least senior justices at the two far ends), and the hour of argument begins. Half of the time goes to the plaintiff, the other half to the defendant. Although a half hour may seem short, the Supreme Court rarely grants exceptions to the time limit. The purpose of oral argument is not to restate the case, but to give the justices a chance to probe specific questions about the record.[43]

The arguments may be short compared to floor debates in the House and Senate, but they appear to matter—in fact, Justice William O.Douglas asserted that "oral arguments win or lose the case."[44] Also unlike the House or Senate, all the members are present. The informal rules governing oral argument are clear: be brief, do not read from a prepared text, and be quick in answering questions. There is no time to waste.

The lawyers who speak before the Court do not all speak with equal authority. First among them is the **solicitor general,** who represents the United States government, which is involved in roughly half of the cases that come before the Supreme Court. Appointed by the president and confirmed by the Senate, the so-

BOX 13-7

Major Supreme Court Decisions of the 1997–1998 Term

Line Item Veto—Congress cannot give the president the power to cancel provisions of bills he has signed into law. Line Item Veto Act of 1996 is unconstitutional. (*President Clinton v. City of New York,* 7–2)

HIV Discrimination—The Americans with Disabilities Act can bar discrimination against people infected with the virus that causes AIDS. (*Bradgon v. Abbott,* 5–4)

Attorney–Client Privilege—The attorney–client privilege survives the death of the client. (*Swidler & Berlin v. United States,* 6–3)

Forfeiture—The government cannot impose a criminal forfeiture that is "grossly disproportionate" to the offense for which the property's owner is being punished. (*United States v. Bajakajian,* 5–4)

Sexual Harassment—Law on sexual harassment in the workplace is clarified and strengthened. (*Faragher v. City of Boca Raton* and *Burlington Industries v. Ellerth,* 7–2)

Same-Sex Harassment—Federal law protects people from being sexually harassed on the job by others of the same sex. (*Oncale v. Sundowner Offshore Services,* 9–0)

Student Harassment—Schools are not liable for a teacher's sexual harassment of a student unless officials actually knew of the problem and refused to intervene. (*Gebser v. Lago Vista Independent School District,* 5–4)

Federal Arts Funding—The law requiring the National Endowment for the Arts to take "decency" into account when making grants to artists does not violate the First Amendment. (*National Endowment for the Arts v. Finley,* 8–1)

Ellis Island—Nearly all of the historic island is under the jurisdiction of New Jersey, not New York. (*New Jersey v. New York,* 6–3)

Private Property—Interest on small, temporary deposits that clients leave with their lawyers is the property of the clients. Such interest is currently channeled to fund state legal aid services. (*Phillips v. Washington Legal Foundation,* 5–4)

Source: Linda Greenhouse, "Supreme Court Weaves Legal Principles from a Tangle of Litigation," *New York Times,* June 30, 1998, p. A20.

licitor general is a senior officer of the Department of Justice. The solicitor decides which cases the government will ask the Court to review, which cases the government will appeal, and what position the United States will take in each case. As former Reagan administration Solicitor General Charles Fried explains,

> . . . the Solicitor General's job has hardly changed since 1870 [when it was created by statute]. He still goes to the Supreme Court in morning coat and striped trousers as the principal spokesman there of the government. It is his job to approve what the government will say in any appellate court in the country. His staff is small (about twenty lawyers), and he takes personal, not just bureaucratic, responsibility for every decision, every brief he signs. In a real sense the Solicitor General is responsible for the government's legal theories, its legal philosophy.[45]

The solicitor general can appear before the court in at least three different roles: representing the defendant when someone sues the federal government, as a plaintiff when the federal government sues a state or individual, or as a friend of the court when the federal government takes a position on a case in which it is neither defendant nor plaintiff. This third role involves filing an **amicus curiae brief,** which literally translates into "friend of the court." (Recall from Chapter 7 that interest groups often submit amicus briefs as part of their efforts to influence Supreme Court decisions on behalf of their members.)

Making the Decision and Writing the Opinion.   The justices do not rely solely, or even primarily, on oral arguments in making their final decisions. They read the original record, consult the law journals, and read the amicus briefs submitted on one side or the other of the case. Although the solicitor general is an important source of these briefs, they can also be submitted by just about anyone with the resources and interest to draft a formal statement.

It is useful to note that the number of amicus briefs has risen dramatically in recent years. In the 1920s and 1930s, for example, less than 2 percent of all Supreme Court cases involved any amicus briefs at all.[46] In 1988 alone, over 80 percent of all cases had at least one amicus brief, and some particularly controversial cases had many more. *Webster v. Reproductive Health Services,* a 1989 case that challenged a Missouri antiabortion law, generated seventy-eight amicus briefs representing over four hundred different organizations.[47]

In addition to careful reading and reflection by individual justices, formal decisions evolve through an ongoing conversation among the justices, whether in ones and twos or in full conferences. The most important votes on a case are taken at these conferences. These votes determine which justices will be in the majority and minority. Although the votes are not absolutely final, they clearly direct the general tone of the Court's final opinion. Under Rehnquist, the chief justice votes first, followed by the most senior justice, moving down one by one to the most junior justice.

These conferences rarely change opinions, however. The docket is just too big to argue each case through in the short time available. As Justice Antonin Scalia remarked after two years on the Court, "To call our discussion of a case a conference is really something of a misnomer. It's much more a statement of the views of each of the nine Justices, after which the totals are added and the case is assigned. I don't like that. Maybe it's just because I'm new. Maybe it's because I'm an academic. Maybe it's just because I am right."[48]

After the conference votes, the most senior member of the majority is asked to either write the opinion or delegate it to another justice. When the chief justice is in the majority, he or she either writes the opinion or assigns it to another justice. Chief Justice Earl Warren decided to write the 1954 *Brown v. Board of Education* opinion that overturned school segregation because of the enormous controversy it involved. As he remembered almost twenty years later,

> I assigned myself to write the decision, for it seemed to me that something so important ought to issue over the name of the Chief Justice of the United States. In drafting it, I sought to use low-key, unemotional language and to keep it short enough so that it could be published in full in every newspaper in the country. I kept the text secret (it was locked in my safe) until I read from the bench.[49]

(Most opinions are still read out loud by the author from the bench. In criminal cases, Rehnquist not only reads his decisions but also recounts the details of the crime.)

Once a majority opinion is drafted, justices have a variety of choices. They can simply sign on to the majority opinion. They can write a concurring opinion that reaches the same conclusion as the majority but through different legal reasoning. They can join with other justices in signing such a concurring opinion. They can write a dissenting opinion explaining why they disagree with the majority. Or they can join with other justices in signing such a dissenting opinion.

Concurring opinions were exceedingly rare until the 1940s, when the proportion began to rise to its current level of roughly 40 percent of all decisions.[50] Dissenting opinions show the same pattern: rare until the 1940s, but now attached to about 60 percent of all decisions. Although roughly two-thirds of the ninety-one *decisions* in the 1997–1998 term were unanimous, and only one-sixth by a 5–4 vote, the Court appears to be increasingly unable to reach consensus on the actual majority *opinions* it writes.[51]

This process definitely produces winners and losers. In the 1993–1994 term, for example, Justice Anthony Kennedy seemed to hold the balance of power on close cases (5–4 and 6–3 votes), joining the winning side on 85 percent of the cases, while Justice Harry Blackmun was the most isolated, appearing on the winning side in just 35 percent of the cases.[52] Kennedy continues to play this balancing role to this day. In the 1997–1998 term, for example, he was the fifth vote in all but two of the 5–4 decisions. As for dissenting votes, Scalia and John

Paul Stevens form the two ends of the ideological spectrum. On the left, Stevens cast twenty-two dissenting votes in the ninety-one cases; on the right, Scalia cast nineteen.

Shortcuts to Decision.   Making a decision and writing an opinion clearly take a certain amount of time—too much time for some cases, such as final appeals from death row inmates about to be executed. Petitions for immediate relief in such cases are sometimes handled under a **Rule of One**—that is, a single justice can decide to issue a writ ordering immediate action that will stand until the rest of the Supreme Court can meet. A **writ of habeas corpus** allows all courts, federal and state, to protect people who are falsely imprisoned. Technically, the term *habeas corpus* means "to produce the body." Legally, it is a request for an immediate review to determine whether a person is being unlawfully imprisoned or detained.

Whatever the writ is called, almost all carry an *injunction* ordering or delaying a specific act. An injunction to stay, or delay action, is particularly important to prisoners on death row seeking to have their cases reviewed at the eleventh hour. Because of the life-and-death nature of these cases, the Court has special procedures for reviewing the requests. As retired Justice Blackmun explained on *Nightline,*

> The justices have scattered and gone home probably. We know in advance about scheduled executions. There is at least one clerk from each chamber who is here, perhaps all night, if necessary. My clerk is on the phone probably several times as papers are being filed and we talk about them. Nearly always the vote is by telephone. On occasion, we have a conference call where we all get on the line. But it is kind of like a death watch.[53]

From the summer of 1993 through January 1994, the Court received fifty-four applications for emergency relief; thirty-six were denied; eighteen were granted, including seven from death row prisoners. The eighteen that were granted involved a stay of some kind until the rest of the Supreme Court could consider the question.

The Conflict over Judicial Activism

One reason for the growing tension on the Supreme Court, which is reflected in the increased number of concurring and dissenting opinions, involves the expanding role of the judiciary in making broad national policy. As all levels of government struggle to deal with an increasingly complex, often divided society, the Constitution is being tested in areas of daily life the Founders could hardly have imagined—from the right to die to genetic testing. The result has been an increasing number of laws and precedents overturned, alongside a growing role for the courts in running everything from schools to prisons.

It is important to note that such judicial activism is not exclusive to either a liberal or a conservative position. The ideological tone all depends on the precedents in place at the start of a given era. Conservative Supreme Courts can be just as active in overturning acts of Congress or precedents if those acts and precedents happen to come from a liberal era. Thus, activism is largely in the eye of the beholder: liberals see conservative courts as too activist, and vice versa. (See Box 13–8 for the history of activism.)

If activism were just a liberal tool, for example, a conservative Supreme Court would never overturn past precedents. But, as Box 13–8 clearly shows, the Rehnquist Court, which is generally seen as conservative, overturned twenty-one precedents in its first five years, many of them eroding liberal precedents established

BOX **13-8**

The Impact of Supreme Court Decisions

Number of Decisions That Overturned . . .

	Past Supreme Court Decisions	Acts of Congress	State Laws	Local Ordinances
1789–1800	0	0	0	0
1801–1835	3	1	18	0
1836–1864	6	1	21	0
1865–1873	3	10	33	0
1874–1888	11	9	7	0
1889–1910	4	14	73	15
1910–1921	6	12	107	18
1921–1930	5	12	131	12
1930–1940	14	14	78	5
1941–1946	24	2	25	7
1947–1952	11	1	38	7
1953–1969	46	25	150	16
1969–1986	52	34	192	15
1986–1991	21	7	46	10

Source: David M. O'Brien, *Storm Center: The Supreme Court in American Politics* (New York: Norton, 1993), p. 63.

under the Warren Court two decades before. The difference between a liberal and a conservative Supreme Court is not in the level of activism, but in ideology.

It is not clear what the Founders would think of this activism. On the one hand, the Founders certainly saw the courts as an important check on legislative power. Recall Hamilton's vision of the courts as a last brake against public passion. Lacking a strong check, Congress would be free to repudiate the Constitution at will.

On the other hand, the Founders also might argue that the lawmaking power clearly resides in Article I and the legislature. Hamilton defended the courts in *Federalist Paper No. 78* as "the bulwarks of a limited Constitution against legislative encroachment," but he also argued that the courts should not "substitute *WILL* instead of *JUDGMENT*," nor "substitute their own pleasure to the constitutional intentions of the legislature."[54]

Some legal scholars interpret this language of "will" and "judgment" to argue that the courts should always interpret the Constitution in the strictest possible terms. If a power or right is not written into the Constitution, this argument goes, judges should not write it now. Others argue that the courts should not become "super legislatures," substituting their judgments for the rightful decisions of duly elected officials. As judicial scholar Henry Abraham argues, however, there is a fine line between Hamilton's "judgment" (sometimes labeled **judicial restraint**) and "will" (often labeled **judicial activism**).[55] Like all fine lines, whether one sees restraint or activism often depends on one's ideological lens. What looks like making laws to conservatives may be restraint to liberals, and vice versa, depending on who happens to be making the decision.

Again, it is hard to know where the Founders would draw the fine line. They might applaud the aggressive use of the courts to protect the rights of minorities. After all, one of the judiciary's prime duties was to protect Americans from each other. But they might also worry that the federal judiciary, by its very decisions, is becoming too intimately involved in actually making the laws.

There is no question, however, that judicial activism has driven some of the key decisions of recent history. A passive judiciary never would have ordered that the Topeka School Board integrate its schools, for example, or ruled that every person charged with a crime is entitled to legal counsel.[56]

No matter what the label, all courts, in effect, make law. As former Chief Justice Earl Warren once remarked, "It doesn't make it consciously, it doesn't do it by intending to usurp the role of Congress but because of the very nature of our job. When two litigants come into court, one says the act of Congress means this, the other says the act of Congress means the opposite of that, and we say the act of Congress means something—either one of the two or something in between. We are making law, aren't we?"[57] Given their embrace of the English common law tradition, and its history of judge-made law, the Founders would likely agree.

 **in a different light** ——— THE IMPORTANCE OF STAYING ANONYMOUS

The federal judiciary is a mystery to most Americans. In an age of *Court TV* and *The People's Court*, Americans know surprisingly little about how the federal courts work, and can do better at identifying the Three Stooges than the nine justices of the Supreme Court. (See Box 13–9 for the name recognition of the nine current justices of the Supreme Court.)

Being anonymous is just fine with the Supreme Court, however. The justices know that the legitimacy of their decisions depends in part on maintaining anonymity. The public's willingness to obey a judicial decision must always reside in the decision itself, not in the personality or appearance of the judge. The less the public knows about a given judge, the better.

BOX 13-9

Members of the Supreme Court, 1998

	Year Appointed	President	Percent Recognized in 1995
Chief Justice			
William H. Rehnquist	1972	Nixon	8%
Associate Justices			
John P. Stevens	1975	Ford	1
Sandra Day O'Connor	1981	Reagan	31
Antonin Scalia	1986	Reagan	6
Anthony M. Kennedy	1988	Reagan	4
David H. Souter	1990	Bush	4
Clarence Thomas	1991	Bush	30
Ruth Bader Ginsburg	1993	Clinton	7
Stephen Breyer	1994	Clinton	1

Source on public recognition: Joan Biskupic, "Has the Court Lost Its Appeal?" *Washington Post,* October 12, 1995, p. A23.

The Supreme Court does not act in secret, however. All Supreme Court decisions are public, and all oral argument occurs in the open. There may not be television cameras in the chamber, but every American is free to wait in line for a turn at watching the nine justices perform without a safety net: "Power and vulnerability exist side by side. No aides hand the Justices follow-up questions to ask the lawyers; no chairman gavels a recess when things get sticky. The atmosphere is businesslike. The Justices make nothing so clear as that every second counts. Showmanship is disfavored; when an inexperienced lawyer makes a florid presentation, a chill almost visibly settles on the bench."[58] The only justice who never speaks during oral argument is Clarence Thomas, who simply believes that the hour of argument is to hear what the lawyers, not the justices, have to say about a case.

What makes Supreme Court justices and other federal judges different from other political leaders is that they seek anonymity, creating a "cult of the robe" in which judges use their anonymity to distance themselves from the public. The justices cannot allow themselves to become celebrities. They would never appear on *The Late Show with David Letterman* to discuss a decision, as Vice President Al Gore did in late 1993 to promote his reinventing government agenda; nor would they show up on one of the Sunday morning talk shows to argue a case.

This anonymity, and the mystery that goes with it, is not necessarily bad for justice. If Americans knew the real justices, or so the notion goes, they would start to think of the Supreme Court as just another collection of politicians and might lose respect for the Supreme Court's decisions. Being anonymous is a fundamental basis for public trust.

The fact is that all courts, from the Supreme Court down to local traffic court, have little else beyond legitimacy to enforce their rulings. They have no army or police force to make the country behave. They can order a Nativity display dismantled, but cannot tear it down; they can order that an African American child be allowed to enter an all-white school, but cannot escort her to class; they can order a convicted child rapist released into the community, but cannot unlock the cell. All the courts can do is issue orders and hope the public will obey.

Obviously, judges can become celebrities despite their best intentions. Supreme Court justices do get noticed from time to time—that is how the public learned that Justice Ginsburg reads her mail by flashlight at the movies; "I don't care much for commercials and previews," she explained.[59] Lance Ito became a public figure merely by being the next superior court judge in line for a murder trial when the O. J. Simpson case came up.

But it is one thing for a judge to become known, and quite another to seek celebrity in the first place. If judges were suddenly to start endorsing political candidates, lending their names to causes, or appearing as regular guests on the Sunday news shows, their courts would lose some of their mystery. And that might weaken their ability to protect Americans from their government and each other, both subjects of Chapter 14.

MAINTAINING THE BALANCE

The federal judiciary has never been more important to maintaining the delicate balance between government action and inaction. It has become a key referee between Congress and the presidency, and has come to use the power of judicial review as a definite check on the other two branches. As the United States continues to grow and divide against itself, the judiciary also plays an increasing role in protecting us against ourselves—assuring our civil liberties and protecting our civil rights. Hence the number of laws, cases, and courts grows steadily.

Despite these changes, the federal judiciary more closely resembles the original constitutional design than either Congress or the presidency does. There are more courts than the Founders could have foreseen, and more women and minority judges than the Founders could have expected. There are more cases and procedure than the Founders could have predicted. But even where the courts have been more active than Hamilton and his colleagues might have liked, they have acted mostly to protect us from ourselves, guarding the Constitution from encroachment and confirming basic rights embedded in the Founders' original design.

This does not mean the courts are immune to criticism. Protecting Americans from each other is often unpopular, as is protecting the rights of the accused. Prohibiting Nativity displays and prayer in school, opening all-male colleges to women, protecting gays and lesbians from discrimination, overturning death penalties, upholding the right to burn the American flag, allowing adult bookstores to stay open, and permitting abortions are hardly the kinds of decisions that make all Americans happy. (Many of these cases will be discussed in Chapter 14.) Every decision makes someone, often many someones, mad.

The more Americans worry about crime, the more the courts will come under criticism. Indeed, it was public anger that led to recent efforts to impose mandatory sentences for a host of federal and state crimes. Not knowing exactly how to solve the crime problem, legislators increasingly see their role as imposing strict limits on judicial discretion—hence the rising tide of laws mandating life sentences for three-time offenders. Such three-strikes-and-you're-out laws give judges little freedom to shape the sentence to the facts of the case.

Ultimately, these efforts are designed to somehow make the judiciary more responsive to public demands for action, which is exactly what the Founders hoped to avoid. They wanted the courts to be perfectly insulated from public opinion and gave federal judges life tenure as one part of the equation. The more Americans pressure the courts, the more they threaten their own freedom. This is one area in which a government *not* of the people is absolutely essential.

JUST THE FACTS

terms to remember

federal judiciary (p. 532)
statutory law (p. 534)
common law (p. 534)
stare decisis (p. 535)
precedents (p. 535)
trial courts (p. 535)
appellate courts (p. 535)
judicial review (p. 537)
justiciable issue (p. 539)
adverseness (p. 539)
standing to sue (p. 539)
ripe for decision (p. 539)

moot (p. 539)
constitutional courts (p. 547)
legislative courts (p. 547)
writ of certiorari (p. 561)
Rule of Four (p. 562)
solicitor general (p. 563)
amicus curiae brief (p. 565)
Rule of One (p. 567)
writ of habeas corpus (p. 567)
judicial restraint (p. 569)
judicial activism (p. 569)

facts and interpretations

- The judicial workload has increased dramatically over the past fifty years, in part because the United States has become a much more complex society and in part because Americans are so concerned about crime. The number of cases at all levels of the federal judiciary and at the state court level has increased. The question is whether the courts can keep up with the deluge of cases while dispensing justice in a timely fashion.

- Appointing judges is one of the most important decisions a president makes. Because federal judges serve for life, a president can influence the courts long after leaving office. George Washington established two precedents for appointing judges that still hold today: judges had to be politically and ideologically compatible with the president, and every state had to be represented by a judge on some federal court somewhere. A third criterion, racial and gender diversity, has been added to the list by modern presidents. The lack of agreement on the level of judicial activism that is acceptable in a judge has resulted in increasing delays in the appointments process, which in turn has added to a growing backlog of court cases.

- The Supreme Court remains the most powerful American court. Its decisions have ripple effects throughout society and are weighed carefully by the nine justices. The Supreme Court makes its opinions through a four-step process: (1) receiving the requests for appeal, (2) deciding which requests to accept, (3) hearing the case, and (4) making the decision and writing the opinion. Although cases reach the Supreme Court primarily on appeal from below, the number of requests, called writs of certiorari, has grown so dramatically that the Supreme Court now accepts just 3 percent of the total.

- The federal judiciary has become increasingly active in shaping public policy (who gets what, when, and how from government). This judicial activism, as it is often labeled, reflects the growing complexity of society. One way to measure activism is to track the number of laws that the federal judiciary declares to be unconstitutional. Whether the courts are regarded as exercising judicial restraint or judicial activism often depends on the ideology of the observer. The fact is that all courts make laws, which is part of the common law tradition that the Founders so heartily embraced.

open questions

- Did the Founders make the right decision in not allowing direct election of federal judges? Would direct election make justice faster? Does it make any sense to have federal judges selected through the nomination and appointment process, when so many state and local judges are elected? If the Founders were so right about protecting judges from public pressure, should states and localities change their systems of selection?

- To what extent has the Founders' final check become too active over time? Would they still see the judiciary as so harmless, so unable to annoy? Does the fact that Congress is passing so many mandatory sentencing laws suggest that the federal judiciary is not working so well or that Congress is working too hard?

- What makes a good judge? Should demographic diversity be part of the answer? What about wisdom and intellect? How much weight should be given to a judge's connection with the ordinary Americans whose lives are affected by what the federal judiciary does? If the weight should be considerable, how might law schools and law firms make such a connection more likely?

- Should the Supreme Court open its oral arguments to television cameras, as the House and Senate do? What are the reasons for giving Americans a closer look at how the Supreme Court works? Do television shows such as *The People's Court* help or hurt the public's confidence in the federal judiciary?

for further study

Bickel, Alexander M. *The Least Dangerous Branch.* New Haven, CT: Yale University Press, 1962.

Coffin, Frank. *On Appeal: Courts, Lawyering, and Judging.* New York: Norton, 1994.

Goldman, Sheldon. *Picking Federal Judges: Lower Court Selection from Roosevelt through Reagan.* New Haven, CT: Yale University Press, 1997.

Katzmann, Robert, ed. *Judges and Legislators: Toward Institutional Comity.* Washington, DC: Brookings Institution, 1988.

O'Brien, David. *Storm Center: The Supreme Court in American Politics.* New York: Norton, 1993.

Rehnquist, William H. *The Supreme Court: How It Was, How It Is.* New York: Morrow, 1987.

Silverstein, Mark. *Judicious Choices: The New Politics of Supreme Court Nominations.* New York: Norton, 1994.

endnotes for chapter 13

1. Roy P. Fairfield, ed., *The Federalist Papers* (Baltimore: Johns Hopkins University Press, 1981), p. 227.
2. Fairfield, *The Federalist Papers,* p. 227.
3. David O'Brien, *Supreme Court Watch 1993* (New York: Norton, 1994), pp. 243–44.
4. Lawrence M. Friedman, *A History of American Law* (New York: Simon & Schuster, 1973), p. 95.
5. Fairfield, *The Federalist Papers,* p. 227.
6. Fairfield, *The Federalist Papers,* p. 231.
7. Fairfield, *The Federalist Papers,* p. 228.
8. See Alexander M. Bickel, *The Least Dangerous Branch* (New Haven, CT: Yale University Press, 1962), p. 1.
9. The figures are from David O'Brien, *Storm Center: The Supreme Court in American Politics* (New York: Norton, 1993), p. 63.
10. O'Brien, *Storm Center,* pp. 210–20.
11. Fairfield, *The Federalist Papers,* p. 233.
12. See O'Brien, *Storm Center,* p. 100.
13. Thurgood Marshall, "Reflections on the Bicentennial of the United States Constitution," *Harvard Law Review,* 101, no.1,(1987), p. 2.
14. Quoted in Neil A. Lewis, "GOP, Its Eyes on High Court, Blocks a Judge," *New York Times,* June 13, 1998, p. A1.
15. See Maeva Marcus and Natalie Wexler, "The Judiciary Act of 1789: Political Compromise or Constitutional Interpretation," in M. Marcus, ed., *Origins of the Federal Judiciary: Essays on the Judiciary Act of 1789* (New York: Oxford University Press, 1992), p. 14.
16. John Frank, *Marble Palace* (New York: Knopf, 1968), p. 9.
17. Most of the statistics on federal workload discussed below are from Harold W. Stanley and Richard G. Niemi, *Vital Statistics on American Politics, 1997–1998* (Washington, DC: CQ Press, 1998), pp. 276–80.
18. Henry J. Abraham, *The Judicial Process,* 6th ed. (New York: Oxford University Press, 1993), p. 156.
19. Robert Kastenmeier and Michael Remington, "A Judicious Legislator's Lexicon to the Federal Judiciary," in Robert Katzmann, ed., *Judges and Legislators: Toward Institutional Comity* (Washington, DC: Brookings Institution, 1988), p. 60.
20. Frank Coffin, *On Appeal: Courts, Lawyering, and Judging* (New York: Norton, 1994), p. 46.
21. Coffin, *On Appeal,* p.56.
22. Stephen Reinhardt, "Are 1,000 Federal Judges Enough? No. More Cases Should Be Heard," *New York Times,* May 17, 1993, p. A11.
23. Stanley and Niemi, *Vital Statistics,* p. 377.
24. See Richard Abel, *American Lawyers* (New York: Oxford University Press, 1989), p. 280.
25. Stanley and Niemi, *Vital Statistics,* p. 279.

26. Margaret Edwards, "Mandatory Sentencing," *CQ Researcher,* May 26, 1995, p. 473.

27. Fox Butterfield, "California's Courts Clogging under Its 'Three Strikes' Law," *New York Times,* March 23, 1995, p. A1.

28. Quoted in David B. Kopel, "Prison Blues: How America's Foolish Sentencing Policies Endanger Public Safety," Cato Institute, Policy Analysis No. 208, pp. 18–19.

29. Edwards, "Mandatory Sentencing," p. 471.

30. Quoted in O'Brien, *Storm Center,* p. 81.

31. O'Brien, *Storm Center,* p. 81.

32. See Mark Silverstein, *Judicious Choices: The New Politics of Supreme Court Nominations* (New York: Norton, 1994).

33. Excerpts of Rehnquist's report were reprinted in the *Washington Post,* January 2, 1998, p. A21.

34. Associated Press, "Report: Judiciary Chairman Says Senate Not to Blame in Judgeship Feud," January 2, 1998, newsfeed.

35. Daniel Meador, "Problems and Uncertainties in the Appointment of Federal Judges," *Miller Center Journal,* (Spring 1998), p. 42.

36. The case can be found at 372 U.S. 335 (1963); see Anthony Lewis, *Gideon's Trumpet* (New York: Random House, 1964), for the story of the case.

37. Abraham, *The Judicial Process,* p. 175.

38. Rule 17 of the Supreme Court's Review Process, in Lee Epstein, Jeffrey Segal, Harold Speth, and Thomas Walker, *The Supreme Court Compendium* (Washington, DC: CQ Press, 1994), p. 53.

39. Quoted in Abraham, *The Judicial Process,* p. 176.

40. William H. Rehnquist, *The Supreme Court: How It Was, How It Is* (New York: Morrow, 1987), p. 264.

41. Linda Greenhouse, "High Court Opens Its Fall Session by Refusing Cases," *New York Times,* p. A10.

42. Steven A. Holmes, "Rights Deal a Pullback to Help Keep Preferences," *New York Times,* November 25, 1997, p. A37.

43. See Abraham, *The Judicial Process,* p. 192.

44. Quoted in the *Philadelphia Inquirer,* April 9, 1963, as cited in Abraham, *The Judicial Process,* p. 191.

45. Charles Fried, *Order and Law: Arguing the Reagan Revolution: A Firsthand Account* (New York: Simon & Schuster, 1991), p. 14.

46. Epstein et al., *The Supreme Court Compendium,* p. 581.

47. See O'Brien, *Storm Center,* p. 45.

48. Quoted in the *New York Times,* February 22, 1988, p. A16.

49. Quoted in the *New York Times,* July 11, 1974, p. A35.

50. Epstein et al., *The Supreme Court Compendium,* p. 158.

51. Linda Greenhouse, "Supreme Court Weaves Legal Principles from a Tangle of Litigation," *New York Times,* June 30, 1998, p. A20.

52. Joan Biskupic, "The Supreme Court's Emerging Power Center," *Washington Post National Weekly Edition,* July 11–17, 1994, p. 31.

53. Joan Biskupic, "11th-Hour Stay Requests Are Business as Usual for the High Court," *Washington Post,* January 16, 1994, p. A10.

54. Fairfield, *The Federalist Papers,* p. 230.

55. Abraham, *The Judicial Process,* p. 316.
56. Walter Murphy and C. Herman Pritchett, *Courts, Judges, and Politics: An Introduction to the Judicial Process* (New York: Random House, 1979), p. 37.
57. Quoted in the *New York Times,* June 27, 1969, p. 17.
58. Linda Greenhouse, "Life and Times," *The New York Times Magazine,* March 7, 1993, p. 84.
59. Linda Greenhouse, "A Talk with Ginsburg on Life and the Court," *New York Times,* July 7, 1994, p. B11.

civil liberties
and civil rights

*protect us from our
government and each other*

American government does not
exist only to defend the nation
from foreign and domestic threats.
It also exists to assure the blessings of liberty for individual
Americans. That means the Constitution must protect citizens
from their government and from
each other by assuring **civil liberties,** which guarantee freedoms
such as speech, press, and religion, and **civil rights,** which protect citizens against discrimination
on the basis of individual characteristics such as race, gender, and
disability. One way to distinguish
the two types of protection is to

remember that civil liberties protect individual citizens against government (government is prohibited from establishing a national religion, for example), while civil rights generally protect individual citizens from each other (businesses cannot discriminate against women or minorities in employment, for example).

Most of the protection resides in the Bill of Rights, the first ten amendments to the Constitution. Recall from Chapter 2 that the Founders did not include a bill of rights in their final draft of the Constitution. They believed that their system of separate powers, interests and layers, and checks and balances would be enough to protect the public against a tyranny of the majority. Moreover, most states already had bills of rights in their constitutions.

Also recall that most citizens of the young nation did not share the Founders' confidence in Articles I, II, and III as their sole sources of protection.[1] Facing opposition to ratification of the Constitution, the Founders promised that the First Congress would enact a bill of rights. Working through a list of nearly two hundred proposals, that Congress eventually proposed twelve amendments, of which ten were eventually ratified by the states. (Recall that one of the two lost amendments, regulating congressional pay, was ratified as the Twenty-seventh Amendment in 1992.)

As noted in Chapter 2, the Bill of Rights is best viewed as a statement of limits, that is, of what the federal government cannot do to the public. As such, it provides a basic list of civil liberties, which protect individuals from their government, not a list of civil rights, which protect individuals from each other.

Americans received additional protections from each other under the Fourteenth Amendment, which was ratified following the Civil War in 1868. Under the amendment, no state shall "deny to any person within its jurisdiction the equal protection of the laws." Under this **equal protection clause**, all citizens, whether former slaveholders or slaves, have the same rights to be protected from each other.

The Fourteenth Amendment also prohibited states from denying any of their citizens life, liberty, property, or any of the privileges granted by the Constitution without **due process of law**, meaning a fair and open process. Each state was also required to ensure that every person within its jurisdiction would be given equal protection under the law, meaning that states could not single out certain groups of citizens for special treatment or punishment.

The challenge in maintaining these protections is that they often frustrate the will of the majority. Indeed, some of the most famous Supreme Court cases have pitted a single individual against the majority of Americans—a single African American who objected to sitting at the back of the bus, a single high school student who objected to a graduation prayer, a single woman who objected to sexual harassment on the job.

Ultimately, this power to frustrate can lead the majority of Americans to long for a government in which no individual citizen can stand in the way of what the majority sees as progress. At the same time, it can also lead minorities to wonder whether government will ever act at all—after all, it took four score and seven (eighty-seven) years for Abraham Lincoln to issue the Emancipation Proclamation freeing the slaves, and another three score years for Congress to grant women the right to vote. And many would argue that the United States has yet to make things right with the Native Americans who occupied this land long before the first foreign immigrants arrived. But even as those delays frustrate majority and minority alike, they also protect. What has taken so long to achieve is also extremely difficult to undo.

Before this chapter turns to separate discussions of civil liberties and civil rights, however, it is important to understand how the Bill of Rights came to involve so much of American life. Originally designed to protect Americans only from their national government, the Bill of Rights was steadily pushed downward to cover every corner of state and local life.

NATIONALIZING THE BILL OF RIGHTS

The most significant events in the evolution of America's civil liberties and civil rights involve what judicial scholars call the **nationalization of the Bill of Rights.** Nationalization is the slow but steady effort to extend the Bill of Rights to cover the actions of state and local governments toward their citizens and the actions of individual citizens toward each other.

For the first one hundred years of the Bill of Rights, the ten amendments did not apply to actions by the states, just the federal government. In 1789, the public did not worry about the states—states were seen as protectors of civil rights and liberties, not as threats. Indeed, many state constitutions at the time contained lists of basic rights, some of which were much more detailed than the Bill of Rights itself. Instead, people wanted a Bill of Rights to protect them from the federal government.

Dual Citizens

Given a chance to expand the Bill of Rights to the states in *Barron v. Baltimore* in 1833, the Supreme Court declined. John Barron owned a prosperous cargo wharf just off the deepest water in Baltimore Harbor—prosperous, that is, until the city of Baltimore dumped so much sand into the water that ships could no longer reach Barron's wharf and his business was ruined.

Barron sued the city under the Fifth Amendment. Although best known for its protections against self-incrimination—individuals cannot be forced to testify against themselves—the Fifth Amendment also protects citizens from unreasonable "takings" of property. Simply put, government may not take something of value from a citizen without providing reasonable compensation. In Barron's view, government (the city of Baltimore) had taken something of very great value (his wharf) without paying anything at all. The trial court agreed with the argument and awarded him $4,500. The city of Baltimore appealed to the Supreme Court.

Barron's case was doomed by one fact: Baltimore was seen as part of the state of Maryland, not of the national government. Under this logic, Barron was a *dual citizen,* first of the state of Maryland and second of the United States of America. If Maryland did not provide protection against takings of property, Barron would have to suffer the consequences. Chief Justice John Marshall made the point in simple terms: "The Constitution was ordained and established by the people of the United States for themselves, for their own government, and *not for the government of their individual states.*"[2] Having concluded that the Bill of Rights did not apply to the states, in part because the states already had their own strong bills of rights, the Marshall Court voided Barron's award.

Fast forward to 1994 and a small business owner in Tigard, Oregon, a tiny suburb of Portland. Florence Dolan wanted to expand her store and pave her parking lot, a relatively simple business decision. But under Tigard's land-use regulations, she could do the work only if she agreed to set aside about one-tenth of her two-acre property for a bike path and small public park. Dolan sued her local government, arguing that the land-use requirement constituted the same kind of taking that had so angered Barron 160 years before. Despite having already lost three times—first at the local planning board, second at an Oregon appeals court, and third at the Oregon Supreme Court—Dolan appealed to the U.S. Supreme Court. There she won a 5–4 decision forcing the city to either reargue its taking or give up.[3] The specifics of *Dolan v. Tigard* are far less important than the simple fact that the Supreme Court felt quite comfortable intervening in a local decision.

A Steady Nationalization

What had happened between 1833 and 1994? The answer is that the federal judiciary had slowly expanded coverage of the Bill of Rights to the states, eventually allowing Dolan to use the federal courts to sue Tigard. Like Barron, Dolan was still a dual citizen, but unlike Barron, she was a citizen of the United States first and of Oregon second.

BOX **14-1**

Nationalizing the Bill of Rights, Step by Step

Year	Right (Amendment)	Case That Extended the Right to the State or Local Level
1897	Fair payment for property (V)	Chicago, Burlington & Quincy RR v. Chicago
1927	Freedom of speech (I)	Fiske v. Kansas
1931	Freedom of the press (I)	Near v. Minnesota
1932	Counsel in capital cases (VI)	Powell v. Alabama
1937	Assembly and petition (I)	DeJonge v. Oregon
1940	Exercise of religion (I)	Cantwell v. Connecticut
1947	Establishment of religion (I)	Everson v. Board of Education of Ewing Township
1948	Public trial (VI)	In re Oliver
1949	Unreasonable search and seizure (VIII)	Wolf v. Colorado
1958	Association (I)	NAACP v. Alabama
1961	Exclusion of evidence from unreasonable search and seizure (IV)	Mapp v. Ohio
1962	Freedom from cruel and unusual punishment (VIII)	Robinson v. California

The breakthrough in Dolan's case actually came with the ratification of the Fourteenth Amendment over one hundred years before Tigard took its action. With the end of the Civil War, southern states became a greater threat to liberty than the federal government. The Reconstruction Era, which lasted until the late 1800s, was one of the most divisive periods in history. It spawned the white-hooded Ku Klux Klan, which spreads its message of hate to this day, and a host of

Year	Right (Amendment)	Case That Extended the Right to the State or Local Level
1963	Counsel in felony cases (VI)	Gideon v. Wainwright
1964	Self-incrimination (V)	Malloy v. Hogan
1965	Confront opposing witnesses (VI)	Pointer v. Texas
1965	Privacy (I, III, IV, V, IX, XIV)	Griswold v. Connecticut
1966	Impartial jury (VI)	Parker v. Gladden
1967	Speedy trial (VI)	Klopfer v. North Carolina
1967	Obtain supporting witnesses (VI)	Washington v. Texas
1968	Jury trial in nonpetty cases (VI)	Duncan v. Louisiana
1969	Double jeopardy (V)	Benton v. Maryland
1972	Counsel in criminal cases involving a jail term (VI)	Argersinger v. Hamlin

Source: David M. O'Brien, *Constitutional Law and Politics: Civil Rights and Liberties* (New York: Norton, 1991), pp. 280–81.

political devices for denying rights to the 4 million former slaves. The Fourteenth Amendment gave them broad outlines of protection as they built new lives.

As this chapter later suggests, the amendment did not suddenly nationalize the Bill of Rights. Rather, it merely laid the groundwork for one hundred years of Supreme Court decisions.[4] The key sentence in the amendment is simple enough: "No State shall make or enforce any law which shall abridge the privileges or immunities of citizens of the United States; nor shall any State deprive any person of life, liberty, or property without due process of law; nor deny to any person within its jurisdiction the equal protection of the laws." The Fourteenth Amendment thus made clear that the Fifth Amendment's due process clause applies to the states.

The nationalization of the Bill of Rights was hardly over with the Fourteenth Amendment, however. The federal judiciary had to decide whether the Fourteenth Amendment applied just to the Fifth Amendment's due process provisions or to the entire Bill of Rights. At least in the beginning, the Supreme Court took the narrow view that the Fourteenth Amendment did not automatically bring the states under any part of the Bill of Rights. Indeed, in its very first decision on the issue, the Supreme Court actually decided not to incorporate the states under the Bill of Rights at all.

Under the *Slaughterhouse Cases,* a collection of cases assembled for a single decision in 1873, the Supreme Court had been asked to apply the equal protection clause to several New Orleans slaughterhouses located along the Mississippi River.[5] The state of Louisiana had passed a law prohibiting the slaughter of livestock near the river to protect the public from the spread of deadly cholera. The slaughterhouse owners sued, arguing that they had been deprived of their livelihood without due process. (Note the similarities to Barron's complaint, the difference being the use of the Fourteenth Amendment, not the Fifth, as the basis for the slaughterhouses' suit.) The Supreme Court disagreed, concluding that the Fourteenth Amendment was concerned only with protecting former slaves, thereby denying the applicability of the amendment to other citizens. The *Slaughterhouse Cases* were the beginning of a long trail of cases leading to nationalization, some that blocked nationalization for a period, others that advanced it.

If the Bill of Rights was to be nationalized, change would have to come one case at a time. Some citizen would have to find a state law that violated some part of the Bill of Rights—say, freedom of speech or the right to a speedy trial—then file a case using the Fourteenth Amendment as a basis to argue that the state law was unconstitutional. Through favorable rulings in such cases, the federal courts could slowly expand the Bill of Rights to incorporate the states. (See Box 14-1, on pages 584–585, for a list of the key nationalization cases.[6])

That is exactly what has happened over the years as cases have come before the Court. Slowly but surely, the Fourteenth Amendment has become the vehicle to nationalize the Bill of Rights. By the late 1920s, the federal judiciary was beginning to accept the notion that every citizen had fundamental rights, regardless of where they lived. States could no longer violate the freedom of speech as of 1927, freedom of the press as of 1931, freedom of religion as of 1940, or the separation of church and state as of 1947. Nor would they be free to deny the accused a public trial as of 1948, deny protection from self-incrimination as of 1964, deny the right to privacy as of 1965, deny a speedy trial as of 1967, try the accused twice for the same crime (double jeopardy) as of 1969, or deny a lawyer in any criminal case involving a jail term as of 1972.[7] By 1972, the expansion was just about complete.

There are still pieces of the Bill of Rights that do not apply to the states. The right to bear arms has never been pushed downward, for example, nor has the right against excessive fines. On the other hand, some states are ahead of the Constitution in granting certain rights to their citizens. For example, the right to privacy is not specifically written into the U.S. Constitution, and the Supreme Court had to infer it from other constitutional amendments in order to establish it in 1965. Some states have included the right to privacy as a separate constitutional amendment.

The Bill of Rights has been almost fully nationalized, but the Supreme Court can still reverse the trend. In 1995, for example, the Supreme Court issued two 5–4 decisions that reflected growing support for reversing decades of federal dominance. One case overturned the Gun Free School Zones Act, which required states to ban the possession of firearms near local schools, while the other rejected a federal law requiring states either to regulate low-level radioactive waste (of the kind produced in medical facilities) or "take title" to the waste and dispose of it properly themselves.[8] Even more recently, as noted in Chapter 3, the Supreme Court overturned the Brady Handgun Violence Prevention Act in *Printz v. United States,* arguing that the federal government cannot order states and localities to do its job for it.

☀ in a different light ——— IS THERE A RIGHT TO DIE?

Until April 2, 1996, thirty-two states prohibited physicians from assisting terminally ill patients to end their lives. On that date, the U.S. Court of Appeals for the Second Circuit (which covers twelve states including New York) voided New York's version of the ban in *Quill v. Vacco.*[9] The defendant was Dennis C. Vacco, who, as the attorney general of New York, was responsible for enforcing the ban. The case was filed by three physicians, one of whom was Timothy Quill, who wrote the *New England Journal of Medicine* in 1991 to admit that he had once prescribed a lethal dose of sleeping pills to a terminally ill patient. "Doctors have been doing this," another of the physicians in the case, Howard Grossman, said of assisted suicide, "but they have been isolated, alone and terrified, afraid to reveal their secret even to the person they sleep next to every night."[10]

The three physicians were joined by three of their terminally ill patients, one of whom was Rita Barrett, a physical education teacher who had thyroid cancer and wanted her doctor to prescribe painless medication to help her end what had been a painful battle with an inevitable outcome. None of the three patients lived to hear the decision. "She had this sense that this would be her legacy," said Barrett's daughter. "When she told me she joined the suit, she told me that it was the right

thing to do, that people shouldn't be made to suffer just because they were terminally ill."

The plaintiffs argued that state restrictions on assisted suicide denied personal liberties without due process and equal protection under the Fifth and Fourteenth Amendments. Under New York law, patients had the right to ask physicians
to stop all efforts to prolong life, such as heroic attempts to resuscitate people suffering a heart attack or stroke. But under the same law, a patient had no right to ask
a physician to hasten death.

By a unanimous decision, the appeals court struck down most of New York's
ban. If a patient can commit suicide by refusing treatment, the appeals court argued, "they should be free to do so by requesting appropriate medication to termi-
nate life during the final stages of terminal illness." The court concluded that bans
on assisted suicide "are not rationally related to any legitimate state interest."
"What interest can the state possibly have in requiring the prolongation of a life
that is all but ended?" the appeals court asked. "And what business is it of the state
to require the continuation of agony when the result is imminent and inevitable?"

New York State appealed the decision to the U.S. Supreme Court, which took
up the right to die in two cases, the first being *Vacco* and the second involving a
challenge to a similar law in Washington State. The Supreme Court chose the Wash-

Dr. Jack Kevorkian, highly visible
advocate of assisted suicide, has
admitted helping 120 incurably
and terminally ill people take
their own lives between 1990
and mid-1998.

ington State case, *Washington v. Glucksberg,* to make its broad statement on the right to die. By the time both cases reached the Supreme Court, all of the patients involved had died. The cases continued because the physicians were also at risk of criminal prosecution for assisting in suicides.

Both sets of physicians based their hopes on a 1990 Supreme Court decision involving Nancy Cruzan, who had been in a vegetative state for seven years following a car accident. In *Cruzan v. Director, Missouri Department of Health,* the Supreme Court had agreed with Missouri in denying the Cruzan family's request to remove their daughter's feeding and water tubes. In doing so, however, the Supreme Court had confirmed a constitutional right permitting people to refuse medical treatment.[11] Only months after the decision, a Missouri state judge decided that Nancy Cruzan would have refused treatment, and the feeding and water tubes were removed. She died on the day after Christmas that year.

The physicians in *Vacco* and *Glucksberg* asked the Supreme Court to extend the permission to refuse treatment to include requests for help in committing suicide. It was a permission the Supreme Court unanimously refused to give. Instead, the Supreme Court allowed each state to decide on its own whether to permit or forbid physician-assisted suicide. The justices clearly understood the issues at stake. As a teenager, Justice Ginsburg had lost her mother to cancer, while Justice O'Connor was a survivor of breast cancer. "Death will be different for each of us," O'Connor concurred in an emotional opinion. "For many, the last days will be spent in physical pain and perhaps the despair that accompanies physical deterioration and a loss of basic bodily and mental functions." But that pain did not justify a deliberate act to help someone take his or her own life. The need to protect individuals who are neither fully competent nor truly facing imminent death, as well as the need to protect individuals whose decisions to hasten death might not be truly voluntary, were sufficient to justify the New York and Washington bans on assisted suicide.[12] With the Supreme Court's decision on June 26, 1997, all thirty-two state bans on physician-assisted suicide were back in full force.

With or without a legal blessing, however, the quiet practice of physician-assisted suicide may go on nonetheless. According to a study released just before the Second Circuit's 1996 decision, requests for such help are not rare and are honored for one out of four patients.[13] Moreover, only months after the Second Circuit's decision, voters in Oregon narrowly approved a "right to die" initiative permitting assisted suicide. Under the Supreme Court's decision, such permission is perfectly legal. It is up to each state to decide whether it will allow or prohibit assisted suicide. But by its decisions in *Vacco* and *Glucksberg,* the Supreme Court clearly declared that a right to die does not exist in the Constitution or its amendments.

CIVIL LIBERTIES: PROTECTING US FROM OUR GOVERNMENT

In launching the Revolutionary War in 1776, the Declaration of Independence asserted the basic right of every American to "Life, Liberty, and the pursuit of Happiness," a right granted not by government, but by the "Creator." In many ways, therefore, the Bill of Rights is best seen as a restatement of what many Americans already held to be "self-evident," that all people are created equal.

The most familiar of these rights are found in the First Amendment, which guarantees freedom of religion, press, and speech. Americans accused of crimes have significant protections under the Bill of Rights, too. And the courts have even found a right to privacy in between the other rights spelled out in the first ten amendments. Each of these rights—religion, press, speech, the rights of the accused, and privacy—is discussed below.

Freedom of Religion

Freedom of religion is the most basic civil liberty guaranteed by the Bill of Rights. It comes before freedom of speech and freedom of assembly in the First Amendment: "Congress shall make no law respecting an establishment of religion, or prohibiting the free exercise thereof. . . ." Indeed, Jefferson called it "the most inalienable and sacred of all human rights."[14]

Americans may not be the most religious people compared to people of other nations, but religion remains prominent in American life nonetheless. Not only do almost two-thirds of Americans say that religion is very important in their own lives, but they also believe that religion is still relevant to all or most of today's problems.[15] Presidents go to church regularly; the Senate and House of Representatives start each day with prayer; the back of every dollar bill carries the motto "In God We Trust"; and between 60 and 70 percent of Americans support some form of school prayer. Moreover, religion has clearly played a prominent part in political history, most recently when southern, white born-again Christians played a major role in lifting Republicans to victory in the 1994 congressional campaigns.[16]

Thus, the question is not so much whether Americans are religious as why there is a wall between church and state. Not surprisingly, the answer goes all the way back to the founding and the evolution of the First Amendment. The amendment actually contains two clauses on religion: the **establishment clause**, which prohibits the establishment of a national religion, and the **free exercise clause**, which prohibits any government interference in the practice of religious beliefs. Each clause has generated its own controversies over the years.[17] Can a public school choir leader require students to sing Christian music? Can a city council start its meeting with a short prayer? Can a high school graduation ceremony involve a moment of silence? The answers involve a balance between protecting individuals against any hint that government favors a particular religion and still allowing them to practice their religion in a way that honors their own traditions. Because Americans seem infinitely capable of inventing new tests of the freedom of religion, it is not always clear just where the Supreme Court stands at any point in time.

What is clear is that the Founders mostly wanted to prohibit creation of a *particular* religion or a *particular* church, not to ban religion from American life. They did not want to separate Americans from their religious beliefs, nor did they want to protect government from religion. Rather, they wanted to protect religion from government.[18]

Toward that end, the Supreme Court has generally argued that government should neither aid nor hinder religion, simultaneously avoiding establishment and promoting free exercise. On the one hand, state legislatures can open their sessions with a prayer, a Nativity scene is fine as part of a larger Christmas celebration at a city park, school districts can lend textbooks to religious schools, and student religious groups can meet in public school buildings. On the other hand, a Christmas creche, or Nativity scene, is not permitted if it is to stand by itself on city ground, a city cannot allow churches to veto liquor licenses, states may not order schools to teach the biblical theory of creation, and public schools cannot give financial aid for field trips taken by religious school students.

These positions are constantly changing with the times. In 1985, for example, the Supreme Court ruled 5–4 that New York City could not provide any instruction to parochial school students on parochial school premises because such aid overstepped the boundary between church and state. Over a decade later, however, the Supreme Court reversed itself in another 5–4 ruling, allowing New York City to provide remedial instruction for parochial school children on parochial school grounds. What had changed? The balance of power on the Supreme Court had shifted. Presidents Ronald Reagan and George Bush appointed four new justices, while Bill Clinton appointed only two, shifting the center of the court exactly one justice to the right.

The line between what is and is not permitted can be blurry at times, in part because the courts can act only when a specific case is presented for decision. The Bill of Rights is not a self-enforcing document; violations can and do occur until they are challenged in the courts. Why is it permissible, for example, to have a Nativity scene in a park, but not in City Hall? Why is it acceptable to lend a religious school textbooks, but not to provide instruction in religious school buildings? The answer rests in the effort to prevent government from promoting a specific religion even as it goes about the business of celebrating holidays and educating students. (See Box 14–2 for a comparison of the two Christmas creche cases.)

It is important to note that the separation of church and state does not ban religious groups from trying to influence government. They have the same rights

BOX 14-2

Rulings on Christmas Creches

A Nativity scene is fine as part of a Christmas celebration. . .

Lynch v. Donnelly, 465 U.S. 668 (1984)

Pawtucket, Rhode Island, set up a Christmas display in a nonprofit-owned park in the heart of the shopping district every Christmas season. It contained all of the usual Santa Claus-related decorations plus a creche. The presence of the creche was challenged as a violation of the Establishment clause. The Supreme Court ruled that "The display is sponsored by the City to celebrate the Holiday and to depict the origins of that Holiday. These are legitimate secular purposes." Furthermore, any benefit to a particular religion from the display is "indirect, remote and incidental."

. . . But not as a single display in a city office building

Allegheny County v. Greater Pittsburgh ACLU, 492 U.S. 573 (1989)

The Roman Catholic Holy Name Society donated a creche that was displayed in the Allegheny, Pennsylvania, County Courthouse. The Court ruled that the display was impermissible as a single display. Without the other, secular seasonal symbols surrounding it (for example, Santa Claus, candy canes, the North Pole), the display "sends an unmistakable message that it supports and promotes the Christian praise to God that is the creche's religious message."

to assemble peacefully and petition government as other Americans.[19] Although some Americans argue that religion has no place in government, even to the point of protesting the morning prayer that opens each day of Congress, the Founders most certainly did not intend religious Americans to be silent on the great issues of the day.

 **in a different light ——— SCHOOL PRAYER**

Freedom of religion involves hard questions about where government ends and religion begins. There is no more controversial issue in the debate than school prayer. The vast majority of Americans see absolutely nothing wrong with opening each

public school day with a moment of silence or spoken prayer. But whether organized prayer in public schools is silent, spoken, printed on a wall (Tennessee once ordered that the Ten Commandments be displayed on school walls), or nondenominational, the Supreme Court has generally ruled that it violates the First Amendment.

The line against prayer in public schools was drawn in a series of cases that began in the 1960s. The first case, *Engel v. Vitale,* came in 1962: the Supreme Court ruled that New Hyde Park, New York, schools could not start the day with the following one-sentence prayer: "Almighty God, we acknowledge our dependence upon Thee, and we beg thy blessings upon us, our parents, our teachers and our Country."[20] A second case quickly followed, striking down a Pennsylvania law requiring a daily Bible reading and the Lord's Prayer.[21] As one case followed another, the courts expanded the protections to prohibit both voluntary prayer and a moment of silence at the start of each day.[22]

One of the most recent affirmations of the ban involved a prayer at a middle school graduation ceremony. The case, *Lee v. Weisman,* was decided in 1992. Deborah Weisman, a student at Nathan Bishop Middle School in Providence, Rhode Island, was about to graduate when her father, Daniel Weisman, found out that a local rabbi had been asked to deliver the opening and closing prayer at the graduation ceremony. Deborah and her father asked a district court to stop the school from including prayers in its graduation ceremony, but the court denied the request. The Weismans attended the ceremony, then filed suit again, this time to prevent school officials from arranging for prayers at future high school graduations, which would someday soon involve Deborah.

What made the prayer a problem was not just that the school had scheduled an invocation and benediction, but that it had also sent the rabbi a pamphlet outlining the elements of a good prayer—for example, that the prayer show "inclusiveness and sensitivity." Although the pamphlet was well-meaning, it meant the school (and, therefore, the state) had a hand in composing the prayer, hence favoring a religion. The district court ruled in the Weismans' favor, prompting the school district to appeal on behalf of the principal, Robert Lee—hence the case title, *Lee v. Weisman.*

In this case, as with the others on prayer, the Supreme Court's concern was clear: government could not endorse prayer because prayer is an expression of religion. Students who did not believe in prayer would be unprotected. As Justice Anthony Kennedy, a Reagan appointee, wrote for the 5–4 majority, "The school district's supervision and control of a high school graduation ceremony places public pressure, as well as peer pressure, on attending students to stand as a group or, at least, maintain respectful silence during the Invocation and Benediction. This pressure, though subtle and indirect, can be as real as any overt compulsion."[23] The Supreme Court prohibited any further prayers at graduation.

According to news reports at the time, Deborah's peers were angered by the controversy. And not just students in Rhode Island, either. The student council president of Penn Laird High School in Virginia vowed to include a prayer and Bible verse in his graduation address in 1993, saying, "It's not an issue of Christianity. It is an issue of free speech. If a Muslim student wants to get up and pray, I'd sit there and listen."[24]

But it was not a majority that was at risk here. For many students, a prayer would have been no big deal, especially if it did not favor one religion or another. Moreover, public opinion is clearly on the side of a little school prayer. Roughly three in five Americans see nothing wrong with reading the Lord's Prayer or Bible verses in schools.[25] The sheer number of Americans who believe in school prayer is not the issue at all. The issue is whether there is a minority, even one composed of but a single student, who might be forced to participate against his or her will.

The school prayer debate is hardly over. Advocates of prayer in public schools have made some progress by defining prayer as freedom of speech rather than free expression of religion. In 1995, the Supreme Court appeared to give the definition some momentum in *Rosenberger v. the University of Virginia.* The 5–4 decision required the university to provide the same financial support to a student religious newspaper as it provides for any other student newspaper. In doing so, the Supreme Court noted the difficulty in knowing when, as Justice Lewis Powell once puzzled, "singing hymns, reading scripture, and teaching biblical principles cease to be singing, teaching, and reading."[26] When a public school schedules a prayer, picks the clergy, and offers instructions on how to write a proper text, it goes over the line into state establishment of religion; but when it makes space available for Bible readings, it may be merely allowing religious students to do what other students already do: engage in free speech.

It is not yet clear where the Supreme Court's next freedom of religion case will come from. It could come from a Jewish high school student named Cheryl Bauchman, who filed suit against the Salt Lake City School District in 1995 for allowing her school choir teacher to include Christian music in its repertory. Although her case was denied at both levels of the lower courts, *Bauchman v. West High School* is just the kind of case that gives the Supreme Court a chance to further define the lines on freedom of religion.

The next case could also come from Yale University, where five Orthodox Jewish students filed suit in 1997 to prohibit the university from forcing all first- and second-year students to live in university dormitories. The students felt that the residential dormitories represented a kind of modern Sodom and Gomorrah built around coed bathrooms, free condoms, unlimited visitation, and easily accessible safe-sex manuals. They did not ask that Yale change the dorms, however. Rather, they only asked to be allowed to live off campus. When Yale refused, in part because of its broader commitment to breaking down barriers between student groups, the students filed suit, asking the courts to declare Yale a public, not private, institution, at least for purposes of protecting freedom of religion.[27]

Freedoms of the Press and Speech

Freedoms of the press and speech also reside in the First Amendment and protect everything from calling for the overthrow of government to distributing pornography. It is important to note, however, that First Amendment protection is not as strong as some of the Founders hoped. James Madison, in particular, was so worried about censorship that he proposed an entirely separate amendment prohibiting the states from interfering with the press.

Like the rest of the liberties guaranteed in the Bill of Rights, these freedoms have been tested and refined over the years. Neither the press nor individual Americans can say anything they wish, for example. Free speech is unprotected when it involves a lie. Both slander, which is a false and defamatory statement by the spoken word, and **libel,** which is a false and defamatory statement by the written or electronic (television, radio) word, are grounds for a lawsuit.

Even here, however, the First Amendment provides some protection. In *New York Times Co. v. Sullivan* in 1964, the Supreme Court ruled that public officials at all levels of government can sue for libel only if they can prove the press published a story that defamed them (that is, harmed their reputations) "with knowledge that it was false or with reckless disregard of whether it was false or not." The case revolved around L. B. Sullivan, a Montgomery, Alabama, city commissioner who argued that the *New York Times* had libeled him by printing an advertisement attacking the city of Montgomery for violating civil rights. The Supreme Court ruled that public officials have much less protection than private citizens against libel, even if they are wronged (which the Court refused to determine in the *Sullivan* case). As Justice William O. Douglas argued, citizens and the press have "an absolute, unconditional privilege to criticize official conduct despite the harm which may flow from excesses and abuses. The prized American right 'to speak one's mind' about public officials and affairs needs 'breathing space to survive.'"[28]

This freedom to speak one's mind was not always so broadly interpreted, however. Until the 1950s, for example, the federal courts had been particularly harsh toward Americans whose free speech created a "clear and present danger" to the nation during wartime. The **clear and present danger test** was established by the Supreme Court in 1919 to uphold the conviction of Charles Schenck. As secretary of the Socialist party during World War I, Schenck took responsibility for discouraging young men from entering the draft. That he was woefully unsuccessful in his work did not matter to the federal government. What mattered, according to the Supreme Court in *Schenck v. United States,* was that Schenck's words were "used in such circumstances and are of such a nature as to create a clear and present danger that they will bring about the substantive evils that Congress has a right to prevent."[29]

Although the ruling appeared to leave room for unpopular speech—if not advocating the overthrow of government, which is often labeled subversive speech, then at least allowing criticism of government—the federal courts allowed states to impose tough restrictions on even limited criticism until the late 1960s. It was not until 1969, in *Brandenburg v. Ohio,* that the Supreme Court finally protected all subversive speech unless it advocated an immediate, violent, and illegal action. Brandenburg was a Ku Klux Klan leader who had told a Klan rally that "it's possible that there might have to be revengeance [sic] taken" if the federal government continued to "suppress the white, Caucasian race." Brandenburg had been convicted of violating restrictions on subversive speech, but the Supreme Court overturned the conviction by requiring that subversive speech involve something more than a vague threat against government.[30]

The federal courts had also been harsh toward free speech (in the form of magazines and books) whose effect was to "deprive and corrupt those whose minds are open to such immoral influences and into whose hands a publication of this sort might fall."[31] This historical test of obscenity was so broad that it led to the banning of books by such noted authors as James Joyce, D. H. Lawrence, and Arthur Miller. It began to unravel in a series of cases starting in 1957. By 1969, the Supreme Court had granted protection even to hard-core pornography, provided that the hard-core pornography meets broadly defined community standards. At the same time, however, the Supreme Court allows communities to ban the sale of pornography to children, limit sexually explicit entertainment, and prohibit the location of adult bookstores in certain areas of cities.

The problem in regulating obscenity starts with defining the term. While the courts have allowed communities to regulate obscenity when "the average person, applying contemporary community standards, would find that the work, taken as a whole, appeals to the prurient interest," the standard is exceedingly difficult to use.[32] Just what is a prurient interest? What is obscene—a nude painting, an adult movie, just certain paintings and movies? The difficulty led Justice Potter Stewart, who served on the Supreme Court from 1958 to 1981, to argue that while he could not define obscenity, "I know it when I see it."[33]

The lack of precise definitions led the Supreme Court to declare the 1996 Communications Decency Act unconstitutional. Enacted to protect children from "indecent" and "patently offensive" material by keeping it off the Internet, the act was so broadly worded that the Supreme Court worried about its impact in limiting access for adults. Writing for a unanimous Court, Justice John Paul Stevens offered a simple balancing test:

> The record demonstrates that the growth of the Internet has been and continues to be phenomenal. As a matter of constitutional tradition, in the absence of evidence to the contrary, we presume that governmental regulation of the content of speech is more likely to interfere with the free exchange of ideas than to encourage it. The interest in encouraging freedom of expression in a democratic society outweighs any theoretical but unproven benefit of censorship."[34]

in a different light ——— CAMPUS HATE SPEECH

The definition of what constitutes free speech continues to evolve on college campuses, where codes against hate speech have proliferated over the past decade. The debate about campus speech codes is intimately related to a little-noticed event in Minnesota that eventually led to a landmark Supreme Court case in 1992, *R.A.V. v. St. Paul.* Just before daybreak on June 21, 1990, a group of teenagers poured lighter fluid on a homemade cross they had planted on the lawn of an African American family in St. Paul and set it afire.

This was not the first time anyone had burned a cross. Cross burnings have a long and ugly history as a way of threatening racial and religious minorities in America. But this was the first time someone had violated a hate crimes law in doing so, for St. Paul had passed its Bias-Motivated Crime Ordinance to punish just such crimes. The law was simple:

> Whoever places on public or private property a symbol, object, appellation, characterization or graffiti, including, but not limited to, a burning cross or Nazi swastika, which one knows or has reasonable grounds to know arouses anger, alarm or resentment in others on the basis of race, color, creed, religion or gender commits disorderly conduct and shall be guilty of misdemeanor.

Actions such as protests, marches, even cross burnings are forms of speech. St. Paul had declared that hate speech, in any form, that was uttered *on the basis of race, color, creed, religion, or gender* was illegal. Many Americans would applaud St. Paul's effort.

However, at least one person did not think so highly of the new law: R.A.V., one of the teenagers charged under the law. His complaint that the ordinance vio-

lated his freedom of speech eventually made it all the way to the Supreme Court. Although government is allowed to regulate certain kinds of speech, including "fighting words" designed to arouse anger, the St. Paul law singled out only certain kinds of fighting words—that is, just fighting words about race, color, creed, religion, or gender.

In a unanimous 1992 decision, the Supreme Court found for R.A.V. and declared the St. Paul statute unconstitutional. The Court ruled that it was not possible to say that one set of fighting words was illegal just because it involved certain people yet other fighting words were perfectly acceptable. St. Paul was free to prohibit all fighting words, but not just the ones that offended certain people.

Writing for the majority, Justice Antonin Scalia, another Reagan appointee, expressed the Supreme Court's disgust with the basic act that it was forced to defend: "Let there be no mistake about our belief that burning a cross in someone's front yard is reprehensible. But St. Paul has sufficient means at its disposal to prevent such behavior without adding the First Amendment to the fire."[35] In other words, states and localities can still stop cross burnings through other laws. Some prosecute cross burners under laws that make trespassing illegal. Others limit cross burning as a fire safety issue. Still others have even stopped cross burning by defining it as a source of air pollution.

How does a single cross burning in St. Paul relate to campus speech codes around the country? The answer rests in the First Amendment. During the late 1980s and early 1990s, many colleges and universities adopted speech codes limiting hate speech in an effort to create a more welcoming learning climate in the classroom. At the University of Michigan, for example, students and professors alike were subject to discipline for any behavior, "verbal or physical, that stigmatizes or victimizes an individual on the basis of race, ethnicity, religion, sex, sexual orientation, creed, national origin, ancestry, age, marital status, handicap or Vietnam-era veteran status," if that behavior threatens or interferes with an individual's academic efforts or creates "an intimidating, hostile, or demeaning environment for educational pursuits. . . ."[36]

Whatever the code and punishment—Yale University gave a student two years of probation in 1986 for ridiculing the gay community—almost all codes shared a singular commitment to eliminating hate speech on campus. By restricting their focus to just those fighting words involving certain students, almost all of the one hundred or so codes in effect in 1992, including Michigan's, were called into question by the Supreme Court's decision on the cross burning in St. Paul.

Once again, the Bill of Rights offers its protection even to those who say and do things many other Americans cannot stand. The result may be anything but a pleasant atmosphere on college campuses, for professors and students have been given much greater latitude to say whatever is on their minds. Yet the decisions may benefit colleges and universities in the long run. Instead of relying on speech codes to merely punish hate speech and possibly drive it underground, institutions of higher learning may have to address the underlying reasons that lead some professors and students to use inflammatory language. If that means tolerating hostile language in the meantime, the Bill of Rights has been interpreted to say, "So be it."

The Rights of the Accused

Having witnessed many of their fellow patriots falsely imprisoned under the British, the Founders were determined to protect the rights of the accused. The accused today are rarely patriots, however, and include some of the most reviled kinds of people—rapists, murderers, drug dealers, child pornographers, kidnappers, and terrorists. Nevertheless, the rights of the accused still hold.

The Fifth Amendment requires government to make a formal charge against the accused, gives the accused the right to remain silent, and assures due process of law, which basically means that every step of the legal process must be fair. The Sixth Amendment requires government to give the accused a speedy and public trial by an impartial jury, full information regarding the nature and causes of the charges, an opportunity to confront witnesses, the power to compel witnesses to testify on his or her behalf, and the right to have an attorney. The Eighth Amendment prohibits excessive bail and cruel and unusual punishments. All three amendments prohibit the kind of practices the British had used to harass the revolutionaries.

Nevertheless, it was not until *Miranda v. Arizona* in 1966 that the Supreme Court ruled that the accused actually have a right to know what these rights are in the first place. Ernesto Miranda was a twenty-three-year-old indigent who had been convicted of kidnapping an eighteen-year-old girl from a candy counter at a movie theater, driving her into the desert outside Phoenix, and raping her. His conviction came largely on the strength of his own confession, which he gave to the police after being identified by the victim. He was sentenced to forty to fifty-five years in prison.

Miranda challenged the conviction on the grounds that he had confessed without being informed of his rights. The American Civil Liberties Union, which represented Miranda all the way to the Supreme Court, argued that such a confession could be considered coerced and was, therefore, a violation of the Fifth Amendment's right against self-incrimination. There was no particular surprise when the Court overturned Miranda's conviction, as Chief Justice Earl Warren noted years later, "except to require police and prosecutors to advise the poor, the ignorant, and the unwary of a basic constitutional right in a manner which had been followed by the Federal Bureau of Investigation procedures for many years. It was of no assistance to hardened underworld types because they already know what their rights are and demand them."[37] As part of its decision, the Supreme Court outlined what quickly became known as the *Miranda* rule:

> [Every American who is arrested] must be warned prior to any questioning that he has the right to remain silent, that anything he says can be used against him in a court of law, that he has the right to the presence of an attorney, and that if he cannot afford an attorney one will be appointed for him prior to any questioning if he so desires. Opportunity to exercise these rights must be afforded to him throughout the interrogation. After such warnings have been given, and such opportunity afforded him, the individual may knowingly and intelligently waive these rights and agree to answer questions or make a statement. But unless and until such warnings and waiver are demonstrated by the prosecution at trial, no evidence obtained as a result of interrogation can be used against him. . . . [38]

Miranda was freed, retried on the basis of new evidence, and convicted a second time in 1966. He was eventually released on parole and died in 1976 of a knife wound incurred during a barroom fight.

Miranda was not the only convict released under the *Miranda* rule, of course. Over the years, an untold number of cases have been dismissed because of the failure to follow the Supreme Court's order. This pattern of dismissals has prompted the more conservative Burger (1969–1986) and Rehnquist (1986 to the present) Supreme Courts to slowly chip away at the precedent. Nevertheless, *Miranda* still holds.

Ernesto Miranda awaits a jury decision in 1966 in his second trial on rape and kidnapping charges. Miranda's first conviction was overturned by the Supreme Court because he had confessed without being informed of his constitutional rights. The jury convicted Miranda on the basis of new evidence.

The Right to Privacy

As noted earlier, there is no explicit right to privacy in the Constitution. Rather, the right resides somewhere in what Supreme Court Justice William O. Douglas called the "penumbras," or shadows, of at least six amendments. Writing the majority opinion in *Griswold v. Connecticut,* Douglas argued that the right to privacy demanded the repeal of an 1879 law that prohibited the distribution of information about the use of contraceptives.[39] The 1965 case involved the director of the Connecticut chapter of Planned Parenthood, Estelle Griswold, who had been convicted of dispensing contraceptives in her birth control clinic.

The Supreme Court found the right to privacy among the First, Third, Fourth, Fifth, Ninth, and Fourteenth Amendments. The First Amendment says people are free to associate with whomever they wish, including counselors at family planning clinics. The Third Amendment says the government cannot force individuals to house soldiers in peacetime, putting a zone of privacy around what happens inside the home. The Fourth Amendment guarantees the people's right to be "secure in their persons, houses, papers, and effects against unreasonable searches and seizures." The Fifth Amendment says people cannot be forced to testify against themselves, creating another zone of privacy around what people do and know. The Ninth Amendment says that the "enumeration in the Constitution, of certain rights, shall not be construed to deny or disparage others retained by the people." The Fourteenth Amendment says that the state cannot deny life or liberty without due process. Mixed in there somewhere, according to the Supreme Court, is a clear right to privacy.

Today's debate about the right to privacy, and the right to abortion that is based on it, is linked to one of the most famous Supreme Court cases of all, **Roe v. Wade.** The case, decided in 1973, overturned dozens of state laws then in effect, and continues to spark political controversy to this day.

Norma McCorvey used the name Jane Roe to remain anonymous. She lived in Texas, she was pregnant, and she wanted an abortion. But Texas allowed abortions only to save the life of the mother, and McCorvey was in no medical danger. Only five states allowed abortion on demand, another thirteen to protect the mother's physical and mental health, and thirty to save the woman's life. Three states did not permit any abortions at all.

Because her pregnancy progressed faster than the courts, Norma McCorvey had her baby and gave it up for adoption before the final decision was made. Along the way, however, she met two young lawyers, Sarah Weddington and Linda Coffee. Together, the three decided to sue Henry Wade, the district attorney in Dallas County, Texas, responsible for enforcing the ban on abortion. The case, *Roe v. Wade,* made it to the Supreme Court in 1971.[40]

The case turned on whether women and men alike had the right to privacy, including the right to control what happened to their own bodies.[41] Building on the *Griswold* decision, the Supreme Court voided the Texas ban on abortion. "We,

Norma McCorvey, also known as Jane Roe, in 1989. For twenty years following the Supreme Court's 1973 decision in *Roe v. Wade,* McCorvey was a strong advocate of abortion rights. In the early 1990s, she became a born-again Christian and re-nounced her support for abortion rights.

therefore, conclude that the right of personal privacy includes the abortion deci-sion," Justice Harry Blackmun wrote for the seven-member majority, "but that this right is not unqualified. . . ." The state had some interest in protecting the health of pregnant women, and in "protecting the potentiality of human life." The question, therefore, was which right to protect at which point in a pregnancy.

The Supreme Court struck what might seem like an awkward solution. It ar-gued that laws regulating abortion were actually of relatively recent "vintage," as Justice Harry Blackmun described them. According to Blackmun's majority opin-ion, antiabortion laws were enacted in part to discourage illicit sexual activity by women, in part to protect women from unsafe abortion techniques, and in part to protect the unborn child's life. The first two reasons were rendered less compelling by the advent of more effective birth control and much safer medical techniques, while the third remained a valid government concern. However, according to Blackmun, past laws had generally regulated abortion after *quickening,* the stage of a pregnancy when the unborn child starts to move inside the womb.

Armed with this history and building on his years as the legal counsel to the Mayo Clinic, Blackmun spent months poring over medical journals. Using his re-search, he convinced six colleagues that quickening, defined with much more precision as *viability,* could still be used to regulate abortion.

Under the Supreme Court's decision, the woman's right to abortion would be the strongest when the fetus was least able to survive, in the first three months of a nine-month pregnancy, while a state's interest in protecting human life would be strongest when the fetus was most able to survive, in the final three months. The state's interest in protecting the health of the mother would also grow over the length of the pregnancy. As of January 23, 1973, abortion became a constitutional right, but one that could be limited somewhat by the states.

The states began testing those limits immediately. In the year after *Roe*, state legislatures considered some 260 abortion bills, of which 39 were passed.[42] Some prohibited public funding of abortions; some forbade abortions in public hospitals; many required waiting periods between requesting an abortion and receiving it; some required abortion clinics to provide patients with information on alternatives to abortion; several required clinics to show pictures of fetuses in various stages of development; and at least two, Minnesota and Ohio, required teenagers to notify one or both parents before getting an abortion. The Supreme Court struck down most of the laws, leaving only the ban on public funding and the statutes requiring parental notification and waiting periods in place.[43] Along the way, the Supreme Court reaffirmed the basic right to abortion at every turn.

Americans remain sharply divided about abortion rights to this day. According to the Gallup poll, roughly one-third support the unqualified right to a legal abortion, another one-sixth say it should always be illegal, while just about half say abortion should be legal only under certain circumstances.[44]

CIVIL RIGHTS: PROTECTING US FROM EACH OTHER

There is absolutely no mention of equality or equal rights in the Constitution or in the first ten amendments. To the contrary, the Constitution itself separated Americans into different groups with distinctly *unequal* rights. Recall that slaves were counted as three-fifths of a person, and women could not vote. Indeed, the story of civil rights in the United States is largely one of eliminating such population classifications, first through the Fourteenth Amendment, then through a tangle of court cases, and finally through civil rights legislation.

Ultimately, of course, all Americans are members of groups and are put into categories all the time: race, gender, marital status, religion, age, region, education, income, sexual preference, size, college major, and so on. However, the classifications become significant only when they are used to give someone a better job, house, mortgage rate, or the like, simply because that person happens to belong to a certain category, such as white or young. This is when the equal protection clause of the Fourteenth Amendment comes into play. It forbids discrimination solely on what the Supreme Court calls "suspect classifications" that place Americans into population categories such as race, gender, and disability.

It is important to understand that the Fourteenth Amendment does not forbid *all* discrimination. The fact is that most laws discriminate against someone in some way: only people over age sixty-two can receive Social Security; married couples pay higher taxes than two single people living together; people who earn more money pay higher taxes; only people with certain college degrees can get certain kinds of jobs.

Some of these population classifications, and the discrimination they produce, are acceptable; others are inherently suspect, meaning that they may lead to unfair discrimination. Consider the use of age as a classification. Obviously, discriminating against young people by giving Social Security benefits only to the elderly makes perfect sense—after all, the program is designed to support retirees. However, discriminating against older people by forcing them to retire at age sixty-five or seventy may not make equal sense. When age has a bearing on job performance—for example, on the ability of airline pilots to make life-and-death decisions—it can be used as a classification; when it has no such bearing, it cannot.

The history of civil rights is best viewed as a series of individual struggles to get certain population classifications declared suspect. What started with the fight to end racial discrimination in the 1950s and 1960s continued to women's rights in the late 1960s and 1970s; to people with disabilities in the 1980s; and to victims of AIDS and same-sex sexual harassment today.

Protection against Classification by Race

The search for protection against racial classification began immediately after the Civil War and continues today. The Thirteenth Amendment (abolishing slavery), the Fourteenth Amendment (creating equal protection), and the Fifteenth Amendment (giving the right to vote to minorities) all contributed to the end of racial discrimination. But, as with so much of the Constitution, mere words were not enough to secure the guarantees.

In fact, ending overt racial discrimination has taken more than a century of protest, three major acts of Congress, dozens of court cases, hundreds of voter registration drives, and countless acts of courage by individuals. It has taken schoolchildren who stood up to police dogs in Birmingham, Alabama; a forty-three-year-old seamstress named Rosa Parks who refused to move to the back of the bus in Montgomery; three young college students who were murdered as they tried to register minority voters in Mississippi during the "Freedom Summer" of 1964; and the civil rights leaders who gave their lives to the cause. Because the effort has lasted so long, it is best viewed in three distinct eras: 1877–1954, 1954–1978, and 1979 to the present.

The Separate but Equal Era (1877–1954).   Although the Fourteenth Amendment was essential to the struggle for civil rights, it was hardly strong enough to ensure success on its own. The Civil War may have ended slavery, but historical

Rosa Parks with her attorney in February 1956 after her arrest on charges of boycotting buses in a mass protest against bus segregation. (Montgomery had passed an antiboycotting ordinance in the wake of her original protest.) Park's refusal to move to the "Negro section" of a bus on December 5, 1955, prompted the boycott.

barriers to full inclusion of African Americans were not so easily removed. Indeed, the equal protection clause was not fully tested as a device for ending racial inequality until 1896, three decades after ratification. And even then, it was easily brushed aside as the Supreme Court endorsed the **separate but equal doctrine,** which allowed American society to satisfy the Fourteenth Amendment's equal protection clause by merely providing separate facilities and services to each race.

The facts of the first test case, ***Plessy v. Ferguson,*** are brief. The Civil Rights Act of 1875 had required public accommodations (restaurants, hotels, railroads, and so on) to allow "the full enjoyment" of their facilities to anyone regardless of race or religion.[45] In 1883, the Supreme Court declared the act unconstitutional, thus encouraging the enactment of **Jim Crow laws,** which were purposely crafted to discriminate against African Americans. In 1892, Homer Plessy, one-eighth African American, bought a train ticket from New Orleans to Covington, Louisiana. Instead of sitting in the car marked "Colored Only," he took a seat in a car reserved for whites only. He was arrested and convicted of violating Louisiana's 1890 Jim Crow law.

Plessy appealed his case all the way to the Supreme Court in 1896, only to find that eight of the highly conservative justices saw nothing wrong with the separate but equal doctrine and accepted the prevailing view of African Americans as somehow below the rest of society. "If the civil and political rights of both races be equal," Justice Henry Brown concluded for the majority, "one cannot be inferior to the other civilly or politically. If one race be inferior to the other socially, the constitution of the United States cannot put them upon the same plane."[46] After all, African American and white train passengers got to Covington at the same time. What difference did it make that they rode in different cars?

BOX **14-3**

Key Events in the Modern Civil Rights Movement

1948   President Truman orders desegregation of U.S. military.

1954   *Brown v. Board of Education I* outlaws segregation of public schools.

1955   *Brown v. Board of Education II* orders integration of public schools.

Interstate Commerce Commission bans segregation in interstate travel.

Montgomery Bus Boycott begins in December after Rosa Parks is arrested for refusing to go to the back of the bus.

1956   Montgomery Bus Boycott ends in December when the U.S. Supreme Court affirms an appellate court ruling that outlawed segregation on the buses.

1957   Southern Christian Leadership Conference forms, with the Reverend Martin Luther King, Jr. as president.

First Civil Rights Act in nearly one hundred years passes Congress, creates the Civil Rights Commission.

President Eisenhower sends troops to enforce desegregation at Central High School in Little Rock, Arkansas.

1960   Student Nonviolent Coordinating Committee forms to organize the sit-ins and boycotts that are occurring all over the South and in some northern cities.

Not surprisingly, *Plessy v. Ferguson* invited states to pass more Jim Crow laws. African American barbers could not give whites haircuts; white nurses could not care for African American patients. Perhaps that is what Justice John Marshall Harlan, the lone dissenter, meant when he warned that the *Plessy* decision would plant the seeds of hate: "What can more certainly arouse race hate, what can more certainly create and perpetuate a feeling of distrust between these races, than state enactments which, in fact, proceed on the ground that colored citizens are so inferior and degraded that they cannot be allowed to sit in public coaches occupied by white citizens?"

1961   Freedom Rides by over three hundred African American and white college students take place across the South to implement the law outlawing segregation on interstate transportation. Many of the students are assaulted or arrested.

1963   Nonviolent demonstrations occur in Birmingham, Alabama, and are met with police violence, including the use of firehoses on children.

1964   Twenty-fourth Amendment bans poll taxes in federal elections.

Freedom Summer: white students travel to Mississippi to register African American voters for 1964 presidential election. Two white students and one African American are murdered.

Civil Rights Act of 1964 passes, forbidding discrimination based on race, color, religion, sex, or national origin.

The Reverend Martin Luther King, Jr. is awarded Nobel Peace Prize.

1965   Voting Rights Act of 1965 passes, sending federal registrars to any district in which less than half of eligible minority voters are registered.

1968   Fair Housing Act bans discrimination in the sale or rental of housing.

Source: Adapted from flyleaf of Juan Williams, *Eyes on the Prize: America's Civil Rights Years, 1954–1965* (New York: Viking, 1987).

The Breakthrough Decades (1954–1978).   The federal courts were reluctant to challenge the separate but equal doctrine for a half century, and even then came late to a prominent role in the civil rights movement. Leadership on civil rights, therefore, fell to the presidency and Congress. (See Box 14–3 for a timeline of key events in the modern civil rights movement.)

It was President Harry S Truman who finally ordered the full desegregation of the U.S. military in 1948, and Presidents John F. Kennedy and Lyndon Johnson who led the fight for the great civil rights legislation of the 1960s: the Twenty-fourth Amendment banning the poll tax in 1964, the Civil Rights Act of 1964, the Voting Rights Act of 1965, the Fair Housing Act in 1968, and along the way a half dozen presidential executive orders forcing integration forward in the federal government. It was an impressive legislative and executive agenda, indeed. The Twenty-fourth Amendment removed one of the last southern barriers facing poor minority voters; the 1964 Civil Rights Act made it unlawful to discriminate against any individual "because of such individual's race, color, religion, sex, or national origin" in housing, schools, public accommodations, and employment; the Voting Rights Act sent federal registrars to the South; and the Fair Housing Act banned discrimination in the sale or rental of housing.[47]

As the list suggests, the civil rights movement used a broad range of legislative and court actions to achieve its goals. As the victories mounted, public attitudes toward discrimination also began to change. The number of African American children who went to school with white students grew from just twenty-three in 1954 to over 2 million twenty years later; the percentage grew from just the tiniest fraction of a percent in 1954 to over 90 percent by 1971.[48] (See Box 14–4 for a sample of changes in white Americans' opinions on race.)

This is not to suggest that the courts played no role at all in desegregation. At least one landmark decision, **Brown v. Topeka Board of Education,** propelled civil rights onto the national agenda in 1954 as never before. The case involved an eight-year-old girl who merely wanted to go to the all-white school just down the street from her home rather than ride a bus to the minority school five miles away.

Bound together in 1951 with three other school desegregation cases (from Delaware, South Carolina, and Virginia), Brown was decided after a three-year wait on the Supreme Court docket. Part of the delay involved the death of Chief Justice Fred Vinson. A new chief justice had to be nominated and confirmed before the case could move ahead.

Part of the wait also reflected the politics of the decision. The justices knew their decision would provoke intense opposition in the South, and they wanted to wait until after the 1952 election to announce their decision.[49] Fear of this backlash clearly influenced the new chief justice, Earl Warren, as he drafted the final opinion on the case. He wanted an opinion short enough to be easily reprinted in newspapers around the country and clear enough to be read and understood by most Americans. Warren also wanted a unanimous opinion so that the nation could hold no illusions about the strength of the Supreme Court's conviction.[50]

Once the Supreme Court turned to making its actual decision, it split the case in two: Brown I came in 1954,[51] and Brown II followed in 1955.[52] Brown I would convey the Supreme Court's decision about the constitutionality of segregation, while Brown II would instruct the states on what to do about segregation in their schools. By breaking the case in two, the Supreme Court divided the substance of the decision from its implementation. Americans would have time to think about the Supreme Court's basic opinion on segregated schools before turning to the actual consequences for educating their children.

BOX 14-4

Evolving Racial Attitudes among Whites

Question: Do you think white students and African American students should go to the same schools or to separate schools?

	Same Schools	Separate Schools	Don't Know
1942	30	66	4
1956	48	49	3
1985	92	7	1

Question: If African American people came to live next door, would you move?

	Would Definitely Move	Might Move	Would Not Move	Don't Know
1958	21	23	56	—
1966	13	21	66	—
1978	4	9	84	3
1990	1	4	93	2
1997	*	1	98	1

Question: Would you move if African American people came to live in great numbers in your neighborhood?

	Would Definitely Move	Might Move	Would Not Move	Don't Know
1958	50	30	21	—
1966	39	31	30	—
1978	20	31	45	4
1990	8	18	68	6
1997	*	18	75	7

*For 1997, the "definitely" and "might move" responses were not separately available.

Source: Harold W. Stanley and Richard G. Niemi, *Vital Statistics on American Politics, 1997–1998* (Washington, DC: CQ Press, 1998), p. 151.

Linda Brown during her first year as the first African American pupil at a previously all-white school.

In the end, *Brown I* confronted a simple question: Could a child get an equal education in a separate but equal system? This time, the Supreme Court unanimously answered no. Although the Court did not reverse *Plessy* nor end segregation in areas of society other than public schools (such as barber shops, hotels, hospitals, and restaurants), it declared the separate but equal doctrine inherently flawed. The opinion came down to two simple sentences in the second-to-last paragraph of the opinion: "We conclude that in the field of public education the doctrine of 'separate but equal' has no place. Separate educational facilities are inherently unequal." Using the Fourteenth Amendment as the basis for its ruling, *Brown I* concluded that Linda Brown had been denied equal protection under the Fourteenth Amendment, and *Brown II* ordered the states to desegregate their schools "with all deliberate speed."

The *Brown* cases provoked intense opposition from the South and lasting political fallout for the Democratic party. Southern politicians, from mayors up to governors, vowed to block schoolhouse doors; southern states encouraged their school districts not to comply with the Supreme Court's order; the governor of Arkansas even put 270 state troopers around Little Rock's Central High School in the fall of 1957 to prevent just nine African American students from entering the building; nineteen senators and eighty-two members of Congress drafted a "Southern Manifesto" attacking the *Brown* decision and giving further aid and comfort to the "massive resistance" back home.

The acts of defiance melted away with repeated court orders and the growing civil rights movement; the governor of Arkansas backed down when President Dwight Eisenhower ordered federal paratroopers into Little Rock. Nevertheless, the overall strategy of delay clearly worked for most of those who opposed integration. Ten years after *Brown,* Justice Hugo Black would complain, "There has been entirely too much deliberation and not enough speed." Forty years later, many public schools remain just as segregated, if not by deliberate action or law (de jure segregation), then by the concentration of minority populations in the central cities. Ending segregation in public schools does not necessarily lead to fully integrated public schools. It can also produce the movement of white students out of the public school system and into private schools, or out of the cities and into the suburbs—both of which frustrate ultimate integration.

The Reverse Discrimination Era (1979 to the Present).   The backlash against civil rights actually began even before the *Brown* decision. It started when southern Democrats bolted the party after the 1948 national convention adopted a platform plank promising action on civil rights. It gained momentum in the 1968 election campaign, when Richard Nixon and Alabama governor George Wallace both courted white votes in the wake of the inner-city riots of the mid-1960s.

Although the backlash was mostly eclipsed by the civil rights movement of the 1960s, it has accelerated in recent years as moderates have joined conservatives in turning against some of the signature programs for eliminating racial discrimination. Americans are not abandoning their support for racial equality, however. As political scientist Seymour Martin Lipset argues, "The old consensus in favor of civil rights and equality of opportunity remains intact. Americans, including many southern whites, categorically reject the kind of racial discrimination that was common in this country only a few decades ago."[53]

Instead, the slippage may be due to lingering resentment toward some of the basic tools of desegregation, none of which has ever been popular. Court-ordered school busing in the 1970s may have fueled white flight to the suburbs; minority "set-asides," or guaranteed shares, of government contracts have created bitterness among owners of firms that are denied the chance to compete; diversity training has been ridiculed as "politically correct."

Of all the tools, **affirmative action,** which gives minorities extra help up the college or job ladder, may be the most controversial. Affirmative action programs give protected classes of Americans, such as racial minorities, special help in advancing through society, whether in getting into college, finding a first job, getting a home loan, or landing a government contract. Some affirmative action programs set goals for the number of women and minorities to be helped; these goals are sometimes converted into quotas that reserve a specific number of slots in a college class or pool of employees for women or minorities.

Most Americans favor some form of affirmative action to help African Americans and members of other minority groups get a fair start in the competition for jobs and education. They also support general goals for helping more women and minorities advance. If that means giving women and minorities access to special job-training programs or extra financial aid in college, the public rarely objects. "But," as Lipset finds, "a large majority of whites and roughly half of all blacks draw the line at preferential treatment, at suspending standards and adopting quotas or other devices that favor citizens on the basis of their membership in groups."[54]

Americans have a particular dislike of quotas, which set aside a specific number of jobs or slots for minorities only. The problem is that quotas appear to fix past wrongs by creating new winners and losers, because reserving a slot for one person means denying one to another. Some argue that the winners are permanently branded as less competent; others believe that the losers are merely new victims of discrimination.

At least one of those "losers" decided to take his anger all the way to the Supreme Court. Twice denied admission to the medical school of the University of California at Davis in the mid-1970s, Allan Bakke sued the school in 1977 on the basis of two facts: first, a quota system had been created because sixteen of the one hundred openings had been reserved in advance for applicants from disadvantaged groups—African Americans, Latinos/Chicanos, and Native Americans; and, second, at least some of the sixteen successful minority applicants had lower test scores and grade point averages than Bakke.

Bakke eventually won his case, **Regents of the University of California v. Bakke,**[55] but he lost his campaign against affirmative action. Although the Supreme Court ordered the University of California to admit Bakke, the final

Allan Bakke's case raised questions about the fairness of quota systems, which set aside a fixed number of jobs or slots for minorities. Bakke eventually won his case and enrolled in medical school in 1978.

opinion did not overturn affirmative action. The bare majority of five justices could agree on only one paragraph of the final opinion: that the university's quota system was unlawful and Bakke should be admitted. As for affirmative action, the complicated opinion seemed to say that government could take race into account as long as it did so only to right past wrongs. At the same time, several justices also worried that affirmative action might damage race relations in the long run.

Ultimately, the mixed signals from *Bakke*—indeed, from most of the affirmative action cases that have followed—merely confirm the Supreme Court's continued ambivalence about how fast and how far to go on racial equality. In late 1994, for example, a federal appeals court rejected a University of Maryland scholarship program that was open only to African Americans, arguing that such a set-aside was going too far. The case was brought by a Hispanic student who was fully qualified for the scholarship but for the fact that he was not African American. In 1996, another federal appeals court rejected the University of Texas Law School's admissions program, which gave special preference to racial minorities. By denying cert. on both appeals, the Supreme Court sent the message that such highly restrictive programs could not survive constitutional review. As a result of the Texas ruling, enrollment of African Americans at the University of Texas Law School dropped from 31 in the 1996 class to just 4 in 1997.[56]

This ambivalence is shared by the American public at large. Americans want integrated schools, but no busing; diverse colleges and universities, but color-blind admissions; equal opportunity in the workplace, but no quotas. According to a March 1995 *Newsweek* poll, 75 percent of Americans think that qualified African Americans should not receive preference over equally qualified whites in getting into accommodations or getting jobs. At the same time, however, just over half of Americans say that cities should give minorities preference in hiring so that the police force would have the same racial makeup as the community, and nearly as many approve of government set-asides under which contracts are reserved for minority-owned businesses.[57]

The debate over the protection of classification by race is far from over. As the U.S. population becomes ever more diverse, the pressure to address the rights of minorities will not abate. Nor will the continuing sense among minorities that race still matters. (See Box 14–5 for a comparison of how whites and African Americans view affirmative action.)

Protection against Classification by Gender

Although the Fourteenth Amendment provides protection against classification by gender, it is not the only protection women have in the quest for equality. Women also benefited from the legislative victories of the 1960s, most importantly the 1964 Civil Rights Act.

BOX 14-5

Views on Affirmative Action among Black and White Americans (percentage of respondents who agree)

	Total	Black	White
Favor special educational programs to assist minorities in competing for college admissions	63%	82%	59%
Favor government financing for job training for minorities to help them get ahead in industries where they are underrepresented	69	95	64
Necessary to have laws to protect minorities against discrimination in hiring and promotion	69	88	65
It is a good idea to select a person from a poor family over one from a middle-class or rich family if they all are equally qualified.	56	65	53
As a result of affirmative action, less qualified people are hired and promoted and admitted to college:			
At least some of the time	79	67	81
Hardly ever or never	15	28	13
Necessary to have affirmative action programs to make sure companies have racially diverse workforces	44	80	38
Preference in hiring and promotion should be given to blacks to make up for past discrimination.	35	62	31
Affirmative action programs should be continued.	41	80	35
Affirmative action programs should be:			
Ended now	12	1	13
Phased out over the next few years	40	17	45
Continued for the foreseeable future	41	80	35

Source: Sam Howe Verhovek, "In Poll, Americans Reject Means but Not Ends of Racial Diversity," *New York Times*, December 14, 1997, p. A32.

Ironically, it was a conservative Virginia Democrat, Howard W. Smith, who added women to the 1964 legislation. He had hoped that bringing women into the statute would defeat the bill. "To the laughter of his House colleagues," writes historian Kenneth Davis, "Smith added 'sex' to the list of 'race, color, religion or national origin,' the groups that the bill had been designed to protect. Assuming that nobody would vote to protect equality of the sexes, Smith was twice struck by lightning. The bill not only passed, but now protected women as well as blacks."[58]

Women won additional protection in 1972, when the original act was amended to deny federal funding to private or public programs that discriminate on the basis of gender. The amendments also required colleges and universities to provide equal facilities and opportunities for female athletes (under Title IX), meaning equal numbers of athletic scholarships.

With these legislative victories in hand, national women's groups made a fateful decision to push for ratification of the Equal Rights Amendment (ERA) to the Constitution. The amendment itself was remarkably simple—"Equality of rights under the law shall not be denied or abridged by the United States or by any State on account of sex"—but the politics were not. Liberals argued that women could not get equal protection without the amendment; conservatives argued that the amendment would require everything from unisex bathrooms to haircuts. As with all constitutional amendments, the controversy favored the status quo. Passed by a two-thirds vote of Congress in 1972, the amendment died in 1982 three states short of the thirty-eight states needed for ratification.[59] (Unlike James Madison's amendment limiting congressional pay, which had been sent to the states without a deadline and thus could be ratified 203 years after it was proposed, Congress limited ERA to a seven-year deadline, which was later extended for an additional three years.)

The defeat hardly ended progress toward women's rights, however. Having been defeated in the court of public opinion, women's groups turned to a legal strategy, bringing case after case forward urging the Supreme Court to broaden women's rights under the equal protection clause and assorted civil rights laws. The strategy resulted in dozens of decisions that protected women in school, at work, and on the athletic playing field. Along the way, the Supreme Court unanimously struck down several laws that favored men—from a Louisiana law allowing a husband to dispose of jointly owned property without his wife's consent to a Utah law that set the age of adulthood at eighteen for females and twenty-one for males, thereby requiring three extra years of child support for male children. During the same period, it also struck down laws that favored women—from a Social Security provision that gave widows more benefits than widowers to a Mississippi nursing school's policy of denying admission to qualified males.[60]

Alongside *Roe v. Wade,* which involves substantial questions of women's rights, the Supreme Court's most visible decisions on women's rights have been in the area of workplace equality. In 1986, for example, the Supreme Court ruled that merely having a formal policy against sexual harassment did not excuse a company from its responsibility to create a climate free of "intimidation, ridicule, and insult."[61] In 1987, the Supreme Court upheld a California law that required companies to provide unpaid maternity leaves for women.[62] And in 1993, the Supreme Court unanimously declared that women need not prove psychological harm or an inability to do their job to win a judgment of sexual harassment.

The 1993 case made a particularly important point: merely uttering an insult in a hallway does not necessarily trigger civil rights protection, but neither do victims of harassment need to suffer an emotional collapse to prove damage.[63] As Justice Sandra Day O'Connor wrote in *Harris v. Forklift Systems,* "A discriminatory abusive work environment, even one that does not seriously affect employees' psychological well-being, can and often will detract from employees' job performance, discourage employees from remaining on the job, or keep them from advancing in their careers."[64] When sexual harassment "pollutes" the job climate, it is covered by both federal law and the Fourteenth Amendment.

In 1997–1998, the Supreme Court term continued the recent tradition by making four major decisions. In *Faragher v. City of Boca Raton,* for example, a 7–2 majority agreed that employers, not just individual employees, are responsible for preventing sexual harassment in the workplace. Even if they do not know that a supervisor is harassing an employee, employers can be held liable for damages. In *Burlington Industries, Inc. v. Ellerth,* another 7–2 majority concluded that an employee could sue for damages without having to show any job-related harm. In *Oncale v. Sundowner Offshore Services,* a unanimous Supreme Court prohibited sexual harassment by members of the same sex, in this case two men who worked on the same offshore oil platform. All three decisions strengthened the ability of adults to bring sexual harassment cases. But in *Gebser v. Lago Vista Independent School District,* a divided Court decided that a student could sue a school district for a teacher's sexual harassment only if the district actually knew of the harassment and was deliberately indifferent toward it. The fourth ruling was at odds with the first three because of the underlying statutes: The first three rulings involved federal workplace and civil rights laws, while the fourth involved federal education law, which set a different standard for harassment suits.[65]

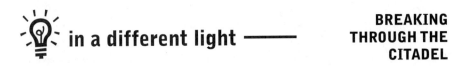

in a different light ——— BREAKING THROUGH THE CITADEL

Although the Fourteenth Amendment was clearly designed to end racial discrimination, it has become an important tool for ending gender discrimination as well. No case better illustrates the point than *Faulkner v. Jones.* Shannon Faulkner seemed to be the perfect candidate for admission to the Citadel, a South Carolina state military academy established in 1842. James E. Jones, Chairman of the Board of Visitors of the Citadel, was the first name on the long list of defendants in the case.

Faulkner was a high school honors graduate with a 4.0 grade point average, a varsity letter, and the kind of recommendations the Citadel admired. Not surprisingly given the file, Faulkner was invited to join the corps of cadets, class of 1997. There was just one problem with Faulkner's application: The Citadel was an all-male school, and Shannon Faulkner happened to be female. The application did not ask whether Faulkner was a male or female, and her name betrayed no clue. Moreover, Faulkner had omitted any reference to gender in her application. On the basis of the facts of her admission file, she was in. But once the Citadel found out her gender, it withdrew the offer of admission.

Faulkner sued the state school and won the first round of her case on July 22, 1994, when a federal district court ordered her immediate admission to the corps. "All classifications based on sex are not unconstitutional," wrote Judge C. Weston Houck in his opinion. "The law recognizes that there are some real differences between men and women and permits different treatment that provides a legitimate accommodation for those differences. What the law will not allow, however, is classifications based on fixed notions, archaic and stereotypical notions, concerning the relative roles and abilities of females and males."[66] On the basis of his reading of

Shannon Faulkner on her third day as a cadet at the Citadel. Faulkner waged a two-year court battle to win admission to the state-run school.

Male cadets celebrate Shannon Faulkner's withdrawal at the end of her first week at the Citadel. Their triumph was short-lived, however. In 1998, thirty-five women enrolled in the Citadel.

the Fourteenth Amendment's protection, Houck ordered Faulkner's immediate admission to the corps.

Faulkner's case was far from over with Houck's decision, however. The Citadel immediately appealed, forcing Faulkner into a two-year court battle. The case was finally resolved when a three-judge panel of the Fourth Circuit Court of Appeals ruled 2–1 that the Citadel had violated the equal protection clause of the Fourteenth Amendment by denying her admission. Faulkner arrived on campus August 12, 1995, to begin orientation as the first woman ever admitted as a cadet.

Six days later, however, Faulkner became one of twenty-four cadets who left after the grueling first week. The male cadets she left behind were overjoyed at their victory over this one young woman, delighted with her failure to survive. To keep Faulkner's experience in perspective, consider the following comment from Army Major Carol Barkalow, who had graduated from the army's West Point Military Academy in its first class that included women twenty years earlier: "Even with all the other women who came, and even though we had Congress on our side, there were plenty of times when you felt very alone and against the world. It's not easy being a pioneer in any situation, and for two years Shannon Faulkner has pretty much fought this alone."[67]

Although she could not reap the rewards of her long struggle, Faulkner made the breakthrough that allowed thirty-five female cadets to enroll in the fall of 1998. In this she resembled another civil rights pioneer, Rosa Parks, who could not reap all the rewards of the whirlwind of liberty she created with a simple decision to refuse to move to the back of the bus.

Protection against Classification by Disability

Over time, the success of minorities and women in breaking down the barriers has spread to other disadvantaged groups. In 1990, for example, Congress passed and President Bush signed the Americans with Disabilities Act (ADA), easily the most sweeping civil rights statute since 1964. More than 13 million Americans have impaired eyesight or hearing, another 8 million have trouble walking, and 1.3 million-plus use walkers or wheelchairs. All told, more than 20 million Americans have some kind of physical or mental disability. Yet, until the ADA, no federal law protected any of them from routine employment discrimination. If a business did not have wheelchair ramps, there was no law requiring it to provide them. If a company wanted to fire someone because he or she happened to have AIDS, epilepsy, or brain cancer, there was no law against doing so.

All that changed with the passage of the ADA. The law's impact is visible in every sector of the economy and public life. All properties open to the public must be accessible to people with disabilities—that means wheelchair access, for example. Employers may not discriminate against qualified people with disabilities in hiring, advancement, pay, or training, and must adjust the workplace to accomodate them if necessary—that means new application procedures, more access, even special computers. All new buses, trains, and subway cars must be wheelchair accessible; and all telephone companies must provide relay services allowing people with voice or hearing impairments to place and receive calls from ordinary telephones.[68]

Because the statute is complicated, the regulations that govern implementation are still being formulated. Nevertheless, the ADA had immediate consequences for American business, not the least of which was a new list of "dos" and "don'ts" for the hiring process. "Don't ask job candidates or even their references about applicants' disabilities," advises the *Wall Street Journal*. "Focus on abilities. Don't ask about the following before you offer a job: medical history; prescription drug use; prior workers' compensation or health insurance claims; work absenteeism due to illness; and past treatment for alcoholism, drug use or mental illness."[69]

Again, passing a law is only the first step toward bringing about change. Complaints must be filed, cases won, court orders enforced, public opinion changed. Compliance with the ADA is so complicated and costly that some firms have even decided to wait to be sued instead of complying voluntarily.[70] And the cases are coming. The first one was filed by the federal government in November 1992 against a small company that had fired its executive director upon learning he had terminal brain cancer. The case was eventually decided in the director's favor.

By 1997, ADA cases had begun to reach the Supreme Court. In *Bragdon v. Abbott*, a 5–4 majority agreed that the law's definition of disability applied to people infected with the virus that causes AIDS, even when there is no evidence of the disease. The case was brought by an HIV-positive woman who was denied treatment by a dentist. In *Pennsylvania Department of Corrections v. Yeskey*, a unanimous Supreme Court also decided that the ADA applied to state prison inmates, who could not be segregated from other prisoners on the basis of disability.[71]

MAINTAINING THE BALANCE

Civil liberties and civil rights do not flow automatically from the delicate balance created by the Constitution. They must be pursued, defended, and won over and over again as times change. The fact that one Supreme Court has declared a basic right is no guarantee that a later set of justices will not change their minds.

Protecting basic liberties and rights is always difficult in a divided society. It has been that way from the very beginning. Recall that the America of the 1790s was deeply divided by race, religious differences, geography, and income. It was more a loose collection of many small communities than one United States. It was also a society trying to define itself in a new world, all the while struggling to manage deep internal divisions.

The future struggle for civil liberties and civil rights will be won or lost on two fronts. The first involves the formal protections embedded in the Constitution and precedent: the Bill of Rights, the Fourteenth Amendment, the Supreme Court decisions, and the assorted laws, executive orders, and regulations that provide the basic protections from government and other individuals. Faced with a threat to their individual rights, Americans can always hope that someone else will invoke the equal protection clause, call on the most recent favorable Supreme Court decision, or exploit one of the many access points that can slow government to a standstill.

Merely invoking court cases and statutes like some ancient prayer is not enough to guarantee protection, however. The cases may be well known and the statutes well established, but they will hardly protect Americans if individuals are not willing to take on the fight. Discrimination will continue unless challenged.

Thus, the struggle for civil liberties and civil rights is also waged on a second front: the courage of individuals to stand up against strong-willed majorities.

The fact is that it does not take much to make an issue of civil liberties and rights. After all, Rosa Parks was just fed up with having to sit at the back of the bus; Shannon Faulkner wanted to attend the college of her choice; Florence Dolan just did not want to set aside a portion of her land without a fair reason; and Homer Plessy just wanted a decent train ride to Covington. None of these individuals were famous before they took their stand, but they most certainly knew many Americans would be angry with the result. So did the African Americans who marched on Washington in the 1960s, and the legion of people with disabilities who literally rolled through the halls of Congress in the 1980s.

Therein lies the true protection for individuals. If Americans are only willing to wait for someone else to act, their rights will slowly wither away. Most of the progress on civil liberties and civil rights has been unpopular at the time. One only needs to ask Rosa Parks, Allan Bakke, or the lawyers who represented R.A.V., the cross-burner from St. Paul, or look back at the picture of the Citadel cadets celebrating Shannon Faulkner's departure. Taking the heat is what being in public life is about. Americans do not need to be president or governor to matter. Nor do they need to be constitutional lawyers. Civil liberties and rights start with simple courage and with a commitment to carry the idea forward against the prevailing public view.

terms to remember

civil liberties (p. 580)
civil rights (p. 580)
equal protection clause (p. 581)
due process of law (p. 581)
nationalization of the Bill of
   Rights (p. 582)
establishment clause (p. 590)
free exercise clause (p. 590)
libel (p. 595)
clear and present danger test
   (p. 595)

Miranda v. Arizona (p. 599)
Roe v. Wade (p. 601)
separate but equal doctrine
   (p. 605)
Plessy v. Ferguson (p. 605)
Jim Crow laws (p. 605)
*Brown v. Topeka Board of
   Education* (p. 608)
affirmative action (p. 611)
*Regents of the University of
   California v. Bakke* (p. 612)

facts and interpretations

- The Constitution and its amendments provide two kinds of protections for individual citizens. They protect individual civil liberties, which guarantee freedoms such as speech, press, and religion, and individual civil rights, which provide protection against discrimination on the basis of individual characteristics such as race, gender, and disability. Some of this protection resides in the basic structure of the Founders' government. Separate powers, separate interests, separate layers, and checks and balances all make it difficult for strong majorities to impose their will on individual Americans. However, most of the protection resides in the first ten amendments to the Constitution. Although the final draft of the Constitution did not contain a bill of rights—most states already had bills of rights in their constitutions—the Founders agreed to offer a bill of rights as the very first item of business in the First Congress.

- For the first one hundred years of American history, the Bill of Rights applied only to actions by the federal government. In *Barron v. Baltimore*, an 1833 case involving the owner of a shipping wharf that was being slowly put out of business as Baltimore filled its waters with sand, the Supreme Court declared that the Fifth Amendment's requirement of due process did not apply to citizens of Baltimore, and by implication to any other state or city. Under the Fourteenth Amendment, however, states were prohibited from denying due process or equal protection to any citizen, whether under state or federal laws. The Fourteenth Amendment has been crucial for the nationalization of the Bill of Rights. Over the years, case by case, most pieces of the Bill of Rights have been extended downward to cover U.S. citizens wherever they live.

- Although the Fourteenth Amendment was a key tool in the fight for civil rights, it was not enough on its own to end all discrimination based on "suspect classifications," which put Americans into population categories such as race, gender, and disability. Many of these categories have been outlawed as a basis for discrimination, either one case at a time or in sweeping federal laws. As the protections have been expanded, Americans have become increasingly opposed to further efforts to help minorities. Several recent Supreme Court cases have restricted the use of affirmative action as a device to give minorities and other protected classes of Americans extra help. Yet Congress did pass the Americans with Disabilities Act, a sweeping law that forces the nation to make facilities more accessible to those with physical or mental disabilities.

- Civil liberties and civil rights are not guaranteed just because the Constitution says so. They must be protected in what are often unpopular cases involving lone individuals who are ready to stand up for their cause. Americans who want to know how they came to have such significant civil liberties and civil rights need look no further than people such as Deborah Weisman (who stood up against school prayer), R.A.V. (who stood up for freedom of speech, no matter how ugly), Jane Doe/Norma McCorvey (who stood up for the right to privacy), Linda Brown (who stood up to fight the separate but equal doctrine), and Allan Bakke (who stood up to challenge racial quotas).

open questions

- What rights have you enjoyed today? Since the beginning of your day, when have you benefited from someone else's fight for protection? What Supreme Court cases listed in this chapter have helped you today? Are there any cases that have hurt you?

- How much courage does someone need to fight for their civil liberties and rights? How can an individual prepare for the public rejection that so often accompanies an effort to guarantee rights such as religious freedom or free speech? Do Rosa Parks and Allan Bakke have anything in common? How would you introduce Shannon Faulkner to R.A.V., the cross-burner from St. Paul?

- How far can the nation go in protecting Americans as individual citizens without eventually weakening its ability to protect the American public as a whole? By letting some Americans use drugs for religious reasons, does government weaken the effectiveness of its war on drugs? Do Americans have too many rights today—that is, do Americans think of themselves too frequently as members of special groups deserving protection rather than as citizens of the nation? Does the focus on individual rights sometimes make it impossible for diverse citizens to work together?

- How effective has the Supreme Court been in balancing the rights of the minority against the demands of the majority over the years? What recent cases seem to have weakened civil liberties and civil rights? How might they be argued differently in the future? Is it right that the retirement of a Supreme Court justice can make such a difference in whether a right is expanded or contracted?

for further study

Abraham, Henry J., and Barbara A. Perry. *Freedom and the Court: Civil Rights and Liberties in the United States,* 7th ed. New York: Oxford University Press, 1998.

Carter, Stephen. *The Culture of Disbelief: How American Law and Politics Trivialize Religious Devotion.* New York: Basic Books, 1994.

Craig, Barbara, and David O'Brien. *Abortion and American Politics.* Chatham, NJ: Chatham House, 1993.

Katzmann, Robert A. *Institutional Disability: The Saga of Transportation Policy for the Disabled.* Washington, DC: Brookings Institution, 1986.

Mansbridge, Jane. *Why We Lost the ERA.* Chicago: University of Chicago Press, 1986.

O'Brien, David. *Constitutional Law and Politics: Civil Rights and Civil Liberties.* New York: Norton, 1991.

endnotes for chapter 14

1. James Roger Sharp, *American Politics in the Early Republic: The New Nation in Crisis* (New Haven, CT: Yale University Press, 1993), p. 2.

2. 7 Peters 243, 246 (1833). Finding the printed record of a Supreme Court case is not difficult. Take each piece of the citation above in order. The number "7" refers to the volume in which the decision is printed. The name, "Peters," refers to the last name of the Supreme Court reporter who recorded the decision. The first 90 volumes of Supreme Court decisions are listed by reporter's name; the rest are simply labeled "U.S.," which stands for U.S. Reports. The number "243" refers to the page number where the case begins in volume 7, and the number "246" refers to the page number where the quotation resides. The last number, which is in parentheses, is the year in which the case was decided, "1833." More recent cases can be found in several additional places. They can always be found in U.S. Reports, which remains the official location of all Supreme Court decisions. Because the official version is printed only after a term is over, private publishers have created several faster ways to get individual decisions out to the legal community, including Lawyers' Edition (L.Ed.) and Supreme Court Reporter (Sup.Ct.). These citations also carry the volume number first, the name of the publisher in the middle, and the page number where the case begins third, page number of a quotation fourth, and the year in parentheses last. Different libraries may have one or more of these sources. For more information on finding Supreme Court and other court decisions, see Albert Melone and Carl Kalvelage, *Primer on Constitutional Law* (Pacific Palisades, CA: Palisades Publishers, 1982).

3. *Dolan v. City of Tigard,* 114 Sup.Ct. (1994).

4. See David O'Brien, *Constitutional Law and Politics: Civil Rights and Civil Liberties* (New York: Norton, 1991), p. 277.

5. *The Slaughterhouse Cases,* 16 Wallace 83 U.S. 36 (1873).

6. The footnotes to Box 14–1 are as follows: *Chicago, Burlington & Quincy RR v. Chicago,* 166 U.S. 226 (1897); *Fiske v. Kansas,* 274 U.S. 380 (1927); *Near v. Minnesota,* 283 U.S. 697 (1931); *Powell v. Alabama,* 287 U.S. 45 (1932); *DeJonge v. Oregon,* 299 U.S. 353 (1937); *Cantwell v. Connecticut,* 310 U.S. 296 (1940); *Everson v. Board of Education of Ewing Township,* 330 U.S. 1 (1947); *In re Oliver,* 337 U.S. 257 (1948); *Wolf v. Colorado,* 338 U.S. 25 (1949); *NAACP v. Alabama,* 357 U.S. 449 (1958); *Mapp v. Ohio,* 367 U.S. 643 (1961); *Robinson v. California,* 370 U.S. 660 (1962); *Gideon v. Wainwright,* 372 U.S. 335 (1963); *Malloy v. Hogan,* 378 U.S. 1 (1964); *Pointer v. Texas,* 380 U.S. 400 (1965); *Griswold v. Connecticut,* 381 U.S. 479 (1965); *Parker v. Gladden,* 385 U.S. 363 (1966); *Klopfer v. North Carolina,* 386 U.S. 213 (1967); *Washington v. Texas,* 388 U.S. 14 (1967); *Duncan v. Louisiana,* 391 U.S. 145 (1968); *Benton v. Maryland,* 395 U.S. 784 (1969); *Argersinger v. Hamlin,* 407 U.S. 25 (1972).

7. This is part of an exhaustive list provided in O'Brien, *Constitutional Law and Politics,* pp. 280–81.

8. See Linda Greenhouse, "Blowing the Dust Off the Constitution That Was," *New York Times,* May 28, 1995, p. D1.

9. All quotes from the appeals court can be found at Docket No. 95-7028—F.3rd—(2nd Cir. 1996).

10. This quote and the one in the next paragraph are from Esther B. Fein, "The Decision Offers Relief to Plaintiffs," *New York Times,* April 3, 1993, p. B5.

11. *Cruzan v. Director, Missouri Department of Health,* 497 U.S. 261 (1990).

12. *Washington v. Glucksberg,* 65 LW 4669; *Vacco v. Quill,* 65 LW 4695.

13. Anthony L. Back, Jeffrey I. Wallace, Helene E. Starks, and Robert A. Pearlman, "Physician-Assisted Suicide and Euthanasia in Washington State: Patient Requests and Physician Responses," *Journal of the American Medical Association,* volume 275, March 27, 1996, pp. 919–925.

14. Quoted in Stephen Carter, *The Culture of Disbelief: How American Law and Politics Trivialize Religious Devotion* (New York: Basis Books, 1994), p. 106.

15. *The Gallup Poll Monthly,* April 1994, p. 3.

16. For an analysis of religion in American politics, see A. James Reichley, *Religion in American Public Life* (Washington, D.C.: Brookings Institution, 1985).

17. For a thorough review of the Supreme Court and freedom of religion, see Henry J. Abraham and Barbara A. Perry, *Freedom and the Court: Civil Rights and Liberties in the United States,* 7th ed. (New York: Oxford University Press, 1998), Chapter 6.

18. Carter, *The Culture of Disbelief,* p. 106.

19. Carter, *The Culture of Disbelief,* p. 106.

20. *Engel v. Vitale,* 370 U.S. 421 (1962).

21. *Abington School District v. Schempp,* 374 U.S. 203 (1963).

22. See, for example, *Wallace v. Jaffree,* 472 U.S. 38 (1985).

23. *Lee v. Weisman,* 112 S.Ct. 2649, 2658 (1992).

24. "Students Challenge Ban on Prayer at Graduation," *New York Times,* May 26, 1993, p. A7.

25. See "Thirty Years After the Supreme Court's School Prayer Decision," *The American Enterprise,* volume 3, number 2 (March/April 1992), for a history of public opinion on the issue.

26. *Rosenberger v. University of Virginia,* 115 Sup. Ct. 2510 (1995).

27. See Samuel G. Freedman, "Yeshivish at Yale," *New York Times Magazine,* May 24, 1998.

28. *New York Times Co. v. Sullivan,* 376 U.S. 254 (1964).

29. *Schenck v. United States,* 249 U.S. (1919).

30. *Brandenburg v. Ohio,* 395 U.S. 444 (1969).

31. The test comes from English common law, cited in O'Brien, *Constitutional Law and Politics,* p. 284.

32. *Miller v. California,* 413 U.S. 15, 24 (1973), quoting *Roth v. United States,* 354 U.S. 476 (1957).

33. Quoted in C. Herman Pritchett, *Constitutional Civil Liberties* (Englewood Cliffs, NJ: Prentice-Hall, 1984), pp. 91–92.

34. *Reno v. American Civil Liberties Union,* No. 96-511.

35. *R.A.V. v. St. Paul,* 112 Sup. Ct. 2538, 2550 (1992).

36. *Doe v. University of Michigan,* 721 F. Supp. 852, 856 (E.D. Mich. 1989).

37. Earl Warren, *The Memoirs of Chief Justice Earl Warren* (Garden City, NY: Doubleday, 1977), pp. 316–17.

38. *Miranda v. Arizona* 384 U.S. 436 (1966).

39. *Griswold v. Connecticut,* 381 U.S. 479 (1965).

40. *Roe v. Wade,* 410 U.S. 113 (1973).

41. O'Brien, *Constitutional Law and Politics,* p. 1160.

42. See Barbara Craig and David O'Brien, *Abortion and American Politics* (Chatham, NJ: Chatham House, 1993), for an excellent history of the issue.

43. For a list of the key decisions, see Robin Toner, "Since Roe v. Wade: The Evolution of Abortion Law," *New York Times,* January 22, 1993, p. A12.

44. *The Gallup Poll Monthly,* January 1992, p. 6.

45. *The Civil Rights Cases,* 109 U.S. 3 (1883). For a brief history of the *Civil Rights Cases,* see O'Brien, *Constitutional Law and Politics,* pp. 1277–78.

46. *Plessy v. Ferguson,* 163 U.S. 537 (1896).

47. For a history of the politics of civil rights in the Eisenhower, Kennedy, and Johnson years, see James Sundquist, *Politics and Policy: The Eisenhower, Kennedy, and Johnson Years* (Washington, DC: Brookings Institution, 1968), Chapter 6.

48. Lee Epstein, Jeffrey Segal, Harold Speth, and Thomas Walker, *The Supreme Court Compendium* (Washington, DC: CQ Press, 1994), p. 621.

49. To read more about the case and the furor it caused, see Richard Kluger's excellent and readable book *Simple Justice* (New York: Vintage, 1973).

50. See O'Brien, *Constitutional Law and Politics,* p. 1306.

51. *Brown v. Board of Education of Topeka, Kansas,* 347 U.S. 483 (1954).

52. *Brown v. Board of Education of Topeka, Kansas,* 349 U.S. 294 (1955).

53. Seymour Martin Lipset, "Affirmative Action and the American Creed," *Wilson Quarterly,* 16, no. 1 (Winter 1992): 53.

54. Lipset, "Affirmative Action and the American Creed," p. 53.

55. *Regents of the University of California v. Bakke,* 438 U.S. 265 (1978).

56. See Abraham and Perry, *Freedom and the Court,* p. 445.

57. Peter Anin, "Race and Rage," *Newsweek,* April 3, 1995, pp. 23–34.

58. Kenneth Davis, *Don't Know Much about History* (New York: Avon Books, 1990), p. 362.

59. For a history of the debate, see Gilbert Steiner, *Constitutional Inequality: The Political Fortunes of ERA* (Washington, DC: Brookings Institution, 1985), and Jane Mansbridge, *Why We Lost the ERA* (Chicago: University of Chicago Press, 1986).

60. See O'Brien, *Constitutional Law and Politics,* pp. 1424–27, for a list of the cases.

61. *Meritor Savings Bank, FBD v. Vinson,* 477 U.S. 57 (1986).

62. *California Federal Savings & Loan Association v. Guerra,* 479 U.S. 272 (1987).

63. "Excerpts from Supreme Court Ruling on Sexual Harassment in Workplace," *New York Times,* November 10, 1993, p. A14.

64. *Harris v. Forklift Systems,* 114 Sup.Ct. 367 (1993).

65. These cases are summarized in Linda Greenhouse, "Supreme Court Weaves Legal Principles from a Tangle of Litigation," *New York Times,* June 30, 1998, p. A20.

66. *Faulkner v. Jones,* 858 F.Supp. 552, 563 (D.S.C. 1994).

67. Debbi Wilforen, "First Female Cadet Leaves the Citadel," *Philadelphia Inquirer,* August 19, 1995, p. A7.

68. For a quick summary of the ADA, see Peter Kilborn, "Big Change Likely as Law Bans Bias toward Disabled," *New York Times,* July 19, 1992, p. A1; for a history of the movement toward rights for the disabled, see Robert A. Katzmann, *Institutional Disability: The Saga of Transportation Policy for the Disabled* (Washington, DC: Brookings Institution, 1986); for a history of the ADA, see Robert L. Burgdorf, Jr., "The Americans with Disabilities Act: Analysis and Implications of a Second Generation Civil Rights Statute," *Harvard Civil Rights–Civil Liberties Law Review,* 26, no. 2 (Summer 1991): 413–522.

69. Joann Lublin, "Disabilities Act Will Compel Business to Change Many Employment Practices," *Wall Street Journal,* July 7, 1992, p. B1.

70. See Julie Janofsky, "Whoever Wrote ADA Regs Never Ran a Business," *Wall Street Journal,* March 15, 1993, p. A10.

71. Greenhouse, "Supreme Court Weaves Legal Principles."

making public policy

artful work

The Founders clearly wanted American government to act. Recall that the Preamble to the Constitution promises that American government will "establish Justice, insure domestic Tranquility, provide for the common defence, [and] promote the general Welfare." Government cannot be so concerned with protecting liberty that it fails to protect the nation as a whole, yet never so obsessed with protecting the nation as a whole that it forgets to protect individual Americans from strong-willed majorities.

When government decides to act, it does so through **public policy,** which involves decisions about who gets what, when, and how from government. The final decision can be conveyed to the public in many ways: in the laws passed by Congress and signed by the president, in opinions issued by the Supreme Court, or in rules written by the federal bureaucracy. Whatever the form, public policy tells the nation what the federal government is going to do about a specific problem.

Making public policy in a government designed to balance action and the obstacles to action is rarely easy. If the Founders ever doubted that their complicated design would make decisions difficult, they learned firsthand as they struggled to make America's first public policies. Even James Madison and Alexander Hamilton, who had worked so closely together on *The Federalist Papers,* soon found themselves locked in a bitter struggle over how to finance the new government.

Hamilton (the first secretary of the treasury) wanted the federal government to create a national bank to fund the costs of the Revolutionary War debt. The war may have been won, but the bills for arms, supplies, and munitions still had to be paid. Much of the debt, which also included IOUs to soldiers who fought in the war, was held by speculators, private banks, and states that had been unwilling to raise taxes to cover the costs of the war. Hence, Hamilton's proposal seemed to favor those who had benefited from others' misfortune by buying up debt at less than full value, even as it appeared to punish states that had worked hard to retire their own debts.

The reactions to Hamilton's proposal reflected geographical and economic divisions that shape the policy debate to this day. Northern states favored a national bank, while southern states opposed it; banking and business interests supported the idea, while farmers and small businesses opposed it; wealthy Americans (including speculators) liked the idea, for it promised a healthy return on their investments, while Americans who had sold their IOUs for a few cents on the dollar saw Hamilton's bank as just another way for the rich to get richer. Because the mostly rural southern states stood to lose the most under Hamilton's proposal, Virginia's James Madison rose in opposition in the House of Representatives. After months of intense debate, which pundits might label gridlock today, Congress finally approved the Compromise of 1790: Southern states would support Hamilton's bank if northern states would move the nation's capital from New York south to its current location on the Potomac River.[1]

Two hundred years later, it is still best not to watch the policy-making process too closely, for it can be messy, confusing, and frustrating. It is also still best to recognize that no public policy is perfect. The process rarely produces works of legislative art, but often involves artful work. Almost every public policy, no matter how carefully drafted, contains flaws. That is the nature of the process and a sign that the delicate balance continues to hold. Although there are times when American government can produce exceptionally clear public policies—for example, in declaring war—the price of action is often a degree of ambiguity. In turn, as noted earlier in this book, that ambiguity can give the federal bureaucracy and the courts a greater role than the Founders might have intended in sorting out the priorities. Nevertheless, the Founders might also agree that a little ambiguity is a small price to pay for the protection of liberty.

This chapter examines these and other challenges in making public policy. First, the chapter describes the different types of public policy (foreign, economic, and social policy) and the general process for making public policy. Then the chapter takes the pieces of the policy-making process examined in earlier chapters (laws in Chapter 10, executive orders in Chapter 11, implementation in Chapter 12, and judicial review in Chapters 13 and 14) and puts them together to form the policy-making chain. The chapter concludes with a broad discussion of the demographic, economic, and social trends that are changing the face of the United States and that will shape the public policy agenda for the coming decades.

TYPES OF POLICIES

The United States barely survived its first thirty years. It had a staggering war debt, was riven by deep internal divisions, and faced a continuing struggle with the British, a struggle that led to the War of 1812. Nevertheless, it seems safe to argue that the foreign and domestic threats the United States faces today are much more complicated, perhaps more unsolvable, than those faced by the Founders two centuries ago.

In large part because of the collapse of the Soviet empire in the late 1980s, the world has become a more volatile place. The United States now faces a host of lesser threats from regional powers such as Iraq (which ignited the 1991 Gulf War with its invasion of Kuwait in 1990) and North Korea (which appears to be well on its way toward building nuclear weapons), not to mention the enormous potential threat from the People's Republic of China.

As for the domestic agenda, there seems to be no shortage of stubborn problems facing government, from America's antiquated air traffic control system to its rising teenage pregnancy rate, declining high school test scores, growing childhood poverty, declining job security, increasing domestic terrorism, aging roads and bridges, and the looming crisis in funding the social safety net for the elderly.

This is not to say that the United States has been unable to make progress toward solving some of its most pressing problems. Gregg Easterbrook argues, for example, that the nation has made great progress in cleaning up the environment. In 1992, he reports, 54 million Americans lived in areas that failed to meet minimum air quality standards. The number is still too high, of course, but it is undeniably lower than the 100 million who lived in dirty air in 1982. Much of this progress occurred because of public policies enacted and implemented by the federal government. "The good news should not scare anyone," writes Easterbrook, "particularly lovers of nature. Consider that recent improvements in air quality came mainly during a decade of Republican presidents—prominently Ronald Reagan, who labored under the garbled impression that trees cause more air pollution than cars."[2]

Nevertheless, American government will always have problems to solve, problems that come in three broad categories: foreign, social, and economic. For ease of discussion, each is treated as a separate concern below, but rare is the foreign problem that does not involve some social and economic impact, and vice versa.

Foreign Policy

Foreign policy is concerned with simultaneously protecting America from foreign threats and promoting American values abroad. As the world has grown more complex, so, too, has meeting these two goals.

In the early years of the republic, America's foreign policy mostly consisted of efforts to protect the nation from economic and military threats. George Washington's farewell address emphasized **isolationism,** the need to keep America as separate from the rest of the world as possible: "The great rule of conduct for us in regard to foreign nations is, in extending our commercial relations, to have with them as little *political connection* as possible. . . . Trust to temporary alliances for extraordinary emergencies, steer clear of permanent alliances with any portion of the foreign world. . . . Such an attraction of a small or weak nation toward a great and powerful nation dooms the former to be the satellite of the latter."[3]

For most of its first 150 years, the United States heeded Washington's warning. This is not to say that the young nation was completely isolated from the rest of the world, however. It occasionally expressed strong concerns about foreign involvement in its corner of the hemisphere, as when President James Monroe issued his Monroe Doctrine in 1823 warning Europe to steer clear of any further efforts to colonize the Americas.

To the extent possible, America wanted to be left alone. Although the nation was drawn into World War I in 1917, it soon returned to isolationism when

President Clinton meets with U.S. peacekeeping troops in Bosnia. The world has become more volatile and foreign policy more difficult to explain since the end of the Cold War.

the Senate rejected President Woodrow Wilson's proposal for a League of Nations. At least in 1919, the United States would have nothing to do with what would become today's United Nations.

Nevertheless, events conspired to make America a critical partner in world affairs. As America grew from being Washington's "small and weak" nation to being a "great and powerful nation" in its own right, its foreign policy became more complicated. In 1781, America had just seven embassies and diplomatic posts located abroad; by 1992, the number had increased to 284.[4] The United States has never been more involved around the world. Along the way, the world has become a more dangerous place. Seventeen international agreements are currently in force just to regulate the spread, testing, or use of nuclear weapons; four more limit the use of poisonous gas, biological, or inhumane weapons; one reduces the risk of nuclear war; one limits conventional weapons in Europe; and one bans the use, development, production, and stockpiling of chemical weapons. The first such agreement came in 1925, when 130 nations signed a treaty banning the use of poisonous gas; the most recent came in 1996, when 45 nations signed the Comprehensive Test Ban Treaty.

America's foreign policy is concerned with four basic goals. The first is *national security,* which involves protecting America from external threats, whether in the form of nuclear weapons or terrorism; the second is *economic interest,* which involves building foreign economic conditions that support American interests back home; the third is to promote *humanitarian or social values,* which involves efforts to project American ideals of human conduct onto other societies, including efforts to encourage democracy and human rights; and the fourth is *world order,* which involves efforts to keep the world from collapsing into the chaos of regional conflict.[5]

The 1991 Gulf War, for example, involved a blend of all four goals. Although Iraq was much too small to threaten the United States directly, its huge army clearly menaced Israel, America's closest ally in the region and largest foreign aid recipient. To the extent that Iraq endangered Israel, it engaged both U.S. security interests and world order. Iraq's 1990 invasion of Kuwait also threatened the American economy, which was and still is highly dependent on oil imports. To the extent that the Iraqi invasion imperiled U.S. oil supplies, it involved U.S. economic interests. Finally, the brutality of the Iraqi invasion called on U.S. humanitarian and social values. These assorted goals came together in the 100-hour war that drove Iraqi forces from Kuwait.

in a different light —— DOES THE UNITED STATES STILL NEED A FOREIGN POLICY?

For much of this century, American foreign policy was shaped by a great battle between democracy and communism. Communism is an ideology in which individual freedom is sharply restricted for the benefit of the nation as a whole. There is no delicate balance in a communist system. All is for the whole, nothing for the individual.

The United States and the Soviet Union emerged from World War II in 1945 both deeply committed to promoting their views of the world. For the better part of the next half century, the two waged a great "Cold War," never firing a shot at each other but constantly sparring through smaller allies. The Soviet Union and its communist neighbor, China, backed the North Vietnamese in the Vietnam War; years later, the United States and its western European allies backed the rebels in the Soviet Union's "Vietnam," Afghanistan.

The Cold War ended abruptly. Under intense economic pressure from the West, the Soviet empire began to crumble, first in Poland and East Germany, then almost overnight in the rest of the Soviet Union. Only Cuba remained committed to the old Soviet communist ideal.

With no great enemy to unite the public behind international involvement, polls showed that Americans were becoming far less worried about foreign policy. Asked for their views of foreign policy in 1997, roughly seven in ten Americans said that the United States "should not think so much in international terms but concentrate more on our own national problems," while just six in ten said that the United States should cooperate fully with the United Nations.[6] These findings suggest that the nation may be entering a new era of isolationism, in which the United States steps back from its role as world leader and global police officer.

For the time being, however, most Americans still believe the nation needs a foreign policy. Americans may not see foreign affairs as a most important problem, but two-thirds want the nation to take an active part in world affairs nonetheless. The majority reject the notion that the United States "should mind its own business internationally and let other countries get along the best they can on their own," while substantial numbers say America should provide food and medical assistance to needy peoples, help needy countries develop their economies, and provide military aid to its allies.[7]

Nevertheless, Americans have become more precise about just when and where their nation should take an active part in world affairs. They no longer want America to be the world's police officer, and believe other nations should rely less on U.S. troops for protection. Less than one in ten Americans believe the United States should be the "single world leader," while three-quarters say the United States should share the leadership role with other nations.

Americans have also become more focused on foreign policy issues that have domestic impacts. Number one is stopping the flow of illegal drugs into the United States (89 percent of the public say that this should be a very important U.S. foreign policy goal), followed by protecting the jobs of American workers (83 percent), preventing the spread of nuclear weapons (82 percent), controlling and reducing illegal immigration (72 percent), securing adequate supplies of energy (62 percent), reducing trade deficits with other countries (59 percent), and improving the global environment (58 percent). The percentages who assigned great importance to traditional Cold War issues such as promoting and defining human rights in other countries, helping bring democratic forms of government to other countries, and helping improve the standard of living in less-developed countries were far smaller.[8]

In short, the United States is becoming a more reluctant partner in world affairs, with limited public support for involvement when the going gets tough or violent. Unless a president can find a clear domestic benefit from engagement abroad, the public is likely to say no, particularly when U.S. troops are at risk.

Economic Policy

Economic policy is concerned with the nation's standard of living, whether measured by inflation, unemployment, the national debt, or gross domestic product. (See Box 15–1 for a brief description of these terms.) The problem is that economic goals are often contradictory. One way to stop **inflation** is to raise federal interest rates, which increases the price people and businesses pay to borrow

BOX **15-1**

Key Economic Terms Defined

Inflation: Measured by the Consumer Price Index (CPI). Shows how much more or less Americans are paying for the same "basket of goods" over time. The major components accounted for in the CPI are food, shelter, household fuel, clothing, transportation, and medical care.

Unemployment rate: Measures the percentage of Americans who are looking for jobs but cannot find them. Does not measure the number who have given up looking for work.

National debt: Measures how much money the government owes; directly tied to the federal budget deficit. When federal spending exceeds taxes and other revenues, the federal government must borrow money, thereby increasing its debt. Like any consumer, the government must pay interest on any money it borrows. A growing percentage of the federal budget is simple interest on the national debt. Paying this interest has several effects. First, if not enough money is available in the economy, government borrowing may drive up the interest rate on money, which is the simple measure of how much money costs (credit cards, for example, often carry an 18 to 22 percent annual interest rate). As interest rates rise, other consumers reduce their spending for a host of goods (houses, cars, clothing) because money is just too expensive. Second, whatever the money costs at the time, government must eventually pay back the money it borrows, meaning that future taxpayers may bear the burden for today's budget deficits.

Gross domestic product: Measures the size of the entire American economy by totaling all the things it produces and sells and subtracting what it buys from other countries. It tells how fast the economy is growing or shrinking. It is reported quarterly by the Department of Commerce.

money, which can reduce new investment by private companies, which cools down the economy, which can increase the **unemployment rate** and reduce **gross domestic product,** which almost always reduces tax revenues (unemployed workers do not have the income to pay taxes), which drives up federal spending for programs to help the needy, which may push up the **national debt,** which may produce even higher interest rates.

The traditional interplay of these economic goals has become even more complicated because the American economy is now part of a vast global network. America no longer controls its own economic destiny, in part because of its own success in rebuilding the devastated economies of Europe and Japan following World War II.[9] Those nations have become major competitors with the United States in the production of such goods as cars, computers, rice, and wine.

Economic policy has always been at or near the top of the federal government's list of problems. It was economic policy, for example, that created the fight over the Revolutionary War debt in the First Congress. For the country's first 150 years or so, however, economic policy was generally left to the private sector. Government stayed out of the business of business, adopting a *laissez faire* (or "leave it alone") philosophy toward the economy.

As the United States moved from being a primarily agricultural, rural economy in the 1800s to a more industrial, urban economy in the early 1900s, government began to take a more aggressive role in regulating the economy, including new rules forbidding child labor, cleaning up the meatpacking industry, improving workplace safety, and breaking up industry monopolies, or trusts. Congress also created the first independent agencies to regulate a variety of economic practices, including interstate commerce. The result of this "progressive era" in American history was a government much more deeply involved in economic life than ever before.

It took the stock market crash in October 1929 and the subsequent Great Depression to drive the federal government toward an even more aggressive role in trying to solve economic problems. Over the ten years leading up to World War II, government became involved in virtually all areas of the economy but one: it never nationalized, or took control of, any industries. Unlike other Western democracies, which have owned everything from airlines to television stations, or communist nations, which generally own all instruments of production from steel factories to farms, the U.S. government has generally resisted the temptation to own whole industries.

Nevertheless, the federal government emerged from the Great Depression and World War II convinced that it could and should manipulate the economy to promote four basic goals. The first is *economic growth,* which involves expanding the standard of living; the second is *full employment,* which involves finding jobs for as many Americans as possible; the third is *price stability,* which involves holding down inflation; and the fourth is *international competitiveness,* which involves keeping the United States a leader in the global economy.

The federal government has two basic options for reaching these four goals: it can use either **fiscal policy,** which involves the adjustment of taxes and spending to stimulate or slow the economy, or **monetary policy,** which involves efforts to change the cost and supply of money.

Fiscal Policy.   Congress and the president control fiscal policy. Whether intended as such or not, any tax or spending decision is a fiscal policy choice. Tax increases and spending cuts, for example, are seen as devices for cooling down a "hot," or inflationary, economy. By taking money away from individual consumers, government reduces demand for products. As demand falls, so do prices. Conversely, tax cuts are seen as devices for stimulating a sluggish economy. By cutting individual and corporate taxes, the government increases demand for products and money for corporate investment. As demand rises, so does production. New jobs should naturally follow.

Monetary Policy.   Despite their considerable influence over fiscal policy, Congress and the president have little control, if any, over monetary policy. That responsibility belongs to the Federal Reserve Board, which is one of the independent regulatory commissions discussed in Chapter 12. Although the seven members of the Federal Reserve Board are appointed by the president and confirmed by the Senate, they serve fourteen-year terms, which makes them mostly independent of political pressure.

The Federal Reserve Board determines the basic price that borrowers must pay for money. The Board sets this price through the *discount rate,* which is the interest rate it charges the member banks of the Federal Reserve system for money. Reducing the discount rate is seen as a device for stimulating a sluggish economy. By lowering interest rates, the Federal Reserve Board puts more money into the economy, thereby increasing demand. Conversely, increasing the discount rate is seen as a device for slowing a hot economy. By raising interest rates, the Board makes consumers pay more for the money they borrow, and thus dampens demand.

The challenge in making fiscal and monetary policy today is that the economy sometimes does not behave as predicted. In the late 1970s the Carter administration confronted a new kind of economic problem in the late 1970s called *stagflation,* which is a combination of unemployment (or economic stagnation) and *inflation,* two problems that are not supposed to exist at the same time. In theory, unemployment is supposed to be high when inflation is low, and vice versa. In reality, stagflation is a symptom of an increasingly complex global economy that does not yield quite so readily to U.S. fiscal or monetary decisions. In fact, much of what happens in the U.S. economy today is determined by decisions made in nations and markets abroad.

Social Policy

Social policy is concerned with protecting Americans' quality of life, while assuring that they have some protection, or a safety net, against personal hardship. Social programs of one kind or another now account for over half of all federal spending, with Social Security for the elderly by far the largest single program in the federal budget.

Until the early 1900s, however, the federal government did little either to protect the quality of life or to create a social safety net. Although the federal government did provide small pensions to veterans and occasional land grants to new settlers, people in need had to rely on the kindness of strangers to find a way through hardship. Education was left to communities; public welfare was left to private charities or religious institutions.[10]

This informal safety net began to fray as America's cities filled with wave after wave of immigrants at the turn of the century; it unraveled completely with the Great Depression. Private charities simply could not meet the enormous need, so greater pressure was put on the federal government to become involved in both managing the economy and preventing poverty. Congress established the Social Security and unemployment compensation programs in 1935 and provided the first federal housing assistance in 1937. Together, these programs—part of President Franklin Roosevelt's New Deal—formed the basis for further expansion under Lyndon Johnson's Great Society, most notably Food Stamps for the poor in 1964 and Medicare for the elderly in 1965.

By the 1960s, America's social policy agenda had grown to cover three broad goals, each an umbrella for dozens of separate programs that endeavor to solve social problems. The first goal is *personal safety,* which involves everything from keeping streets safe to environmental protection, from access to decent housing to at least minimal access to health care, primarily for the elderly (through Medicare) and the poor (through Medicaid), though not yet for the working poor, who often hold jobs without health insurance. The second goal is *income security,* which involves providing protection against downturns in economic performance through programs such as unemployment insurance, job training, disability insurance, Food Stamps, and Tempory Assistance for Needy Families, as well as support for the elderly through programs such as Social Security and regulations to protect pensions. The third goal is *protection of civil liberties and civil rights,* which has become so important over the past thirty years that it warrants its own chapter in this book (see Chapter 14).

One way to distinguish among the many income security programs that now exist is to ask who gets the benefits. Some programs provide benefits only to

Americans who have earned a right to participate through contributions earlier in life, either in the form of taxes (a financial contribution) or service to the nation (a personal contribution). These programs are called **contributory social programs.** For example, veterans of the armed services receive substantial benefits for putting themselves in harm's way, including help paying for college, government-subsidized home mortgages, special medical care, and special preferences in getting a federal civil service job. They also receive low- or no-cost health care at America's 172 Veterans Health Centers, including everything from eyeglasses to heart transplants.

Other programs provide benefits only to Americans who need government help because of accidents and events mostly outside their control, whether an act of God such as a hurricane or a personal crisis such as a divorce or teenage pregnancy. These programs are labeled **noncontributory social programs** and include everything from disaster relief to job training. Some of these programs require proof that recipients are poor enough to merit government support. To qualify for such **means-tested programs,** recipients must prove that they lack the means to provide for themselves. To qualify for federal Food Stamps, which poor families can use to purchase groceries, a recipient must prove that he or she has no other sources of income, including savings accounts or certain kinds of property (cemetery plots, second homes or apartments) that could be sold for cash.

Although most income security programs are either contributory *or* noncontributory, the Social Security system provides both kinds of benefits. Americans cannot qualify for Social Security unless they have paid at least some amount

President Bill Clinton swears in a class of Americorps volunteers in 1995. Americorps is an example of a contributory program in which voluntary service entitles the contributor to funding for college.

of taxes into the system over a certain number of years, making access to the program contributory. At the same time, the formula for calculating payments once an individual actually applies for benefits is designed so that those with lower incomes (who paid in less) receive a greater proportion relative to those with higher incomes (who paid in more), thereby making a portion of each Social Security check noncontributory.

THE POLICY-MAKING PROCESS

As the types of public policies have become more complicated over time, so has the process for making those policies. There are more participants at the policy table—witness the dramatic increase in the number of interest groups over the past half century—and there are more "tables," or places, where policy gets made—more subcommittees in Congress, more White House staffers, more presidential appointees, more media outlets, more political consultants. Indeed, there are more of just about every kind of participant imaginable (except, it seems, individual citizens). The result is a fragmented, often messy process that confirms the Founders' desire to counteract ambition with ambition.

Where Policy Is Made

The final decisions on who gets what, when, and how from government are usually made under formal rules—only senators can vote in the Senate, only the president can issue an executive order, and so on. And they produce formal outcomes—a public law, a verdict.

The fact that the process for making final decisions looks formal does not make it so, however. Final policy decisions usually involve a long string of informal decisions made by collections of political leaders and interest groups that join together on behalf of a specific cause. Some of these collections exist for decades, while others come together for a specific cause, then disband.[11] The former are often called *iron triangles,* while the latter are labeled *issue networks.*

Iron Triangles.   An **iron triangle** has three sides: (1) a federal department or agency, (2) a set of loyal interest groups, and (3) a House and/or Senate authorizing committee. Each side supports the other two. Congress gives money to the agency, for example, and gets campaign money and endorsements from the interest groups in return; the interest groups give money and endorsements to Congress and gets special services from the agency in return; the agency gives special services to the interest groups, and gets money from Congress in return.

BOX 15-2

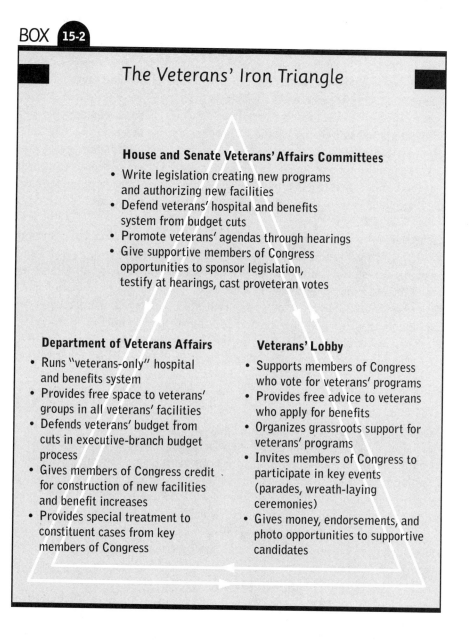

The Veterans' Iron Triangle

House and Senate Veterans' Affairs Committees
- Write legislation creating new programs and authorizing new facilities
- Defend veterans' hospital and benefits system from budget cuts
- Promote veterans' agendas through hearings
- Give supportive members of Congress opportunities to sponsor legislation, testify at hearings, cast proveteran votes

Department of Veterans Affairs
- Runs "veterans-only" hospital and benefits system
- Provides free space to veterans' groups in all veterans' facilities
- Defends veterans' budget from cuts in executive-branch budget process
- Gives members of Congress credit for construction of new facilities and benefit increases
- Provides special treatment to constituent cases from key members of Congress

Veterans' Lobby
- Supports members of Congress who vote for veterans' programs
- Provides free advice to veterans who apply for benefits
- Organizes grassroots support for veterans' programs
- Invites members of Congress to participate in key events (parades, wreath-laying ceremonies)
- Gives money, endorsements, and photo opportunities to supportive candidates

Making veterans policy is a classic example of how iron triangles work. (See Box 15–2 for the veterans' iron triangle.) Composed of the House and Senate Veterans' Affairs Committees, veterans' groups, and the Department of Veterans Affairs, the triangle has been able to protect the $17 billion a year health care system for veterans in spite of a 56 percent drop in the number of inpatients since the late 1960s. "We have the moral high ground," Veterans Affairs (VA) Secretary Jesse Brown explained in 1995. "We have God on our side. We're right. And we have the American people on our side."[12]

Brown might have added that the VA has the House and Senate Veterans Committees and the veterans' groups on its side, too. "There is no anti-veterans group," argues Brown's predecessor, Edwin Derwinski, who was fired by the president after proposing changes in the VA hospital system. "It's just a one way street. Now we're not talking about a hell of a big army, but it's unopposed."[13] With thousands of local posts across the United States, the veterans' groups (American Legion, Veterans of Foreign Wars, Disabled American Veterans) are able to generate huge volumes of mail for or against particular policy proposals.

Issue Networks.   Most of the old iron triangles have been replaced by **issue networks**, which come together to make a specific decision or two, then disband. Issue networks have flourished with the growth in the number of narrowly focused interest groups, discussed in Chapter 7. The increasing number of small, highly specialized interest groups has meant that Congress and federal agencies can no longer identify an ongoing occupant for the third corner of an iron triangle. They have to find temporary allies, depending on the issue. There is nothing "iron" about such coalitions of smaller groups: They last only as long as a given issue is hot.

The 1993–1994 debate over a national health care system produced a remarkable pair of issue networks. (See Box 15–3 for just a sampling of the members involved.) The network in favor of reform ("pro") included organized labor (including the twenty union presidents who created the Committee for National Health Insurance), a variety of "good government" organizations (including a coalition called Healthright), smaller collections of physicians, consumers, and even the League of Women Voters. The network opposed ("anti") included large physician groups, tobacco companies (which feared that health care reform would be financed by a tax on cigarettes), small businesses, hospital organizations, a variety of insurance groups, and huge pharmaceutical companies. In between were an assortment of lone insurance companies and health care groups that hoped for a compromise on the issues.

Such issue networks may weaken government's ability to act by forcing presidents and leaders of Congress to build separate majorities for every issue that arises, a time-consuming and often frustrating process that raises the cost of passing legislation. Given the decline of the large groups that once dominated the policy-making process, the only way to create a majority in support of passage is to build coalitions of narrowly focused interest groups. As British political scientist Anthony King argues, "The materials out of which coalitions might be built simply do not exist. Building coalitions in the United States today is like building coalitions in the sand. It cannot be done."[14]

BOX 15-3

The Health Care Issue Network

COMPROMISERS

Medical Schools
American Association of Medical
  Colleges

Insurance Companies
National Association of Life
  Underwriters
American Council of Life Insurance
AFLAC, Inc.
Prudential Insurance

Other Health Care Providers
American Podiatry Association
American Dental Association
American Chiropractic Association
American Nurses Association
American Optometric Association

PROREFORM

Consumer Groups
Families USA
AIDS activists
Child Welfare League
National Council of Senior
  Citizens

Doctors
American Academy of
  Family Physicians
Physicians for a National
  Health Program

ANTIREFORM

Hospitals
American Hospital Association
American Health Care Association

Doctors
American Medical Association
American College of Emergency
  Physicians
American Academy of
  Ophthalmology
American College of Physicians

Tobacco Companies

**Pharmaceutical
Manufacturers**
Eli Lilly & Co.
Pfizer Inc.
Shering-Plough Corp.

Business Associations
National Association of
  Manufacturers
National Federation of
  Independent (Small) Business
U.S. Chamber of Commerce

PRIMARY

House Ways and Means
  Committee
House Education and Labor Committee
House Energy and Commerce Committee
Senate Finance Committee
Senate Labor and
  Human Resources Committee
Hillary Clinton's Health Care
  Reform Task Force

POLICY MAKERS

Private Companies
American Airlines
United States Surgical
  Corporation

Reform Groups
Health Care Reform Project
League of Women Voters
Healthright

Organized Labor
AFL-CIO
United Auto Workers
Committee for National
  Health Insurance

**Department of Health
and Human Services**
Health Care Financing
  Administration

Department of Labor

SECONDARY POLICY MAKERS

Department of Veterans Affairs
Veterans Health Administration

Other Congressional Committees
House and Senate Appropriations
House and Senate Budget
House and Senate Veterans Affairs
House Energy and Commerce
House Science, Space, and Technology
Senate Commerce, Science, and
  Transportation
Senate Aging

☀ in a different light ——— HOW ISSUE NETWORKS FIGHT: THE TOBACCO WARS

Issue networks have pioneered the use of issue advocacy to make their case to the American people. As noted in Chapter 7, issue advocacy is designed to shape public opinion and was invented in 1993–1994 by opponents of the Clinton health care reform plan. Using a series of clever ads that were aired off and on for almost a year on cable television, the health insurance industry exploited public distrust of big government to stop the administration's complicated proposal.

Building on lessons learned in the health care debate, the tobacco industry mounted a much more intensive issue advocacy campaign against a Senate tobacco bill in 1998. The original proposal would have settled all the lawsuits that had been brought by smokers against the tobacco companies by imposing a one-time $516 billion penalty on the industry, increased the price of a pack of cigarettes by $1.10 total over a five-year period to pay for medical research and a government-sponsored media campaign to reduce youth smoking, given the tobacco companies financial incentives for mounting their own campaign against youth smoking, banned billboards advertising tobacco products within 1,000 feet of schools, and protected the tobacco companies from future lawsuits. Supported by Democrats and Republicans alike, the bill would have made smoking a more expensive habit, but would not have destroyed the tobacco industry. The tobacco companies also agreed to the deal, launching an advertising campaign urging Americans to accept it.

Something happened as the bill worked its way toward final passage, however: it got tougher. First, the Senate dropped the legal protection against future lawsuits. Then it began to attract legislative freight, including parts of the old Republican Contract with America and $3 billion to help veterans cope with smoking-related illnesses. Only a month after its original advertisements had asked the nation "Isn't it time to move forward?" the tobacco companies began a new, $40 million campaign to stop the legislation it had just accepted.[15]

The campaign was impossible to miss. It ran week after week nationwide, and included at least fourteen different television commercials, at least as many radio spots, and dozens of newspaper and magazine advertisements. One television advertisement featured an off-key cuckoo clock and closed with the line "Washington wants to raise the price of cigarettes so high, there would be a black market in cigarettes with unregulated access to kids." Another spelled out its message in black letters against a stark white background: "Huge new taxes for working people; cigarettes at $5 a pack, $50 a carton, a black market in cigarettes with unregulated access to children, jobs at risk for thousands of Americans." Still another, featuring an elaborately decorated Christmas tree that fell over, closed with the line " ... lots of money for new government bureaucracy.... But remember, it is your money they're giving away." Viewers were invited to call a toll-free telephone line to express their outrage. Of the nearly 500,000 who did call, well over one-third were patched through to their member of Congress.

The results were immediate. Although most Americans supported the anti-tobacco bill, an intense minority of smokers, tobacco farmers, and other angry citizens made its opposition known. Unable to find the sixty votes needed to break a pending filibuster by tobacco-state senators, the Senate gave up in early June, pushing action into an uncertain future.

The campaign itself set several important, possibly dangerous, precedents for the future. First, it worked primarily by exploiting public anger toward big government and high taxes. Despite what the tobacco advertisements claimed, most Americans would not have paid a cent in increased taxes under the settlement. Second, it worked by being misleading. Claims that the Senate bill would have created seventeen new government bureaucracies were clearly false, as were fears of a new black market in cigarettes. Finally, it worked because supporters of the bill never fired back, except for a tiny, poorly funded counterattack by the American Cancer Society and the Campaign for Tobacco-Free Kids.

The primary advertisement in the counterattack was just as misleading as the tobacco company spots, however. It urged the public to support the Senate bill to "stop the lies, stop the killing, and stop big tobacco." How a bill that merely raised the price of a pack of cigarettes and funded more research would "stop the killing" was never explained.

The danger was that both sides had learned how easy it is to manipulate public opinion through issue advocacy. It has always been difficult to pass a law, but modern issue advocacy may have made it nearly impossible. Because distrust of government will always be part of the American political character, interest groups may now have the capacity to create permanent stalemate. As if to make the point, the tobacco companies continued their issue advocacy campaign after the Senate bill was withdrawn just to make sure it did not come back to life. Their last advertisement showed that fallen Christmas tree and reminded viewers that Washington would try to put it back up unless Americans said no.

How Policy Is Made

Every policy reflects a series of separate decisions leading to final implementation and action. From start to finish, making public policy involves at least eight decisions: (1) making assumptions about the world, (2) choosing the problem to be solved, (3) deciding whether to act at all, (4) deciding how much to do, (5) choosing a tool for solving the problem, (6) finding someone to deliver the services, (7) making the rules for implementation, and (8) running the program. The first four decisions are mostly made by Congress, the presidency, or the courts, while the last four are mostly made by the federal bureaucracy.

What makes the process both exciting and frustrating is that it does not always start at the beginning. In fact, it is more appropriate to depict the eight decisions as spokes of a wheel. (See Box 15–4 for a simple diagram of the process.) A

BOX 15-4

Decisions in the Policy-Making Wheel

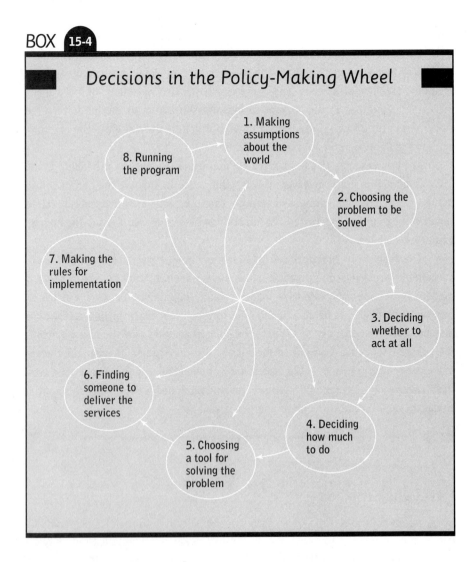

1. Making assumptions about the world

8. Running the program

2. Choosing the problem to be solved

7. Making the rules for implementation

3. Deciding whether to act at all

6. Finding someone to deliver the services

4. Deciding how much to do

5. Choosing a tool for solving the problem

specific problem gets identified, a solution gets passed, implementation occurs; the problem may worsen, an amendment to the old solution gets passed, further implementation occurs, and so forth.

It is important to note that the process does not always flow neatly from decision to decision. Indeed, it is quite possible that a solution will exist *before* a problem is identified, or that the decision about how much to do will influence the assumptions that Congress and the president use to describe the size of the problem, or even that an agency will exist to run a program before that program exists (which is one reason why so many federal departments and agencies are immortal). In the 1998 transportation funding bill, for example, members of Congress decided that they wanted to spend a lot of money on new highways and roads long before they held the hearings to define the size of the problem. It is best, therefore, to think of making public policy as an often unpredictable process in which problems and solutions are loosely connected. It can start anywhere in the circle and skip back and forth at will. The result is a policy-making process that is often unpredictable and almost always in flux.[16]

Making Assumptions about the World.   Every government decision involves assumptions about how the world works. Is the economy going to get stronger? If so, perhaps employment will go up, and the costs of supporting the unemployed will go down. Is teenage pregnancy going to increase? If so, perhaps childhood poverty, which increases as more single teenagers have babies, will continue to grow. Is world terrorism going to increase? If so, perhaps the United States needs to strengthen its border security.

The problem with making even short-term assumptions about the world is that they are often wrong. David Stockman, director of the Reagan administration's Office of Management and Budget (OMB), once despaired of making assumptions even a year into the future. "I'm beginning to believe that history is a lot shakier than I thought it was," he remarked in late 1981 as the federal budget deficit began to rise. "In other words, I think there are more random elements, less determinism, and more discretion in the course of history than I ever believed before."[17]

Making short-term assumptions is easy, however, compared to creating the seventy-five-year forecasts needed to run the Social Security program. Because most Americans pay into the program for thirty or forty years of working life and draw out their benefits for another twenty or thirty years of retirement, the program is very slow to change, meaning that policymakers must plan for possible problems decades in advance. Knowing how well Social Security will be doing in 2070 involves guesses about how many children will be born (more children born today means more taxpayers tomorrow), inflation (in indexed programs such as Social Security, higher inflation means higher benefit checks), and unemployment (higher unemployment means fewer people working, which means less Social Security tax being paid).

Because there is no sure way to choose among competing assumptions about such a distant future, policymakers often make choices that help sell their particular views of the world. They are often pessimistic about the future when they define problems, but optimistic when they announce specific proposals to fix the problems. The result is that problems may look much worse than they truly are, while solutions may seem likely to work better than they possibly could.

Choosing the Problem to Be Solved.   Choosing the problem to be solved is the essential decision in setting the **policy agenda.** The policy agenda, as political scientist John Kingdon defines it, "is the list of subjects or problems to which governmental officials, and people outside of government closely associated with those officials, are paying some serious attention at any given time."[18]

Problems reach the agenda from a variety of sources. Many arise from events: an American passenger jet crashes; an earthquake hits California; a tanker runs aground and spills oil in Alaska. Others reach the agenda because of the government's own numbers: the economy slows down; the number of children immunized against illness falls; crime rates increase.

The source of the problem clearly matters to policymakers. Some sources, particularly interest groups, have a great stake in making sure their cause reaches the agenda. That is why they exist in the first place, and most certainly why they make campaign contributions. Problems that arise from a crisis are difficult to ignore. Nevertheless, as noted below, the public's attention span for a crisis may be very short. Problems that are identified through numbers and analysis may be the easiest to ignore, in part because there always seem to be numbers to refute one analysis or another.

The number of problems competing for a place on the agenda has grown, in large part because of the proliferation of interest groups. In response, policymakers have increasingly come to rely on a small number of think tanks to help winnow the list. Recall from Chapter 7 that a think tank is a research organization that employs scholars and experts to study problems, write books and papers, and generally provide expertise to the government and media. Ideas are the main products of a think tank.

Think tanks tend to rise and fall with the party in power. One of the most visible think tanks during the 1980s was the Heritage Foundation. Populated largely by conservative scholars and funded mostly by conservative foundations, Heritage was deeply involved in supporting the Reagan administration's effort to shrink government. The closer it worked with the White House, the better it seemed to do in raising money from conservatives. It grew from an initial funding of just $250,000 when it was created in 1973 to $10 million ten years later. Along the way, Heritage was able to finance a $9.5 million headquarters building located near Capitol Hill.

Although most think tanks employ a rather small number of scholars, they have a significant impact. Think tanks distill information, translating raw numbers on foreign, economic, and social trends into meaningful advice. They often lay the intellectual and research groundwork for major legislative proposals. They supply many of the witnesses who testify before key committees, many of the authors who write the op-ed pieces that endorse or oppose action, and many of the "talking heads" who show up on the network news. Think tanks may not come up with every proposal enacted into law, but the fact that they are studying a particular issue is an important sign that the issue is high on the policy agenda.

Deciding Whether to Act at All.   The fact that a problem exists does not automatically mean Congress and the president will try to solve it. Sometimes they make a *nondecision,* which is simply a deliberate decision not to act. Government may not have the money to do much of anything substantive, and a delaying device such as a commission or study may not be appropriate.

Other times, issues will simply fade from the public's mind. In fact, writes political scientist Anthony Downs, "American public attention rarely remains sharply focused upon any one domestic issue for very long—even if it involves a continuing problem of crucial importance to society." According to Downs, attention to problems follows an **issue-attention cycle** in which each problem "suddenly leaps into prominence, remains there for a short time, and then—though still largely unresolved—gradually fades from the center of public attention."[19] (See Box 15–5 for a list of the steps in the issue-attention cycle.)

Ultimately, nothing forces presidents, members of Congress, or judges to choose a problem if addressing that problem does not further their reelection, place in history, or good policy. Some problems help policymakers achieve one or more of these goals; others do not.

Deciding How Much to Do.   Once Congress, the president, or the courts decide to act, the process of actually finding a solution to a given problem is enormously complicated in its own right—recall the discussion in Chapter 10 of how a bill becomes a public law. Even before a bill is introduced, however, policymakers make two basic decisions.

The first involves the size of the proposed solution. Will it be a small step from current practice, which political scientists call an **incremental program,** or a major policy reform? Major policy reforms are generally much more difficult to pass, sometimes because they cost much more and sometimes because they cut long-established federal programs. Because they are so sweeping, however, they allow Congress and the president to claim much greater credit for solving a problem.

BOX 15-5

The Issue-Attention Cycle

The Preproblem Stage

This first stage in the cycle prevails when some highly undesirable social condition exists but has not yet captured much public attention.

Alarmed Discovery and Euphoric Enthusiasm

Stage two comes about when, as a result of some dramatic series of events. . . , or for other reasons, the public suddenly becomes both aware of and alarmed about the evils of a particular problem.

Realizing the Cost of Significant Progress

The third stage consists of a gradually spreading realization that the cost of "solving" the problem is very high.

Gradual Decline of Intense Public Interest

In stage four, as more and more people realize how difficult, and how costly to themselves, a solution to the problem would be, three reactions set in. Some people just get discouraged. Others feel positively threatened by thinking about the problem, so they suppress such thoughts. Still others become bored by the issue.

The Postproblem Stage

In the final stage, an issue that has been replaced at the center of public concern moves into a prolonged limbo—a twilight realm of lesser attention or spasmodic recurrences of interest.

Source: Anthony Downs, "The Issue-Attention Cycle," *The Public Interest* 28 (Summer 1972), pp. 38–50.

The second decision involves how benefits are to be distributed across the various groups in society. A **distributive program** is a solution that generally offers new benefits to most groups in society and shares the costs evenly. National parks, air traffic control, the interstate highway system, education funding, national defense, and Social Security are all defined as distributive in nature.

If, instead, the solution takes wealth (in the form of taxes) from one group in society and converts it into benefits for another, it is called a **redistributive**

The Head Start program, designed to help poor preschool children get a head start on education, is a redistributive program.

program. Such a solution tends to concentrate benefits on the less fortunate in society, and often provokes conflict between the haves and have nots. Welfare, poverty programs, Head Start for poor preschool children, and special programs to help minority groups are often characterized as redistributive. Some political scientists call these programs *zero-sum games,* meaning that one group's gain (the program's benefits) is another's loss (the program's cost in taxes).

If, as is often the case today in cutting the federal budget, the solution asks all Americans to give up benefits they once enjoyed, it is called a **dedistributive program.** Because of its controversy, such a program is the most difficult to pass. It is always easier for Congress and the president to sell a program that distributes benefits than to sell one that reduces them. The 1983 Social Security rescue is one example of a dedistributive program. It cut benefits for older Americans, raised taxes on all workers, and increased the retirement age for future retirees—all exceedingly unpopular ideas, but essential if the program was to continue to pay benefits on time.[20]

Choosing a Tool for Solving the Problem.   Policymakers are not finished with formulating a solution until they choose a tool for actually solving the problem. Although there are literally thousands of federal programs now on the statute books, public policy scholars argue that there are four basic tools available to solve most public problems: (1) making outright money payments, (2) providing goods or services directly, (3) providing protection against risk, and (4) enforcing restrictions and penalties.[21]

Outright money payments are made either directly to individuals or to agencies that provide services to them. Social Security is a direct payment to individuals; Head Start, which provides early-childhood education for disadvantaged children, is funded by the federal government and delivered by local schools.

Goods and services are provided either completely free to the public or for a price. National parks such as Yosemite and the Grand Canyon generally charge an admission fee; the National Air and Space Museum on the Washington Mall is open to the public for free; and Americans do not pay anything directly for national defense. Ultimately, of course, nothing the government does is completely free—the National Air and Space Museum is supported by general taxes, as is defense.

Protections against risk involve a range of devices to encourage activities where the private sector might otherwise not go. The most familiar protections are federal loan guarantees, under which the government promises to cover the losses in the event that a student, farmer, small business, or other borrower fails to repay a debt. The federal government also provides protection against risk in the form of special exemptions from certain laws. Major league baseball, for example, is exempted from federal antitrust law. The exemption was designed to encourage the expansion of the national pastime, but was never given to professional football, hockey, or basketball.

Restrictions and penalties are designed to encourage or discourage certain behaviors. The list of laws and regulations that affect Americans is seemingly endless, and includes everything from criminal laws to cancer warnings on cigarette packages, which are required under federal law.

Finding Someone to Deliver the Services.   Once a tool is selected, Congress, the president, or the courts must decide who will actually deliver the services. The answer is no longer always federal employees.[22] With federal employment actually in decline, policy success increasingly depends on **third-party federal government,** which is defined as the use of nonfederal employees to deliver services on behalf of the federal government.

There are three major sources of third-party delivery of government services today: (1) private companies who work for the federal government under contracts; (2) state and local governments who work for the federal government under mandates; and (3) nonprofit organizations, which are sometimes called part of the independent sector, that fill in the gaps where private contractors or state and local governments are unwilling or unable to go.

Private Companies.   Private companies are a first alternative to delivery of services by federal employees. Paid under contracts with federal agencies, these profit-making businesses provide an increasing share of federal services. These services include everything from performing laboratory tests for the National Institutes of Health to writing congressional testimony for the secretary of the Department of Energy.[23]

As of 1998, almost one-fifth of the federal budget went to private contractors. Recall from Chapter 12 that the Defense Department accounted for over two-thirds of the government's nearly $200 billion contracting budget, the Department of Energy one-tenth, NASA one-fifteenth, and the rest of the domestic agencies about one-sixth. However, the share going to jets, parts, and weapons is clearly falling as more of the federal budget gets spent on services—computers, telephones, consulting, and so forth.

As the amount of contracting grows, so does the number of "shadow" federal employees—people who are basically federal employees without the ID cards. Thus, promises to shrink government by merely cutting the total number of full-time federal employees are misleading. The number of employees who work for the federal government may be going down, but the number who work under federal contracts has been rising steadily for two decades.

State and Local Governments. The state and local governments are a second source for the delivery of services on behalf of the federal government. As noted in Chapter 12, state and local governments are growing much faster than the federal government. State and local employment has ballooned from roughly 3 million in 1950 to 16 million today, rising from just one state and local employee for every forty Americans to one for every sixteen.

The growth of state and local government is one of the most dramatic, yet least visible trends shaping American government today. The federal government may get the attention, but state and local governments deliver an increasing share of the services. As the National Commission on the State and Local Public Service observed in making its final report to President Clinton on the condition of state and local government in 1993:

> These employees do much of the real work of domestic governance. We literally could not live without them. They provide our water, collect our trash, vaccinate our children, police our communities, and administer traffic safety, airports, and the vital systems we need to communicate with each other and other nations. They do much of the teaching, training, and counseling in our public schools, universities, and community colleges to prepare our children for fulfilling careers. They are responsible for environmental cleanup and protection programs. They design and carry out programs to lift our most needy out of poverty and into jobs and housing. They operate the hospitals that are the last hope of the uninsured. They staff most of our prisons, as well as our court system. Not a day passes during which their work does not touch and shape our lives.[24]

Recall from Chapter 3 that part of this role involves federal mandates to the states. A mandate is quite simple: the federal government orders a state or local government to accept some responsibility it might otherwise not accept. Because most mandates come attached to federal grants, state and local governments are hard-pressed to refuse the added responsibility.[25] Although states can always refuse the funds if they do not like the strings attached, the money has become irresistible, even habit-forming.

Not all mandates come from federal legislation, however. The Supreme Court mandated that states integrate the public schools under *Brown v. Board of Education* in 1954, for example. As political scientist Martha Derthick explains,

> Until the mid-1950s, federal courts interpreting the Constitution had habitually told the states what they might *not* do. . . . But they had refrained from telling the states what they *must* do. This changed with school desegregation. . . . Once courts and litigants discovered what could be done (or attempted) in the schools, other state institutions, especially prisons and institutions for the mentally ill, became targets.[26]

The Independent Sector. The final alternative to service delivery by federal employees is the **independent sector,** which is composed of tax-exempt agencies such as the Red Cross, Salvation Army, and Catholic Charities. By law, these agencies are prohibited from making a profit from their work.

The kindness of strangers. The United States has always relied on private charities, such as the American Red Cross and the Salvation Army, to help the victims of hurricanes and other crises. In recent years, the federal government has come to rely on such groups to deliver services on its behalf under federal contracts and grants.

The growth of the independent sector is another one of the most important trends in public policy. The number of charities is growing, as is their role in addressing many of the tough problems that now plague American society. By 1990, there were over 130,000 charitable organizations providing services in the United States. Over one-third of these agencies provided human or social services—from marriage counseling to crisis prevention. One-fifth provided health care services, one-sixth education, and one-tenth arts and culture.[27]

Charitable agencies play two important roles as third-party providers of services. First, many small social service agencies receive grants to administer federal programs of one kind or another. Second, many charitable agencies provide services in the absence of federal programs, filling the gaps in the government's safety net. These agencies are particularly important in addressing some of the nation's most difficult problems, such as drug abuse, inner-city crime, AIDS, and joblessness among able-bodied adults.[28]

Making the Rules for Implementation.   Almost everything the federal government does involves a **rule**. A rule is a precise legal statement about what a policy actually means. It lays out the details on exactly who gets what, when, and how—for example, by specifying the amount of sulfur dioxide that can be released from a smokestack, the required height of a wheelchair ramp in a private building, or the number of life jackets that must be on a ferryboat. As such, rules are essential for turning even the most detailed legislation into action, and rule making is the central device used to execute the laws.[29]

Technically, rule making comes at the very end of the policy-making process, and is almost invisible to most Americans. Nevertheless, it is in ironing out the details that the federal bureaucracy converts the abstract ideas and language of laws, presidential orders, and court rulings into precise rules governing what individual members of the public, companies, or agencies can or must do.

There is no question that rules have become more important since the 1950s. Although government has been making rules since the Revolutionary War, it was not until the 1950s that the explosion in rule making began, driven largely by implementation of new civil rights and labor laws. The greatest growth in rule making occurred in the 1970s. Congress passed 130 laws requiring some form of social or economic regulation during the decade, leading to a vast increase in the number of rules governing American society.[30] The number of pages published in the *Federal Register,* a weekly newspaperlike report that lists all new and proposed rules, jumped from just 5,000 a year in 1940 to 87,012 in 1980.[31] By the 1990s, the OMB estimated that Americans were spending 6.6 billion hours each year filling out paperwork required under those rules—whether IRS tax forms, Census Bureau surveys, or environmental and occupational safety and health reports.

The growth of regulation is clear in the *Code of Federal Regulations,* which contains every rule issued by the federal government. The *Code* grew from 121 chapters in 1938 to 221 in 1969 to 313 in 1989. In 1938, there were no pages devoted to environmental protection; by 1990, there were 8,250 pages. In 1938, there were just 39 pages on labor law; by 1990, there were 5,726.[32]

The number of rules is not growing because it is easy to make a rule, however. It is just as complicated to draft, review, and issue a rule as it is to draft, debate, and pass a bill. The process of rule making involves eight separate steps. (See Box 15–6 for a quick review of how the eight steps came into play for the Department of Transportation's rule on the transport of hazardous materials, such as volatile chemicals, by air, sea, truck, or train.)

Step 1. The rulemaking process starts when a bill is signed into law, and is sent to the appropriate agency for rulemaking. No bill, no rule.[33]

Step 2. The agency starts a rulemaking process, basically deciding what to decide. This is no simple decision. The fact that a law is passed does not mean it is converted into a rule—not immediately, at least. Some agencies, such as the Environmental Protection Agency, have so many laws that need to be converted and so little staff that some rulemaking gets delayed far into the future.

Step 3. A draft of the rule is written, including a preamble that states the basic purpose of the rule, the specific language of the rule itself, and whatever research backs up the decision.

Step 4. The agency must post a formal "Notice of Proposed Rulemaking" in the *Federal Register.* Under federal law, those affected by the rule must be given a chance to raise their concerns.

Step 5. The people affected by the rule have between thirty and ninety days to register their concerns through a process called *notice and comment.* All letters and formal reactions become part of the rulemaking record.

Step 6. The formal rule is finished in response to the notice and comment.

Step 7. The formal rule is published in the *Federal Register.*

Step 8. The rule goes into effect thirty days after it is published.

The process involves a number of smaller steps along the way, including a detailed review of proposed rulemaking by the OMB.[34] And it does not necessarily end after Step 8. Some of the people affected by the rule may decide to sue, blocking final implementation until a court of appeals acts.

The rulemaking process is so time-consuming that it can make how a bill becomes a law seem simple. Even a small delay in a federal rule—say, one that requires private companies to clean up toxic waste dumps faster—may save an industry millions of dollars. Indeed, it was meat producers who slowed down the new food labels in 1991 and 1992. Because some meats contain a high percentage of fat, producers worried that the new labels would cut sales. They fought the process at every step, and most certainly delayed final government action.

BOX **15-6**

Making an Explosives Rule

Step 1. The Explosives and Combustibles Act of 1908 is passed, giving the federal government authority to regulate dangerous and hazardous materials as they are transported.

Step 2. Over the next eighty years, regulations enforcing the act are adopted, resulting in 1,400 pages in the *Code of Federal Regulations,* known as the Hazardous Materials Regulations (HMR).

Step 3. As society changes, the regulations become harder to follow and enforce. By the 1970s, there is a general agreement that the existing HMR is inadequate. Work on the revised HMR begins in 1981.

Step 4. The first Notice of Proposed Rulemaking appears in the *Federal Register* in April 1982. Numerous other public notices appear in the *Federal Register* inviting further comment as the process moves ahead.

Step 5. Interested parties take full advantage of the comment period as their primary chance to shape the final rules. More than 2,200 written comments are received. Each comment must be read, analyzed, and answered somewhere in the rulemaking process. The rule must also be negotiated with other departments and agencies in the federal bureaucracy. This step takes ten years.

Step 6. Twenty federal employees are engaged full-time in drafting the final rule, including analyses of the impact of the rule on the environment, small business, occupational health and safety, paperwork burdens on the public, and general cost.

Step 7. The final rule is published in the *Federal Register* on Friday, December 21, 1990.

Step 8. The rule becomes effective on October 1, 1991, over ten years after the process begins. The length of time is not unusual even for rules implementing routine legislation.

Source: Cornelius Kerwin, *Rulemaking: How Government Agencies Write Law and Make Policy* (Washington, DC: CQ Press, 1994), pp. 39–42.

Running the Program.   Implementation of public policy does not end with publication of the formal rule. It continues in the day-to-day tasks of running public agencies, evaluating how programs work, and dealing with ordinary citizens.

These tasks are all part of what the founder of the Children's Defense Fund, Marian Wright Edelman, once called the "nitty-gritty steps of implementation":

> Passing a law or drafting a regulation or issuing an RFP [request for proposal for federal funding] is the easiest part of a change process. Making it work. Informing the public. And assisting and monitoring local enforcement, protecting budgets in a sustained manner, and getting and training sensitive and skilled personnel to administer it in a compassionate way are all important parts of the change process.[35]

Implementation involves a variety of tasks that policymakers often leave to the career public service, and includes everything from hiring the staff to do the work to writing the checks, enforcing the laws, evaluating success, and reporting to Congress. The reason most policymakers ignore implementation is that it is rarely as glamorous or exciting as actually passing the laws, but, as the old saying goes, "the devil is in the details." Implementation is where many programs fail, in part because Congress and the president often write such vague and uncertain laws that no bureaucrat or third-party provider can figure out just what government wants.

 **in a different light** ———————   **COUNTING AMERICANS**

Under Article I, Section 2, a national census was the Founders' chosen device for counting the number of Americans. Conducted every ten years by the U.S. Census Bureau, the census was to be an "enumeration," which means a strict head count, of every last person living in the United States. In turn, that head count would determine how many representatives each state would get. Recall that the census is also used today as a tool for spending federal money.

The only problem with counting every last head today is that every last head is not always countable. With more and more Americans on the move, and a substantial number of homeless people, it is no longer possible to be sure that the census catches everybody. The Census Bureau estimated that in 1990 it missed about 8.4 million people, most of them renters and many of them African Americans or Hispanics. Because renters are more likely to live in cities than suburbs or rural areas, and because cities lose billions in federal funding as a result of undercounts,

big-city mayors and their congressional representatives have become strong advocates of a new way of making sure the census is fair. They also want to make sure they keep as many seats in Congress as possible.

Their proposed solution for 2000 was simple: Conduct the formal census as always by sending field workers to every home in the United States, but add a second mini-census that would check the formal census in 750,000 randomly selected homes. Once the results of the mini-census were in, the Census Bureau would adjust the final totals to add more people to the rolls, most likely in the cities.

Because the result would almost certainly have given an advantage to cities, where more Democrats live, and reduce the relative strength of suburbs and smaller cities and towns, where more Republicans live, the solution created sharp party divisions. It produced a major backlash in Congress, where the Republican majority cut the Census Bureau's 1999 budget in half, forcing the president to return to Capitol Hill for the money to conduct the 2000 census. Republicans argued that the Constitution demands an "actual Enumeration," which it certainly does, while Democrats argued that the meaning of the term had changed with the times, which it certainly had. Republicans also argued that even a sample of 750,000 homes would carry its own margin of error, which it certainly would, while Democrats argued that strict enumeration would undercount minority groups, which it certainly would. In August 1998, a federal district court ruled that the proposal violated the Constitution, setting the stage for a battle that will likely reach the Supreme Court.

This controversy is not about to be solved by a statistics book or a dictionary. Like so much else in American government, determining who gets what, when, and how is very much a political debate. With Republicans holding a slim eleven-seat majority, the word "enumeration" actually means power. Ultimately, no census is going to be completely accurate. As with most of the underlying assumptions used in the policy-making process, conducting a census involves a mix of politics and science.

THE FUTURE POLICY AGENDA

It is not difficult to imagine the kinds of policy issues the United States will confront in the future. Indeed, the shape of the policy agenda of the future is already clear in five demographic and economic trends that are changing the face of the country: (1) the population is getting older, (2) more women are working, (3) the nation is becoming more diverse, (4) the gap between rich and poor is widening, and (5) the American family is changing.

The Aging of America

The U.S. population is getting older every year. In 1990, the average American was thirty-three years old; by the year 2020, the average American will be thirty-eight. No one knows yet whether the Rolling Stones and the Eagles will still be on tour. The population is getting older for two reasons: fewer children are being born per woman, and Americans are living longer. More older people living longer plus fewer children means that the age of the average American must go up.

The birth rate declined largely because of the birth control pill. At the height of the postwar "baby boom" in the 1950s and 1960s, for example, 20 percent of all births were unwanted; by 1980, the proportion was down to 7 percent.[36] Over the period, birth rates fell from 3.4 births per woman to roughly 1.8 births per woman (2.1 is considered the number necessary for zero population growth). The result was a "baby bust." The children born during this baby bust are often labeled Generation X.

As the number of children fell, the number of elderly increased. In 1900, only one out of every twenty-five Americans was over the age of sixty-five. By 1950, the number was one in twelve and by 1985, one in nine. By 2030, it will be one in five. In 1900, the average American lived to age forty-seven; by the year 2000, the average will be up to seventy-nine.

The increase in life span is largely due to a decline in death at early ages. More children are surviving childhood as vaccinations and better nutrition and sanitation now prevent many of the illnesses that killed so many children in previous generations. More of today's middle-aged Americans will live to retirement age as medical research renders once-deadly diseases manageable. And more sixty-five-year-olds will live into their eighties and beyond as heart attacks no longer kill quite so easily and survival rates from cancer inch upward.

The fact that more Americans now survive the early and middle years of life ensures that more will live past their seventies and eighties. Indeed, the number of "oldest old," which is defined as people over age eighty-five, is expected to grow from just over 3 million today to almost 17 million by 2050; the number of people over 100 will jump from 45,000 today to over 1 million.[37] By the year 2020, many states will look like Florida looks today.

This rising tide of older Americans influences economic and social policy in many ways. By 2030, with the baby boomers mostly retired, the number of Americans eligible for Social Security and Medicare will more than double from 40 million today to 80–90 million.[38] That means the government will have to figure out how to cover the huge increase in the cost of these two entitlement programs.

Women and Work

The past three decades have witnessed a dramatic increase in the number of women who work full- and part-time outside the home. By 1992, three out of five women were working, compared with two out of five in the early 1960s. As the number of working women has grown, the face of many professions has changed. Half of the Secret Service agents who protect the president are now women.[39]

It is not as if women suddenly discovered work in the 1970s, however. "The mythical American family of the 1950s and 1960s was comprised of five people, only one of whom 'worked'—or at least did what society called work," writes sociologist Juliet Schor. "Dad went off to his job every morning, while Mom and the three kids stayed at home. Of course, the 1950s-style family was never as common as popular memory has made it out to be. Even in the 1950s and 1960s, about one-fourth of wives with children held paying jobs."[40]

Most women went to work for a simple reason: they needed the income. But many women soon found that they could not earn as much as men even for comparable work. In 1997, women still earned only about 74 cents for every dollar earned by men. Some of this gap results from the tendency of men and women to work in different jobs—women tend to get caught, or segregated, in lower-paying positions. But some of the gap results from simple discrimination. Even in similar jobs, women earn less. Women doctors, lawyers, secretaries, and construction workers all earn less than their male co-workers.[41]

The pay gap, as it is sometimes called, continues up the educational ladder. Women with high school degrees earn less than men with high school degrees, women with bachelor's degrees earn less than men with bachelor's degrees, and women with law or medical degrees earn less than men with law or medical degrees. Women did catch up somewhat during the 1980s, in part because of longer hours worked and increasing seniority.[42] Nevertheless, equal pay for either equal work (the same job) or comparable work (jobs that use similar skills) is not likely to be achieved any time soon.

Even as more women enter the workforce, they still provide most of the care to their elderly parents and to their children.[43] It should be no surprise, therefore, that economic and social policy issues such as maternity leave, day care, and elder care are primary concerns for women who work.

Increasing Diversity

The United States is well on its way to becoming the most diverse nation on earth. The changes are already clear in the workplace, where only 15 percent of new workers are white males, compared to almost 50 percent in the early 1980s.[44] The United States can no longer be thought of as a white male, or even white, country. In some border states, such as California and Texas, the term *mi-*

The United States is becoming the most diverse nation on earth, in large part because so many of the world's people still believe in the basic call to freedom enshrined in the inscription to the Statue of Liberty.

nority no longer has any meaning. In one out of every four California cities, for example, no racial group is a majority.[45]

America is becoming more diverse for two reasons: birth rates among white Americans have declined faster than birth rates among minorities and the number of minority immigrants continues to rise.

Although Americans have become more tolerant toward racial minorities over the past three decades, immigration remains a particularly controversial public policy issue. Although America has always been a nation of immigrants, the country has been tightening its borders in recent years. The tightening began in the late 1970s in response to the unexpected flood of Cuban "boat people" into the Miami area, and heightened a decade later due to the rising number of illegal immigrants entering the United States from Mexico. Florida, California, and Texas have all complained about the high cost of supporting illegal immigrants who arrive in the country with limited education and job skills. These concerns have prompted proposals to deny public support to illegal immigrants and their children, even though those children are legal citizens if they are born in the United States.

Still, America admits more immigrants than all of the other industrialized nations in the world combined. From 1971 to 1991, America greeted 12.5 million immigrants. Roughly half the immigrants came from Latin America and South America, while another third came from Asia. (One hundred years ago, nine out of ten came from Europe.) Seven out of ten of the 1991 immigrants went to just seven states, with California, Texas, New York, and Florida the largest gainers.[46]

It is important to understand that all parts of the U.S. population are growing, but that some are growing faster than others. According to the Census Bureau, the nation's white population grew the slowest between 1980 and 1990, at 6 percent, while the Asian and Pacific Islander population grew the fastest, at 108 percent. In between were Hispanics at 53 percent, Native Americans-Eskimos-Aleuts at 38 percent, and African Americans at 13 percent. The white population is also growing in actual numbers—11 million of the 22 million total Americans added during the 1980s were white—but the minority population is increasing faster.

These trends are particularly visible in America's schools. By the year 2000, nearly one-third of all school-age children will be students of color. Already, forty-nine of the nation's one hundred largest public school districts report majorities of nonwhite children. Most of the change mirrors the population growth discussed above, but some involves white flight to the suburbs and a growing number of mostly white private schools.

Even as schools struggle to face these changes, diversity is creating conflict in foreign, economic, and social policy. Americans are debating dozens of issues surrounding race. Should everyone speak English? How far should affirmative action go? Are the public schools worth saving? Should ballots be bilingual? Who should be fired first as corporations downsize? What about immigration reform? These and many other questions are being confronted in today's policy process.

At the same time, however, diversity remains America's strength as a world economic power. Even as it creates conflict in a deeply individualistic nation, diversity is a source of enormous economic creativity. This lesson has been learned by many of America's leading corporations, which have embraced diversity as a tool for innovation and for access to new markets. Changing the face of their workforces is one path to changing the size of their profit margins.

The Gap between Rich and Poor

The 1980s were very good years for wealthy Americans. Tax rates on the richest Americans went down, as did tax rates on corporate earnings and investment. According to the Internal Revenue Service, the number of millionaires grew 1,400 percent over the decade. In 1980, only 4,400 Americans reported $1 million in adjusted gross income (the figure listed at the bottom of the tax return); by 1990, the number was up to 63,642.[47] By 1998, the New York Times bestseller list included a book titled *The Millionaire Next Door.*[48]

Just as the number of rich people increased, so did the number of poor people. The rich got richer, and the poor got poorer. According to the Center on Budget and Policy Priorities, a liberal think tank, the average income for the top one-fifth of Americans grew by nearly $14,000 over the 1980s, rising from $83,000 to $97,000, while the average income for the bottom one-fifth dropped by $600, from $10,900 to $10,300.[49]

The gap between rich and poor is widening for two reasons: first, the rich are keeping more of their earnings, and, second, the jobs that once supported the middle class are disappearing. The rich got richer largely because of economic policies enacted during the early 1980s. According to Donald Bartlett and James Steele, the Pulitzer Prize–winning reporters who wrote *America: What Went Wrong?*, the very wealthy got the largest tax cuts of anyone: their taxes actually fell 31 percent under the 1986 tax cut, amounting to an average saving of $281,033 in 1989. Those with $10,000 to $20,000 in annual income got the smallest cuts: their taxes fell just 6 percent, for an average of $69. The middle class got a tax cut between 11 and 16 percent.[50]

The middle class not only got a smaller tax cut than the rich, but lost over 300,000 relatively high-paying manufacturing jobs over the decade. Those jobs were mostly replaced by relatively low-paying service and retail jobs. By the end of the 1980s, more Americans were working in service and retail than in manufacturing, a dramatic turnaround from the 1950s and 1960s. Many of the old manufacturing jobs that once supported America's middle class have moved abroad as global economic competition has led corporations to find cheaper sources of labor.

At the bottom of the economic ladder, government statistics show that the poor have gotten poorer. By 1996, the U.S. Census Bureau reported that the number of people in poverty was growing faster than the population itself.[51] (In 1996, a family of four was considered below the poverty line if it had cash income less than roughly $15,911, which is not even enough to pay the annual tuition at most private colleges.) Children were particularly hard hit by the increase in poverty. By the end of the 1980s, nearly one in five children lived in poverty; more than one in eight were being raised by mothers on Temporary Assistance for Needy Families, the federal income support program that replaced AFDC (Aid to Families with Dependent Children) in 1996. (Box 15–7 shows the distribution of poverty by race, family status, and region.)

The growing gap between rich and poor influences economic policy in several ways. It clearly shapes tax policy, which involves discussions about who pays what (a *progressive tax,* such as the federal income tax, is one whose rate increases as income goes up; a *regressive tax,* such as a sales or gasoline tax, is one that lays the burden equally on all income groups). It also shapes welfare policy, which establishes the level of support that society is willing to give to those in need.

BOX 15-7

Persons below the Poverty Line, 1995

Group	Percentage of Group That Is Poor	Group as a Percentage of All Poor People
Race/ethnicity		
White	8.5%	44.7%
Black	29.3	27.1
Hispanic origin	30.3	23.5
Family status		
Female householder, no husband present		
White	29.7	19.3
Black	48.2	18.0
Hispanic	52.8	8.4
All other families		
White	6.6	29.0
Black	10.8	4.5
Hispanic	22.1	11.8
Location		
City	13.4	77.8
Noncity (suburb, rural area, small town)	15.6	22.2
Region		
Northeast	12.5	17.7
Midwest	11.0	18.6
South	15.7	39.7
West	14.9	24.0
All persons	13.8	100.0

Source: Harold W. Stanley and Richard G. Niemi, *Vital Statistics on American Politics, 1997–1998* (Washington, DC: CQ Press, 1998), p. 359.

One way to narrow, if not eliminate, the gap is to increase wages, which is exactly what Congress and the president agreed to do in raising the minimum wage to $5.15 in 1996, a jump of 90 cents in one year. Although the increase clearly helped move poor Americans upward, it had no effect on the middle class, which has seen its earnings decline for nearly ten years in a row.[52]

The Changing American Family

There is no such thing as a "traditional" American family anymore. The two-parent, two-child, mom-at-home, dad-at-work family celebrated in such 1950s television shows as *Leave It to Beaver* and *Father Knows Best* is increasingly rare. Most children today would say their families are much more like the Simpsons than the Cleavers.

The numbers prove the point. In 1960, at the height of the baby boom, there were just over 50 million American families. About half were married couples with children; another 37 percent were married couples without children; just 6 percent were single women with children; and fewer than 1 percent were single men with children. By 2000, the numbers will look very different: Of 72 million families, only 35 percent will be married couples with children; 43 percent will be married couples without children; 10 percent will be single women with children; and 3 percent will be single men with children.[53]

This general movement away from the traditional family reflects a host of other trends in marriage, childbearing, and divorce: the number of people who will never marry is up; divorce rates are high; the number of babies born outside of marriage is up; gays and lesbians are having or adopting more children. People are getting married later in life. Once people do get married, the odds of divorce are high. Roughly 2.4 million people got married in 1990, but 1.2 million got divorced. Almost half of the people who got married in the late 1960s and early 1970s had already been divorced by 1990, and current projections show that the numbers will remain high far into the future.

These statistics on marriage, divorce, and single parenthood have created their own political divisions. Indeed, the 1992 presidential campaign helped fuel what may have been the first "family gap" among the U.S. electorate. Married voters with children between the ages of eighteen and thirty-four gave almost half their votes to President George Bush versus just 29 percent to Bill Clinton, while single voters in the same age group gave 58 percent to Clinton and only 20 percent to Bush.

Family policy is a growing focus of debates in Congress, whether in proposals to increase federal support for day care to ease the caregiving burden on women or in efforts to keep families with children together by making divorce more difficult. Family policy also involves debates over gay and lesbian rights, foster care for children, education reform, and a host of other issues that directly or indirectly touch on family life.

-Ö- in a different light —— THE FUTURE OF SOCIAL SECURITY

The Social Security program, which provides income support to millions of older Americans, will enter a funding crisis in the next century as the huge baby boom generation retires. Although Social Security is often viewed by the public as a savings program to which taxpayers contribute throughout their working lives, it is, in fact, a modified "pay-as-you-go" program. Most of the money that comes in by way of taxes from working Americans and their employers immediately goes out in the form of benefit checks to the current beneficiaries.

At the start of the program in 1940, there were almost 160 workers paying their taxes into the program for every one beneficiary receiving monthly Social Security checks. By 1998, there were 3.3 workers for every beneficiary. But by the year 2030, when the baby boom generation is fully retired, there will be just two workers for every beneficiary.

The result is a serious and growing gap between the money taxpayers put into the program and the money they take out in monthly benefits. Looking far into the future and assuming that benefits will stay at their current levels, the Social Security system faces a $12 *trillion* shortfall in meeting its obligations. Somewhere in the 2020s, the program will start taking in less money each year than it pays out.

There are only two ways to fix a pay-as-you-go system: increase revenues or cut benefits. One way to increase revenues is to raise the amount workers pay in FICA (Social Security) taxes, thereby putting more money into the system. Another is to allow the Social Security system to invest part of its current reserves in the stock market; under current law, Social Security taxes are invested in federal treasury bonds, which pay a very low interest rate. Neither option is particularly popular on Capitol Hill. Workers are already paying 6.2 percent of their paychecks into Social Security (plus another 1.45 percent into Medicare), and they might revolt at the kind of tax increase needed to address the future crisis. And allowing Social Security to invest in the stock market is risky: the stock market looks good when it is going up, but what goes up must sooner or later come down—as the stock market did in the summer and fall of 1998.

The options for cutting benefits are just as unpopular. One way to cut benefits is to raise the retirement age, which is already scheduled to increase from age sixty-five today to age sixty-seven in the early 2020s. Some experts argue that the retirement age should be set at seventy years. After all, Americans are living longer. However, the extra years of life are not necessarily good ones. Raising the retirement age means trading the very healthiest years of retirement (which come at the beginning) for the very worst (which come just before death). Another way to cut benefits is to freeze or reduce the annual cost of living adjustment, which indexes Social Security benefits to inflation. (See Chapter 12 for a discussion of indexing.)

However unpopular the solutions are, Social Security simply cannot survive without some kind of reform. The question for the moment is whether Congress and the presidency have the political courage to act now, when there is more time for the revenue increases and benefits cuts needed to close the gap to build up, or will wait until the very last minute, when the increases and cuts will have to be deeper.[54]

If Congress and the president wait to act, much of the burden of paying for reform will fall squarely on Generation X and its younger brothers and sisters. Americans plan for retirement decades in advance and will not tolerate a last-minute change in retirement age or Social Security investment policy. By waiting, Congress and the president also create an inevitable preference for tax increases, rather than benefit cuts, as the tool for closing the shortfall.

The question is whether the members of Generation X will be able to pay the tax increase needed to close the gap in Social Security funding. Most Generation Xers are not doing very well to begin with. They are trailing previous generations in home ownership, starting salaries, and savings rates, but leading in college debt. "After graduation," write Neil Howe and William Strauss, "they're the ones with big loans who were supposed to graduate into jobs and move out of the house but didn't, and who seem to get poorer the longer they've been away from home—unlike their parents at that age, who seemed to get richer."[55] This poor performance clearly poses a problem for the future of Social Security. Even if they are willing to pay higher Social Security taxes, the members of Generation X may not have the income to pay as the baby boomers go.

MAINTAINING THE BALANCE

It is no surprise that making public policy is so difficult. Obstacles are built into the Founders' original design. Separated powers create doubts about just who is in charge at every step of the policy-making process. Their separate interests put Congress, the presidency, and the judiciary on radically different timetables, and make agreement on the policy agenda difficult. Separate layers have created a patchwork of federal, state, and local delivery units. And checks and balances keep the entire system just a little off balance.

American government can still act, however. Congress, the president, and the courts are quite capable of making decisions, even during periods of sharply divided government. Although making policy to deal with the changes in American society described above will be frustrating at times, there is ample evidence to suggest that the nation and its government will be able to respond. The policies will not be perfect, if only because the problems of the future are complex. But the past suggests that American government will continue to produce artful work in the making of policy.

Indeed, the challenge for the future is to avoid becoming discouraged by a government that makes patience a virtue. After all, each decision in making policy contains its own perils for those who want quick government action. Assumptions create impossible expectations, problems get defined out of existence, decisions to act get delayed, tools are misplaced, finding someone to deliver the program becomes fuzzy, rules are always hard to make, and implementation is often ignored. Given the number of access points along the way, it is something of a miracle that policy ever gets made at all.

Even though danger signs are emerging from issue advocacy and changes in how interest groups do their work, there are parallel dangers in altering the Founders' design to make government more efficient. Those who argue for a more powerful presidency or a faster Congress may underestimate the continuing threats to liberty that reside in the numerous divisions that characterize American society. They may also lose sight of the essential purpose of American government, which is not just to protect the nation as a whole.

The Founders could have made government very efficient indeed by creating a monarchy or dictatorship. Instead, they created a government that would be strong enough to protect the young nation from foreign and domestic threats, but never so strong as to threaten Americans as individual citizens. It is far better to build delay and frustration into the process of making policies for the future than to jeopardize freedom. Success in the American system of government is all about maintaining the delicate balance, even when doing so frustrates and delays.

terms to remember

facts and interpretations

- The Constitution deliberately makes the public policy-making process difficult. Separated powers create doubts about who is in charge of everything from making assumptions about the world to the day-to-day decisions in running programs. Separate interests make agreement on the policy agenda difficult, and often create conflicts in deciding to act, deciding how much to do, and choosing a tool to use. Separate layers have created a vast inventory of federal, state, and local delivery units. And checks and balances keep the entire system just a little off balance as it tries to reach judgments at every step of the process.

- Final policy decisions usually involve a long string of informal decisions made in issue networks, which are composed of temporary collections of political leaders and interest groups. Issue networks are a looser version of what political scientists call iron triangles of influence. An iron triangle consists of a federal department, a set of loyal interest groups, and a House and/or Senate authorizing committee. As most of American government's iron triangles rust away, issue networks have become increasing powerful in shaping public policy, particularly in using public anger toward government to create stalemate in the legislative process.

- Once Congress, the presidency, or the judiciary have decided to act and chosen a tool for solving a problem, they must decide who will deliver the program. Often, the answer is not federal employees. Recent decades have witnessed an increase in what public administration scholars call third-party government, which involves the delivery of services by private companies who work for the federal government under contracts, state and local governments who work for the federal government under mandates, and nonprofit organizations that deliver services for the federal government that neither private contractors nor state and local governments are willing or able to provide. As a result, Americans often receive government services from people who do not work for government.

- The policy agenda of the future is already emerging in five demographic, economic, and social trends that are changing the face of America. First, the U.S. population is getting older, in part because women are having fewer children and in part because Americans are living longer. Second, more women are working full- and part-time outside the home. By the year 2000, women will compose roughly three-fifths of all new workers hired. Third, American society is becoming much more diverse, in part because the number of immigrants is growing and in part because birth rates among minority populations are higher than among whites. Fourth, the gap between rich and poor is growing. Fifth, the American family is changing. Barely one-third of the families of the future will be married couples with children, while almost half will be married without children. These trends are already having important effects on the policy agenda. The question is whether the policy-making process is capable of crafting timely responses.

open questions

- What is the best way to stop a policy from happening? Is it to change the assumptions so as to make the world look better than it already is? Push for a nondecision that takes a problem off the agenda? Stop the rulemaking process from producing an effective rule? Reduce funding for the agencies that must implement the law? Does the fact that the process has so many places where a stand can be taken against action support or undermine the delicate balance?

- Is American government becoming too inefficient? What kinds of problems do you think government should be solving that it is not? Does the fact that interest groups seem able to grind the process to a stop undermine the delicate balance discussed throughout this book? Would it make Americans more or less trusting to know that government was designed to be easily stalemated?

- What kinds of changes could be made to help the policy-making process become more efficient? What kinds of authority would make the president a stronger leader when times get tough? How might Congress be strengthened? Would proposals such as limiting the number of terms a member of Congress can serve help or hurt the policy-making process? What are the potential costs of having the policy process work more efficiently?

- Which of the demographic, economic, and social trends described in this chapter have affected you personally? How could American government help you deal with the changes more effectively? Or would you be better off if government just left you alone to deal with the changes on your own? Is it government's job to make sure that individual Americans are protected from the hardships created by economic and social troubles? Or is it government's job just to make sure everyone has a fair start?

for further study

Bartlett, Donald, and James Steele. *America: What Went Wrong?* Kansas City, MO: Andrews and McMeel, 1992.

Kerwin, Cornelius. *Rulemaking: How Government Agencies Write Law and Make Policy.* Washington, DC: CQ Press, 1994.

King, Anthony. "The American Polity in the 1990s," in A. King, *The New American Political System,* 2nd ed. Washington, DC: American Enterprise Institute, 1990.

Kingdon, John. *Agendas, Alternatives, and Public Policy.* Boston: Little, Brown, 1984.

Salamon, Lester, ed. *Beyond Privatization: The Tools of Government Action.* Washington, DC: Urban Institute Press, 1989.

Schor, Juliet B. *The Overworked American: The Unexpected Decline of Leisure.* New York: Basic Books, 1992.

Skocpol, Theda. *Protecting Soldiers and Mothers: The Political Origins of Social Policy in the United States.* Cambridge, MA: Harvard University Press, 1992.

endnotes for chapter 15

1. See James Roger Sharp, *American Politics in the Early Republic: The New Nation in Crisis* (New Haven, CT: Yale University Press, 1993), pp. 33–38.
2. Gregg Easterbrook, *A Moment on the Earth: The Coming Age of Environmental Optimism* (New York: Viking, 1995), p. xv.
3. The quotation can be found in Daniel Boorstin, ed., *An American Primer,* vol. 1 (Chicago: University of Chicago Press, 1966), pp. 192–210; emphasis in the original.
4. Harold W. Stanley and Richard G. Niemi, *Vital Statistics on American Politics* (Washington DC: CQ Press, 1995), p. 347.
5. Barbara Kellerman and Ryan J. Barilleaux, *The President as World Leader* (New York: St. Martin's Press, 1991), p. 20.
6. See Jeremy Rosner, "The Know-Nothings Know Something," *Foreign Policy,* 101 (Winter 1995–1996), p. 124.
7. Steven Kull, "What the Public Knows That Washington Doesn't," *Foreign Policy* 101 (Winter 1995–1996), p. 103.
8. See John Reilly, "The Public Mood at Mid-Decade," *Foreign Policy* 98 (Spring 1995), pp. 76–93, for an inventory of public opinion on foreign policy.
9. The Pew Research Center for The People & The Press, *Post-Cold War Era Looks Better* (Washington, DC: Pew Research Center, October 1997), p.16.
10. For a history of this period, see Theda Skocpol, *Protecting Soldiers and Mothers: The Political Origins of Social Policy in the United States* (Cambridge, MA: Harvard University Press, 1992).
11. Hugh Heclo, "Issue Networks and the Executive Establishment," in A. King, ed., *The New American Political System* (Washington; DC: American Enterprise Institute, 1978), pp. 87–124.
12. Bill McAllister, "VA Hospitals Refuse to Sound Retreat," *Washington Post National Weekly Edition,* May 29–June 4, 1995, p. 31.
13. McAllister, "VA Hospitals," p. 31.
14. Anthony King, "The American Polity in the 1990s," in A. King, *The New American Political System,* 2nd ed.(Washington, DC: American Enterprise Institute, 1990), p. 296.
15. This material is based on Kathleen Hall Jamieson, *"Tax and Spend" vs. "Little Kids": Advocacy and Accuracy in the Tobacco Settlement Ads of 1997–1998* (Philadelphia: Annenberg Public Policy Center of the University of Pennsylvania, August 1998).

16. See John Kingdon, *Agendas, Alternatives, and Public Policy* (Boston: Little, Brown, 1984), for a description of the policy-making process.
17. William Greider, "The Education of David Stockman," *Atlantic*, 248, no. 12 (December 1981), p. 39.
18. Kingdon, *Agendas, Alternatives, and Public Policies*, p. 3.
19. Anthony Downs, "The 'Issue-Attention Cycle,'" *The Public Interest* 28 (Summer 1972), p. 38.
20. See Paul Light, *Still Artful Work: The Continuing Politics of Social Security Reform* (New York: McGraw-Hill, 1994), p. 13, for a discussion of Social Security reform as a dedistributive issue.
21. Lester Salamon and Michael Lund, "The Tools Approach: Basic Analytics," in L. Salamon, ed., *Beyond Privatization: The Tools of Government Action* (Washington, DC: Urban Institute Press, 1989).
22. Frederick Mosher, "The Changing Responsibilities and Tactics of the Federal Government," *Public Administration Review*, 40, no. 6 (November/December 1980), p. 541.
23. See Donald Kettl, *Sharing Power: Public Governance and Private Markets* (Washington, DC: Brookings Institution, 1993).
24. National Commission on the State and Local Public Service, *Hard Truths/Tough Choices* (Albany, NY: National Commission on the State and Local Public Service, 1993), p. 1.
25. See John DiIulio and Donald F. Kettl, *Fine Print: The Contract with America, Devolution, and the Administrative Realities of American Federalism* (Washington, DC: Brookings Institution, 1995), p. 17.
26. Martha Derthick, "Federal Government Mandates: Why the States Are Complaining," *Brookings Review*, 10, no. 4 (Fall 1992), p. 52.
27. Virginia Hodgkinson, Murray Weitzman, Stephen Noga, and Heather Gorski, *A Portrait of the Independent Sector: The Activities and Finances of Charitable Organizations* (Washington, DC: Independent Sector, 1993), p. 10.
28. See Michael Lipsky and Steven Rathgeb Smith, "Nonprofit Organizations, Government, and the Welfare State," *Political Science Quarterly*, 104, no. 4 (Winter 1989–1990), pp. 625–48.
29. See Cornelius Kerwin, *Rulemaking: How Government Agencies Write Law and Make Policy* (Washington, DC: CQ Press, 1994).
30. Kerwin, *Rulemaking*, p. 14.
31. Stanley and Niemi, *Vital Statistics*, p. 253.
32. Kerwin, *Rulemaking*, p. 19.
33. Kerwin, *Rulemaking*, p. 75.
34. See Gary Bryner, "Restructuring Review in OMB," *The Bureaucrat*, 18, no. 3 (Fall 1989): 45–51, for a discussion of the OMB process.
35. Quoted in Richard Nathan, *Turning Promises into Performance: The Management Challenge of Implementing Workfare* (New York: Columbia University Press, 1993), p. 133.
36. See Paul Light, *Baby Boomers: A Social and Political Reappraisal* (New York: Norton, 1988), pp. 149–52.
37. These figures are drawn from U.S. Department of Commerce, Bureau of the Census, *Population Projections of the United States, by Age, Sex, Race, and Hispanic Origin: 1992–2050* (Washington, DC: U.S. Government Printing Office, November 1992).
38. For a discussion of these key programs, see Eric R. Kingson and Edward D. Berkowitz, *Social Security and Medicare: A Policy Primer, Governance* (Montclair, CT: Auburn House, 1993).

39. "President's Safety Is Now Often a Woman's Work," *New York Times,* July 6, 1993, p. A7.

40. Juliet B. Schor, *The Overworked American: The Unexpected Decline of Leisure* (New York: Basic Books, 1992), pp. 24–25.

41. Marie Cocco, "There's Still a Way to Go on Pay Equality, Baby," *Newsday,* April 3, 1998, p. A56.

42. See Sylvia Nasar, "Women's Progress Stalled? Just Not So," *New York Times,* April 16, 1996, p. F1.

43. See Betty Sancier and Patricia Mapp, "Who Helps Working Women Care for the Young and Old?" *AFFILIA,* 7, no. 2 (Summer 1992) pp. 61–76.

44. These figures come from William Johnston and Arnold Packer, *Workforce 2000: Work and Workers for the 21st Century* (Indianapolis: Hudson Institute, 1987), p. xxi.

45. Peter Morrison, "Testimony before the House Subcommittee on Census and Population," May 26, 1992, p. 3, draft, author's files.

46. The numbers are from Tom Morganthau, "America: Still a Melting Pot?" *Newsweek,* August 9, 1993, pp. 16–25; for an excellent analysis of how immigration helps American society, see Thomas Muller, *Immigrants and the American City* (New York: New York University Press, 1993).

47. See Paul Farhi, "They're in the Money," *Washington Post National Weekly Edition,* July 20–26, 1992, p. 21.

48. Thomas J. Stanley and William D. Danko, *The Millionaire Next Door: The Surprising Secrets of America's Wealthy* (New York: Longstreet, 1998).

49. Numbers are rounded; see Spencer Rich, "The Rich Got Richer, Again," *Washington Post National Weekly Edition,* September 14–20, 1992, p. 37.

50. Donald Bartlett and James Steele, *America: What Went Wrong?* (Kansas City, MO: Andrews and McMeel, 1992), p. 6.

51. These figures come from data available from the U.S. Census Bureau at <www.census.gov>.

52. See Louis Uchitelle, "The Middle Class:Winning in Politics, Losing in Life," *New York Times,* July 19, 1998, p. D1.

53. Dennis Ahlburg and Carol J. De Vita, "New Realities of the American Family," *Population Bulletin,* August 1992, reprinted by the Population Reference Bureau Social Issues Resources Series, 4, article no. 96.

54. For a discussion of how Congress and the president solved the most recent Social Security crisis, see Light, *Still Artful Work.*

55. Neil Howe and William Strauss, "The New Generation Gap," *Atlantic,* 270 (December 1992): 78–79.

the declaration of independence

When in the Course of human events, it becomes necessary for one people to dissolve the political bands which have connected them with another, and to assume among the Powers of the earth, the separate and equal station to which the Laws of Nature and of Nature's God entitle them, a decent respect to the opinions of mankind requires that they should declare the causes which impel them to the separation.

We hold these truths to be self-evident, that all men are created equal, that they are endowed by their Creator with certain unalienable Rights, that among these are Life, Liberty and the pursuit of Happiness. That to secure these rights, Governments are instituted among Men, deriving their just powers from the consent of the governed. That whenever any Form of Government becomes destructive of these ends, it is the Right of the People to alter or to abolish it, and to institute new Government, laying its foundation on such principles and organizing its powers in such form, as to them shall seem most likely to effect their Safety and Happiness. Prudence, indeed, will dictate that Governments long established should not be changed for light and transient causes; and accordingly all experience hath shown, that mankind are more disposed to suffer, while evils are sufferable, than to right themselves by abolishing the forms to which they are accustomed. But when a long train of abuses and usurpations, pursuing invariably the same Object evinces a design to reduce them under absolute Depotism, it is their right, it is their duty, to throw off such Government, and to provide new Guards for their future security.—Such has been the patient sufferance of these Colonies; and such is now the necessity which constrains them to alter their former Systems of Government. The history of the present King of Great Britain is a history of repeated injuries and usurpations, all having in direct object the establishment of an absolute Tyranny over these States. To prove this, let Facts be submitted to a candid world.

He has refused his Assent to Laws, the most wholesome and necessary for the public good.

He has forbidden his Governors to pass Laws of immediate and pressing importance, unless suspended in their operation till his Assent should be obtained; and when so suspended, he has utterly neglected to attend to them.

He has refused to pass other Laws for the accommodation of large districts of people, unless those people would relinquish the right of Representation in the Legislature, a right inestimable to them and formidable to tyrants only.

He has called together legislative bodies at places unusual, uncomfortable, and distant from the depository of their public Records, for the sole purpose of fatiguing them into compliance with his measures.

He has dissolved Representative Houses repeatedly for opposing with manly firmness his invasions on the rights of the people.

He has refused for a long time, after such dissolutions, to cause others to be elected; whereby the Legislative Powers, incapable of Annihilation, have returned to the People at large for their exercise; the State remaining in the mean time exposed to all the dangers of invasion from without, and convulsions within.

He has endeavoured to prevent the population of these States; for that purpose obstructing the Laws of Naturalization of Foreigners; refusing to pass others to encourage their migration higher, and raising the conditions of new Appropriations of Lands.

He has obstructed the Administration of Justice, by refusing his Assent to Laws for establishing Judiciary powers.

He has made Judges dependent on his Will alone, for the tenure of their offices, and the amount and payment of their salaries.

He has erected a multitude of New Offices, and sent hither swarms of Officers to harass our People, and eat out their substance.

He has kept among us in times of peace, Standing Armies without the Consent of our legislature.

He has affected to render the Military independent of and superior to the Civil power.

He has combined with others to subject us to a jurisdiction foreign to our constitution, and unacknowledged by our laws; giving his Assent to their acts of pretended Legislation.

For quartering large bodies of armed troops among us:

For protecting them, by a mock Trial, from punishment for any Murders which they should commit on the inhabitants of these States:

For cutting off our Trade with all parts of the world.

For imposing taxes on us without our Consent:

For depriving us in many cases, of the benefits of Trial by Jury:

For transporting us beyond Seas to be tried for pretended offences:

For abolishing the free System of English Laws in a neighbouring Province, establishing therein an Arbitrary government, and enlarging its Boundaries so as to render it at once an example and fit instrument for introducing the same absolute rule into these Colonies.

For taking away our Charters, abolishing our most valuable Laws, and altering fundamentally the Forms of our Governments:

For suspending our own Legislature, and declaring themselves invested with Power to legislate for us in all cases whatsoever.

He has abdicated Government here, by declaring us out of his Protection and waging War against us.

He has plundered our seas, ravaged our Coasts, burnt our towns, and destroyed the lives of our people.

He is at this time transporting large Armies of foreign Mercenaries to compleat the works of death, desolation and tyranny, already begun with circumstances of Cruelty & perfidy scarcely paralleled in the most barbarous ages, and totally unworthy the Head of a civilized nation.

He has constrained our fellow Citizens taken Captive on the high Seas to bear Arms against their Country, to become the executioners of their friends and Brethren, or to fall themselves by their Hands.

He has excited domestic insurrections amongst us, and has endeavoured to bring on the inhabitants of our frontiers, the merciless Indian Savages, whose known rule of warfare, is an undistinguished destruction of all ages, sexes and conditions.

In every stage of these Oppressions We have Petitioned for Redress in the most humble terms: Our repeated Petitions have been answered only by repeated injury. A Prince, whose character is thus marked by every act which may define a Tyrant, is unfit to be the ruler of a free People.

Nor have We been wanting in attention to our British brethren. We have warned them from time to time of attempts by their legislature to extend an unwarrantable jurisdiction over us. We have reminded them of the circumstances of our emigration and settlement here. We have appealed to their native justice and magnanimity, and we have conjured them by the ties of our common kindred to disavow these usurpations, which, would inevitably interrupt our connections and correspondence. They too have been deaf to the voice of justice and of consanguinity. We must, therefore, acquiesce in the necessity, which denounces our Separation, and hold them, as we hold the rest of mankind, Enemies in War, in Peace Friends.

We, therefore, the Representatives of the United States of America, in General Congress, Assembled, appealing to the Supreme Judge of the world for the rectitude of our intentions, do, in the Name, and by Authority of the good People of these Colonies, solemnly publish and declare, That these United Colonies are, and of right ought to be Free and Independent States; that they are Absolved from all Allegiance to the British Crown, and that all political connection between them and the State of Great Britain, is and ought to be totally dissolved; and that as Free and Independent States, they have full Power to levy War, conclude Peace, contract Alliances, establish Commerce, and to do all other Acts and Things which Independent States may of right do. And for the support of this Declaration, with a firm reliance on the protection of divine Providence, we mutually pledge to each other our Lives, our Fortunes and our sacred Honor.

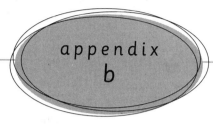

the constitution of the united states of america

We the People of the United States, in Order to form a more perfect Union, establish Justice, insure domestic Tranquility, provide for the common defence, promote the general Welfare, and secure the Blessings of Liberty to ourselves and our Posterity, do ordain and establish this Constitution for the United States of America.

[THREE BRANCHES OF GOVERNMENT]

[The legislative branch]
Article I

[Powers vested]
SECTION 1 All legislative Powers herein granted shall be vested in a Congress of the United States, which shall consist of a Senate and House of Representatives.

[House of Representatives]
SECTION 2 The House of Representatives shall be composed of Members chosen every second Year by the People of the several States, and the Electors in each State shall have the Qualifications requisite for Electors of the most numerous Branch of the State Legislature.

No Person shall be a Representative who shall not have attained to the Age of twenty-five Years, and been seven Years a Citizen of the United States, and who shall not, when elected, be an Inhabitant of that State in which he shall be chosen.

[Representatives and direct Taxes shall be apportioned among the several States which may be included within this Union, according to their respective Numbers, which shall be determined by adding to the whole Number of free Persons, including those bound to Service for a Term of Years, and excluding Indians not taxed, three fifths of all other Persons.][1] The actual Enumeration shall be made within three Years after the first Meeting of the Congress of the United States, and within every subsequent Term of ten Years, in such Manner as they shall by Law direct. The Number of Representatives shall not exceed one for every thirty Thousand, but each State shall have at Least one Representative; and until such enumeration shall be made, the State of New Hampshire shall be entitled to chuse three, Massachusetts eight, Rhode-Island and Providence Plantations one, Connecticut five, New York six, New Jersey four, Pennsylvania eight, Delaware one, Maryland six, Virginia ten, North Carolina five, South Carolina five, and Georgia three.

When vacancies happen in the Representation from any State, the Executive Authority thereof shall issue Writs of Election to fill such Vacancies.

The House of Representatives shall chuse their Speaker and other Officers; and shall have the sole Power of Impeachment.

[The Senate]

SECTION 3 The Senate of the United States shall be composed of two Senators from each State, [chosen by the Legislature thereof],[2] for six Years; and each Senator shall have one Vote.

Immediately after they shall be assembled in Consequence of the first Election, they shall be divided as equally as may be into three Classes. The Seats of the Senators of the first Class shall be vacated at the Expiration of the Second Year, of the second Class at the Expiration of the fourth Year, and of the third Class at the Expiration of the sixth Year, so that one-third may be chosen every second Year; [and if Vacancies happen by Resignation, or otherwise, during the Recess of the Legislature of any State, the Executive thereof may make temporary Appointments until the next Meeting of the Legislature, which shall then fill such Vacancies][3]

---

[1] Changed by Section 2 of Amendment XIV.
[2] Changed by Amendment XVII.
[3] Changed by Amendment XVII.

No person shall be a Senator who shall not have attained to the Age of thirty Years, and been nine Years a Citizen of the United States, and who shall not, when elected, be an Inhabitant of that State for which he shall be chosen.

The Vice President of the United States shall be President of the Senate, but shall have no Vote, unless they be equally divided. The Senate shall chuse their other Officers, and also a President pro tempore, in the absence of the Vice President, or when he shall exercise the Office of President of the United States.

The Senate shall have the sole Power to try all Impeachments. When sitting for that Purpose, they shall be on Oath or Affirmation. When the President of the United States is tried, the Chief Justice shall preside: And no Person shall be convicted without the Concurrence of two-thirds of the Members present.

Judgment in Cases of Impeachment shall not extend further than to removal from Office, and disqualification to hold and enjoy any Office of honor, Trust, or Profit under the United States: but the Party convicted shall nevertheless be liable and subject to Indictment, Trial, Judgment, and Punishment, according to Law.

[Elections]

SECTION 4 The Times, Places and Manner of holding Elections for Senators and Representatives, shall be prescribed in each State by the Legislature thereof; but the Congress may at any time by Law make or alter such Regulations, except as to the Places of chusing Senators.

The Congress shall assemble at least once in every Year, and such Meeting shall be on the first Monday in December, [unless they shall by Law appoint a different Day][4]

[Powers, duties, procedures of both bodies]

SECTION 5 Each House shall be the Judge of the Elections, Returns, and Qualifications of its own Members, and a Majority of each shall constitute a Quorum to do Business; but a smaller Number may adjourn from day to day, and may be authorized to compel the Attendance of absent Members, in such Manner, and under such Penalties as each House may provide.

Each House may determine the Rules of its Proceedings, punish its Members for disorderly Behavior, and, with the Concurrence of two thirds, expel a Member.

Each House shall keep a Journal of its Proceedings, and from time to time publish the same, excepting such Parts as may in their Judgment require Secrecy; and the Yeas and Nays of the Members of either House on any question shall, at the Desire of one fifth of those Present, be entered on the Journal.

---

[4]Changed by Section 2 of Amendment XX.

Neither House, during the Session of Congress, shall, without the Consent of the other, adjourn for more than three days, nor to any other Place than that in which the two Houses shall be sitting.

[Compensation, privileges, limits on other government service]

SECTION 6 The Senators and Representatives shall receive a Compensation for their Services, to be ascertained by Law, and paid out of the Treasury of the United States. They shall in all Cases, except Treason, Felony and Breach of the Peace, be privileged from Arrest during their Attendance at the Session of their respective Houses, and in going to and returning from the same; and for any Speech or Debate in either House, they shall not be questioned in any other Place.

No Senator or Representative shall, during the Time for which he was elected, be appointed to any civil Office under the Authority of the United States, which shall have been created, or the Emoluments whereof shall have been encreased during such time; and no Person holding any Office under the United States, shall be a Member of either House during his Continuance in Office.

[Origin of revenue bills; presidential approval or disapproval of legislation; overriding the veto]

SECTION 7 All Bills for raising Revenue shall originate in the House of Representatives; but the Senate may propose or concur with Amendments as on other Bills.

Every Bill which shall have passed the House of Representatives and the Senate, shall, before it become a Law, be presented to the President of the United States; if he approve he shall sign it, but if not he shall return it, with his Objections to that House in which it shall have originated, who shall enter the Objections at large on their Journal, and proceed to reconsider it. If after such Reconsideration two thirds of that House shall agree to pass the Bill, it shall be sent, together with the Objections, to the other House, by which it shall likewise be reconsidered, and if approved by two thirds of that House, it shall become a Law. But in all such Cases the Votes of both Houses shall be determined by Yeas and Nays, and the Names of the Persons voting for and against the Bill shall be entered on the Journal of each House respectively. If any Bill shall not be returned by the President within ten Days (Sundays excepted) after it shall have been presented to him, the Same shall be a Law, in like Manner as if he had signed it, unless the Congress by their Adjournment prevent its Return, in which Case it shall not be a Law.

Every Order, Resolution, or Vote to which the Concurrence of the Senate and House of Representatives may be necessary (except on a question of Adjournment) shall be presented to the President of the United States; and before the Same shall take Effect, shall be approved by him, or being disapproved by him, shall be repassed to two thirds of the Senate and House of Representatives, according to the Rules and Limitations prescribed in the Case of a Bill.

[Powers granted to Congress]

SECTION 8 The Congress shall have power To lay and collect Taxes, Duties, Imposts and Excises, to pay the Debts and provide for the common Defence and general Welfare of the United States; but all Duties, Imposts and Excises shall be uniform throughout the United States;

To borrow money on the credit of the United States;

To regulate Commerce with foreign Nations, and among the several States, and with the Indian Tribes;

To establish an uniform Rule of Naturalization, and uniform Laws on the subject of Bankruptcies throughout the United States;

To coin Money, regulate the Value thereof, and of foreign Coin, and fix the Standard of Weights and Measures;

To provide for the Punishment of counterfeiting the Securities and current Coin of the United States;

To Establish Post Offices and post Roads;

To promote the Progress of Science and useful Arts, by securing for limited Times to Authors and Inventors the exclusive Right to their respective Writings and Discoveries;

To constitute Tribunals inferior to the Supreme Court;

To define and punish Piracies and Felonies committed on the high Seas, and Offences against the Law of Nations;

To declare War, grant Letters of Marque and Reprisal, and make Rules concerning Captures on Land and Water;

To raise and support Armies, but no Appropriation of Money to that Use shall be for a longer Term than two Years;

To provide and maintain a Navy;

To make Rules for the Government and Regulation of the land and naval Forces;

To provide for calling forth the Militia to execute the Laws of the Union, suppress Insurrections and repel Invasions;

To provide for organizing, arming, and disciplining the Militia, and for governing such Part of them as may be employed in the Service of the United States, reserving to the States respectively, the Appointment of the Officers, and the Authority of training the Militia according to the discipline prescribed by Congress;

To exercise exclusive Legislation in all Cases whatsoever, over such District (not exceeding ten Miles square) as may, by Cession of particular States, and the acceptance of Congress, become the Seat of the Government of the United States, and to exercise like Authority over all Places purchased by the Consent of the Legislature of the State in which the Same shall be, for the Erection of Forts, Magazines, Arsenals, dock-Yards, and other needful Buildings;—And

[Elastic clause]

To make all Laws which shall be necessary and proper for carrying into Execution the foregoing Powers, and all other Powers vested by this Constitution in the Government of the United States, or in any Department or Officer thereof.

[Powers denied to Congress]

SECTION 9 The Migration or Importation of Such Persons as any of the States now existing shall think proper to admit, shall not be prohibited by the Congress prior to the Year one thousand eight hundred and eight, but a tax or duty may be imposed on such Importation, not exceeding ten dollars for each Person.

The privilege of the Writ of Habeas Corpus shall not be suspended, unless when in Cases of Rebellion or Invasion the public Safety may require it.

No Bill of Attainder or ex post facto Law shall be passed.

[No capitation, or other direct, Tax shall be laid, unless in Proportion to the Census or Enumeration herein before directed to be taken.][5]

No Tax or Duty shall be laid on Articles exported from any State.

No preference shall be given by any Regulation of Commerce or Revenue to the Ports of one State over those of another: nor shall Vessels bound to, or from, one State be obliged to enter, clear, or pay Duties in another.

No money shall be drawn from the Treasury, but in Consequence of Appropriations made by Law; and a regular Statement and Account of the Receipts and Expenditures of all public Money shall be published from time to time.

No Title of Nobility shall be granted by the United States: And no Person holding any Office of Profit or Trust under them, shall, without the Consent of the Congress, accept of any present, Emolument, Office, or Title, of any kind whatever, from any King, Prince, or foreign State.

[Powers denied to states]

SECTION 10 No State shall enter into any Treaty, Alliance, or Confederation; grant Letters of Marque and Reprisal; coin Money; emit Bills of Credit; make any Thing but gold and silver Coin a Tender in Payment of Debts; pass any Bill of Attainder, ex post facto Law, or Law impairing the Obligation of Contracts, or grant any Title of Nobility.

No State shall, without the Consent of the Congress, lay any Imposts or Duties on Imports or Exports, except what may be absolutely necessary for executing its inspection Laws: and the net Produce of all Duties and Imposts, laid by any State on Imports or Exports, shall be for the Use of the Treasury of the United States; and all such Laws shall be subject to the Revision and Control of the Congress.

No State shall, without the Consent of Congress, lay any duty of Tonnage, keep Troops, or Ships of War in time of Peace, enter into any Agreement or Com-

---

[5]Changed by Amendment XVI.

pact with another State, or with a foreign Power, or engage in War, unless actually invaded, or in such imminent Danger as will not admit of delay.

[The executive branch]

Article II

[Presidential term, choice by electors, qualifications, payment, succession, oath of office]

SECTION 1 The executive Power shall be vested in a President of the United States of America. He shall hold his Office during the Term of four Years, and, together with the Vice President, chosen for the same Term, be elected, as follows:

Each State shall appoint, in such Manner as the Legislature thereof may direct, a Number of Electors, equal to the whole Number of Senators and Representatives to which the State may be entitled in the Congress: but no Senator or Representative, or Person holding an Office of Trust or Profit under the United States, shall be appointed an Elector.

[The Electors shall meet in their respective States, and vote by Ballot for two persons, of whom one at least shall not be an Inhabitant of the same State with themselves. And they shall make a List of all the Persons voted for, and of the Number of Votes for each; which List they shall sign and certify, and transmit sealed to the Seat of the Government of the United States, directed to the President of the Senate. The President of the Senate shall, in the Presence of the Senate and House of Representatives, open all the Certificates, and the Votes shall then be counted. The Person having the greatest Number of Votes shall be the President, if such Number be a Majority of the whole Number of Electors appointed; and if there be more than one who have such Majority, and have an equal Number of Votes, then the House of Representatives shall immediately chuse by Ballot one of them for President; and if no Person have a Majority, then from the five highest on the List the said House shall in like Manner chuse the President. But in chusing the President, the Votes shall be taken by States, the Representation from each State having one Vote; A quorum for this Purpose shall consist of a Member or Members from two-thirds of the States, and a Majority of all the States shall be necessary to a Choice. In every Case, after the Choice of the President, the Person having the greatest Number of Votes of the Electors shall be the Vice President. But if there should remain two or more who have equal Votes, the Senate shall chuse from them by Ballot the Vice President.][6]

The Congress may determine the Time of chusing the Electors, and the Day on which they shall give their Votes; which Day shall be the same throughout the United States.

---

[6]Changed by Amendment XII.

No person except a natural born Citizen, or a Citizen of the United States, at the time of the Adoption of this Constitution, shall be eligible to the Office of President; neither shall any Person be eligible to that Office who shall not have attained to the Age of thirty-five Years, and been fourteen Years a Resident within the United States.

[In case of the removal of the President from Office, or of his Death, Resignation, or Inability to discharge the Powers and Duties of the said Office, the same shall devolve on the Vice President, and the Congress may by Law provide for the Case of Removal, Death, Resignation or Inability, both of the President and Vice President, declaring what Officer shall then act as President, and such Officer shall act accordingly, until the Disability be removed, or a President shall be elected.][7]

The President shall, at stated Times, receive for his Services, a Compensation, which shall neither be encreased nor diminished during the Period for which he shall have been elected, and he shall not receive within that Period any other Emolument from the United States, or any of them.

Before he enter on the Execution of his Office, he shall take the following Oath or Affirmation:—"I do solemnly swear (or affirm) that I will faithfully execute the Office of President of the United States, and will to the best of my Ability, preserve, protect and defend the Constitution of the United States."

[Powers to command the military and executive departments, to grant pardons, to make treaties, to appoint government officers]

SECTION 2 The President shall be Commander in Chief of the Army and Navy of the United States, and of the Militia of the several States, when called into the actual Service of the United States; he may require the Opinion, in writing, of the principal Officer in each of the executive Departments, upon any subject relating to the Duties of their respective Offices, and he shall have Power to grant Reprieves and Pardons for Offenses against the United States, except in Cases of Impeachment.

He shall have Power, by and with the Advice and Consent of the Senate, to make Treaties, provided two-thirds of the Senators present concur; and he shall nominate, and by and with the Advice and Consent of the Senate, shall appoint Ambassadors, other public Ministers and Consuls, Judges of the Supreme Court, and all other Officers of the United States, whose Appointments are not herein otherwise provided for, and which shall be established by Law; but the Congress may by Law vest the Appointment of such inferior Officers, as they think proper, in the President alone, in the Courts of Law, or in the Heads of Departments.

---

[7]Changed by Amendment XXV.

The President shall have Power to fill up all Vacancies that may happen during the Recess of the Senate, by granting Commissions which shall expire at the End of their next Session.

[Formal duties]

SECTION 3 He shall from time to time give to the Congress Information of the State of the Union, and recommend to their Consideration such Measures as he shall judge necessary and expedient; he may, on extraordinary Occasions, convene both Houses, or either of them, and in Case of Disagreement between them, with Respect to the Time of Adjournment, he may adjourn them to such Time as he shall think proper; he shall receive Ambassadors and other public Ministers; he shall take Care that the Laws be faithfully executed, and shall Commission all the Officers of the United States.

[Conditions for removal]

SECTION 4 The President, Vice President and all civil Officers of the United States, shall be removed from Office on Impeachment for, and Conviction of, Treason, Bribery, or other high Crimes and Misdemeanors.

[The judicial branch]

Article III

[Courts and judges]

SECTION 1 The judicial Power of the United States, shall be vested in one supreme Court, and in such inferior Courts as the Congress may from time to time ordain and establish. The Judges, both of the supreme and inferior Courts, shall hold their Offices during good Behaviour, and shall, at stated Times, receive for their Services a Compensation which shall not be diminished during their Continuance in Office.

[Jurisdictions and jury trials]

SECTION 2 The judicial Power shall extend to all Cases, in Law and Equity, arising under this Constitution, the Laws of the United States, and Treaties made, or which shall be made, under their Authority;—to all Cases affecting Ambassadors, other public Ministers and Consuls;—to all Cases of admiralty and maritime Jurisdiction;—to Controversies to which the United States shall be a Party;—to Controversies between two or more States;—[between a State and Citizens of another State;—]8 between Citizens of different States;—between Citizens of the

---

8Changed by Amendment XI.

same State claiming Lands under Grants of different States, [and between a State, or the Citizens thereof, and foreign States, Citizens or Subjects][9]

In all Cases affecting Ambassadors, other public Ministers and Consuls, and those in which a State shall be Party, the supreme Court shall have original Jurisdiction. In all the other Cases before mentioned, the supreme Court shall have appellate Jurisdiction, both as to Law and Fact, with such Exceptions, and under such Regulations as the Congress shall make.

The trial of all Crimes, except in Cases of Impeachment, shall be by Jury; and such Trial shall be held in the State where the said Crimes shall have been committed; but when not committed within any State, the Trial shall be at such Place or Places as the Congress may by Law have directed.

[Treason and its punishment]

SECTION 3 Treason against the United States, shall consist only in levying War against them, or, in adhering to their Enemies, giving them Aid and Comfort. No Person shall be convicted of Treason unless on the Testimony of two Witnesses to the same overt Act, or on Confession in open Court.

The Congress shall have power to declare the Punishment of Treason, but no Attainder of Treason shall work Corruption of Blood, or Forfeiture except during the Life of the Person attainted.

[THE REST OF THE FEDERAL SYSTEM]

Article IV

[Relationships among and with states]

SECTION 1 Full Faith and Credit shall be given in each State to the public Acts, Records, and judicial Proceedings of every other State. And the Congress may by general Laws prescribe the Manner in which such Acts, Records and Proceedings shall be proved, and the Effect thereof.

[Privileges and immunities, extradition]

SECTION 2 The Citizens of each State shall be entitled to all Privileges and Immunities of Citizens in the several States.

A Person charged in any State with Treason, Felony, or other Crime, who shall flee from Justice, and be found in another State, shall on demand of the executive Authority of the State from which he fled, be delivered up, to be removed to the State having Jurisdiction of the Crime.

---

[9]Changed by Amendment XI.

[No Person held to Service or Labour in one State, under the Laws thereof, escaping into another, shall, in Consequence of any Law or Regulation therein, be discharged from such Service or Labour, but shall be delivered up on Claim of the Party to whom such Service or Labour may be due.][10]

[New states]

SECTION 3 New States may be admitted by the Congress into this Union; but no new State shall be formed or erected within the Jurisdiction of any other State; nor any State be formed by the Junction of two or more States, or parts of States, without the Consent of the Legislatures of the States concerned as well as of the Congress.

The Congress shall have Power to dispose of and make all needful Rules and Regulations respecting the Territory or other Property belonging to the United States; and nothing in this Constitution shall be so construed as to Prejudice any Claims of the United States, or of any particular State.

[Obligations to states]

SECTION 4 The United States shall guarantee to every State in this Union a Republican Form of Government, and shall protect each of them against Invasion; and on Application of the Legislature, or of the Executive (when the Legislature cannot be convened) against domestic Violence.

[MECHANISM FOR CHANGE]

Article V

[Amending the Constitution]

The Congress, whenever two-thirds of both Houses shall deem it necessary, shall propose Amendments to this Constitution, or, on the Application of the Legislatures of two-thirds of the several States, shall call a Convention for proposing Amendments, which, in either Case, shall be valid to all Intents and Purposes, as part of this Constitution, when ratified by the Legislatures of three-fourths of the several States, or by Conventions in three-fourths thereof, as the one or the other Mode of Ratification may be proposed by the Congress; Provided that no Amendment which may be made prior to the Year One thousand eight hundred and eight shall in any Manner affect the first and fourth Clauses in the Ninth Section of the first Article; and that no State, without its Consent, shall be deprived of its equal Suffrage in the Senate.

------

[10]Changed by Amendment XIII.

[FEDERAL SUPREMACY]

Article VI

All Debts contracted and Engagements entered into, before the Adoption of this Constitution shall be as valid against the United States under this Constitution, as under the Confederation.

This Constitution, and the Laws of the United States which shall be made in Pursuance thereof; and all Treaties made, or which shall be made, under the Authority of the United States, shall be the supreme Law of the Land; and the Judges in every State shall be bound thereby, any Thing in the Constitution or Laws of any State to the Contrary notwithstanding.

The Senators and Representatives before mentioned, and the Members of the several State Legislatures, and all executive and judicial Officers, both of the United States and of the several States, shall be bound by Oath or Affirmation, to support this Constitution; but no religious Test shall ever be required as a Qualification to any Office or public Trust under the United States.

[RATIFICATION]

Article VII

The Ratification of the Conventions of nine States shall be sufficient for the Establishment of this Constitution between the States so ratifying the Same.

Done in Convention by the Unanimous Consent of the States present the Seventeenth Day of September in the year of our Lord one thousand seven hundred and eighty seven and of the Independence of the United States of America the twelfth. In witness whereof We have hereunto subscribed our Names.

[BILL OF RIGHTS AND OTHER AMENDMENTS]

Articles in addition to, and amendment of, the Constitution of the United States of America, proposed by Congress, and ratified by the several States, pursuant to the fifth Article of the original Constitution.

Amendment I [1791]

[Freedoms of religion, speech, press, assembly]

Congress shall make no law respecting an establishment of religion, or prohibiting the free exercise thereof; or abridging the freedom of speech, or of the press; or the right of the people peaceably to assemble and to petition the Government for a redress of grievances.

Amendment II [1791]

[Right to bear arms]

A well regulated Militia, being necessary to the security of a free State, the right of the people to keep and bear Arms, shall not be infringed.

Amendment III [1791]

[Quartering of soldiers]

No Soldier shall, in time of peace be quartered in any house, without the consent of the Owner, nor in time of war, but in a manner to be prescribed by Law.

Amendment IV [1791]

[Protection against search and seizure]

The right of the people to be secure in their persons, houses, papers, and effects, against unreasonable searches and seizures, shall not be violated, and no Warrants shall issue, but upon probable cause, supported by Oath or affirmation, and particularly describing the place to be searched, and the persons or things to be seized.

Amendment V [1791]

[Protection of citizens before the law]

No person shall be held to answer for a capital, or otherwise infamous crime, unless on a presentment or indictment of a Grand Jury, except in cases arising in the land or naval forces, or in the Militia, when in actual service in time of War or public danger; nor shall any person be subject for the same offence to be twice put in jeopardy of life or limb; nor shall be compelled in any criminal case to be a witness against himself, nor be deprived of life, liberty, or property, without due process of law; nor shall private property be taken for public use, without just compensation.

Amendment VI [1791]

[Rights of the accused in criminal cases]

In all criminal prosecutions, the accused shall enjoy the right to a speedy and public trial, by an impartial jury of the State and district wherein the crime shall have been committed, which district shall have been previously ascertained by law, and to be informed of the nature and cause of the accusation; to be confronted with the witnesses against him; to have compulsory process for obtaining witnesses in his favor, and to have the Assistance of Counsel for his defence.

Amendment VII [1791]

[Rights of complainants in civil cases]

In suits at common law, where the value in controversy shall exceed twenty dollars, the right of trial by jury shall be preserved, and no fact tried by jury, shall be otherwise reexamined in any Court of the United States, than according to the rules of the common law.

Amendment VIII [1791]

[Constraints on punishments]

Excessive bail shall not be required, nor excessive fines imposed, nor cruel and unusual punishments inflicted.

Amendment IX [1791]

[Rights retained by the people]

The enumeration in the Constitution, of certain rights, shall not be construed to deny or disparage others retained by the people.

Amendment X [1791]

[Rights reserved to states]

The powers not delegated to the United States by the Constitution, nor prohibited by it to the States, are reserved to the States respectively, or to the people.

Amendment XI [1798]

[Restraints on judicial power]

The Judicial power of the United States shall not be construed to extend to any suit in law or equity, commenced or prosecuted against one of the United States by Citizens of another State, or by Citizens or Subjects of any Foreign State.

Amendment XII [1804]

[Mechanism for presidential elections]

The electors shall meet in their respective states and vote by ballot for President and Vice-President, one of whom, at least, shall not be an inhabitant of the same state with themselves; they shall name in their ballots the person voted for as President, and in distinct ballots the person voted for as Vice-President, and they shall make distinct lists of all persons voted for as President, and of all persons voted for as Vice-President, and of the number of votes for each, which lists they shall sign and certify, and transmit sealed to the seat of the government of the United States, directed to the President of the Senate;—The President of the Senate shall, in presence of the Senate and House of Representatives, open all the certificates and the votes shall then be counted;—The person having the greatest number of votes for President, shall be the President, if such number be a majority of the whole number of Electors appointed; and if no person have such majority, then from the persons having the highest numbers not exceeding three on the list of those voted for as President, the House of Representatives shall choose immediately, by ballot, the President. But in choosing the President, the votes shall be taken by states, the representation from each state having one vote; a quorum for this purpose shall consist of a member or members from two-thirds of the states, and a majority of all the states shall be necessary to a choice. [And if the House of Representatives shall not choose a President whenever the right of choice shall devolve upon them, before the fourth day of March next following, then the Vice-President shall act as President, as in the case of the death or other constitutional disability of the President.—][11] The person having the greatest number of votes as Vice-President, shall be the Vice-President, if such number be a majority of the whole number of Electors appointed, and if no person have a majority, then from the two highest numbers on the list, the Senate shall choose the Vice-President; a quorum for the purpose shall consist of two-thirds of the whole number of Senators, and a majority of the whole number shall be necessary to a choice. But no person constitutionally ineligible to the office of President shall be eligible to that of Vice-President of the United States.

Amendment XIII [1865]

[Abolishment of slavery]

SECTION 1 Neither slavery nor involuntary servitude, except as a punishment for crime whereof the party shall have been duly convicted, shall exist within the United States, or any place subject to their jurisdiction.

---

[11]Superseded by Section 3 of Amendment XX.

SECTION 2 Congress shall have power to enforce this article by appropriate legislation.

Amendment XIV [1868]

[Citizens' rights and immunities, due process, equal protection]

SECTION 1 All persons born or naturalized in the United States, and subject to the jurisdiction thereof, are citizens of the United States and of the State wherein they reside. No State shall make or enforce any law which shall abridge the privileges or immunities of citizens of the United States; nor shall any State deprive any person of life, liberty, or property, without due process of law; nor deny to any person within its jurisdiction the equal protection of the laws.

[Basis of representation]

SECTION 2 Representatives shall be appointed among the several States according to their respective numbers, counting the whole number of persons in each State, excluding Indians not taxed. But when the right to vote at any election for the choice of electors for President and Vice-President of the United States, Representatives in Congress, the Executive and Judicial officers of a State, or the members of the Legislature thereof, is denied to any of the male inhabitants of such State, being twenty-one years of age, and citizens of the United States, or in any way abridged, except for participation in rebellion, or other crime, the basis of representation therein shall be reduced in the proportion which the number of such male citizens shall bear to the whole number of male citizens twenty-one years of age in such State.

[Disqualification of Confederates for office]

SECTION 3 No person shall be a Senator or Representative in Congress, or elector of President and Vice-President, or hold any office, civil or military, under the United States, or under any State, who, having previously taken an oath, as a member of Congress, or as an officer of the United States, or as a member of any State legislature, or as an executive or judicial officer of any State, to support the Constitution of the United States, shall have engaged in insurrection or rebellion against the same, or given aid or comfort to the enemies thereof. But Congress may by a vote of two-thirds of each House, remove such disability.

[Public debt arising from insurrection or rebellion]

SECTION 4 The validity of the public debt of the United States, authorized by law, including debts incurred for payment of pensions and bounties for services in suppressing insurrection or rebellion, shall not be questioned. But neither the United States nor any State shall assume or pay any debt or obligation incurred in aid of insurrection or rebellion against the United States, or any claim for the loss or emancipation of any slave; but all such debts, obligations and claims shall be held illegal and void.

SECTION 5 The Congress shall have power to enforce, by appropriate legislation, the provisions of this article.

Amendment XV [1870]

[Explicit extension of right to vote]

SECTION 1 The right of citizens of the United States to vote shall not be denied or abridged by the United States or by any State on account of race, color, or previous condition of servitude.

SECTION 2 The Congress shall have power to enforce this article by appropriate legislation.

Amendment XVI [1913]

[Creation of income tax]

The Congress shall have power to lay and collect taxes on incomes, from whatever source derived, without apportionment among the several States, and without regard to any census or enumeration.

Amendment XVII [1913]

[Election of senators]

The Senate of the United States shall be composed of two Senators from each State, elected by the people thereof, for six years; and each Senator shall have one vote. The electors in each State shall have the qualifications requisite for electors of the most numerous branch of the State legislatures.

When vacancies happen in the representation of any State in the Senate, the executive authority of such State shall issue writs of election to fill such vacancies: *Provided,* That the legislature of any State may empower the executive thereof to make temporary appointments until the people fill the vacancies by election as the legislature may direct.

This amendment shall not be so construed as to affect the election or term of any Senator chosen before it becomes valid as part of the Constitution.

Amendment XVIII [1919]

[Prohibition of alcohol]

SECTION 1 After one year from the ratification of this article the manufacture, sale, or transportation of intoxicating liquors within, the importation thereof into, or the exportation thereof from the United States and all territory subject to the jurisdiction thereof for beverage purposes is hereby prohibited.

SECTION 2 The Congress and the several States shall have concurrent power to enforce this article by appropriate legislation.

SECTION 3 This article shall be inoperative unless it shall have been ratified as an amendment to the Constitution by the legislatures of the several States, as provided in the Constitution, within seven years from the date of the submission hereof to the States by the Congress.][12]

Amendment XIX [1920]

[Voting rights and gender]

The right of citizens of the United States to vote shall not be denied or abridged by the United States or by any State on account of sex. Congress shall have the power to enforce this article by appropriate legislation.

Amendment XX [1933]

[Terms of executives, assembly of Congress, presidential succession]

SECTION 1 The terms of the President and Vice President shall end at noon on the 20th day of January, and the terms of Senators and Representatives at noon on the 3d day of January, of the years in which such terms would have ended if this article had not been ratified; and the terms of their successors shall then begin.

SECTION 2 The Congress shall assemble at least once in every year, and such meeting shall begin at noon on the 3d day of January, unless they shall by law appoint a different day.

SECTION 3 If, at the time fixed for the beginning of the term of the President, the President elect shall have died, the Vice President elect shall become President. If a President shall not have been chosen before the time fixed for the beginning of his term, or if the President elect shall have failed to qualify, then the Vice President elect shall act as President until a President shall have qualified; and the Congress may by law provide for the case wherein neither a President elect nor a Vice President elect shall have qualified, declaring who shall then act as President, or the manner in which one who is to act shall be selected, and such person shall act accordingly until a President or Vice President shall have qualified.

SECTION 4 The Congress may by law provide for the case of the death of any of the persons from whom the House of Representatives may choose a President whenever the right of choice shall have devolved upon them, and for the case of the death of any of the persons from whom the Senate may choose a Vice President whenever the right of choice shall have devolved upon them.

---

[12]Repealed by Amendment XXI.

SECTION 5 Sections 1 and 2 shall take effect on the 15th day of October following the ratification of this article.

SECTION 6 This article shall be inoperative unless it shall have been ratified as an amendment to the Constitution by the legislatures of three-fourths of the several States within seven years from the date of its submission.

Amendment XXI [1933]

[Repealing of Prohibition]

SECTION 1 The eighteenth article of amendment to the Constitution of the United States is hereby repealed.

SECTION 2 The transportation or importation into any State, Territory, or possession of the United States for delivery or use therein of intoxicating liquors, in violation of the laws thereof, is hereby prohibited.

SECTION 3 This article shall be inoperative unless it shall have been ratified as an amendment to the Constitution by conventions in the several States, as provided in the Constitution, within seven years from the date of the submission hereof to the States by the Congress.

Amendment XXII [1951]

[Limits on presidential term]

SECTION 1 No person shall be elected to the office of the President more than twice, and no person who has held the office of President, or acted as President, for more than two years of a term to which some other person was elected President shall be elected to the office of the President more than once. But this Article shall not apply to any person holding the office of President when this Article was proposed by the Congress, and shall not prevent any person who may be holding the office of President, or acting as President, during the term within which the Article becomes operative from holding the office of President or acting as President during the remainder of such term.

SECTION 2 This article shall be inoperative unless it shall have been ratified as an amendment to the Constitution by the legislatures of three-fourths of the several States within seven years from the date of its submission to the States by the Congress.

Amendment XXIII [1961]

[Voting rights of District of Columbia]

SECTION 1 The District constituting the seat of Government of the United States shall appoint in such manner as the Congress may direct:

A number of electors of President and Vice President equal to the whole number of Senators and Representatives in Congress to which the District would be entitled if it were a State; but in no event more than the least populous State; they shall be in addition to those appointed by the States, but they shall be considered, for the purposes of the election of President and Vice President, to be electors appointed by a State; and they shall meet in the District and perform such duties as provided by the twelfth article of amendment.

SECTION 2 The Congress shall have power to enforce this article by appropriate legislation.

Amendment XXIV [1964]

[Prohibition of poll tax]

SECTION 1 The right of citizens of the United States to vote in any primary or other election for President or Vice President, for electors for President or Vice President, or for Senator or Representative in Congress, shall not be denied or abridged by the United States or any State by reason of failure to pay any poll tax or other tax.

SECTION 2 The Congress shall have power to enforce this article by appropriate legislation.

Amendment XXV [1967]

[Presidential disability and succession]

SECTION 1 In case of the removal of the President from office or his death or resignation, the Vice President shall become President.

SECTION 2 Whenever there is a vacancy in the office of the Vice President, the President shall nominate a Vice President who shall take the Office upon confirmation by a majority vote of both houses of Congress.

SECTION 3 Whenever the President transmits to the President pro tempore of the Senate and the Speaker of the House of Representatives his written declaration that he is unable to discharge the powers and duties of his office, and until he transmits to them a written declaration to the contrary, such powers and duties shall be discharged by the Vice President as Acting President.

SECTION 4 Whenever the Vice President and a majority of either the principal officers of the executive departments, or of such other body as Congress may by law provide, transmit to the President pro tempore of the Senate and the Speaker of the House of Representatives their written declaration that the President is unable to discharge the powers and duties of his office, the Vice President shall immediately assume the powers and duties of the office as Acting President.

Thereafter, when the President transmits to the President pro tempore of the Senate and the Speaker of the House of Representatives his written declaration that no inability exists, he shall resume the powers and duties of his office unless the Vice President and a majority of either the principal officers of the executive department, or of such other body as Congress may by law provide, transmit within four days to the President pro tempore of the Senate and the Speaker of the House of Representatives their written declaration that the President is unable to discharge the powers and duties of his office. Thereupon Congress shall decide the issue, assembling within 48 hours for that purpose if not in session. If the Congress, within 21 days after receipt of the latter written declaration, or, if Congress is not in session, within 21 days after Congress is required to assemble, determines by two-thirds vote of both houses that the President is unable to discharge the powers and duties of his office, the Vice President shall continue to discharge the same as Acting President; otherwise, the President shall resume the powers and duties of his office.

Amendment XXVI [1971]

[Voting rights and age]

SECTION 1 The right of citizens of the United States, who are eighteen years of age, or older, to vote shall not be denied or abridged by the United States or by any state on account of age.

SECTION 2 The Congress shall have the power to enforce this article by appropriate legislation.

Amendment XXVII [1992]

[Congressional pay raises]

No law varying the compensation for the services of the Senators and Representatives shall take effect, until an election of Representatives shall have intervened.

appendix C

from the federalist papers, nos. 10 and 51

FEDERALIST NO. 10 [1787]

To the People of the State of New York: Among the numerous advantages promised by a well-constructed union, none deserves to be more accurately developed than its tendency to break and control the violence of faction. The friend of popular governments, never finds himself so much alarmed for their character and fate, as when he contemplates their propensity to this dangerous vice. He will not fail, therefore, to set a due value on any plan which, without violating the principles to which he is attached, provides a proper cure for it. The instability, injustice, and confusion introduced into the public councils, have, in truth, been the mortal diseases under which popular governments have everywhere perished; as they continue to be the favourite and fruitful topics from which the adversaries to liberty derive their most specious declamations. The valuable improvements made by the American constitutions on the popular models, both ancient and modern, cannot certainly be too much admired; but it would be an unwarrantable partiality, to contend that they have as effectually obviated the danger on this side, as was wished and expected. Complaints are everywhere heard from our most considerate and virtuous citizens, equally the friends of public and private faith, and of public and personal liberty, that our governments are too unstable; that the public good is disregarded in the conflicts of rival parties; and that measures are too often decided, not according to the rules of justice, and the rights of the minor party, but by the superior force of an interested and overbearing majority. However anxiously we may wish that these complaints had no foundation, the evidence of known facts will not permit us to deny that they are in some degree true. It will be found, indeed, on a candid review of our situation, that some of the distresses under which we labour have been erroneously charged on the operation of our governments; but it will be found, at the same time, that other causes will not alone account for many of our heaviest misfortunes; and, particularly, for that prevailing and increasing distrust of public engagements, and alarm for private rights, which are echoed from one end of the continent to the other. These must be chiefly, if not wholly, effects of the unsteadiness and injustice, with which a factious spirit has tainted our public administrations.

By a faction, I understand a number of citizens, whether amounting to a majority or minority of the whole, who are united and actuated by some common impulse of passion, or of interest, adverse to the rights of other citizens, or to the permanent and aggregate interests of the community.

There are two methods of curing the mischiefs of faction: The one, by removing its causes; the other, by controlling its effects.

There are again two methods of removing the causes of faction: The one, by destroying the liberty which is essential to its existence; the other, by giving to every citizen the same opinions, the same passions, and the same interests.

It could never be more truly said, than of the first remedy, that it was worse than the disease. Liberty is to faction what air is to fire, an ailment without which it instantly expires. But it could not be a less folly to abolish liberty, which is essential to political life, because it nourishes faction, than it would be to wish the annihilation of air, which is essential to animal life, because it imparts to fire its destructive agency.

The second expedient is as impracticable, as the first would be unwise. As long as the reason of man continues fallible, and he is at liberty to exercise it, different opinions will be formed. As long as the connection subsists between his reason and his self-love, his opinions and his passions will have a reciprocal influence on each other; and the former will be objects to which the latter will attach themselves. The diversity in the faculties of men, from which the rights of property originate, is not less an insuperable obstacle to an uniformity of interests. The protection of these faculties is the first object of government. From the protection of different and unequal faculties of acquiring property, the possession of different degrees and kinds of property immediately results; and from the influence of these on the sentiments and views of the respective proprietors, ensues a division of the society into different interests and parties.

The latent causes of action are thus sown in the nature of man; and we see them everywhere brought into different degrees of activity, according to the different circumstances of civil society. A zeal for different opinions concerning religion, concerning government, and many other points, as well as of speculation as of practice; an attachment to different leaders ambitiously contending for preeminence and power; or to persons of other descriptions whose fortunes have been interesting to the human passions, have, in turn, divided mankind into parties, inflamed them with mutual animosity, and rendered them much more disposed to vex and oppress each other, than to cooperate for their common good. So strong is this propensity of mankind, to fall into mutual animosities, that where no substantial occasion presents itself, the most frivolous and fanciful distinctions have been sufficient to kindle their unfriendly passions and excite their most violent conflicts. But the most common and durable source of factions, has been the various and unequal distribution of property. Those who hold, and those who are without property, have ever formed distinct interests in society. Those who are creditors, and those who are debtors, fall under alike discrimination. A landed interest, a manufacturing interest, a mercantile interest, a moneyed interest, with many lesser interests, grow up of necessity in civilized nations, and divide them into different classes, actuated by different sentiments and views. The regulation of these various and interfering interests forms the principal task of modern legislation, and involves the spirit of the party and faction in the necessary and ordinary operations of the government.

No man is allowed to be a judge in his own cause; because his interest will certainly bias his judgment, and, not improbably, corrupt his integrity. With equal, nay, with greater reason, a body of men are unfit to be both judges and parties at the same time; yet what are many of the most important acts of legislation, but so many judicial determinations, not indeed concerning the right of single persons, but concerning the rights of large bodies of citizens? And what are the different classes of legislators, but advocates and parties to the causes which they determine? Is a law proposed concerning private debts? It is a question to which the creditors are parties on one side, and the debtors on the other. Justice ought to hold the balance between them. Yet the parties are, and must be, themselves the judges; and the most numerous party, or, in other words, the most powerful faction, must be expected to prevail. Shall domestic manufactures be encouraged, and in what degree, by restrictions on foreign manufactures? are questions which would be differently decided by the landed and the manufacturing classes; and probably by neither with a sole regard to justice and the public good. The apportionment of taxes, on the various descriptions of property, is an act which seems to require the most exact impartiality; yet there is, perhaps, no legislative act, in which greater opportunity and temptation are given to a predominant party to trample on the rules of justice. Every shilling, with which they overburden the inferior number, is a shilling saved to their own pockets.

It is in vain to say, that enlightened statesmen will be able to adjust these clashing interests, and render them all subservient to the public good. Enlightened statesmen will not always be at the helm: nor, in many cases, can such an adjustment be made at all, without taking into view indirect and remote considerations, which will rarely prevail over the immediate interest which one party may find in disregarding the rights of another, or the good of the whole. The inference to which we are brought is, that the *causes* of faction cannot be removed; and that relief is only to be sought in the means of controlling its *effects*.

If a faction consists of less than a majority, relief is supplied by the republican principle, which enables the majority to defeat its sinister views, by regular vote. It may clog the administration, it may convulse the society; but it will be unable to execute and mask its violence under the forms of the constitution. When a majority is included in a faction, the form of popular government, on the other hand, enables it to sacrifice to its ruling passion or interest, both the public good and the rights of other citizens. To secure the public good, and private rights, against the danger of such a faction, and at the same time to preserve the spirit and the form of popular government, is then the great object to which our inquiries are directed. Let me add, that it is the great desideratum, by which alone this form of government can be rescued from the opprobrium under which it has so long laboured, and be recommended to the esteem and adoption of mankind.

By what means is this object attainable? Evidently by one of two only. Either the existence of the same passion or interest in a majority, at the same time, must be prevented; or the majority, having such coexistent passion or interest, must be rendered, by their number and local situation, unable to concert and carry into effect schemes of oppression. If the impulse and the opportunity be suffered to coincide, we well know that neither moral nor religious motives can be relied on as an adequate control. They are not found to be such on the injustice and violence of individuals, and lose their efficacy in proportion to the number combined together; that is, in proportion as their efficacy becomes needful.

From this view of the subject, it may be concluded, that a pure democracy, by which I mean a society consisting of a small number of citizens, who assemble and administer the government in person, can admit of no cure for the mischiefs of faction. A common passion or interest will, in almost every case, be felt by a majority of the whole; a communication and concert, results from the form of government itself; and there is nothing to check the inducements to sacrifice the weaker party, or an obnoxious individual. Hence, it is, that such democracies have ever been spectacles of turbulence and contention; have ever been found incompatible with personal security, or the rights of property; and have in general been as short in their lives, as they have been violent in their deaths. Theoretic politicians, who have patronized this species of government, have erroneously supposed, that by reducing mankind to a perfect equality in their political rights, they would, at the same time, be perfectly equalized and assimilated in their possessions, their opinions, and their passions.

A republic, by which I mean a government in which the scheme of representation takes place, opens a different prospect, and promises the cure for which we are seeking. Let us examine the points in which it varies from pure democracy, and we shall comprehend both the nature of the cure and the efficacy which it must derive from the union.

The two great points of difference, between a democracy and a republic, are, first, the delegation of the government, in the latter, to a small number of citizens, elected by the rest; secondly, the greatest number of citizens, and greater sphere of country, over which the latter may be extended.

The effect of the first difference is, on the one hand, to refine and enlarge the public views, by passing them through the medium of a chosen body of citizens, whose wisdom may best discern the true interest of their country, and whose patriotism and love of justice, will be least likely to sacrifice it to temporary or partial considerations. Under such a regulation, it may well happen, that the public voice, pronounced by the representatives of the people, will be more consonant to the public good, than if pronounced by the people themselves, convened for the purpose. On the other hand the effect may be inverted. Men of factious tempers, of local prejudices, or of sinister designs, may by intrigue, by corruption, or by other means, first obtain the suffrages, and then betray the interest of the people. The question resulting is, whether small or extensive republics are most favourable to the election of proper guardians of the public weal; and it is clearly decided in favour of the latter by two obvious considerations.

In the first place, it is to be remarked that, however small the republic may be, the representatives must be raised to a certain number, in order to guard against the cabals of a few; and that however large it may be, they must be limited to a certain number, in order to guard against the confusion of a multitude. Hence, the number of representatives in the two cases not being in proportion to that of the constituents, and being proportionally greatest in the small republic, it follows, that if the proportion of fit characters be not less in the large than in the small republic, the former will present a greater option, and consequently a greater probability of a fit choice.

In the next place, as each representative will be chosen by a greater number of citizens in the large than in the small republic, it will be more difficult for unworthy candidates to practise with success the vicious arts, by which elections are too often carried; and the suffrages of the people being more free, will be more likely to centre in men who possess the most attractive merit, and the most diffusive and established characters.

It must be confessed, that in this, as in most other cases, there is a mean, on both sides of which inconveniences will be found to lie. By enlarging too much the number of electors, you render the representatives too little acquainted with all their local circumstances and lesser interests; as by reducing it too much, you render him unduly attached to these, and too little fit to comprehend and pursue great and national objects. The federal constitution forms a happy combination being referred to the national, the local and particular, to the state legislatures.

The other point of difference is, the greater number of citizens, and extent of territory, which may be brought within the compass of republican, than of democratic government; and it is this circumstance principally which renders factious combinations less to be dreaded in the former, than in the latter. The smaller the society, the fewer probably will be the distinct parties and interests composing it; the fewer the distinct parties and interests, the more frequently will a majority be found of the same party; and the smaller the number of individuals composing a majority, and the smaller the compass within which they are placed, the more easily will they concert and execute their plans of oppression. Extend the sphere, and you take in a greater variety of parties and interests; you make it less probable that a majority of the whole will have a common motive to invade the rights of other citizens; or if such a common motive exists, it will be more difficult for all who feel it to discover their own strength, and to act in unison with each other. Besides other impediments, it may be remarked, that where there is a consciousness of unjust or dishonourable purposes, communication is always checked by distrust, in proportion to the number whose concurrence is necessary.

Hence, it clearly appears, that the same advantage, which a republic has over a democracy, in controlling the effects of faction, is enjoyed by a large over a small republic,—is enjoyed by the union over the states composing it. Does this advantage consist in the substitution of representatives, whose enlightened views and virtuous sentiments render them superior to local prejudices, and to schemes of injustice? It will not be denied that the representation of the union will be most likely to possess these requisite endowments. Does it consist in the greater security afforded by a greater variety of parties, against the event of any one party being able to outnumber and oppress the rest? In an equal degree does the increased variety of parties, comprised within the union, increase the security? Does it, in fine, consist in the greater obstacles opposed to the concert and accomplishment of the secret wishes of an unjust and interested majority? Here, again, the extent of the union gives it the most palpable advantage.

The influence of factious leaders may kindle a flame within their particular states, but will be unable to spread a general conflagration through the other states; a religious sect may degenerate into a political faction in a part of the confederacy; but the variety of sects dispersed over the entire face of it, must secure the national councils against any danger from that source: a rage for paper money, for an abolition of debts, for an equal division of property, or for any other improper or wicked project, will be less apt to pervade the whole body of the union than a particular member of it; in the same proportion as such a malady is more likely to taint a particular county or district, than an entire state.

In the extent and proper structure of the union, therefore, we behold a republican remedy for the diseases most incident to republican government. And according to the degree of pleasure and pride we feel in being republicans, ought to be our zeal in cherishing the spirit, and supporting the character of federalists.

JAMES MADISON

FEDERALIST NO. 51 [1788]

To the People of the State of New York: To what expedient then shall we finally resort for maintaining in practice the necessary partition of power among the several departments, as laid down in the constitution? The only answer that can be given is, that as all these exterior provisions are found to be inadequate, the defect must be supplied, by so contriving the interior structure of the government, as that its several constituent parts may, by their mutual relations, be the means of keeping each other in their proper places. Without presuming to undertake a full development of this important idea, I will hazard a few general observations, which may perhaps place it in a clearer light, and enable us to form a more correct judgment of the principles and structure of the government planned by the convention.

In order to lay a due foundation for that separate and distinct exercise of the different powers of government, which to a certain extent, is admitted on all hands to be essential to the preservation of liberty, it is evident that each department should have a will of its own; and consequently should be so constituted, that the members of each should have as little agency as possible in the appointment of the members of the others. Were this principle rigorously adhered to, it would require that all the appointments for the supreme executive, legislative, and judiciary magistracies, should be drawn from the same fountain of authority, the people, through channels, having no communication whatever with one another. Perhaps such a plan of constructing the several departments would be less difficult in practice than it may in contemplation appear. Some difficulties however, and some additional expense, would attend the execution of it. Some deviations therefore from the principle must be admitted. In the constitution of the judiciary department in particular, it might be inexpedient to insist rigorously on the principle; first, because peculiar qualifications being essential in the members, the primary consideration ought to be to select that mode of choice, which best secures these qualifications; secondly, because the permanent tenure by which the appointments are held in that department, must soon destroy all sense of dependence on the authority conferring them.

It is equally evident that the members of each department should be as little dependent as possible on those of the others, for the emoluments annexed to their offices. Were the executive magistrate, or the judges, not independent of the legislature in this particular, their independence in every other would be merely nominal.

But the great security against a gradual concentration of the several powers in the same department, consists in giving to those who administer each department, the necessary constitutional means, and personal motives, to resist encroachments of the others. The provision for defense must in this, as in all other cases, be made commensurate to the danger of attack. Ambition must be made to counteract ambition. The interest of the man must be connected with the constitutional rights of the place. It may be a reflection on human nature, that such devices should be necessary to control the abuses of government: But what is government itself but the greatest of all reflections on human nature? If men were angels, no government would be necessary. If angels were to govern men, neither external nor internal controls on government would be necessary. In framing a government which is to be administered by men over men, the great difficulty lies in this: You must first enable the government to control the governed; and in the next place, oblige it to control itself. A dependence on the people is no doubt the primary control on the government; but experience has taught mankind the necessity of auxiliary precautions.

This policy of supplying by opposite and rival interests, the defect of better motives, might be traced through the whole system of human affairs, private as well as public. We see it particularly displayed in all the subordinate distributions of power; where the constant aim is to divide and arrange the several offices in such a manner as that each may be a check on the other; that the private interest of every individual, may be a sentinel over the public rights. These inventions of prudence cannot be less requisite in the distribution of the supreme powers of the state.

But it is not possible to give to each department an equal power of self defense. In republican government the legislative authority, necessarily, predominates. The remedy for this inconveniency is, to divide the legislature into different branches; and to render them by different modes of election, and different principles of action, as little connected with each other, as the nature of their common functions, and their common dependence on the society, will admit. It may even be necessary to guard against dangerous encroachments by still further precautions. As the weight of the legislative authority requires that it should be thus divided, the weakness of the executive may require, on the other hand, that it should be fortified. An absolute negative, on the legislature, appears at first view to be the natural defense with which the executive magistrate should be armed. But perhaps it would be neither altogether safe, nor alone sufficient. On ordinary occasions, it might not be exerted with the requisite firmness; and on extraordinary occasions, it might be perfidiously abused. May not this defect of an absolute negative be supplied, by some qualified connection between this weaker department, and the weaker branch of the stronger department, by which the latter may be led to support the constitutional rights of the former, without being too much detached from the rights of its own department?

If the principles on which these observations are founded be just, as I persuade myself they are, and they be applied as a criterion, to the several state constitutions, and to the federal constitution, it will be found, that if the latter does not perfectly correspond with them, the former are infinitely less able to bear such a test. There are moreover two considerations particularly applicable to the federal system of America, which place that system in a very interesting point of view.

First. In a single republic, all the power surrendered by the people, is submitted to the administration of a single government; and usurpations are guarded against by a division of the government into distinct and separate departments. In the compound republic of America, the power surrendered by the people, is first divided between two distinct governments, and then the portion allotted to each, subdivided among distinct and separate departments. Hence a double security arises to the rights of the people. The different governments will control each other; at the same time that each will be controlled by itself.

Second. It is of great importance in a republic, not only to guard the society against the oppression of its rulers; but to guard one part of the society against the injustice of the other part. Different interests necessarily exist in different classes of citizens. If a majority be united by a common interest, the rights of the minority will be insecure. There are but two methods of providing against this evil: The one by creating a will in the community independent of the majority, that is, of the society itself; the other by comprehending in the society so many separate descriptions of citizens, as will render an unjust combination of a majority of the whole, very improbable, if not impracticable. The first method prevails in all governments possessing an hereditary or self appointed authority. This at best is but a precarious security; because a power independent of the society may as well espouse the unjust views of the major, as the rightful interests, of the minor party, and may possibly be turned against both parties. The second method will be exemplified in the federal republic of the United States. While all authority in it will be derived from and dependent on the society, the society itself will be broken into so many parts, interests and classes of citizens, that the rights of individuals or of the minority, will be in little danger from interested combinations of the majority. In a free government, the security for civil rights must be the same as for religious rights. It consists in the one case in the multiplicity of sects. The degree of security in both cases will depend on the number of interests and sects; and this may be presumed to depend on the extent of country and number of people comprehended under the same government. This view of the subject must particularly recommend a proper federal system to all the sincere and considerate friends of republican government: Since it shows that in exact proportion as the territory of the union may be formed into more circumscribed confederacies or states, oppressive combinations of a majority will be facilitated; the best security under the republican form, for the rights of every class of citizens, will be diminished; and consequently, the stability and independence of some member of the government, the only other security, must be proportionally increased. Justice is the end of government. It is the end of civil society. It ever has been, and ever will be pursued, until it be obtained, or until liberty be lost in the pursuit. In a society under the forms of which the stronger faction can readily unite and oppress the weaker, anarchy may as truly be said to reign, as in a state of nature where the weaker individual is not secured against the violence of the stronger: And as in the latter state even the stronger individuals are prompted by the uncertainty of their condition, to submit to a government which may protect the weak as well as themselves: So in the former state, will the more powerful factions or parties be gradually induced by alike motives, to wish for a government which will protect all parties, the weaker as well as the more powerful. It can be little doubted, that if the state of Rhode Island was separated from the confederacy, and left to itself, the insecurity of rights under the popular form of government within such narrow limits, would be displayed by such reiterated oppressions of factious majorities, that some power altogether independent of the people would soon be called for by the voice of the very factions whose misrule had proved the necessity of it. In the extended republic of the United States, and among the great variety of interests, parties and sects which it embraces, a coalition of a majority of the whole society could seldom take place on any other principles than those of justice and the general good; and there being thus less danger to a minor from the will of the major party, there must be less pretext also, to provide for the security of the former, by introducing into the government a will not dependent on the latter; or in other words, a will independent of the society itself. It is no less certain than it is important, notwithstanding the contrary opinions which have been entertained, that the larger the society, provided it lie within a practicable sphere, the more duly capable it will be of self government. And happily for the *republican cause,* the practicable sphere may be carried to a very great extent, by a judicious modification and mixture of the *federal principle.*

JAMES MADISON

glossary

adverseness A test used to determine whether a court case involves an actual dispute between two or more parties; used by the Supreme Court to determine whether to hear a case. (See **writ of certiorari**)

affirmative action Programs designed to help women and minorities in areas where they have experienced discrimination, such as getting into college or finding a job.

amicus brief Background information provided to courts by individuals and groups who have an interest in a case.

Anti-Federalists Opponents of ratification of the Constitution.

appellate courts The second tier of the federal courts; appellate courts can hear appeals only from courts of original jurisdiction.

Articles of Confederation America's first constitution, adopted by the thirteen colonies in the midst of the Revolutionary War; the national government consisted of a weak president and a unicameral legislature, and most of the power remained in the states.

association A formal or informal collection of individuals who come together for some purpose.

attentive policy elites Those who follow news coverage and have the ability to set the policy agenda.

Australian ballot A voting system introduced in the late 1800s in which the ballot names all candidates and the vote is cast in secret; also known as the *secret ballot*.

autocracy A government in which a single person has absolute power to decide who gets what, when, and how from government.

baseline polls Measures of public opinion taken early in a campaign to assess a candidate's strengths and weaknesses and test possible campaign themes.

bicameral legislature A two-chambered legislative body.

Bill of Rights The first ten amendments to the Constitution.

bills Legislative proposals in the form of a draft law that are considered by Congress.

bimodal distribution In public opinion polling, a situation in which opinion is distributed heavily toward two extreme ends of the possible range of opinions. The midpoint does not represent the average American opinion.

blanket primary An election in which the ballot lists all candidates of both parties and voters are free to move back and forth across party lines all the way down the ballot. (See **open primary**)

block grant A grant of money from the federal government to the states with broad instructions about how to spend the money. (See **categorical grant**)

broadcasting Messages that are transmitted by the media to all viewers on a single network.

Brown v. Topeka Board of Education The 1954 Supreme Court decision that ended the widespread practice of providing "separate but equal" facilities for blacks and whites and led to desegregation of public schools.

Budget and Impoundment Control Act A 1974 act of Congress that strengthened congressional influence over the federal budget.

budget resolution A congressional statement that sets broad revenue and spending targets that govern the revenue and spending committees as they adopt the federal budget; a resolution is passed by both chambers of Congress but is not signed by the president.

bundling A technique for raising money that involves collecting large numbers of individual checks and turning them over en masse, or bundled, to a candidate.

cabinet An executive body composed of the heads of the fourteen departments of government and selected agencies; members are appointed by the president and confirmed by the Senate.

candidate-centered campaign An election campaign that is run by the candidate with little reference to party. (See **party-centered campaign**)

casework Efforts made by congressional staff to help their representative's constituents.

categorical grant A grant of money from the federal government to the states with specific instructions about how to spend the money. (See **block grant**)

caucus system A process for nominating candidates in which delegates to the party conventions are selected through a series of meetings that usually begin at the local level.

caucuses Informal committees that individual members of Congress join to promote their legislative interests.

censorship Reviewing material with the intent to prevent or punish publication or broadcast of whatever may be found objectionable.

central clearance The process by which the Office of Management and Budget approves legislation and testimony that an agency sends to Congress.

checks and balances The constitutional powers given to the legislative, executive, and judicial branches of government to prevent the other two branches from threatening liberty.

chief of staff A key member of the White House staff and of the president's inner circle; supervises the White House staff.

civic journalism An effort by some journalists to strengthen the media's role in promoting citizen participation; also known as public journalism.

civil liberties Freedoms such as speech, press, and religion guaranteed to protect citizens against government.

civil rights Protections against discrimination on the basis of individual characteristics such as race, gender, and disability.

civil service The federal employment system that seeks to fill federal jobs on the basis of employee merit without regard to political affiliation.

civil society The informal associations that bind communities.

clear and present danger test   A standard used to determine whether speech is protected under the First Amendment; it takes into consideration the circumstances under which words are spoken.

closed primary   An election in which only party members are allowed to cast ballots; voters must declare their party preference when they register to vote.

cloture   A vote by sixty of the one hundred members of the Senate to end a filibuster; a successful vote is known as invoking cloture.

Code of Federal Regulations   A compilation of all rules issued by the federal government.

collective benefits   Benefits that are available to all people regardless of their membership in an interest group.

commerce clause   The section of Article I, Section 8, of the Constitution giving Congress the power to regulate commerce among states, nations, and Indian tribes.

committee on committees   The separate committee selected by the members of each party in each chamber of Congress to assign all committee and subcommittee seats.

common law   Laws that come from the judicial interpretations of statutory law and previous judicial opinions; also known as *judge-made law.*

concurrent powers   Those powers given to both the states and the national government under the Constitution, such as the power to raise taxes.

confederation   A form of governance in which the states dominate and the national government has only those responsibilities given to it by the states.

conference committee   A temporary committee formed to resolve the differences between the House- and Senate-passed versions of a particular bill.

confidence level   The likelihood that the results of a poll are correct.

congressional campaign committee   The separate committee appointed by each party in each chamber to raise money for the election of its members and candidates.

congressional case workers   Staff of members of Congress who handle constituent requests, such as applications to West Point or lost Social Security checks.

conservatives   Americans who believe that government should play a limited role in solving the nation's problems. (See **liberals**)

constituents   People who live and vote in an elected official's district or state.

constitutional courts   Courts that are created by Congress under Article III of the Constitution.

contributory social programs   Programs that provide benefits to people who have earned the right to participate by contributing to the programs earlier in their lives.

conventional participation   Forms of civic activity that Americans find acceptable.

cooperative federalism   A structure of government in which the federal, state, and local governments work together to solve problems.

critical election   An election that produces a lasting shift in the underlying party loyalties of voters; also known as a *realigning election.*

crosscutting requirements   Federal laws that state and local governments must abide by after they accept federal grant dollars.

crossover sanctions   Obligations that state and local governments must fulfill before receiving federal grant dollars.

cycle of decreasing influence   The tendency for presidents to lose public and congressional support over time.

cycle of increasing effectiveness   The tendency for presidents to learn more about their jobs and become more effective over time.

dealignment   A situation in which the strength of the dominant political party declines but no other party rises to take its place, so that no party is dominant.

Declaration of Independence   A list of grievances against the British that announced the colonies' intent to be free; written by Thomas Jefferson and signed on July 4, 1776. (See Appendix A)

dedistributive program   A government policy that requires all Americans to give up government benefits. (See **distributive program; redistributive program**)

delegates   Legislators who do only what their constituents want them to do.

democracy   A system of government in which the power resides with the people.

demographics   Personal characteristics such as race, gender, age, education, and income.

departments   The most visible organizations in the federal bureaucracy: thirteen of the fourteen departments are headed by secretaries; the fourteenth is headed by the attorney general.

direct democracy   A form of democracy in which every citizen has a say in every decision that government makes.

distributive program   A government program that generally helps all groups in society and spreads the costs evenly. (See **dedistributive program; redistributive program**)

disturbance theory   The view that most interest groups emerge from social or economic upheaval.

dual federalism   A structure of government in which the federal and state levels of government do not work together to solve problems.

dual sovereignty   A distribution of power between the states and national government under which states are independent except where the Constitution specifies otherwise.

due process of law   Fair and open legal procedures guaranteed by the Fifth and Fourteenth Amendments.

earmarks   Grants that members of Congress set aside for specific projects in their home districts.

elastic clause   Found in Article I, Section 8, of the Constitution; gives Congress the power to make any laws needed to carry out its express duties and is the source of Congress's implied powers; also known as the *necessary and proper clause.*

electoral college   Created by the Founders to elect the president. The people of each state vote for slates of delegates to the electoral college, who, in turn, elect the president.

elitism   An option for representative democracy in which educated, often wealthy individuals speak for the people.

entitlements   Federal programs that provide benefits to everyone who is eligible.

enumerated powers   The responsibilities specifically given to Congress in the Constitution.

equal opportunities rule   The requirement that radio and television stations that give or sell advertising time to one political candidate must provide an equal amount of time to all opposing candidates.

equal protection clause   Found in the Fourteenth Amendment; declares that all citizens of the United States and the states are to be treated equally under the law.

establishment clause   Found in the First Amendment; prohibits the establishment of a national religion.

ex post facto laws   Laws declaring an act criminal after the act has occurred.

exclusive powers   Those powers given only to the national government under the Constitution, including the power to declare war, make treaties with other governments, and create money.

executive agreements   Agreements between the president and heads of countries that do not require Senate approval.

executive branch   The part of government created to implement the laws.

Executive Office of the President (EOP)   The small number of offices that serve the president directly; includes the Office of Management and Budget, the White House staff, and the National Security Council.

executive orders   Presidential orders that carry the same force as an act of Congress except that (1) they apply only to the executive branch and (2) they can be overturned by a future president.

fairness doctrine   The requirement that radio and television stations must discuss public issues and offer opposing points of view; repealed in 1987.

feature news   Media coverage devoted to stories about people and celebrities.

federal bureaucracy   The components of the executive branch—departments, independent regulatory commissions, agencies, and government corporations—that do the work of implementing the laws.

Federal Communications Commission (FCC)   The federal agency that regulates the airwaves, including radio and television.

Federal Election Commission (FEC)   The federal agency that administers the laws limiting campaign contributions.

federal judiciary   The part of government created to interpret the laws.

Federal Register   A weekly newspaperlike report that lists all new and proposed rules of the federal government.

federalism   The division of power among the national, state, and local layers of government.

Federalists   Supporters of ratification of the Constitution.

federation   An interest group that has membership organizations as members.

filibuster   The practice that allows a single senator to hold the floor indefinitely in order to block a particular piece of legislation; can be ended only by cloture.

First Continental Congress   The national legislature convened by the Founders in Philadelphia in September 1774.

fiscal policy   Decisions to use taxes or spending in order to slow or stimulate the economy.

focusing skill   A president's ability to use timing and lobbying to focus public attention on top legislative priorities.

formula grants   Funds awarded proportionally, often on the basis of population, to ensure that each state or locality gets its share.

free exercise clause   Found in the First Amendment; prohibits any government interference in the practice of religion.

free media   News coverage of a candidate in a campaign. (See **paid media**)

free rider problem   A problem faced by interest groups in recruiting members; by providing benefits that anyone can enjoy, whether a member or not, an interest group reduces incentives to join the group.

gatekeepers   The editors and producers who decide which stories are covered in the media and which are not.

gender gap   Differences in the opinions and voting behavior of men and women; related to childhood socialization as well as to the generally poorer economic situation of women.

general election   The election contest that determines who will hold a particular office. (See **primary election**)

general revenue sharing   A new federalism program under which states and localities receive revenues from the federal government to use with no strings attached.

general welfare clause   The section of Article I, Section 8, of the Constitution giving Congress the power to impose taxes to provide for the general welfare of the Untied States.

generational theory of participation The theory that people born into the same generation learn the same lessons about the costs and benefits of participation.

gerrymandering Redrawing of election district lines to favor one party over another.

government A set of institutions (Congress, the presidency, executive branch, and courts in the United States) for managing politics.

government corporations Organizations in the federal bureaucracy designed to act more like businesses than traditional governmental departments and agencies.

grant-in-aid Movement of money from one layer of government to another.

Great Compromise The agreement by the Constitutional Convention that the American government would have a two-house, or bicameral, legislature.

gross domestic product A measure of the size of the American economy that totals all the things the economy produces and subtracts what it buys from other countries.

home style The way in which members of Congress develop trust with their constituents and explain their votes in Congress.

horse race coverage The aspect of an election campaign that involves which candidate is ahead or behind; tends to dominate media coverage at the expense of campaign issues.

hyperpluralism The trend among interest groups to divide into ever smaller, more specialized organizations.

ideology Underlying views of how much government should be involved in the day-to-day activities of American society.

impeachment A process used to remove duly elected and appointed officials from office; in presidential impeachments, the House of Representatives votes the articles of impeachment, and the Senate votes to acquit or convict.

implied powers Those powers given to Congress under the necessary and proper clause of the Constitution; implied powers allow Congress to carry out its enumerated powers.

incremental program A small change from current practice in a public policy.

incumbent A current officeholder. Incumbents may have advantages in running for office, including name recognition.

independent agencies Usually small federal bureaucracies that either serve specific groups of Americans or work on specific problems; their heads report to the president.

independent counsel The official appointed by the Justice Department and the federal courts to investigate the president and senior members of the administration.

independent regulatory commissions Federal agencies established to protect Americans by overseeing and regulating various industries; governed by boards or commissions that serve for fixed terms and cannot be removed by the president or Congress without cause.

independent sector The tax-exempt organizations that perform social services, sometimes in the absence of federal programs and sometimes with federal funding.

independent spending Money spent on behalf of a federal candidate that is not coordinated with a campaign and is not, therefore, subject to campaign finance limits.

independents Individuals who do not identify with a political party.

indexing The practice of increasing the dollars spent on a benefit program automatically with inflation.

inflation An increase in the cost of living, commonly measured by the Consumer Price Index.

infotainment News that is clearly designed more to entertain than inform.

initiative An election question that is placed on the ballot by citizen petition; a form of direct democracy.

inner circle The president's most loyal and trusted advisors.

institutional presidency   The leadership, organizations, and advisors who help presidents do their jobs.

interest group   An organization that exists for the purpose of influencing government for the benefit of its members.

iron triangles   A tight relationship involving a federal department or agency, a set of loyal interest groups, and a congressional authorizing committee; most have been replaced by *issue networks.*

isolationism   A foreign policy that seeks to avoid involvement with the rest of the world, to which the United States largely adhered until well into the twentieth century.

issue networks   Political leaders and interest groups that form alliances around a specific policy decision and then disband.

issue voting   A method by which voters choose a candidate whose views on the issues come closest to a voter's own, which requires a clear understanding both of the issues and of candidates' views on them.

issue-attention cycle   A pattern in which the public becomes alarmed or enthusiastic about an issue, realizes the cost of action, and loses interest even though the issue may remain serious and unresolved.

Jim Crow laws   Laws that discriminated against African Americans, specifically by requiring separate facilities for whites and blacks.

judicial activism   A term used to describe broad interpretation of the Constitution and congressional intent in making judicial decisions. (See **judicial restraint**)

judicial branch   The part of government created to interpret the laws and protect individual rights.

judicial restraint   A term used to describe narrow interpretation of the Constitution and faithful adherence to congressional intent in making judicial decisions. (See **judicial activism**)

judicial review   The power of the courts to overturn an act of Congress or of the president as unconstitutional.

justiciable issue   A test used to determine whether a court case involves issues that are within federal court jurisdiction and whether the case can be resolved by either the legislative or executive branch.

leadership PAC   A political action committee controlled by a member of Congress.

legislative branch   The part of government created to make the laws.

legislative courts   Courts that are created by Congress under Article I of the Constitution.

legislative hold   A senator's personal objection to a given proposal. Because the Senate operates largely by unanimous consent, a hold can delay or even kill a bill.

legislative record   The formal hearings, legislative reports, and debates about a bill as it works its way through Congress; used by executive agencies and courts to interpret congressional intent.

libel   A false and defamatory statement made by the written or electronic (television, radio) word.

liberals   Americans who believe that government should play an active role in solving the nation's problems. (See **conservatives**)

libertarians   People who favor a limited government that is directed by the people.

life-cycle theory of participation   The theory that people become more active in political participation as they age.

line item veto   Authority given to the president (and many state governors) to strike specific items from a spending bill.

lobbying An effort to influence government; includes providing information, building public support, and influencing elections.

majoritarian representative democracy A government in which the people choose their representatives and decisions are made by majority rule.

majoritarianism The decision rule in government that determines the outcome of elections (a majority vote is required to elect representatives) and that determines which decisions are made by representatives (a majority vote of representatives is required to make a choice).

majority leader The member elected to lead the majority party in each chamber of Congress.

majority rule A way to make public decisions that allows the majority (50 percent plus one) the greatest say. (See **minority rights**)

majority-minority districts Election districts created to improve the odds that minority candidates will be elected.

mandate An order by the federal government to state or local governments to perform some action. Also refers to the president's ability to claim broad public support for specific public policy initiatives.

means-tested programs Noncontributory social programs that require proof that recipients are poor enough to merit government support.

media The print, electronic, and cybernetic sources of information that exist between the government and the people, interpreting events, shaping opinions, and sending messages in both directions.

media event A situation created specifically to provoke media coverage.

military-industrial complex The combination of the United States military and the private-sector arms industry, first identified by President Dwight Eisenhower.

minority leader The member elected to lead the minority party in each chamber of Congress.

minority rights Constitutional protections designed to ensure that minorities are not oppressed by majority rule. (See **majority rule**)

Miranda v. Arizona A 1966 Supreme Court decision that stated that all accused persons have a right to know their rights.

moderates Americans who see the benefits of government activism on some issues and of limited government on others.

monarchy A government in which a single person, because of membership in a royal family, has absolute power to decide who gets what, when, and how from government.

monetary policy Decisions to alter the supply of money in order to stimulate or slow the economy.

moot A test used to determine whether a case has already been resolved outside the judicial proceeding; used by the Supreme Court to determine whether to hear a case. (See **writ of certiorari**)

motor voter law A 1993 statute that requires states to allow citizens to register to vote at the same time they apply for other state and local services, such as a driver's license.

multimember districts Electoral districts in which a large group of candidates compete for several seats in an election, such as a park board election. (See **single-member districts**)

narrowcasting Messages transmitted by specialized media to select viewers.

nation-centered federalism A view of the relationship between the state and federal governments that sees the federal government as the more important voice.

national debt How much money the federal government owes.

national party conventions Meetings of party delegates every four years to nominate each party's presidential and vice presidential candidates.

nationalization of the Bill of Rights   The extension of the Bill of Rights to cover the actions of state and local governments.

necessary and proper clause   Found in Article I, Section 8, of the Constitution; gives Congress the power to make any laws needed to carry out its express duties and is the source of Congress's implied powers; also known as the *elastic clause*.

New Deal coalition   The groups that supported the Democratic party from the 1930s through the 1960s, including workers, southern farmers, southern Democrats, liberals, Catholics, Jews, and African Americans.

new federalism   A term first used in the early 1970s to describe efforts to shift federal responsibilities and dollars back to the states and localities.

New Jersey Plan   A plan for organizing the new federal government offered in response to the Virginia Plan; outlined a weak national government, leaving most power to the states.

nomination   A party's formal endorsement of a candidate for office.

nonattitudes   Public opinion based on a lack of information; often created when the public is asked polling questions about which little is known.

noncontributory social programs   Programs that provide benefits to Americans according to their circumstances, such as a personal emergency or a flood or other act of God.

normal distribution   In public opinion polling, a situation in which opinion is distributed equally up and down the range of opinions. The midpoint is a good indicator of the average American opinion.

norms   Informal congressional rules that govern behavior; include apprenticeship and specialization.

nullification   The theory that states may ignore, or nullify, national laws that they feel violate the Tenth Amendment.

oligarchy   A government in which a small number of people have the power to decide who gets what, when, and how from government.

open primary   A primary election in which voters are allowed to choose the party primary in which they will vote at the time of balloting; voters may not switch back and forth to the other party on specific contests. (See **blanket primary**)

oversight   Presidential and congressional monitoring of the day-to-day decisions and activities of the federal bureaucracy.

paid media   Campaign advertising on radio and television designed to reinforce public liking of the candidate or disliking of the opponent. (See **free media**)

partial preemption   The federal government's practice of setting a minimum standard for the states that the states may exceed.

party committees   The national, state and local organizations that recruit candidates, register voters, raise money, campaign for the party slate, and get out the vote on election day.

party eras   Periods in which either one political party is dominant or the competition between the parties is stable.

party identification   A voter's sense of attachment to a particular political party.

party machines   Organizations consisting of a party boss, workers, and money to buy votes; once dominated big-city politics and were key to successful local, state, and national campaigns.

party platforms   Statements of the policies that the national political parties support.

party-centered campaign   An election campaign in which the candidate runs as a representative of the party. (See **candidate-centered campaign**)

peak business association An interest group that has individual corporations or small businesses as members.

Plessy v. Ferguson An 1896 Supreme Court decision endorsing the "separate but equal" doctrine that divided Americans by race; overturned by *Brown v. Topeka Board of Education.*

pluralism An option for representative democracy in which interest groups speak for the people.

pluralistic representative democracy A government in which the people allow interest groups to make decisions about representatives and policies.

plurality The number of votes received by the leading candidate, no matter how many candidates are on the ballot.

pocket veto The president's power to kill legislation passed by Congress by allowing ten days to expire without having signed or vetoed the measure; can be used only if Congress formally adjourns during the ten-day period.

policy agenda The issues to which Congress and the president are paying attention.

political action committee (PAC) Formal organizations that raise and contribute money to election campaigns and political parties.

political capital The assets that presidents have when they take office, such as public approval and the number of seats held by their party in Congress.

political consultants Major advisers in political campaigns who are hired by candidates and operate independently of the political parties.

political efficacy An individual's sense that he or she can influence government.

political party A broad membership organization designed to win elections, organize government, and influence voters.

political socialization The process by which children and adolescents form underlying beliefs about politics and government.

politics How people decide who gets what, when, and how in society.

polling The collection of public opinion by questioning a random sample of individuals who represent the public as a whole.

populists People who favor an activist government that is directed by the people.

precedents Judicial decisions made in previous cases.

preemption The federal government's practice of taking a responsibility away from the states.

president's agenda Informal list of the president's top legislative priorities.

presidential appointee An employee of the executive branch who is either subject to confirmation by the Senate or appointed on the sole authority of the president.

presidential ticket The joint listing of presidential and vice presidential candidates on the same ballot, as required by the Twelfth Amendment.

primary election The election that determines who will run as a party's nominee for a particular office in the general election. (See **general election**)

priming effects The power of campaigns to influence the issues that voters think are important in an election.

prior restraint Censorship that occurs before material is published or broadcast in the media.

procedural theory of democracy The notion that the success of a democracy can be determined by whether or not it has procedures associated with the possibility of giving consent; the focus is on how government makes decisions.

professional association An interest group that has individual members of a specific profession as its members.

project grants Funds awarded for specific purposes through competition.

proportional voting system A system of counting votes in which delegates are split among all candidates according to the final votes in a primary or caucus. (See **winner-take-all system**)

public administration Government's implementation and management of public policy once the decisions about what to do are made.

public interest group An interest group whose members have joined because they support a specific cause.

public opinion The collective views of Americans on government, politics, and society.

public policy Decisions about what government does.

rally points The increase (and occasional decrease) in public approval that presidents tend to experience during periods of foreign crisis.

random sample A small number of people who are chosen by pure chance to represent the views of the entire population in an opinion poll; each person in the population must have an equal chance to be selected.

ratification The final stage in adopting the Constitution or its amendments. Three-fourths of the states must approve the proposal, either in the state legislatures or in constitutional conventions.

realigning election An election that produces a lasting shift in the underlying party loyalties of voters; also known as a *critical election*.

reasonable access rule The requirement that radio and television stations must give air time to candidates for public office.

recall The process by which voters may call a special election by petition to remove elected officials from office.

redistributive program A government program that takes wealth from one group in society and transfers it into benefits for another. (See **dedistributive program; distributive program**)

referendum A specific election question placed on the ballot by the state legislature; a form of direct democracy.

Regents of the University of California v. Bakke A 1978 Supreme Court decision that stated that quotas were not permissible even to achieve affirmative action goals.

representative bureaucracy A method to increase the federal bureaucracy's responsiveness to the public by making it look like the nation in terms of race and gender.

representative democracy A form of democracy in which the people vote for leaders who make the decisions on their behalf.

republic A society in which the people give their consent to be governed through the election of representatives.

republican form of government A form of governance in which people govern themselves through the election of representatives.

reserved powers Those powers specifically given to the states under the Constitution, including the power to regulate commerce within state borders, police the public, and prosecute most crimes.

response rates The percentage of people who agree to answer a pollster's interview questions.

responsible party theory The notion that a party's platform will accurately describe what the party will do once in office, so that voters can choose the party that comes closest to their views, trusting that the party will implement the platform.

retrospective voting A form of voting in which voters choose between candidates on the basis of past performance. Voters ask whether they are better off since the last election; if "yes," they vote for the incumbent; if "no," they vote against the incumbent.

retrospective voting Choosing a candidate on the basis of how well things have been going over the last couple of years: When things are going well, the incumbent party's candidates benefit; when things are not, the opposing party benefits.

Revolutionary War The war that established America's independence from England; lasted from 1775 to 1783.

ripe for decision   A test that asks whether an injury claimed in a case is imminent and whether judicial action is the last likely obstacle; used by the Supreme Court to determine whether to hear a case. (See **writ of certiorari**)

Roe v. Wade   A 1973 Supreme Court decision that legalized abortion.

rule   A precise legal statement from the federal bureaucracy about what a policy actually means.

Rule of Four   The Supreme Court requirement for granting a petition for writ of certiorari: four of the nine justices must agree to hear a case in order to grant cert. (See **writ of certiorari**)

Rule of One   The Supreme Court rule allowing a single justice to order immediate relief until the rest of the Court can consider the request; most visibly used in death penalty cases.

salience   A measure of public awareness of an issue.

sampling error   A measure of the potential for inaccuracy in polling data: the percentage by which the opinions of the random sample might differ from the opinions of the entire population.

Second Continental Congress   The national legislature convened by the Founders in Philadelphia in May 1775, which ultimately produced the Declaration of Independence.

secular realignment   A steady erosion in one political party's power and a corresponding increase in the power of another party.

selective benefits   Benefits that are available only to members of an interest group—for example, discount insurance and travel clubs.

senior executives   The federal employees who occupy the most senior posts in the career civil service.

seniority   Length of service by a member of Congress in the House or the Senate; used as one of several criteria for selecting party leaders and committee and subcommittee chairs.

separate but equal doctrine   An interpretation of the equal protection clause that permitted separate facilities and services for blacks and whites; confirmed in *Plessy v. Ferguson* (1896) but overturned in *Brown v. Topeka Board of Education* (1954).

separate interests   Used in the Constitution to ensure that the three branches of government would remain independent of each other by giving the branches different sets of voters and terms of office.

separate layers   Used in the Constitution to limit the power of the national government by dividing power between the state and national governments, creating what is called a federalist system of government.

separate powers   Used in the Constitution to ensure that no single branch of government is able to control decisions about who gets what, when, and how from government.

shadow government   The nearly 13 million nonfederal employees who work for the federal government under contracts and grants.

Shays's Rebellion   A 1786 protest led by Daniel Shays that helped convince the Founders of the need for a stronger national government.

single-issue groups   Interest groups formed around one specific issue, such as abortion rights or gun control.

single-member districts   Electoral districts in which there can be only one winner for each election, no matter how many candidates there are. (See **multimember districts**)

skewed distribution   In public opinion polling, a situation in which opinion is strongly weighted toward one extreme position on the possible range of opinions. The midpoint does not represent the average American opinion.

socioeconomic status   A person's standing in society, based on education and income.

soft money Money donated to the national party committees for "party-building activities" under federal campaign finance laws; includes money for voter registration and get-out-the-vote campaigns.

solicitor general The Justice Department appointee who represents the federal government before the Supreme Court.

sound bite The very brief blocks of time in which a candidate is actually heard speaking in a news story.

Speaker of the House The member of the House of Representatives elected as its leader; presides over the business of the House.

special district A government body usually created to manage a single service for more than one locality.

spin control Attempts to get the media to cover an event or story in the most favorable light.

split-ticket voting Voting for candidates of different parties for different offices on the same ballot. (See **straight-ticket voting**)

spoils system The practice of political patronage, started by President Andrew Jackson, under which the victorious party gives government jobs to its faithful operatives after the election.

standing committees The permanent congressional committees created to manage legislation.

standing to sue The legal status to bring a lawsuit; the individuals who bring a case must be truly injured or subject to injury.

stare decisis Literally, "let the decision stand"; the doctrine that every judicial decision made today must be linked to a decision made in the past.

State of the Union address Annual presidential statement to Congress on how the country is doing and what the president plans to do about various issues.

state-centered federalism A view of the relationship between the state and federal governments that sees the states as the more important voice.

states' rights A view of federalism that emphasizes the states as having the primary role in a federal system. (See **dual federalism**)

statutory law Laws that come from Congress and the president.

straight news Media coverage devoted to accounts of events.

straight-ticket voting Voting for the candidates of one party for every office on the ballot. (See **split-ticket voting**)

straw polls An inaccurate way of measuring public opinion by having movie theater patrons toss their drinking straws into trash cans marked for various candidates.

substantive theory of democracy The notion that the success of a democracy can be determined by whether the outcomes of government decisions appear democratic.

substitution effect The transfer of dollars from one state or local program to another because the federal government has funded the original program. The federal dollars replace dollars that the state or local government would have spent, allowing it to direct those funds elsewhere.

supply-side economics The theory that cutting taxes on wealthy Americans will stimulate greater investment, which will increase economic growth, which will increase wages, which will generate additional tax revenue.

supremacy clause The clause in Article VI of the Constitution that gives federal laws precedence over state or local laws when they conflict.

take care clause The clause in Article II of the Constitution that gives the president ultimate authority to implement the laws.

tax expenditures Items that taxpayers are allowed to deduct from their annual income tax, such as charitable contributions or mortgage interest.

third-party federal government The use of nonfederal employees (private companies, state and local governments, and nonprofit organizations) to deliver services on behalf of the federal government.

three-fifths compromise An agreement reached by the Constitutional Convention that calculated each slave as three-fifths of a person toward the total population of a state in determining the allocation of seats in the House of Representatives.

trade association An interest group that has individual corporations or small businesses from the same industry as members.

trial courts Courts of original jurisdiction; the first courts in the judicial system to hear a case.

trustees Legislators who vote for the greater good even when their constituents are opposed.

uncontrollable spending Money spent on programs that Congress or the president have been unwilling to cut and that rise in cost nearly automatically.

unconventional participation Socially unacceptable forms of civic activity, such as breaking the law to advance a cause.

unemployment rate The percentage of Americans who are looking for jobs but cannot find them.

unicameral legislature A single-chambered legislative body.

unitary government A form of governance in which the national government dominates and state and local governments play very minor roles, reporting directly to the national government.

veto The power to reject laws passed by another branch of government. Presidents exercise the veto by returning a bill to Congress with a message stating the reasons for not signing it.

veto override The legislative branch's overturning or rejection of a veto by a two-thirds vote in each chamber.

Virginia Plan Drafted by James Madison as a model for the new government; outlined a government with three branches: legislative, executive, and judicial.

voter turnout The number of registered voters who actually vote in a particular election.

War Powers Resolution A 1973 act of Congress adopted to restrain the president's war-making power.

whip A party position filled in each chamber of Congress to win support for and "whip" members into line behind party legislation on the floor of Congress.

White House staff The members of the Executive Office of the President who work in the White House and serve the president's daily needs.

winner-take-all system A method of counting votes that gives all the delegates or electors at stake to the candidate who gets the most votes, even if by the narrowest margin. (See **proportional voting system**)

writ of certiorari An order by the Supreme Court to a lower court requesting the record of a case that the Supreme Court has agreed to review. Granting a petition for a writ of certiorari (also known as *granting cert.*) places a case on the Supreme Court's calendar to be heard. (See **adverseness; moot; ripe for decision**)

writ of habeas corpus An order by the Supreme Court to a lower court requesting the record of a case to determine whether a person is being unlawfully imprisoned or detained.

yellow journalism The outrageous and sensational newspaper coverage of the late 1800s.

illustration credits
and acknowledgments

PHOTO CREDITS

Title page: Corbis Digital Stock.

Chapter 1: Chapter opener photos: Corbis Digital Stock; 4: AP/Wide World Photos; 15: UPI/Corbis; 18: Dan Lamont Photography; 21: (top photo) Culver Pictures; (bottom photo) Reuters/Corbis; 26: Corbis Digital Stock.

Chapter 2: Chapter opener photos: National Archives and Records Administration; 37: AP/Wide World Photos; 41: Culver Pictures; 55: (left photo) AP/Wide World Photos; (center photo) Corbis; (right photo) Corbis; 58: Janice Jacobs/Texas Accalade; 68: National Archives and Records Administration.

Chapter 3: Chapter opener photos: AP/Wide World Photos; 88: AP/Wide World Photos; 96: New York City Department of Environmental Protection; 101: Sybil Dodson/NYC Department of Design & Construction; 108: AP/Wide World Photos.

Chapter 4: Chapter opener photos: AP/Wide World Photos; 125: UPI/Corbis; 130: (top photo) AP/Wide World Photos; (center photo) AP/Wide World Photos; (bottom photo) UPI/Corbis; 135: AP/Wide World Photos; 140: Lawrence Migdale/Stock, Boston; 148: AP/Wide World Photos.

Chapter 5: Chapter opener photos: Franklin D. Roosevelt Library; 158: Historical Pictures Services/Stock Montage; 185: (left photo) Reuters/Corbis; (right photo) AP/Wide World Photos; 188: Karen Cooper/Gamma Liaison; 192: Franklin D. Roosevelt Library.

Chapter 6: Chapter opener photos: Joseph Sohm: ChromoSohm Inc./Corbis; 204: AP/Wide World Photos; 215: (left photo) Gamma Liaison; (right photo) AP/Wide World Photos; 231: AP/Wide World Photos; 234: Joseph Sohm: ChromoSohm Inc./Corbis.

Chapter 7: Chapter opener photos: AP/Wide World Photos; 243: Corbis; 257: Reuters/Corbis; 266: Halstead/Gamma Liaison; 274: (left photo) AP/Wide World Photos; (center photo) Reuters/Gerald Reed Schumann/Archive Photos; (right photo) AP/Wide World Photos; 278: AP/Wide World Photos.

Chapter 8: Chapter opener photos: AP/Wide World Photos; 290: (top photo) UPI/Corbis; (bottom photo) Sygma; 297: UPI/Corbis; 302: ROCK THE VOTE (& Design)® is a registered servicemark of Rock the Vote Education Fund; (right photo) Rock the Nation (& Design)® is a registered servicemark of Rock the Vote Education Fund; 317: AP/Wide World Photos; 321: Gamma Liaison; 324: AP/Wide World Photos.

Chapter 9: Chapter opener photos: AP/Wide World Photos; 335: UPI/Corbis; 339: Reuters/Corbis; 348: AP/Wide World Photos; 350: AP/Wide World Photos; 363: AP/Wide World Photos; 365: UPI/Corbis; 376: AP/Wide World Photos.

Chapter 10: Chapter opener photos: AP/Wide World Photos; 391: (top photo) Corbis; (bottom photo) Reuters/Stephen Jaffe/Archive Photos; 398: Reuters/Corbis; 403: AP/Wide World Photos; 426: AP/Wide World Photos.

Chapter 11: Chapter opener photos: AP/Wide World Photos; 439: (top photo) AP/Wide World Photos; (bottom photo) AP/Wide World Photos; 443: AP/Wide World Photos; 447: AP/Wide World Photos; 449: Corbis; 453: Corbis; 454: AP/Wide World Photos;

456: AP/Wide World Photos; 461: (left photo) AP/Wide World Photos; (right photo) Reuters/Corbis; 466: (left photo) AP/Wide World Photos; (right photo) AP/Wide World Photos; 478: AP/Wide World Photos.

Chapter 12: Chapter opener photos: Steve Winter/Black Star/PNI; 490: Gamma Liaison; 504: Sygma; 518: AP/Wide World Photos; 524: Alan F. Singer; 526: © Steve Winter/Black Star/PNI.

Chapter 13: Chapter opener photos: Corbis Digital Stock; 538: AP/Wide World Photos; 540: AP/Wide World Photos; 541: © John Dessarzin Studio Inc.; 551: (top photo) Gamma Liaison; (bottom photo) AP/Wide World Photos; 574: Corbis Digital Stock.

Chapter 14: Chapter opener photos: Mike Zens/Corbis; 588: Reuters/Corbis; 600: AP/Wide World Photos; 602: AP/Wide World Photos; 605: UPI/Corbis; 610: AP/Wide World Photos; 612: AP/Wide World Photos; 617: AP/Wide World Photos; 618: AP/Wide World Photos; 622: Mike Zens/Corbis.

Chapter 15: Chapter opener photos: AP/Wide World Photos; 632: AP/Wide World Photos; 639: Diana Walker/Gamma Liaison; 651: Paul S. Conkin/Monkmeyer; 654: AP/Wide World Photos; 662: Brown Brothers; 670: AP/Wide World Photos.

ACKNOWLEDGMENTS

Box 1-1: From "Washington Leaders Wary of Public Opinion," from The Pew Research Center for The People & The Press News Release, April 17, 1998, pp. 26, 28.

Box 2-4: Adapted from the *New York Times,* June 21, 1998, p. 5. Copyright © 1998 by The New York Times Company. Reprinted by permission.

Box 3-2: From "Deconstructing Distrust: How Americans View Government," from The Pew Center for The People & The Press News Release, 1998, p. 82.

Box 3-3: Adapted from *Understanding Intergovernmental Relations* by Deil S. Wright. (Pacific Grove, CA: Brooks/Cole Publishing, 1988).

Box 4-3: From "Clinton Ratings Hold: Balanced Budget a Public Priority, But Few See Personal Payoff," from The Pew Research Center for The People & The Press News Release, January 18, 1996, pp. 11–12; 16–17.

Box 4-4: From "Reality Check: The Politics of Mistrust (Polities Quiz)," from the *Washington Post,* January 29, 1996, p. A6. Copyright © 1996 Washington Post Writers Group. Reprinted with permission.

Box 4-5: From *Vital Statistics on American Politics, 1997-1998,* by Harold W. Stanley and Richard G. Niemi. (Washington, DC: CQ Press, 1998), p. 112, and the General Social Survey of the National Opinion Research Center, University of Chicago.

Box 5-3: From "Internet News Takes Off: Pew Research Center Biennial News Consumption Survey," from The Pew Research Center for The People & The Press News Release, June 1998, pp. 35–53.

Box 5-4: From "A Guide to Leaks in Government" by Stephen Hess, in *Governing* by Roger H. Davidson and Walter J. Oleszek. (Washington, DC: CQ Press, 1992), pp. 212–213.

Box 5-5: From "Internet News Takes Off: Pew Research Center Biennial News Consumption Survey," from The Pew Research Center for The People & The Press News Release, June 1998, p. 8.

Box 6-1: From "Win or Lose, Perot Proves One Can Run without Major Parties," by James M. Perry. From the *Wall Street Journal,* July 14, 1992, p. A11. Copyright © 1992 Dow Jones & Company, Inc. All rights reserved worldwide.

Box 6-2: Adapted from *Politics, Parties, and Elections in America* by John Bibby. (Chicago, IL: Nelson-Hall Publishers, 1992), p. 22.

Box 6-3: From the *New York Times,* August 26, 1996, p. A12. Copyright © 1996 by The New York Times Company. Reprinted with permission.

Box 6-4: From *Vital Statistics on American Politics, 1997–1998,* by Harold W. Stanley and Richard G. Niemi. (Washington, DC: CQ Press, 1998), p. 108.

Box 6-5: From *Vital Statistics on American Politics, 1997–1998,* by Harold W. Stanley and Richard G. Niemi. (Washington, DC: CQ Press, 1998), p. 111.

Box 7-1: From "Executive Compensation, Washington Style" from the *National Journal,* April 26, 1997. p. 804.

Box 7-2: From "A Web of Ideological and Financial Ties" by Paul Starobin, from the *National Journal,* January 28, 1995, p. 220.

Box 7-3: From *Voice and Equality: Civic Voluntarism in American Politics* by Sidney Verba, Kay Lehman Schlozman, and Henry E. Brady. (Cambridge, MA: Harvard University Press, 1995), pp. 190, 218, 233, and 255. Reprinted with the permission by The President and Fellows of Harvard College.

Box 7-4: From "Washington's Power 25" from *Fortune,* December 8, 1997.

Box 7-5: Adapted from *Interest Group Politics in America,* 3rd ed., by Ronald J. Hrebenar. (Armonk, NY: M.E. Sharpe, 1998), p. 48.

Box 7-6: From *Issue Advocacy Advertising during the 1996 Campaign* by Deborah Beck, Paul Taylor, Jeffrey Stanger, and Douglas Rivin. (Annenberg Public Policy Center, 1997).

Box 7-7: From *Vital Statistics on American Politics, 1997–1998,* by Harold W. Stanley and Richard G. Niemi. (Washington, DC: CQ Press, 1998), p. 94.

Box 8-1: Modified from "Citizen Activity: Who Participates" What Do They Say?" by Sidney Verba, Kay Lehman Scholzman, Henry E. Brady, and Norman Nie, as it appeared in *American Political Science Review,* vol. 87, no. 2 (June 1993), p. 315.

Box 8-3: From *Voice and Equality: Civic Voluntarism in American Politics* by Sidney Verba, Kay Lehman Schlozman, and Henry E. Brady. (Cambridge, MA: Harvard University Press, 1995), p. 51. Reprinted with permission by The President and Fellows of Harvard College.

Box 8-4: From "The People, the Press, and Politics—Campaign '92: 'The Generations Divide.'" (Survey VIII), from the Times Mirror Center for the People and the Press News Release, July 8, 1992, p. 44.

Box 8-5: From *Voice and Equality: Civic Voluntarism in American Politics* by Sidney Verba, Kay Lehman Scholzman, and Henry E. Brady. (Cambridge, MA: Harvard University Press, 1995), p. 190. Reprinted with permission by The President and Fellows of Harvard College.

Box 8-6: Adapted from *The Politics of American Government* by Stephen J. Wayne, G. Calvin Mackenzie, David M. O'Brien, and Richard L. Cole. (New York: St. Martin's Press, 1995), p. 349.

Box 9-1: Adapted from *A Brief History of Money in Politics: Campaign Finance and Campaign Finance Reform in the United States* by the Center for Responsive Politics. Copyright © 1995.

Box 9-3: From *The Big Picture: Money Follows Power Shift on Capitol Hill* by the Center for Responsive Politics. Copyright © 1997.

Box 9-4: Adapted from *Parties and Elections in America,* 2nd ed., by L. Sandy Maisel. (New York: McGraw-Hill, 1993), p. 190.

Box 9-5: From *The 13 Keys to the Presidency* by Allan Lichtman and Ken DeCell. (Lanham, MD: Madson Books, 1990), p. 7.

Box 9-6: From "How Clinton and Dole Spent $232 Million" by Ira Chinoy, from the *Washington Post,* March 31, 1997, p. A19. Copyright © 1997 Washington Post Writers Group. Reprinted with permission.

Box 9-8: From "Voter Anxiety Dividing GOP: Energized Dems Backing Clinton," from the Times Mirror Center for the People and the Press News Release, November 14, 1995, p. 22.

Box 9-9: From CNN/TIME All Politics and Voter News Service, November 5, 1996.

Box 10-2: Adapted from "Congress: The First and the 100th" from the *New York Times,* January 5, 1987, p. A14, and "The 105th Congress: A Study in Sameness" from the *New York Times,* January 19, 1997, p. E5. Copyright © 1987, 1997 The New York Times Company. Reprinted with permission.

Box 10-4: Updated from *Thickening Government: Federal Hierarchy and the Diffusion of Accountability* by Paul C. Light. (Washington, DC: Brookings Institution/Governance Institute, 1995), p. 157.

Box 10-6: From *Congress A to Z.* (Washington, DC: CQ Press, 1993), p. 233.

Box 11-2: From *Presidential Leadership: Politics and Policy Making* by George C. Edwards III and Stephen J. Wayne. (New York: St. Martin's Press, 1997), p. 181.

Box 11-3: Adapted from the *Washington Post,* February 5, 1993, p. A23. Copyright © 1993 by The Washington Post Writers Group. Reprinted with permission.

Box 11-4: From "Presidential Support and the Military Option" by Anne Cronin. From the *New York Times,* September 18, 1994, pp. 4-5E. Copyright © 1994 by The New York Times Company. Reprinted with permission.

Box 11-5: From "States of the Union: Then and Now" by Mark Murray, from the *National Journal,* January 24, 1998, p. 154. Copyright © 1998 by the National Journal, Inc. All rights reserved. Reprinted by permission.

Box 12-2: From *The Federal Machine: Beginnings of Bureaucracy in Jacksonian America* by Matthew Crenson. (Baltimore, MD: The Johns Hopkins University Press, 1976), pp. 77–78.

Box 12-3: From *The Shadow of Government: The Changing Shape of the Public Service* by Paul C. Light. (Washington, DC: Brookings Institution, 1999).

Box 12-6: From "Takin' on the Bacon" by Kirk Victor, from the *National Journal,* May 16, 1995, p. 1084. Copyright © 1995 by the National Journal, Inc. All rights reserved. Reprinted by permission.

Box 12-7: From "Deconstructing Distrust: How Americans View Government," from The Pew Center for The People & The Press News Release, 1998, p. 16.

Box 12-8: From "Deconstructing Distrust: How Americans View Government," from The Pew Center for The People & The Press News Release, 1998, p. 33.

Box 12-9: From *Stupid Government Tricks* by John Koht. Copyright © 1995 by John Kohut. Used by permission of Plum Books, a division of Penguin USA, Inc.

Box 13-1: From "Clinton's Legal Policy and the Courts: Rising from Disarray or Turning Around and Around?" by David M. O'Brien, from *The Clinton Presidency: First Appraisals,* edited by Colin Campbell and Bert A. Rockman (Chatham, NJ: Chatam House Publishers, 1996), p. 137; and *Vital Statistics on American Politics, 1997–1998,* by Harold W. Stanley and Richard G. Niemi (Washington, DC: CQ Press, 1998), pp. 272–273.

Box 13-3: From *Vital Statistics on American Politics, 1997–1998,* by Harold W. Stanley and Richard G. Niemi (Washington, DC: CQ Press, 1998), p. 280.

Box 13-4: From *Vital Statistics on American Politics, 1997–1998,* by Harold W. Stanley and Richard G. Niemi (Washington, DC: CQ Press, 1998), pp. 272–273.

Box 13-6: From *Storm Center: The Supreme Court in American Politics,* 3rd ed., by David M. O'Brien, p. 209. Copyright © 1993, 1990, 1986 by David M. O'Brien. Reprinted by permission of W.W. Norton & Company, Inc.

Box 13-8: From *Storm Center: The Supreme Court in American Politics,* 3rd ed., by David M. O'Brien, p. 209. Copyright © 1993, 1990, 1986 by David M. O'Brien. Reprinted by permission of W.W. Norton & Company, Inc.

Box 13-9: From "Has the Court Lost Its Appeal?" by Joan Biskupic. From the *Washington Post,* October 12, 1995, p. A23. Copyright © 1995 by the Washington Post Writers Group. Reprinted with permission.

Box 14-1: From *Constitutional Law and Politics: Civil Rights and Civil Liberties,* vol. II, by David M. O'Brien, pp. 280–281. Copyright © 1991 by David M. O'Brien. Reprinted by permission of W.W. Norton & Company, Inc.

Box 14-4: From *Vital Statistics on American Politics, 1997–1998,* by Harold W. Stanley and Richard G. Niemi (Washington, DC: CQ Press, 1998), p. 151.

Box 14-5: From "In Poll, Americans Reject Means but Not Ends of Racial Diversity" from the *New York Times,* December 14, 1997, p. A32. Copyright © 1997 by The New York Times Company. Reprinted by permission.

Box 15-5: From "The Issue-Attention Cycle" by Anthony Downs. Reprinted with permission of the author and *The Public Interest,* (Summer 1972), vol. xx, no. 28, pp. 38–50. Copyright © 1991 by National Affairs, Inc.

Box 15-6: From *Rulemaking: How Government Agencies Write Law and Make Policy* by Cornelius Kerwin. (Washington, DC: CQ Press, 1994), pp. 39–42.

Box 15-7: From *Vital Statistics on American Politics, 1997–1998,* by Harold W. Stanley and Richard G. Niemi (Washington, D.C.: CQ Press, 1998), p. 359.

index